imago
CHRONICLES BOOK SEVEN
the broken covenant

L.T. Suzuki

Book Cover, graphic design and layout:
Scott White
Shinobi Creative Services
www.shinobicreativeservices.com

imagine...

There is a secret place that exists; unknown to most, forgotten by many, and lives on only for the few who believe.

Though you cannot look to a map to find this magical realm, it is still very real. In this world, lost on a plane that hangs in the twilight where one enters a dream as sleep takes over the mind and body, Imago lives on.

Here, as in all places where man dwells, the eternal struggle between good and evil plays out. In this land, there are places fair and foul, heroes that are larger than life and villains that one hopes exists only in our nightmares.

In this mystical world, life is an extraordinary adventure where revenge and redemption, betrayal and salvation, and love; lost and found, are woven together to create this rich tapestry of life.

Where is this realm you ask? To find Imago, all you must do is close your eyes and believe...

*This book is dedicated to Scott,
for boldly surviving nine novels
and all the countless hours of
proofreading, book cover designing,
formatting, and so on!*

With much love & gratitude…

contents

in shadow and light

"*RUN!*"

This single word raked at Goren's nerves like never before.

Dodging behind a tree, he wheezed, gasping for each painful breath he gulped down. Squinting from the salty sting of perspiration, he brushed the sweat and thinning strands of hair from his eyes with the back of his trembling hand. How was a man his age to run for this hard and for this long? Though not grossly obese and fitter than most, he was used to doing the hunting, not being hunted.

With his heart thundering in his chest, resonating clear through his quaking body, this frantic order squeezed Goren's very being with unyielding fear as his comrade urged him on, "You can't stop now, ya lazy bugger! Run!"

"I jus'- I jus' need ta catch my breath," groaned Goren, clutching his aching side with one hand as the other clenched his bow.

"You won't need ta catch yer breath if you're dead!" argued Dagor. Pressing his back to the tree trunk, he goaded his fellow Talibarrian on. "Now, move! That damned thing is comin'."

"But I don't hear it anymore," whispered Goren, as he listened for what his eyes could no longer make out in the growing darkness. "Suppose it gave up on us or we jus' out ran it?"

"Out ran it? Are ya crazy? You saw how that thing moved! I've never seen anything like it before."

"Maybe we were lucky an' it found somethin' else ta chase after," said Goren, his terrified eyes glancing about, searching the deep shadows of the forest for signs of danger.

"Look at us! We ain't never been lucky!" snapped Dagor. He swallowed down a deep breath to calm his shattered nerves so his trembling hands could nock an arrow onto his bow. "Our stars ain't about ta change now."

"I was jus' wishin'," groaned Goren, still struggling to catch his breath.

"Wishin' ain't gonna save our lives, but runnin' jus' might. Now arm yourself, jus' in case."

"In case of what? So we can kill each other first than ta let that beast rip us ta shreds while we're still alive?" grunted Goren, reluctantly pulling an arrow from the quiver.

"We can't panic. We gotta believe that we're jus' huntin' down a cunnin' wolf or a stinkin' huge boar – the mother of all boars."

"But it ain't no wolf or boar chasin' us! Did ya see the size of that creature? It's enormous!"

"Ya dolt! Of course I know how big it is! Jus' trust me," urged Dagor, his fingertip testing the barbed, steel bodkin arming the tip of the arrow.

"I did, an' look at the fix we're in now! I told ya we should've never come huntin' here so close ta Spirit Wood," snarled Goren. "That forest is still haunted, I tell ya!"

"Haunted my arse! That ain't no ghost comin' fer us," argued Dagor, his hushed words rising with his mounting anger and impatience.

"We're suppos'd ta be the hunters! We ain't the ones that's suppos'd ta be chased down like common prey," snapped Goren, angrily shaking his bow at his younger, leaner comrade.

"That's why we gotta stay calm, Goren. We gotta turn the tables on that creature before it gets the upper hand."

"We already tried killin' that *thing*. We ain't hit it yet, not once!"

"We must've! My quiver's half empty!"

"Well, if ya made a hit, it hasn't made a diff'rence," stated Goren, with an incredulous snort. "It might not be a ghost, but there ain't nothin' natural 'bout it, if ya ask me."

"I ain't askin' you what it is! I'm askin' you ta help me kill it before it kills us!" growled Dagor, praying for the moon to show its face to shed some light on their gloomy surroundings. Instead, the sliver of moon taunted them, its cold, silver light remaining cloaked behind a growing layer of cloud cover.

"Listen... I think it's gone," whispered Goren, pressing a finger to his lips for Dagor's silence.

Standing perfectly still, their ears strained to hear above the sounds of their anxiously pounding hearts and ragged breath. The deep forest was engulfed in an unnatural quiet. An eerie hush settled thick and heavy all around them. There was no hooting of owls or the peeping of tree frogs; only dead silence as a thin mist swirled along the forest floor.

A pair of glowing eyes suddenly peered through a thick stand of trees as the still of the night was shattered by a blood-curdling sound. It was unlike anything they had ever heard. Neither a growl nor a roar, it was a strange, visceral rumble erupting from deep within a tortured body.

"Bloody hell!" cursed Dagor. He leapt away from the safety of cover to take aim as Goren struggled to nock his arrow; his hand shaking so violently, the notched end of the projectile kept slipping off the string of sinew.

Moving with the speed and agility of a cat, but the ferocity of a ravenous wolf intent on a kill, the creature charged straight for them, bounding with enormous strides before leaping at its prey.

Driven more by sheer panic than skilled precision, Dagor unleashed his arrow. Though it was too dark to see, by the sharp crack echoing through the night, he could tell immediately the shaft of the arrow had shattered on impact. He hit the beast, but it did nothing to slow it down, only serving to infuriate the creature all the more.

Running in fear, Dagor abandoned his friend as the beast vaulted into the air to leap at Goren. The terrified man screamed, falling back as he let the arrow fly. With a hard *'thunk'* the projectile struck the monster on its chest. The creature snarled, veering off as it sailed over Goren's prostrate body to disappear into the shadows once more.

"Get up!" shouted Dagor, waving his friend on to follow.

Goren lay frozen in fear. Momentarily in shock, he was unable to believe he survived this encounter and his arrow had actually hit its mark.

"Get the hell up! Run, ya fool!"

"B- but I got it!" stammered Goren, scrambling up onto his shaking legs. "I got that wretched beast right in the heart!"

"Are ya sure?"

"It came right o'er top of me. I got it spot on. Pierced its heart, I did!" bragged Goren. "I killed the bloody monster!"

"Then where is it?" questioned Dagor, his wary eyes searching the forest for the beast's presence.

"It skulked off ta die, I bet. That's where it went! That creature is dead an' gone."

Dagor's eyes opened wide in horror. He stumbled, backing away as his terrified gaze remained fixed over Goren's shoulder. Dagor's trembling finger pointed behind his friend.

"Wh- what?" asked Goren, frowning in confusion.

Dagor's mouth gaped open. He couldn't squeeze out the words of warning stuck in the back of his throat. His finger frantically pointed while his feet continued to place greater distance between him and his friend.

"Bloody hell," gulped Goren, trembling in absolute fear. "It's behind me, ain't it?"

"Get outta there!" hollered Dagor.

Instead, Goren froze in his tracks as the ominous crackling and snapping of dried twigs sounded in the darkness behind him.

"Run!" shouted Dagor, as he dashed away. "Don't look back, ya fool!"

As though these words caused an instinctive reaction, Goren's head whipped about to glance behind him as the rustling of leaves grew louder. Suddenly, those sinister, amber eyes gleamed in the darkness once more.

Racing away in a blind panic, Goren's fear was so overwhelming he was almost able to catch up to his comrade. Crashing through the forest, they dashed across a clearing, heading southward.

"Almost there!" hollered Dagor, knowing their village was just beyond the distant rise; nestled at the edge of the forest bordering the Plains of Fire.

"We ain't gonna make it!" puffed Goren, gasping for his breath as he forced his legs to pump even as the muscles burned, aching with exhaustion.

"Gotta make it! We gotta warn the others," huffed Dagor, his own feet beginning to drag after enduring this relentless pursuit they were forced to engage in.

"Can't – can't take another step." Goren groaned in pain, his chest heaving as he dodged behind a tree for a momentary reprieve from this torture.

"Then stay here an' distract the beast. I'll run fer help," suggested Dagor, unwilling to sacrifice himself up so easily to this fearsome predator.

"Yeah, right! You ain't leavin' me behind ta die jus' so you can escape!"

The men shrieked in fright as a deep growl rumbled from the darkness behind them.

"It's comin'!" hollered Dagor, his frightened eyes searching for the precise location of this menacing cry now echoing all around them.

Pushing off against the tree they were resting against, the men were forced to run once more. With hearts hammering in their chests and the cold night air catching in the back of their throats as they fought to fill their aching lungs, the Talibarrian hunters sprinted with all their waning might, utterly exhausted by this terrifying ordeal.

Unable to endure any more, the men staggered to a stop, spinning about to face the creature. Taking up their bows once more for a final stand, they armed it with their dwindling supply of arrows. If not to kill the rampaging beast, they hoped to hold it at bay until they could regain their strength to resume the last, desperate sprint to the safety of their village.

Taking up the weapons in their trembling hands, the two men braced for the assault. They stared into the darkness. Instead of spying the monster, their frightened eyes were greeted by nothing more than fleeting glimpses of a shadow moving within the shadows, and then, there was an all-consuming silence that droned in their ears.

For the longest moment, Goren and Dagor stood there, watching and listening.

Without warning, the creature attacked, charging straight for them.

Releasing a torrent of arrows, the men heard some of the projectiles flying astray to pierce earth and foliage while others met their mark, striking the beast, only to shatter or ricochet off hard, spiny protrusions and its incredibly tough hide that seemed invincible.

Veering off, not so much as to avoid this assault as it was to prolong the chase, the creature vanished into the forest, blending into shadow and light.

"Run! Run before it comes back," urged Dagor, throwing down his bow and empty quiver.

Goren did the same, discarding this extra bit of weight as he forced his legs to carry him on. It didn't take a fool to know that in a chase, a man need only be as fast as the one behind him to avoid certain death.

"In here!" hollered Dagor, motioning Goren to the safety of a large, hollow log lying on the forest floor.

Just as Dagor was about to clamber inside, the sounds of the beast rushing up behind them caused Goren to panic. Seizing his comrade by the scruff of his neck, Goren yanked the lighter, leaner Dagor from the mouth of the log, pushing him aside so he could scramble in first.

In fear and desperation, Dagor shoved Goren away as the older man dropped down onto his hands and knees to crawl inside this sanctuary. Clambering over his downed companion, Dagor dove into the hollow, taking immediate cover.

Goren scrambled in behind his friend, dragging, pulling and pushing his less-than-svelte body into the tight, dark confines Dagor easily fit into. Grunting, huffing and wheezing as he wedged himself in as far as he could to avoid the long reach of this enraged creature, Dagor's muffled words ordered him to be silent.

For the longest moment, as they lay frozen in terror within this dark hollow, the men listened. Their hearts jumped to their throats as the silence was broken by the heavy *thump* of massive paws landing atop this log. The decaying wood creaked, moaning beneath the weight of this behemoth.

Goren peered through a knothole. His eyes squeezed shut as a loud, snuffling snort followed by a jet of spent air as rancid as a dragon's curdled breath puffed through the hole. He dare not breathe as a snout pressed up against this small opening, forcing Goren to throw his hand over his mouth to prevent from gagging on the stench of decaying flesh.

As the creature hopped off the log, they heard the leathery pads of its feet patting along the soft earth as it circled the log.

The men lay silent, praying this danger would pass.

After a torturously long wait that was in reality less than a minute, a sense of calm returned to the forest. In the distance, an owl's haunting call echoed through the tranquil night as the tree frogs resumed their chorus.

Goren wiped the sweat from his brows as he breathed a sigh of relief: "Thank goodness, there is a God!"

'Not for you!' thought Dagor, launching himself from the opening just as their hiding place was ripped apart. Huge, curved claws raked through layers of bark and rotting wood.

As he watched his friend flee, snarling lips curled back to expose a set of sharp, gnashing teeth to fill Goren's frightened eyes. Never in his life had he seen such massive fangs!

Ramming its head into the opening, its snapping jaws stopped just short of grazing the mortal's scalp. A row of sharp spines rising up from the crown of the creature's head, down the length of its neck and along its back prevented the beast from thrusting its entire head into this narrow opening.

Screaming in terror, Goren tried to wriggle his body backward to evade these monstrous fangs. Unable to retreat fast enough, the last thing Goren saw was the vicious rows of deadly teeth clamping down around his head to forcibly yank him free from the shattered log.

The rancid odour of decay rising from the beast's throat caused

Goren's stomach to churn. He grimaced in pain as the creature's saliva ate away at his skin and a rough, powerful tongue rasped the flesh from his cheek.

Surrendering his partner to the beast, Dagor fled in terror, not even glancing back as Goren's muted screams raked at his nerves. He did not see as the monster wrenched Goren's body free to easily toss it up into the air. Catching the helpless man by his throat, the creature's powerful jaws locked down as it slammed its prey to the earth, easily snapping Goren's neck.

Fuelled by a fear he never imagined possible, the rush of adrenalin coursing through Dagor's veins propelled him forward with a sudden burst of energy. He raced away from the carnage of this grisly scene.

Darting behind a tree in hopes of eluding the beast, Dagor remained concealed. He fought to compose himself in preparation for the final, desperate sprint to his village.

Not wanting to draw the creature's attention, his trembling hands slapped over his mouth. He tried to muffle the sounds of his ragged breath, sucking the cold air in between the gaps of his fingers to fill his lungs. As he attempted to calm his breathing and slow his thundering heart, he noticed how the heat of the exertion from this frantic run manifested into steam rising from his burning skin and weary, trembling muscles. Hot and exhausted, Dagor prayed for redemption from this hellish ordeal as he blinked away the sweat dripping into his eyes.

Dagor's breath caught in the back of his throat. An icy drop splashed down on his arm to send a shiver down his spine. He breathed a sigh of relief as another cool, revitalizing drop pelted his face as the gentle patter of rain sounded against the tree canopy.

Listening to the comforting sounds of raindrops, Dagor breathed easier as he came to realize the beast could no longer be heard. It had either left to find shelter from the rain or it was still preoccupied with his undoubtedly deceased comrade, dragging off Goren's body.

Taking another deep breath before venturing off to his village, Dagor felt a sense of calm return to the forest. It was as though the heavens were opening up to drive off the creature, its cleansing rain promising to wash away all evidence of the bloody carnage. Dagor breathed a great sigh of relief. He finally relaxed, leaning wearily against the tree trunk.

Just as he pushed off from the tree to resume his trek, a heavy drop splashed onto his shoulder. Dagor took no notice, until he gasped in pain. What he thought was nothing more than a heavy drop of rain, burned through his cloak and raiment to eat into his flesh.

"What the…" gasped Dagor, carefully lifting the smoldering fabric off from his shoulder as he sniffed at this strange, thick liquid that ate through layers of clothing to sear his flesh.

The sudden downpour drenched his raiment to ease the burning sensation, but it made the night suffocating and unnaturally dark. Squinting through this curtain of rain, a damp heat prickled down the back of his neck.

Dagor slowly peered up into the tree.

Before he could scream, a sickening *'crrrunch'* echoed through his head as a tremendous pressure engulfed him, crushing his skull. Dagor could feel his blood, hot and pulsating. It gushed from these wounds as powerful fangs sank in, puncturing the temporal bones to stab through his eyeballs as his limp body was hoisted high into the branches. His world faded into a black abyss, but Dagor's ears continued to ring as the wretched screeching of a horn sounded in the distance, causing the creature to momentarily release its grip.

"My liege, it has happened again!" announced a harried knight, rushing into the throne room to address King Sebastian. In his haste, he barely acknowledged the royal guards posted at the double doors as they respectfully saluted their Captain's presence.

Sebastian's curious eyes peered over the scroll he was reading as Cullen Bristow barged into the chamber. Raising his hand for a moment of silence, the King accepted a goblet of wine from a servant first, before addressing the young Captain's concerns.

Cullen stopped in his tracks, biting his lower lip to resist speaking out of turn.

"That will be all, Marda," said Sebastian, nodding in gratitude as she delivered his midday beverage of choice. "Take your leave."

"As you wish, Your Highness." Marda bowed politely as she exited the room. The young woman swept past the Captain, not even glancing in his direction as she left under the scrutiny of Cullen's suspicious eyes.

"Pray tell, *what* has happened again, Captain Bristow?" queried Sebastian, waving Cullen forward as he inhaled deeply to admire the fragrant bouquet of the wine before indulging in a sip.

"That rampaging creature has left a path of carnage in its wake!" The words rushed out of Cullen's mouth as he spoke.

"Slow down, Captain," urged Sebastian. "What creature do you speak of? Did Farmer Wilton's new hound attack his neighbor's flock of sheep again?"

"I am not speaking of Wilton's mangy mongrel. I am speaking of that damned beast in Talibarr everyone is talking about!"

"*Everyone,* meaning you?" questioned Sebastian, knowing how much of this self-absorbed man's world revolved around him.

"Everyone, *including* me," corrected Cullen. "The beast has attacked another settlement to the north."

"Odd... Your words confound me, Captain!" gasped Sebastian, almost gagging on a mouthful of wine. He was momentarily stunned that Cullen would feel some sense of compassion for those he long regarded as the enemy.

"How so?"

"It would appear you are suddenly concerned for the welfare of the Talibarrians."

"Concerned for *those* barbarians? I think not! What concerns me is that the creature in question is roaming about. In fact, its movements are bringing it ever closer to our borders, my liege. For this reason, we should be prepared to act; to protect our people in case that beast makes its way over the Aranak Mountains to lay siege on the citizens of Darross."

"And this beast you speak of, exactly what manner of animal is it?"

"That is yet to be ascertained, Your Highness." Cullen's shoulders arched up in a shrug as he answered, "Some say it is the work of a pack of marauding wolves; others say it is a rogue brown bear; while others claim it to be a large mountain cat on the prowl."

"Disregard the rumours, Captain Bristow. What are the facts? What do the survivors of these attacks say it is?"

"Strangely enough, there have been no survivors to speak of," answered Cullen.

"*None?*"

"Yes!"

"If as many have come under attack as you claim, you would think there would be at least one person who lives to tell about it."

"As I understand it, my liege, those who lived long enough to speak of the creature were delirious; absolutely deranged from the trauma of the attack," explained Cullen. "These people were so hysterical they spoke nothing more than indiscernible gibberish before dying. Nothing they said made any sense. Mind you, they were Talibarrian so what more can one expect?"

"So there are no reliable eye-witness accounts of these attacks?" queried Sebastian.

"As troubling as this is, at this point, I believe the disturbing rumours of the *sane* are more reliable than the delirious words of the *insane*."

"Troubling, indeed," sighed Sebastian, nodding in agreement as his eyes shifted from Cullen to the doorway of the throne room as his two sons appeared, only to suddenly retreat upon seeing he was engaged in conversation with the Captain.

"Come in," invited Sebastian, waving Garrick and Carstian to step forward. "Perhaps one of you can help shed light on this matter."

"What matter, father?" asked Garrick, approaching the throne as his younger sibling followed close behind.

"The matter of the strange happenings in Talibarr," replied Sebastian.

"Oh, you mean the mysterious creature to the north," responded Garrick, "the one that is on the loose."

"Yes! That is the creature in question."

"I heard the animal comes out to hunt only at night," disclosed Garrick; "preferring the shadows to the light of day."

"I understand it is no animal at all, but a monster – a dragon to be exact!" claimed Carstian.

"And how would you know this, Carstian?" questioned his father. "You have not stepped beyond the courtyard since your return to the castle."

"Though I have not ventured from these walls since that madman Draven Eldard had kidnapped me, I still hear news," admitted Carstian. He was unmoved by the fact that it had been almost five months since his rescue and safe return to the castle, but he still refused to leave the protection of Darross Castle after surviving his terrifying ordeal. "I still share in information pertaining to the world beyond these castle walls."

"From a trusted source, I pray," hoped Sebastian.

"If you consider those in your service to be trustworthy, then yes!" answered Carstian, nodding with confidence. "I suppose they can be regarded as a trusted source."

"Go on then," urged his father, motioning Carstian to step forward. "What have you heard of this matter, my son?"

"Well, according to the scullery maid whose grandfather lives on the outskirts of Heathrowen –" answered Carstian, only to be interrupted by Captain Bristow.

"Aah, hearsay from an old codger looking for attention or wishing to stir up some excitement," disputed Cullen, already dismissing this news he now regarded as nothing more than idle gossip shared by domestic staff.

"Yes, an *old codger* whom, by the way, befriended a Talibarrian he trades with. This fellow told her grandfather that the beast in question is a dragon," continued Carstian. "By the way it moves and the ferocity of the attacks, it can be nothing else but a dragon."

"Be it a bear, a wolf... or a dragon. It must be one or the other, it cannot be all of the aforementioned," sighed Sebastian.

"No disrespect to you, my lord," responded Cullen, his head bowing to the younger Prince, "but your father is quite correct. I believe we can rule out that the creature is indeed a dragon."

"You are quick to dismiss this possibility, Captain," determined Carstian, his voice prickling with annoyance as he stared at Cullen.

"If you are not already aware, aside from that wretched beast the Wizard of the North had insisted on befriending and adopting as a pet, there are no other dragons to speak of in this realm. In time, even the Wizard's dragon will be nothing more than a creature of legend."

"And no disrespect to you, Captain, but after that harrowing adventure late of last year, there is not too much I am reluctant to believe in after all we had witnessed and endured," countered Carstian.

The Prince held up his maimed left hand as a less than subtle reminder of their shared escapade. It almost ended tragically had it not been for the help they received from the four Wizards, Nayla Treeborn as well as the surviving members of the Order.

"No need to thank me for sparing you the loss of your entire hand," smiled Cullen. He thoughtlessly flexed his left pinkie finger at the Prince, the small digit that was brutally amputated from Carstian's hand by the deranged Draven Eldard. "But keep in mind, Prince Carstian, much of what you had witnessed was conjured up by the powers of the forbidden arts."

"And what makes you say black magic is not at work now?" countered Carstian. "What makes you believe magic was not used to conjure up this beast, a dragon, even?"

"For one, the dreaded Book of Spells had been completely and utterly destroyed," reminded Cullen, his words terse. "Unless there is another copy lying about, and that is highly unlikely, the book is no more."

"You sound so confident," assessed Garrick, listening intently to this exchange between his younger brother and the Captain of his father's army.

"There is more, my lord. Secondly, I am well acquainted with Tor Airshorn and his behemoth dragon," continued Cullen. "As uncouth as that Wizard is, he would never allow his *pet* to run amok. The Wizard has complete control over Mutton."

"You mean *Button,*" corrected Carstian.

Cullen's face contorted into a frown of curiosity as he pondered the Prince's words.

"The dragon's name is Button," reiterated Carstian, "as in, as cute as a button."

"That is what I said; Button his *mutton-eating* dragon," responded Cullen, pretending to be personally acquainted with the Wizard and his gargantuan, flying reptile. "The whole matter being; a dragon, it is not! Besides, a creature of such size and destructive power would leave no question as to what it is."

"Then, in all your wisdom, Captain Bristow, what do you suppose this creature is?" questioned Garrick.

A momentary hush settled on the throne room as Cullen scratched his head in thought. He mulled over the possibilities based upon the limited information he had sifted through so far.

"Yes, Captain Bristow, any thoughts on the identity of this mysterious animal?" probed Carstian. He was eager to hear what bizarre manifestation Cullen would contrive to explain the manner of beast.

"Based on what I have heard, it is safe to assume the creature is some kind of hybrid."

"Say again! " responded Sebastian, baffled by Cullen's suggestion.

"You know, my liege? A species of animal crossbred with another creature. A *mongrel* to the uneducated. Like a dog of no definable breed."

"A hybrid you say?" pondered Garrick. "Pray tell, a hybrid of what?"

"Consider this," replied Cullen, "it is rumoured to have the strength of the great brown bear found only in the northern reaches of Talibarr and Orien."

"Go on," urged Sebastian, intrigued by these words.

"It is said to possess the speed and agility of a mountain cat, moving like a phantom through the forest. And, it had been described to have the cunning of a wolf."

"So it is a…?" asked Carstian, waiting for Cullen's answer.

"It is only logical this beast is a hybrid of all three creatures," concluded Cullen.

"*What?*" The royal family gasped in unison.

"You heard me! It is a true abomination of nature – a monster, I tell you!"

"How can this be, Captain Bristow?" grunted Sebastian, thoroughly annoyed by Cullen's outrageous suggestion. "I can accept an overgrown wolf or mountain cat, even a rogue bear, but a collaboration of all three animals? Preposterous!"

"Impossible, really!" added Garrick, shaking his head vigorously as he attempted to stifle his laughter.

"Aah, but think on it, Your Highness. Such a thing is possible," insisted Cullen, turning to Sebastian to solicit his agreement. "You breed a female horse to a male donkey and the end result is a mule."

"Or an *ass*," grumbled Carstian, speaking under his breath as he rolled his eyes in disbelief at Cullen.

"I will give you that, Captain. However, a horse and a donkey are quite similar creatures; a cat, a bear and a wolf are not," contested the King. "All three are very different animals."

"Well, anything can potentially happen," insisted Cullen, unwilling to back down from his claim. "I figure if it is possible for an Elf to breed with a mortal to produce that halfling warrior woman Prince Arerys has taken as his wife, the possibilities are endless!"

"You are obviously not a man of science," sighed Sebastian, unwilling to entertain Cullen's cockamamie conclusions.

"I will be the first to admit I am not academically inclined as your wise and scholarly sons are, Your Highness," responded Cullen, unashamed to verbalize this declaration. "My expertise is in the battle-field. My skills rest with the longbow and my sword."

"It is a good thing then, for now, it will be wise to continue honing your skills, Captain," advised Sebastian. "There is a chance you will be called upon to hunt down this beast."

"You do not intend to do anything about it?" gasped Cullen, frowning in curiosity at the King's seeming indifference. "You will allow that beast to continue its rampage, venturing closer to our borders?"

"There is no reason to do anything," answered Sebastian. "With all due respect to those in Talibarr, until they come forth with a formal request asking for me to intervene, we have no business barging into their territory."

"Those people know nothing of respect," grunted Cullen. "I say, intervene for their own good!"

"Captain Bristow, I have no intention of jeopardizing the current state of affairs between our two nations. The peace accord we have in place will only hold true if the Talibarrians come to understand we will not impose our will or demands upon them. That being the case, we will not interfere unless we hear from a representative of Talibarr to do so."

"But we did," insisted Cullen. "That is how I received the latest news of this attack."

"*You* did?" gasped Garrick, stepping forward to confront him. "Why did you not say so?"

"I thought I did." Cullen tugged pensively on his beard as he contemplated this oversight.

"You rushed in with *news*. You said nothing about speaking to a representative of Talibarr," corrected Sebastian.

"By *news*, I meant to say it came from this representative," explained Cullen, his shoulders shrugging in response.

"And just where is this man now?" queried Sebastian.

"I sent him on his merry way."

"You did *what*?" asked Carstian, staring in disbelief. "That was for my father to decide, not you."

"I merely spared you all the time and grief of dealing with that ruffian of a man by questioning him on your behalf. There was no need to allow his kind into the castle for an audience with the King."

"And exactly what is his *kind*?" questioned Sebastian, slumping in his throne as he listened to Cullen defend his actions.

"Talibarrians tend to fall into the category of rogue, scoundrel, thief, murderer, miscreant, or ne'er-do-well. You are welcome to choose, but by the ill-favoured look on his face, this man, in all likelihood, was a thief, if not a murderer. I will tell you now, he looked as unscrupulous as they come."

"And you would know *unscrupulous*, Captain," retorted Carstian, shaking his head in dismay.

"After your first-hand experience with these people, you know how untrustworthy they truly are, my lord," warned Cullen, stunned that Carstian was not in complete agreement with him.

"You cannot make such a sweeping statement about an entire nation of people," denounced Carstian. "True, some sought to take advantage of my situation to better theirs. Contrary to what you believe, they were not all motivated by avarice, nor are all Talibarrians bent on revenge."

"Granted the Talibarrian woman and her daughter did remain true to their promise to you, delivering word to your family of your incarceration and whereabouts, you must admit; Marda was rewarded for this deed. It was not as if she did not stand to gain something in doing so."

"Marda Dreysoon asked for nothing more than to seek sanctuary in Darross; to be away from those wishing to do her harm so she may grant her daughter, Freya a better life," argued Carstian. "It was my father who decided to give her this opportunity to work in our castle. Think of it as a gesture of goodwill so all will see that those who are law-abiding, whatever their nationality or belief, have an equal opportunity to prosper in our fair country."

"Lucky for her that your father was feeling so generous, my lord," sniffed Cullen, nodding his head in feigned approval.

"Well, what little Marda gained was done so at great risk to her life to deliver much needed news to my family," countered Carstian.

"It was a gamble she was willing to take, and in doing so, she reaped the rewards of this undertaking," stated Cullen, unwilling to change his mind or attitude toward the people of Talibarr.

"Really, Captain Bristow, you must learn to be more compassionate to those less fortunate," insisted Sebastian.

"Is that an order?"

"Where you are concerned; yes! It is. Now, where is this man from Talibarr?"

"I shooed him away," explained Cullen. "Once I extracted the pertinent information from him, I told him to be off. Unfortunately, he was rather persistent, insisting on an audience with you, Your Highness. Undoubtedly, he loiters about the courtyard waiting for word."

"Good gracious, send the man in!" demanded Sebastian. "Do not leave the representative of his people standing out there like an unwelcome guest."

"Are you positive, Your Highness?" queried Cullen, cringing under Sebastian's scathing tone.

"Of course, I am! Now deliver this man to me."

"Allow me, father," offered Carstian, rushing past Cullen. "There is no point in offending this man twice over."

"Well, then… I suppose there is no need for me to be present if you are intent on listening to the old codger drivel on," decided Cullen, bowing as he turned away from the King. "It is old news to me, after all."

"Remain right where you stand, Captain," ordered Sebastian, as he rang the bell to summon a servant.

Cullen turned about to face the throne as Marda rushed in.

"What is your wish, Your Highness?" asked Marda, bowing

respectfully as she entered the room.

"I am expecting a guest. I have no doubt he will be thirsty and hungry after his long journey. Deliver food and drink to the throne room immediately."

"Yes, Your Highness." Marda curtsied politely as she backed away to fulfill the King's request.

As she departed under Cullen's condescending stare, Sebastian addressed him once more, "Though undoubtedly your intentions were honest, Captain Bristow, in the future, I insist that you refrain from taking it upon yourself to decide whom I shall, or shall not, grant an audience to. As conscientious as you attempt to be in your quest to prevent those of dubious character from entering my inner sanctum, please allow me to have the final word. Is that understood?"

"Yes, my liege." Cullen's head bowed in obedience.

Carstian returned, and just as Cullen suspected, as a fly hovers over horse dung even after numerous attempts to shoo it away, this Talibarrian had remained in the courtyard even after he was dismissed. He followed behind the Prince, tattered hat in hand as he humbled himself before the King of Darross.

"Up on your feet, my good man. What is your name and who sent you?"

"My name's Taegus Arpoth, Yer Highness. I'm the leader of a village jus' south of Spirit Wood near the Plains of Fire. I was sent by the governin' council of Talibarr."

"You were not sent by the people of your village?" questioned Garrick.

"They're all dead, save fer the men that were with me when our village was attacked!" responded Taegus. "There's not a single survivor – all killed by the beast. The council was thinkin' I was the most likely representative in respect ta this treachery."

"And how is it that all in your village died, but you?" queried Cullen, gazing at the Talibarrian with a notable degree of suspicion. "Perhaps *you* were the one who killed them?"

"*Me?* Kill all those people? Are ya mad?" snapped Taegus, sweeping his unkempt hair from his eyes as he glared at Cullen.

"Just answer my question, sir," demanded Cullen, pacing impatiently before him. "Were you responsible for these killings?"

"I was away with four of my men. We were doin' sum tradin' with a neighbourin' village. When we returned, ain't one person was found alive. They were all dead; sum ripped ta shreds, I tell ya!"

Sebastian motioned for Marda to enter as she appeared at the doorway. She discreetly wheeled the tray of food and hot tea into the throne room, delivering it to the famished man.

"Bless you, my dear woman!" exclaimed Taegus. His mouth watered at the sight and smell of the steaming hot biscuits smothered in warm, melted butter and sweet strawberry preserves. "Thank you fer this fine meal!"

"You are quite welcome, sir," responded Marda, nodding politely as she poured tea into a delicate, porcelain cup.

"Say... you're Talibarrian!"

"What difference does it make if I am, sir?" questioned Marda, not even making eye contact with Taegus as she served him this modest meal.

"I may be a simple man, but I ain't stupid. I can see through ya. You're dressed all fancy an' speakin' all proper, but you're still soundin' like yer country-folk," determined the stranger, noting her distinct accent that set her apart no matter how impeccable her speech. "So, the King's got ya here as a slave, eh?"

"Gracious, no! I will have you know I am duly employed. I am part of King Sebastian's staff." Marda took care to enunciate each word than to digress to her former speech pattern of using contracted words the Talibarrians were infamous for. "King Sebastian would never enslave our people."

The man scratched his head as he pondered Marda's claim. "I'm supposin' it could be true..."

"Whether I am Talibarrian, or not, if you cannot treat the King with the respect he is due, it is best that you leave than to be a sorry example of the people of Talibarr," hissed Marda, incensed by his insinuation.

"No need for concern, Marda," responded Sebastian, motioning her to calm down. "This man is here for good reason. He just needs to come to terms with the fact that all Darrossians are not as barbaric as he assumes."

"Meant no disrespect, Yer Highness," apologized the man, his head bowing down as he stuffed a biscuit into his hungry mouth.

"Get to the point, sir," urged Cullen. "What is the purpose of this visit to Darross Castle? What do you want from my King?"

Slurping loudly as he guzzled down the honey-sweetened tea he had filled to the rim with fresh cream, the man wiped his mouth with the back of his hand before answering, "With that blasted beast runnin' amok, the people of Talibarr can sure use yer people's help in killin' that creature before it kills again."

"So, you are in need of an organized hunting party; those with the expertise to conduct an expedition to chase down and capture such a quarry?" queried Sebastian.

"Capture the quarry? We need someone ta *kill* that beast!" declared Taegus, speaking in no uncertain terms.

"So, the creature must die," surmised Cullen.

"That's exactly what I'm sayin'," said the Talibarrian, barely looking up as he dragged the final morsel of biscuit around the plate to sop up the last of the creamy butter and sweet strawberry preserves so nothing would go to waste.

"Answer me this, Master Arpoth," requested Sebastian. "Just what manner of beast are we faced with?"

"Don't quite know fer sure, Yer Highness," responded Taegus, drinking directly from the creamer now that his tea was done. "Jus' from what we can tell, it looks ta be some kind of bear-dog."

"*Bare* as in a *naked* dog?" questioned Cullen, perplexed by this Talibarrian's strange words.

"No, I'm sayin' bear as in *b-r...*" Remembering he couldn't spell to save his life, the man rose up, tottering about like a bear walking on its hind-legs as he growled and slashed at the air. "Ya know? It's a bear that somehow got mixed up with a big dog or a wolf. Could even be a tad bit of mountain cat mixed in there somewhere by the way it takes ta the trees."

The Princes exchanged quizzical glances as Garrick whispered to Carstian, "This is too bizarre... Could this man and Bristow be in cahoots?"

"So, you are telling me that you do not know for certain what manner of beast this is?" determined Sebastian.

"I'm certain it ain't no ordinary animal."

"Well, lo and behold! I told you it was some kind of hybrid monster – an aberration of nature!" concluded Cullen. "This creature must be killed before it takes any more lives!"

"Tell me, Master Arpoth, you have not seen the beast with your own eyes. Is that correct?" asked Carstian.

"Yes, my lord. But it don't take a fool ta see it ain't no ordinary wolf or bear that can tear a grown man clean in half."

"And you are not exaggerating?" questioned Cullen, doubting this man's horrific claim.

"What's the point of doin' that? I don't gain anythin' by exaggeratin' to you good folks. I jus' want ya ta be aware of what you're gettin' yerselves inta, that's all," insisted Taegus, using the back of his hand to wipe the cream moustache from his stubbly, upper lip.

"Well, I think it would be foolish for us to assume it is some monstrosity of a *hybrid* creature," dismissed Sebastian. "Nonetheless, we cannot overlook the fact that it is no ordinary animal we are confronted with."

"So, does that mean you're willin' ta help my people, Yer Highness?" questioned Taegus. "Cause we're at our wit's end. We don't know who else ta turn to fer help."

"We would not be decent neighbours if we did not aid you and your fellow Talibarrians to be rid of this beast."

"I'm tellin' ya now, Yer Highness, we can sure use yer help. As skilled as we are at huntin', we ain't never encountered a beast like this one. Some say it's a ghost or a phantom that can't be killed!"

"Nonsense! How absolutely preposterous!" dismissed Cullen, waving off this warning. "If it is an animal of this world, it can be killed and made to leave this world, too."

"But what if it is not, Captain Bristow?" queried Carstian.

"My lord, I know you have yet to fully recover from the trauma of the ordeal you endured in Talibarr at Draven's hands, but now you are sounding as superstitious as those people," admonished Cullen. "You are the Prince of Darross, it is best that you act accordingly."

"And you are the captain of my army," reminded Sebastian. "As such, *you* shall act accordingly by investigating all the possibilities surrounding this strange creature and the circumstances of these horrific deaths."

"So, I am to take measures to ensure our people's safety once the beast crosses over into Darross?" assumed Cullen.

"No, you will take the necessary measures to kill that beast in Talibarr long before it comes anywhere near to the borders of our country," instructed Sebastian. "Capture that creature before it can take any more innocent lives."

"Now that's very noble of ya," praised Taegus, his head bowing in gratitude as he polished off his empty plate, his fingertip chasing the last few crumbs of biscuit. "My people will be forever grateful ta ya."

"It is kind of you to say, however, I believe in helping those who are willing to help themselves. While I rally my men to engage in this hunt, I shall offer up a grand bounty to any man able to kill the beast," promised Sebastian.

"A bounty, ya say?" Taegus' eyes glazed over with the prospects of great financial compensation for this risky undertaking.

"A sizeable bounty," assured Sebastian. "As you return to Talibarr, spread the word to your people."

"Ooh… Now I'm thinkin' that I can easily inspire sum of my countrymen ta rally together fer this cause," responded Taegus, with a thoughtful nod.

"Ah, monetary incentive to encourage the Talibarrians to take the initiative to fend for themselves," assessed Cullen.

With the longstanding belief that the Talibarrians were inherently lazy, the young Captain could only interpret this spark of hope to rise above a life of poverty as nothing more than the embers of greed igniting in this man's eyes.

"You are mistaken, Captain," countered Garrick. "My father is attempting to encourage these people to be resourceful, to rely on their skills and to devise their own strategy so they may have the opportunity to be rewarded for their hard work and to be acknowledged for their efforts."

"I take it then, we will not be needed to venture into Talibarr to partake in the hunt or to orchestrate it?" questioned Cullen.

"Oh, indeed we shall be travelling to the north, Captain Bristow," promised Sebastian. "If the Talibarrians are unable to capture this beast, they will have the backing of my forces to aid them. If they are fortunate enough to kill the beast without our assistance, all the better for them, I say. Whatever the case, I am most curious as to the manner of beast on the loose. I wish to dispel with the rumours, to see for myself exactly what this creature is. Perhaps, it is a great and rare creature whose head will be worthy of mounting on the wall of this very room!"

"Well, now! That's soundin' like a fair offer, Yer Highness." Taegus bowed deeply as he prepared to take his leave. "The beast's head fer a kingly bounty, that's soundin' more than fair! I'll make sure those in council hear of yer grand offer."

"You best be on your way, Master Arpoth," ordered Sebastian. "As I rally my men and prepare for this trek to Talibarr, take advantage of this time. It shall give your people a head start by a good day or two in capturing the beast."

"You're a generous man, Yer Highness, ain't no doubtin' that! Maybe I'll be the one ta claim that bounty from ya."

"Perhaps luck will be with you, sir," nodded Sebastian. "If you are fortunate enough to capture the creature first, then you will indeed be the one to claim the reward."

"Carstian and I will escort Master Arpoth out," offered Garrick. He was quick to intervene before Cullen could step in, offering to toss the Talibarrian from the castle keep in a bid to hasten his departure.

"Very well, Garrick. See to it, and make sure this gentleman has some food and drink for his journey home," ordered Sebastian.

"Thank you, Yer Highness!" Taegus bowed enthusiastically as he left the room. "You're most generous indeed!"

"Be careful, Master Arpoth. Have a safe journey," bade Sebastian, as he turned his attention to Cullen. "Now, Captain Bristow, summon my best huntsmen and their hounds. Rally a good dozen of your best men for this little adventure. Have them ready to depart at first light the day after tomorrow."

"As you wish, my liege," responded Cullen, bowing to the King as he departed the throne room. "That will be more than sufficient time to ready a hunting party."

Watching as the brothers escorted the Talibarrian through the main hall, Cullen grunted his acknowledgement to the royal guards posted at the entrance of the throne room. He suddenly darted around the corner, his hand coming up to conceal Marda's mouth as she gasped in surprise.

"So what do we have here?" Cullen whispered into her ears. "And do not tell me you were dusting the stands of armour."

Marda's nerves bristled with anger upon hearing these scathing words and accusing tone.

"Spying on us, were you?" grunted Cullen, leaning closer to breathe in the perfume clinging to her long, dark tresses.

"*Spying?* I saw nothing, Captain Bristow," protested Marda, prying his hand from her mouth as she recoiled from his handsome, but intrusive face coming in close to hers.

"Even if that were so, I am certain your Talibarrian ears heard plenty," countered Cullen, his hands coming up against the wall on either side of Marda's head to trap her.

"I assure you, I heard no more than you did."

"But I was privy to that conversation with King Sebastian and those in his company. You were not. Now, I ask again; what business do you have skulking about, listening to our meeting with this man from Talibarr?"

"If you must know, it has been long since I have heard news from that country. I was just hoping to hear news of happenings from…"

Her voice trailed off as she thought on her past.

"Home," concluded Cullen, as he nodded in understanding. "I see. Once a Talibarrian, always a Talibarrian. Though the good Queen was quick to groom you for this role and graciously educated you so you can function proficiently within the castle, you still long for *home.*"

"You misunderstand, Captain Bristow. Talibarr is no longer my home. *This* is my home," insisted Marda, staring into Cullen's hazel eyes.

"Well, sneaking about like this will see you ejected from *this home* faster than you can say Talibarr."

"Are you threatening me?"

"No. Consider it a warning. There is only one person permitted to sneak about this castle, sticking his nose into the affairs of others."

"King Sebastian?"

"No! That person would be *me*. It is my business to know what is going on within these walls. It allows me to be in a better position to protect the royal family," snapped Cullen, annoyed by her impudence.

"I see."

"So tell me, how is it that Taegus Arpoth recognized you?" queried Cullen, refusing to allow Marda to resume her business as he continued with his inquisition. "How does this man know you?"

"I hate to disappoint you, but he does not know me," countered Marda, scowling with annoyance. "That fellow only recognized my accent as being Talibarrian, nothing more."

"Well, he certainly seemed pleased to see one of his own."

"After his encounter with you, can you blame him?"

"I am confident he can be blamed for something," decided Cullen. "Just what it is, is yet to be determined."

"You are much too suspicious for your own good. That is all it was, the comfort of familiarity in a strange place."

"I suppose that is plausible."

"Even if that man recognized *me*, I certainly didn't recognize *him*," snipped Marda.

"*Did not.*"

"What?" asked Marda.

"The proper words are, you *did not recognize him*," corrected Cullen, noticing how she squirmed with discomfort at his close proximity as he took certain pleasure in the power he had over her.

"That was what I meant to say, Captain Bristow. I *did not* recognize that man though he was from Talibarr."

"Provided that I decide to believe your words to be true; based on what you have heard, what do you make of this creature terrorizing those to the north?"

"Truth be told, Captain, I find that man's words of these events and the possible existence of this creature to be very disturbing and rather astounding."

"Astounding as in… you do not believe him?"

"I do believe he was sincere in his claim and in what he believes to be the honest truth."

"But…" probed Cullen, eager to learn more.

"But Master Arpoth's description of this beast is what I find rather remarkable."

"And just what do you think it is?" queried Cullen.

"Do you want my honest opinion?"

"If it is possible from a Talibarrian, an honest opinion from you would be appreciated."

"Are you saying I am a liar?"

"You are not a true citizen of Darross. You are Talibarrian. Honesty and integrity are not exactly the traits your people are known for," answered Cullen, in his own defense.

"And you claim to be a knight, yet chivalry and honour are as foreign to you," hissed Marda, glaring with obvious contempt.

"How would you know? You have yet the pleasure of knowing me on a more intimate level, to know how chivalrous I truly am."

"You have a reputation, Captain Bristow. I hear what the women say about you."

"Do tell! Just what are the ladies saying about me?"

"Plenty! And if there is a single grain of truth to it, it would serve you well to be concerned, Captain."

"Ha! I hardly think so," scoffed Cullen. "They have only words of high praise for a knight of my standing."

"It is obvious to me that you have overheard them speaking of another, for where you are concerned, I would have to say the most notable, oft-said comments centered around your lack of moral scruples."

"Oh, that is absolute balderdash!" dismissed Cullen. "You are ill-advised to listen to the idle gossip of these women, particularly the ones who believe they had been scorned."

"Scorned?"

"Indeed! These ladies have had a fleeting taste of my manly attributes and are now made to suffer; deprived of my affections once I set my sights on fresher fare. They bicker and squabble for my attention. They will even smear my good name and character to dissuade other young lovelies from falling for my charms. It is nothing more than a campaign to lessen the competition, if you get my meaning?"

"No, I do not, Captain Bristow. I am inclined to lean toward caution. The warnings I have heard pertaining to you is reason enough to question your morals and ethics."

"Well, enough about me. We digress," responded Cullen, wishing to change the subject. "I was asking about what you believe that creature in question to be. What conclusions have you drawn?"

"As I was saying, that man's description of the beast was rather far-fetched, however, I did sense his desperation and sincerity. What concerns me is if his words are true, this is no ordinary animal he was speaking of."

"So you agree with me?"

"Agree with what?"

"That the rampaging creature is some kind of deviant, hybrid beastie. It is an abomination of nature that must be done away with."

"I never said I agreed with you," corrected Marda. "All I am saying is this animal, at least its abilities and behaviour, certainly does not make it natural."

"Are you trying to say dark magic is at work here to conjure up such a horrific creature?"

"As strange as it sounds, there are some in Talibarr who cling to the old ways. They still believe in controlling the forces of nature and work to harness the powers of the forbidden arts," revealed Marda, speaking in a whisper.

"You are speaking of witches!"

"Indeed," confirmed Marda.

"They still exist?" Cullen frowned in doubt.

"When did they ever stop existing? Look at it this way, Captain Bristow, until five months ago the whole world believed that Fairies no longer existed in this realm. And yet, lo and behold, you were the one to first come across that infamous Fairy named Bug – the one who jeopardized your quest to rescue Prince Carstian from Draven Eldard."

"Fair enough, but you expect me to believe this monstrosity was conjured up by a coven of witches?"

"You asked what I thought it might be. I answered. You are entitled to believe whatever you want, Captain."

"Well, in my opinion, and you are more than entitled to accept it, that creature is nothing more than a manifestation of nature gone terribly awry."

"Terribly awry thanks to the powers of the witches to the north," interjected Marda.

"You Talibarrians are so bloody superstitious and simple-minded to believe such things are still possible! If you are attempting to unnerve me with tales of dark magic, it is not working."

"No, I am not attempting to do that. Just consider it a warning," snipped Marda, her dark eyes smoldering with resentment. "You do not know what dangers still lurk far to the north, Captain Bristow."

"Please, dispense with formality. Just call me Captain," invited Cullen, laughing lightly as he whispered, "And the only magic at work here is between you and me, my lovely."

As his body brushed up against hers, Marda lashed out, slapping Cullen across his startled face.

"You, sir, are a cad - a lecherous cad!" She ducked beneath the arms meant to trap her in an embrace, dashing away from his unwanted attention.

"But I am ever-so charming!" Cullen called after her in his own defense as Marda stormed off.

"Hmph!" grunted Cullen, rubbing the prickling heat of this unexpected assault from his reddened cheek. "She may be Talibarrian, but she still behaves like a typical woman."

As she disappeared down the corridor, Cullen turned, jumping with a start as he came face-to-face with Prince Carstian.

"Do you make it a habit of harassing the domestic staff, particularly those of the feminine persuasion?" questioned the Prince, a look of condemnation etched clearly on his face.

"It is not as it appears, my lord," explained Cullen, his face flushed with embarrassment.

"Then please, Captain, explain your actions and what had just transpired."

"I make it my business to know the business of others, my lord; the comings and goings of those in your father's service. The mere fact that woman is Talibarrian leaves me to question everything she says and does."

"How can you say that?" snapped Carstian, thoroughly annoyed by this man's prejudicial feelings. "When she ventured into Darross on my behest, though revenge was in her heart for all those who had wronged her, she did not seek my parents out for personal gains."

"And yet, look how much she had gained in doing so," reminded Cullen, his skeptical eyes glancing about the grand surroundings of Darross Castle.

"She asked for no money, no restitution whatsoever. The only thing that woman asked for was permission that she and her daughter be allowed to live in Darross without the constant fear of threat for once in their lives. That was her one and only request. It was my father who insisted she stay on and be gainfully employed here."

"Well, your father is a generous man, however, I am afraid there are times King Sebastian's heart is too soft for his own good."

"And yours is not soft enough, Captain Bristow. Where is your sense of compassion for those less fortunate?"

"It is reserved for those deserving of it," replied Cullen.

"Well, I tend to agree with my father. Ironically, Marda feels privileged to be in our service, and yet, I am the one truly indebted to her."

"Given that she and her child had found sanctuary in Darross Castle, your debt to her had been repaid many times over, my lord. Just do not lose sight of this woman's background and her true nature. She is Talibarrian and you know she cannot be truly trusted."

"And I know *you*, Captain Bristow. I believe your interest and disdain for her are rooted in the fact that Marda Dreysoon is Talibarrian, and a very attractive one at that. Plus, she is wise to your ways where the ladies are concerned."

"I admit she is strangely fetching… comely even for a northerner, but I am a professional," stated Cullen, holding his head up high. "I mean to uncover unscrupulous characters wherever they lurk. To do so, one must sometimes force oneself to endure the unsavoury task of getting to know the subject in question on an intimate level to understand their true nature and motives."

"I will personally vouch for Marda's good character, for she is above reproach. And if you cannot deal with her with a degree of compassion, then I strongly recommend you learn to treat her with utmost respect," demanded Carstian.

"As you wish, my lord," Cullen replied with a bow of his head.

"I *do* wish, Captain. In fact, consider it an order. And I suggest you turn your attentions to other more questionable characters skulking about these halls than to focus your efforts on entrapping an innocent."

"There are other questionable characters lurking about?"

"Yes, you best ferret them out, Captain, but do so on your own time," advised Carstian. "Your first duty is to prepare for this trek to Talibarr."

"King Sebastian is quite intent on participating in this hunt," noted Cullen. "I anticipate that you and Prince Garrick will be joining us?"

"My brother will. As for me, I have had quite enough adventure in that country to last me for a good, long while - if not for a lifetime."

"But I assure you, you will be quite safe by my side," promised Cullen, his hand patting the hilt of his grand, ornate sword that hung conspicuously from his baldric.

"You said that the last time," responded Carstian, glancing down at his maimed hand. "Besides, someone must remain here in the castle. My mother does not wish to be left on her own anymore."

the killing spree

"It is a terrible thing the blessings of an early spring are now tainted by the arrival of that murderous beast," noted Sebastian, dismounting from his steed as his men made ready to establish a temporary camp in the shadows of the Aranak Mountains.

"Terrible indeed," responded Cullen, nodding in agreement. "And yet, it is somehow befitting that such a creature should be unleashed in these northern lands than in our fair country."

"Your insensitivity astounds me, Captain. You make it sound as though these poor people deserve to be under attack," commented Garrick, scowling with disapproval.

"Your assessment of my words sound rather harsh, my lord," stated Cullen, surprised by Garrick's irate tone. "I mean to say, no one deserves to live under such threat and fear. However, when all is said and done, better them than us, I say."

Garrick heaved a weary sigh, for no matter how Cullen wished to rephrase his sentence; ultimately, it would still mean the same thing. There was no love lost between Cullen and those he held responsible for his father's death when their two countries were at war, even after all these years.

"Then it is a good thing you are a son of Darross, Captain Bristow," responded Garrick, handing his horse's reins over to his squire. He watched as his father wandered over to where one of the hunters pounded stakes into the ground upon which the hounds would be tethered to until called upon to scent out their quarry.

"Oh, yes," Cullen agreed wholeheartedly. "Heaven forbid had I been cursed with the misfortune of being born in this god-forsaken country. I would sooner poke out my eyes with a burning stick than to be subjected to life as one of these barbarians."

"Your compassion overwhelms me," grunted Garrick, surveying the lands that were to play host to this unusual hunt. "For your sake, I shall remember to think twice before ever considering to wed a Talibarrian woman."

"Come now, my lord, you are the heir apparent to the throne of Darross," reminded Cullen, cringing at the mere thought of such a union. "You have impeccable taste and a predilection for cultured women of refined breeding. The only women you will find in Talibarr are loathsome and homely, not to mention uneducated and uncivilized."

"You seem so sure," snorted Garrick, annoyed by Cullen's sweeping generalization that he obviously held to heart.

"Of course, I am sure, my lord. I am quite positive. It is a well known fact the females of this country are rather brutish, smaller versions of the men, save for obvious physical differences."

"Then how do you account for Marda Dreysoon and her charming little daughter?" queried Garrick. "Unless my eyes deceive me, Marda is quite beautiful."

"True, that woman can easily be mistaken for a fine Darrossian lady, but Marda is an anomaly; a rare and beautiful flower amongst a field of horrid weeds," explained Cullen. "Being the exception, overall, the vast majority of Talibarrian women are left wanting in the way of looks, charm and social graces. I swear, if these women grew facial hair, and some do, they can easily pass for men-folk."

"You are exaggerating, Captain Bristow," scoffed Garrick. He laughed lightly. Unwilling to believe Cullen's unwavering animosity toward these people, he dismissed the Captain's discriminatory words.

"This is no exaggeration, my lord. In fact, I can prove this to be so, if you desire."

"Perhaps I am the one who should prove you wrong," offered the Prince. "What say you if I should chance upon a Talibarrian woman I wish to take as my bride?"

"You jest!" snorted Cullen. "Perish the thought! A Talibarrian as the future Queen of Darross? I think not!"

"When you consider the social and political implications, Captain, this act can prove to be beneficial for both our countries. It would certainly guarantee an end to the tensions between the nations."

"Now you are scaring me, my lord," gasped Cullen, grimacing at the very notion. "There are better pairings *and* better nations to be paired with!"

"That may be so, Captain Bristow, but the relationships we share with the other nations of Imago are not strained, not as it is with Talibarr."

"If you think it is a prudent move, then I suppose I should applaud the lengths you are willing to go to for the sake of diplomacy, my lord."

"You must not forget, Captain, the power of the crown comes with a duty to the country."

"Just be advised, my lord, if you decide to allow this *duty* to preside over good sense and personal taste, you should at least bed a Talibarrian woman first so you will know exactly what you will be condemning yourself to for your remaining days."

"This is your advice to me? To bed the woman first?" questioned Garrick.

"No, *this* is my advice to you should you decide to bed one of those hags. When the shadow of night is not enough to diminish the true level of her homeliness, a sack over her head will help. However, just keep in mind should you decide to wed, you cannot ask the woman to wear this sack in public. The crown will not sit right on her slovenly head, so at the very least, do your best not to select the ugliest runt of the litter."

"Sage advice from one who had undoubtedly found a need to *sack* a woman or two in his many conquests," sighed Garrick, dismally shaking his head as he digested these troubling words hatched by a mind that was just as troubled when it came to matters concerning members of the opposite sex.

"Contrary to popular belief, for a member of the royal family, you do have a fine sense of humour, my lord," noted Cullen, with a congenial grin. "However, you best heed this sound advice for the women-folk of this country are homely at best and unabashedly ugly at their worst."

"Are you aware that you are prone to great exaggeration, Captain?" queried Garrick, staring with raised eyebrows at Cullen.

"I protest! I am merely stating the obvious. Talibarrians in general are not an attractive race of human beings, if they can even be regarded as such."

"Come now, could it be that you measure these aesthetic qualities against your own *perfection*?"

"Against me, it would be an unfair comparison," confided Cullen, speaking with all seriousness. "I am referring to the average citizen south of these mountains."

"That is very generous of you."

"It is more generous than the Talibarrians deserve," sniffed Cullen, gazing over to the edge of the clearing as the hounds barked, howling to warn of an impending intruder.

"I prefer to keep an open mind, Captain. Besides, if all the women are as ugly as you claim, the Talibarrian men would be just as inclined as you are to steer clear of these *ladies*. For this reason, I shall consider your harsh criticism of these people with a rather large grain of salt."

Staring through the trees, Cullen spotted the object of the hounds' agitation. It was a local denizen wandering through the forest and heading in their general direction.

"You doubt my words now, my lord, but here is a friendly wager. Just what do you assess *that* to be?" questioned Cullen, as he pointed at the person approaching the clearing. "Is that individual a man or a woman?"

Garrick's eyes squinted as he stared at the bedraggled human weaving through the stand of trees to meet his party.

From where the Prince stood, a positive identification was impossible. The clothes, ragged trousers topped by a dirty, long-sleeved shirt and a torn cape tossed loosely over the shoulders gave no clue as to this person's true form. To complicate the whole matter, from this distance, Garrick could swear the bushy, unkempt eyebrows knitted together to form a single brow each time this person frowned. This lush growth and the straggly, matted head of hair were as nondescript as this individual's bland facial features.

"Well, go on, my lord. Is it a very *ugly woman* or a rather *unhandsome man*?" asked Cullen, a smug smile curling his lips as he watched Garrick struggle to come to some kind of conclusion.

Where manner of attire and outright physical appearances failed, Garrick relied on body language. He thought that surely the manner of walk would ascertain the gender of this individual. Unfortunately, for Garrick *and* the person in question, the gait, this heavy, plodding stride hampered by the weight of a hefty pack did not allow for the graceful sway of the hips. There was not even a hint of feminine movement as this person trudged along.

Just as Garrick was about to declare this person to be a man, a high-pitched voice, at least high by manly standards, chirped out a friendly greeting, "G'day, kind folks of Darross!"

Garrick frowned in confusion, reconsidering his tentative answer.

"Quickly, Prince Garrick, decide now," urged Cullen, delighting in the dilemma facing his royal charge as he whispered discreetly, "are those pathetic mounds concealed beneath that shabby attire a sorry excuse for female bosoms or are they nothing more than flabby man-breasts?"

"*He* is a *man*," whispered Garrick to Cullen, confident of his decision as he called out in greeting, "And a good day to you, too, sir!"

The Talibarrian stopped, lowering the pack before glancing about with great curiosity upon hearing this greeting.

"Are ya speakin' ta me, m'lord?"

"Of course. Why do you ask?" Garrick was suddenly mortified. Perhaps he was wrong?

"Jus' thought I heard ya callin' me a *sir*," responded the unkempt woman.

"Oh, you misunderstand me!" replied Garrick, most apologetically. "I said, a good day to you, for *sure* – not *sir*."

"No worries," the woman responded with an affable smile comprised of yellow, crooked teeth that seemed too large for her mouth. "It ain't nothin' more than that strange accent you folks from the south speak with."

"How right you are," nodded Garrick, embarrassed by his call as he turned away to join his father.

"See… Told you," teased Cullen, speaking in a whisper as he suppressed the urge to laugh. "Ugly woman – ugly *Talibarrian* woman."

"By the way," called the stranger, sitting down to take a breather, "my husband sent me ahead while he an' the men-folk took down our camp. He an' his comrades will be comin' ta claim the bounty."

"They caught the killer beast?" questioned Garrick, stunned by this unexpected news.

"Caught it? They gone an' killed the bloody creature!" declared the woman, rummaging through her pack for a pipe. "Jus' give it time, they're on their way as we speak an' they'll be bringin' the carcass with 'em!"

"Begging your pardon, Your Highness," called Cullen, his head appearing from behind the tent flap. "I have some news."

"What is it, Captain Bristow?" responded Sebastian, peering up from the map he was studying to determine the most logical course to travel should they be made to engage in the hunt.

"A man has arrived with his cronies. They bring a dead animal."

"Is it *the* beast?" questioned Sebastian, rolling up the large parchment outlining the sprawling lands of Talibarr.

"It is a beast, but whether it is the one that had been rampaging about killings people, that is yet to be determined," answered Cullen, motioning for the Prince and King to follow him.

"Yer Highness!" called the man, eagerly dashing forward to greet Sebastian. "We heard of yer grand offer of a bounty fer the head of the creature causin' all the killings."

"That is correct. Step forward. Let me see this animal of yours."

With a wave of his hand, the man motioned his two comrades to deliver their catch. Mounted on a long pole, the opposite ends resting on their shoulders, a dead mountain cat with its front and hind feet bound together hung from this carrier. The men grunted, struggling as they hoisted the weight off their shoulders onto the ground as the hounds bayed, excited by the scent of fresh blood.

"Here ya go, Yer Highness," offered the man. He and his hunting companions bowed respectfully as they made their presentation. "The beast is dead an' we're ready ta claim that generous reward, if ya don't mind."

"What makes you say this is the creature responsible for the killings?" questioned Sebastian, inspecting the bloodied carcass.

"Meanin' no disrespect, Yer Highness, but look at the size of this animal. It's gotta be the biggest mountain cat to ever roam this region! Look at these paws. Jus' take a gander at these huge claws. They were definitely made fer killin'!"

The man squeezed the toe pads of one of the front paws. Retractable claws, each neatly curved and terminating with a deadly sharp point sprang out from its protective sheathe to reveal its true danger.

Picking the pole up by one end, Cullen lifted it up to determine the dead animal's bulk. "I would say this cat weighs a good ten stone, if not more."

Scrutinizing the carcass, from the tip of its nose down the length of its long, sinewy body to the end of its thick, long tail, Garrick estimated the creature's length. Measuring well over eight feet long, it was certainly the largest specimen he had ever seen.

"Granted these are mighty big claws and this mountain cat is exceedingly large for its species, it still does not mean it is the *monster* everyone has been ranting about," stated Cullen, still skeptical of this man's claim.

"I'll tell ya now, Cap'n, it's the beast all right!" insisted the man, his friends' vigorously nodding their heads in confirmation. "We caught the critter red-handed – in the middle of killin'!"

"This cat was seen killing a human?" questioned Sebastian, his gloved hand pulling up on the animal's upper lip to examine the teeth. His eyes were greeted by imposing fangs measuring over an inch long. Set between these long fangs and the molars positioned far to the back of the mouth, the carnassial teeth, flattened molars designed specifically for shearing flesh and administering the killing bite revealed the true potential for a deadly encounter with such an animal.

"Well… actually, it killed my friend's hound that had treed it," the man admitted sheepishly; "but we could tell it was intendin' on killin' us next!"

"You dolt!" admonished Cullen, kicking at the carcass in anger. "Even I would have killed your damned mutt if it had treed me. This cat was behaving as any animal would, if cornered."

"Alrighty then! How do you account fer the way it moved?" argued the Talibarrian. "Cause there weren't anything natural 'bout it."

"What do you mean, sir?" asked Garrick.

"This cat leaped clear 'cross a gully that spanned from here ta there!" explained the leader of this hunting expedition. Unable to incorporate the formal method of measurement, the Talibarrian's grubby finger pointed from where he stood over to the entrance of the King's tent, a good fifteen feet away. "Plus, I swear, it jumped straight up a rock face ta land on top of it. It had ta be as high as three men of my height standin' one atop the other."

"For pity's sake, look at this creature's hind legs," ordered Cullen, the toe of his boot impatiently poking the cat's haunches. The powerful muscles enhanced by the springy design of strong bones augmented by tough, resilient tendons and ligaments permitted not only for rapid forward movement, but allowed this animal to leap great heights and distances with relative ease. "Of course it can handle large spans and jump great heights! That was what this animal was designed to do."

"So ya think you were clever 'nough ta explain that away, Cap'n. Well, how 'bout this?" offered the Talibarrian. "This killer cat was near impossible ta track! It moved about like a ghost. First it was in front of us, an' then it was behind us."

"Half the times we didn't know where it was comin' from," interjected one of his comrades.

"Yeah… This creature moved about in silence. It crept about like a – like a…" the leader of the trio struggled for an appropriate comparison.

"A *cat*?" offered Cullen, his tone smug.

"Exactly!" the three men chirped in unison as they nodded in agreement.

"That is because it *is* a cat, albeit a very large one!" snapped Cullen, thoroughly annoyed by their ignorance.

"Well, it don't change the fact that this is the beast responsible fer the killin' spree," argued the Talibarrian; adamant that he and his hunting colleagues collect the bounty.

"There is only one way to ascertain if this mountain cat is indeed responsible for all the killings," said Sebastian.

"What are you suggesting, my liege?" asked Cullen.

"Cut this animal open. Gut it to see if there are human remains in its stomach, Captain Bristow."

"*Me?*" groaned Cullen, his face grimacing in revulsion. "I would willingly oblige you, my King, however the blade of my sword is not meant to be soiled in this manner."

Sebastian rolled his eyes in frustration as Cullen's hand lovingly fondled the hilt of his new sword. It was a special weapon he had commissioned; a sword forged and presented to Cullen in appreciation for his efforts in aiding in the rescue of Prince Carstian when he was taken hostage. Though this weapon was meant more for ceremony, this Captain chose to wear this sword wherever he went, proudly displaying it for all to admire.

"If it means collectin' the bounty, I'll do it," offered the Talibarrian, eagerly taking up his hunting knife.

"By all means," invited Cullen, stepping aside to make room. "Go to it, my good man!"

Cutting the rope that bound the dead animal to the post, the leader ordered his two comrades to hold the cat steady by its paws as his dull, rusted knife sawed through hair, skin and flesh to delve into its belly. He jumped away as the expanding gases trapped within this cavity suddenly forced the entrails to spill out before him as a stomach-churning stench tainted the air.

The Talibarrian immediately pressed his nose and mouth into the crook of his elbow as he gagged from the stink.

"Well? What do you see?" questioned Cullen, talking through the fabric of his cloak he used to filter out the foul air.

"Jus' give me a moment, Cap'n," grunted the Talibarrian, annoyed by Cullen's impatience. "No point in rushin' me. Ain't as if this cat's gonna up an' walk away on us."

"Just get to it," urged Cullen. "King Sebastian is a busy man. He does not have all day."

"Gotta find the stomach in all this mess first." The man rolled up his sleeves for the next step of this gruesome task. "If you're in such a hurry though, you're welcome ta join me, Cap'n."

"That is quite fine," declined Cullen, taking a step back. "It is better that I supervise this little operation."

"Suit yerself," grunted the man, reaching into the abdominal cavity. With the squelching sounds of internal organs pushed about by his bare hands, the Talibarrian grumbled as he haphazardly tossed the liver at Cullen's feet. "Nope, that ain't no stomach."

"Be careful!" scolded Cullen, his face contorting in disgust as he stared at the bloody mess. "I just had these boots cleaned."

"Sorry 'bout that, Cap'n."

"I just bet you are."

"Here we go!" announced the Talibarrian.

Yanking at the membrane and tissues anchoring this organ into place, he pulled. A wet, tearing sound was followed by a squishy sound as another internal organ plopped unceremoniously at Cullen's feet.

"Oops! Those things can't be the stomach," decided the man. "There's two of 'em!"

"I do believe those would be the kidneys," determined Garrick, frowning in disgust at the growing mess.

"Found it!" declared the Talibarrian, taking a moment to blot the beads of sweat from his forehead.

"And none too soon," grumbled Cullen.

"I jus' have ta cut it open an' then we'll see what goodies are lurkin' inside these guts."

Piercing the stomach lining, the unpleasant sound much like gas passing from a flatulent goat, escaped this bloated organ.

"Hold on, I think I got somethin' here!" Fishing about, the man pulled on some partially digested flesh. "It looks ta be a baby..."

"A baby?" Sebastian and his son gasped in unison, bracing for this gruesome sight to be presented to them.

"Yep, a baby rabbit," concluded the Talibarrian, tossing aside the mangled mess of fur, bone and flesh. "But hold on... There's more."

Rummaging about, the man could feel that the only thing the mountain cat had eaten of late was this bunny. He leaned over, whispering to his comrade, "There ain't nothing else."

"Gotta be," his friend whispered back. "How are we gonna collect the bounty if there ain't nothin' else in there?"

"There's nothin' an' the King needs ta see somethin' *human*," the

Talibarrian whispered beneath his breath as he blindly groped about, pretending to continue his search for necessary proof.

"What're we gonna do?" whispered his friend, as he held open the flap of skin for the leader to continue his futile quest for evidence.

"How badly do ya want the bounty?"

"*Real* bad," answered his friend.

"Good. Then ya won't be minding this," said the leader, not even asking for permission. In one swift movement, he lopped off his friend's index finger.

The man yelped in pain. Falling backward, he immediately buried his maimed hand into his armpit, squeezing to staunch the flow of blood as their comrade, holding the cat steady by its front paws, frowned in momentary confusion over this sudden commotion.

"Here ya go!" announced the Talibarrian, proudly holding forth the bloodied finger for the King's inspection. "Human remains jus' like I promised."

"Do you take me for a fool?" Sebastian growled with indignation. "That finger was not inside the beast."

"Sure it was, Yer Highness," insisted the Talibarrian, using the dismembered digit to point at the stomach protruding from the dead animal. "How else would it have gotten in there?"

"You imbecile!" scolded Cullen, snatching the still-warm finger from the man's grasp. "*You* put this in there. In fact, this belongs to your friend."

Cullen threw it at the man favouring his wounded hand. Without a word, the fellow, obviously still in shock from this unexpected assault exacted by his comrade, picked up the dismembered finger. He placed it into his pocket for safekeeping.

"Are you callin' me a liar?" growled the Talibarrian, scowling in resentment at the Captain.

"Amongst a myriad of other things!" snapped Cullen, his patience at its end. "If you know what is good for you, you and your cronies will take this carcass and that *thing* claiming to be your wife and leave immediately! You have wasted enough of our time."

"Are ya sure 'bout this?" queried the man, looking hopefully to Sebastian.

"What do you not understand? I said leave!" demanded Cullen, angrily pointing the way.

The Talibarrian's shoulders drooped in dejection as he sulked, "We were so sure it was the killer beast. We spent all of last night huntin' it down. Now, all that work ended up bein' fer nothin'!"

"Serves you bloody right! Crooks and scoundrels, each and every one of you." denounced Cullen, waving a fist at them. "The three of you will get exactly what you are deserving of: Nothing!"

"Though it is not the beast we seek, I shall give you one gold piece," offered Sebastian, tossing a coin to the leader.

The man's eyes gleamed, lighting up as he and his comrades stared at the gold shining in the palm of his grimy, blood smeared hand.

"Oh, you're more than generous, Yer Highness!" praised the Talibarrian. His hand clutched tightly to the first gold piece he and his friends had ever had the good fortune of owning. "Word shall spread far an' wide of your generosity an' fairness!"

"Do not reward these men for their act of duplicity," urged Cullen, watching with bitter resentment as this small hunting party, including the man made to part with his finger, gleefully whooped and hollered in celebration. They scurried off with their gold just in case Cullen was able to convince the King to rescind his offer.

"Hold your tongue, Captain Bristow," warned Sebastian, his words terse. "Let it be known I am not rewarding them for attempting to deceive me. Though they had opted to be *creative* in their efforts to collect the bounty, I will not be accused of theft by taking their catch without properly compensating them for their hard work."

"You *want* this dead animal?" questioned Cullen, staring at the eviscerated carcass on the ground before him.

"There is no point in letting it go to waste. Though it is not the beast we seek, it is certainly a specimen of extraordinary size. This pelt, once properly cured, will make for an impressive rug in the library," explained Sebastian, abruptly turning away. He abandoned Garrick and Cullen to return to the solitude of his tent.

"I hate to be the one to say this, my lord, but I do believe your father's declining years affects his thinking. He has been tricked by those despicable sods," noted Cullen, speaking in a whisper as he watched Sebastian disappear inside his temporary abode. "The good King cannot be in his right mind to dole out financial compensation to those barbarians in exchange for their act of deceit."

"Captain Bristow, it is obvious to me that you do not understand my father's motives. As he said, he does not reward them for their dishonesty. He is paying them for the animal they had worked so hard to catch and kill. My father, just as I do, believe these men truly thought they had the correct creature. Their desperation, going as far as amputating a perfectly good finger, only served to prove how desperate these people truly are."

"I cannot deny that it was a desperate act, alright."

"You must admit, Captain, there was a time when the Talibarrians would outright steal from us, thinking nothing of killing to collect anything they deemed of value. These people actually attempted to work for the reward than to steal from my father."

"Now that is a matter of opinion, my lord."

"If you do not understand his reasons, then consider this, Captain Bristow. By paying those men for the opportunity to purchase the skin of that mountain cat, for the sake of diplomacy and good relations, such a seemingly trivial act can be perceived as a grand gesture to these people. News of this will spread to ease tensions of our presence here."

"That may be so, my lord, but these people do not deserve to be trusted," grunted Cullen. "In fact, I would trust them as far as I could throw one of those rotters, and believe me, I can throw far."

"Even with this peace accord in place, the Talibarrians have no more reason to trust us than you have to trust them. Consider it a gesture of goodwill, a political statement that my father and those of Darross can be trusted and can be expected to act in an exemplary manner when dealing with them."

"Well, in the name of diplomacy, I believe King Sebastian bends over backwards to accommodate them than to enforce his power and will upon those miscreants."

"Better to bend a little than to break entirely," disclosed Garrick. "And that is why he is the king and you are not."

"I am a knight and a knight I will always be. However, I believe your father's elevated status in life has everything to do with his royal bloodline. My liege is entitled to this power whether they trust him or not."

"True, Captain, but what good is power if it is abused? Do you not think a king who flaunts his power and cares not for the well-being of his subjects will be permitted to oversee the rule of the country if he does not hold favour amongst his people? Without question, anarchy will be the order of the day."

"Speaking of anarchy… Here comes trouble," announced Cullen, glancing over his shoulder as the hounds yelped and howled. They strained at their leads that kept them tethered to the stake as a noisy party of a half-dozen Talibarrians advanced in their direction.

With great commotion, the boisterous men heralded their arrival with bold claims of their harrowing adventure, one that ended with the capture and death of the killer beast.

Cullen promptly marched over to issue an icy salutation to the men, "Do not tell me. Let me guess… You killed the animal and it happened to be a huge mountain cat."

"We killed the beast, alright, Cap'n!" responded the leader of this hunting party. He gave Cullen a knowing wink and gnarled smile through a mouthful of black and broken teeth. "But it's no stinkin' mountain cat. What we got here are the *creatures* responsible fer all the killin' in these parts."

"Hmph!" grunted Cullen, his curiosity piqued as Prince Garrick stepped forward to inspect their kill. "Creatures, you say?"

"Oh, yeah, Cap'n," nodded the man, motioning the Prince and Cullen to follow him. "In fact, a whole pack of 'em! If you jus' get the King, he can come see fer himself."

"King Sebastian will be summoned when he has good reason to be called," retorted Cullen. "As far as I am concerned, at this point, what you bring is merely hearsay and dead animals, nothing more. My liege already had his time wasted by unscrupulous maggots wishing to reap the rewards of the bounty he offers."

"But I speak the truth," swore the Talibarrian, hand over his heart. "My men an' I killed them murderous animals."

"I will be the judge of that," sniffed Cullen. "Show the way."

Escorting the Prince and the Captain to the edge of the camp where the other hunters proudly stood over their kill, the leader motioned his men to stand aside.

"Here ya go, m'lord," said the man, pointing to the great mound of bloody carcasses.

"Wolves?" asked Garrick, staring at the dead animals.

There were seven animals of varying age and size, both male and female. To lend emphasis to the real danger these animals posed, the alpha male, the largest, fiercest and smartest animal of the pack lay in a lifeless heap, sprawled on top of the others.

"Oh, these ain't jus' any ordinary wolves, m'lord," promised the leader. "These wolves are real killers, the whole pack of 'em! I mean, look at the size of this beast!"

Grabbing the dominant male by its bloodied snout, the Talibarrian pried open the wolf's stiffening jaws to reveal a nasty set of teeth. "Look at these monstrous fangs! You can't tell me these can't kill a man."

"Monstrous indeed," agreed Garrick, examining the ferocious display of a true carnivore. "However, it does not make this, or any one of these other wolves, the beast responsible for all the killings."

"What even makes you think these creatures are the ones?" queried Cullen.

"We saw these wolves at their worst," insisted the Talibarrian, his eyes wide with fear as his mind replayed the terrifying moments leading up to their encounter with the deadly pack. "We saw 'em on a kill; tore their prey clean apart, they did!"

"You saw these wolves attack and kill a man?" questioned Garrick.

"We saw it kill, alrighty!" declared the Talibarrian, his eyes breaking contact with the Prince.

"We are speaking of a *man*," reiterated Cullen. "Did these wolves kill a man – a human being to be exact?"

"We saw this pack kill something much bigger than any man," replied the leader, his arms outstretched wide to lend emphasis to his words.

"Here we go!" groaned Cullen, his eyes rolling about in utter frustration. "Let the story begin."

"Ya mock me now, Cap'n, but I'll have ya know I'm speakin' the truth," snarled the leader of the hunting party, his voice curdling with resentment under Cullen's scathing tone.

"Look here, if these wolves were not responsible for the taking a human life, then Prince Garrick and I are not interested in hearing any of this cock and bull story you are about to contrive," sniffed Cullen, turning away from the Talibarrian hunters.

"Are ya sayin' I'm a liar?" growled the leader, grabbing Cullen to prevent his departure.

Cullen glared at the filthy hand gripping his arm, then he snapped, "Do *not* touch me!"

"Sorry, Cap'n," apologized the leader, his hand instantly releasing its hold on him. "I jus' want you ta hear 'bout these vicious creatures an' what these animals did ta make us believe they're the culprits."

"As I said, if these wolves did not kill a human, do not waste our time," ordered Cullen.

"Believe me, Cap'n, if they can kill what they did so easily, they can certainly kill a man. In fact, it wasn't so much what they killed, but how they killed it! It was the savagery of it all."

"You Talibarrians have a distinct penchant for exaggeration, if not telling an out-and-out lie," dismissed Cullen.

"There you go with your generalizations once again, Captain," admonished Garrick. "What makes you think this man is lying to us?"

"He is Talibarrian and his lips are moving," replied Cullen, speaking with all seriousness. "Need I say more?"

"For pity's sake, Captain Bristow, it will not hurt to hear what this man has to say," urged Garrick, attempting to diffuse a potentially volatile situation. "It is obvious they went through a great deal of effort to capture and kill these wolves."

"Thanks, m'lord," said the Talibarrian, bowing his head in gratitude. "We certainly did go through plenty of trouble ta do jus' that."

"Go on then," coaxed Garrick. "What did these wolves kill and what did you mean by *how they killed it*?"

"Well, m'lord, me an' my men were followin' the fresh tracks of a brown bear down by the river early this morn," started the Talibarrian, his thumb jabbing over his shoulder to the west. "It was then that we heard the bayin' of wolves."

"Lots of wolves," interjected one of his comrades.

"They were on the hunt an' the animal these wolves were chasin' down almost bowled us over!" continued the leader.

"I say again, the prey pursued by these animals was *not* a man," ascertained Cullen, the toe of his boot impatiently tapping the ground as he was forced to listen to this tale.

"Indeed, Cap'n! But what's most important is that it was much bigger than any man!"

"Go on… Pray tell, what could it had been?" groaned Cullen, gesturing the Talibarrian to hasten on the telling of this tale.

"We were almost trampled down by a huge bull elk. Though there was only the start of its spring growth of antlers, I swear, the top of the stag's shoulders stood higher than the top of my head! It was as tall as a draft horse!"

"Taller!" chimed in another of his hunting companions, to the agreement of the members of the hunting party who had witnessed the drama unfold.

"It might have been great in size, but the stag could have been well past the prime of its life," disputed Cullen. "It was probably old and weak or sick and starving, making it easy prey to begin with for a pack of ravenous wolves."

"I assure you, Cap'n, that was definitely a stag in its prime," swore the man, his frustration mounting as he endured Cullen's skeptical tone. "In fact, if ya don't believe me, after the wolves killed the stag an' then we finished those vermin off, there was no point in lettin' all that perfectly good meat go ta waste. We took what venison we could."

"So you and your men will be dining well on this eve," sniffed

Cullen, his shoulders shrugging with indifference.

"An' a long time ta come, Cap'n," promised the Talibarrian. "You can see fer yerself jus' how large that stag really was. I got a whole hindquarter still hangin' up in a tree not far from here for when we're done with this business of claimin' the bounty. You'll be able ta see with yer own eyes jus' how massive an' fit that elk was before those wolves did it in."

"I have heard tales of wolves on the hunt," recalled Garrick.

"If it's 'bout their viciousness an' cunnin' on the hunt, then it's all true, m'lord," vowed the leader.

"Some say these predators are such skilled, methodical hunters, where individually they would never attempt to hunt such an imposing prey, in a pack, they have been known to attack and do so with great efficiency," continued Garrick. "Working in collaboration, they are able to stalk and take down prey much larger than they are."

"Efficient indeed, m'lord, but as I said, it wasn't so much the size of the stag these wolves took after, it was the way they killed the poor beast. That's what gave us good reason ta believe without a shadow of a doubt that these wolves were the killers you've been lookin' fer."

"Go on, good sir, tell us more," coaxed Garrick.

"Well, with all the commotion an' this great stag crashin' through the forest, comin' straight at us, all we could do was ta jump inta the bushes ta get outta the way. As the stag bounded by, these wolves came barrellin' up right behind the poor thing."

"They were movin' so fast an' were so intent on killin' the stag, they didn't even take notice of us," interjected another hunter.

"Yeah, an' jus' as the stag was pacin' the river's edge lookin' for a safe crossin', those damned wolves surrounded it," continued the leader.

"Of course they would! They are wolves, after all," grunted Cullen, his face contorting in frustration. "It makes perfect sense to surround the elk so it cannot escape."

"But listen, Cap'n," urged the Talibarrian; "there's more. These wolves didn't jus' go an' kill the stag; they took their own sweet time doin' it. If I didn't know better, I'd say they had great sport tormentin' the trapped animal. They were takin' turns snappin' at the stag's feet and nippin' at its rump. They had the poor animal skitterin' all 'bout, prancin' an' kickin' until it was ready ta drop from exhaustion."

"As savage as it appears, it would make perfect sense to tire the stag before attempting to down such large prey," said Garrick, listening to this tale with keen interest.

"The stag was puffin' an' snortin', tryin' ta catch its breath," continued the hunter; "an' no sooner than the animal lowered its head ta turn its stumpy antlers on 'em wolves, those animals ripped inta the stag."

"So they killed the animal? It's natural," grunted Cullen, dismissing this news. "Even wolves must eat."

"True 'nough, Cap'n, but there weren't nothin' natural 'bout what these wolves did ta the stag. It was beyond savage!"

Picking up the alpha male by the scruff of its neck, the hunter shook the wolf at Cullen as he continued his grim tale, "This big brute clamped its jaws on the stag's snout, suffocatin' it. In a blink of an eye, its mate lunged up, grabbing the stag by its throat while the other wolves each latched onta a leg. They were pullin' the stag in all directions tryin' ta rip it apart. Next thing ya know, one of the young wolves jumped up, sinkin' its teeth inta the elk's balls."

With graphic, animated gestures, the hunter used his free hand, curling his fingers in liked curved fangs as he pretended to mimic the wolf as it tore off the elk's testicles.

"With that, the stag dropped straight ta the ground," said the hunter, throwing the alpha male back onto the heap of carcasses. "It was a gruesome sight ta behold! I swear ya could see the whites of the stag's eyes as the wolves tore inta its belly. They were feedin' on the poor animal while it was still alive – its guts hangin' out as they ripped inta it."

"Oh, that is horrific!" agreed Garrick, hoping the trauma of the attack was enough to send the elk into shock so it felt little in the way of pain as the wolves dove into the hot entrails and choicest organs as the wounded animal clung to life. "It would be a terrible way to die!"

"I assure you, m'lord, it was terrible indeed. But like I was sayin' before, it was the manner that these wolves took ta killin' the stag that made us believe this pack was the guilty culprit responsible fer all the killin' in our country. There was somethin' evil in the way they took ta tearin' the poor animal apart, feedin' even while the prey was still strugglin' ta live. And now that ya know what these wolves could do to a full-grown elk in the prime of its life, you can jus' imagine what these creatures can do to a human being!"

"If the great size of this elk did not serve as a deterrent to sway this pack of wolves to pursue smaller, easier prey, then even a large man has little hope of surviving such an attack," determined the Prince.

"Well, m'lord, as I was tellin' you before; what was truly disturbin' was the way these wolves seemed ta take great sport in chasin' the stag down, torturin' the poor beast once they had it cornered."

"Disturbing, but true. Wolves are like their domesticated cousins," assessed Garrick. "Dogs are one of the few predators that will hunt and kill for sport. They have been known to kill prey animal only to abandon the carcass, completely uneaten, after having their *fun* with it."

"I suppose you have a point, my lord," agreed Cullen, thinking back to an incident during his childhood. "When I was a boy, I had a dog that took certain pleasure in killing rabbits, squirrels and cats. Actually, anything that mutt could fit into its jaws was considered fair game."

"Maybe you didn't feed it 'nough," offered one of the Talibarrians.

"To the contrary, sir; that dog was well-fed, so it had no need to hunt for food, but that little bugger would chase down any animal it would find, throwing the carcass about and ripping it to shreds with obvious glee. When he grew tired of it, that mutt thought nothing of abandoning the kill without taking so much as a single bite to eat."

"So, do you believe these wolves are responsible for all the killings, Captain Bristow?" questioned Garrick.

"I do believe these wolves were responsible for killing the stag. And I do believe they were quite capable of killing a man if they had chosen to do so, but I hesitate to blame them for taking the lives of so many villagers."

"But do not forget, Captain Bristow, throughout history, both in western and eastern Imago, there have been tales of wolves attacking men," reminded Garrick. "Usually, it is a lone wolf banished from a pack and forced by sheer hunger and desperation to settle for helpless prey to victimize."

"True, but it very rarely happens. And more often than not, there was no substantiated proof a wolf did the deed," contested Cullen. "In fact, if I remember correctly, it has been close to half a century since there was a verified report of such an attack on a human being."

"Perhaps this is one of those rare occasions?" offered Garrick, his eyes studying the small hill of dead wolves heaped before him.

"I'm tellin' you, m'lord, in life these wolves were more than capable of tearin' a grown man ta pieces," insisted the Talibarrian. "These creatures are the killers you've been lookin' fer."

"So, you saw these wolves kill a large, robust stag. The fact remains you never did see them attack a single human being," argued Cullen, his voice still as skeptical as ever.

"Ta be perfectly honest, Cap'n, that's true," admitted the man.

"We've seen these wolves plenty of times. They roamed the forest on this side of the Aranak Mountains usually huntin' fer deer an' sometimes they were seen huntin' for rabbits and voles in the open on the Plains of Fire."

"And in all the times you have seen this pack, had any of these animals attacked you or any of your people? Did they ever show signs of aggression?" interrogated Cullen.

"Usually, the wolves would act timid whenever we were about, shyin' away 'cause they know we've killed one or two of 'em in the past fer stealin' from our cache of meat," revealed the Talibarrian hunter. "But that don't mean these wolves ain't the ones that's been doin' all the killin'. They're cunnin' creatures an' we saw firsthand the level of their ferocity. In fact, I'm so sure of it, I'll bet my life these wolves are the killers."

"If you are going to make a wager, I would believe you more if you had bet on something with actual value," sniffed Cullen.

"You're a cruel man, Cap'n," groaned the hunter, rolling his eyes in frustration. "But ignorin' yer sorry insult; me an' my men know these wolves are the killers."

"Prince Garrick hopes it to be so and you can wish it to be true, but I am still leery of your claim," disputed Cullen.

"Why? Because these wolves don't look big 'nough or ferocious 'nough ta do such damage?" queried the Talibarrian.

"No," answered Cullen. "More than I question the size and ferocity of these creatures, I question more your integrity and motivation, being that you are a Talibarrian."

"Are ya sayin' I'm a liar jus' 'cause I'm from these parts?" growled the hunter, his hands curling into balled fists as he glared at Cullen with growing contempt.

"Takes one to know one," grunted the young Captain, daring the man to incite a physical altercation. "And even if you had spoken the truth about the wolves and the nature in which they hunted the stag, you are only speculating these wolves were responsible for the human deaths in Talibarr."

"You bastard!" snapped the hunter, raising his fists to Cullen as Prince Garrick stepped in between them.

"Now see here, my good man! What Captain Bristow means to say is that we already had some of your countrymen attempting to claim the bounty under false pretenses," interjected Garrick, motioning for calm to prevail. "The Captain merely wishes to ascertain the credibility of your claim."

"One of my own countrymen tried ta steal away with the bounty?" gasped the leader, as his comrades released a collective gasp of surprise. "We're shocked an' appalled!"

"Now *that* is funny!" scoffed Cullen, offering the Talibarrians a smug smile. "I am confident you meant to say, *indifferent and delighted.*"

"Come now, Cap'n, such underhanded shenanigans are usually unheard of! Mind you, I suppose there's a few of 'em out there that's willin' ta lie an' swindle from the honest if it helps to eke out a livin'. But I promise you when I say me an' my men are honest folks. It's the only reason we bothered killin' these wolves ta begin with. In our guts, we have a feelin' these wolves are the culprits."

"And if you are wrong, sir, it will be *your guts* lying all about with these dead animals," sneered Cullen, his hand resting on the hilt of his sword.

"Well, there's one way ta prove if these wolves are man-killers, or not," offered the hunter. "Cuttin' these wolves open will reveal what they've been feastin' on of late."

"By all means, go right ahead," invited Cullen, his hand sweeping out before him as an invitation to the Talibarrians to undertake this grisly task. "Show us what is inside."

"You're the one doubtin' our words," argued the hunter. "You're the one who should be gettin' his hands dirty, not us."

"Look here, I have already accused you and your kind of being liars. Do not have me label you as being lazy to boot!" countered Cullen, his tone scathing as he shamelessly berated the Talibarrians.

"We aren't lazy! We jus' don't think it's fair that we hunted down an' killed these wolves an' now you're the one refusin' ta believe these are killer wolves," contested the hunter, his insulted cohorts nodding in agreement with their leader. "If anything, you should be the one ta gut 'em if you're lookin' fer proof."

Once again, Garrick was forced to intervene between the bickering adversaries. "As King Sebastian is the one offering the bounty, it is up to the individual wishing to claim the reward to prove his kill is the beast in question. It is not that I question your words, sir, I just require proof these animals are the man-killers we are looking for."

"Well, why didn't ya jus' say so, m'lord," responded the leader, his head bowing apologetically to Garrick. With a wave of his hand, he motioned his men to take up their hunting knives and to claim a carcass to begin this internal inspection on the Prince's behalf. "We'd be happy ta oblige ya."

"Hold on!" ordered Cullen, stepping before the Talibarrians as they were about to proceed with this grim task. "First, a show of hands."

"Why? What're we votin' on, Cap'n?" questioned the bewildered leader of the hunting party.

"You misunderstand me, sir," replied Cullen, motioning for the men to step forward. "I mean to inspect your hands."

The men frowned in confusion, but complied nonetheless, presenting their dirt encrusted hands to the Captain for his scrutiny.

"There is nothing missing now. There better be nothing missing later," snapped Cullen, noting the fact that all these men, aside from the scratches and cuts inflicted during the hunt, had all their fingers intact.

"My, you're not a very trustin' fella are ya, Cap'n?" grunted the leader, as he sank his knife in the wolf's belly.

"We already had one man cut off his friend's finger, trying to pass it off as human remains just to claim the bounty," retorted Cullen. "I shall leave nothing to chance where you and your cohorts are concerned."

"Now that's jus' plain silly, cuttin' off a lousy, little finger," moaned the Talibarrian, his hand squishing about the abdominal cavity. "That fella should've gone fer a whole hand an' stuffed it inside first before presentin' it ta ya."

"Well, I suppose not all Talibarrians are as crafty as you, my crooked, little friend," grumbled Cullen. "At least you served to reaffirm my suspicions where your people are concerned."

In a matter of minutes, all the carcasses were disemboweled. Each stomach was removed, dissected and found to contain only partially digested grasses and freshly consumed venison.

"As convincing as your tale of the hunt was, good sir, I am afraid there are no human remains to speak of," announced Garrick, as the ever-doubtful Cullen continued his inspection, using a stick to probe the stomach contents in search of human bones, flesh or even hair and clothing.

"Good gracious, m'lord, we jus' gone an' wasted a good part of yer day all fer nothin'! My men an' I are terribly sorry," apologized the Talibarrian, cleaning his hands on some grass as his cohorts wiped clean their knives before sheathing the blade.

"No harm done. I am confident that had I been the one to see these wolves take down a great stag, I undoubtedly would have had reason to believe as you did," nodded Garrick, offering the men a consoling smile.

"Well, I suppose we best be on our way," said the leader, motioning his men to follow. "That creature's still out there, so that means the bounty's still up fer grabs."

"Hey, hold on here," ordered Cullen, staring suspiciously at the departing Talibarrians. "What is the meaning of this?"

"Of what, Cap'n?"

"You are just going to walk away? You are not going to try and finagle the Prince of some coins for these useless pelts?"

"We ain't all dishonest jus' 'cause you'd wish ta believe we are, Cap'n. You're welcome ta do what ya want with those carcasses. Right now, me an' my men got us a killer beast ta hunt down if we're gonna be the ones ta rightfully claim that bounty."

"It would be a pity to let these skins go to waste," sighed Garrick, his fingers parting the wiry guard hairs to reveal the soft fur beneath. "I tell you what, my good man; I will give you a single gold piece for the whole lot of them."

The leader of the hunting party stopped in his tracks. He and his comrades were momentarily dumbfounded by Garrick's unexpected, generous offer.

"A gold piece, ya say, m'lord?" questioned the Talibarrian, his grubby fingers pensively rubbing his stubbly chin.

"That is the most I will offer," confirmed Garrick. "These wolves have already lost much in the way of their soft winter coat, but I am confident there is still some good use for these pelts."

"Well, on behalf of my men, I'd be a fool ta turn ya down an' I'd be a fool ta ask fer more when one can see that ya have a keen eye fer quality, m'lord," stated the Talibarrian, holding out his dirt-encrusted hand to accept this payment. "An' I certainly don't want ta be accused of insultin' royalty by turnin' my nose up at such a generous offer."

"Well then, here you go, my good man," said Garrick, placing the coin into his trembling hand. "Remember, the reward will be greater still if you be the one to catch and kill the beast."

"You'll be seein' us again, m'lord," promised the Talibarrian, his eyes gleaming with delight. He stared at the shiny, embossed coin as his cronies hovered about their shared reward to see what they only ever heard about. "We'll be back ta claim the bounty."

"Good luck," called Garrick, watching as the men scurried off, eager to resume the hunt for the creature that was still at large.

"Good gracious, my lord, I can somewhat understand your father's motives for rewarding those ne'er-do-wells that brought the mountain cat to us, for even if it was done as a token of his generosity, at least the cat's hide was in better shape than these scabby, mangy wolf carcasses."

"I am no fool, Captain Bristow. I am perfectly aware of the condition of these skins. My action was prompted by other reasons."

"You wish to follow suit with your father: another notable act of generosity to be appreciated by the locals," determined Cullen.

"Not really, Captain. What I chose to do was to reward those men for their honesty."

"*Honesty?* Are we speaking of the same people, my lord?"

"We most certainly are. Those men did not attempt to contrive a false explanation for what was *not* inside the stomach of any one of these wolves. They could have easily demanded some type of restitution for their work in hunting them down; but they did not. Instead, they were ready to walk away with nothing and to resume their hunt in an effort to earn the right to claim the bounty. For their honesty, I chose to reward them in the hopes they will come to understand that sincerity and integrity in itself has its own rewards."

"This, I fail to understand," groaned Cullen, giving his head a dismal shake as he pondered the Prince's words. "I suppose diplomacy is not one of my strong points."

"And that is why you are a knight and why, one day, I will be king." teased Garrick.

"With this in mind, this lowly knight shall ready our hunting party before another one of the locals shows up with a killer squirrel or deranged rabbit they will try to pass off as the man-killer. In the meantime, I'll have some of the men take care of the carcasses before they attract unwanted scavengers."

Garrick turned in the direction of their camp as the hounds began to howl. The vicious barking of an approaching dog set them off again.

"You spoke too soon, Captain," sighed Garrick.

Against the clamour of the hounds' agitated howling as they struggled to be free of their tether, they could hear the high pitched yelp of a dog's bark to announce its approach. Cullen and Garrick watched as this dog and two bickering men emerged from the forest.

Immediately, they could see these Talibarrians had nothing more than a big, brute of a hound on a short leash. There were no dead carcasses or live animals, save for this highly aggressive dog that frothed at its slobbering mouth as it lunged and surged against its leash as one of the men struggled to maintain control of the canine.

"It would appear we have another contender for the bounty," determined Garrick.

"Or perhaps these *gentlemen*, and I do use the term loosely, and their mutt wish to join us on the hunt," suggested Cullen, staring suspiciously at the strangers as they pushed and jostled for control of the dog.

As Cullen and Garrick stepped forward to greet the Talibarrians, the older man called out in warning, yanking back on the course rope looped around the dog's thick, muscular neck as it bounced about on its hind legs to lunge at the Prince, "Ya best step back, m'lord. This is one dangerous hound I got here."

"If that creature is as dangerous and difficult for you to control as it appears to be, it is better that you leave that mutt behind than to allow it to accompany us on the hunt," recommended Cullen, motioning Garrick to take another precautionary step away from the snapping, growling dog. "It will prove to be more trouble than a benefit to us."

"Oh, this ain't no huntin' hound, Cap'n. Oh, no! This is the killer beast you've all been lookin' fer," declared the older man.

"Say again," gasped Garrick, staring at the black and tan dog straining against the man's tenacious hold.

Not only was this vicious animal imposing in size and threatening in demeanor, but its physical appearance made it obviously clear this creature was a pugilist; a ferocious, bellicose fighter that eagerly challenged any animal unwilling to immediately submit in its presence. Torn ears and nasty scars across its snout, under its right eye and throat along with its lower right lip that permanently sagged after being ripped were all painful reminders of the battles with neighbouring dogs and wolves.

"You heard me, m'lord, this is the killer beast."

"You lyin' bastard!" cursed the younger man, struggling to wrench the leash from the older Talibarrian's hand. "You know that ain't so! You're jus' jealous cause my dog beat yers in the bear-baitin' contest!"

"That may be so, but don't you go denyin' that this crazy hound of yers ain't dangerous!" argued the older man, pushing the younger one off. "You know it's a killer."

"So, this dog is not yours?" questioned Garrick, watching as the man continued to struggle with the dog and its rightful owner.

"That's so, m'lord," admitted the older man. "I'd never be crazy 'nough ta keep a killer hound like this deranged mutt."

"My hound ain't crazy," insisted the true owner. "It jus' acts crazy 'round you an' strangers 'cause it's been ill-treated fer most of its life. It jus' don't trust no one except me!"

"Well, this dog looks and acts rather demented, but it does not necessarily make it the killer beast," grunted Cullen, scrutinizing the animal from a respectable distance.

"But it *is* a killer – *the* killer!" argued the older man.

"And just what has this ugly mutt killed? A rabbit? A squirrel?" scoffed Cullen, his voice oozing with cynicism. "Maybe it bit a donkey's ass?"

"Yeah, right!" snorted the rightful owner, tussling with the older man. "There ain't no donkeys or *asses* in these parts, if ya don't count him!"

"Never mind," sighed Cullen.

"Listen up! This bloodthirsty hell-hound killed a human!" declared the man, smacking the dog across its snout as it snapped at him. "Bad 'nough it'd run amok killin' my pig an' the neighbourhood goats, but when it gone an' took a human life, that was the last straw!"

"Is this a rumour?" questioned Cullen, staring at the man and the dog with obvious skepticism. "Or an out-and-out lie?"

"What do I have ta gain in lyin' ta ya?" snapped the man, pushing the owner of the dog off yet again.

"The bounty, perhaps?" offered Garrick.

"Sure, I'd be lyin' if I said I weren't interested in collectin' the reward, but I'll tell ya right now, m'lord, as God is my witness, I ain't lyin'. This dog is a killer – *the* killer."

"What a bunch of malarkey!" scoffed Cullen. "You Talibarrians do not even believe in God, however, you do have lying down to a fine art."

"Okay, if I believed in such a thing, then He'd be my witness that I'm speakin' the God's honest truth," insisted the Talibarrian. "This dog killed a human being. I saw it with my own eyes! This savage creature is evil – pure evil, I tell ya!"

"It was an accident!" disputed the owner. "My hound didn't mean ta go an' kill. It was an accident."

"Are you saying your dog *did* indeed kill a human?" queried Garrick, gazing at the animal with newfound respect as it gnashed its teeth in his direction.

"Yes, m'lord," confessed the owner, his voice meek as he realized he had just revealed his dog's greatest sin.

"See! I told ya so!" gloated the older man, wishing to turn the dog in for the bounty.

"It is bloody well about time we had a legitimate claim," responded Cullen. "Where is proof of this body? In the mutt's belly?"

"No, Cap'n, the body's been buried," confessed the owner of the dog. "I can show ya where it's at, but the boy's folks won't be happy if we go an' disturb his grave, if ya get my meanin'?"

"The boy, as in a child? Not an adult?" questioned Garrick.

"Yes, m'lord," admitted the owner, his head hanging low in shame. "Damned fool kid was teasin' my pet. My dog jus' acted as any dog would that was bein' taunted like that."

"Hold on!" ordered Cullen. "So it was not a grown man that was attacked and killed by this mangy mongrel of yours?"

"No, Cap'n, it was a young boy."

"But the boy was big fer his age," insisted the older man. "Ya should've seen the damage! This killer mutt mauled the boy beyond recognition. Almost tore off one of the boy's arms."

"Let me get this straight," said Garrick. "This dog is responsible for the death of *a* child?"

"That is so, m'lord," said the older man. "An' there's probably more dead bodies in the wake of this dog rampagin' about! It went on a killin' spree, I tell ya!"

"My dog wasn't rampagin' about," argued the owner. "So it got off its rope once or twice before it gone an' killed the boy, but my dog's been by my side since then. Only now, after hearin' that the King of Darross was offerin' a bounty fer the killer beast did ya turn yer stinkin' attention on my pet."

"When did your dog kill the boy?" queried Garrick.

"Had ta be a good fortnight since that accident," answered the owner, scratching his dog's ears as the animal drooled from its sagging, flappy jowls. "But since then, he's been by my side. I've got people who'll vouch fer my good word."

"Yer word ain't good fer nothin' an' neither is that damned dog of yers," cursed the older Talibarrian.

"This dog could have very well killed a human, but if this animal had been tethered for this duration, it cannot be the killer beast," determined Garrick.

"Yes," agreed Cullen, recalling news of the latest attack. "The last killings took place about four nights ago. This is not the animal."

"But – "

"But nothing!" snapped Cullen, pointing an accusing finger in the Talibarrian's face before waving the older man off. "Your bid to claim the bounty failed. You best be on your way if you do not want to be charged for making a false claim."

"King Sebastian does not take lightly to such foolhardy antics," warned Garrick. "My father will be displeased if you attempt to pursue this matter."

"An honest mistake, m'lord," apologized the older man, bowing in respect and defeat to the Prince. He thrust the coarse rope tethering the agitated dog into the rightful owner's eager hands as he backed away.

"Thank you, m'lord," gasped the owner, taking a firm hold of his struggling pet. "I'm ever so grateful ya saw fit ta have my dog returned to me."

"You do not deny your dog has killed livestock and had taken a human life?" questioned Garrick.

"I won't be denyin' it, m'lord," admitted the man, bowing his head in regret. "An' I'll tell ya now, my hound won't be doin' such a thing again. I promise."

"No need to make such a promise," decided Garrick.

"No?" queried the dog's owner. "Why not?"

"Because it is obvious this animal is a danger to livestock and poses a further threat and danger to your neighbours. As you admitted the dog had killed a child, you will take this animal and do away with it before it harms another person."

The younger man's hands squeezed around the rope as he gulped, "Ya want me ta kill my pet?"

"That is correct, good sir," nodded the Prince. "And if you fail to do so, I will have my men confiscate your dog and do the deed for you to make sure no others come to harm should this dog escape again."

"But it was an accident," protested the dog's owner, rubbing his mutt's scabby, scarred head as the animal drooled, completely oblivious to its intended fate.

"An accident that will have no chance of occurring again if that dog no longer poses a threat," assured Garrick. "Now, abide by this order or I shall be the one to see it done."

"Yes, m'lord," sighed the younger man, tugging at the dog's lead to take it back home. "I'll see to it."

"Good," responded Garrick, nodding in approval.

"And you better not be lying or you will answer to me," warned Cullen, glaring at the Talibarrians as they departed. "If we see that dog again and it is still alive, I will see to it myself to kill that mutt."

"Yes, Cap'n," responded the younger man, pulling at his dog as it stubbornly strained at its leash to challenge the hounds waiting for the hunt to commence.

"You bloody idiot," grumbled the older man, cuffing the dog's owner on the back of his head. "Had ya played along with me, I'd have shared the bounty with you. Look at yer sorry self. Now, you won't even have a dog ta speak of!"

Watching the two Talibarrians trudge away, Cullen had endured more than enough. What little patience he held for these people had finally wore thin. "If one more person attempts to make a false claim for the King's reward, I will have him drawn and quartered."

"I must admit, these people have been rather zealous in their efforts to reap the rewards of this hunt," sighed Garrick.

"Well, it is obvious to me, if we expect to see an end to these killings and the wanton butchering of animals not responsible for the human deaths, we have no choice but to capture this creature."

"Then we shall waste no more time," recommended Garrick. "Let us get this hunt under way while the day is still young."

unnatural solitude

"The latest word has it that a trio of hunters were attacked and killed as they entered the Valley of Shadows," disclosed Cullen, shooing away the distraught Talibarrian bearing this terrible news.

"The Valley of Shadows?" repeated Garrick, staring quizzically at the Captain as he mulled over this surprising bit of information.

"That is far removed from the northern forests surrounding Spirit Wood," noted Sebastian, his eyes determining the distance between the killings Taegus Arpoth had informed them about and the site of the latest attack. "The creature is moving with unexpected haste. Unless there are two at large, it appears to be capable of covering great distances in a short span of time."

"That is clear, but, I fail to understand the randomness of the attacks," stated Garrick, scrutinizing the parchment detailing the country of Talibarr. This scroll was now marred with a growing cluster of 'x' ink marks to indicate the verified locations of the beast's many victims.

"Well, the random attacks scattered across the country leads me to believe this animal has not established a defined territory as its own," assessed King Sebastian.

"If the people's words are true that this creature's movements do not reveal a set pattern, it will prove to be most difficult to track the animal," determined Garrick.

"And even more difficult to establish where it will strike next," added Sebastian.

"When it comes right down to it, this is nothing more than a lowly animal we are speaking of," reminded Cullen. "How is a simple creature capable of thinking to the extent that it can methodically set a pattern? As far as I am concerned, the beast is running about willy-nilly as animals do."

"Then how do we account for the victims?" questioned Sebastian.

"Those unfortunate souls were at the wrong place at the wrong time," decided Cullen. "Fate was unkind to them."

"Am I wrong to assume that you *do not* have extensive experience in hunting game, big or small?" queried the King.

"You assume correctly, my liege. If it is absolutely necessary for me to hunt when I am away from the castle, then the occasional deer, boar and other such animal will fall victim to my hunting prowess. However, I am not keen on hunting for the predators that compete against me for a meal."

"I will tell you now, Captain," said Sebastian; "it takes a certain level of skill and experience to hunt predatory animals."

"The only predators I have extensive experience in hunting are enemy soldiers and rabble-rousers looking to bring unrest to our lands."

"Well then, Captain Bristow, allow me to educate you in the art of the hunt and the nature of these so-called *lowly animals*," offered Sebastian.

"By all means, Your Highness, I am always willing to learn from one as experienced as you," responded Cullen, his head bowing in respect and appreciation.

"Then listen up, Captain. It is quite normal for animals that hunt, whether it is a wolf, a mink or a mountain cat, to establish territories – a tract of land they claim and mark as their own so rival animals will know to move on or face a potentially fatal encounter," explained Sebastian. "Whether it is to lay claim to prey animals or to assert the right to mate with a female of their species entering this territory, predatory animals will protect their territory fiercely against unwanted competition."

"So, are you saying this creature we hunt may be a female because it has not staked out a specific territory?" queried Cullen.

"That is a very real possibility," responded Sebastian. "But consider this, Captain Bristow, based upon what we know so far about the way this animal kills, in nature, it is often the male of the species that is greater in size, strength and aggression."

"Mind you, a mother bear or wolf, even a mountain cat will aggressively defend its young when its offspring is threatened," interjected Garrick. "A female protecting its young will have no hesitation in attacking even a group of people to drive them away."

"That is quite true, but the very nature of these attacks suggests a rogue male acting on its own," countered Sebastian.

"But what kind of rogue male do you speak of, Your Highness?" questioned Cullen, listening with keen interest.

"That is what we are here to find out, Captain. And in order to uncover the answer, we must somehow anticipate where the beast will attack next."

"Did you not say this animal's movements do not suggest a set pattern?" asked Cullen, deliberating on the available evidence. "That there was no rhyme or reason to where it has shown up thus far?"

"That is very true," nodded the King. "Even if the creature we are searching for did not have an established territory, most animals have a set pattern in terms of their daily movements: Where they hunt; when they hunt; even where and when they sleep or relieve themselves especially for scent-marking purposes."

"I have always thought that animals, being what they are, lead a carefree, vagabond lifestyle; going wherever they want, whenever they want. Care to elaborate, Your Highness?" asked Cullen, intrigued by Sebastian's knowledge of wildlife behaviour.

"That I can do, Captain. Take the northern foxes," offered Sebastian, stroking the white fur trim of his cloak; "with the arrival of fall, when migratory waterfowl fly south for the winter, these foxes venture south to warmer climes that will ensure at least an adequate diet of vole, quail and grouse. With the warm days of spring, as the ducks and geese return to the north, the foxes follow. And quite deliberately, the foxes arrive when these waterfowl are at the height of the molt and are unable to fly. As such, it makes these birds easy prey for the cunning little predators."

"So the predator we search for is following its prey?" deduced Cullen.

"Even animals larger than the fox will follow its next meal," reasoned Garrick. "Just as the bears will congregate at the rivers to dine on salmon each autumn, so, too, do the wolves follow deer and elk."

"Well, that would certainly account for the randomness of this killer's movements," noted Cullen, nodding judiciously as he considered the facts. "If it has chosen to dine exclusively on man-flesh, the Talibarrians are scattered far and wide. They can be found almost everywhere. No longer forced to follow herds for sustenance, they have established settlements from here to the Shadow Mountains and beyond."

"These are all elements to be considered as we undertake this hunt," said Sebastian. "However, what I find most disturbing is why this creature would turn to killing man in the first place. Granted, an unarmed individual can make for easy pickings, but from what we know, those who came under attack fought valiantly. They had engaged spears, bows, knives and swords in vain to fight off the beast. With this in mind, why does this creature continue to target human victims than to hunt prey that would not fight back with weapons?"

"Obviously, we are faced with more questions than answers," sighed Cullen, rolling up the parchment detailing Talibarrian landmarks, and now, the scattered sites of the many killings.

"Yes, and I am a man in dire need of answers. I must sate my curiosity," stated Sebastian. "Let us head northeast."

"To the last known location of the attacks?" questioned his son, thinking back on the Talibarrian's desperate words issued to Cullen as he stumbled into their camp with the terrible news of the hapless hunting trio he had found.

"At this time, it is the most logical destination," confirmed Sebastian, motioning for the hunt master to set his hounds toward the Valley of Shadows.

From the dense forest hugging the shoulders of the Aranak Mountains, Sebastian and his royal hunting party steered their mounts toward the open expanse of the Plains of Fire to cut a straight course to the valley surrounding Mount Hope, the last location of a rumoured attack.

King Sebastian found certain thrill in this most unusual hunt. He reigned in his steed as the constant baying of their hounds came to an abrupt halt as a loud, screeching vibrato raked at the air and their nerves. By the high-pitched trumpeting, they knew it was a Talibarrian goat horn sounding in the distant.

"It is obvious we are not the only ones on the hunt," assessed Garrick, gazing to the east in the direction of the ear-piercing call used to summon a hunter's pack of hounds.

"With the promise of a hefty bounty, I believe we can safely assume every Talibarrian and his dog is out and about hunting the killer beast," groaned Cullen, releasing a dismal sigh. He was in no mood to contend with yet another citizen wishing to make a false claim for the reward.

"There is no harm in inspiring these people to take the incentive to protect their own," said Sebastian, ignoring the Captain's cynicism.

"Of course," conceded Cullen, glancing through the stand of trees in the direction of the squealing horn and the frantic howling of distant hounds travelling with the approaching hunting party. "Remain behind my steed. Allow me to ascertain the identity of those heading in our direction – make sure they do not inadvertently take to unleashing their arrows at us."

As Cullen took the lead, escorting his party eastward, the jubilant chorus of men celebrating a triumphant hunt grew louder as they neared.

Sebastian, Garrick and Cullen immediately recognized the leader of this small band. It was the Talibarrian who had arrived at Darross Castle a few days earlier with word from the governing council requesting aid in dealing with the killer beast.

"What do you know? It is our old *friend*, Taegus Arpoth," grumbled Cullen, raising his hand in cold salutation as this man and his comrades emerged from the thick of the forest. "Fancy meeting you in these parts."

"I'm Talibarrian. Where else would I be?" grunted Taegus, motioning one of his men to restrain the hounds as he stepped forward to meet with Cullen and his royal party.

"I suppose this forest is as good a place as any for a Talibarrian to be skulking about," responded Cullen.

"We're here fer good reason. Me an' my men were on a mission an' I'll have ya know, Cap'n, we were successful!"

"As was everyone else we have met up with thus far," muttered Cullen, reluctant to believe this news.

"Care to elaborate, Master Arpoth?" asked Sebastian.

"We come bearin' wonderful news, Yer Highness!" announced Taegus, leaning against his walking stick as he took a moment to catch his breath.

"Let me guess," offered Cullen, eyeing this man with a degree of suspicion, "you and your cronies have caught the killer beast."

"How right you are, Cap'n!" nodded Taegus, glancing over his shoulder as he waved his friend forward. In response, his comrade yanked at the horse's reins as the old nag struggled to pull a decrepit cart heavily loaded down. "But how did ya know?"

"Every Talibarrian we have met since coming across Rock Ridge Pass has made this very claim. Why would you be any different?"

"Well, those fellas have been lyin' to ya if they said they killed the *real* beast. We're the ones that got the genuine creature."

"Do tell," sighed Cullen, his eyes rolling in frustration.

Sensing the Captain's doubt, Taegus turned instead to address the King and his son, "I can tell ya this, Yer Highness; me an' my friends killed the animal. It was no easy feat, but we did it!"

"And what is this beast?" questioned Sebastian, dismounting from his steed to examine Taegus' quarry.

"Right this way, Yer Highness," invited Taegus, bowing respectfully as he motioned them to the back of the horse-drawn cart. "Come see fer yerself. It's a regular monster!"

As he motioned one of his men to throw back the soiled, tattered tarp concealing their prize, Sebastian and Garrick gasped in astonishment as the carcass of the dead animal filled their eyes as well as the full-to-bursting cart.

"Now this holds some promise!" declared Sebastian, nodding in approval of Taegus' admirable catch.

Cullen casually sauntered over to inspect the specimen. Crammed onto the cart and bulging over the sides, a huge brown bear, the biggest the Captain had ever seen dead or alive, made the horse's task of transporting the behemoth all the more difficult.

"I must admit, I am truly impressed," conceded Cullen, poking the bear's snout with a stick. "It is dead, right?"

"Deader than dead!" assured Taegus, climbing onto the cart to show off their quarry. "Took plenty of spears an' arrows ta do the deed an' one of my men gettin' hurt in the process, but we killed it alright."

"So, Master Arpoth, what makes you so sure this is the animal responsible for killing your people?" questioned Sebastian.

"We returned ta the last place the creature had done its killin'," explained Taegus.

"That makes perfect sense," nodded Garrick. "That is exactly where we were heading; to the Valley of Shadows."

"Valley of Shadows?" queried Taegus. "Well, I'll be! We just saved you a lengthy journey, m'lord."

"How so?" queried the Prince.

"We caught the bear in this very forest, just a little east of here. It killed a party of five hunters who were probably headin' to the last known place in the Valley of Shadows where they heard that an attack had takin' place."

"If this is indeed the killer animal, it was journeying south," noted Garrick.

"Yes, and too close to the borders of Darross, for my liking," muttered Cullen.

"When we came 'cross the five hunters, they were dead. It appeared ta be that they were the latest victims to fall prey to the beast," informed Taegus, shaking his head with regret. "It was a bloody mess, not unlike the killin' that took place at my settlement."

"They were dead for how long?" questioned Sebastian.

"By the blood an' how it was dryin', I'd say the men were killed not more than an hour before we stumbled across 'em."

"The three hunters we had heard about in the Valley of Shadows were most likely killed very late last night," said Garrick, glancing up to check the position of the sun in the sky. "That would indeed make these unfortunate souls Master Arpoth had come across the latest victims."

"Well, we were right in assumin' the beast might still be lurkin' about," said the Talibarrian, standing proudly over the massive hump of the bear's mountainous shoulders. "No sooner than we showed up ta find all those dead bodies that we heard these loud snufflin', snortin' sounds comin' from the edge of the camp."

"So, the bear returned to dispense more carnage," assessed Cullen, admiring the impressive size of this enormous brown bear.

Garrick stared in disbelief at Cullen. "This is a surprise! Where is the doubt? Where is the skepticism, Captain Bristow?"

"I understand your cynicism, my lord," acknowledged Cullen. "However, I am more inclined to believe this hulking beast is the guilty culprit because of its sheer size when you compare it to the other contenders we have been subjected to so far."

"But you had stated the size of the beast has nothing to do with whether it is the man-killer," argued Garrick.

"Yes, I did say that," admitted Cullen; "but that was before these *gents* presented us with this big brute of a bear. And I do not believe it was a mere coincidence this animal was at the site of this latest killing. It probably worked up a monstrous appetite and returned looking for an easy meal."

"That's exactly so, Cap'n!" exclaimed Taegus, using his walking stick to prop up the bear's snout so all could set their sights on the deadly fangs protruding below the drooping lips. "We came across this bear jus' as it was makin' off with a body."

"A human body?" queried Sebastian, seeking confirmation.

"You're bloody right, Yer Highness. It would seem this bear has a penchant for the portly, ignorin' the other men it killed. The poor fella he was draggin' off had ta weigh more than the Prince and the Cap'n put tagether!"

"See! It was not a baby rabbit or a scrawny, little child to fall victim to the beast!" declared Cullen. "It killed a strapping, large man."

"Let us not jump to any conclusions just yet, Captain Bristow," ordered Sebastian, turning to address the Talibarrian. "Master Arpoth, help me to better understand. Did you not say these men where already dead when you came across their camp?"

"Yes, Yer Highness. That's exactly what I said."

"So... If I understand correctly, you did not actually see this bear commit the killings?"

"Truth be told, Yer Highness, we didn't actually *see* this bear do any real killin', but we did see it tryin' ta make off with the dead body it was feedin' on. Fer sure, we were witness to that," explained Taegus.

"This bit of information changes everything," stated Sebastian, mulling over this news. "Feeding is not the same as killing."

"Whoa! Hold on here, Yer Highness," urged the Talibarrian. "Jus' 'cause we didn't actually see this old bear do the deed, it don't mean this beast didn't do the killin'. In my way of thinkin', if it was eatin' it, then in all likelihood, it killed it."

"The man does have a good point, my liege," said Cullen. "In all likelihood, this bear returned to finish where it had left off."

"That would certainly simplify matters if it was true," responded Sebastian. "However, it serves us, and these people, no good if we abandon the hunt in accepting this creature to be the killer when in reality, the real culprit prowls about, waiting to attack again."

"I can understand this concern, Yer Highness," agreed Taegus, "but you're a wise man. Consider this; the very fact this creature was skulkin' about at the scene of the last killin' an' it jus' happened ta have a man in its jaws makes me believe this bear has a taste fer human blood."

"I will give you that, sir, but it still does not prove this animal is the one. Yes, I believe it when you say it had a man in its jaws; however, it still does not mean this bear was responsible for killing him."

"It could very well have been scavenging, as bears are known to do," added Garrick.

"Ya say that now, m'lord," grunted Taegus, as he used both hands to pry open the bear's jaws. "But look here! See this tooth?"

Garrick and Sebastian recoiled as a stomach-churning stench rising from the abscessed gum wafted into the air to assault their senses.

"This tooth is broken. It's rotten all the way inta the gums. It's no wonder this animal had taken ta killin' an' eaten easy prey like man. An' look at these monstrous paws."

The Talibarrian pressed his dirt-smudged hand against the pad of this bear's front paw. Even with his fingers spread wide apart, this paw was still wider than the span of his hand.

"See these claws," pointed out Taegus, each one measuring as long as his own fingers. "The marks left on those dead bodies back there were long, deep gashes made by claws jus' like these. An' see... that's blood in there."

"As much as this fellow is Talibarrian, his words are making sense to me," stated Cullen. "This bear must be the creature responsible for all the killings."

"You perplex me, Captain," groaned Garrick, frowning in bewilderment at Cullen.

"How so, my lord?"

"Why are you now so eager to see that this animal is the killer beast when before, you demanded proof, substantiated evidence the animal in question did commit the deed?" queried Garrick. "Suddenly, you are willing to accept this man's words, a Talibarrian no less, as being the truth. You do not even question if there are human remains within this dead animal."

"I know it seems contrary to everything I have said in the past," reasoned Cullen, his shoulders rolling in a shrug.

"It *is* contrary," insisted Garrick. "If we had gone as far as asking the others to prove the animals' guilt in the way of gutting the carcasses for evidence of consumed human bodies, then surely we should ask the same of this man."

"I suppose it is only right," sighed Cullen. "There's no harm in being consistent."

"Of course it is the right and proper thing to do," averred Sebastian, agreeing with his son.

"That won't be hard ta prove, Yer Highness," said Taegus.

"You are willing to do that?" questioned the King, staring at the Talibarrian and his hunting comrades.

"If it helps ta secure the bounty, sure I will. I'm bettin' the dead man's arm that was chewed off is still inside this creature's belly."

Taegus hopped down as he motioned for his men to help dump the massive carcass from the cart onto the ground.

"You sound so confident, Master Arpoth," noted Cullen, stunned by this level of cooperation from a Talibarrian.

"Of course I'm sure. An' rightfully so," declared Taegus. "In fact, the man this bear mauled an' ate ain't buried yet if you wanna see fer yerself that the arm inside belongs to that dead fella."

"In fact, if ya need ta see more, none of the bodies are buried yet," chimed in the man holding the horse's reins as the others removed the hitch from his nag so the cart could be tipped to unload the grizzled looking bear.

"Well, I suppose that is unfortunate for those poor souls, but fortunate for us," decided Cullen, inwardly relieved that he and the hunters in their company would not have to be burdened with the task of exhuming the bodies for the King's inspection if that was to be his request.

"Why were the dead not cremated or given a proper burial before you had set off to find us?" questioned Garrick.

"We were gonna get around to it eventually. It wasn't as if those dead men were goin' anywhere," reasoned Taegus, unsheathing his dagger as his men rolled the bear carcass from its stomach onto its side. "The bounty was another matter though. If I remember correctly, the reward goes to the first person who can prove they killed the beast."

"Master Arpoth, before you commence with gutting this bear, answer me this," requested Sebastian.

"Of course, Yer Highness," said Taegus, the calloused pad of his thumb testing the sharpness of his dagger's blade before setting to this grisly task. "What would ya like ta ask?"

"When you had delivered word of those killed at your settlement, if I remember correctly, you stated that you were greatly disturbed by the manner in which your people were killed," recalled Sebastian.

"That's so, Yer Highness. As I said before, those folks weren't jus' killed; they were butchered! Sum of 'em were missin' limbs or their bodies were ripped in half! It was somethin' only a creature this big an' powerful could've done."

"As horrific as these memories are, do you recall if any of the dead were actually consumed by the beast?" questioned Sebastian, attempting to piece together this mystery.

"I was the first ta arrive back at my settlement," replied Taegus. "These men that are with me now, I met up with 'em as I fled. There was no point in them goin' back 'cause there was nothing ta go back ta. Plus, none of us wanted ta take a chance the killer beast was still skulkin' about. We were comin' back from tradin' with a neighbouring village so we were ill-prepared ta undertake a huntin' expedition."

"So you were only there to see the dead bodies scattered about. You did not even stay long enough to check if any of your people actually survived the attack?" probed Cullen.

"I'm tellin' ya now, Cap'n, you didn't need ta go checkin' fer a heartbeat ta see these folks were dead. If you call an' they don't answer, as far as I'm concerned, they're dead."

"So, you fled and may have left a survivor or two behind?" determined Sebastian.

"No one could've survived what I saw. At least, I've never heard of a man torn in half stayin' alive fer any length of time," answered Taegus, justifying his actions. "One glance at their poor bodies an' any old fool, even you, could've seen these people were long dead."

"It is clear the extent of their injuries were massive, Master Arpoth. We need to know if during your brief glimpse of the victims, were you able to determine if any of the dead were actually *eaten* – not just mauled or clawed, but actually consumed by the beast?" queried Garrick.

"Mauled, clawed, or all eaten up... What's the difference? All those people are dead," stated Taegus, his voice grim. "Knowin' this ain't gonna bring none of 'em back."

"True, but we must determine if there is some kind of pattern with respect to how and why the creature in question has taken to attacking people," answered the Prince.

"I'm speakin' the truth, m'lord, an' you might take it that I was bein' cowardly," responded Taegus, "but I wasn't about ta stick around ta count the arms an' legs ta see who was missin' what. As fer those who were ripped clean apart, I suppose the creature might have dined on their innards, but I was so terrified by what I saw, I never thought ta check. I jus' ran... I ran as fast as I could from there."

"I suppose the shock of stumbling upon such a horrific scene is enough to send a person's senses reeling – to cause them to flee in sheer panic," sympathized Garrick.

"That kinda carnage was too much fer me ta handle, m'lord. I jus' wanted ta get outta there as fast as I could – ta warn my friends before they headed back home an' got themselves killed runnin' smack-dab inta the monster."

"Well, that is a pity," sighed Sebastian. "If we knew for certain, it would have helped to determine if the killings at these two very separate locations, as well as the others, were committed by the same creature."

"If it's of any consolation, Yer Highness, the dead at my settlement weren't buried either," disclosed Taegus. "I left them were they lay so it'd be easy fer you ta see the damage done, if it pleases ya."

"That was rather *indecent* of you," snorted Cullen, rolling his eyes in disgust and ridicule. "Mind you, it seems typical for a Talibarrian like you to bugger off without even bothering to bury or cremate your own people in your haste to flee."

"So I admit I was bein' cowardly," confessed Taegus. "But had you been in my shoes, I'd hardly think you'd be the one ta stick 'round ta take care of the dead if ya thought the beast was still lurkin' about, waiting ta attack so you'd be one more carcass ta add ta the pile."

"I will have you know, I would have remained, if not to properly do away with the bodies, then to confront the killer beast," retorted Cullen. "I would have stayed to kill the rampaging monster myself just to end its reign of terror."

"Right…" nodded Taegus, his tone tainted with doubt. "Those are mighty bold words, Cap'n."

"Coming from a bold knight, they are more than mere words," grunted Cullen, angered by the Talibarrian's insolence. "I recommend you take this opportunity to prove this bear is the killer you claim it to be. Let us see this arm you say is inside this beast."

"If it proves me right, then ya best stand aside, Cap'n," advised Taegus, as he motioned for his comrade to control one of the dogs.

The man yanked at the lead of an indiscriminate male hound as it proceeded to shamelessly mount and mate with the dead bear's hind leg before present company.

With the whining mutt pulled out of the way, Taegus eagerly plunged the tip of his dagger into the bear's belly as he grunted, "Let's see what's inside."

"Well, I have seen enough." Cullen groaned in disgust, turning away as Taegus and his cohorts quickly bury the mangled arm they had extracted from the bear's stomach. Mauled to the bones and liberally coated in saliva, gastric juices, mulched grass and partially digested tubers the bear had previously consumed, the dead man's arm was barely recognizable. "That was a rather gruesome exercise."

"Gruesome, yes," agreed Sebastian. "However, we are now one step closer to ascertaining whether this creature was indeed the killer beast."

"And another step closer to awarding the bounty to the rightful person; a matter you have had grave concerns about, Captain," reminded Garrick.

"It is a matter of principals, my lord."

"Yes, and as a matter of principals, we shall conduct this investigation with some consistency," responded Garrick.

"It was very evident that mangled limb was not placed into the bear by Taegus or his cronies," confirmed Cullen. "Aside from the very real danger an animal of this size and power can pose, not to mention the human remains it had consumed, as well as the fact it was preparing to drag the body off for later consumption, what more proof do you need?"

"Though there is strong indication this bear is guilty for the deaths, there is still the remote chance it just happened to come across the dead bodies and simply chose to take advantage of an easy meal," stated Garrick.

"It would not be by chance such a creature would stumble across such an easy banquet," commented Sebastian. "Bears have an excellent sense of smell; much better than their ability to see."

"So, this big, old bear either sniffed out this main course or it was indeed returning to its kill," responded Cullen.

"That is why we have asked Master Arpoth to guide us back to the scene of this attack," said Sebastian. "There must be some kind of evidence left behind, some indication as to the culpability of this animal as the perpetrator of the killings."

"Well, if we were to engage in a friendly wager, I'd bet that Taegus Arpoth and his cohorts already have the killer beast," decided Cullen, glancing up ahead where the Talibarrian and his comrades moved through the forest with haste, even though they travelled by foot.

"And I would only hope that you'd win this wager because I would like to believe this animal is the beast in question and the killings have come to a stop," responded Garrick. Speaking in a whisper, his gaze turned to his father as Sebastian followed behind Taegus' hurried footsteps. "Not to mention that I do not relish the idea of my father, being the avid hunter of large game that he is, becoming deeply embroiled in the physical, not to mention potentially deadly aspects of confronting such a formidable creature."

"You worry all for naught, my lord." Cullen whispered back so the King would not hear him addressing Garrick's concerns. "Your father is in excellent health. In fact, he is fitter than most men his age. Do not forget, he is as skilled a hunter with the bow as he is a swordsman. And it is obvious to me that he is extremely knowledgeable when it comes to the animal he is hunting."

"Your words ring true, Captain Bristow," agreed Garrick. "However, at this time, how can he be knowledgeable when we do not even know for sure what animal it is that has taken to hunting men?"

"Good point," responded Cullen, speaking in a hushed tone. "I will keep the King close to me at all times."

"I am counting on you to do exactly that," stated Garrick.

"Not much further now, Yer Highness," called Taegus, staring through the lengthening shadows creeping across the forest floor. "It's 'bout another league or so from here, headin' due east."

"Will we arrive at this place before sundown?" questioned Sebastian, urging his steed on to follow the Talibarrians.

"Should do, Yer Highness, if we keep this pace," replied Taegus, drawing another deep breath as he plodded on, not even stopping to properly address the King.

As they journeyed on, racing against the sun to reach the site of the latest attack before the land was engulfed in darkness, Taegus' crooked finger pointed before him. "There ya go, Yer Highness. Right on ahead."

A small flock of ravens squabbled over choice bits of the dead body that was now devoid of an arm. The ebony scavengers cawed in protest as one of the Talibarrians unleashed a hound to chase them off. In an agitated cloud of black feathers, the ravens greedily yanked at a beak full of flesh before abandoning their find. They brazenly dined while perched on overhanging tree branches, impatiently waiting and watching for their next opportunity to feed.

Garrick grimaced at the ghastly sight of the corpulent corpse. The crimson splash of dried blood was all the more vivid against the man's ashen skin; a deathly pallor made all the worse by the massive loss of blood. With a face permanently contorted in a look of utter fear, and vacant, bloodied orbs that once housed the eyes, but now sat empty upon feeding the marauding ravens, it was a terrifying reminder of what this man had endured before, during and after his untimely demise.

Long, sharp claws had slashed clean through several layers of clothing. Upon closer examination, Cullen could see the claws had torn through fabric to easily carve into skin and flesh, clear through to expose the man's ribcage. It left no doubt it was the handiwork of a very large, powerful predator.

Using the toe of his boot, Cullen pushed back the man's dangling scalp, more skin and blood than hair. He loosely positioned it back on the corpse's head as he assessed the carnage.

"Look at these bite marks," noted Cullen, pointing to the many puncture wounds that helped to loosen the scalp from the man's head where powerful jaws crushed the skull. "Huge fangs bit clear through, sinking into the skull bone to break it."

"But these bite marks look much bigger than any teeth in the bear's mouth," determined Garrick.

"Quite right," nodded Sebastian, scrutinizing the morbid evidence.

"True enough," agreed Cullen. "But I have seen bears in the midst of devouring their kills. What cannot be immediately bitten off is twisted and shaken until the flesh comes loose. There is nothing to say Arpoth's bear did not do just that; shook this man about in its jaws to create these misshapen, excessively large teeth marks."

"An' don't ferget, this fella's arm was in the bear's belly," reminded Taegus, pointing to the remaining limb that had been mauled off just above the elbow.

"There is no mistaking the arm once belonged to this man," confirmed Garrick, seeing how the torn flesh and shattered bone was a match to the dismembered arm removed from the bear's stomach.

"You must admit, these wounds are unnecessarily brutal, even by animal standards," appraised Sebastian. "It is one thing to kill, but to continue such a savage assault when the victim is dead? It is basically unheard of."

"Well, as unlikely as it may seem, it's all here fer you ta see, Yer Highness," said Taegus, pointing to the four other bodies scattered less than ten paces from where this corpse lay.

"And to wantonly attack so many?" wondered Sebastian. "I know female bears, both black and brown, have been known to attack anyone coming between a sow and her cub, but that bear was an older boar. Aside from an abscessed tooth, it was in relatively good shape."

"What's odd is that when we first spotted the bear, it was draggin' this body off. It didn't stay an' fight," revealed Taegus. "In fact, we were made ta chase it down."

"Perhaps it had become all too familiar with weapons, choosing to flee than to confront a hostile hunting party it was unable to take by surprise," reasoned Cullen.

"Yeah, well, it gets odder still," insisted the Talibarrian, recalling moments of this terrifying hunting expedition. "When we took off after the beast, it dashed away. Fer a time, we lost sight of the bear. Didn't know which way it had buggered off ta. Suddenly, the crafty critter circled 'round, comin' up behind us to attack."

"Now that *is* a very cunning creature, indeed," agreed Sebastian, his eyes squinting as he stared at the other dead bodies through the impending darkness of night.

"Cunning bear or exceptionally stupid hunters." Cullen grumbled beneath his breath.

"Cunning indeed, Yer Highness! The bear even outsmarted our hounds," stated Taegus. "That animal crept up behind us so quick an' so quietly it almost snuck right up on one of my men."

Cullen, Sebastian and Garrick glanced over to the man standing by the flea-bitten hounds. He continued to favour his broken arm that rested in a dirty rag of a sling to alleviate some of the pain.

"So, your man was attacked by the bear?" questioned Garrick, voicing concern for the man's well-being.

"Almost, but nah, he jus' got scared an' tried ta run away. Careless fool tripped an' fell over his own feet, hurtin' his arm in the process," confessed Taegus, "but the bear would've killed him if our hounds didn't turn on the big brute ta hold him at bay 'til we were ready to attack it with our spears an' arrows."

"And this is where you killed the bear?" questioned Garrick, as he crept through the forest, following the trail of blood to examine the other bodies that were slashed and mangled by a powerful force.

"Nope. It was about thirteen paces that way," replied Taegus, his thumb jabbing over his shoulder. He pointed out the location where broken twigs and branches from shrubs and trees lay scattered over the trampled moss and disturbed earth where the bear ferociously fought for its life. "An' I'm tellin' ya now, m'lord, that bear didn't go down easy. The damned thing put up a real battle. It was determined ta kill us!"

Sebastian scrutinized the site of the bear's demise. It was apparent by the amount of damaged vegetation and soil marred by heavy paw prints the cornered beast had put up a desperate fight. However, as huge as this creature was, between Taegus Arpoth and the six armed men in his company, as well as the pack of hounds snapping at the bear's feet, this animal had no chance. Undoubtedly, the bear was weary; its energy already spent on its attack of the five hunters.

"I know for a fact a predator of this size and strength, not to mention its temperament when antagonized, requires aggressive action to bring it down," acknowledged Sebastian, his tired eyes struggling to focus on the muted details of the life and death battle between man and beast. With the sun withdrawing its waning light from the forest, the lengthening shadows darkened to blur all it touched as the twilight sky deepened.

"Perhaps we should wait until the morning to inspect this carnage and to bury the bodies," suggested Garrick, his eyes glancing nervously about to penetrate the impending darkness waiting to engulf them. "I recommend we set up camp immediately. Do so well away from here and return by the light of day to finish the task."

"Nonsense, my lord, if you are concerned the killer beast will return to wreak havoc on us, the creature is dead," assured Cullen, his voice ringing with confidence as Taegus vigorously nodded his head in agreement. "As much as I prefer not to believe in Arpoth, he being a Talibarrian and all, after what we have been made to witness, it is evident the behemoth of a bear is responsible for the deaths across this land."

"I would prefer to reserve judgment until after we have had ample opportunity to examine the other dead bodies, but only when we have sufficient light to do so," countered Garrick. "And the flickering flames of a torch will not suffice, Captain."

"I understand your concern, my son," responded Sebastian. "However, based on the circumstances and the evidence we have seen thus far, I am inclined to side with Captain Bristow. I believe the bear is the culprit. There will be no more wanton killings. It is over."

"I wish for you to be correct, father; that there will be no need to be wary while we are in this place," conceded Garrick, his head bowing in respect. "I just have a bad feeling about this…"

"I have a tendency to side with caution, especially where the lives of others are concerned, my son," confided Sebastian. "I am confident any precautions to keep us safe that Captain Bristow had in mind will be unnecessary on this eve."

"Very well, father, I only pray you are correct," said Garrick, not wishing to go against his father's will. "I shall have our men set up camp for the night."

"Of course your father is correct," added Cullen. "And there is no point in the men setting up camp half a league away from here when we shall only be forced to make this trip again to finish our inspection and to bury the dead. We will set up right here."

"Here, amongst the dead?" gasped Garrick, glancing over to the cold, lifeless bodies scattered along the forest floor.

"Perhaps not smack-dab over top of them, but close enough that our presence and the light of our campfire will drive away any scavenging animals sniffing about for an easy meal," recommended Cullen. "After all, what is the point of this overnight exercise if marauding beasties destroy whatever proof you and your father are looking for?"

"Point well taken," said Garrick. "But let us do so quickly; get a roaring fire underway before darkness consumes us."

"Better the darkness than the beast, I say," smiled Cullen, pulling a piece of flint from his pocket. He glanced up to the twinkling stars alighting the sky one by one as the day finally surrendered to the night. "Mind you, on this eve, there will be no need for us to contend with either."

"The night is strangely quiet," noted Garrick, his wary gaze turning up high. He spied a brilliant dusting of stars sparkling against the deep cobalt sky; the tiny lights dancing between the branches of the tree canopy as an invisible wind rustled through the leaves.

"I believe it only seems so to you because you are used to the sanctuary of Darross Castle, where every step echoes through the keep and even hushed voices carry through the halls and corridors," stated Cullen. "If it is tranquility you seek, there is no such thing as *quiet* in that grand palace of mortar and stone."

"It is more than just the constant presence of knights and servants moving through the keep," explained Garrick. "I urge you, Captain Bristow, take a moment to listen. There is something bizarre about this solitude. It is not natural."

Cullen humoured the Prince. Cupping his hands up to his ears he strained to hear through the ambient sounds of the forest at night.

"I hear nothing untoward; nothing that would give me cause for concern, my lord," decided Cullen, listening over the hushed words shared between the King's huntsmen speaking with Taegus and his cohorts. They were clustered around a separate fire near to the hounds as their gregarious, slobbering dogs sniffed and licked each other as they settled down for the night. "As far as I am concerned, all is peaceful."

"Peaceful as in *eerily silent*," corrected Garrick, feeling claustrophobic as an unnatural veil of darkness and quiet cloaked this forest, numbing it in an artificial serenity. "If all was well, why do I not hear the chorus of frogs or even the chirping of a single cricket on this night? There is not even the cry of an owl to be had."

"We are north of the Aranaks. It is too early for frogs, too cold for crickets and the resident owl is undoubtedly off somewhere on the hunt," replied Cullen, his tone matter-of-fact.

"My! You seem to have an answer for everything, Captain," noted Garrick, his ears still struggling to pick up even one familiar, comforting sound that would put his mind at ease.

"Only if an answer is solicited," responded Cullen, placing a log onto the heart of the fire. "You asked, I merely answered to the best of my abilities."

"Perhaps I should ask my father what he thinks of this strange solitude?" suggested Garrick, glancing over to the tent where Sebastian had retired for the night.

"Why worry him over such mundane matters, my lord? Your father is weary from the day's travel and made all the more so contending with the locals bickering for the right to claim the bounty he offers. Let the King sleep."

"I suppose you are right. Perhaps such is the state of nights in this strange land away from our beloved country."

"Strange indeed!" snorted Cullen. He fished about his pack to retrieve a bottle of wine. Twisting off the cork seal with his teeth, he passed it first to the Prince to allow him a drink.

"Red wine from my father's private collection," assumed Garrick, sniffing the distinct, aromatic bouquet. "If I did not know better, I would say it is a vintage stock from King Augustyne's vineyard at Land's End."

"Before I am accused of pilfering from my liege, this wine was indeed made from grapes grown at Land's End. However, it was given to me by Lando Bayliss. It was his attempt at convincing me that he took as much pride in producing this wine as he did in protecting his King. He called it the *fine and exquisite fruits of his labour* and I am man enough to give credit where credit is due. In my humble opinion, this is one of the best wines I have ever had the good fortune of drinking."

Garrick's brows arched up in surprise as he recalled tales from his youth when his father and the allied forces of Carcross, Cedona and Wyndwood united their military might in a campaign to defeat the Dark Lord Beyilzon a decade ago.

"You are speaking of *the* Lando Bayliss? *Sir* Lando Bayliss of the famed Order?"

"Yes, that miserable, old curmudgeon is still a surviving member of the *prestigious Order*. However, how *famous* is that retired knight? That is up for debate. I will tell you now, my lord, in my humble opinion a knight loses his credibility when he chooses to wield a lowly pruning shear over a magnificent sword."

"I see there is no love lost between you two," noted Garrick. "I thought being that you are members of the knighthood, you would have plenty in common with him."

"With that old gaffer?" scoffed Cullen, motioning for Garrick to drink. "I think not! We are as different as a purebred stallion and a worthless ass. And there is no need to tell you who qualifies as the ass."

"Such animosity," scolded Garrick, wiping the dribble of wine from his chin with the back of his hand. "I would think you would be more respectful and appreciative of that man after all he and his friends had done to help rescue my brother from the hands of Draven Eldard."

"I admit Bayliss had a minor hand in executing Prince Carstian's rescue. However, he was not *instrumental* in the success of that mission."

"I beg to differ, Captain," disputed Garrick, handing the bottle to Cullen. "I have heard accountings of this adventure."

"Hearsay and rumour, my lord," dismissed Cullen, taking a quick swig of wine. "A fabrication of the truth to cast the retired knight in a more favourable light in his declining years."

Garrick laughed lightly as he responded, "I will have you know, Captain Bristow, King Markus does not deal in rumour or hearsay. Both he and Prince Arerys are not one for fabricating the truth."

"Oh… those two," grunted Cullen.

"And they are as credible as they come."

"All I can say is, the King of Carcross and the Prince of Wyndwood are the best of friends. As such, they continue to hold that miserable, old do-gooder close to their hearts. Of course they will say things to boost Lando's battered ego and diminished pride since the old man was deemed useless and forced to retire from Augustyne's court."

"An old man? Am I to assume my father, *your King*, a man almost two decades senior to Sir Bayliss is now regarded as old and useless in your eyes, Captain?"

"Make no mistake, my lord, had your father been a commoner he would quickly lapse into decay, much like Lando Bayliss does now. However, King Sebastian's royal blood keeps him youthful for his years and indispensable to his loving family and loyal subjects. In Lando's case, that miserable old goat had outlived his usefulness to the King and was forced to relinquish his place in the knighthood."

"Sir Bayliss was not forced to retire," reminded Garrick. "King Augustyne granted him his request to be released from service so he may pursue a life more suitable and accommodating for a man with duty to wife and responsibility to a young family."

"Well, there you go then," snorted Cullen. "A true knight knows his place. His loyalty and duty is reserved first and foremost to his liege, not a wife who waits at home to hen-peck him and a litter of runny-nosed brats latching onto his legs, clamouring for attention when no one else will give it to him."

Garrick chuckled, "Perhaps you will think differently once you commit to marriage and have a family of your own."

"*Marriage?* Bite your tongue! That word has no place in my vocabulary or life," responded Cullen, cringing at the thought of an eternal union. "What man in his right mind would want to be shackled and fettered to the same female for the rest of his natural life? He would have to be utterly mad to even consider subjecting himself to this misery."

"That is odd," commented Garrick. "I have always thought my father was quite sane and rather content."

"No disrespect to your father, my lord, but as the King, he is expected to marry and produce an heir," reminded Cullen, taking another swig before handing the bottle back to Garrick. "However, just because he is married, it does not mean the King does not indulge in the company of other desirable women."

"Your words border on scandalous, Captain! Are you saying my father is cheating on my mother?" queried Garrick, staring through suspicious, narrowed eyes at Cullen.

"No, no, no! I am saying that he is the King of Darross. As such, he can do whatever his heart desires, including being a philandering husband if that is what he wishes. Not that he is... But for now, I strongly recommend you refrain from using your father as a comparison. My words were meant for the common man. You and your father are far from common."

"Grant you that, Captain, but if you believe the common man willing to subject himself to a life of matrimonial bliss is a man gone mad, how do you account for your best friend, first officer Brandis Blackmer and his recent wedding?"

"Temporary insanity," grumbled Cullen. He shuddered at the thought as the memory of Brandis' early spring wedding, celebrated with much joy, played out in his mind. As guests made merry at the reception, Cullen sulked, seeking refuge in drink. He overindulged to the point of utter intoxication, drowning his sorrows as he lamented his friend's fate. "In my mind, the poor man was overcome by momentary madness."

"Mad, indeed! I was there and I can honestly say Brandis was *madly in love.* He only had eyes for Lady Catherine."

"And I was ready to poke them to do Brandis a great service," groaned Cullen, holding his hand out for the shared bottle of wine. "I still lament that sorry day. In fact, on the eve before his wedding, I took Brandis to my cousin's fine drinking establishment in Beckham on the guise of celebrating his impending nuptials."

"This sounds like the start of a sad and sordid tale," noted Garrick, handing the bottle over to Cullen's eager hands.

"Sad, indeed! A rousing night of drinking and carousing to be topped off in the company of several comely maidens ended in a sorry way."

"This sounds intriguing. Go on! What happened?"

"Even inebriated to the point of falling down drunk, Brandis still had the gall to keep his moral compass on the straight and narrow," sighed Cullen, shaking his head in disappointment. "I was shocked and appalled when he turned down the grand offer to spend the night with a pair of lovely twins. I even offered to have my way with their mother to keep that woman occupied on Brandis' behalf, as I hardly think he could have handled three women all at once."

"The girls' *mother*?" gasped Garrick, spewing out a mouthful of wine as the repulsive thought of a gray-haired, matronly woman with the sags and wrinkles to match lewdly licked her lips as she stared enticingly with bloodshot, come-hither eyes at Cullen. "Now that is a ghastly image if there ever was one!"

"Oh, you were not there, so you do not know," responded Cullen, unmoved by the Prince's reaction. "Truth be told, so the mother was a little long-in-the-tooth compared to her nubile daughters, but she was mighty fine on the eyes nonetheless. And being more mature, she was much more knowledgeable and experienced in the ways of pleasing a man, if you get my meaning?"

"You introduced Brandis, your best friend, to a tart and her harlot daughters on the eve before his wedding? What kind of man are you, Captain Bristow?"

"You have it wrong, my lord. The mother was the *harlot*, her daughters were the *tarts*," laughed Cullen. "And what kind of man would I be if I did not try to intervene on behalf of my dear friend and act in his best interest."

"Obviously, Brandis was not interested in your type of intervention," decided Garrick, shaking his head in disgust.

"Well, even if he was sober enough to have his *old boy* stand at attention and salute the ladies, I do believe his moral fiber would have gotten in the way of that. In fact, Brandis is so full of *moral fibre*, it would probably come out his back side if he took a moment to relax and enjoy the bounty that is available to hot-blooded men like us."

"I have seen the *bounty* you speak of, and like Brandis, I prefer to be selective. After all, some of us do have standards," stated Garrick. "Being as such, I would rather sink my teeth into one sweet, crisp, perfectly unblemished apple than to wallow in a keg full of runny, lumpy apple sauce on the edge of fermentation."

"I *like* apple sauce," Cullen sighed longingly, his muscles unwinding with the warmth of the wine seeping through his body. For a moment, his mind strayed to a place that undoubtedly the Prince would have no business or desire to wander to.

"Admittedly, you like too many things, Captain," retorted Garrick, yanking the bottle from Cullen's hand. "Just keep in mind, that does not mean all these *things* are good for you. It is one thing to indulge, another entirely to overindulge, especially when we are speaking of vices."

"To overindulge implies the inability to resist when faced with excess," reasoned Cullen.

"That is so."

"Well, in my way of thinking, I have yet to be faced with excess. Therefore, I have yet to overindulge."

"There is no arguing with you, is there?"

"Only because we both know I am right," responded Cullen, giving Garrick a small, knowing smile.

"You say that now and you can even believe you are right for the time being, but I sense your attitude will change drastically when you are ready to settle down and embrace the unspeakable *M* word."

Cullen glanced over at the Prince, his face frowning with confusion. "You are being facetious, right?"

"Oh, I am being quite serious, Captain. You immerse yourself in the frivolity of many dalliances, convincing all – you included, just how thrilling and emotionally and physically uplifting these affairs can be."

"My lord, I assure you, I need no convincing. It *is* thrilling and *uplifting*, if you get my meaning?" said Cullen, playfully thrusting his hips forward in a provocative gesture.

"Yes, that is until you return to your bedchamber all alone," countered Garrick, grimacing at this lewd display as he pondered the libidinous Captain and his carefree lifestyle.

For a moment, Cullen almost blundered, letting it slip that on more than one occasion, in spite of Brandis' objections, he had discreetly shuttled a bevy of beauties into the castle keep so he would not have to be alone.

"There are worse things in life than to be alone in one's bedchamber," responded Cullen, his shoulders shrugging with indifference. "Besides, who in his right mind would want to put up with all the snoring? To be deprived of a good night's sleep?"

"If the lady loves you, she will overlook your snoring, no matter how loud, just to be with you."

"I was not speaking of me doing the snoring," grumbled Cullen.

"Oh yes! How dare I be the one to make such an assumption, Captain Bristow?" sighed Garrick, rolling his eyes in dismay. "You do need your beauty sleep after all."

"Though it is true being well rested helps to enhance my dashing good looks, I was speaking of being well rested for the purpose of being alert and fit to keep the King safe," stated Cullen.

"Of course." Garrick nodded in understanding. "One must be completely fit and alert to protect my father."

A warm swell of light from a coal oil lamp illuminated the tent to silhouette the King's form. Sebastian stood, stretching as he rose up from his cot. As his head peered out from beneath the tent flap, his huntsmen as well as Taegus and his comrades abruptly ended their dice game to bow in his presence, politely acknowledging him. Garrick and Cullen immediately rose to their feet, bowing in respect to Sebastian as he stepped forward, lamp in hand.

"As you were," ordered the King, waving at the men to resume their friendly wager.

"I thought you were asleep, father."

"I was, but nature calls and it is a call even a king must answer"

"Allow me to summon your squire, my liege," offered Cullen, glancing over at the young man asleep in his bedroll by the fire. "He can hold the lamp steady for you."

"It has been a long day. Let the boy sleep," responded Sebastian, pressing a finger to his lips for quiet. "I am perfectly capable of relieving myself while holding a lamp."

"Are you positive?" asked Cullen.

"Absolutely, Captain! It is not as though I am venturing off deep into the night," responded Sebastian, pointing to an old, gnarled tree just far away enough from the camp to give him some privacy. "That tree over yonder shall do quite nicely."

"Just be careful, father," cautioned Garrick. "Keep that lamp lit and do not wander off."

"Worry not, I will be back in a shake… or two," said Sebastian, with a wry smile as he rushed off for his appointment with a tree.

With that said, Garrick and Cullen sat back down before the fire. The Prince handed the bottle back to Cullen, motioning him to resume imbibing.

"We are fortunate the rain held off for another day," said Garrick, his eyes turning to the deep sky as tiny stars continued to shine brightly.

"Fortunate indeed," agreed Cullen, raising the bottle to his lips. "Though Darross is known for its copious quantity of spring rain, against these mountains, the clouds seem to unleash a deluge. Not only is it wet, it becomes dreadfully cold."

"Well, as you are so confident the killer beast is no more, I suppose we will be returning to Darross tomorrow morn, well before the rains come," determined Garrick. Leaning his back against a log, he sighed contentedly, breathing in deeply as he absorbed the tranquility of this forest.

This solitude was suddenly shattered as a loud burp rumbled forth, escaping Cullen as the men sharing the fire erupted into laughter as the force of the belch caught the Captain by surprise.

Garrick bolted upright. "Did you hear that?"

"Terribly sorry," apologized a red-faced Cullen, his hand fanning the reek of alcohol that wafted from his stale breath. "I drank too quickly."

"No, not that," whispered Garrick, slowly rising to his feet as he motioned for the others to be silent. "Listen."

"I already told you about the frogs and crick-"

Cullen's sentence was cut short as a loud *whoosh,* like the rush of air sounded behind them. Cullen and Garrick spun about just as bright amber flames swelled to peel back the darkness of the forest.

"Your Highness!" hollered Cullen, tossing the bottle aside as he leapt over the log to the tree Sebastian was last seen heading to.

Yanking off his cloak, Cullen beat the flames down as Taegus snatched up the bucket used to water the hounds. Tossing its content onto the stubborn fire, the combination of being smothered by the cloak and drowned by the water, the flames were extinguished.

As the smoke rolled into the night sky, Cullen knelt down to examine the charred earth and the scorched tree.

"Over here!" shouted Garrick, motioning the now-awake squire to deliver a torch to shed some like on this strange situation.

As the bright flames of the torch illuminated the immediate area, Garrick knelt by Cullen's side.

"What do you see?" asked Garrick, staring at his reflection shining off a fragment of broken glass. A cold fear suddenly seized his heart.

The realization this shattered glass was the remnants of the lamp his father was using hit him hard.

Cullen stared at the blackened earth. Prints from a pair of hands were clear to see. The long, narrow depressions created by fingers raking at the soil and clawing at roots and clumps of grass to secure a desperate hold was all that was left of his father.

"The hounds, release the hounds!" hollered Cullen, racing to his tent to retrieve his sword and bow. "The creature is back! The King is gone!"

"This is futile," groaned Garrick, his frantic eyes sweeping the forest for a sign of his father or the beast. "We have searched through the night and my father has all but vanished. There has been nary a trace of this creature except a drop of blood here and there."

"Do not lose hope, my lord," said Cullen, motioning for the huntsmen to spread out with the dogs.

Pressing their sensitive snouts to the ground, the dogs skittered to and fro, yelping at every turn in a bid to scent out the King.

"Do not speak to me of hope, Captain. This is a fool's errand we have embarked on. Not even these bloody dogs can pick up a scent. This creature continues to elude us."

"I know you are exhausted, my lord, we all are," said Cullen, using his forearm to mop the beads of sweat from his brows as the sun continued to climb. "But we cannot abandon this search now. Though we have yet to find the King, neither have we found evidence that he is dead."

"Your words offer little comfort."

"I know, but it is true. We cannot stop now," ordered Cullen. "Precious time is wasting away!"

"I am painfully aware of that, Captain Bristow!" snapped Garrick, dogged by frustration, worry and fear for his father's life. "That is why we must stop. We head back now."

"And leave your father for dead?" gasped Cullen, appalled by the Prince's order.

"If, by God's good grace he is still alive, we must rally those with the ability to search him out or my father will most certainly die."

an early spring

"What a beautiful morning!" declared Markus. He turned his face skyward to revel in the radiant light of the morning sun dancing through the lacey, emerald leaves. "Another perfect day in our lovely realm."

"That statement holds true for Wyndwood," agreed Arerys; "but who knows what trouble lurks beyond the borders of the enchanted forest."

"A warm spring wind, a glorious golden sun, an endless blue sky and nary a cloud in it. It *is* perfect! Nothing can possibly go wrong on a spectacular day like this."

"Speaking of wonderful, it was wonderful to play host to you and your son once more," said Arerys, "but the time has gone by much too quickly. Are you positive you must be leaving tomorrow? If you wait for a few days Nayla should be back."

"As much as I would love to see your beautiful wife again, by all rights, I should have left for Carcross yesterday. Since my coronation last fall the duties and responsibilities I had inherited from my father have been many and unending. However, I have but one son. I find it difficult to refuse his request that I stay for an extra day or two."

"Yes, it is amazing how our children have us so well trained," chuckled Arerys, listening to the delightful laughter wafting up from the forest floor. "All Carys must do is look at me with those big, blue eyes and purse her lower lip into a sad pout. Lo and behold, she has me wrapped around her little finger."

"It is ironic that we rule our great countries, and yet, our children rule our hearts and control our actions," stated Markus, marvelling on this strong and loving bond shared with his son.

"The things we are willing to do for the love of our children."

"Yes, all the sacrifices we must make," sighed Markus, nodding in empathy.

"And yet, we would never want it any other way."

"Absolutely," responded Markus.

"Well, for however long you decide to stay and whenever you choose to depart, you know you are always welcome in Wyndwood."

"That is good to know, for this forest has been a second home to me," said Markus. He admired the sunlight dancing like diamonds cast upon the emerald waters of the Lake in the Woods as the powerful energy emanating from the heart of the Elf kingdom braced his soul, revitalizing body and mind each time he returned to this magical realm. "I hope Mark will come to feel the same way in time."

"He is his father's son," remarked Arerys, giving his good friend a knowing smile. "Given time, Mark will feel right at home."

"I am confident he will. Plus, Mark's eagerness to come to Wyndwood is motivated by his desire to rekindle his friendship with Carys."

"Carys was absolutely beside herself with excitement when we told her the news that Mark would be coming for a prolonged visit. I must admit, they do enjoy each other's company immensely," confided Arerys, smiling with delight as he gazed down to the courtyard where his daughter and her playmates engaged Markus' son in a boisterous game of tag.

"It is more than that. It would seem their shared ordeal was the inspiration of their bond. Most of all, they share a kindred spirit that is the mainstay of their friendship."

"Very true. And I cannot help but notice Mark continues to grow in measurable spurts. It astounds me each time I see your son," said Arerys. "He grows straight and tall, just like his father."

"I suppose it is all the more startling when you see him standing next to Carys. Though she has barely changed since their first meeting, she is transforming into an amazing young lady, much older and wiser than other children of comparable age, both mortal and Elf."

"She comes by this quality quite honestly," smiled Arerys. "Carys takes after Nayla in many respects."

"In all the most positive ways," assured Markus.

"I suppose if intelligence and charm balanced with a good measure of strong-mindedness and a self-deprecating sense of humour are positive qualities, then Carys will navigate through her life with the same grace and determination her mother does. And that is not such a bad thing."

"No, it is not! And I do hope this is not too much of an imposition on you and your father for Mark to spend the summer in Aspenglow," said Markus, searching Arerys' eyes for the truth.

"Longer if you will allow it," responded Arerys. "However, I know my heart cannot bear to be away from Carys for any great length of time. It would be no different for you."

"Yes, I would miss Mark and there is still much catching up we have to do. After all, I had missed the first eight years of his life. I have no intention of missing another day if I can help it."

"You must cherish this time. A mortal's life is fleeting in comparison. You must make the most of your time together."

The old friends glanced down as Carys giggled. Her voice floated up to the walkway, tinkling like the delightful sounds of silver bells.

"Tell me something, Arerys. Does Carys still have nightmares?" asked Markus. His heart was warmed to see this little girl's contagious smile, but perhaps behind this smile, Carys was still troubled by the nightmarish ordeal that led to her abduction from the enchanted forest, a terrifying ordeal that ultimately resulted in the discovery of his son.

"The nightmares have all but stopped," disclosed Arerys. "However, there are times when she will cry out, waking with a start from her sleep."

"Sounds disturbing."

"Yes, and yet, Carys claims she does not recall these troubling dreams."

"Residual memories that are best forgotten," assessed Markus, watching as his son dodged to miss being tagged by Carys' hand.

"And Mark?"

"If he has nightmares, he denies it. And if he does, I am confident his denial is his way of putting on a brave face."

"Does he ever speak of his mother?"

"He made it perfectly clear from the start, the Sorceress was *not* his mother. His cruel keeper perhaps, but not his mother, even though she did give birth to him," stated Markus. "But no, he does not even mention Taiko Saikyu's name in passing, at least, not any more."

"That is for the better – to let go of the past in order to boldly face the future," decided Arerys.

"Yes, but I sense Mark will never forget that woman's cruel treatment. As painful as his young life had been, though he no longer speaks of her, his mind is scarred by the ordeal he had endured. I am sure of it."

"Mark will never forget, but at least his young heart bears no scars," stated Arerys. "And that is only because the positive influence you have had on his life has been more profound than that woman's harsh dealings. When you rescued him, Mark was old enough to know good from evil, but not so old that his mind and heart could not be touched and reshaped for the better to allow him to determine what fate he would choose for himself."

"That is why we are here," disclosed Markus.

"You feel that by allowing Mark to learn about my people and culture, this, too, will serve to be a positive influence on his life?"

"How can it not? Though I admit that as a youngster, I had at first balked at the very idea of spending a good portion of my formative years in Wyndwood amongst strangers, it worked out well for me," confided Markus.

"Oh, yes, I remember that day like it was only yesterday," nodded Arerys, thinking back on how Markus, as a young boy, wept bitterly at the prospect of being abandoned by his father King Bromwell in this strange forest to live amongst the Elves.

"That is because, from an Elf's perspective, it *was* like only yesterday," commented Markus, smiling at his long-lived friend. In almost four decades that he had become personally acquainted with the Elves, Arerys and his people had barely aged two years, while this Elf watched him grow from young boy to a man into his middle years of life. And during this span of time, Arerys had become mentor and friend, seeing Markus through some of the defining moments in his comparatively short lifespan.

"I have some wonderful memories indelibly etched in my mind of your time in Wyndwood," said the Elf, reminiscing back on teaching Markus the fine art of archery the Elven way when the young Prince thought he knew everything he needed to know to be a great marksman.

"As I do, too, and the experience was invaluable on so many levels. I hardly believe I would be the person I am now if it had not been for your influence and that of your father's."

Arerys smiled as he recalled the first time King Bromwell delivered the young Markus to his father Kal-lel Wingfield. As diplomatic envoys originally established to enlighten and educate the mortals were no longer sent forth from Wyndwood since the days of Arerys' grandfather, Lord Galan Wingfield, those of royalty wishing to enhance their studies and establish strong political ties with the nation of Elves would send a child, usually the heir apparent to the throne, for this enhanced education.

"So, you feel the time has come for your son to learn our ways?"

"I wish for him to be enlightened by your people, to learn of the values and traditions you hold dear, so there will always be a level of understanding and compassion between our races," stated Markus. "If you will have him, that is?"

"You had spent much of your young life in my father's domain learning the ways of the Elf-kind. Consider it a tradition, and who am I to break with tradition?" responded Arerys, with a congenial smile as he and Markus gazed down to the courtyard below. "Besides, if Mark is anything at all like you, he will be an absolute delight to have around."

"I admit I was a handful at times, testing the boundaries of your patience, but my son is eager to begin his lessons. And, unlike me, he has the pleasure of a ready-made friend in Carys."

"The experience can be much less intimidating when you feel you are not alone," agreed Arerys.

"Yes, and what Mark stands to learn from you can be beneficial for my subjects and for the well-being of Imago as a whole."

"What your son learns can also be beneficial for my people, too. Consider it our legacy," stated Arerys. "Once we depart from this realm, the stewardship of the lands and all its wealth and the bounty of Imago's great forests must be placed into responsible hands. There are few humans left willing to listen to the teachings of an Elf. Where you have proven to be a great steward of your lands, learning to benefit from it than to blindly plunder its wealth until the resources are exhausted, when your time is done, then who will be left, if not your son?"

"Mark holds much promise. I am confident he will prove to be an apt pupil," said Markus, smiling with pride.

"Already his lessons begin and he does not even realize it," noted Arerys.

The children's energetic game of tag stopped as Carys led the way, tiptoeing to the edge of puddle where a dozen butterflies with iridescent blue wings basked in the warmth of the spring sun. Their slender proboscis sipped on moist, rich mud to extract nutrients to supplement a steady diet of nectar.

Markus and Arerys watched and listened with fascination as Carys explained to Mark and her other young companions how the drab, mottled exterior of the wings when the butterflies were at rest allowed them to remain camouflaged, blending into the sylvan colors of the forest. She went on to explain how some butterflies are brightly colored as a warning to potential predators that they are poisonous or foul-tasting, therefore, should not be eaten.

As Mark crept closer to this puddle to better examine the object of Carys' interest, his heavier footfalls sent small tremors through the earth causing the butterflies to scatter. In a dazzling explosion of sapphire blue, the winged insects took to the air in an eye-catching aerial display that caused Mark to gasp at this wondrous spectacle.

Mark groaned with embarrassment, his mortal steps were much more cumbersome than the Elves'.

"I was just like him," recalled Markus, empathizing with his red-faced son. He remembered how his heavy footfalls caused more than a deer or two to bound away upon his less than stealthy approach.

"And just like you, Mark, too, will learn to step lightly through the forest," assured Arerys, motioning his friend to follow him along the walkway to his father's residence. On the balcony, a pot filled with hot, fragrant tea perfumed with jasmine flowers awaited them. On this table next to the teapot, a small crock of freshly churned butter lay nestled in a basket brimming with hot, fresh biscuits waiting to be served with sweet, juicy strawberries; the first crop of the year.

Here, the Prince of Wyndwood invited the King of Carcross to join him for breakfast. From this balcony, they could enjoy a private conversation while still keeping their children in full view as they played in the courtyard below.

"I must say; I was rather surprised to learn Nayla had departed for Orien, especially so early in the year," admitted Markus, inhaling deeply to truly appreciate the tantalizing aroma of the tea before taking a sip. "Mind you, it has been almost a decade since she had last set foot in the east. She must have been missing her home."

"I do not believe she was feeling even the slightest pangs of homesickness for the Kagai village of Anshen, however, she did miss her old master. With Hunta Saibon in failing health, she felt compelled to pay her final respects. She hoped to return before Master Saibon passed from this realm."

"In many ways, he was the father Nayla never had in Dahlon Treeborn," said Markus. "I suppose it is only natural Nayla would feel compelled to see him one last time."

"Master Saibon loved Nayla like she was his own daughter," reminded Arerys. "As such, it was understandable that the old man would worry about her. Even though she had outlived him by over two centuries and she had been taught in the ways of the Kagai Warrior by his predecessors, Master Saibon worried about her well-being and happiness nonetheless."

"Do you know if Nayla made it back to Anshen in time?"

"I received word shortly after her arrival to the secret enclave that it was as though Hunta Saibon knew she was coming. And, as fate would have it, the time they shared, as brief as it was, was all Master Saibon required. As soon as he had ascertained that Nayla was truly happy with her life outside of Orien, he seemed to have found the peace he desired, passing from this realm on that very night."

"I take it, she made the trek fully prepared?" questioned Markus.

"You know as well as I do that Nayla is an ardent believer in always being prepared. She was, and will always be, a Kagai Warrior. She is armed to the teeth and donning her battle regalia, at least, for the duration of the trek."

"Well, it is a fortunate thing that spring came unseasonably early this year to permit Nayla a safe crossing through the Iron Mountains," said Markus.

"Even if the weather permitted it, I would have balked at the prospect of having Nayla embark on this trip with only two council members of Talibarr's fledgling government by her side. If Lando had not offered to make this excursion, I would be making this trip with her."

"Lando Bayliss is in her company?" queried Markus, his startled eyes peering up from his cup of tea. "*Our* Lando Bayliss?"

"Indeed!"

"Odd… I thought our friend stated he was getting much too old for high adventure."

"Lando does not view this excursion as *high adventure,*" explained Arerys. "It was quite by accident, or rather through a strange twist of fate, but our old friend was planning a journey to the east on King Augustyne's behalf even before Nayla received news of Master Saibon's ill health. He was going as Augustyne's royal envoy to promote trade with those to the east. Think of it as a wine for silk mission."

"I suppose that makes sense," responded Markus, nodding thoughtfully. "Ever since he retired his sword, Lando has garnered a reputation as a shrewd businessman. Plus, his role of captain to the King's army has made him diplomatic by necessity. He was the perfect choice for King Augustyne to promote commerce between the two countries."

"Of course, part of the deal to embark on this trade mission was that Augustyne includes wine produced from Lando's vineyard at Land's End as part of the business transaction," explained Arerys, passing the biscuits to his friend.

"A clever bit of negotiation on Lando's part," praised Markus.

"With this in mind, Lando's motivation to travel to the east was two-fold. Not only did he intend to accompany Nayla to Orien, he wanted to promote sales of his country's goods, most notably the wine, prior to the fall harvest and before those in the east turned to other sources, thereby skewing their chance for shared commerce. Hence, the presence of the *diplomats* from Talibarr, for even they understood the potential for trade with their neighbors to the east."

"So Lando wanted to take advantage of the favourable conditions through the Iron Mountains to use the opportunity to promote trade between their countries?" determined Markus.

"Nayla required little in the way of convincing him to make the arduous trek through Deception Pass. With the good weather conditions, the promise of a lucrative business venture to the east, the chance to see that the Talibarrian delegates remained on their best behavior, not to mention allowing Lando to do the knightly thing by keeping Nayla safe, was his motivation."

"Since when did Nayla need anyone to keep her safe?" questioned Markus. "In all likelihood, she keeps a wary eye out for Lando."

"True, but I feel safer for her knowing she travels in the company of our dear and trusted friend."

"So, Joval Stonecroft does *not* journey with them?" queried Markus, stunned that Nayla's life-long friend and protector was not by her side.

"He offered, but Nayla turned him down. She assured Joval that she would be safe to make this trip and he should use this time with Dania and their infant son."

"I take it, Dania is still upset with Joval for his involvement in helping to rescue Prince Carstian last fall," decided Markus.

"Even though our lives were in jeopardy in confronting Draven Eldard, Joval's dear wife was rather traumatized in learning how close we all came to meeting an untimely demise. Mind you, Dania is not like Nayla."

"There is *no* woman quite like Nayla," corrected Markus.

"Yes, but what I mean to say is that Dania is a delicate flower. She does not hold up well to pressure and the dangers of what we are sometimes faced with beyond the safety of this forest. Dania was more than a little upset when she learned how Joval risked his life to save Nayla when that bridge we crossed collapsed."

"Yes, that was quite the bizarre quest," recalled Markus. He thought back on their harrowing encounter with a huge unicorn, dragon, gargoyles and giant knights made of solid ice that came to life under the power of the forbidden arts at a frozen palace far to the north.

"Dania was rather mortified when Joval revealed the details of that adventure to her," stated Arerys. "Where Nayla would merely be concerned and would regard such creatures and situations as being no more than the hazards one might encounter on such a mission, I believe Dania would have been quite traumatized had she been in Nayla's stead."

"I suppose being that Joval is her husband and the father of her child, she was understandably upset by the news. It hit a little too close to home. Or perhaps, it was too close to…" Markus' voice trailed off as he considered the other possibility.

"*He* was too close to Nayla, you mean to say," finished Arerys, sensing his friend's concern.

"You know the history between Nayla and Joval," responded Markus, squirming uncomfortably in his chair. "And where you are secure in your relationship with your wife, trusting her completely, perhaps it is Joval's wife who is not as secure as she should feel with her husband?"

"Joval Stonecroft can be honest to a fault, if that is possible. Knowing this, I am confident he disclosed to Dania his past relationship with Nayla – their continued friendship; the loyalty and devotion that cannot be simply discarded or disregarded after the many battles they survived together."

"Well, Dania knows Joval can be trusted, or at least, she *should* know that by now," said Markus.

"It is her own insecurities that cannot be trusted. But whatever the case, Joval remains in Wyndwood, establishing a home in Elmgrove, away from Aspenglow – and Nayla, for Dania's sake."

"And just how does our friend fare?" questioned Markus.

"Joval has a lovely wife and a delightful infant boy," responded Arerys, leaning back in his chair with a cup of tea; "all in all, he adapts well to life as a family man."

"Somehow, *adapting* was not quite the word I expected to hear."

"What can you say about an Elf who has spent a good portion of his life devoted to captaining an army or serving as a steward to a bustling city like Nagana? By divine forces, it would appear Joval was destined for a life of service from the start; protecting the weak and the innocent. Now he must devote his time and energy to serving and protecting his wife and the most innocent of all innocents, his son."

"I suppose it is quite the drastic change in his life," determined

Markus, thinking back on the first time he saw this Elf on the slope of Mount Hope when all seemed lost. Joval had journeyed far with a battalion of Taijin and Elven Warriors in his company. Guiding them over the Iron Mountains, they answered Nayla's call for help as they faced the Dark Lord Beyilzon in a desperate stand against evil.

"Do not mistake my words, my friend. Joval seems very content, but a quiet life in the enchanted forest is far removed from the life he once knew and undoubtedly had grown accustomed to."

"And your father, how does he fare?" queried Markus, taking the opportunity to catch up on other news. "I have seen little of Kal-lel during these past few days."

"I must apologize on my father's behalf. He did not mean to be rude to you," said Arerys. "He has been distracted of late."

"When I arrived in Aspenglow, I met with him, but only briefly. He was gracious as usual, but his mind seemed taxed by other matters."

"Well, speaking in confidence, my father has been meeting with the elders. He is faced with what our friend Lindras Weatherstone would refer to as a *conundrum*."

"How so?"

"My father ascended to power when my grandfather, Lord Galan of the WestHaven, abdicated from the throne to leave for the Twilight, so he may return to the home of our forefathers."

"Yes, I recall that much of Elven history. In fact, your father was the mortal equivalent of a young man in his twenty-fifth year when your grandfather abdicated the throne."

"That is correct."

Markus sat forward on his chair as he gasped, "Do not tell me your father wishes to retire to the Haven?"

"It is something he seriously contemplates, even as we speak," revealed Arerys, his words spoken in a hush.

"But why? He is of sound mind and body. He still has many centuries for which he can administer to his land and devote to his people."

"My father assumed the power of the throne when he was a young man even by mortal standards. He did so willingly, even as the threat of a great war loomed on the horizon. When my grandfather sought refuge from the toil and turmoil of this realm, my father accepted this burden, becoming the youngest Elf King to lead a major military campaign and to do so successfully."

"Though I pray to God we never face such evil again and the chance of such a battle unfolding is minimal since the peace accord instituted with those to the north, even if Kal-lel never leads another army into war, he is still more than capable of administering to the wants and the needs of his people. And never mind his role as diplomat when it comes to peacefully settling the contentious issues arising from matters of foreign affairs where the other nations are concerned."

"I have already spoken to him about that."

"And your words fell on deaf ears, I presume?" asked Markus.

"My father listened, carefully weighing and balancing all the issues involved. However, in the end, I sensed in his heart, his mind was made up."

"So Kal-lel plans to retire to the Haven."

"That is his desire."

"And there is no changing this decision?" questioned Markus.

"My father said that throughout his reign, he did what he always deemed necessary for the good of our people and the safety of this realm. Though some of his decisions and actions caused him internal conflict, he said he has made amends in his life, atoning for the issues that truly mattered to him."

"What did he mean by that? Atone for what?"

"He merely said it was a matter that concerned no one else in this realm but his own conscience. What truly matters is the nation of Elves is united once more and most importantly, my father claimed he had made peace with himself, at long last."

"Hmph!" grunted Markus, pondering his friend's troubling words. "I suppose if one was to leave this existence, it is good to have a sense of accomplishment and to be at peace with one's self."

"It is a blessing only a few can truly claim," said Arerys, thinking of all the Elves cut down in battle. Some became one with the energy of this forest, never to see their loved ones again, while others departed from this realm with much of their lives unfinished, forced to retire to the Haven with what life experiences they had endured thus far.

"So, this *conundrum* you spoke about was when Kal-lel plans to step down and allow you to ascend to the throne?"

"No. The real bone of contention between him and the elders is in allowing Artel to assume this power."

"You do not wish to become king?" Markus scrutinized Arerys' face, uncertain if his friend was speaking in jest.

"Why do you sound so surprised, Markus? I had told you long ago it was not my desire," responded Arerys.

"Well, when you first mentioned that on the eve we were to commence our campaign against the Dark Lord, I thought perhaps it was nothing more than the words of a Prince burdened with an overwhelming task. I sensed the difficulties in being made to salvage a bearable life for your people should Beyilzon's cruel reign grip these lands set the underlying tone for your words."

"Like you, I had no intention of losing to that deviant soul, so it was never a question of contending with life under the Dark Lord's rule."

"Then why?" probed Markus.

"I am a warrior and the time of the warrior has come to pass. Artel, on the other hand, is the true diplomat. Though skillful with bow and sword, he is a true sylvan Elf. His heart belongs in this forest and besides; he loves the underpinnings of a truly functional government. He is the one who enjoys rubbing shoulders with kings and princes on both social and political levels. He was born for this role and better suited for it than I am. Artel enjoys the pomp and circumstance; I prefer my trusty sword and a reliable steed."

"But do you not want more?"

"I can handle remaining a prince indefinitely and doling out advice should Artel ask for it."

"And that is it?"

Arerys smiled as Markus' face vacillated between doubt, confusion and surprise.

"What more can I want or ask for? I am blessed. I have a loving, devoted wife in Nayla. We share a beautiful, spirited daughter. I have friends I care for dearly, and they care for me. My life is complete."

"You lead a full life and you want for naught, that is true," admitted Markus.

"If my life was somewhat lacking, perhaps I would think twice, however, I have all that I need. As much as I am content, I am very happy. And it is a kind of happiness that can be complicated by matters such as inheriting the duties and responsibilities of governing a land and its people."

"I cannot deny you speak the truth," acknowledged Markus. "But assuming these responsibilities can also be quite rewarding."

Arerys gazed over at Markus, only to chuckle at the seriousness of his expression.

"Markus, my friend, I have known you since you were a young boy. I know you so well. Though your words and by that grave expression on your face, you come across oh-so sincere, can you honestly tell me that if you had a brother, you would not pass this title on to him?"

"You are asking a hypothetical question."

"Yes, and you are a human. I am an Elf. We are different and yet, we are both alike in so many ways. You would rather lead the fight for your people's freedom than spend your days sequestered in great meeting halls with ambassadors, trade commissions and the various guilds all attempting to negotiate trade agreements in their best interest."

"True, there is nothing more frightening and yet, so very exhilarating about charging into battle. Somehow, it does not compare to fighting off the noddsies in one of those stuffy, drawn-out meetings," conceded Markus, his head drowsily bobbing, and then jerking up as he pretended to ward of sleep. "But just as I was destined to wield the sword to defeat the Dark Lord, so too, am I fated to rule the lands of Carcross."

"And if fate had nothing to do with it, can you honestly tell me that you do not wish King Bromwell was still alive and entrusted with these duties while we are free to roam the country, engaged in another one of our grand adventures?"

"If I can fool my mind and body into believing I can still endure one more adventure, then that would be so. But, unlike you, my long-lived friend, I continue to age where you have remained relatively unchanged in all these years I have known you."

"How right you are, Markus! I feel *old* just watching you age before my very eyes," chuckled Arerys, pretending to gum his buttered biscuit like a toothless, old man.

"Go ahead! Mock me if you wish, Arerys. For a friend, you are not very sympathetic to my plight."

"You are not in need of sympathy, my friend. Another rousing adventure to get your blood flowing, perhaps, but sympathy? No!"

"Well, where the mind would be more than willing, my old body would be lagging two steps behind while the chape of my sword drags in the earth. It is better I wield a quill of ink for signing agreements to end a war than to actively embark on quelling a war or uprising with one of these," sighed Markus, his hand patting the hilt of his sword. "Just give yourself a few more centuries and you will come to understand my situation."

"When that time comes, I will bow down to old age with grace," responded Arerys.

"That is what I am attempting to do, but you insist on making this process difficult," grumbled Markus.

"Words… Nothing more than words," teased the Elf, dismissing his friend's complaint. "You are as young as you believe in your heart to be."

"See these gray bits?" asked Markus. His fingers held up the silvery strands peppering his head of chestnut hair before rolling up a sleeve to expose his arm. "See these scars that take much longer to heal than when I was a young man?"

"Yes, but only because you have taken the time to point them out, otherwise, who would have known."

"I will have you know, my heart cannot be fooled by what my eyes see in the looking glass, nor can it ignore the aches and pains of old wounds inflicted during our little adventures."

Arerys sat back in his chair, quietly contemplating Markus' words.

After an awkward pause, Markus felt compelled to break the silence, "Where are your words of Elven wisdom that you usually have at the ready?"

"It dawned on me that since Mark's arrival into your life, I noticed your steps are lighter. Your energy and enthusiasm for life abounds in dealing with your son."

Markus smiled as he thought on his young progeny. "I will be the first to admit I have found renewed strength and energy, even a second chance at youth, in sharing my experience and knowledge to shape Mark from a boy into a fine, young man."

"But there is more," determined Arerys. "It is not the business of aging that bothers you. It is death itself that is the vexation to your spirit."

"Unfortunately, death has always been a constant with me since my mother's passing," admitted Markus. "And with my wife's death during childbirth – losing both Elana and our son, it is a constant reminder of the frailty of life. Since my father's passing last autumn, it is a very real warning that death is inevitable no matter how well you live your life. In many ways, I curse the passing of each year, knowing a little more of my mind and strength yields to age until my body decays, ravaged by time."

"Do not take my words lightly just because I am long-lived, my friend," urged Arerys. "Though death is indeed inevitable, the one thing you should have learned in the passing of those dear to you is in not how they died, but rather how they had lived. It is an utter waste to lament the passing of the years. Do you not think your wife would have cherished a life growing old by your side? Do you not ever think what Elana would have done just to live for even one more year with you? It does not take a fool to see that only the living have the privilege of growing old."

Markus grew silent as he absorbed Arerys' stern words.

"Though I will eventually age just as surely as you do for as long as I remain in this realm, I will treasure this time now," said Arerys. "If I were you, I would choose to cherish the time you have with Mark and those you care about. Make the very best of this time you have been given. Do not wallow in self-pity, lamenting for the passing of another year and the arrival of the next. Be grateful when the dawn of a new year comes."

"That is easy for you to say," sighed Markus.

"You feel this way now, but take the time to think of all those who will learn that through illness or circumstance, they will not see it to the end. And not even a prayer will give them one more year or another month to heal old wounds, to make amends with those they had wronged or to forgive those who had wronged them. You know you get but one chance in this realm, and once it is done, there will be no second opportunity to make amends. It is a life unfinished."

Markus drew another deep breath, reflecting on the Elf's wisdom.

"That was harsh! Spoken like a true friend... but harsh nonetheless," commented Markus.

"I am sorry if I came across that way," apologized Arerys. "However, you have never been one to sit back and complain, feeling sorry for yourself. It is a side of you I am not well acquainted with and prefer to keep at a distance if I can help it."

"You are correct, my friend, in the big scheme of things, I have nothing to complain about and no reason to wallow in self-pity. I hope to see Mark grow to manhood, but that cannot happen unless I grow along side with him, even if it is only in age."

"How right you are, Markus," agreed Arerys, topping up his friend's cup with fresh tea. "And besides, you are the King of Carcross. Self-pity does not sit well with a nobleman like you. It is rather unbecoming, if you get my meaning?"

"I do. And the next time you hear a complaint from me, it will be legitimate," vowed Markus, his right hand over his heart in solemn promise.

"Fair enough," acknowledged the Elf. Gazing down into the courtyard where the children played, he spied a young page with a small scroll in hand, darting over to the sanctuary where his father and the elders continued their meeting. The page pounded on the door, to be ushered inside by the elder Tor-rin Greenshield.

"I take it, the elders are reluctant to allow Kal-lel to abdicate the throne," assessed Markus.

"It is more than that," confided Arerys. "Though my father had been successful in his appeal, there is the matter of allowing Artel to assume the role. The title had always been handed down to the eldest son. They are in a quandary as to what they are to do about me stepping aside to make way for my little brother."

"It is just like you to break with tradition and complicate matters," teased Markus, imagining poor Artel in the center of this maelstrom as the debate raged on as to what is the right and proper thing to do.

"Though it is a time-honoured tradition among your people and mine that the title of king, as well as all its vested powers, be handed down to the first born, there is nothing wrong with change. I believe it is time to pass this role and its corresponding duties on to the one more qualified and enthusiastically willing to undertake this challenge. Though it is a privilege to rule my father's domain, it should not be done with only half a heart and half the intention."

"So you really do not want this?" responded Markus.

"What I truly want, I already have. I do not feel it is the proper thing to do, to ask for more than what one needs or desires. Plus, I have my reasons for wanting Artel to assume this title."

"Now I am intrigued! Pray tell, for what reason?"

"My little brother is yet to announce his betrothal. As the new King of Wyndwood, I believe he will make for a worthy catch for a fair maiden and if he does not decide on a bride, the elders will be more than happy to intervene on his behalf to ensure a future heir to the throne of Wyndwood."

"Hold on! I know where this conversation is leading," declared Markus, giving his friend a scornful look of reproach.

"You do?" queried Arerys, looking and sounding all very innocent. "Where?"

"You were going to ask me if I had set my sights on a maiden – a potential bride," determined Markus.

"I was?"

"You always do. You are worse than the village matchmaker," snorted Markus. "If you are not hinting at arranging a meeting for me, then you are probing about, trying to find out if I am already courting a woman."

"Are you? It would be grand if you were."

"You are my dear friend and you are also impossible!" grumbled Markus, his face flushed with embarrassment.

"Ah-ha, there is someone!" declared Arerys, scrutinizing Markus' face.

"You only wish."

"Well, in all honesty, I do," responded the Elf, sounding hopeful. "Your letter writing campaigns to keep me abreast of news from Whycliffe Castle suffers at the best of times. I am left to speculate and worry about you. And besides, I have not seen you since last autumn when we embarked on that quest to rescue Prince Carstian. Anything could have happened since then."

"Well, I am sorry to be the one to disappoint you, Arerys, but no, I am not yet betrothed."

Arerys sat back, contemplating the tone and choice of Markus' words. His eyes suddenly gleamed with excitement as he announced, "Aah, but there *is* a lady!"

"No…" said Markus, his voice incredulous as his eyes seemed to glance everywhere else but at Arerys as he made this denial.

A broad smile spread across Arerys' face as he declared, "You *are* courting a lady! Do not deny it. And being your closest friend, do not deny me of the details."

"See! I was right! You *are* worse than the village matchmaker!"

"If I admit to the world that I am, will you share in the details?" asked Arerys, leaning forward to learn more of this juicy bit of unexpected news.

"That sounds rather desperate."

"I *am* desperate. Desperate to learn about your ladylove. So, do tell!"

"Now you sound like a gossipy, old woman," denounced Markus, staring with raised eyebrows at his inquisitive friend. "Have you no shame?"

"Not in this respect! And that is why I will never make for a good king," confided Arerys, urging his friend to update him on the personal matters of his life. "Now go on, who is she?"

"If you must know, it is Lady Anne of Kalispel."

Arerys brows arched up in surprise. "A descendent of Queen Cordelia, the wife of the long departed King Brannon?"

"Yes, a noblewoman of refined breeding and culture," revealed Markus, his face red with embarrassment.

"I take it, she is beautiful?"

"She is near-sighted, as wide as she is tall and she has a severe overbite, if you must know."

"Say again!" gasped Arerys, stunned by Markus' description.

"Of course she is beautiful! But more than she is pleasing to the eyes, Lady Anne has a fair and kind heart."

"So, she is like Elana?" assumed Arerys, thinking Markus would gravitate to the familiar.

"No, she has flaxen tresses and dazzling green eyes set against her fair skin, but I suppose her gentle manner, gracious demeanor and compassionate heart make her similar to Elana in some ways."

"And just how did you happen to come together? Was it an arranged meeting or was it by accident?"

"It was quite a happy coincidence, really," reminisced Markus. "I was familiar with her name and reputation, for she is well known in the social circles for her work in tutoring the privileged in Carcross and for providing educational opportunities for children less fortunate."

"A woman with a social conscience," praised Arerys, smiling in approval.

"With her noble lineage, it afforded her a comprehensive education most can only dream of. She chose to devote her life to educating others."

"So, I take it, you had solicited her skills and vast knowledge to tutor your son?"

"You know I want only the best for Mark. Because of the recommendations to back her concise and intimate knowledge of my country's history, she was the most qualified candidate for this posting."

"An academic! Intelligent and beautiful," surmised Arerys, nodding in admiration. "That is a winning combination."

"The irony of it all was that when she accepted the posting to tutor Mark in history, mathematics and the language arts, I was expecting a bookish spinster – a strict, matronly type to show up at the castle gates. Instead, into the throne room glides this lovely and charming woman."

"You are smitten by her!" declared Arerys, a broad smile spreading across his face.

Markus momentarily flushed with embarrassment as he responded, "More important than how I feel, Mark is very fond of her. And just as important, she is quite fond of Mark. They share a mutual admiration and respect for each other."

"Is there potential for a family in the making?"

"Yes, there is that potential," confided Markus. "But do not breathe a word of this to anyone, not even my son. If I choose to propose to her, I would very much like it coming from me first, not some well-meaning friend wishing to expedite the matter."

"I get your meaning," said Arerys. "My lips are sealed. I will not even share this news with Nayla."

"You will truly keep this secret, even from her?" asked Markus, wondering if this was something Arerys could accomplish.

"Mind you, if she asks, I *am* her husband. I cannot lie to her."

"Why did I open my mouth?" groaned Markus, his hand slapping his forehead.

"To lie to my wife would be low, dishonest even," stated Arerys, considering the consequences of his actions. "Besides, even if I tried, she will know I am not telling her the truth."

"You would divulge a secret shared amongst friends? Between you and me?"

"Not willingly, but you know Nayla. She still carries a mean sword. I would be forced to reveal what I know, but I can swear her to secrecy; make Nayla take one of those Kagai oaths she still abides by."

"I suppose that will have to do," sighed Markus, resigning to the fact that whatever secret Arerys was privy to, so too, was Nayla. "If I cannot trust my two dearest friends, then who in this world is there left to trust?"

"Well said, Markus, and quite true! I must say, Nayla will be absolutely delighted to hear there is finally a woman in your life."

"Whoa! Hold on there, Arerys. How involved she will be in my life is yet to be determined."

"What are you speaking of? This sounds absolutely promising!"

"I admit I do enjoy her company. Lady Anne is charming, witty and capable of sparkling conversation. However…" Markus' voice trailed off as he thought on how best to explain their budding romance.

"Go on," urged Arerys.

"As much as I enjoy her company, I cannot say the same for her."

"Oh, come now, my friend. It has been a long time, too long really, since you had spent quality time with those of the feminine persuasion. I sense it is your confidence that is lacking, nothing more."

"I admit I am out of form in this respect, however, Lady Anne seems, for a lack of a better word, *uncomfortable* in my immediate presence."

"Nonsense!" declared Arerys. "The good woman is merely overwhelmed by your greatness. After all, it is not everyday one is in the company of royalty, a king no less. And remember, you were the one to defeat the Dark Lord Beyilzon."

"You are too kind, Arerys."

"You know I speak the truth."

"I wish it were so, but I sense she is too polite to speak her mind where I am concerned."

"I do believe you are fishing for compliments in order to boost your ego," teased the Elf. "And you should know; it is completely unnecessary."

"Then listen to this. I am fast approaching my forty-eighth year."

"So? For a mortal of your age, you still possess striking good looks."

"Says who? I am not about to take a man's word for it, even if he were my best friend," scoffed Markus, laughing lightly.

"Fair enough, but according to Nayla, she believes so."

"Nayla said that?" gasped Markus, pleasantly surprised by this unexpected bit of information. "Are you positive?"

"Indeed!"

"In what context did she say this?"

Arerys rolled his eyes in exasperation as Markus' tone became tinged with suspicious.

"She said, and I quote, *'Why does Markus forestall marriage? He is a charming, handsome man and more than he is a king, he is a gentleman'*. So take that in whatever context you wish."

The suspicious frown on Markus' face melted away as he smiled upon digesting this news.

"As pleased as I am that at least one woman of taste and sound judgment finds me to be attractive, even if Lady Anne agreed, it does not change the fact that I am years her senior."

"How old is she?"

"I would never dream of asking a lady such a personal question, but from what I have been able to uncover, I believe I can safely place her age at approximately thirty-three years."

"She is too young for your liking?" queried Arerys, puzzling over this mystery.

"Goodness, no! But I sense I am the one too old for her liking."

"And how did you come to this conclusion? Did she tell you this? Does she recoil in disgust when you come near her?"

"No, she does not. Though she graciously accepts dinner invitations and willingly accompanies me to social functions, I believe I have put her in an awkward position. I sense Lady Anne feels she cannot refuse me because I am the King of Carcross."

"Granted it is a prestigious title you bear, why do you think she remains a spinster to this day? Is she too homely to find a husband?"

"Bite your tongue, Arerys! She is a strong-willed woman, one who chose to defy convention by pursuing a profession as an educator in order to do away with ignorance."

"Aah, I see! She is strong-willed enough to take control of her life and do what she considers is the best for her, and yet she lacks the will to say *no* to a king. Mind you, the threat of losing one's head for refusing the king is enough to sway anyone."

"How dare you? I would never make such a threat to Lady Anne, or any other person, for that matter."

"Did it ever occur to you that perhaps Lady Anne truly enjoys your company and has never declined an invitation because she finds you to be charismatic and dashing for an *old man*?"

"Do you think that is possible?"

"You are looking to have your ego stroked, but you are turning to the wrong person for this attention. I suggest you ask the lady yourself."

"Is that not too forward?"

"Lady Anne seems to be a woman before her times. I hardly think she would consider it as such."

"I suppose you could be right on this account, but how does one go and ask such a thing? I would be like a giddy, awkward adolescent boy asking the prettiest girl in the village if she is fond of me."

"If it is too difficult for you, I can ask the lady on your behalf," offered Arerys.

"Oh, wonderful! Then I will be reduced to a little boy with a childlike infatuation. I am sure she will find that appealing."

"And I say, if you do not ask, you will never know. And since you had been lamenting about aging before your time, perhaps you should be proactive? Do something about it. Or are you waiting until you are so old; with a balding head, a toothless smile and suffering from dementia that you will be reduced to a blithering man-child she will feel compelled to adopt as a baby that requires coddling?"

"Now *that* is a disturbing thought," groaned Markus. "It is a good thing I know you have quite the sense of humour."

"Who said I was speaking in jest?"

"Now you are scaring me!"

"Enough to make you take decisive action?" queried Arerys. "For if not, I am more than willing to act on your behalf."

"Thank you, but no," responded Markus. "I am quite capable."

"I knew you would say that!" proclaimed Arerys, his hands clapping together in delight. "So… when do you plan to take action?"

"Some things cannot be rushed."

"That is a strange thing coming from a man, who only moments ago, whined about time and age; and not having enough time as he ages before my very eyes," teased the Elf.

"It has been many years since Elana's passing and it has taken me as many years to finally come to terms with my grief. I believe I am entitled to a little time to ensure this budding romance has the opportunity to blossom as it should."

"I suppose I should cut you some slack in this matter," agreed Arerys, gazing down into the courtyard.

He watched as the doors of the sanctuary opened and the page who had delivered a message to his father reappeared. Behind the boy came Kal-lel and Artel, followed by the three elders; Tor-rin Greenshield, Sol-lel Amberwood and Ansat Graystone.

"I wonder if they have come to some kind of resolution?" said Markus, glancing down to see Kal-lel leading the way back to this royal residence.

"I doubt it, but they definitely have news to share with us," determined Arerys, rising up from the table.

As the golden shafts of sunlight flooded into the great meeting hall, following Arerys into this room, Markus could see that Kal-lel and Artel were already seated at the table as the elders took their place.

Kal-lel motioned for Markus to join them for this impromptu conference.

"I sense this has nothing to do with your father's abdication," Markus whispered to Arerys.

"That is correct, Markus," confirmed Kal-lel, his keen ears easily detecting this mortal's hushed words. "It has nothing to do with affairs of my kingdom, however, it very much affects our neighbours to the north."

"Talibarr?" queried Markus, taking a seat next to Tor-rin Greenshield.

"Though the events leading up to this matter unfolded in Talibarr, it concerns the King of Darross," revealed Kal-lel, his hand unrolling the scroll. "Only moments ago, a falcon arrived with urgent word from King Sebastian's son, Prince Garrick."

"It did not come from King Sebastian himself?" questioned Arerys.

"I wish it did," replied Kal-lel. "However, Prince Garrick is faced with a desperate situation."

"Go on," urged Arerys, eager to learn more. "What is this situation you speak of?"

"On the request of the governing body in Talibarr, King Sebastian was called upon to provide the men and the resources to help them capture a killer," explained Kal-lel.

"A killer? If the criminal had not committed a murder within King Sebastian's jurisdiction, why are the Talibarrians seeking his help?" asked Markus.

"The fledgling council in Talibarr is at a loss for what to do. They mean to serve those they represent, however, they did not have the ways or the means to orchestrate a proper search in an organized fashion to hunt down this killer," explained Kal-lel. "But at the heart of this matter, in the process of helping the Talibarrians to hunt down and capture the killer at large, King Sebastian has gone missing."

"Missing as in abducted? Taken for ransom?" queried Markus, wishing to better understand the implications.

"If it were only something as simple as a kidnapping for ransom," stated Arerys' brother. "A kidnapping would imply a human perpetrator, but there is nothing human about the instigator of this crime."

"Your words are strangely ominous, Artel," noted Arerys.

"And rightfully so, Prince Arerys, for this is no ordinary killer we speak of," said Tor-rin. "Those to the north are faced with a creature that has been rampaging through Talibarr on a killing spree."

"So, this killer is an *animal*," determined Arerys. "Exactly what kind of animal are they dealing with?"

"That is the mystery," replied Kal-lel. "According to Prince Garrick, they were at first under the assumption the killer beast was a bear."

"A bear?" repeated Markus.

"Yes, a great brown bear," confirmed Kal-lel. "However, after a bear was found at the sight of one of the latest killings, all in King Sebastian's company, the King included, were under the firm belief this animal was the culprit. It was finally captured and killed."

"Whatever made off with King Sebastian was definitely not this bear," said Artel.

"I take it, King Sebastian has yet to be found, dead or alive," assessed Arerys.

"That is so, my son," responded Kal-lel. "And that is why Prince Garrick has made this appeal for our help. He believes where he and the royal huntsmen failed in recovering his father, those with our skills will succeed where the others have not."

"There is no time to waste," decided Arerys. "I will ready my bow and horse."

"You will not undertake this task alone, my son," said Kal-lel. "I shall accompany you on this search."

"You have a kingdom to tend to, father," responded Arerys. "I will go in your place."

"I know you mean well, Arerys, however, not only do I owe the King of Darross my allegiance in a political sense, but Sebastian is a loyal and trusted friend. For this reason, I will actively engage in the hunt to see him returned home."

"But you know I am capable of undertaking this mission," contested Arerys. "And you should use your time to revel in the peace we now enjoy in this realm."

"You are very capable indeed, Arerys. However, if this is to be my last, meaningful act before I retire to the Haven, then please allow my actions to have greater meaning to someone other than myself," countered Kal-lel, seeking his son's understanding. "Besides, Wyndwood will be in good hands. I will leave Artel in charge during my absence."

Arerys nodded in agreement. He now realized his father's decision was two-fold. Not only did he mean to come to the aid of a close, personal friend, it was to allow his younger son the opportunity to prove to the elders that Artel was more than capable of administering to the needs of their people without constant supervision. Such a demonstration will prove to the elders that Artel is a promising candidate, ready to take over the duties of the throne.

"Then it is decided," said Arerys, his head bowing in respect and agreement to his father. "Let us prepare to leave immediately."

As the elders hurried out of the meeting hall to deliver word for the staff to ready the horses for this trek, Artel departed with Kal-lel. He was to help his father prepare for this journey to the north as well as receive final instructions for the administrative duties he was to undertake.

Markus rose up from his chair. He looked pensive as he contemplated this strange news Kal-lel had shared with them.

"I do not mean to be rude, Markus, but I must ready for this task," said Arerys. "You are free to return to Carcross, if you wish."

"I will be leaving promptly," confirmed Markus. "But I will not be returning to my castle."

"Oh?"

"I do believe my sword and this old body of mine is up for one last adventure, Arerys," said Markus, his hand patting the hilt of his weapon. "And it is only right that a king come to the aid of a fellow king."

chasing a mystery

"There they are!" announced Garrick, staring through the trees at the trail leading down from Rock Ridge Pass. "They must have departed from Wyndwood immediately upon receiving my message."

Cullen glanced up from the campfire to spy upon Joval Stonecroft, escorting the royal party. Following behind his personal guard, King Kal-lel arrived in person to aid in the search for the King of Darross.

"Well, this is a surprise," muttered Cullen, rising up from the fire as he quickly came to notice Garrick's call was answered not by one king, but two. "King Markus is in their company."

Markus' rode in on his black stallion. He proceeded behind Arerys as the Elf Prince urged his gray-dappled mare to follow his father's steed. In their company, a dozen Elven warriors prepared to help in the hunt for the missing King dismounted on Joval's command. These warriors took control of the horses, allowing the meeting to commence immediately.

"Thank goodness you have come, King Kal-lel!" exclaimed Garrick, relieved to see help arrive in such a timely manner considering the distance this party was made to travel. "I was not expecting to see you for another day or two, if you even chose to come to my aid."

"Of course I would come, Prince Garrick. I have known King Sebastian since before you were born. And throughout our shared history, my father and I had cultivated and maintained a strong ally in the House of Northcott, but more importantly, your father is a friend. How can I not answer your call for assistance at this desperate time?"

"I am most grateful!" Garrick bowed his head in respect and appreciation. "And I see you have not come alone."

Markus and Arerys stepped forward, clasping Garrick's wrist in greeting as Joval bowed in respect to the Prince.

"This is not the best of circumstances, however, it is always a pleasure to see you again," greeted Arerys. "I suspect you will need all the help you can muster to find your father."

"Absolutely," nodded Garrick. "Your assistance is most appreciated and desperately needed."

"That is why I had come along with King Kal-lel and Prince Arerys," explained Markus. "Understandably, time is of the essence; another experienced in tracking and hunting can only help the cause."

"I do appreciate your involvement, King Markus, especially after all you, Prince Arerys and Master Stonecroft had done to help Captain Bristow in rescuing my brother last autumn. And should my father lay wounded, perhaps Prince Arerys and Master Stonecroft can do for him what they did for me," said Garrick, thinking back on when he lay gravely injured in the infirmary during Draven Eldard's mad bid to take control of Darross Castle.

"I pray it does not come to that. However, it is better to hope for the best while anticipating the worst," responded Arerys. "But more than our combined powers, my father possesses the healing powers of a high Elf. Where Joval and I may fail, my father will be in a better position to aid King Sebastian."

"If such aid is even necessary," Kal-lel was quick to add.

"Oh, yes! Of course," nodded Garrick, bowing to the Elf King once more before motioning them to the safety of the campfire.

Cullen glanced through the party that had arrived with Kal-lel, searching for another familiar face or two as Garrick escorted them to their camp.

"Good evening, Captain Bristow," greeted Arerys, not surprised to see Cullen in the thick of things. "Are you expecting someone?"

"Indeed, my lord," admitted Cullen. He bowed to Markus and Joval as they nodded in polite acknowledgement. "It would appear that your lovely wife and your friend, the fat one, are not in your company on this occasion."

"The *fat one*?" repeated Arerys, frowning with curiosity.

"I speak of Lando Bayliss. The last time we were together, the old gaffer was not in the best of shape," explained Cullen, deliberately protruding his belly to appear portly as his hands pretended to pat a rotund midsection. "More often than not, for a knight retired, he seems to spend more time than he should being involved in quests a fellow his age should really consider refraining from."

"Well, thank you for being so concerned about Lando's health and well-being, but at this moment, he and Nayla are in Orien," responded

Arerys, stepping past Cullen as he follow behind Markus and Joval.

"Orien? This early in the spring?" wondered Cullen. "It must be a matter of grave importance for them to chance a trek through Deception Pass this early in the year."

"It was of grave importance, for their own separate and personal reasons," said Arerys. "So, if that was your *discreet* way of asking if Nayla and Lando were to be joining us on this mission? The answer is no, not this time."

"Pity!" exclaimed Cullen, hoping he sounded sincere as he snapped his fingers in feigned disappointment.

"Pity, indeed," sighed Arerys, taking a seat between Markus and Joval as Garrick motioned for the King's squire to deliver wine to his esteemed guests. "But at this moment, we have more pressing matters to be concerned about than the whereabouts of my wife and my dear friend."

"Yes! Of course, let us get to the business at hand," nodded Cullen, taking his place next to Prince Garrick. "I suppose I should rally my men immediately to resume the search."

"In due time, Captain Bristow," said Kal-lel, motioning Cullen to remain seated. "First, we must have a better grasp of exactly what we are faced with and how best to conduct this search. There is no point in venturing out into these great forests, running haphazardly in all directions. We must organize a thorough and methodical search. This will only happen with some planning."

"What was I thinking, Your Highness?" apologized Cullen, his knuckles rapping his forehead as he cursed his forgetfulness. "I suppose my concern for my liege and our exhaustive search have taken its toll on my mind. Of course, we must devise a worthy plan."

"Very good. Now, Prince Garrick, the message I received from you was brief and concise," stated Kal-lel, politely accepting a goblet of wine from the squire. "However, based on this note, am I correct in assuming the killer beast you had referred to has yet to be properly identified? You have not ascertained what manner of creature is responsible for the numerous killings as well as your father's disappearance?"

"You assume correctly, King Kal-lel. The only thing we know for certain is that we have been chasing a mystery," answered Garrick. "Upon issuing a bounty for the capture of the murderous animal, we had been inundated by Talibarrians delivering all manner of beasts, great and small, they claim to be the killer."

"Yes, we even went as far as ordering the most likely contenders of this bounty to disembowel their catch in an effort to prove their animal was indeed the one," added Cullen, barely acknowledging the squire as he took up a goblet of wine.

"You were looking for proof in the way of human flesh that had been consumed?" determined Arerys.

"Yes," answered Garrick. "We had to be sure."

"And what did you find?" questioned Markus.

"When all was said and done, the only animal that did indeed eat a man – or at least a part of one, was a massive brown bear," replied Garrick.

"That creature sounds to be a likely candidate," responded Markus, nodding judiciously. "They have a reputation as being ferocious when accosted or provoked and there are a few verified accounts of brown bears killing men."

"This knowledge and the irrefutable proof that it was a man-eater gave us reason to believe this *was* the creature," said Garrick.

"I will tell you now, it was the largest brown bear any of us had ever seen," added Cullen, speaking with all certainty. "A Talibarrian hunting party came across five dead men not far from here. And lo and behold, settling down for a warm meal was this great beast. This bear was swift and cunning! It took the hunting party much effort to down the creature."

"The Talibarrians willingly gutted the bear, and before our eyes, they produced a mutilated arm from the animal's stomach," continued Garrick.

"We were so confident this bear was the guilty culprit – the creature responsible for all the deaths across this country that we made the unfortunate mistake of lowering our guard," admitted Cullen. "In the single moment my liege stepped not but a few paces from the glow of our campfire, it was all the killer beast needed to seize him – to make off with his body."

"Do not speak of my father as though he is already dead!" admonished Garrick.

"I am sorry, my lord," apologized Cullen, bowing his head in regret. "I should not assume the worst has happened to him."

"There is still a chance my father is alive!" snapped Garrick. "As slim as it is, I refuse to believe otherwise; not until it is proven he had been killed."

"Of course, my lord," responded Cullen, his voice contrite. "I had no right to even consider this possibility."

Sensing the Prince's guilt for what had happened to his father, Kal-lel quickly piped in, "Alas, given such convincing evidence, I believe it is fair to say any one of us would have come to the same conclusion, Prince Garrick."

"And feelings of guilt and sorrow will do nothing to bring your father back," added Arerys. "Your energies should be devoted completely to finding him. Our collective efforts should be focused on retreiving King Sebastian."

"That being said, Prince Garrick, what has been done up to now to locate your father?" questioned Markus.

"As of this morning, an army of knights and soldiers dispatched by my brother Carstian arrived to aid in the search," replied Garrick.

"They have joined with the citizens of Talibarr to assist in the search," added Cullen. "Needless to say, the local inhabitants are more than willing to help, however, they did require some persuasion to actively and enthusiastically partake in this exercise."

Joval stared at the mortal as he responded matter-of-factly, "Coming from you, Captain Bristow, I take it that you had threatened the locals by the point of your sword to gain their cooperation."

Cullen snorted in laughter as he replied to the Elf, "These Talibarrians are lazy dolts and not known for their intelligence! And I hardly think the majority of them are even smart enough to know what the point of a sword can do to them. When I spoke of *persuasion,* I meant monetary kind. Prince Garrick had more than doubled the original bounty to be awarded to the first person able to deliver King Sebastian to him. And four times that if he is returned alive!"

"So, there is no bounty for the capture of the killer beast?" queried Kal-lel, attempting to understand the reasoning behind this decision.

"Originally there was," replied Cullen. "But it was an exercise in futility."

"Unfortunately, we had already wasted too much time with the locals. They delivered every creature imaginable, *except* for the one responsible for the killings," explained Garrick. "I chose to offer this reward specifically for my father's return, for there is no mistaking the King of Darross."

"A prudent move," Kal-lel nodded with approval.

"And your knights and soldiers, where are they now?" questioned Arerys, his eyes searching the forest as dusk settled thick and velvety on this clear night. "Do they continue the search?"

"With the coming darkness, they have ended their search for the day," answered Garrick.

"They do not search on into the night?" asked Markus, stunned by this unexpected news.

Garrick heaved a beleaguered sigh as he felt the weight of this decision bear down upon his weary shoulders.

"Allow me to answer for my lord," offered Cullen.

"Please do, Captain Bristow," said Markus.

"Although my men are ready, willing and prepared to engage in this search throughout the night until King Sebastian is found, we are in Talibarr, not Darross."

"I understand that," responded Markus, "but that should not get in the way of delaying the search."

"If you are dealing with the people of Talibarr, it most certainly does," countered Cullen. "Not only are these people lazy, imbecilic gadabouts, they are bloody superstitious to boot! As much as they would love to get their grubby little paws on the reward Prince Garrick has generously posted, they adamantly refuse to partake in the search during the darkness of night as this is when the creature is most active."

"I see," said Markus, mulling over these words.

"Not to mention the fact that if I should send my men out into the dark of night, I also place them in potential danger. Not only is that creature lurking about, but every jumpy Talibarrian with spear and bow is out there, waiting for an excuse to *accidentally* assault my men."

"Even if that were so, I find it difficult to believe that a handsome reward is not enough to motivate the Talibarrians to continue the search with your men," stated Arerys.

"These people are scared out of their puny, little minds!" retorted Cullen, his tone curdling with malice as his obvious contempt for the Talibarrians was made clear to all in his presence. "They prefer to huddle by the safety of a blazing campfire and dream of what they would do with this money than to venture forth into the night to earn it."

"It is clear to see that whatever this creature is, the Talibarrians are truly frightened by its presence," assessed Arerys.

"How many have fallen victim to this beast?" queried Joval.

"Since the Talibarrians first reported the killings far to the north near to Spirit Wood, in these two weeks, over four dozen lives had been taken," answered Garrick.

"However, there is nothing to say more killings have occurred farther to the north beyond the Shadow Mountains, and we have yet to receive this news to add to the body count," added Cullen.

"And the killings have continued unabated?" questioned Joval.

"Strangely enough, the last reported killings occurred on the very day my father was taken. He is the last confirmed victim," informed Garrick.

"If any more had died since then, we have yet to hear about it."

Joval appeared pensive. He rubbed his chin in thought as he mulled over this bit of information.

"I recognize that look on your face, Joval," noted Markus. "What are you thinking, my friend?"

"I am thinking on the manner of beast we are faced with," replied Joval, turning to Garrick and Cullen for more details. "What do you, based on what you have seen, believe this creature to be?"

"We, my father included, believed the creature was a rogue brown bear," answered Garrick. "Unfortunately, we were tragically wrong."

"There is a chance the killer beast is indeed a brown bear, just not the one the Talibarrian hunters had killed," said Arerys.

"But what makes you believe it was even a bear to begin with?" inquired Joval.

"Judging by the extent of damage inflicted to the bodies of the victims that were strewn all about from Spirit Wood to here, it had to be an animal of great size and power," answered Cullen.

"What type of damage do you speak of?" queried Kal-lel. "Bite marks? Clawing? Were they mauled to death?"

"Biting, clawing, dismembering of limbs, decapitations, bodies literally torn in half..." replied Cullen, thinking back on the last grisly scene they had inspected. "I believe I have covered it all."

"It sounds like absolute carnage!" gasped Markus. "Why would any creature go on such a bloodletting rampage?"

"That is a very good question," said Kal-lel, turning to his hosts once more. "Assuming that the beast had good reason to kill, just how many of the dead were consumed by this creature?"

"From the bodies we have had the ill-fortune of inspecting, aside from the man whose arm was recovered from the dead bear, all the other victims, as maimed and mutilated as they were, this fellow was the only one we could ascertain had been eaten," responded Garrick.

"And this large, brown bear you speak of had only consumed one arm?" asked Joval.

"It would have been more than just a little snack if the Talibarrian hunters did not interrupt its supper when they did," explained Cullen. "The bear attempted to make off with the corpse when the men turned on it."

"But you are quite certain of the state of the other bodies?" pressed Joval, looking to better understand their quarry.

"As cursory as our inspection was, for the bodies were quickly falling to decay, we were able to determine that all other detached limbs and one decapitated head were accounted for," replied Garrick. "They were mauled to varying degrees, but definitely not eaten."

"And other than scavenging minks, foxes and ravens feasting on an easy banquet," added Cullen; "as best as we could tell, the animal that did the actual killing might have drank some spilled blood, but flesh and entrails were not eaten by a large carnivore."

"What do you make of all this, Joval?" questioned Kal-lel.

"I was just thinking that if Nayla was here, she would be able to help unravel this mystery," replied the Elf. "Being that she is so familiar with the study of wild creatures and their behavior, Nayla would undoubtedly have immediate insight as to the animal we are faced with."

"I wish she were here, too, Joval, but we are not afforded this luxury. In all your wisdom, what do you believe this creature to be?" asked Arerys.

"The type and level of carnage Prince Garrick and Captain Bristow had described are the hallmarks of a rogue brown bear – a very large and powerful brown bear, to be sure," determined Joval. "However, these giants consume more vegetation in the way of grasses, roots, tubers and berries, than flesh."

"But it is a well-known fact that these bears, even the small black bears, do eat meat," contested Cullen.

"Yes, they do," agreed the Elf. "However, more often when they do consume prey in the way of deer, it is usually a kill stolen from a pack of wolves. Although these bears have been known to actively and successfully hunt such game, they are far more likely to scavenge for meat than to hunt for it."

"So you are saying that if there is an easier source of meat than to hunt for it themselves, they would rather steal it away from another animal?" questioned Garrick.

"Yes," confirmed Joval.

"Then are we faced with an exceptionally clever bear that has learned to hunt with great efficiency?" queried Cullen.

"Even if a bear became as efficient a hunter as this, it does not explain this sudden and prodigious killing spate. And why kill, but not consume?" asked Joval. "In all honesty, the only animal I know of that will, on occasion, kill for sport are wolves, dogs and, no offense to the mortals in our company, the odd human being."

"We had considered this possibility," responded Garrick. "However, I sense by now, the last wolves in Talibarr are either dead or running north for their lives. None have been seen for the past two days."

"Yes, and from the carnage we have been witness to, there is no way a pack of wolves could tear apart a man the way this creature did," stated Cullen.

"Perhaps a bear follows these marauding wolves?" suggested Markus. "Driving off the pack, it would be free to inflict horrible damage to the already dead body."

"There is a possibility," agreed Joval. "But why does everyone assume this is the work of an animal? There is a remote, but very real chance this is the work of a man gone mad; a deranged soul bent on murder."

"That is absolutely preposterous!" retorted Cullen, quickly denouncing Joval's suspicions.

"Why do you say that, Captain Bristow?" questioned Joval.

"Because nobody in his right mind would run about the countryside to engage in such a bloodbath!" sputtered the Captain. "That is why!"

"That is just it. It could well be a person *not* in his right frame of mind," argued Joval. "We all wish to believe the human race is not capable of such madness, but in my lifetime, I have had the misfortune of being witness to a number of atrocious acts of cruelty inflicted on man by man."

"Before you go washing my kind as horrible monsters capable of such heinous acts, perhaps you should consider other potential candidates," grunted Cullen, insulted by the Elf's words.

"We are open to suggestions if you can back them with plausible reasons, Captain Bristow," responded Markus.

"If you choose to believe the killer is something other than an animal, the only *thing* that comes immediately to my mind is a powerful entity that has had a long history of indiscriminately killing both human beings and Elves!" snapped Cullen.

"Dare we ask?" groaned Markus, rolling his eyes in dismay as he endured the Captain's caustic tone.

"The better question is, dare you consider my words with an open mind?" challenged Cullen. "Are you willing to consider the possibilities even if you do not want to believe it can be so?"

"As Markus said, we are willing to consider all possibilities," stated Arerys. "However, you must be able to back your claim with legitimate reasons, not haphazard speculations that make no sense."

"Well, here is a possibility for your esteemed consideration," offered Cullen. "Instead of pointing an accusing finger at a human being as Master Stonecroft so willingly and eagerly does, did it ever occur to any one of you that the real villain is a *Wizard*?"

There was a moment of profound silence as Cullen searched the faces of those in his company, waiting for a response.

"Well?" prompted Cullen, squirming with discomfort as they mulled over his suspect.

Everyone, the staid Elves included, suddenly burst out in laughter after considering Cullen's words.

"Now, *that* was preposterous!" chuckled Markus, shaking his head in dismay.

"How can you even come to such a bizarre conclusion, Captain Bristow?" queried Arerys, perplexed by Cullen's insinuation.

"If you want to consider a killer that is *not* an animal, then why not a Wizard?" Cullen responded with a question of his own. "After all, it is obvious a powerful Wizard is far more capable of committing such monstrous acts against humanity than a mere mortal, and to do so in quantity without an ounce of remorse."

"I take it, you already have a particular Wizard in mind to blame for these atrocities, Captain?" determined Arerys.

"I most certainly do! The Wizard of the East, Eldred Firestaff to be exact, was once an evil Sorcerer. He is the mostly likely suspect. How do we know this necromancer has not turned to evil once more?"

Between chuckles and guffaws, Markus responded, "Why would Master Firestaff do such a thing? He has no desire to revert to his past. That is the last thing that Wizard would do!"

"Oh, you say that now, but how do you know what truly lurks in the heart of that Wizard?" replied Cullen. "Besides, it is a very well documented fact what Master Firestaff had done to those on either side of the Iron Mountains. He has a long history of torturing, killing and maiming a countless number of human beings and Elves, burning entire villages to destroy innocent lives."

"Right there is pause for thought," countered Arerys. "Yes, the Wizard used the element of fire to inflict the very worst of his damage. But think on this, Captain Bristow. Why in the world would Eldred Firestaff take to dirtying his hand by engaging in such brutal, physical acts of murder than to use his powers? It makes no sense whatsoever!"

"I beg to differ, my lord," argued Cullen.

"How so?" asked Arerys.

"By using a method far different than incorporating the powers he had been vested with, the Wizard means to confuse those he knows will be hunting him down for these murders," reasoned Cullen.

"I assure you, Captain Bristow, we have absolutely nothing to fear from this Wizard," promised Kal-lel.

"No disrespect to you, Your Highness," responded Cullen. "However, I am sure you were witness to some of the Wizard's most despicable acts committed at the height of his treachery. How can you believe otherwise?"

"True, I had engaged in many expeditions with Lindras Weatherstone to capture the rogue Wizard when Eldred delved into the forbidden arts to vent his wrath. However, as reluctant as I was to believe Firestaff had truly turned his back on evil after his capture and expulsion into the Painted Desert; I believe Lindras' assessment of his brother Wizard is very reliable. Eldred has done nothing of late to cause me to question his integrity."

"For one so long-lived, you have a short memory," grumbled Cullen, unmoved by the Elf's claim. "I would not be so quick to forget what that Sorcerer had done – the vile acts he had committed."

"If anything, Eldred Firestaff has become the very bastion of compassion and humanity since his bout living a mortal's life," reminded Markus. "He has definitely changed his ways for the better."

"And do not forget, Captain Bristow," added Arerys; "Eldred Firestaff helped us to defeat Draven Eldard when that deranged Captain took Prince Carstian hostage."

"Yes, if it was not for Eldred Firestaff doing away with that giant knight of ice conjured up by Draven, it probably would have been to our doom," stated Markus, remembering the massive ice sculpture come to life as they searched Draven's ice palace for Garrick's brother.

"I am inclined to believe the Wizard of the East used that opportunity, this grand gesture of coming to our rescue, as a way to earn our trust under false pretenses," explained Cullen. "It was merely a ploy to lull us into a false sense of security. I believe it was nothing more than a clever ruse to divert our attention from the fact that he was up to no good."

"*No good?* It is not as though you are accusing the Wizard of petty crimes, Captain Bristow. You are accusing Eldred Firestaff of committing numerous, gruesome murders throughout Talibarr!" gasped Markus.

"What can I say? As far as I am concerned, old habits are hard to break. The Wizard has fallen back on his old, deviant ways in grand fashion," stated Cullen, growing more confident of his claim.

"If you thought Master Firestaff was behind all of this, why did you not say so from the start?" questioned Garrick, scowling at Cullen for making this brazen accusation.

"Truth be told, it did not occur to me until after Master Stonecroft had asked that we consider other possible culprits other than an animal," responded Cullen. "The more I think on it, the more my suspicions turn to that Wizard."

"Well, keep your suspicions to yourself," grunted Markus. "You have no proof to back your claim."

"Not yet," responded Cullen, shrugging his shoulders with indifference. "Just give me some time."

"It is best not to speculate," warned Arerys.

"I agree with my son," stated Kal-lel. "At this moment, until we have had an opportunity to examine the victims of these attacks, I recommend we reserve judgment rather than to cast false blame, whether it is directed at an animal, mortal man or Wizard."

"Shall I have my soldiers prepare to leave for the site where King Sebastian was abducted? Have them exhume the bodies?" asked Cullen.

"Abduction would imply the King was taken for revenge or ransom by something other than an animal," noted Joval. "Aside from your assumption that it was Eldred Firestaff, is it safe to assume you are now willing to consider it can possibly be something other than an animal?"

"Yes, I am willing to consider it, but I still hold fast to my suspicions where the Wizard of the East is concerned," admitted Cullen. "I never did trust him. He has beady, little eyes that shine of evil."

"As I said before, dispense with the speculations and assumptions," ordered Arerys. "We must base the identity of the killer on facts – on conclusive findings, not ridiculous assumptions or vague rumours."

"Even if we were to leave now, by the time we get there, night shall be well upon us," warned Garrick. "My need to rescue my father tells me to take you there this very minute, but my concern for those of you willing to aid in his search forewarns me of the potential dangers. Soon, it will be darker than dark in this forest."

"And out there, every frightened, superstitious Talibarrian huddled down for the night with a spear or bow in his hand are scattered between here and there," determined Kal-lel.

"That is so," admitted Garrick.

"We are no good to you or King Sebastian if we are killed on our way to this site," stated Arerys.

"I know." Garrick nodded in understanding.

"We shall leave for this place at dawn," vowed Markus. "At least we will be able to survey the carnage and look for potential clues by first light without being mistaken for the killer beast by those on the hunt."

"This is profoundly disgusting," gagged Cullen, drawing the edge of his cloak over his mouth and nose to filter out the putrid stench of decay as the soldiers worked quickly to exhume the bodies while the cool of the morning air served to slightly dull the stink. "Are you sure this is absolutely necessary, Master Stonecroft?"

"Do you honestly think I would disturb the dead if it were not," replied Joval, kneeling down by the first of the cadavers laid out on the forest floor before him to begin this grim and grisly inspection.

"Master Stonecroft, do you wish to examine the dismembered limbs, too?" asked one of the soldiers.

"Definitely," responded Joval. "Match them up to the bodies if you can."

With faces contorted in repulsion and distaste, the soldiers fought against waves of nausea as their stomachs churned with this unpleasant undertaking.

"You heard the Elf, go to it!" ordered Cullen, grimacing in disgust. "I will stand by; oversee this task to ensure it is done right."

"Of course, Captain," grumbled the soldier, nodding to his comrades to proceed with unearthing the rest of the remains.

While Joval searched for clues among the dead and the Elven warriors fanned out into the forest, Arerys, Markus and Kal-lel inspected the sight of King Sebastian's mysterious disappearance. At the burned tree, the broken coal oil lamp used by the King remained exactly where he had dropped it.

"This is the very spot I last saw my father," disclosed Garrick, holding up one of the blackened shards of glass that once housed the flame of the lamp.

Arerys examined the charred earth and scorched tree where the fuel from the lamp had spilled and burned.

"And where were you and Captain Bristow when your father disappeared?" asked Markus.

"We were sitting right over there, by that cold fire pit," answered Garrick, pointing to the rocks encircling a pile of ashes and blackened pieces of wood.

"Just a stone's throw away from here," noted Kal-lel, carefully brushing aside the leaf litter in the immediate area to see what clues waited to be discovered. "And yet you saw and heard nothing?"

"It all happened so abruptly," replied Garrick, thinking back on that fateful night. "There were no screams, no cries for help... Only the sound of breaking glass; a terrible noise as the coal oil spilled and this tree suddenly burst into flames to do this damage."

"Look at the clawed earth," said Kal-lel, pointing at the disturbed soil that was raked by the nails on curved fingertips of human hands. "King Sebastian did not go willingly, that is for certain."

"It is obvious King Sebastian was dragged away from here," assessed Markus, following the long, linear claw marks until they became trampled into the earth by the footprints of those dispersing into the night in search of the missing King. As well as these footprints, a scattering of paw prints belonging to the hounds set loose to track the beast down, not to mention the myriad of hoof prints stamped into the soft earth by the horses, served to compromise what evidence there was.

"By all indications, King Sebastian had been taken eastward," determined Arerys, his keen eyes sifting through the assortment of tracks to distinguish those left by the King as he fought to hold his ground.

"Apparently so," agreed Garrick. "The hounds followed the scent until they came to a creek. Crossing to the other side, they lost the scent. It was as though the creature and my father vanished. Try as they might, the hounds have had no success in tracking either one from this point on."

"Is it possible that the creature was clever enough to move through the creek, using the flowing water to disperse its scent than to cross to the other side and leave an obvious trail on land?" queried Arerys.

"I suppose it is possible, but I do not know of a single creature with this type of intellect or cunning to do so," responded Garrick.

"Perhaps Joval's suggestion that it was something other than an animal being the perpetrator of this crime was not so outlandish," said Markus, considering the evidence.

"I sense it is not presumptuous to say that your father was singled out from your company only because he left the immediate area of the camp," determined Arerys.

"Yes, I believe because the rest of us were in groups huddled around the campfires and my father strayed away from our encampment, this alone made him vulnerable and a likely target for attack," responded Garrick.

"All others were killed immediately. Why was the King *taken* instead?" pondered Arerys. "Why was King Sebastian not killed right away as the others were?"

"Well, I am beginning to suspect that it is one extremely clever beast," determined Garrick. "Obviously, from where my father was attacked, the creature could see and hear us. It did not want to chance a hostile encounter with the hounds and the huntsmen, choosing to make off with my father to, God bless his soul, do the deed elsewhere."

"But this is what makes no sense," stated Kal-lel. "By all accounts, the killer beast had no qualms in laying siege on hunting parties, large and small. There was no hesitation in terrorizing and killing those in various settlements no matter the number. Why now, would it decide to make off with only *one* when there was at least a half dozen more waiting to be slaughtered? Where before, it would kill indiscriminately and with no hesitation, why now would it change its behavior and pattern of killing so drastically?"

"Perhaps the creature was killing indiscriminately before, but with King Sebastian, he was a deliberate target?" offered Markus. "What if the creature knew exactly whom it was looking for and the others were just hapless victims killed in the search for the King of Darross?"

"Are you suggesting that it was a creature capable of complex thought? It was intelligent enough to distinguish my father from all other men it encountered?" gasped Garrick.

"It was either a very motivated mortal with an insatiable appetite for murder, or a very obedient creature following the commands of a mortal with murder on his mind," suggested Kal-lel.

"But for what reason?" pondered Arerys.

"It is no secret there are a few dissidents; malcontents and usurpers that roam Talibarr," stated Garrick. "They are vehemently opposed to the peace accord proposed by my father and approved by those now forming this country's fledgling government, but this is utter madness. Even if they were violently opposed to this peace treaty, why kill so many of their own people before absconding with my father?"

"Another mystery to unravel," decided Markus.

"Joval could have some answers by now," said Arerys. "Let us see what he has uncovered."

"The dead do not speak, however, these bodies had plenty to reveal," disclosed Joval, washing his hands clean as Cullen tipped the water from a drinking flask.

"This sounds intriguing, Joval, do tell," urged Markus, his hand fanning the rancid air as the soldiers worked swiftly to bury the corpses before the cool brace of the morning air gave way to the heat of the midday sun.

Joval led the party away from the burial sight before he decided to share in his findings.

"So, I take it the grim undertaking yielded results?" queried Kal-lel.

"Yes, and it was most fascinating what I had learned," replied Joval. "All five men were indeed killed by the same creature in a relatively consistent manner."

"Go on," coaxed Arerys. "What else have you learned?"

"By the massive amount of blood loss experienced by each body, it is evident that the creature actively pursued each man, chasing him down, inflicting terrible slashing wounds and then allowing the poor soul a chance to escape, only to take him down again."

"How can you tell these deep lacerations were not inflicted on them after they were dead?" questioned Cullen.

"These men, each one of them, were very much alive during most of the assault," assured Joval. "Their terrified hearts were pumping away. This is what accounted for the great quantity of blood loss when they were being chased down and slashed repeatedly."

"In other words, Captain Bristow," explained Arerys; "if these men were already dead, the loss of blood would be minimal compared to if it was gushing out thanks to a heart working under great stress."

"I see… So these men bled to death?" assumed Cullen, imagining hot crimson jets of blood spurting rhythmically from the stumps of flesh where arms and legs were once attached. He shook his head to erase this disturbing thought.

"Eventually, that would have been the case," responded Joval. "However, these men did not bleed to death."

"Not even the fellow that was basically pulled in two?" asked Garrick.

"That unfortunate fellow was torn apart only after he was good and dead," replied Joval.

"Thank goodness for that, I suppose," groaned Cullen.

"Then what do you believe was the cause of death for these men, Joval?" questioned Kal-lel.

"As best as I can determine, each of the men received a killing bite that in effect broke their necks. The force was so powerful, for one man, his head remains attached only by threads of tissue anchoring his skull to what remained of the spinal bones in the neck."

"By your estimation, what kind of animal can dispense this type of death?" queried Markus, greatly disturbed by the gruesome details.

"An animal we are all familiar with," answered Joval.

"Do tell!" invited Cullen.

"It was a cat. In this case, a cat-like creature."

Cullen's face reddened as he stifled his laughter. "How can a lowly cat inflict this type of injury on a grown man?"

"For one, if it was indeed a cat, it would make it an exceedingly large cat of monstrous proportions," explained Joval, unfazed by Cullen's incredulous tone. "Second of all, surely you have seen a barn cat hunting for mice and rats, Captain Bristow?"

"Of course," replied the Captain. "Who has not?"

"The point being, cats will play with their quarry, especially if it is a she-cat with kittens she wishes to teach how to hunt," continued Joval. "It is only once they are ready to dispatch their terrified prey will they inflict the quarry with a killing bite; one that will break the creature's neck resulting in instant death if it had not already died of shock."

"I will grant you that, Master Stonecroft," responded Cullen. "But what other proof do you have that it is a *cat-like creature*, as you so eloquently put it."

"Aside from the manner of death that was dispensed, the claws that shredded these bodies could not have been inflicted by any type of canine animal, not even the largest of wolf," stated Joval.

"A wolf's claws are too dull," determined Markus.

"Exactly," confirmed Joval, with a nod of his head. "Wolves, and all dogs for that matter, have claws that are constantly exposed and subject to wear as they walk and run."

"While cats, when they are not using their claws, keep them sheathed in their toes, regularly honing them to a needle-sharp point," added Arerys.

"That is correct," said Joval.

"But how about a bear?" asked Cullen. "Brown bears have massive claws. I have seen them using these formidable weapons to dig up earth and turn over massive rocks and logs in search of food."

"Very true, Captain Bristow," acknowledged Joval. "However, a bear's claws are designed for just that; digging. Yes, they can deliver a deadly blow with a single swipe of a paw. And yes, those claws can inflict lethal damage. However, upon close examination to better understand the wounds inflicted, it became quite obvious the initial puncture to break the skin and enter the flesh was administered by something that was needle-sharp. By the tearing of the flesh, I could determine it was a curved claw much stronger and sharper than any possessed by a wolf or bear."

"I have had the ill-fortune of being scratched by a cat on more than one occasion," said Markus. "They tend to sink their claws in, and then tear, sometimes latching on with their front paws while kicking with the claws on their hind feet as though they mean to disembowel a prey."

"The other clues that has me leaning in this direction are the signs of the use of dewclaws on the men," added Joval.

"Dewclaws?" questioned Cullen, baffled by this term. "Just what are dewclaws?"

"They are present on both dog and cat species. They are like vestigial toes situated high on the inside of the animal's front legs. In the case of feline species, some cats will use the dewclaw to trip up fleet-footed prey, pouncing on their quarry when the animal takes a tumble."

"So the animal that killed these men had such a thing – this dewclaw?" asked Cullen.

"As sharp as a dagger and just as big," assured Joval.

"This sounds rather nasty," commented Cullen, thinking on how the terrified men had ran for their lives, only to be tripped up by this weapon.

"To be sure; it is. But what was truly interesting were the bites inflicted on these men," commented Joval.

"From what I saw, those men were quite literally stabbed by the fangs of a carnivore," offered Garrick.

"Fangs of a carnivore indeed, but fangs of a size I have never seen before," stated Joval, the tip of his index finger and thumb barely touching together to represent a single tooth mark of over two inches in diameter. "They are remarkably huge."

"If what you say is true, then there is a very large cat with a massive overbite roaming these forests," gasped Cullen. "That would mean it has fangs as big as ice picks."

"Bigger," corrected Joval. "By the depths of the canine teeth sinking deep into the skulls and torsos I have examined thus far, each upper canine must measure a good hand-length to mine, if not more."

Cullen's eyes opened wide in surprise as Joval held forth his hand for a visual comparison. From the tip of his middle finger down to his wrist, the Elf's large hand easily dwarfed his.

"That big?" gulped Cullen, squirming nervously as he considered the size of the killer beast.

"Unfortunately, yes."

"So definitely, this is no ordinary creature we are up against," surmised Kal-lel.

"That is correct, Your Highness," confirmed Joval. "It is a creature I have no familiarity with. All I know for certain is that it is an efficient hunter and a ruthless killer; an exceptionally large beast of tremendous strength and cunning for none to have tracked down as of yet."

A sudden commotion caught their attention as the soldiers who had finished burying the bodies and now kept watch for danger, tried to subdue an intruder. These men physically blocked the way as a frantic Talibarrian fought this imposing barrier to approach Prince Garrick, at first pleading, and then angrily throwing himself bodily against this human barricade.

"What is going on over there?" called Garrick, watching as the small Talibarrian attempted to squeeze between two of the soldiers in a bid to approach him.

Pushing the man back, one of the soldiers answered, "This fellow wishes to have a word with you, my lord. He claims it is about the killer beast."

"Good gracious, allow the man to pass!" urged Garrick, motioning for the harangued Talibarrian to step forward.

"Thank goodness ya have the decency ta hear me out, m'lord!" praised the man, dropping to his knees before the Prince more from exhaustion than respect. "I travelled all through the night ta get here."

"What is it, good sir?" asked Garrick, motioning the weary man to rise before him. "What news do you have?"

"Ain't good news, that's fer sure, m'lord!" exclaimed the man, as he drew a deep breath to compose himself.

"Go on? Have you seen my father, King Sebastian?"

"Sure wishin' I had, m'lord, but all I've seen were more dead bodies!" declared the Talibarrian, using the back of his hand to blot away the beads of sweat trickling from his forehead into his eyes.

"Where?" asked Arerys.

"And when?" added Markus.

"That a-way," answered the man, his finger pointing northeast across the Plains of Fire. "Jus' as ya enter the Valley of Shadows. They had ta be dead fer a good two days, if not longer."

"It must be the men we first heard about prior to these killings," determined Garrick, "the ones we were on our way to investigate before Master Arpoth and his men arrived with the bear."

"How many dead?" questioned Cullen.

"Three that I know of fer sure," replied the man.

"There could be more?" queried Kal-lel.

"I wasn't stickin' 'round there ta find out. I ran away as fast as I could. Ran all through the night ta get here – away from that horrible thing."

"You are aware there is a bounty to be rewarded for King Sebastian's return?" asked Garrick.

"No disrespect ta you or yer old man, m'lord, but there ain't no amount of money worth dyin' fer, if ya get my drift?"

"Did you see any sign of my father?" probed Garrick, desperately hoping for some news.

"Like I said, didn't stick around. As soon as I stumbled upon 'em dead bodies, I got me outta there as fast as these old legs could carry me!" confessed the Talibarrian, completely unashamed of his decision to flee for his life.

"Can you take us to this place?" asked Garrick.

"Bloody hell, no! I ain't goin' nowhere near there again," declared the man. "I'm headin' west an' I intend ta keep headin' that way."

"How about for a generous sum of money to compensate for your time and effort?" offered Garrick.

"Heck no! I'm plannin' on puttin' as many leagues as I can between me, that damned place and the killer beast. That ain't gonna happen if I head back east."

"How about a little monetary incentive for a detailed map revealing the exact location?" negotiated Garrick, holding up a silver coin to bribe the man for his co-operation.

"I suppose if ya have some ink an' parchment, I can scribble a map fer ya," accepted the man, greedily eyeing the shiny coin.

"For a man incapable of spelling and can barely speak the common speech properly, the fellow can certainly draw," praised Cullen, gazing up from the map to identify the corresponding landscape where the Plains of Fire ended and the Valley of Shadows began.

"This way," ordered Kal-lel, recognizing the distinctly gnarled and stooped pine tree that had been forced down by powerful winds long ago, but continued to survive. This conifer now grew bent and twisted over the ground before reaching skyward again. "I would guess about half a league due east from this tree."

Sure enough, as Kal-lel and his party urged their horses on, they located the distinct landmarks noted on the Talibarrian's map. Along the way, they also found the man's rushed footprints. It told the tale of his mad sprint; where he stumbled and fell as well as the places he scrambled on all fours to flee from this terrifying place. There was a sinister foreboding about this region, even without the immediate presence of the killer beast.

"Do you smell that reek?" asked Arerys, motioning all to stop.

"Do not look at me!" exclaimed Cullen, thinking the Elf was accusing him of being flatulent.

"I was not speaking of you this time," dismissed Arerys. "There is a smell hanging heavy in the air."

"Blood?" inquired Markus, reining Arrow in as he sniffed the air in a bid discover what it was that Arerys smelled.

"No… smoke," answered Arerys, steering his horse eastward, following the faint, acrid odour. "There was a fire not far from here."

"I smell it," said Kal-lel.

"As I do, too," agreed Joval, nodding in confirmation. With a wave of his hand, the Elven warriors spread out. Six positioned themselves to the front, while six took up the flank to protect the royal party as they ventured deeper into the Valley of Shadows.

"It is an *Elf thing*." Cullen whispered discreetly to Garrick as he pointed to his nose. "These woodland beings have a sense of smell that is far better than any animal."

"And the hearing to match," stated Arerys, hearing the mortal's muted exchange with Garrick.

These unexpected words caused Cullen to jump with a start in his saddle.

"How did you think we found you so easily in Talibarr, Captain Bristow?" informed Arerys, giving the mortal a knowing wink before urging RainDance on.

Cullen frowned as he thought on the Elf's words.

"I do believe Prince Arerys means to say not only are you loud, but you stink, too," decided Garrick, smiling in amusement.

"I stink?" repeated Cullen, in an incredulous tone as he discreetly raised his arm to sniff his armpit.

"Oh, yes," teased Markus, coaxing Arrow on to follow Arerys' mare. "I am not even downwind from you and I would still be able to find you if I was blindfolded, and I am not even an Elf."

"You are mistaken! I believe it is my horse that smells badly," insisted Cullen, patting his stallion's withers. "I have been working him hard with no time to properly groom him."

"Well, if not your foul odour, then it must be your wretched mind-set I detect, for I can definitely smell a *bad attitude* from ten paces," teased Markus, laughing inwardly at the Captain's embarrassed and flustered expression.

"Oh... You were only making fun," hoped Cullen.

Neither confirming nor denying this, Markus quickly changed the subject, "Just as you said Arerys; a fire."

A disturbing sight greeted their eyes as they rounded the bend of the trampled trail left by the Talibarrian who had provided them with the detailed map to this place. An abandoned camp left in shambles; one tent lay crumpled and burned, the other tattered to shreds. Bits and pieces of fabric fluttering in the breeze were situated near the remnants of a long-cold campfire.

Large, fist-sized rocks once neatly arranged around this fire pit lay in a jumble. It was clear to see the logs that originally burned in this pit were scattered about during some kind of scuffle or clash that ended badly. The area immediately around this fire pit that was originally cleared of leaf litter and other flammable materials left telltale clues. Beyond the scattering of firewood, several large and distinct patches revealed where dried grasses, shrubs and trees were set ablaze. The black soot and a thin layer of gray ash showed the precise extent of damage.

"What say you, Joval?" asked Kal-lel, surveying the destruction caused by the fire. "What do you make of this?"

"If it was a simple matter of an unattended fire jumping the rock surround, the wind would dictate the direction and volume of the burn," offered Joval, dismounting his horse to better inspect the clues left by the fire. Glancing up from the broken circle of rocks, he could see where several other fires began a distance away from this fire pit.

"Well, it must have been one hell of a gust to send burning embers over there," decided Cullen, pointing to the patch of burned over forest floor where dried pine needles seemed to vaporize from the intense heat to leave a fine dusting of ash.

Arerys dismounted from RainDance to better scrutinize the damage and the irregularity of the direction and placement of the scorched areas.

"Captain Bristow, it was no ember that was carried by the wind to set this particular fire," disclosed Arerys, inspecting the farthest burn on the outskirts of the camp. "It was a piece of wood taken from the fire pit itself that ignited this blaze."

"How do you know?" called back Cullen, using the toe of his boot to poke around the fire pit for clues the others could have overlooked.

"Because the person who took this burning wood is still holding onto it," revealed Arerys, kneeling over the charred remains of a human body.

"Here is another one!" hollered Markus, recoiling from the grotesque sight of the broken and battered corpse that lay in a bloodied heap beneath a shrub. By the stench alone, he could tell the man had been dead for some time.

"I take it, he is no more?" presumed Kal-lel, smelling the distinct, malodourous reek of death hanging heavy in the air.

"I recommend that we stay together," suggested Garrick, nervously glancing about for signs of the killer beast. "In another hour or two, the sun will set and the creature will be on the prowl once more."

"Whether the creature is in close proximity or not, it will serve us well to keep our guard up and our wits about us," recommended Kal-lel, as he and Joval joined Arerys to inspect the burned body.

"Yes, my lord, you best remain close," advised Cullen, drawing his sword to protect Prince Garrick.

Without a word, even after Cullen's suggestion that he remain close, Garrick automatically gravitated toward Joval Stonecroft. The Prince stood near to this large, imposing Elf as Joval motioned his warriors to fan out to search for other bodies and possible survivors.

"Hmph! That does not speak well of Prince Garrick's confidence in your ability to protect him," Markus whispered to Cullen. "Are you not offended by this?"

"Why would I be offended?" responded Cullen, his shoulders shrugging with indifference. "Given the choice, in this particular situation, I would do the same if I were the Prince."

"You would?" asked Markus, in an incredulous tone.

"If it is not obvious to you, Your Highness, Master Stonecroft is large for an Elf and he is most definitely a house of a man next to me. With this in mind, of course Prince Garrick will want a larger, more physically imposing barrier coming between him and potential danger. And do not forget that Master Stonecroft and Prince Arerys had restored Prince Garrick's health once before when he lay wasting away in the palace infirmary."

"I suppose I can see your point," responded Markus, contemplating the Captain's candid admission.

"You should, Your Highness! After all, is it not for this very reason that you associate with the Elf-kind?" probed Cullen. "Even if you were wounded, your chances of survival will be increased by many fold if you kept an Elf close to you at all times."

"My reasons for *associating* with the Elf-kind have little to do with this. However, I sense there is no point in explaining my motives or the meaning of friendship to you, Captain Bristow," sighed Markus, giving his head a dismal shake. He cleared the debris from around the body to prepare for the Elves' inspection while Joval finished examining the first corpse.

"This man was definitely burned by the fire he started," noted Joval, upon cursory examination of the body they first discovered at this site. "However, it is too difficult to determine if the fire was the actual cause of his death."

"I agree," nodded Arerys. "Though there are deep lacerations across his back and chest, the burned flesh refuses to yield any real clues."

"If not the depth, at least the lengths of these slashes are consistent with those on the bodies we initially inspected," determined Kal-lel.

"Over here!" called Markus, as he waved the Elves over. "I am confident this body will reveal what that one did not."

Their large strides quickly delivered them to Markus' side. This body he had discovered was now meticulously picked clean of leaves, grasses and twigs that clung to the dead man's raiment. Brushed aside, it allowed the others an unobstructed view of the corpse in all its grisly glory.

Garrick, remaining close to Joval, followed in the Elf's great footsteps. But just as the body came into view, the breeze suddenly shifted in their direction. The rancid stench of decay combined with the gruesome sight of the maggot-riddled cadaver overwhelmed the Prince. Garrick promptly reeled to one side as his stomach churned. Falling to his knees, he retched as a wave of nausea engulfed him.

"Sorry, my lord, I should have warned you," apologized Cullen, turning away as the Prince heaved.

"Give me a moment... I will be fine," gasped Garrick, fighting to regain his composure.

"It is too bad these maggots infest this body," said Cullen, grimacing in revulsion. The dead man's flesh seemed to undulate with the writhing of the translucent, white fly larvae. "It makes it impossible to determine anything other than the fact this man is dead and is now a heaping big serving of supper for these disgusting little creatures."

"As disgusting as you find them to be, these maggots can help to determine when, approximately, this man died," countered Joval, gently picking up the largest of the squirming fly larva for the others to inspect.

"How can that be?" questioned Garrick, still fighting off the queasy feeling in his stomach.

"These grubs grow at an incredible rate," answered Joval. "This particular specimen will begin its transformation into a pupa sometime tomorrow, hatching as an adult fly three days later."

"So based on the size of this specific grub, you can estimate when this man died?" asked Garrick, fascinated by this morbid claim.

"That is correct," confirmed Joval. "Within minutes of dropping dead, this body attracted a host of flies. They lay their eggs directly into the wounds where hatching maggots can easily feast on the flesh."

"Based on the size of the maggots, how long do you estimate this man has been dead?" queried Markus.

"I would say approximately five days – perhaps six, but no longer than that," assessed Joval, flicking the squirming maggot from his fingertip before picking up a stick to scrape away the thick blanket of fly grubs from the wounds.

"Five days?" repeated Garrick. "So these men died before that creature made off with my father."

"If that is so, and as we have yet to receive news of any other killings, there is a distinct possibility whatever has been committing the killings stopped once it found what it wanted," determined Arerys.

"So my father was abducted by this animal?" queried Garrick, attempting to make sense of it all. "It was a deliberate act?"

"It is the only explanation for why the killings had suddenly stopped and why your father was not immediately killed when he first encountered the beast," replied Kal-lel.

"But first, we should ascertain if this man did indeed meet the same death as the others," stated Markus.

"Hence this investigation," responded Joval, probing into the festering flesh to determine the exact length and depth of the lacerations.

Cullen's face contorted in utter repulsion. He gagged as Joval's examination caused the distended stomach, bloated with gases, to suddenly and noisily deflate.

"Now *that* was disgusting," groaned Cullen, drawing the edge of his cloak over his mouth and nose to mask out the putrid stink as his other hand fanned the air. "Perhaps you should stop poking about like that."

"This body has more to reveal to us," countered Joval, motioning Cullen to help him roll the corpse from its back onto its stomach.

To Cullen's horror, just as the body flopped over, the blood stained earth beneath squirmed with life. A carpet of carrion beetles, worms and more maggots perfectly outlined where the man had fallen dead. They struggled to flee the sudden brightness of daylight. Cullen yelped in surprise and disgust, falling back with a start as Garrick leapt out of the way to resume gagging and heaving; the sight and smell sending his senses reeling once more.

"I know you have a morbid fascination for all things dead, Master Stonecroft," denounced Cullen, glancing over his shoulder to the retching Prince; "but perhaps you should cease with this examination. Not all of us are as enthralled with this as you are."

"If it bothers you so, perhaps you should wait elsewhere, Captain Bristow," suggested Joval. "This body deserves further inspection and we are in need of concise answers."

"You best go to it then," invited Cullen, taking several steps back to allow the Elf to resume with this gruesome task. "Prince Garrick and I will maintain a respectable distance from that *thing.*"

Pulling up on the blood-soaked shirt, Joval discovered similar wounds raking the man's back.

"These lacerations are identical to those inflicted on the dead at the first camp," noted Arerys.

"So are these," stated Joval, pointing to the large puncture wounds where huge fangs sank into the base of the man's neck and the top of his skull. "Death was instant."

"One thing is for certain," said Markus, examining the marks left by teeth that had clamped around the man's upper torso, "the creature's bite radius suggests it was delivered by something far greater in size than the largest wolf and much more powerful than the biggest brown bear."

"This is what I find rather curious," noted Kal-lel. "The flesh where the bite marks were inflicted looks as though infection had set in after death."

Joval scrutinized the entry of the deep puncture mark and the surrounding area where skin and flesh were blistered.

"It appears to be burned, not infected," decided Joval.

"What would cause such a thing?" questioned Garrick, peering over the Elf's shoulder at the puzzling wounds that were reminiscent of a severe burn from a searing.

"The mystery deepens," said Arerys. "The only thing we are sure of is what this killer is *not.*"

"I have my suspicions," stated Cullen, nodding his head with conviction as he mulled over the evidence.

"You do?" asked Garrick.

"Of course," responded the Captain. "All one must do is consider the evidence we have uncovered thus far. Just take a look around us... at the dead bodies... the fire ravaged grounds."

"And what has your brilliant mind deduced, Captain Bristow?" probed Markus.

"Consider this: How do you account for the fire?" questioned Cullen, his eyes glancing about at the charred and burned forest floor that expanded out from the fire pit.

"Most animals are naturally fearful of fire," explained Arerys. "Where traditional weapons failed, perhaps these men attempted to ward off the beast with the flames?"

"I suppose that is plausible, but here is another suggestion for your consideration," offered Cullen, looking pensive as he mulled over the evidence. "There is a bloody good chance this fire was started by the killer beast."

"And how did you come to this conclusion, Captain Bristow?" queried Kal-lel, as he surveyed the carnage. "I do not know of one creature that exists, other than Elf or man, capable of using a firestick or utilizing flint."

"Your Highness, even if the creature did not start the fire, it certainly had no fear of it," replied Cullen. "Those men are dead and if they had used the fire in an attempt to ward off the creature, it did them no good."

"As my son said, most animals are innately afraid of fire," responded Kal-lel. "The only creature I know of that shows no fear of heat or flame because it is capable of producing fire is a dragon."

"There you go then! A dragon it is!" insisted Cullen; pleased he and the Elf King were of like mind. "Either that, or it was a creature spat up from the bowels of hell, therefore explaining why it is unfazed by fire."

"You change your idea of what or whom is to blame for these killings as quickly as the wind shifts directions," noted Arerys.

"It is called being adaptable. My answer changes according to the evidence I am presented with," grunted Cullen. "But what difference does it make? I would think you'd be pleased Eldred Firestaff was no longer at the top of my list of suspects. If anything, better a Wizard's dragon than a Wizard himself, I'd say!"

"King Kal-lel!" called out one of the Elven warriors sent out to search for survivors. "We have found others just east of here. You will want to see this for yourself, my liege."

6

pulled and broken

"I take it, we will be contending with more dead bodies," assumed Kal-lel, following the warrior beyond the outskirts of the camp.

"I am afraid so, Your Highness," responded the Elf.

"Does it appear these men were part of the hunting party killed back there?" questioned Arerys, as he glanced over his shoulder.

"I can only say with confidene that it would appear both were savagely attacked in a like manner, my lord."

"Are they far from here?" asked Markus.

"Just over there, King Markus," answered the Elf, pointing through the trees where two fellow warriors stood over the dead, as the others continued their search in the general vicinity. "So far, we have found one body where they stand and another over yonder."

"Where that massive tree grows?" asked Garrick, following the direction of the Elf's finger.

"Yes, my lord."

"While you examine that unfortunate victim, Master Stonecroft, I will investigate the condition of the other one," offered Cullen, quickly veering away from the corpse that reeked from the onset of decomposition. It was his hope the second body was in better condition.

"Very well," agreed Joval. "However, I intend to inspect both, so do not disturb the body."

"As you wish," responded Cullen, inwardly pleased that he was now relegated to merely ascertaining the location of the body in question.

"And under no circumstance should any one of us be alone, you included Captain Bristow," warned Arerys.

"I mean to spare us some time, so more can be devoted to the finding of King Sebastian," stated Cullen.

"Then I will go with you, Captain," offered Garrick.

"Very well, then," approved Arerys. "Just stay together. Be sure you both remain within our sights. Keep your weapons at the ready, just in case."

"Of course," agreed Garrick, his hand patting the hilt of his sword as he hastened his pace to catch up to Cullen.

As the warriors stood aside to make way for their King and his party, Joval ordered them to continue the search.

"If you chance upon a survivor, summon us immediately," instructed Kal-lel.

"I will do so, Your Highness," acknowledged the Elf who had escorted them to the dead man.

"This poor fellow looks like he has been dead for longer than the others we had just examined," assessed Markus, noting how the body was incredibly bloated from the gases trapped inside as the soft organs deteriorated faster than muscle. This man lay in eternal slumber on his right side, the right arm trapped beneath the swollen corpse as the left arm was unnaturally twisted, the elbow pointing painfully forward rather than back.

"By his condition, it would appear so," agreed Joval, "however, the body you had found was somewhat protected by shade. This one is in the wide open, fully exposed to the heat of the sun for the better part of the day."

"So warmer temperatures will accelerate the rate of decomposition," determined Markus, cringing as the squirming maggots angrily writhed about upon being disturbed by the stick Joval wielded.

"Yes," answered Joval, clearing off the rapacious fly larvae to better examine the wounds these invertebrates were clustered around. "As you can see, the largest grub is no bigger than the ones on the body you had discovered earlier, Markus."

"Since you established that both men were killed roughly around the same time, can you also confirm how he met his demise?" queried Markus.

"Unfortunately for this fellow, he died the same horrific death – dispatched in the identical manner," confirmed Joval, peering through the rips in the bloodied apparel.

He recognized the long, deep claw marks that created linear tears on skin and flesh as well as the same strange puncture marks inflicted by massive canine teeth that easily pierced the skull as well as the man's once muscular neck and shoulders.

With Markus' help, Joval turned the corpse over from his side onto his back to complete his inspection.

"A hunting knife…" announced Joval, spying the oak handle attached to a steel blade that had been concealed beneath the body until now.

"This man died fighting," determined Arerys, watching with interest as Joval removed the knife from the earth that squirmed with carrion beetles, maggots and worms busily devouring the juices left by the rotting flesh.

"The question is, what was he fighting?" queried Joval, holding up the blade for all to see. "If this is blood staining the blade, why is it black?"

"How do we even know if it is blood?" wondered Kal-lel, inspecting the black residue that coated the blade from the tip to its hilt. Whatever it was, it had coagulated and dried.

"Look… it left a mark on the ground and against the man's vest," noted Joval, pointing out the dark, shrivelled grasses and a scorching on the deer hide vest that perfectly outlined where the blade of the knife had come to rest.

"If I did not know better, it appears to be burned," assessed Markus, "like it was some kind of acrid substance."

"Wrap it up," ordered Arerys. "We shall take this knife with us. Perhaps one of the Wizards can shed some light on this."

Before rolling it into a sheath of cloth, Joval shook off the maggots that stubbornly clung to the knife.

"Let us see what Captain Bristow has learned from the other corpse," suggested Arerys, glancing up to see Cullen circling a large tree as Garrick traced his footsteps, undoubtedly searching for clues the Captain had missed.

"I believe Master Stonecroft's warrior was mistaken," grumbled Cullen, annoyed that the body they were led to believe rested beneath this tree was nowhere to be found.

"Perhaps he meant in the general vicinity?" suggested Garrick, using a long stick to probe beneath the low branches of surrounding shrubs growing in the shadow of this tree.

"If that were so, being an Elf, you'd think he would have been more precise," grunted Cullen, the toe of his boot sifting through layers of fallen leaves in search of the dead.

"It must be close to here," stated Garrick, grimacing in disgust as he tried not to gag as the foul stench grew heavier each time he neared the trunk of the tree.

"What makes you say that, my lord?"

"This very place reeks of death," replied Garrick, taking in a shallow breath through his cloak so as not to be overwhelmed by the putrid odour permeating the air around them.

"I agree, but where is it?"

"Just keep looking," ordered Garrick, glancing up to see Kal-lel and the others marching over. "I do not think Master Stonecroft's warrior made an error when he said to look in this vicinity."

Cullen drew in a deep breath, sniffing the air to scent out the body in question.

"It does smell something fierce around here," agreed the Captain, sniffing and pacing about as he allowed his nose to home in what was not obvious to his eyes. "The stink grows stronger the closer you are to the tree trunk."

Following his nose, the rancid stink led Cullen directly beneath the great boughs of this tree. "It is the worst right over here."

"But there is nothing." Garrick frowned in confusion as he searched the ground.

"Perhaps the beast concealed the body?" suggested Cullen. "Some creatures do bury their prey to consume later."

"I suppose you are right."

The Prince began to probe the earth for a soft spot that would betray the presence of a body rotting beneath it as Cullen brushed aside a layer of leaf litter with the edge of his boot.

"Well look here," noted Cullen, flicking aside a fly larva. "It is one of those maggoty things."

"We must be close."

No sooner than Cullen disposed of the maggot, another appeared on the ground before him. Its pale, translucent body undulated against the dark, loamy soil.

"Revolting little pest, I thought I had gotten rid of you."

"You did," informed Garrick, gazing over to where the first maggot landed, wiggling away to take cover before a bird swooped down to devour it.

"Well this is truly bizarre," Cullen grunted in disgust. "Either these filthy, little grubs are crawling up from the earth or we are cursed and it is now raining maggots."

Garrick watched as a plump maggot at the verge of pupating fell onto Cullen's shoulder. Glancing up, the Prince's eyes opened wide in horror as he stumbled back.

"What?" asked Cullen, seeing the colour drain from Garrick's face as another maggot fell, landing on his head.

"Bugger me…" groaned Cullen, his face grimacing in disgust as his hand reached up to the crown of his head to feel the cold, moist body of a fat, wiggling maggot worming its way through his hair.

"Listen to me, Captain, just step over here!" ordered Garrick, continuing to back away. "Come toward me. Do not look up."

As though the Prince's words fell on deaf ears or his warning caused an instinctive reaction, Cullen could not fight the urge to look. He glanced up. His mouth gaped open in shock as his eyes took in the horrible sight.

High on the tree's branch dangled a body, snagged onto a broken limb. Torn almost in two at the midriff, entrails and organs exposed to the drying winds were festooned with a swarm of hungry maggots with the sole intention of filling their guts on the dead.

This momentary lapse of good judgment was abruptly broken as a plump grub fell from the corpse, landing into Cullen's mouth that drooped open in shock.

"*Aargh!*" roared Cullen. Spitting out maggot and saliva, his dirty hands frantically wiped his tongue in a bid to remove all traces of the fly larva. He collided into Garrick as the Prince turned away to heave.

"What are you doing?" asked Markus, frowning in bewilderment as he watched Cullen dance about, spitting and shaking his raiment in case other maggots had found a home on his person as Garrick fell to his knees, retching loudly in utter revulsion.

"Where is the body?" questioned Arerys. Choosing to ignore the Captain's antics, he glanced about, looking for the second cadaver that was supposed to be at this tree.

Joval helped Garrick back onto his unsteady legs as the Prince explained, "When your warrior said the body was *at* this tree, he should have been more specific and said *in* the tree. Look up!"

"Good gracious! How did the poor soul get all the way up there?" gasped Markus, staring in disbelief.

"He certainly did not climb," said Kal-lel, gazing up at the mangled human form dangling overhead.

With incredible agility that left Garrick and Cullen gawking in stunned silence, Joval hoisted himself up into the tree. He easily maneuvered between the branches until he reached the dead man.

As his weight caused the branch supporting the body to bow down, Joval called out, "Look out below!"

There was the ripping of fabric and the snapping of leather as the belt that had snagged onto the branch and kept the body suspended in the tree suddenly broke.

Those on the ground promptly leapt aside as the upper torso snapped off where the spinal column finally rotted away, no longer able to support this weight. Instantly, the remainder of the corpse followed, falling to the ground with a sickening *thud* and a squishy *splat* that sent maggots flying in all directions.

As Joval made his way back down from the overhead branches, the others gathered around the broken body.

"It is quite evident how this man died," stated Kal-lel, assessing the nature of the wounds inflicted on the corpse.

"Yes," agreed Arerys. He dragged the lower half of the body off the torso to better inspect the dead.

"It looks like the birds feasted well on this poor fellow," noted Markus, seeing how clawed feet scratched at the skin as crows and ravens braced themselves as they tugged on chunks of flesh and internal organs. "I suppose from up there, there were no other creatures to drive them off. They were free to feed without harassment."

"Why must those damned birds always do that?" Garrick groaned in disgust, pointing at the vacant sockets that once housed the eyeballs. "Why must they always go for the eyes?"

"Tasty, little morsels, I suppose," offered Cullen, recoiling in repulsion as he stared at the bloodied orbs that now housed a multitude of feasting maggots.

"Actually, Captain Bristow, these birds generally go for the eyes, not because they are easy pickings, but because once removed, their beaks have easy access to the soft tissue beneath," explained Joval, peering into the hollows. "Birds lack the teeth possessed by true carnivores, so they must take advantage of what is easily accessible to them."

"Thank you for that gruesome bit of information, Master Stonecroft." Cullen nodded in feigned appreciation. "I feel somehow enlightened."

"As we have established the cause of death, the question remains: How did his body get up into the tree?" pondered Kal-lel.

Joval knelt down by the dead man. Gently lifting the head, the Elf tilted it from side to side; noting how the head flopped unnaturally to rest squarely on either shoulder only to loll backward to give the appearance the body had no head at all when looking at it straight on.

"You can stop now, Master Stonecroft," urged Cullen, grimacing in disgust as he watched the Elf deliberate on the cause and condition of the dead body. "You are really putting us off with your morbid fascination for the dead."

Ignoring Cullen's comment, Joval shared in his observation, "Not only was this man's neck broken, it is as though each bone in his neck separated."

"Like the weight of his body pulled the bones apart when he was being hoisted up into the tree by his head," surmised Markus.

"Exactly," nodded Joval. "The dead weight, no pun intended, and the lack of muscle strength to resist such strenuous abuse caused the neck bones to separate, popping apart much like the beads of a necklace when the string is pulled and broken."

"It would certainly explain the condition of this particular body," determined Arerys, nodding in agreement.

"Could this have happened to my father?" questioned Garrick, thinking back on Sebastian's abrupt and strange disappearance. "Perhaps he was hauled up high into a tree to go undetected?"

"It would definitely account for why the hounds lost the scent and how the creature managed to vanish without a trace with King Sebastian," decided Kal-lel, recalling the large trees overhanging the creek where the hounds ended their futile search for an olfactory clue to guide them on.

"How can that be possible for a creature to move about in this fashion?" queried Garrick.

"It is *not* possible!" denounced Cullen, speaking with great conviction. "Think on it, my lord. What kind of animal has the strength to drag a grown man high into the trees and move about like that? There is not one creature I know of that can accomplish such an incredible feat."

"Based on what we have seen, we can definitely rule out wolves and bears now," offered Kal-lel.

"That makes sense," agreed Cullen. "I have yet to see even one wolf that can climb a tree to save its life."

"And as strong as the great brown bears are, unless they are small cubs, they cannot haul the sheer bulk of their own bodies up into a tree, at least not to that height, never mind attempting to carry the weight of a grown man to boot," added Markus.

"Look over there," said Arerys; pointing to the base of the tree they stood beneath. There, shreds of bark and a scattering of small branches that once grew from the trunk littered the ground.

"What in heaven's name do you suppose did that?" queried Garrick, staring up the side of the tree to scrutinize the scarred trunk. The deep lacerations were now sealed with hardening pitch that had oozed forth from the tree to heal the assault it had endured.

"I can tell you now, a large brown bear can most certainly reach up that high," assessed Markus. "A large male standing up on its hind legs has been known to carve up the sides of trees within their territory for all other rival males to know its size."

"Yes, and the higher the marks, potentially the greater the size and strength of the bear. Consider it a warning to all others wishing to challenge it for this space," added Arerys.

"So this marking of one's territory is used to ward off potential competition?" queried Cullen. "It is to give rival males the opportunity to size up the resident male and to avoid a confrontation they are destined to lose if they are smaller and weaker?"

"Precisely," answered Joval. "However, bears tend to tear off great chunks of bark. Whatever manner of creature did this, there are long, linear claw marks of the identical width and length as the slashes on the dead men."

"I have seen the barn cats sharpening their claws on the hitching posts in the stable," noted Markus. "Those marks up there are very reminiscent of the clawings made by cats, but on a much grander scale."

"There are some cat species that will drag their kills into trees so other carnivores such as wolves and bears cannot steal away with their food," added Kal-lel, thinking back on a clever mountain cat he had observed dragging half a deer carcass up into a tree as a pack of wolves closed in to steal away with what they had anticipated would be an easy meal, only to find the deer well out of their reach.

"As astute as these observations have been, if these killings were done by a very large cat with monstrous fangs, it is an unavoidable fact that such a creature does *not* exist," insisted Cullen.

"Until now," countered Arerys.

"If that were so, why would it suddenly appear, coming from out of nowhere after all this time to create such havoc?" argued Cullen, unwilling and unable to accept the existence of such a monster.

"Perhaps this creature ventured over the Iron Mountains?" offered Garrick, turning to Arerys for his opinion. "Could there be a chance this animal came far from the east in Orien and in a spate of killings, the Taijins drove it over those mountains to be rid of it?"

"There is always that possibility," responded Arerys. "However, our nations share a peaceful existence with those in eastern Imago. Even now, Nayla maintains close, personal ties with the Kagai Warriors. If anything, those Taijins would warn us of such danger or at the very least, they would have declined their invitation to her and the trade delegates from Cedona and Talibarr. They would have prevented them from making the journey if their lives were put in deliberate peril."

"I suppose that makes sense," said Garrick.

"At this moment, what makes sense is to be rid of these bodies before the coming of the night," suggested Joval. "It is bad enough that creature is still at large. We do not need to contend with a host of bears, wolves and other beasts sniffing about, looking for an easy meal."

"Good idea," agreed Cullen, staring up to the leaden sky that was growing dark. Heavy, brooding clouds massed above them to warn of an impending storm. "We best bury these poor buggers where they lay."

Two Elven warriors suddenly came bounding through the stand of trees to deliver urgent news to their King.

"Your Highness," called one of the warriors. "There is another body, northeast of here!"

"How far away?" asked Kal-lel.

"Just a little less than half a league from where we stand now."

"So, another dead body, probably not unlike these others?" assumed Arerys, with a weary sigh.

"That is so, my lord, however, the one we found was obviously in pursuit of the killer beast. He made a valiant attempt to slay the animal before the creature turned on him," revealed the Elven warrior.

"Perhaps we should leave now before we lose daylight entirely?" suggested Markus.

"Even if we leave now and buried these bodies later, we will not get there before darkness comes," warned Joval. "The forest in the Valley of Shadows is deep and dark, even on a full moon night."

"If the creature is lurking about, it will be even more difficult to detect," stated Kal-lel, his eyes taking in the deepening sky.

"And it may be even more inclined to attack," determined Joval.

"Then we best retire for the coming of the night. I will leave at first light," decided Garrick. "And I shall go on without you if this is as far as you are willing to go."

As night passed by peacefully to surrender to the coming of dawn, an unusual sight greeted Markus' bleary eyes.

"What are you doing?" questioned Markus, his brows furrowing in curiosity as he watched King Sebastian's squire assist Cullen with donning a full stand of armour. "Are you going to war, Captain?"

"Against the beast, I am," explained Cullen. He raised his arm so the boy could fasten the pauldron, the articulated piece of steel protecting him from his shoulder down to his forearm.

"This is rather drastic, is it not?" queried Markus, securing the scabbard of his sword to his belt as he readied to resume their search.

"That is a matter of opinion. If you asked one of the many dead the beast had killed so far, I am sure if they were able to speak, they would not think so. And if I were you, I'd take similar precautions."

Tossing his quiver over his shoulder, Markus responded, "I do believe my sword and bow will provide adequate protection."

"That is just it," argued Cullen, standing still as the squire secured the steel and leather greaves designed to guard his shins against an assault. "We do not know what we are protecting ourselves from."

"I will take my chances," said Markus, taking up his bow.

"I have already seen too much to take such a chance. That is why I don my armour now, even before I take in my morning sustenance. There is no telling what that beast is, where it is lurking about or when it will strike next. The only thing I know for certain is what those monstrous fangs will do if I am not properly outfitted to confront that creature."

"Just judging by the size of the puncture wounds, it is fair to assume teeth of that size will easily stab through your skin of steel," assessed Markus, his knuckles rapping against Cullen's metal-shroud chest.

"Well, those are comforting words," groaned Cullen, in a dismissive tone as he held in place the vambrace made of double-boiled leather that he wore on each forearm as his squire adjusted and secured the buckles.

"They were not said to comfort you. I say this so you will not be lulled into a false sense of security that your armour will protect you completely."

"I will grant you that," acknowledged Cullen. "However, if by some strange twist of fate, I should end up in the maw of that killer beast, at least I stand a better chance with a shell of steel protecting my body than to present scantily-clad flesh and bones to that creature. Armour, no matter the quality, will always hold up better than ordinary mortal skin."

"That is true. Just keep in mind, it is apparent this creature moves with incredible speed and great agility. There is a chance the heft and the rigidity of your armour will only serve to slow you down, hamper your movements in countering an assault."

"I am willing to sacrifice a bit of mobility if this armour will provide me some resistance against teeth and claws."

"It will provide some, but as I said before, do not come to rely totally upon it."

"Fear not, for I keep my trusty sword always by my side," stated Cullen, his hand patting the hilt of the weapon hanging from his baldric.

"That fancy thing?" questioned Markus, frowning in curiosity. He glanced at the garishly ornate scabbard and the matching hilt decorated with the brass detailing of a dragon, the heraldic symbol of Darross.

"It is kind of you to notice." Cullen smiled as his fingers proudly fondled the brass pommel of the sword.

"How can one not?" commented Markus, scrutinizing the grand weapon that was obviously beyond Cullen's draw-length. "Tell me if I am wrong, but is that sword not designed more for ceremony than combat?"

"Though King Sebastian presented this magnificent weapon to me during a ceremony to recognize my exemplary service in rescuing Prince Carstian late of last year, I assure you, the blade is exceptionally sharp and capable of dispensing a quick death."

"You say that now, but what difference does it make how sharp the blade is if you cannot draw it with speed to counter an assault? Even your old sword would serve you better than that lovely piece of decoration."

"Do not be deceived by its loveliness, Your Highness," responded Cullen. "I assure you, once it is drawn, the sheer beauty of the hilt and blade will be enough to leave an attacker awe-struck; enough that I will be able to draw first blood."

"That is just it, Captain Bristow, the sword must be *drawn* in the first place," stated Markus. He suddenly unsheathed his sword, pressing the flat edge of the cold blade against Cullen's throat.

The Captain gulped. His face reddened with embarrassment as he struggled to unsheathe the very tip of his ornate, but cumbersome weapon from its scabbard as Markus made his point with this impromptu demonstration.

"I see what you mean." Cullen admitted sheepishly as he thrust his sword back into its protective housing. "Though this weapon does exceed my draw-length, it is nothing that cannot be rectified with a little practice. I just haven't had the opportunity to get used to it yet – to practice the art of drawing this exceptional sword."

"Now is hardly the time to do so," retorted Markus, reaching to the small of his back to remove a dagger and its holster. "In your most desperate moment, a sharp blade will prove to be your closest ally, but only if you can use it."

"I can and I will," insisted Cullen, growing agitated as he struggled to remove the last inch of the blade's tip from the scabbard as he practiced his draw once more. "I just need a bit of time."

"There is no time," argued Markus, thrusting his dagger into Cullen's hand. "I suggest you borrow this, just in case."

Cullen glanced down at the white oak handle. Drawing the dagger from the sheath, by the sweeping curve of this elegant blade he could tell it was crafted by the Elf-kind.

"Now this is a lovely dagger," remarked Cullen, admiring the unique craftsmanship.

"It is indeed. And for now, I shall entrust it to you. Take care of this weapon and it will take care of you."

"This dagger was gifted to you by King Kal-lel, I take it?" assumed Cullen, motioning for the squire to secure the holster and its weapon to the small of his back.

"I consider it an heirloom," replied Markus. "It was gifted to my descendent, King Brannon by Arerys' father when they, and the original members of the Order appointed to defeat the Dark Lord Beyilzon, first went to war against evil."

"That was over one thousand years ago!" gasped Cullen. "That would make it is as old as King Kal-lel."

"Older," responded Markus. "In fact, it once belonged to his father, Lord Galan Wingfield."

"That would be Prince Arerys' grandfather."

"Indeed, and he often relied on this dagger when his sword failed him."

"It is the weapon of kings, therefore, I shall treat it accordingly," promised Cullen, feeling noble with the knowledge he had been entrusted with this legendary dagger. "I shall wear it with pride and wield it with skill until it is returned to you when this task is done."

"I will hold you to your word, Captain Bristow. Now, let us join the others for a hasty breakfast before we depart."

"Now that is a brilliant idea! I am feeling rather peckish," agreed Cullen, the hilt and scabbard of his sword clanging noisily against the articulated skirting of armour. He hastened his pace to keep up as he followed Markus to the campfire where mortals and Elves gathered for a quick meal and conversation to discuss matters pertaining to this morning's search.

"What I find truly baffling is that with all the dead we have so far inspected, not one showed signs of having been eaten," commented Joval, munching on a piece of Elven bread. "*Nibbled* on by small scavengers, yes; but not truly devoured the way the killer beast would do if its intention was to hunt and kill for food."

"So we are back to considering that the animal, if it is indeed an animal, was being selective," responded Markus. He blew on the hot tea, sending wisps of aromatic steam rising from the cup swirling to vanish with his breath. "That it actually sought out King Sebastian while the others merely happened to be at the wrong place at the wrong time."

"I would say the condition of the dead bodies speak for themselves," commented Arerys. "As Joval said, as badly mangled and ravaged as some of the men were, not one of them showed true signs of being consumed. They were killed for sport."

"If anything, it would appear the birds and maggots are the only ones to have done any real feasting," added Joval.

Garrick's face took on a sickly pallor as he suddenly tossed aside his breakfast. "Well, that put me off my meal."

"My apologies, my lord," said Joval, truly contrite as he bowed his head in regret to the Prince. "That was not my intention to do so."

"I know," nodded Garrick, passing the empty plate to the squire. "I suppose I am not used to such gory breakfast conversation. However, I do understand we are up against a creature we must fully understand before we confront it. So go on, what were you saying of the dead, Master Stonecroft?"

"Though it is true, the dead men were badly mauled and their flesh had been pecked at," continued Joval. "It is evident to me that whatever committed all those killings did not eat a single man."

"All the victims, save for King Sebastian, were Talibarrians," reminded Cullen. "Perhaps it is like the difference between dining on a plump, young pheasant and being made to eat a stringy, old rabbit? I know one certainly would be more appealing than the other."

All in his company grew momentarily silent as they digested Cullen's bizarre analogy.

"Just what are you insinuating, Captain Bristow?" queried Arerys.

"What I am saying is that these barbarians to the north do smell particularly foul, so it would stand to reason they probably taste as bad as they smell."

"Interesting summation as usual, Captain," grunted Markus, almost gagging on his tea as he listened to Cullen's less-than-thought-provoking commentary.

"So, Captain Bristow, are you saying my father was killed because he was not a Talibarrian?" groaned Garrick, staring at Cullen in disbelief. "Because he valued good, personal hygiene, he had been devoured?"

"We do not know your father's fate as of yet," responded Cullen, speaking with all seriousness. "But given the choice between eating something that reeks of an old, unwashed sock that had been stuffed into a smelly riding boot for an eon, or something that is pleasantly perfumed with the sweet fragrance of rose or the fresh scent of lavender, I know which one I would choose."

"And we are to seriously entertain this notion?" questioned Kal-lel, staring with raised eyebrows at Cullen.

"I am just offering my personal opinion in case the killer beast has refined tastes and prefers quality over quantity."

"Then why the full stand of armour?" queried Arerys, eyeing Cullen decked out in his full battle regalia well before they were ready to depart.

"It is a precaution I would strongly advise the rest of you to follow," suggested Cullen, not realizing that the Elf had just insulted him. Instead, the young captain's knuckles rapped on the steel cuirass that shielded his torso front and back. "There is nothing wrong with being prepared."

"I agree, however, your definition of preparedness obviously differs from mine," countered Arerys, preferring his light, flexible Elven vest of mail to that of the mortal's cumbersome armour. "I suppose it is better that we each prepare in the manner that best suits us."

"And on this note, let us ride," suggested Kal-lel, motioning for Joval to gather their warriors. "We have another body to investigate and a creature still to capture."

"The most obvious trail begins over here," announced the Elven warrior who had first delivered the news of the mutilated corpse found a distance from the camp and his departed comrades. "There are broken arrows littering the way to the body."

Joval dismounted from his steed, as did the others, to investigate the scene that would eventually deliver them to where the man was killed.

"This is most unusual," commented Joval, holding up one of the arrows for closer scrutiny.

"What is unusual?" queried Garrick, examining the projectile the Elf held forth for all to see.

"This arrow struck against something so hard and at such a great speed, the tip of the bodkin is slightly flattened while the shaft shattered upon impact," observed Joval. His fingertip tested the steel, barbed tip that had lost its sharp, defined point and the fray of wood splinters pushed out behind it. "This arrow hit against something at close range – something that was exceptionally hard."

"Like a dragon's scale…" surmised Cullen, his head nodding judiciously as he inspected the projectile.

"Whatever it was, it was as hard as armour," determined Joval.

"What is for certain, this arrow struck against something much harder than any tree," noted Arerys, pointing to two other arrows that had lodged into a tree trunk.

"It would appear the poor sod was a terrible marksman," decided Cullen.

"Either that, or the creature he was shooting at possesses an impenetrable hide, impervious to the traditional weapons we use," assessed Kal-lel.

Arerys glanced down at the footprints left behind by the dead man. It was obvious by the length of these strides and the depths of each impression, this fellow was forced to engage in an all out sprint - to run like his very life depended on it.

At almost regular intervals, the man had slowed down, but just long enough to take aim and fire an arrow or two.

"The victim was not so much a poor marksman as he was a terrified soul made to take aim while forced to run for his life," responded Arerys.

"That would account for why some of these arrows strayed to pierce into trees or the earth while others are damaged," surmised Garrick.

Kal-lel ventured several paces ahead of the others where he found another arrow.

"Whatever manner of beast this was intended for, one side of the bodkin is worn and slightly bent to one side," assessed Kal-lel, holding forth this projectile for the others to scrutinize. "It is apparent it had glanced off a very hard, smooth surface."

"Like armour… or a dragon's scale," offered Cullen, feeling confident he had done the right thing in donning a full stand of armour when all others dismissed his advice.

The shape of the steel cuirass conforming to his chest, its smooth lines and curving shape were designed to allow arrows to glance off as long as the projectile did not strike him straight on from close range.

Cullen often took to parading around in his armour, for he knew that not only did it make him look more physically imposing, but to the ladies, it allowed him to cut a dashing form. However, on this day, his armour had taken on a very practical purpose.

"Look at this one!" called Markus. He held up the remnants of another arrow that was only identifiable because of the bits of feathers that fledged what remained of the shaft. "It appeared to have struck something at close range to shatter completely like this."

"The last time I saw arrows damaged in this manner was when I used my arrows against an attacking dragon," commented Joval.

"Aah-ha! So I was correct!" bragged Cullen, boastfully puffing out his armoured chest. "Did I not say the killings were committed by a dragon?"

"That you did," admitted Joval. "However, before you jump to the wrong conclusion, I did not say the creature *was* a dragon, I merely said that whatever these arrows struck up against, it was as tough as dragon scales – just like armour."

"Oh, come now, Master Stonecroft! Consider the evidence," urged Cullen. "Huge fangs capable of inflicting massive wounds; the burned area around that camp; and let us not forget the body up in the tree! There is nothing to say a dragon attempting to fly off with that dead man got the body snagged up in the branches, abandoning it there."

"It is an interesting supposition, Captain Bristow, one we shall keep in mind," responded Kal-lel, motioning Joval to resume his inspection than to engage this mortal in a nonsensical debate.

"Supposition?" gasped Cullen; perturbed his theory was so casually dismissed. "How do you know for certain that it was not a dragon that made off with King Sebastian? You know as well as I do we have yet to find definitive proof, irrefutable evidence to discount the possibility of a dragon."

"Let us not jump to any conclusions, Captain," recommended Kal-lel.

"I mean no disrespect to you, Your Highness, but let it be known, the only conclusions I ever jump to are the ones I am right about. Why do you and the others refuse to believe the creature is a dragon? The evidence we have found thus far speaks more and more in favour of my suspicions. What else can it be, but a bloodthirsty, rampaging reptile on wings?"

"I tend to agree with my father," stated Arerys. "Do not allow your fertile imagination to get the better of you, Captain Bristow. There is no sense in assuming it is a creature that it's not."

"What makes you say I am wrong, my lord?" countered Cullen, scowling in resentment. "As far as I am concerned, my assumptions *are* based on facts, not on my imagination."

"So tell me then, just how many dragons are you familiar with?" questioned Arerys, his tone cynical as he addressed Cullen. "How many have you personally encountered, Captain?"

"I am acquainted with only one, the Wizard of the North's dragon to be exact. And that is quite enough."

"So, you are saying Tor Airshorn's dragon is suddenly on the loose and rampaging about killing human beings?" rebuked Arerys.

"Come now, my lord, now that is absolutely ludicrous! We all know *Glutton* or *Mutton*, or whatever that crazy, old Wizard calls his behemoth pet reptile, is much too large to be the perpetrator of *these* killings. A dragon of that immense size would not go by unnoticed, not even from a distance. I am certain there is another dragon roaming these parts, and it is smaller than Airshorn's *pet*, but just as capable of dispensing a horrible death."

"The dragon belonging to Tor Airshorn is named *Button* and I will have you know that if that dragon was responsible for all these killings, it would have no hesitation in devouring those bodies," interjected Joval.

"Well, as I said, you can discount Master Airshorn's beastly pet because of its sheer size. And do not forget, the Wizard claimed he had taken great pains to wean the dragon off of man-meat," countered Cullen. "But mark my words, gentlemen, there is another dragon lurking about, waiting to kill again."

"There was a time not so long ago when that dragon indulged on human flesh," stated Joval, wandering ahead to search out other clues. "I have seen it consume human bodies in the past and I suspect it would take little more than the taste of blood to whet its appetite for this flesh again, but I highly doubt Tor Airshorn's dragon committed these killings."

"I agree with you, Master Stonecroft. Even if that blasted dragon took to eating man and Elf once more, it is much too large to be the culprit," insisted Cullen. "This is the work of a smaller, craftier dragon, I tell you."

"You pose an interesting argument," acknowledged Kal-lel. "We shall keep this in mind as we continue our search for King Sebastian and the creature that absconded with him."

"This is the last of the arrows," stated Arerys, following the trampled trail that continued on from where the broken projectile lay.

"And this is where the poor fellow threw his empty quiver at his pursuer," remarked Joval, pointing to the empty, wood and deer hide arrow holder that was smashed into several, flattened pieces.

"He must have been absolutely terrified; desperate to escape," decided Markus, seeing where the man had fallen and scrambled on his hands and knees to get away from the purveyor of death that gave unrelenting chase.

"The body is just up ahead," disclosed the Elven warrior, pointing to the bend of the trail made by the man in his frantic bid to escape. "It appears he had returned to camp to find it under attack. His attempts to flee led him here where the creature caught up to him."

Following the man's footprints, the putrid smell of decay grew ever stronger with each step they advanced. As they neared the corpse, Garrick's steps lagged, faltering behind the others as they gathered around the dead.

"It is not my father, is it?" asked Garrick, hanging back as he waited for confirmation.

"No, my lord," answered Cullen, after drawing back the man's tattered cloak that had fallen over his head to conceal his face. "Thankfully, it is not King Sebastian."

"By the type of wounds and the rate of decay, this man met his demise on the same day as the others did," assessed Joval.

A quick glimpse of the injuries sustained, plus the amount and size of ravenous maggots and those pupating that congregated on the wounds told the Elf all he needed to know as he presented his conclusion, "This unfortunate man just happened to run farther than his comrades did before he was killed."

"Take a look at this!" called Arerys, waving the others over to where he knelt. "I have never seen anything like this before."

"Whoa! What the hell would make a print like that?" gasped Cullen, his eyes opening wide in disbelief as he stared at the spoor left behind on the soft earth as Arerys removed his hand, his fingers spread wide apart to provide a scale as comparison for his comrades.

"It was certainly not made by any kind of dragon," determined Joval, nodding judiciously. "A dragon's print is much more elongated; its toes much longer and its claws more pronounced than what can be seen here."

"Whatever it is, the animal is heading east," stated Kal-lel, gazing toward Mount Hope.

Thinking back on details of the first reported attacks and the seemingly random pattern at which the beast struck, it suddenly dawned on Garrick. "The creature has been roaming north to south and north again, travelling back and forth, but always moving eastward."

"Like it is searching something out," determined Joval.

"But why east?" questioned Cullen, gazing over his shoulder to the mount peering ominously just over the trees. "What is the relevance?"

"The relevance is, beyond the Valley of Shadows is the place where I confronted the Dark Lord Beyilzon," responded Markus.

"Oh… I do not like where this is going," groaned Cullen, a chill running down his spine.

"It was almost ten years ago that we defeated evil," continued Markus. "And now, it appears we are being drawn back to that very place."

"Damn it! I knew you were going to say that," grumbled Cullen, yanking the helmet from his head.

"As of yet, we do not know why, but I sense we must proceed with utmost caution," warned Kal-lel. "We do not even know what kind of animal we are faced with."

"One thing is for certain, whatever this creature is, it is not natural," stated Joval, speaking with conviction.

"Whether the beast was spawned from Hell or just happened to wander over from some far and distant country, it does not belong here," insisted Cullen, speaking with absolutely certainty. "I suggest we do away with it immediately."

"I believe we are all in agreement with you, Captain Bristow," responded Kal-lel, nodding in approval.

"You are?" queried Cullen, momentarily baffled that his recommendation did not meet up with immediate opposition or ridicule.

"Even if we should be fortunate enough to find King Sebastian alive and we are able to rescue him from that beast, none will be safe if that creature is allowed to roam free," replied Kal-lel.

"And that is why we are here, Captain Bristow, we will hunt that animal down and destroy it," vowed Arerys.

"Well, no time like the present, I say," responded Cullen, pulling his helmet onto his head. "Let us see where these paw prints take us."

the lair of the beast

"King Kal-lel, do you honestly believe my father can still be alive after all this time?" asked Garrick, as he steered his mount next to the Elf King's steed. "It has been five days now, if I had not lost count."

Kal-lel could feel the burn of this mortal's intense stare. Garrick's worried eyes searched his soul for an answer he might not be prepared to accept.

"What say you, King Kal-lel? Do you believe he is still alive?"

For a lingering moment, Kal-lel thought on how best to answer this sensitive question, wondering whether it was better to give Garrick some reason for hope, even if it was false hope, or to brace him for the worst possible outcome.

"In your heart, what do you believe?" responded Kal-lel, urging his horse on to follow the warriors travelling in a procession behind Joval.

"My heart grows sick with worry. It grows weary with grief for each sleepless night and exhausting day that separates us."

"Then King Sebastian is still alive," answered Kal-lel, speaking with great conviction.

"How did you come to this conclusion?"

"A heart does not grow sick with worry enduring sleepless nights for those who had already passed on," replied Kal-lel. "I sense in your heart, you feel your father is still alive. That is why you suffer as you do."

"It could be nothing more than my sense of hope – a false sense of hope, that my father is alive," responded Garrick, shaking his head in sadness.

"If your father is alive, it is because he clings to this hope that you will search him out. This alone should be enough for you to keep going; to remain motivated until you have reason to no longer do so, Prince Garrick."

Joval suddenly raised his hand, motioning for horses and riders to come to a stop. The Elf dismounted to better scrutinize the signs.

"What is it, Master Stonecroft? Have you lost its tracks?" questioned Garrick, peering through the contingent of Elven warriors appointed to protect the royal search party by riding between them and Joval as he led the way.

"Patience, my lord," urged Cullen, watching as the Elf searched for signs of the beast's movements against this twilight sky. "They do not call this the Valley of Shadows for no reason. Even before the sun hides its face completely, it becomes disturbingly dark in this forest."

"Fear not, my lord, I have not lost the creature's tracks. The soft earth and the layer of pine needles upon the forest floor continues to yield clues, betraying the creature's movements," replied Joval. "I merely spied upon something that I believe will interest you."

"What is it?" asked Garrick, frowning with curiosity.

"Does this look familiar to you?" questioned Joval, presenting the Prince with a torn and frayed shred of fabric.

Garrick held the tattered fragment of cloth, inspecting the pulled threads of gold that once served to embroider a distinct pattern. Along one frayed edge, a trace of a stain marred the material.

"This came from my father's vest! I am sure of it," confirmed Garrick, recognition sinking in as he scrutinized the ragged bit of detailing. He could not help but notice the dark substance that had dried, staining the fabric. "But what is this? Can it be blood?"

"It looks too dark to be blood," determined Cullen, leaning in closer to better inspect the evidence in the diminishing light.

Joval took up the shred of material. Sniffing it first, he then spat on it, working his saliva in with the stain.

"Was that really necessary?" groaned Cullen, his face contorting with disgust as he watched the Elf.

"Master Stonecroft means to determine what this substance is," explained Kal-lel, knowing that Joval was attempting to reconstitute the dried residue. "Allow him to do his work."

As the stain moistened, the Elf took another whiff. His nose wrinkled as the sharp smell of iron assaulted his olfactory senses. Pressing this dampness, it left a distinct, red smudge on the pad of his fingertip.

"This stain is most definitely blood," confirmed Joval, holding up the fabric for the others to see the deep reddish-brown stain soiling the frayed edge of this cloth. "But what is this?"

The Elf pointed to a tiny hole, its edge outlined by a blackish residue as though it was burned through.

"It is reminiscent of the substance we found earlier," noted Arerys.

Joval spat on this small stain. His fingertip worked at the residue to moisten it for possible identification. Suddenly, he cursed in pain, dropping the tattered cloth. "It burns!"

He hastily wiped the seared pad of his finger on the damp moss growing from the trunk of a nearby tree.

"I do not know what it is, but judging by Joval's reaction, it appears to be the same substance that was on the dagger," stated Markus. "Whatever it is, it had marred the earth and the hunter's vest wherever it made contact."

"Any ideas, Joval?" queried Kal-lel.

"At this point, it is a substance foreign to me."

"Foreign or not, it is a definite clue whatever manner of beast it was that killed those hunters back there, it must be the one and the same creature that made off with King Sebastian," decided Cullen.

"So this is a sign my father is dead," lamented Garrick, his heart sinking as he assumed the worst as the sight of this small smear of blood became a terrible omen.

"It is nothing more than a sign that your father's raiment is torn and he was bleeding," assured Arerys. "For now, that is all it means."

Garrick said nothing in response. He merely nodded his head to show he heard Arerys' words, but there was nothing to indicate if he truly accepted it to be true. Taking the shred of cloth that once formed a bigger piece of something his father once wore, the Prince carefully tucked it into his vest pocket in case this was to be all that remained of his father.

"Night will be upon us very soon. We should stop for now," suggested Cullen. "We should rest until first light."

"No! We continue the search," demanded Garrick. "This is the first time we have had a sign we are heading in the right direction. This fragment of clothing is the only clue we have found of my father. We must move on!"

"And move on, we shall," vowed Kal-lel.

"Gentlemen, ready your bows! You six remain up front with me," ordered Joval, pointing to the warriors forming the line to protect the royal party. "The rest of you, take to the rear. Keep your eyes and ears open. Be aware the creature can approach from behind or even above."

The Elven warriors nodded in understanding, removing the bows from their backs to have it ready in their hands in case of an attack.

"Do we continue eastward?" questioned Markus, his eyes no longer able to make out the faint tracks his Elven comrades were still able to detect in the growing darkness.

"Where I had discovered that bit of cloth, I also found some fresh tracks. They are no more than a day old," disclosed Joval.

"Then it is even more reason to continue on," stated Kal-lel. "Lead the way, Joval."

"Be forewarned," cautioned Joval; "stay close, do not stray away. It is easy to get lost in this forest."

Instead of remaining within the protective circle of Elven warriors, Cullen steered his mount to the front where Joval escorted the party.

"There is no need to be up here, Captain Bristow," said Joval, as he mounted his steed. "It does not take two to lead the way."

"I do not mean to steal your thunder, Master Stonecroft, however, keep in mind this is *my King* we are searching for," whispered Cullen, steering his horse before Joval's as the Captain thrust his thumb over his shoulder. "If you had forgotten, your King is back there and it is *your* job to keep *him* safe."

"I intend to do just that by detecting danger before it has a chance to strike, hence my position at the front of the vanguard," explained Joval.

"Ooh, how very noble of you," smirked Cullen, nodding his head in feigned approval. "It will certainly sit well with those you wish to impress if your grand gesture of self-sacrifice comes to fruition. There is nothing like going down in the annals of history for a bold and selfless act of courage."

"I do not seek fame or glory," growled Joval. "I mean to keep those in my charge as safe as possible under these circumstances. And I have every intention of doing just that. If you have a sudden urge to subject yourself to danger and possible death for the sake of fame, your foolishness can well lead to an act of infamy for which you shall forever be remembered. Is that what you desire, Captain Bristow?"

"What I *desire* is to lead the search as it was first intended to be," argued Cullen, muttering beneath his breath so Garrick would not hear.

"I suppose since you were the one to lose King Sebastian in the first place, it is only fair you would want to lead the search in finding him," grunted Joval, shrugging his shoulders with indifference.

"I did not *lose* the King! He was stolen away from me," retorted Cullen, glaring angrily at the Elf.

"Is there a problem, Master Stonecroft?" queried Garrick.

"No, my lord, it is nothing to be concerned about. Your Captain is merely being vocal about his desire to lead this search."

Garrick glanced about the ever-darkening forest before his eyes settled on Cullen.

"Well, go to it then, Captain Bristow," urged Garrick. "Obviously, your sight is better than mine and as good as Master Stonecroft's if you claim to see the tracks in these deepening shadows. Time is wasting away. Let us continue on before we lose all light and whatever chance we have of finding my father on this eve."

"As Master Stonecroft's keen eyes spied this scant proof your father came by this way and he also spotted these fresh tracks, I suggest we allow him to continue on," recommended Cullen.

"A splendid idea, Captain," agreed Garrick, coaxing his horse on to follow. "Master Stonecroft, lead the way."

As day became night, a velvety dusk dissolved into a suffocating darkness made all the deeper by the thick canopy of the forest. This cover served to block out what little there was of the celestial light strong enough to pierce the growing layer of clouds.

"We are at the foot of Mount Hope," announced Joval, speaking in a whisper as he held forth a torch to light the way.

"Any other signs of my father?" Garrick asked hopefully as he stared up the slope looming before them.

"No, but there are numerous signs of the creature's presence in this immediate area," alerted Joval, his fingertip testing the dryness of the track pressed into the earth. "And they are fresh."

"How fresh?" questioned Cullen, his grip tightening around the hilt of his sword as his anxious eyes nervously darted about. They scanned the eerie surroundings that seemed to close in around them as the hour grew late and the search dragged on into the night.

"Fresh as in the beast could be breathing down your neck as we speak," whispered Arerys, inspecting the latest paw prints Joval had uncovered.

"Oh… that close," whispered Cullen, his words hushed as the Elf's warning sent an involuntary shiver down his spine. It was enough to cause him to secure his helmet to his head in case of a surprise attack.

The sudden crackling of dried leaves under foot sounded in the distance. It was followed by ominous silence.

"Did you hear that?" asked Cullen, straining to listen over the beating of his heart resounding in his metal helmet.

"Of course we did," answered Arerys, his eyes probing the darkness. "However, the denseness of this forest and our proximity to Mount Hope makes it difficult to ascertain the exact location of that sound."

"One thing is for certain," determined Kal-lel, "that noise we heard was made close to us."

Again, the rustling of leaves and the crackle of snapping twigs, this time from the opposite direction, caused the horses to prance about, nervously snorting and pawing at the earth.

"Something evil is near to us," warned Joval, calming his steed as it anxiously pulled at its reins as though sensing the approach of danger.

"Abandon your horses. Pair up and spread out from this point to search for signs of King Sebastian!" instructed Arerys. "Keep your arrows pointed out. You do not want to turn your weapons on a friend."

"And do not hesitate to kill the beast if you should come across it," added Cullen. "Just kill the bloody thing!"

With this command, the warriors immediately dismounted from their horses. Pairing off, they moved with stealth, weaving between trees and shrubs as they set off from this point in an expanding radius.

"Where to, Joval?" questioned Markus, nocking an arrow onto his bow just in case.

Joval glanced up to ascertain the direction the other warriors were heading to ensure there would be no overlap and the potential to be downed by a friendly arrow.

"This way," ordered Joval. "We shall follow these prints. See where they take us."

"Stay close," advised Cullen, motioning for Garrick to remain by his side.

For a moment, the Prince watched as the Captain struggled to unsheathe his cumbersome sword.

Without a word, Garrick chose to discreetly position himself between Joval and Arerys.

"Your actions do not exude a sense of confidence in me, my lord," whispered Cullen, embarrassed that the Prince chose to find safety amongst the Elves in their company.

"I do not question your ability with your sword, *when* you are able to draw it," admitted Garrick. "At this moment, I am inclined to believe our Elf friends are in a better position to hear and see danger before you do, at least in this consuming darkness."

"I see," sighed Cullen, clutching his sword close to his body as he followed the Prince.

"Hush!" ordered Joval. "I hear something."

"What?" whispered Cullen. His eyes stared through the darkness. "What did you hear?"

"There it is again," noted Arerys, glancing over to the right.

"What is it?" Cullen's voice tightened with fear as the invisible presence, unseen and unheard by him, caused genuine concern for the Elves.

"Shut it, Captain," ordered Markus, straining to hear above Cullen's nervous chatter.

"This way," whispered Joval, motioning with his head as he nocked an arrow onto his longbow.

Creeping through the darkness, they advanced with caution. They whipped about as a loud *snap* sounded behind them. The tip of every arrow and sword turned in the direction of this noise. Again, it was followed by an eerie silence that smothered the forest and gnawed at their nerves.

For Markus, Garrick and Cullen, their collective breath caught in the back of their throats. Beads of sweat began to form on their foreheads as the tension became palpable. Their hearts thundered in their chests as the invisible danger stealthily maneuvered in the darkness, steadily closing in on them.

Kal-lel's words broke this unnatural silence as he cautioned his comrades, "Remember, refrain from unleashing your arrows unless it is absolutely necessary."

All understood this order was meant to protect one of their own or King Sebastian, in case he was stumbling about, dazed and lost in the forest.

"What the?" gasped Garrick, jumping with a start as he turned.

All eyes glanced to the treetop where leaves and branches thrashed about in the darkness, only to grow strangely still.

Their attention was immediately drawn to a neighbouring tree as its branches violently shook and rattled, forcing them to turn their weapons once more.

"*FIRE!*" ordered Joval, unleashing his arrow.

This abrupt hail of projectiles ended as suddenly as it started. It soon became evident by the whine of arrows slicing through the air or the hard *thunk* of those striking against the trunk of the tree, whatever was up there had now vanished.

"Where did it go?" asked Cullen, spinning about in a bid to locate the creature lurking in the shadows. The strangest sensation, the unsettling feeling they were being watched and stalked, crept uneasily into his mind. "What just happened?"

"Quiet!" snapped Markus. "That is what we are trying to figure out."

"Whatever it is, it's circling around us," whispered Joval, glancing over Cullen's shoulder as he nocked another arrow.

"Then what is that?" queried Cullen, pointing with his sword behind the Elf.

Joval, Arerys and Kal-lel spun about, following the sound of a falling leaf brushing against foliage as it settled onto the ground.

"Never mind..." sighed Cullen, relieved to see it was nothing more than a leaf floating down to earth. "As you were."

A horrific roar abruptly rattled through the night air. Before they could turn to face the noise, a monster charged straight for them. Kal-lel and Garrick were instantly bowled over as the creature pounced on Cullen. Driving him face first into the ground before launching itself off his back. In a blur of shadow against darkness, the beast sailed through the air. Just as Arerys raised his bow to take aim, he was knocked backwards, his bow and arrow flying from his hands.

Arerys screamed in pain as the creature snagged him, sinking a powerful fang high into his right shoulder to drag him off into the night.

Instinctively, Markus pivoted, avoiding a head-on collision as he dove away. Too close to use his bow, he rammed the arrow into the side of the beast's neck as Joval struggled to take aim without hitting either Arerys or Markus.

As the arrow sank into its flesh, with a guttural snarl, the creature dropped Arerys from its mouth. Bounding into the forest, the beast dissolved into the shadows. It was in this instant, as Markus fell back to the ground, he caught a fleeting glimpse of a bizarre and horrifying sight as the monster vanished. He could have sworn he saw what appeared to be monstrous dewclaws, like the curved blades of harvesting sickles, protruding from the inside of the front legs. And what was as strange as these protrusions appeared deadly, Markus was sure he spied a flash of what looked to be overlapping plates of scales and sharp spikes on the shoulders that continued down its rump before the spike-tipped tail whipped about, slashing Markus across his forehead.

In a momentary daze, Markus lay gasping on the ground. He used the back of his hand to wipe the blood seeping from the gash as it trickled down his face and into his eyes. Gazing over, he squinted through the blood to see Joval kneeling by Arerys as his friend groaned in pain.

Kal-lel knelt by Markus' side only to have the mortal wave him off, "Go see to Arerys."

"You are bleeding... and quite badly," stated Kal-lel.

"It looks worse than it is," assured Markus, slowly sitting up with Garrick's help. "I can wait. Go see to Arerys."

"Can't... breathe! Can't... breathe!" wheezed Cullen. He frantically flailed about, motioning for someone, anyone, to help him as he struggled to roll onto his back.

The tremendous weight of the creature as it launched its body off of this mortal's back effectively compressed the cuirass. The metal shell that was once contoured to perfectly fit and protect his torso was compressed. The front and back of the cuirass were flattened so his ribcage could not expand with each breath he fought to inhale. The leather ties and buckles that held the armour in place now strained, pulling with the unsightly shape the cuirass had taken on.

Garrick dashed over to Cullen's side. The Captain's eyes watered, bulging as the shallow breaths he managed to gulp down failed to deliver a sufficient amount of life-giving oxygen his body was in need of. Garrick yanked off his gloves. His fingers frantically worked to untie the leather straps and undo the tight buckles, but to no avail.

"Armour... Cut it off..." wheezed Cullen, squeezing out these words as he struggled to remove the dagger Markus had lent him.

Garrick snatched up the weapon. The Elven blade easily sliced through the leather straps. Cullen's ribcage suddenly expanded, the cuirass popping off his chest and falling from his back with the first full breath of air he inhaled. As the cool night air filled his lungs, Cullen flopped to the ground, thankful he was still alive after this ordeal.

Seeing that Cullen was destined to recuperate once he caught his breath, Garrick abandoned him to see how Arerys fared after the attack. He watched as Joval and Kal-lel worked with haste to loosen Arerys' raiment to inspect the level of damage inflicted by the beast.

"The mail," groaned Arerys, wincing in pain as his father and Joval peel it off from his shoulder. "It could not stand up to the pressure of the creature's bite."

Immediately, the hot blood seeping through from the wound was clear indication the links of the Elven mail separated.

"It would have been much worse if you had not been donning your vest," stated Kal-lel. He positioned the palm of his left hand over the front of the wound just below the right collarbone as Joval slipped in his left hand to heal the puncture on Arerys' back where the fang sank in, striking up against his shoulder blade to crack this bone.

Joval's hand suddenly recoiled from the wound as he examined the palm of his hand. Where it came up against the creature's saliva that still lingered on Arerys' skin, the dark slime seemed to eat away at his skin.

"This substance burns!" exclaimed Joval, staring as wisps of smoke rose from his flesh.

"It most certainly does," acknowledged Arerys, through gritted teeth as his father set to work on a healing incantation.

The saliva coating the creature's fangs that sank into his shoulder burned like a red-hot poker that had been thrust deep into the wound.

Joval's hand hovered, just barely making contact with the wound as he set to work to relieve Arerys pain and to mend this injury. With their combined powers to heal, in a matter of several minutes, all traces on the wound had disappeared.

Arerys rolled his arm and shoulder, testing its flexibility and strength as Kal-lel turned his attention to Markus.

"Let me see how bad it is," said Kal-lel, prying Markus' hand from the gash on his forehead.

Where the steady pressure Markus applied helped to staunch the flow of blood, the hot crimson wept from the wound once more as the Elf inspected the damage.

Pressing the palm of his left hand to the injury, the high Elf set to work. Immediately, Markus felt relief. Where before, this nasty slash seemed to throb with agony, the blood seemingly gushing forth with each beat of his heart, it now tingled as flesh and skin mended, fusing together to bring this liberal flow of blood to an end.

"You will be fine," promised Kal-lel, removing his hand from the newly healed wound. "I am afraid you will be left with a small scar, but other than that, you will recover nicely."

"One more scar on my body will not be the death of me, at least, not yet," responded Markus, nodding in appreciation to Kal-lel. "Thank you for your help."

"I would be grateful for a little of that healing Elven magic, too," groaned Cullen. He staggered up onto his unsteady legs as the damaged cuirass dangling from his body fell free with a loud clatter.

"Where are you bleeding?" questioned Kal-lel, his eyes quickly inspecting the mortal for obvious injuries.

"I need not be spouting blood to be injured," moaned Cullen. His arms wrapped about his trembling body, clutching his aching ribs as he fished about for a little sympathy.

"Allow me," offered Joval. His left hand hovered over Cullen's chest as he assessed the damage.

"Am I wounded or what?" whined Cullen, waiting expectantly for the Elf's prognosis.

"You are wounded, but it is really not that bad," stated Joval. "These ribs are badly bruised."

"Ouch!" yelped Cullen, wincing in pain as Joval's finger poked him on the ribcage. Here, deepening contusions marked the points of impact with the metal cuirass. The bruising was most obvious where the armour folded beneath the creature's weight as it bodily launched itself off from his back to attack Arerys.

"Fear not, Captain Bristow, this can be easily remedied," assured Joval, his hands resting lightly over the damaged area to initiate healing. After whispering a healing incantation, the Elf announced that his work was done.

Cullen drew a full, deep breath to fill his lungs. There was not even a dull ache to remind him of the trauma he had endured.

"Much better, Master Stonecroft!" praised Cullen. "I am as good as new. Thank you."

"You are welcome," said Joval. "And as you are fit enough to continue on, let us resume the search."

"You want to go look for that *thing* at this very moment?" gasped Cullen, staring off into the darkness that engulfed the forest. "It almost killed us!"

"*Almost* being the operative word, Captain," responded Joval. He picked up his bow once more. "We must stop that creature before it attempts to kill again."

"And let us not forget my father," reminded Garrick. "There is a chance he is close by. And before you even hint that he is dead, Captain Bristow, I do not care. I want him recovered, dead or alive. Is that understood?"

"Of course, my lord," Cullen replied with a curt bow as he inspected his armour to see if it could be salvaged.

"This way," ordered Joval, pointing in the direction the animal had fled. "Stay close and keep your weapons at the ready."

"Somehow, this does not surprise me," whispered Markus, staring into the mouth of the cave where the large paw prints disappeared inside.

"We were told the creature moves by night," reminded Garrick, holding forth the torch to illuminate the entrance. "I suppose it makes sense it would seek refuge in the darkness of a cave with the coming of daylight."

"There is a foul stench in the air," noted Joval, sniffing the stale odour wafting from the cave.

"It smells like brimstone," said Cullen.

"Hush, I hear something," whispered Arerys, listening for an unusual noise emanating above the resonating sounds of water dripping steadily into a pool deep within this cave.

"Say... Look at this," said Kal-lel. He spied upon what appeared to be the regular edge of a boot's heel pressed into the sandy soil. The light of the torch Cullen carried served to illuminate this print.

"A button," announced Joval, picking up the small, gold piece that glistened in the torchlight. Brushing off the sand, he held it before Garrick for his inspection.

"The golden dragon," noted the Prince, recognizing the embossed image of this heraldic symbol. "This came from my father's vest."

"He is in there," decided Markus, his eyes tracing the large paw prints that tracked in and out of the cave.

"Whether he is dead or alive, I will not leave him here," declared Garrick, boldly brandishing his sword to confront the beast. "I must bring him home to Darross."

Before Garrick could march in, Cullen seized him by his shoulder. "You cannot go traipsing into that black hole like it is nobody's business, my lord. The beast could very well be inside, waiting."

"Then are you going to do that for me, Captain?" questioned Garrick, offering the torch to him.

All eyes turned to scrutinize Cullen as they waited for his answer. After a discomforting moment of silence, he responded, "I was appointed by King Sebastian to captain his army. It is only right that I be the one to oversee his rescue."

"Go on then," urged Joval, shoving Cullen to the mouth of the cave. He then whispered to the Captain, "Here is your chance to be a hero –

to steal my thunder as you so eloquently put it."

"A hero? I am only going first because I am the one with the torch," Cullen grumbled beneath his breath, his apprehensive steps inching him through the entrance of the cave.

"Draw your swords. Keep your voices down," whispered Joval, stepping before Cullen.

"And if you should see the beast, do not hesitate to kill it," added Arerys, more than ready to confront his attacker.

As the torch peeled back the darkness in their immediate area, its flame was not enough to illuminate the high ceiling of this cave.

For a moment, they stood absolutely still as their eyes adjusted to the suffocating darkness waiting to engulf them should the torch lose its light.

"What is that sound?" whispered Arerys, straining to hear as everything, including the beating of their own hearts, seemed to resonate and amplify in this chamber.

Glancing about, Cullen spotted a small pool in the center of the cave where drops of water forming on overhanging stalactites dripped loudly to accumulate in this subterranean reservoir.

"It is nothing more than water gathering in that pool," responded Cullen.

"No..." countered Arerys, cocking his head to one side as his sensitive ears tried to identify this particular noise. "That was not what I heard."

"I hear it, too," insisted Joval, his keen ears attempting to home in on the strange, muffled sounds echoing around them. It was as though something was attempting to stifle its breathing in hopes of going by unnoticed.

"Over there," whispered Kal-lel, pointing with the tip of his sword to the deep shadows clinging to the north side of this chamber.

"I cannot hear it," responded Garrick, straining to see and hear what the Elves did.

"But they can," assured Markus, glancing over to Arerys, Kal-lel and Joval as they slowly advanced to the dark corner.

"There is something alive in here?" gulped Cullen, his eyes darting about nervously to search out the creature.

"Most definitely," whispered Joval, his sword poised before him as crept in closer.

"Then kill the beast!" roared Cullen, thrusting the torch up high to challenge the creature. His bellow reverberating off the ceiling of the cave launched a colony of roosting bats into flight.

Markus, Arerys and Joval's groans of anger and frustration directed at Cullen was drowned out as the deafening clatter of thousands of leathery wings in frenetic flight swelled and echoed all around them.

"Bugger me!" gasped Cullen, ducking low to the cave floor as the winged mammals swirled around them like a black tornado.

The Elves threw their hands over their ears as the high-pitched squeaks emitted by the bats played havoc with their sensitive hearing. Undetected by mortal ears, the mammals' repetitive calls were piercingly shrill to them.

The thunderous flapping of wings quickly died out as the bats exited, winging out into the night.

"Do you wish us dead?" grunted Markus, glaring at Cullen as the glow of the torch served to diminish the true level of the Captain's embarrassment.

"Of course not, but if that creature is about, I refuse to be taken by surprise again," snapped Cullen, in his own defense. "I was daring the beast to come get me."

Markus snatched the torch from Cullen's hand as he ordered him along, "This way."

"Up ahead... I see something," cautioned Joval, gripping his sword as he pressed on.

As the flames pushed back the darkness, Garrick gasped, "Father!"

In a dishevelled, bloodied heap cowering low to the ground, King Sebastian trembled in utter fear, mumbling incoherently as he shrank away from the bright glare of the torch.

Garrick rushed toward him, but this sudden movement and the touch of his son's hand on his shoulder caused Sebastian to recoil, shrieking in fright.

"Father, I am your son, Garrick," whispered the Prince. He tried to console the King, only to have him retreat farther into the cave.

"It is coming... It is coming," muttered Sebastian, his eyes were wild as he crawled away from his son.

"What is coming?" questioned Cullen, glancing about the chamber.

Instead of answering his question, Sebastian backed off, whimpering in fear. But as Garrick and Cullen neared, the King snarled like a deranged and wounded animal.

"Bloody hell, the King has gone mad!" groaned Cullen, staring at the almost unrecognizable man in tattered, bloodied clothing.

"Can you blame him after this ordeal?" responded Markus, watching the pitiful family reunion, as father no longer recognized son.

"We must leave this place immediately," ordered Joval. "The beast may be lurking about."

"Father, come with me," coaxed Garrick, extending his hand to the King. "You are safe now."

Instead, Sebastian retreated. Withdrawing deeper into the cave, his voice tightened as he whined, "It is coming."

"We must leave *now*," urged Arerys, his words hushed. "And we must do so with as little commotion as possible."

"I agree," nodded Cullen. With that said, he marched straight over to where Garrick knelt.

The Prince's words of comfort did nothing to console the King. Failing this, Garrick resorted to pleading to his father for his cooperation.

"You must hurry, my lord. We must leave this place immediately," insisted Cullen.

"I am trying, but my father is much too hysterical to be reasoned with."

"There is no reasoning with the King," argued Cullen, growing more impatient the longer he was made to endure these dark, dreary surroundings. "I mean no disrespect to your father, but the man has lost his mind. Now, make him come along."

"I am trying," snapped Garrick, "but he is too frightened to move."

"Allow me, my lord," offered Cullen, pushing past the Prince.

Cullen abruptly and unceremoniously seized Sebastian by his arm, but his bid to physically extricate the King from this cave was met with violent retaliation. Sebastian snarled, hurling himself at his tormentor. Bowling him over, the King straddled Cullen's body, his filthy hands wrapping around the Captain's neck to throttle him.

Markus and Joval lunged forward, grabbing Sebastian by his arms to restrain him. Struggling to haul him off the winded Captain, their actions only served to set the King spinning off in a greater rage. Sebastian bellowed, ranting like a man possessed.

"If he does not quiet down, he will draw the beast's attention, if it is not already here," warned Arerys, motioning for calm.

As Markus and Joval hoisted the struggling man onto his quaking legs, Kal-lel approached.

Unable to recognize a long-time friend, Sebastian growled, throwing his head back to scream. Suddenly, the distraught mortal fell silent under the Elf's touch. His body went limp as Kal-lel placed a hand, the thumb on one side of his windpipe and the fingers on the other, to apply steady pressure on Sebastian's throat.

"Elven magic?" queried Cullen, watching in stunned silence as Sebastian was rendered unconscious. The King's body flopped in Markus and Joval's hold, his head lolling on his chest.

"No magic," responded Kal-lel, "just a little pressure to momentarily deprive his brain of its blood supply. He will come around soon enough."

"We leave now!" demanded Markus, lifting one of Sebastian's arms over his shoulder as Cullen took the other to help support his weight.

"Arm yourselves and take the lead," ordered Joval, waving Arerys and Kal-lel on. "I will take up the rear in case the creature is hiding somewhere in this cave."

"A brilliant idea," nodded Cullen. Dragging Sebastian along, he was secure in the fact he was protected from a surprise assault.

As they neared the mouth of the cave, the light of the torch sputtered, dying out to send a swirl of gray smoke into the night. Garrick tossed it aside, sighing in relief that at least this darkness was not as intense as the all-consuming blackness of the cave.

Joval's head slowly turned. Somewhere deep in the bowels of this cave, there was a presence. It was not the sudden movement of shadow in darkness or a telltale growl or snarl, instead, it was a soft sound indiscernible to mortal ears, but quite apparent to Joval's. It was like the sound of a cat creeping up on its prey, the pads of its paws pressing into the sandy soil as it carefully inched its way forward.

"Run!" shouted Joval.

As his comrades raced to safety, Joval's warning spurred the creature to attack. The Elf spun about, sword in hand as he braced for the assault. With no time to think and barely enough time to act, Joval fell backwards as the beast pounced at him. As he fell, the creature flew over his body. Joval rammed the tip of his sword up into the creature's belly. A nerve-raking roar rumbled from the animal as the power of its forward momentum freed it from the Elven blade. It bounded away, disappearing into the forest.

Just as Joval's sword was wrenched from the wound it had inflicted, the creature's hot blood splash across the Elf's chest and face as noise, like steam escaping from a boiling kettle, hissed.

"Bloody hell!" cursed Joval. His skin burned on contact with the thick, black liquid; his raiment smoldering as the blood ate away at leather and fabric. "It burns like its saliva."

Arerys dashed over to Joval, pulling him onto his feet. Placing his left hand over the wound, he winced in pain as his palm brushed lightly on the creature's blood. With an incantation, Joval's face was healed.

"What in heaven's name was that?" asked Markus, watching the branches and leaves sway in the creature's wake. "My second glimpse was no better than my first. It moved with such speed."

Flicking the blood from his sword, Joval replied, "It behaved and sounded like a cat. It most definitely moved with the stealth of a cat, but exactly what kind? I cannot even hazard a guess."

"I have never encountered such a beast," responded Markus.

"One thing is for certain, it was an exceptionally large cat," surmised Arerys, listening as the creature charged off into the night as the high-pitched squeal of a horn sounded far off in the distance.

"How can that monstrosity be a *cat*?" questioned Cullen. "Not even the largest mountain cat has ever grown to these behemoth proportions!"

"The better question is, since when did cats take to wearing armour?" questioned Joval. In the split second the creature was over him and his sword plunged into its belly, it was one of the few unprotected parts not shielded by this strange, spike-studded shell.

"For now, we are safe," determined Kal-lel. "That noise seemed to have driven the creature off."

"Or it has called the beast home," decided Joval, as he wiped his blade clean.

the broken covenant

"It's been almost a full cycle of the moon an' we still don't have a single crystal ta speak of," grumbled a young Talibarrian woman. She stared impatiently at the near-full moon peeking out from behind the clouds before she pulled the rickety door closed behind her. "This just ain't workin' fer ya, is it, Gran?"

"Ya gotta be patient, Druen," scolded Ratha, dismissing her granddaughter's skeptical words as the old witch carelessly tossed an old, battered goat horn onto the cluttered table. "Our people have waited fer an eon - over a thousand years fer such an opportunity. We ain't gonna ruin it now jus' 'cause you're gettin' a bit antsy."

With her left eye clouded by cataracts and no longer trusting her one functioning eye to identify the items she required, Ratha sniffed at the contents stuffed into an earthenware jar. With a grunt, she straightened her stooped back, reaching up to shove the container back onto the dusty, tilted shelf. Feeling the shape of the one next to it, her grubby, gnarled fingers wrapped around this jar, but the stiff, swollen joints of her fingers prevented her from prying off the tight-fitting lid.

"This jus' won't do," groaned Ratha, as she tried to flex her knotted fingers ravaged by the onset of arthritis.

With a grimace of pain, she used an index finger that could not quite straighten out to point to the old, cracked jar behind the young woman. "Fetch me those bees, Druen. Bring 'em over here. I need at least three of those little buggers ta do the trick."

"There's only two of 'em left. The others are dead," announced the young woman, inspecting the survivors through the hazy glass that served to distort the bee's features. Their wings buzzed angrily even as they crawled about, exhausted by their futile search for a way out of this prison. "Maybe they stung each other ta death?"

"In all this time, have ya learned nothin' from me, girl?" snapped the wizened, old hag. "Bees live in hives with a whole bunch of other bees. Jus' like wasps, they don't fare well separated from their colony fer long."

"I learned that… I jus' fergot, that's all," sulked Druen, as she untied the rough bit of twine that held the thin cloth over the mouth of the jar to keep the bees contained within. "So… whatcha gonna do with these bees again?"

The old woman's one working eye rolled in exasperation as she impatiently snatched the glass jar from the girl's hands.

"Watch an' learn," grunted Ratha, thrusting her right hand into the container to remove a bee. Trapping the insect between her thumb and index finger, she pinned its wings down against its thorax. Careful to subdue the bee without killing it, Ratha held it up for Druen to inspect.

"Wouldn't it be easier if ya jus' killed the thing first?" She watched as the bee struggled. Its tiny legs flailed about as the stinger on the very tip of its abdomen attempted to swivel around to prick its tormentor.

"Ya know, you're my gran'daughter an' all, but you're still a dolt," grumbled Ratha, frustrated by the failed efforts to educate her young apprentice. "I told ya before, dead bees don't sting. They'd be useless ta me."

With that said, Ratha began administering the homeopathic remedy to the worst of her arthritic knuckles. Pressing the agitated bee to the swollen joint, the insect did not hesitate to jab its tiny stinger into the inflamed knuckle. As the barbs of the stinging apparatus set into her flesh, the stinger remained lodged as the venom sac tore free of the bee's posterior to create a lethal wound on the insect.

"Look here," ordered Ratha, flicking the dying bee over her shoulder as she held up her arthritic hand to the candlelight for her granddaughter to see. "If ya look closely, you'd see how the stinger continues ta work. Now, this wouldn't be happenin' if the bee was already dead."

Sure enough, Druen watched as the poison sac attached to the stinger pulsated with life even as the bee died. It worked to deliver the venom into Ratha's arthritis ravaged joint. As the burning sensation from the injected bee venom spread into this inflamed knuckle, it eased the stiffness and pain. Ratha flexed her finger as she mumbled, "Better… Much better."

Seizing the last bee with the same care and regard as the first, the old woman strategically administered a sting to another finger that was swollen and knotted by this crippling disease.

"I thought it was honey that ya used fer this pain," said Druen, shuddering as she watched the second stinger pumping away, injecting the last of its venom into the swollen knuckle.

"Honey's fer minor burns, scratches an' cuts," Ratha snapped impatiently; "ta heal an' ta fight infections, ya fool!"

"There's jus' so much ta remember, but at least I knew it had somethin' ta do with bees," groaned Druen, scratching her head in thought as she attempted to memorize this bit of information. "I should really write it all down."

"Ya don't know how ta write, ya ninny," sniffed Ratha, slowly flexing her digits to help the venom circulate through the ravaged joints. Satisfied with the temporary results, she was ready to resume her work. "And had I taught ya how ta read an' write before my sight went on me, I'd doubt you'd be able ta remember any of it ta save yer own life."

"Sure I would," argued Druen.

"Even after all my tutorin' ya still don't remember the diff'rence between the properties of the deadly nightshade an' the dead man's bell," growled Ratha, pointing to the jars containing the dried and crushed plant parts kept on opposite sides of the shelf so Druen would not mix the two containers up.

Picking up the earthenware jar whose lid refused to budge under her crippled grip, Ratha was now able to pry the cover off. She recoiled as a small cloud of dust and the sharp odour of decay erupted into the air before her. Though she could see objects from a distance adequately, she could no longer rely on her right eye to distinguish small items held up close. As this puff of dust dissipated, Ratha took a whiff only to gag as the pungent stench assaulted her nostrils.

"Aah! Here we go! I knew I still had some dried newts," the woman cackled with delight.

With a gleeful snort, Ratha blew the wiry gray strands of hair from her face so it floated off from her good eye to stray over the one clouded with cataracts. Now that her vision was not quite as impaired, she prepared to make her selection, gently shaking out the contents of the jar onto the only space on the table that wasn't occupied by dirty, food-encrusted dishes, pots, pan or eating utensils.

Druen observed in silence; the delicate features of her face contorting in disgust. She watched her grandmother sorting through the amphibians that had been dried out in the heat of the summer sun until each animal was hard and shrivelled almost beyond recognition.

"They're all dead an' they're all newts," grumbled Druen, her nose wrinkling as she grimaced in revulsion. "What diff'rence does it make which ones ya choose?"

"Were you asleep when I was readin' out the ingredients fer this potion?" snapped Ratha, her fingers carefully separating the good ones from the rejects. "We gotta use only *whole* newts fer this spell ta work. Can't go using ones with their tails, legs an' especially their heads broken off. They gotta be perfectly whole newts, an' the bigger, the better it'll be."

Ratha selected thirteen of the best newts. Each black body was adorned with a fire-red pattern on its underbelly. One by one, she carefully placed each stiff, little corpse into a soot-blackened, iron cauldron suspended over a slow burning fire. Inside this vat, the newts disappeared, sinking into in a strange concoction blended with the blood of a goat. These ingredients had been simmering over the flames for a good part of the day.

"Do ya remember what the newt is used fer, girl?"

"It makes ya dream strange dreams, even when you're awake?" guessed Druen, hoping she was correct.

"Bloody hell! My efforts are wasted on ya! You're thinkin' of the slime of a toad," groaned the old woman. She glanced over at the bloated, old amphibian squatting on the corner of the table; its sticky tongue flicking forward to deliver the discarded bee Ratha had tossed aside into its wide, gaping mouth. "Perhaps I should make ya lick the toad so ya don't ferget it."

Remembering the others who had experienced the hallucinogenic properties of the secretions extruded from the pores of this toad's rough skin when it was agitated or frightened, Druen shuddered in disgust. She was more repulsed by the whole notion of licking the creature's warty back than being made to endure the results of sampling this milky-white substance.

"I won't ferget," promised the girl, shrinking away from her grandmother's scowl of disapproval.

"Let's hope not! So, what's the next symbol on there?" asked Ratha, the lid of her cloudy eye closed as she strained to focus on the ancient rune with her working eye.

Druen scrutinized the yellowed parchment. Picking up a stick, she etched the identical symbol into a large platter filled and levelled with sand, copying the image many times larger than it was inscribed on the aged parchment.

"Ooh! We're in luck. I've got some me of *that!*" exclaimed the old woman, giving her granddaughter a pleased smile comprised mostly of shrinking gums lined with a few broken, blackened teeth.

"Some of what?" asked the girl, watching as Ratha scanned the shelves in search of this particular ingredient.

"Here we go! It's the blowfish," announced Ratha. "But what part of this fish am I speakin' of, girl?"

"The slime?" replied Druen, in a meek voice. Her response sounded more like a question than an actual answer.

"Ya good-fer-nothin' dolt! The fish slime don't do nothin'," cursed Ratha. "It's the *liver* that's deadly – even jus' a pinch of it in this dried state will kill a grown man."

"But why would ya use poison that kills when the idea is ta restore life with this potion?" wondered Druen; staring up at the dead blowfish her grandmother was drying in the rafters of this cottage.

"This ain't no ordinary life we're tryin' ta restore. With this special incantation, the effects of this poison are reversed if ya do it exactly right," explained Ratha, using the tip of a wooden spoon rather than her fingers to measure out the proper quantity of this powder. "But why am I tellin' ya, anyway? It's all wasted on yer feeble mind."

"My mind ain't feeble. It's just preoccupied with other stuff."

"Other stuff that's makin' ya feeble-minded," assessed her grandmother.

"You can always find yerself another apprentice more eager ta learn the craft," invited Druen, hoping the old woman would take her up on this offer that she never wanted in the first place.

"True enough, but witchery is in our blood. Ya can't deny yer kinfolk an' the fine, time-honoured traditions we're tryin' ta uphold."

"If it's so fine a tradition, then why are we shunned by our fellow Talibarrians?" questioned Druen, recalling how, when she was a little girl, other children would throw stones at her to drive her away if she came too close to their village.

"Those ignorant sods are scared of anythin' they don't understand," grumbled Ratha, spooning in the equivalent of four pinches of the highly toxic, dried fish liver into the brewing concoction where the dehydrated newts slowly softened as they soaked in the goat blood as it reached a sluggish boil. "They strayed away from our teachin' an' now, everythin' we do that was once natural an' part of a long-standin' tradition is considered ta be strange an' evil."

"Well, you gotta admit, conjurin' up strange magic an' dispensin' hexes an' spells ain't somethin' jus' anyone would take ta doin'," argued Druen.

"Strange magic, indeed!" Ratha snorted with indignation as her one good eye shot a baleful glance in Druen's direction. "Way back in the early days, our kind – our order was the religion of choice in these parts. Our magic wasn't strange; it was powerful! We were a-tuned ta nature an' understood its true powers. Witches back then knew how ta use it; jus' how ta harness it. These days, it's all but a forgotten art remembered only by those of us descended from the original four witches that once dwelled here when Mount Hope was known as the Witch's Hold."

"Why were there only four witches ta begin with?" questioned Druen. "Maybe this art would have lasted fer longer if there were more than jus' four ta spread the word an' keep the tradition goin' on."

"Ya fool!" cursed Ratha, glaring impatiently at her granddaughter. "There were four 'cause four was all that was needed. The four witches, the leaders of the most powerful covens, represented the four seasons an' the four elements – "

"I ain't no genius, but even I know four an' four makes eight," interjected Druen, hoping to impress her mentor and guardian with fundamental math skills.

"Oh, shut yer gob, you imbecile!" snapped the old woman. "Let me finish."

"Sorry…"

"As I was sayin'; these four seasons combined with the powers of the four elements; fire, water, air an' earth bring balance ta this world. There was a time our ancestors were as wise and more revered by our kind than the great Wizards. The Wizard of the North, the one known as Tor Airshorn, was feared for the powers he possessed, but even at that, he had little influence over our people's beliefs. The four witches though… now they had the Talibarrian folks' true respect."

"An' the Dark Lord Beyilzon knew the kind of power the witches had an' the kind of authority they had over the people. That's why that evil soul was in cahoots with those witches in the first place," added Druen, recalling this crucial bit of family history.

"Oh yes, the Dark Lord knew all right," agreed Ratha, her gaunt, haggard face contorting with bitterness as she remembered the tales of yore, when her kind once wielded true authority over the Talibarrians. "He knew the four leaders possessed great powers indeed. And he knew when they'd congregate fer annual rituals conducted at the sacred site once known as the Witch's Hold. They had powers vested to 'em of this realm – of the natural world; powers the Dark Lord wasn't that familiar with, havin' been cast from his high place by his

Father's throne."

"So, with the wisdom an' knowledge the witches of old possessed of the natural forces, workin' tagether with the Dark Lord's forbidden magic, it made Beyilzon even more powerful," remembered Druen.

"I see ya finally recall somethin' of my teachings," sighed Ratha, her filthy, gnarled finger tapping on the parchment for her granddaughter to copy and enlarge the characters so she could decipher them.

"But if the witches were all so powerful, why are there so few of us now?" questioned Druen, her hand running lightly over the sand to smooth it out. "You'd think we'd be flourishin' an' runnin' this country if that was the case."

"Pay close attention, 'cause I ain't gonna repeat it again!" snapped the old woman. "When the four witches made a pact with the Dark Lord, Beyilzon had promised them greatness an' power that'd extended beyond the borders of Talibarr. Some say he even promised 'em immortality if they shared in their knowledge an' aided the Dark Lord in his quest for dominion over this realm."

"Of course, those poor, old witches must've had ta do somethin' in return fer this promise."

"Ain't nothin' fer free, Druen. Those witches had ta prove they had the power ta convince thirteen of the most powerful warlords that roamed these lands ta unite their people under Beyilzon's banner; ta fight as a united front fer the Dark Lord."

"It couldn't have been that hard ta do," decided Druen, unimpressed by this news, "especially if those witches had that kind of influence over the people."

"But there was more. These witches had ta show they had the power ta enslave the warlords ta do the Dark Lord's biddin' in his cursed name so their armies would confront those ta the south under *his* orders. Beyilzon demanded absolute control over these thirteen men – the kind of obedience an' loyalty that can't be bought with riches or bribed with promises of power."

"But how do ya know that there were really thirteen of 'em warlords?" questioned Druen. "How do we know if this number changed over all these many years? After all, it's human nature fer people ta exaggerate if it makes fer a better story ta tell."

"This ain't no *story* I'm speakin' of, ya silly girl. It's historical fact!" snapped Ratha, her voice tightening with bitterness.

"Yeah, but it could be nothin' more than facts that got twisted 'bout over time ta make an old tale more excitin' fer the next generation ta want ta hear it. Ya gotta admit, thirteen warlords sound a lot more scary than jus' one or two of 'em comin' at ya."

"You're testin' my patience, Druen!" growled Ratha, her deeply creased face contorting with even more and deeper wrinkles as she scowled in frustration at her apprentice.

"But this war happened so many centuries ago. How'd ya know this fer sure – that there were thirteen of these warlords? Thirteen bein' such an odd number an' all."

"I know fer sure 'cause I can count past ten!" snarled the old woman, angrily fishing about beneath her tattered smock to pull up on a thin, leather string. The gloomy hut suddenly glowed with an eerie green light as a small, sealed vial dangled before Druen's surprised eyes. "See! Look closely fer you'll see thirteen souls bound to an eternity in this puny hell!"

"These specks of glowin' light are the souls of men?" gasped the girl.

"There were fourteen at one time, but the light of one of 'em was much weaker than the others. It was as though the others ganged up on him. His light eventually faded out some time ago after an eon of torment."

"Was it the soul of a Talibarrian warlord?" queried Druen, wondering of its fate. "I bet he challenged the Dark Lord an' was punished fer his actions. His soul got tossed in there with the lot of 'em ta teach 'em all a lesson if they disobeyed their master."

"No, legend has it this particular soul belonged to a mortal man of royal blood."

"A king? From what country?" asked the girl.

"Actually, the soul belonged to an emperor from a land far ta the east in Orien. It's been said that he made the mistake of defyin' an' betrayin' the Wizard, Eldred Firestaff when he was better known as a Sorcerer. The story that's been passed down was that the Sorcerer trapped this mortal's soul to be forever tormented by the Dark Lord's minions. I suppose whatever they had done ta him was jus' too much fer his soul ta bear."

The infinitesimal beads of light floated about, dodging each other in this miniscule prison Ratha wore around her neck.

"So, jus' what did the Dark Lord use if the offer of power and wealth couldn't sway 'em warlords ta join his cause?" questioned Druen.

"Oh, make no mistake, Beyilzon did bribe 'em with all the trappings of greatness. But what the Dark Lord offered these men was somethin' none but he could offer. It was somethin' that ta this very day, all mortal men crave, but could never have."

"What's that?"

"That vile soul bribed those thirteen warlords with the promise of eternal life! An' those damned fools bein' ambitious to a fault, they failed ta consider the terms of this offer."

"But if they were granted immortality, what are they all doin' in this vial?" questioned Druen.

"During the first great war to confront the allied forces to the south, nine warlords were killed in battle," revealed Ratha.

"Hold on here, how can they be killed if they were immortal?"

"Remember, I said that to our folks the Dark Lord became known as Beyilzon the Deceiver?"

"Yeah…"

"Well, it wasn't fer nothin' he earned that name. These men became nothin' more than ghosts of their former selves; rotten husks made ta endure a life of servitude while their souls were trapped fer an eternity in this vial," explained the witch, holding forth the tiny prison.

"So their bodies were killed, but their souls are made ta endure an eternity in this hell?"

"Yes, ya see… the warlords failed ta consider the Dark Lord's idea of immortality was quite different from theirs."

"So they were lied to?"

"In the worst possible way," confirmed the witch.

"So, nine warlords were killed in battle… What happened to the others?"

"If you had let me finish, I'd 've told ya that nine were felled in the first great war, while the others scurried off at the height of the battle," continued Ratha. "Four escaped, fleein' deep into the Shadow Mountains. Abandoned by the Dark Lord in his defeat an' shunned by those who were once their people, they were forced ta live a hollow existence trapped between this realm an' the netherworld."

"So, those four warlords still exist?"

"Let me finish," snapped the old woman. "Eldred Firestaff, when he turned against those he swore ta protect an' guide, called upon dark powers ta summon the four. Ten years ago, he promised these warlords a chance ta die a mortal's death, freein' 'em from their earthly shackles an' releasin' their souls from this realm."

"So the Sorcerer lied ta them," determined Druen.

"The four remainin' warlords were so desperate, they were driven ta act on the rogue Wizard's behalf. Unfortunately fer them, they learned the hard way that Firestaff was no better in his dealings than the Dark Lord was."

"But how can these dots of light be the thirteen warlords?" wondered Druen, her eyes staring in fascination at the tiny orbs of light floating about inside. "You'd think a mortal's soul would at least be bigger an' brighter than the largest firefly."

"As I understand it, the four witches combined their knowledge of the natural forces at work in this world with Beyilzon's dark magic. Makin' little figures of straw an' twine ta be burned on a great fire, the powers of the forbidden arts was unleashed ta harvest the souls of the warlords that had come ta pledge their allegiance to the Dark Lord in exchange fer his promises."

"How did ya come ta find this thing, anyway?" questioned Druen, never before hearing about this strange vial her grandmother wore about her neck.

"I'd like to believe this wonderful thing came ta find me. Discovered it near ta where the Dark Lord once held court," revealed Ratha, her bony finger pointing in the direction of Mount Hope.

"In that old, deserted cave near the top of the Witch's Hold?" questioned Druen. She shuddered, recalling the first time she was forced to harvest some skulls from the Dark Lord's abandoned lair for her grandmother.

Deep within this chamber, a huge and grisly throne built of bones from the men who had challenged Beyilzon and failed, sat in a dusty heap stacked high. Taking one of the skulls used to decorate the top of this gruesome seat of power, its removal sent an avalanche of bones cascading down upon her. That was the first and last time Druen had entered that dark and dreary place. Even in memory, it was still a frightening place; its walls seemed to crawl and weep with the tormented ghosts trapped in another time.

"Yes, yes! It was in the Dark Lord's lair," nodded Ratha, her calloused fingertip thoughtfully tapping on the hairy wart protruding from her chin. "I had heard rumours that Eldred Firestaff, in his bout as an evil Sorcerer, would take refuge in there from time ta time when his brother Wizards were huntin' him down. One autumn night not so many years ago, I went snoopin' up there ta see what I could find."

"But jus' what were the other Wizards huntin' that Firestaff fellow down fer?" questioned Druen.

"Ta face the charges of the crimes against humanity that crazy bugger was accused of committin' against the mortals an' the Elves."

"But why'd the Sorcerer leave this vial behind? It must've been worth somethin' ta him?"

"No doubt! But as I understand it, Firestaff was forced ta steal away in haste one night," explained Ratha. "He took his most prized possession an' left the rest behind, hidin' the tools of his trade in a box beneath that dreadful throne. He thought no mortal would be brave or fool 'nough ta enter the lair that once played host to the Dark Lord. An' he was right, bein' that most Talibarrians are so bloody superstitious, fearin' anythin' ta do with Beyilzon. But what that Wizard wasn't countin' on was me venturin' inta that place, not fearin' the dark nor the supernatural!"

"I take it; when ya spoke of the Sorcerer's most prized possession, you were referrin' to the Book of Spells?"

"You ain't a lost cause yet, dearie!" Ratha cackled in delight. "Yes, Firestaff fled in the dead of the night with the Book of Spells – its parchments filled with ancient curses an' spells, potions an' incantations unlike any you've ever seen or will ever have a chance ta conjure up lest ya take to yer lessons in earnest."

"But there's other things I'm more interested in than becomin' a witch, no disrespect ta you, Gran."

"Oh, now you are disrespectin' me an' all our kin that came before us," grumbled Ratha, glaring at the young woman fidgeting nervously before her. "An' jus' what's wrong with being a witch? You've got the brains fer it if you'd only apply yerself. An' don't ya go fergettin', you've got my beauty an' charms, too. You'd certainly make fer a beautiful enchantress capable of winnin' over the heart of any man you desire."

Druen's mouth drooped in dismay as she stared at the weather-beaten, stooped hag of a woman with a mop of tangled gray hair and a wrinkled, warty face not even a blind mother could love.

"Don't you go lookin' at me like that!" snapped Ratha. She proudly straightened her back to minimize the size of the dowager's hump rising from between her shoulders as she primped her grizzled head of hair, forcing a little bat nesting in this tangled mess to vacate its warm roost. Its leathery wings delivered the bat up into the rafters of the dark, dreary hut.

The young woman snickered, her hand coming up over her mouth in a bid to stifle her laughter.

"I know what you're thinkin', girl! I'll have ya know, I was once as beautiful as you are now! Maybe even more so!"

"I know, I know!" whined Druen, dreading the thought that one day she, too, would inherit the disturbing features that practicing witches gradually succumbed to after years of testing their potent spells and disgusting potions on themselves and each other. "I ain't doubtin' it."

"Then what're ya gripin' about, Druen?"

"It's jus' that I know what testin' all those potions have done ta ya," responded Druen, shrinking away from the glare of Ratha's one evil eye. "I just don't welcome turnin' inta a wrinkled, old prune before my time if I intend on snaring a half-decent man."

Ratha's one good eye rolled around in frustration as she groaned in disgust, "Men! Men! Men! Is that all you can think about? An' if ya set yer sights on a Talibarrian, that's about all yer gonna get: A half-decent man, if ya can even call him that!"

"What's wrong with that? It ain't like we're high society in this country or any other country fer that matter. Besides, I'd like a child of my own one day – maybe even a whole bunch of 'em."

"That'll happen in time an' probably when ya least 'xpect it, but you should at least set yer sights higher. Don't go settling fer less than ya deserve when there's some choice men fer the pickin'!"

"What choice men?" questioned Druen. "There ain't none here in Dreymoor I'd consider *choice*. An' if you're speakin' of Terat or Krygor, I'd hardly consider either one ta be even half-decent by Talibarrian standards. In my way of thinkin', they're definitely not marriage material."

"You're such an ignerant simpleton," sighed Ratha, shaking her head in disappointment. "Haven't ya figured out how me an' yer momma got in a family way even with no decent-lookin' men ta choose from in our clan?"

"I jus' figured you killed 'em an' got rid of their bodies when ya finished havin' yer way with 'em. That way, the other fellas in our village wouldn't get jealous," responded Druen, her face blushing with embarrassment for not knowing the answer to something that had perplexed her for so long.

Ratha's crippled hand smacked the young woman across the back of her head as she scolded Druen, "You're as dense as you're beautiful! Any fool knows a man can't do his manly duties if he's bein' coerced with the threat of death or made ta bed a hag of a woman he can't stand ta look at, let alone touch."

"I didn't know that. You always gave me the impression that men really didn't care," groaned Druen.

"Well, I suppose there are some men in our clan that jus' don't care an' will take ta beddin' anything that moves, but ya gotta be more selective in choosin' a mate if ya want ta make somethin' of yerself in this world."

"I can be selective, but I haven't been allowed with a man, so how am I supposed ta know these things?"

"You're still a young woman, there'll be time enough fer that silliness later," dismissed Ratha.

"Well, if I'm ta devote my life ta becomin' like *you*, there better be great rewards fer endurin' this long-sufferin' apprenticeship," decided Druen, seeking some kind of compensation for all her troubles.

"Look here, young missy, once ya learn how to make potions an' weave our kind of magic, there ain't no man ya can't have," promised Ratha. "Why'd ya think our young ones are as lovely as they are? We don't go choosin' jus' any ordinary man ta father our children. In fact, some of the most handsome men come from south of the Aranak Mountains, if ya get my meanin'?"

Druen's eyes opened wide in surprise. "We're of mixed blood? I thought we were pure Talibarrian."

"What's so pure about it? An' jus' whom did ya think you inherited those eyes from? Sure as hell wasn't from me or yer momma. An' there ain't one man in our village with eyes ta match."

"I've got me some Darrossian blood runnin' through my veins?" gasped Druen. She was flabbergasted by this knowledge, but finally understood why she did not possess the dark brown eyes that were typical of the people living to the north.

"Jus' think of it as boostin' the quality of our stock," replied Ratha, her bony shoulders arching up with a shrug.

"Then who's my father?"

"Who cares who sired ya?"

"I do!"

"If ya really need ta know, it was some knight from Darross yer momma happened ta come across. He got separated from his battalion when they chased a bunch of our folks back over Rock Ridge Pass after raiding a village in Darross," informed Ratha.

"His name! What was his name?" questioned Druen, eager to learn more about this man's identity.

"It wasn't as if they exchanged howdy-dos or anythin' like that, if ya get my drift?" grunted Ratha, coyly winking her cloudy eye at her granddaughter. "Besides, why's it so important ta know? It's always been the women in power in our coven, not the men. When it comes right down to it; men are good fer only one thing. Sadly, half 'em aren't even good at doin' what they're intended fer!"

"I think you're 'xaggerating, Gran," decided Druen.

"Think what ya like, girlie! Jus' be warned, ta bind yerself in wedlock jus' means ta have a man hangin' around so you'd be stuck pickin' up after the lazy sod; cookin' an' cleanin' fer a no-good oaf when we've got more important things ta do than tendin' to one of 'em lazy buggers."

"I'll tell ya right now, I'd be really choosy 'bout who'd I take fer a husband," insisted Druen. "No lazy bugger fer me! One day I'm gonna have me a decent man."

"Yeah, yeah! That's what they all say!" scoffed Ratha. "Jus' as soon as he says *I do,* then *he won't.* They go puttin' their best foot forward an' once ya bind ta them in matrimony, they go an' try trippin' ya up with it!"

"They can't all be like that."

"You're jus' so young an' gullible, Druen. Mark my words; honest an' hard-workin' decent men are a rare commodity in these parts. Even with yer fine features you inherited from yer momma an' the knight that sired ya, you'd be lucky ta find a half-decent man in these parts."

"What man, Talibarrian or Darrossian, would want me now, knowin' I'm a half-blood?"

"Who says anyone's gotta know?" sniffed Ratha. "Besides, men are stupid creatures when it comes right down ta it. If ya look pretty, that's all they care about."

"That's really shallow."

"But it's the truth. When it comes ta women, 'specially pretty women; men have puny, little brains. When they use it, they don't think with this head," grunted Ratha, her finger tapping the crown of her grizzly mane. "Oh, no… they think with this."

The witch's gnarled hand grabbed her crotch, lewdly gesturing as though she was a man proudly cupping his manhood.

Druen blushed with embarrassment as she turned away from her grandmother's graphic display. "I jus' always believed we were of pure Talibarrian blood…"

"As witches, we gotta stay one better than even our own people if we're ever ta get ahead in this world."

"You're makin' it sound like *all* of our men are ugly, stupid, lazy boors," argued Druen.

"Maybe only a handful aren't, but the vast majority of Talibarrian men are brutish lookin' thugs with the brains ta match. Given the choice, who'd you rather bed? Delectable, handsome man-meat with the smarts ta boot? Or would ya rather conceive a child with a run-of-the-mill Talibarrian oaf with a forehead that protrudes farther than his chin?" sniffed Ratha, her aged face scowling in a dreadful frown as she jutted out her lower jaw like some primitive being, ready to drag her knuckles along the ground.

"But how can that happen?"

"Didn't yer momma teach ya nothin', girl?" grumbled Ratha, in a disgruntled huff as her grubby hand smacked her forehead in frustration. "First ya gotta get him ta drop his trousers, and then – "

"No, that's not what I'm askin'," groaned the young woman, her burning cheeks flushed with embarrassment. "I'm wonderin' how ya get men from Darross ta do, ya know... the *deed*? After all, we're in Talibarr an' its common knowledge most of those ta the south hate us."

"During the warring years, there were always a few stragglers that strayed away from their battalions in the commotion of the fightin'. An' men are men, no matter where they're from or what their breeding. They're easily seduced when enticed by the charms of a comely, young maiden," explained Ratha, one hand on her bony hip, the other on her head as she struck a provocative pose as best she could for a woman of her advanced years with a noticeable dowager's hump to contort her less-than-elegant stance.

Druen's eyes watered. She held back her laughter as she tried to imagine her grandmother attempting to seduce a handsome knight or soldier from another land. Suddenly, she burst out laughing, unable to contain herself as Ratha seductively batted the lashes of her one good eye at her.

"You're too much, Gran!" giggled Druen, her face reddened as she began to cough, choking on her merriment as she laughed at the witch.

"Drink this, it'll fix ya," offered the old woman, handing her a vial of liquid as thick and dark as molasses. "Jus' a little dollop on yer tongue will do the trick."

Druen reluctantly took a small swig, but as the viscous potion slithered over her tongue. Her eyes squeezed shut as the liquid burned, trickling down her throat. When she opened her eyes once more, as the blur of tears cleared, she jumped back with a start. Druen gazed upon a willowy beauty with flowing tresses of raven hair, perfect alabaster skin and startling violet eyes that were hypnotically entrancing to say the least.

"Hey... Where's my granny?" Druen demanded to know as she backed away from this striking beauty she had never seen before. "What did ya do with her?"

"Ya fool! I *am* yer granny!" The woman struck her provocative pose once more for the sake of her granddaughter's memory.

"The voice sounds the same, but you're definitely ain't no granny of mine, so stop messin' with me!" argued Druen, picking up a broom to keep this stranger at bay. "My grandma is all gray-haired an' hunched over. Her face looks like a chewed up old boot."

"How dare ya speak of me like that? I oughta slap you silly, Druen!" snarled the lovely woman, her eyes glaring in anger.

"Alright, now you're definitely soundin' like Gran, but you sure as hell don't look like her," decided Druen, lowering her broom, but only slightly.

"It's the potion I made you drink, ya dimwit! In a minute or two, it'll wear off an' you'll see me as I truly am."

"No… So you're really my granny?" Druen stared in the pair of dazzling, violet eyes glaring at her.

"How do ya think we've been able ta seduce the men we've been breedin' with?" growled Ratha, putting the vial of magical potion away for another time. "It's either administer a bit of this potion or cast an enchantment while they're fast asleep – fast asleep meanin' ta hit 'em on their heads, knockin' 'em unconscious."

"Well, that certainly explains plenty!" exclaimed Druen. She watched in fascination as her grandmother gradually transformed back to her normal appearance. As the power of the potion wore off, Ratha shrivelled up before Druen's very eyes to assume her hunched, grizzled form once more. "Before that, I really couldn't figure out how these men were made ta cooperate."

"A drop of that potion an' you'll have 'em doin' everythin' yer little heart desires, fer it makes the drinker see true beauty rather than the potential of it even if there ain't none. An' now that ya know my secret, ain't it worth all the testin' of our magic, even if ya come out lookin' like me in the end?"

Druen gave these words serious consideration before responding, "I suppose lookin' like you've been run down by a wagon several times over an' then left ta dry out in the infernal sun fer a month ain't so bad if these powers ta do what ya like an' ta get what ya truly want really works."

"Now you're comin' to yer senses, my girl!" praised Ratha, nodding her head with approval.

"An' you'll teach me how ta make this potion?"

"Druen, my dearie, I'll teach ya this an' more," promised the old woman. "An' believe me, you're beautiful now, but I can mix up a batch of potion that can make any man ya desire, even a great knight or a wealthy prince, fall in love with ya ferever, not jus' fer one night!"

"A knight... or a prince?" gasped Druen, her eyes sparkling as these prospects served to entice. "Wonderful..."

"Does that sound like incentive 'nough fer you ta get crackin' on yer lessons?" tempted Ratha, giving the young woman a sly wink of her one good eye.

"Hmm... Sounds temptin', but I'd rather have a man that truly loves me than havin' ta trick him into it."

"Damn it all!" cursed Ratha. "You're definitely more Darrossian than Talibarrian. What's up with all this common sense?"

"I'd like ta believe in true love, not in a love concocted by a magical potion or spell."

"You keep on dreamin' yer little dreams, dearie, 'cause that's all *true love* is: A dream an' a big, fat lie. It doesn't happen ta ordinary folks like us, only ta the rich an' the privileged."

"Well, I can always hope," sighed Druen.

"Why don't ya hope fer somethin' that can actually come true?" mocked the old woman.

"Say what ya want, but I'm thinkin' it's too ambitious ta believe I'd ever snag a prince ta marry ta begin with."

"Not if you're willin' ta use some magic," countered Ratha.

Ignoring her grandmother's words, Druen continued on, truly believing she was being sensible in her choices.

"I believe a noble, chivalrous knight is more ta my likin', but when it comes right down to it, I'd much rather have a kind, decent ordinary fella who'd treat me well, than a royal or nobleman who'll treat me badly," stated Druen, nodding her head judiciously after giving this some serious thought.

"What's wrong with ya, child?" scolded Ratha. "It's fine ta have realistic expectations, but ta have none at all? That jus' won't do ya any good if ya mean ta make somethin' of yerself in this world. At least settle fer a man with some social standing! It'll serve ta improve your lot in life."

"What's wrong with wishin' fer an ordinary man that'll treat me well an' love me fer real?"

"Fer one, there ain't no such thing as a kind, decent man; ordinary, royal or otherwise," retorted Ratha. "Secondly, that being so, if ya plan ta get yerself a man, you're better ta set yer sights on one that'll at least offer a promise of a wealthy life than ta be stuck with a fella who's poor an' is gonna treat ya like a worthless dog in the end anyway."

"Oh my! You're soundin' kinda bitter," assessed Druen.

"I may be soundin' bitter, but you're soundin' like a silly, little girl who needs ta get her head out of the clouds. Jus' mark my words, Druen; all men are the same. Royal or commoner, Talibarrian, Darrossian or whatever, they're all alike. They're all dogs, but they'll be the one treatin' you like a worthless mutt in the end."

Druen fell silent. She knew her grandmother was set in her ways as well as her thoughts and ideas. There was no point in arguing with her.

"Now, if you're smart, at the very least, you'd settle fer a knight. But don't settle fer jus' an ordinary knight, get yerself one of some social standing or rank!"

"If I can get my hands on a decent man – a man of means, maybe I won't have ta become a witch anymore!" exclaimed Druen, her hands clapping together in excitement.

"What? Give yer head a shake, girl!" admonished Ratha. "Once a witch, always a witch. It's in yer blood, there's no denyin' it."

"But what if I didn't want to become a witch?" questioned Druen, her young mind daring to entertain this possibility. "Suppose one day I jus' up an' walked away from this life."

"Then I'd have ta hunt ya down an' make you *change* yer mind."

"And if ya couldn't change my mind?" probed Druen.

"There are some secrets that should be kept as jus' that. There are secrets worth dyin' fer ta keep it from fallin' inta the wrong hands," growled Ratha. "The knowledge ya hold of our craft is such a secret, if you ain't gonna conform, then I guess I'll jus' have ta kill ya."

"You're speakin' in jest, right?" asked the girl.

"Nope."

"Oh…" gulped Druen.

"Besides, it's up ta us ta make things right. Our people had been persecuted fer too many years. Now, it's time ta fix those bastards who did us wrong."

"What bastards are ya talkin' of? The folks to the south?" queried Druen, thinking that Ratha was referring to those in Darross.

"Oh, those rotters will get their comeuppance in time, but I'm speakin' of all those Talibarrians who thought their combined efforts would lead ta the defeat of the people ta the south. When things fell apart, they turned on those witches that had promised 'em victory through an alliance with the Dark Lord."

"Can ya blame 'em? I know I'd be feelin' pretty let down if I was promised somethin' I didn't get."

"Ya fool! The Talibarrians' loss was due ta Beyilzon's own treacherous ambitions. Once the Dark Lord broke his covenant with my ancestors, in revenge, those witches cursed Beyilzon ta damnation."

"I thought the Dark Lord was already damned by his own father," said Druen.

"Alright then, so Beyilzon was twice damned," grunted Ratha. "But no matter, fer in the end, it was our own countrymen that turned against those witches. They drove 'em an' their kin from place ta place. They became pariahs, shunned by their fellow Talibarrians. Ta this very day we're still treated as outcasts; no longer are witches honoured an' revered as in the days of old."

"Is that why, through the ages, our numbers have been on the decline?" questioned Druen, knowing they had been ostracized for as long as she could remember. "Because our own people fear bein' associated with us?"

"Eventually, with all the fightin' that happened within the clans, it caused the covens ta break up, goin' their own separate ways."

"So our craft was forgotten," determined Druen.

"It was worse than that! The original four were reduced ta conjurin' up curses an' hexes, offering up herbal remedies or fortune-tellin' fer pay."

"An' the four witches? Whatever became of them after their clans fell apart?" asked the girl.

"They remained strong; committed to their craft 'til the day they died. They shared their wisdom with those few who stayed loyal to 'em," explained Ratha. "We're the last known livin' relations an' it's our duty ta make sure our traditions lives on. It's our job ta seek redemption fer our kin who suffered because of the Dark Lord an' this broken covenant."

"Ain't it a little too late ta be thinkin' of revenge fer those four?" questioned Druen, scratching her head in bewilderment. "They are dead, after all."

"What's wrong with ya, girl? Don't you know there's a diff'rence between redemption an' revenge? I mean ta restore their good name an' status in society; ta give 'em what they were deservin' of ta begin with."

"Even if they were worthy of this, all I'm sayin' is; it's too late for those witches. They're dead an' long gone. Even if ya spared their name or reputation, or whatever it is you're thinkin' they're deservin' of, it won't make any diff'rence ta any one of those witches 'cause they've passed on."

"They're dead, but we're not!" snapped Ratha. "Our people had been made ta suffer fer an eon 'cause of Beyilzon the Deceiver. He broke his promise to our ancestors, castin' 'em aside once he gained control of the warlords. Those witches were tricked. The Dark Lord deceived them. He held the key ta their rise ta ultimate power – a promised, shared power that in the end, they were denied. This is our chance ta set things right. Our time has come ta claim what should've been ours from the very start."

"So, you're thinkin' that conjurin' up more magic will do that?"

"Conjurin' the *right* kind of magic will do 'xactly that, my dear," nodded Ratha, her finger tapping impatiently on the worn parchment with its singed border. "Now, what's the next symbol look like?"

Druen's hand skimmed lightly over the platter of dry sand, smoothing it out. With the tip of a stick, she carefully retraced the symbols large enough for her grandmother to see clearly.

"Why are we doin' all this anyway?" Druen grumbled with boredom. She ran her slender fingers through her long, dark tresses, idly playing with her hair as she watched the old woman's stooped form hover over the sandy impression; deciphering its meaning.

"I already told ya. If you weren't listenin' with those cloth ears of yers, I ain't about to go an' repeat myself jus' ta have you ferget everythin' I said, again," grunted Ratha, inspecting her granddaughter's perfect copy of the mysterious characters that were inscribed on the parchment.

"You barely even read or write the common speech. How do ya even know what these symbols mean?" queried Druen.

"This is an ancient language you're lookin' at. It's so old, it's been long forgotten by most an' spoken by only a select few," answered Ratha, her good eye following the flowing strokes left in the sand. "Only the witches of highest standin' in our coven were ever taught ta read this."

"But what language is this?"

"It's Elvish."

"*Elvish?*" repeated Druen, her voice tightened with cynicism. "How can that be? I always thought that all the Elves dwelled in a forest far to the south, beyond Darross – never in Talibarr?"

"That's so," agreed Ratha. "But this is *old Elvish* I'm speakin' of, an arcane dialect known these days only to Wizards, Elven royalty an' the elders of Wyndwood."

"You're jus' makin' me more confused," groaned Druen, contemplating these words. "What diff'rence which Elven language it is, old or new? It still doesn't explain how ya learned ta read it."

"Way back before the Dark Lord was forced ta dwell amongst the mortals he so despised, there was one Wizard appointed to provide wisdom an' guidance to those of us in Talibarr."

"That'd be Tor Airshorn, also known as the Wizard of the North, I do believe," responded Druen.

"How right you are, young missy," confirmed Ratha. "The Wizard of the North tried *enlightening* our people. He thought it prudent ta start with the four witches, fer if they could be swayed ta learn from him, then they had the power to influence the other Talibarrians to follow an' benefit from his teachings."

"But what happened? No one here speaks Elvish an' only some of the old warlords left ta buck against the new governing council are able ta read the common speech properly."

"Yes, an' to this very day only those in positions of privilege have access ta that kind of education, but only our ancestors still remember how ta decipher this ancient language," revealed Ratha, her one good eye quickly scanning the shelves for a specific jar. Finding the one she wanted, she pulled it down from the shelf. She blew off the thick coating of dust and cobwebs smothering this earthenware container.

"But why bother remembering a language no one but the Wizards an' a few hoity-toity Elves rarely even speak themselves?"

"There's good reason fer it. Amongst only the highest rankin' witches in our covens, we kept this language alive 'cause it's a crucial part of our history an' power," explained Ratha, her ragged nails prying at the sealed lid of the jar. "It was believed that one day, the ability ta read this old language would be the one thing that would redeem us; ta restore us ta our true an' venerated place in Talibarrian society."

"That's all fine an' dandy," nodded Druen, pretending to believe her grandmother's words, "but I still don't understand what brewin' up this potion of shrivelled up newts, poison fish liver an' whatever else you're thinkin' of throwin' in there has to do with any of this."

"You're young an' you're only an apprentice – a crappy one at that," grunted an irate Ratha, scooping a heaping spoonful of the jar's content into the bowl of a granite mortar. "If ya paid even half the attention ta my teachings as ya do ta yer looks, then you'd be able ta figure it out. Now pick up that darned pestle an' get ta work. Grind this down 'til it's a fine powder."

"What is this stuff?" Druen poked the coarsely ground, brittle substance into the center of the stone mortar.

"Bones."

"Oh… Deer bones? Or bones from a goat?"

"Human bones," replied Ratha. "Now, get ta work. I don't have all day ta hear ya talk."

"Whoa! It's from a *human?*" gasped Druen, dropping the pestle in disgust. "Whose bones? It better not have belonged ta someone I knew!"

"Nah, it's from the grave of a dead soldier an' he's been dead long before you were even born."

"A Talibarrian soldier or an enemy soldier?"

"Fer this potion ta work, the bones gotta be from one of our own soldiers," answered Ratha, glaring impatiently at her granddaughter. "Now, fer the last time, stop with the questions an' get ta work. This special potion's gotta be ready well before the full moon that's ta rise during the spring equinox."

With an obvious degree of reluctance, the young woman's face screwed up in disgust as she picked up the stone pestle. Holding the mortar with the other hand, she proceeded with the distasteful job of grinding the broken bits of bone into a powdery substance.

After pounding and grinding the fragments into dust, Druen passed the heavy mortar and its contents to her grandmother for her inspection.

"That'll do," grunted the old woman. Taking the powdered bones, she limped toward the cauldron.

"So now what?" asked Druen, watching as her grandmother carefully shook the substance into the iron pot.

On contact with the ingredients simmering in this cauldron, the concoction suddenly bubbled, hissing as it erupted to send a puff of foul smelling, gray smoke swirling into the dank air.

As the smoke dissipated, to Druen's astonishment, one by one the dried newts that had been soaking in this magical brew suddenly crawled out of the cauldron. Some fell into the fire, only to die a terrible death after coming back to life while others managed to push off against the rim of the cauldron to fall to the floor, scurrying away from the heat and the flames.

"Those newts were dead!" exclaimed Druen, staring with fascination as the amphibians bobbed to the surface, frantically swimming to the edge of the blackened pot to escape. "I swear they were!"

"That means this batch of potion is workin' perfectly," stated Ratha, giving the brew a stir. "Once it's done, it'll be very potent indeed."

"So, now what?"

"Now, we must be patient, Druen," instructed Ratha, watching as yet another hapless newt fell to die in the fire while another crawled away. It squirmed between a crack in the loose floorboards to take refuge beneath in the damp, earth. "We keep this fire burnin' nice an' slow 'til the goat's blood is reduced. If ya copied those runes jus' right an' I deciphered 'em properly, we jus' need ta top it up with some rejuvenatin' spring water."

"That's easy 'nough ta do. There's plenty of water ta be had," said Druen, thinking of the creek running just behind this ram-shackled hut.

"Oh no, it can't be jus' any water," cautioned Ratha, using a great wooden ladle to blend the contents in the pot. "It's gotta be water from a special spring at the place we still call the Witch's Hold."

"What's so special about it?" queried Druen.

"When the time is right, you'll be seein' with yer own eyes, my dear," promised Ratha, giving the magical potion a gentle stir. "You'll be comin' with me an' I promise you, you'll be absolutely astounded by what you're gonna be witness to."

"That sounds downright excitin'," sighed Druen, dreading the idea of returning to the place now referred to, even by most of her fellow Talibarrians, as Mount Hope.

"Now, be a good girl an' put that page back where it belongs," ordered Ratha, her talon of a finger pointing to the large, heavy book that lay open on the table. "Make sure ya put it in its proper place."

Druen nodded in understanding. Taking the tattered, yellow parchment with its singed edges she slowly leafed through the volume of pages inscribed with what appeared to be blood.

"Say, Gran, this ink… did it turn this dark red with age?" questioned Druen, her fingertip gently tracing the ancient runes written on the parchment.

"It was always red," answered Ratha, not even gazing up from the cauldron as she continued to stir.

"Oh… must've been the juices of crushed berries ta give it this colour. I swear, it's so dark red, it looks like dried blood."

"That's 'cause it *is* blood."

"Real blood?" gasped Druen, her hand recoiling from the yellowed pages that had become warped with age as well as heat and moisture damage. "As in human blood?"

"Not just any human blood," revealed Ratha; "but the blood from the four witches combined with a drop of the Dark Lord's ta give these spells true power ta last fer an eternity."

"You jus' had ta tell me that, didn't ya?" groaned Druen, shuddering involuntarily as a cold chill ran down her spine. She resumed her search to place the piece of parchment in its proper place without touching the traces of blood.

"You're a witch! Why do ya have ta be so bloody squeamish about these things?" scolded Ratha, waving the wooden ladle at her granddaughter. "It should be a natural thing ta you!"

"Well, as far as I'm concerned, there ain't nothing natural 'bout this old book. Did ya ever think that you weren't meant ta dredge this thing up?" countered Druen.

"Bite yer tongue, missy!" snarled the old woman. "It was meant ta be. An' this is where it belongs; in the hands of our people once more."

Druen shook her head in disagreement, recalling how she was made to brave the bitter elements during the dead of winter to help her grandmother. They stood on the shores of the Sea of Storms to cast out their nets.

She glanced up at the half-dozen spiny, puffed up fish they had caught that blustery morning nearing the last day of the last month of the year. Bloated like air-filled bladders, the small harvest of fish festooned the smoky rafters of this hut.

In these frothing, angry waters, it was only during the cruel months of winter did small schools of these fish dare to venture this close to land. Feeding in the shoals, these fish were quickly snared in nets as the powerful thrust of the incoming tide drove them to shore. But on that fateful day, it was more than just fish that had become tangled in their nets.

"I think that if it was really meant fer you ta have it, ya wouldn't have almost drowned tryin' ta haul it onto dry land," argued Druen.

"I told ya before an' I'll tell ya again, by divine powers – the natural forces us witches delve in an' the powers we were gifted with, did it come back ta its rightful owner," disputed Ratha, raising her gnarled hand for silence to prevent Druen from continuing this argument. "An' if I really wasn't meant ta have it, then I would've drowned, but I'm alive, so there! That's proof enough of who it belongs ta now."

Carefully inserting this tattered, warped parchment into its rightful place, a cloud of dust erupted from pages of the heavy, worn book as the red, leather-bound cover slammed shut. The ancient runes branded onto the cover of this Book of Spells were now barely visible in the candlelight.

a creature of legend

High in the tree canopy, songbirds flitted from branch to branch. Their cheerful warbling broke the solitude to herald the start of a new day as the light of the morning sun crept into the clearing. Its radiant energy bathed the tent in its warm glow as slivers of golden light seeped in through the seams. And inside this tent, King Sebastian convalesced in a warm cot. By the grimace on his face, it was obvious he was immersed in a troubling sleep.

"Miraculously, your father's physical injuries were not life-threatening," disclosed Kal-lel. "We were able to heal his wounds and stave off infection where the creature's saliva appeared to have burned his skin and flesh."

"So, those were bite marks?" questioned Garrick.

"Yes, but the pressure applied was meant to restrain, not kill him," explained Kal-lel. "Fortunately, in time your father will recover completely."

"Thank goodness for that! But why does he not wake after all you had done for him?" whispered Garrick, glancing over to see his father's nervously twitching form.

Sebastian seemed to be fighting through a terrible nightmare. And even covered by layers of wool blankets to warm his chilled, weary body, the King continued to tremble either from utter fear or a consuming cold that refused to release its grip on him.

"It would seem that thirst, hunger and exhaustion has wreaked more havoc on his body and soul than the physical injuries inflicted on him," replied Kal-lel.

"Not to forget the horrific ordeal he was subjected to over the days of his disappearance," added Arerys.

Just as he spoke these words, Cullen arrived with some sustenance in the way of a bowl brimming with warm, rich broth to nourish Sebastian's wanting body.

"How does the King fare, my lord?" whispered Cullen, as Garrick accepted the broth to feed to his father.

"How does he look to you?" replied the disheartened Prince.

"I would say King Sebastian is better than when we had first found him," responded Cullen.

"Given time, he will recover completely from his injuries…" Kallel's words faltered.

"But?" queried Cullen. "I sense there is more."

"In all honesty, I have concerns about his mental state when we found him," answered Arerys, speaking candidly for his father.

"So the King was a little emotional," dismissed Cullen, trying to sound optimistic for Garrick's sake. "I think, given the circumstances and the nature of his disappearance, even a short time spent trapped by that murderous beast would cause any man to go a bit loopy."

"He was more than just a *little emotional*, Captain, he was hysterical – on the verge of madness," reminded Arerys, recalling his shattered state of mind when they found him. "My father was forced to *sedate* King Sebastian just so we could remove him from the cave. And believe me, it is not something my father does lightly to a mortal man when you consider the risks involved in doing so."

"Are you saying my father's state of mind is a permanent condition?" gasped Garrick.

"Only time will tell," answered Kal-lel.

With the whispering of voices drifting around him, Sebastian stirred from his sleep. His eyes were squeezed shut as he groaned, mumbling as his hands batted away at an invisible assailant.

"Father!" called Garrick, gently lifting his head to offer him some much needed sustenance. "Wake up, father."

Sebastian's eyes slowly opened, only to squint beneath the bright glare of the morning sun burning through the walls of the tent.

"You are safe now," assured Garrick, raising the bowl of broth to Sebastian's dried and cracked lips. "Drink this."

Hearing the murmuring of voices and the blur of shapes and movement through his half-closed eyes, they suddenly flew wide open; fear and terror burning within.

Bolting upright, the King knocked the bowl from Garrick's hand, its contents splattering across Cullen's startled face and raiment. Shoving Garrick away, he wrestled to be free of the blankets tucked around his body. Struggling from the cot, Sebastian tumbled to the floor in a dishevelled heap. In a bellow of fright, the King scrambled on his hands and knees; crawling to the farthest corner of the tent where he proceeded to frantically scratch and claw at the canvas to be free of these confines.

"Father!" Garrick cried out, his hand resting lightly on Sebastian's shoulder to console and comfort him. "I promise you, you are safe now." Sebastian snarled. Bowling his son over, his hands lunged forward, squeezing around Garrick's throat.

Markus and Joval burst into the tent upon hearing this commotion, just in time to see Cullen dive onto the King to restrain him.

"By God!" groaned Cullen, taken by complete surprise as he fell backwards with the impact of Sebastian's elbow slamming hard into his chest. "For an old bugger, he is as strong as a bull!"

Seizing Sebastian by his arms, Joval and Markus wrenched him off of Garrick as the Prince coughed and gasped for his breath, rolling away as his father thrashed about, violently kicking at him. Kal-lel and Arerys quickly pulled the Prince back onto his feet, preventing him from getting too close to the demented King.

"Father, do you not know me?" asked Garrick, peering into his Sebastian's confused and frightened eyes.

Instead of words, the Prince was greeted with a visceral snarl. Sticky threads of saliva spewed from the King's mouth as he continued to rage in fear and defiance, struggling to be set free.

"Bloody hell! King Sebastian is only fit to rule a town of crazies!" declared Cullen, watching as Markus and Joval fought to control him. As the Captain approached to help contain the King, Sebastian's foot struck out, kicking Cullen hard in his midriff.

Moaning in pain, Cullen doubled over. His arms wrapped around his waist as he slumped over to one side, whimpering pathetically as he was still recuperating from last night's attack, "I did not need this..."

Once more, Kal-lel was forced to sedate Sebastian, temporarily cutting off the flow of blood to his brain. In response, the King's body fell limp, his chin flopping onto his chest as he crumpled in Markus and Joval's hold. Lifting him up, they eased Sebastian back onto the cot.

"Captain Bristow, fetch some rope," ordered Arerys. "Preferably, a fine cord that will not chafe."

"Rope? For what reason?" questioned Cullen, slowly picking himself up from the floor of the tent.

"It is obvious King Sebastian is in an altered state of mind," answered Arerys. "If you wish to get him home to recuperate, I strongly recommend some measure of restraints to prevent him from fleeing or hurting himself in the process."

"Good idea," said Cullen, ducking beneath the tent flap as he limped away.

"This is not good," lamented Garrick, rubbing his throat as he stared down at his unconscious father. "What do we do now?"

"He needs to rest," advised Kal-lel. "You must continue to administer water and nourishment to restore his health."

"But what of his mind?" asked Garrick, glancing over his shoulder as Cullen reappeared with some rope in his hands. "Surely there is some kind of magic a high Elf can administer to remedy this condition."

"The trauma he suffered during his ordeal was so great, there is no telling if he will ever recover completely," warned Kal-lel. "What wounds his mind is not physical. That being said, it is something I have no power to heal."

"I suggest returning him back to the familiar comforts of Darross Castle to facilitate his recuperation," recommended Arerys. "It will only do him good to recover in the presence of his loved ones."

"And what if he never recovers?" asked Garrick, staring dismally at his father as Cullen proceeded with the undignified task of tying the King's wrist down to the frame of the cot.

"You know what will happen if your father does not recuperate," responded Kal-lel, his words matter-of-fact. "He will be forced to abdicate from the throne. You will have to be ready to take up the crown and scepter in his place."

"I hope this does not come to pass," sighed Garrick. "This is not how I ever imagined taking over the rule of Darross."

"Do not lose hope, my lord," urged Cullen, trying to sound positive as he worked quickly to secure the knot. "There is nothing to say the King's state of mind is a permanent condition. He may be absolutely fine in a day or two, especially if he were to leave this god-forsaken land and be allowed to recuperate back in his castle with his beloved family by his side."

"I do believe you are being overly optimistic, Captain," warned Arerys. "I suggest taking this day by day. Time will be his greatest ally as he recovers from the trauma of this ordeal."

As Cullen maneuvered around the cot to secure Sebastian's other wrist, Garrick took the lengths of rope from the Captain's hands. "Allow me to do this. I want to make sure my father is secured, but comfortable."

"I understand," said Cullen, bowing in respect as he backed away.

"Let us step outside," suggested Markus. "Allow the King some peace and to rest without us milling about in his tent."

Joval led the way out, holding up the tent flap as the others followed, ducking beneath it. Under the brilliant glare of the morning sun, they gathered in the clearing as a squire delivered a flask of water and more warmed broth.

"Now what, father?" asked Arerys, turning to Kal-lel. "Do we abandon the search for that creature to escort Garrick and his father home?"

"The Prince will be fine under the protection of the soldiers and knights that made the journey from his castle," answered Kal-lel. "I am confident they will be safe as they leave Talibarr."

"So you wish to resume the search?" asked Cullen.

"Absolutely. We are hardly in a position to allow a killer beast to roam the countryside," replied Kal-lel. "We are here now. There is no point in returning home with the task only half done."

"There is also the very real danger that creature will expand its range, venturing over the Aranak Mountains to terrorize and kill the citizens of Darross and beyond," warned Joval.

"I am inclined to agree. This creature must be stopped – preferably killed," responded Markus, understanding the true potential for danger this rampaging animal posed.

"Here, here!" chanted Cullen, nodding in agreement. "That beast has shown no mercy; neither will we!"

"*We?*" repeated Arerys, as he stared at the Captain. "I thought you would be escorting King Sebastian back to Darross."

"One would think, being the captain of his army and all. However, that beast must answer to me for all the suffering – that hellish ordeal my liege was forced to endure. I owe it to my King to kill the beast in his good name."

"So, vengeance will be yours," determined Markus.

"You're bloody right it will be mine… and a hell of a lot more!" grunted Cullen. "That murderous creature has done more damage than one can imagine. Mark my words when I say I will not have it crossing over the Aranaks to defile my country and terrorize my people."

"Bold words, Captain Bristow," responded Arerys. "Are you positive you would rather not see to your King's safe return?"

"My men will keep him and Prince Garrick safe. Besides, that beast has an appointment with destiny," said Cullen, his hand patting the hilt of his grand weapon; "and destiny will be dealt by the tip of my sword."

"Perhaps you are better to escort your men and the royal party back to Darross," suggested Markus. Having endured Cullen's company on past missions, this was not a prospect he was looking forward to. "After all, we are in Talibarr. It does not fall within your jurisdiction, Captain."

"True enough," agreed Cullen, his shoulders shrugging with indifference. "And no disrespect to you, King Markus, but is this *not* Carcross, so neither does it fall under *your* jurisdiction. And you should know, my liege was requested by the new council of this country to aid in the capture of this creature. With this in mind, I intend to finish what King Sebastian could not."

"Your intentions are honourable, Captain Bristow," acknowledged Kal-lel. "I suppose it would not hurt to have an additional man to aid in this hunt. I shall bid farewell to Prince Garrick; inform him of our plans to resume the hunt."

"Very good, Your Highness," responded Cullen, bowing in respect to the Elf King as Kal-lel returned to Sebastian's tent. "While you do so, I shall make ready for the hunt."

There was an uneasy hush as Cullen raised his head. He could feel the burn of several pairs of eyes scrutinizing him.

"What?" snapped Cullen, noticing how Arerys, Markus and Joval eyed him in stony silence.

"What say you that *we* capture that creature and *you* can take the credit for it?" offered Markus, attempting to strike up a bargain with the Captain.

"I am no fool! There is always a catch. So what is it?"

"You must return with your battalion to escort King Sebastian home," answered Markus. "Leave us to complete this task so we can do so unfettered."

"I dare say, you speak as though I will be a hindrance on this mission!" Cullen grunted with indignation.

"Perhaps not so much of a hindrance as you might prove to be a total encumbrance to us," explained Arerys, coming to Markus' defense.

"Well, I am going on this hunt whether you like it or not!" declared Cullen, glaring at Arerys. "But if you insist that I do not accompany you on this quest, then perhaps you should take it up with your father, Prince Arerys. After all, King Kal-lel graciously *invited* me to come along. Perhaps you should defy your father; ask that he change his mind where I am concerned."

"It is not my place to challenge my father or change his mind. My intention is to change *yours*," responded Arerys, his words terse as he addressed Cullen. "My father does not know you as we do. I encourage you to return to Darross, for the sake and safety of all concerned."

"I believe you are mocking me!" gasped Cullen, his brows furrowing in resentment. "I get the distinct impression you are implying that I am incompetent."

"It is better to say that you can be rather zealous in your actions," reasoned Joval, having experienced firsthand the chaos this Captain seemed to instigate, even unintentionally.

"Just for that, I will prove you all wrong!" snapped Cullen, his arms crossing his chest in defiance. "One day, you will be pleading for me to join your esteemed little *Order,* begging me to impart my noble name on this prestigious group that seems to still hold some reverence amongst the citizens of Imago, almost a decade after the fact. Perhaps, I will be the one to bring renewed greatness to your cloistered little society."

"Oh, you wish!" scoffed Markus, rolling his eyes in dismay.

"Oh, I will," insisted Cullen. "In fact, I better make ready for this hunt while the three of you wait for instructions from King Kal-lel."

Markus, Arerys and Joval watched as Cullen confidently strutted away, disappearing into his tent to gather his weapons and belongings required for this mission.

"I will tell you now, this does not bode well for any of us," sighed Arerys, dreading this undertaking if the obstinate mortal was permitted to tag along with them.

"That goes for Captain Bristow, too. He just does not know it yet," said Markus.

"If we are forced to undertake this task with Captain Bristow, at least there is one good thing we should not overlook," offered Joval.

"You jest, right?" queried Markus. "How can there be anything good in this situation?"

"At least Nayla and Lando had been spared his company," reminded Joval, knowing how there was a love-hate relationship between Lando and the brash, young captain. He also knew there was a strained relationship between Nayla and Cullen, having both endured his insolence and petty animosity during their last quest to rescue Prince Garrick's brother Carstian from the clutches of the deranged, escaped prisoner Draven Eldard.

"You are quite correct, Joval!" exclaimed Arerys, nodding in thoughtful agreement. "Nayla and Lando would be fit to be tied if they were here now and made to endure his company on another treacherous mission."

"Thank goodness for that!" agreed Markus. "They chose the most opportune time to venture to Orien."

"There you go… It could have been much worse," stated Joval.

"What could have been much worse?" asked Cullen, tripping as he stumbled out of his tent, his excessively long sword somehow becoming trapped between his legs.

"Never mind," answered Joval. "It does not concern you."

"You do not lie very well, Master Stonecroft," grunted Cullen, tossing down his pack. "You were speaking about me."

"I assure you, Captain Bristow, not *everything* is about you," responded Joval. "We were merely discussing the possibility of heading out before the weather should change."

"Oh," said Cullen. "Good idea. If King Kal-lel is ready to leave now, unlike the rest of you, at least I am prepared."

"But not in every sense," countered Arerys.

"What do you mean?" grunted Cullen.

"You seem intent on rushing headlong to a confrontation with a creature we still have little knowledge of," answered Arerys.

"I know it will die, most likely by my hands. But why over think this when the end results will be the same?"

"What still has me utterly baffled is why that creature did not kill King Sebastian from the start," commented Joval, as he and those in his company waited for Kal-lel to give his orders. "The beast had ample opportunity to do just that, and yet, the King is the only person, aside from Arerys, to survive an attack."

"The creature's change in behaviour leaves more unanswered questions than anything else," responded Arerys, rubbing his shoulder where the animal sank its fangs into his body. "I swear; when that animal charged out of nowhere to knock me down, that monster had incredibly powerful jaws, strong enough to easily crush my bones. And yet, it seemed apparent by its very actions – the nature of the bite inflicted, it was obvious the creature meant to drag me off, not to kill me then and there."

"Perhaps it meant to drag you off to kill you later?" offered Cullen, fidgeting impatiently as he waited to embark on this hunt. "It wanted to do the deed where and when it pleased."

"You could be right, Captain Bristow," conceded Arerys, nodding in agreement.

"I am?" Cullen's eyes narrowed in suspicion as he scrutinized the Elf's pensive face.

"I was closer to the beast than I would ever want to be. With teeth that large set in such a powerful mouth like that, it could have easily seized me by the neck to break it in one small move."

"I agree," nodded Markus. "When I managed to sink my arrow into its neck, there was no denying its power and its capacity to kill. It was not by luck that Arerys survived that attack."

"So, you are saying this creature can recognize its prey?" questioned Cullen, his tone incredulous. "It can distinguish commoner from royalty – mortal man from Elf?"

"It does not seem as impossible as it sounds," decided Joval, thinking on this creature's actions. "Take the hounds used for the hunt; they can easily distinguish the scent of the prey they are ordered to track just as easily as they can distinguish each other by scent alone."

"So the creature has an excellent sense of smell," determined Cullen.

"I am inclined to say it has an *excellent trainer*, one that has taught it well for whatever nefarious reasons," responded Arerys.

"But even if this is true, it still does not answer the question of why," stated Cullen; "nor do we know who this *trainer* is."

"And neither does it answer the question of the identity of this animal," added Markus. "I was up close, as close as Arerys, to that wretched thing and I am no closer to resolving what nature of beast it was."

"That is why we must summon the Wizard of the West," announced Kal-lel, appearing with one of his white falcons perched on his forearm. "I believe if there is anyone who can shed light on this matter, it will be Lindras Weatherstone."

"Hold on here!" demanded Cullen, rising up from his seat. "I thought you said we were going to resume the hunt, not call for a meeting to further discuss matters of this quest?"

"Captain Bristow, I understand your need to rush out and confront the beast," sympathized Kal-lel. "However, what is the point of a hurried confrontation if it only means to hasten your death? We are all aware of what that creature is capable of. And I refuse to recklessly endanger the lives of any man or Elf committed to engaging in this hunt."

"I suppose a meeting with the Wizard would do no harm," sighed Cullen, sitting himself back down.

"If the Wizard's knowledge can possibly aid us in this matter, a little patience can mean the difference between success and failure, life or death," responded Kal-lel.

"I take it, the falcon is ready to go?" assessed Arerys, noting the small metal vial secured to the leather jesses on the bird's ankle.

"Indeed, my bird will speed home to Wyndwood. Once there, the elders will receive word to disperse our warriors to search for Lindras and deliver words of instructions to meet us here."

"And just how long do you anticipate it shall take for the venerable, old Wizard to show his face?" questioned Cullen. "A day? A week? A fortnight? These are great and sprawling lands. That old coot could be anywhere."

"I am exactly where I should be! And you should know, Captain Bristow, I resent your tone and choice of words."

All turned with a start to see a tall, hooded figure draped in a flowing, blue-gray cloak. He urged his steed on, weaving through the stand of trees.

"Lindras Weatherstone!" welcomed Kal-lel, glancing over his shoulder to see the great Wizard approaching to meet them. He was riding high on the back of his great grey stallion Tempest. "I was about to release my falcon with orders to search the lands for you. Your timing cannot be better!"

"My timing was rather impeccable, if I do say so myself," said the Wizard, bowing in respect to the Elf King as Markus, Arerys and Joval crowded around to greet their old friend as he dismounted from his steed.

"Welcome, my friend!" smiled Markus, embracing the Wizard in a warm hug.

"How did you find us all the way out here?" queried Cullen, mystified the Wizard would know exactly where they'd be. "We are in the middle of nowhere!"

"I would like to amaze you by saying that it was by magic, but alas, it was nothing more than common sense," replied Lindras. "In my travels, I had come across many in the vicinity who knew of your presence in Talibarr and the route you travel. I merely asked for directions."

"Hmph!" grunted Cullen. "Come to think of it, I would have preferred to have been amazed by your magic. At least that way, I would know your powers were still intact."

"Intact and highly potent," promised the Wizard, lowering the crystal orb of his staff to the mortal. "Care for a demonstration?"

"We have other matters more pressing to contend with, my friend," said Kal-lel, turning the crystal away from Cullen in case the Wizard discharged his magic, accidentally or otherwise.

"I take it, you had heard the news of the creature attacking and killing those in Talibarr?" questioned Arerys, motioning the Wizard to join them by the campfire for some tea.

"Who has not? I was in the Emerald Forest when I first heard the news. It is most disturbing," disclosed Lindras, easing his weary body onto the log next to Cullen. "Everyone is speaking of this mysterious creature."

"Who did you hear it from?" asked Markus.

"The hunters of your forest," replied the Wizard, nodding to the King of Carcross. "In fact, they were debating on whether they should make ready in case you were in need of their assistance in tracking down the beast."

"And just what is it that have you heard, my friend? Did these hunters know what manner of beast it is?" queried Kal-lel, passing the falcon on to one of his warriors before taking his place at this meeting.

"How much truth to this news I have heard thus far remains to be seen, as the truth has the tendency of being stretched the more it is passed on," responded Lindras. "However, what I did hear was enough to prompt me to make my way to the north."

"You must have come across Prince Garrick and his party on your journey," decided Cullen.

"Indeed, I did."

"Had they made it safely back into Darross when you came upon them?" asked Cullen.

"Oh yes!" nodded the Wizard, rummaging through his leather pouch for his trusty pipe. "In fact, when I happened upon them, Prince Garrick and his party had crested Rock Ridge Pass and were well on their way down the mountain."

"I take it, you saw King Sebastian?" wondered Kal-lel.

"I did," answered Lindras, taking a smoldering twig from the fire to ignite the contents compressed into the ceramic bowl of his pipe. With a deep draught, a puff of aromatic smoke escaped his lips as he spoke, "Needless to say, I was alarmed by the King's presence of mind; for it was quickly evident his mind was not present at all! The man was rambling incoherently. I could not make sense of his words."

"So he has improved," noted Cullen, nodding in approval.

"*Improved?*" questioned Lindras, his brows furrowing in curiosity. "How can that be an improvement?"

"Believe me, rambling incoherently is a vast improvement to ranting like a lunatic," assured the Captain.

"Aah, that explains why the soldiers were carrying King Sebastian secured to a cot," responded the Wizard, recalling the ropes used to tie the man down, restraining him for this long trek home.

"Did Prince Garrick inform you as to what had happened?" queried Markus.

"The poor fellow was quite distraught, but yes, Prince Garrick did share in the dreadful details of what had happened to his father."

"Perhaps you can shed some much needed light on this matter, Lindras," probed Kal-lel. "We are at a quandary as to exactly what nature of beast we are faced with and just how to kill it."

"Prince Garrick told me, as best he could, details of this creature. As close as he had come to that beast, he said that the creature travelled by night and moved with such speed, none had been able to ascertain exactly what it is."

"I was held in that creature's jaws, but only briefly. And I will tell you now, Lindras, I have *never* seen an animal of this size and strength, with such cunning and agility in all of my life," disclosed Arerys.

"Considering you are many centuries old, my lord, that cannot be a good sign," noted Cullen.

"You are longer lived than any of us here, Lindras," said Kal-lel. "In your long life and many travels, have you ever been witness to a creature such as this?"

"Oddly enough, I have."

Their backs straightened upon hearing this unexpected news as they waited to hear more.

"Where? When?" probed Arerys.

"It was long before you were born and when your father was just a small lad that your grandfather King Galan and I had encountered a strange beast that once roamed through Talibarr."

"The range is identical," noted Joval, thinking on the commonalities that could betray this mysterious animal.

"Whoa! It cannot be the one and the same creature," argued Cullen, his mind attempting some quick calculations. "It would make it older than old! And I know for a fact there are no beings longer lived than Elves and Wizards – and it was definitely not that!"

"I assure you, Captain, it is not the same beast, nor would you wish it to be," responded Lindras, the wooden mouthpiece of his pipe clenched firmly between his teeth.

"How do you know?" queried Kal-lel.

"For one, based upon the information I had gleaned from Prince Garrick, this creature moved with the speed and agility of a great cat, easily taking to the trees. Is that not so?"

"That is very true," confirmed Kal-lel, as those present nodded in agreement.

"Plus, King Galan had killed the original creature, as best as I can recall, about two centuries before the great war that pitted King Brannon and the original members of the Order, myself and Kal-lel included, against the Dark Lord Beyilzon."

"And just what was this creature my father had killed?" asked Kal-lel, searching his memory for stories of old shared by King Galan that had included tales of this peculiar beast. "And why do I not recall tales of this strange animal? You would think I'd remember my father telling me of this encounter."

"In true Elven fashion, your father did not crow about his deeds," reminded Lindras. "However, it was me, I was the one who told you the tale of this hunt and the ensuing battle, much to the chagrin of your dear mother. The good Queen felt you were too young and impressionable to hear such tales of deadly entanglements with dangerous creatures. She was worried about your youthful mind being plagued by nightmares. But as I said, it was a very long time ago. I am sure it merely slipped your mind being that you were so young at the time."

"Then remind me again," urged Kal-lel. "What was this animal?"

With a contemplative puff on his pipe, Lindras gathered his thoughts, mulling over the best way to describe this creature of legend.

"I take it, it was not a rogue brown bear or a killer wolf?" queried Cullen.

"Oh, no! It was nothing at all like one of these run-of-the-mill animals," confirmed Lindras. "In fact, there was something very extraordinary, or at the very least, something very *unnatural* about the creature King Galan had killed."

"Details, Lindras, we are in need of details," urged Kal-lel.

"About two centuries prior to the first great war that led to the defeat of the Dark Lord, Beyilzon roamed the lands of Talibarr. At first, he killed the mortals he encountered only to discover he had more to gain in enslaving them to do his bidding. It was during these violent and tumultuous times a terrible creature roamed these lands. It willfully and wantonly killed all it came upon."

"It killed men or livestock?" asked Markus.

"Both," responded Lindras. His eyes suddenly darkened with dread as his mind recalled the horrific details of the carnage left in the wake of this terror. "That beast indiscriminately maimed, mutilated and killed all manner of livestock, however, it was most savage in its dealing with men, women and children! And it seemed to kill for sport, never devouring those it attacked."

"This cannot be a mere coincidence," decided Joval. "By the very nature of these attacks, we are dealing with a similar beast."

"When you said there was something *unnatural* about this animal, exactly what did you mean, Lindras?" questioned Kal-lel.

"Yes, and what manner of beast was it?" probed Arerys.

"It was a dog," responded Lindras, his words matter-of-fact.

"A *dog*? A dog is as ordinary, as run-of-the-mill, a creature as they come!" scoffed Cullen, rolling his eyes in dismay.

"Oh, this was no ordinary dog I speak of. It was at least three times the size of the largest wolf-hound."

"So it was an extremely large brute of a dog. It was still a dog, nonetheless," grunted Cullen, his shoulders shrugging with indifference.

"Yes, but it was a creature conjured up by the dark magic of Beyilzon himself. It was said, but never confirmed, as the Dark Lord preferred taking credit even where credit was not due, that the witches of the north had a hand in raising this creature."

"If it was indeed a beast conjured up by the forbidden arts, then it must have been one hell of a hound!" determined Cullen.

"That is correct," said Lindras. "To be exact, it was a hound from Hell; the Dark Lord's loyal and deadly pet."

"Who in his right mind would want a pet with a taste for blood and a penchant for maiming and killing?" wondered Cullen, truly disturbed by this news.

"This is the Dark Lord Lindras speaks of, Captain," reminded Kal-lel. "Why dirty his hands when Beyilzon can have someone, or in this case, something else do the deed for him?"

"Beyilzon's cherished pet, a creature with no rivals in ferocity and loyally obedient to one master, terrorized those the Dark Lord set it on," informed the Wizard. "More treacherous and deadly than a well-armed man, this animal served its purpose where Beyilzon was concerned."

"But you did say my grandfather killed this beast, did you not?" queried Arerys, looking to Lindras for more answers.

"Indeed, my friend. Once Beyilzon felt he had adequately tormented the people of Talibarr, striking fear in their hearts by unleashing that bloodthirsty animal, he turned his attention on those to the south."

"That beast roamed Darross?" asked Cullen, never recalling tales from the past of such a creature terrorizing his people.

"One dark, autumn night, it slunk down from the Aranak Mountains to attack a small settlement just outside of Heathrowen to kill four people before it was driven off," responded Lindras.

"Why have I never heard of this?" questioned Cullen.

"By human standards, it happened so long ago this animal had faded from memory to become nothing more than a mythical creature to your people," explained Lindras. "Before it could be sent to attack once more, King Galan and I had organized a hunting party to track the creature down. For over a week, we searched for that murderous dog, hunting for it at night when it was on the move. It almost managed to return to Talibarr, reaching Rock Ridge Pass when we caught up to that dreadful beast."

"And there, my father killed the creature?" asked Kal-lel, only now having vague childhood memories of this tale.

"King Galan did kill the beast, but it was not without a great deal of effort. Spears and arrows did nothing but enrage it. The powers of my crystal merely stunned it," revealed the Wizard, his chin resting on his tented fingers as he recalled the terrifying events of this hunt.

"Tell me something, Lindras. Did this *dog* seem impervious to weapons?" queried Joval.

"If I remember correctly, that creature was decked out in a form of armour made of tough, doubled boiled leather. I distinctly recall how wide strips of this leather; overlapping and articulated, especially over its neck, shoulders and down its back seemed to move as one with the animal. It served to absorb the brunt of our assault. But even with this armour, it was apparent conventional weapons, arrows and such, that did indeed penetrate its body did nothing more than to hamper its movements and anger it all the more. No matter how well placed the weapons, traditional means of defense did nothing to kill the beast."

"Were there steel spikes and studs protruding from this armour, Lindras?" queried Arerys.

"Why do you ask?"

"The creature we encountered was protected by armour which is why it made it all the more difficult to identify, but this one had a protective coat embellished with nasty looking adornments," replied Arerys, remembering how he narrowly escaped being stabbed in the chest by a deadly spike protruding from the beast's neck. "In fact, Markus was cut by one."

"Hmph!" grunted Lindras, chewing on the stem of his pipe as he contemplated this information. "It seems the times have changed and this creature has had an upgrade of sorts in terms of armour."

"Now, I am thoroughly and completely confused," groaned Cullen, his hand slapping his forehead in frustration. "First you say that King Galan had killed the beast, and then you say that conventional weapons, no matter how well placed, could not kill it. Care to clarify, Wizard?"

"My words are true on both counts, Captain Bristow. No weapon we used could kill the beast, nor could my magic defeat it. Mind you, this creature was already dead to begin with."

"Good gracious, Master Weatherstone, you speak in riddles!" snapped Cullen, wallowing in his impatience and mounting frustration. "You were trying to kill something that was already dead? This is madness! Complete and utter madness, I say!"

"That is exactly what King Galan and I were thinking when it became evident the creature would not yield to our weapons, nor die when impaled upon King Galan's sword."

"But in the end, it was defeated, was it not?" asked Kal-lel, seeking confirmation from the Wizard.

"Yes. That savage creature was eventually dispatched, but not without an equal measure of effort and luck."

"But how?" asked Markus. "If a mighty Elven sword could not do it in, nor could your magic, I hardly think a man, mortal or Elf can take on an animal of such ferocity and strength, especially without a weapon."

"And what did luck have to do with any of this?" wondered Cullen.

"It was by luck that King Galan had killed the beast with a dagger," answered Lindras.

"And once more, you speak in riddles, Wizard," groaned Cullen, scratching his head in thought. "You said no weapons could kill the monster, now you are telling us the creature was dispatched with a little dagger; something no bigger than a large hunting knife."

"Please, Captain Bristow, allow Lindras to finish," urged Arerys, motioning Cullen for silence.

"Thank you, my friend," said the Wizard. "This was where luck or perhaps divine intervention played into the scheme of things. And I suppose it is better to say that *what was on* the blade of the dagger was to be credited for the demise of the creature."

"A poison?" queried Kal-lel.

"Blood, to be exact."

"*Blood?*" repeated all those in the Wizard's presence, baffled by his response.

"Yes, and it was like poison to that beast," disclosed Lindras.

"As soon as the blade of that bloodied dagger was plunged into the creature's heart, it died where it stood."

"What kind of blood?" questioned Arerys, eager to learn more about this bit of history he had no prior knowledge of.

"It was your grandfather's blood, Arerys. When my bid to down the beast with the power of my crystal failed, the creature turned on me. Just as it lunged, King Galan intervened, plunging his sword all the way to the hilt into its belly. Before he could retract the blade, the beast suddenly veered away, making off with the king's sword in its body, only to return to attack once more."

"And my father's quiver was empty – the arrows spent," recalled Kal-lel, a small piece of this memory rekindled in his mind with the retelling of this tale.

"Yes," nodded Lindras. "Just as that monster rushed in to attack, knocking the staff from my hands, King Galan came to my aid once more, throwing himself bodily onto its back. With one arm wrapped around the creature's throat, he used the other to repeatedly plunge his dagger into its neck and chest, but to no avail."

"But you said that it was Galan's dagger that killed the beast," reminded Cullen, frowning with bewilderment at the Wizard.

"Indeed, I did, but allow me to finish! In a fit of rage, the creature whipped about, throwing King Galan from its back. Turning its wrath away from me, the beast lunged at the King. I will never forget how its teeth snapped as its mouth frothed in its madness. Pinning King Galan to the ground, just as it was going to sink its fangs into his face, the King forcefully rammed his fist down the creature's throat."

"Good gracious, the beast could not have cared too much for that!" exclaimed Cullen, listening with keen fascination.

"How correct you are, Captain!" agreed Lindras. "The creature gagged, its head instantly recoiling upon receiving this brazen, unexpected blow. But in doing so, its teeth raked against King Galan's forearm, shredding his flesh from elbow to hand. The King's blood was everywhere."

"And some had spilled onto his dagger," remembered Kal-lel.

"Precisely! In the ensuing struggle, King Galan's own blood had spilled onto the blade of his dagger. When the creature bore down on him once more to finish him off, it was by luck that when King Galan had plunged the blade into the beast's heart, this time, it was coated with his blood. It was the contact with this Elven blood, still warm from the assault that the creature succumbed to the wound inflicted unto it."

"So the creature met its demise," determined Arerys.

"Yes," confirmed Lindras.

"Are you absolutely certain it was dead, Wizard?" interrogated Cullen. "The beast was not just terribly wounded, limping away to its master to recuperate in Talibarr?"

"I was there! Of course the creature was dead."

"It was dead as in taking an eternal-slumber-in-the-dirt dead?" queried Cullen, still doubting his words.

"I assure you, Captain, as soon as the bloodied dagger pierced the beast's heart, the creature died instantly."

"That was what my father meant," recalled Kal-lel, thinking back to when his father abdicated from the throne of Wyndwood to retire to the Haven.

"What do you speak of?" questioned Arerys, gazing over to his father.

"When your grandfather left for the Haven, prior to his departure he gifted me with his dagger. It was an exquisite weapon with a white oak handle and an elegant, sweeping blade," explained Kal-lel. "He said that on more than one occasion this dagger was his greatest ally in his most desperate hour; that it saved his life when his sword could not."

"That would be the dagger you had gifted to King Brannon on the eve you had departed with him and the men of the Order to begin your quest against evil over one-thousand-years ago," stated Markus, recalling this moment in their countries' shared history. "To this day, it has been a cherished heirloom handed down from father to son through the generations."

"I remember gifting it to King Brannon, because like you, Markus, he was unable to wield the sword of power against anyone except the Dark Lord," explained Kal-lel. "He needed to be armed with a weapon he could use in case of an attack."

"And to this day, I carry this dagger with the same reverence and honour it is deserving of," Markus bowed his head in respect and gratitude to the Elf King. "And that is why Captain Bristow will do the same as he keeps it safe for me. Is that not so, Captain?"

"Absolutely, Your Highness," promised Cullen, responding with a respectful bow. "I will guard it with my life."

"How is it that you are in possession of this particular dagger?" questioned Arerys, staring suspiciously at the mortal.

"To make an exceedingly long story short, King Markus felt this dagger would serve me better than the sword I bear now," explained Cullen, his hand patting the ornate scabbard of his precious weapon.

"You must admit, Captain Bristow, a hunt for a killer animal is hardly the place for a ceremonial sword," remarked Joval, glancing over at the garish weapon hanging from Cullen's baldric.

"It was only in hindsight that I realized I had erred in donning this sword, thinking it would appease my liege to know that this weapon he had gifted to me was appreciated. I never had the opportunity to use it in battle or to defend myself. Therefore, I never realized the blade *slightly* exceeded my draw-length."

"In other words, King Markus thought it was better to lend the dagger to you than to witness your untimely demise as you struggle to unsheathe this sword in a life-threatening situation," determined Joval.

"And King Markus' kind gesture is appreciated," responded Cullen, nodding politely as he quickly attempted to deflect attention away from him and his new sword. "Now, getting back to the matter at hand. This creature we have been hunting, the one that had attacked King Sebastian, I get the distinct sense we are dealing with a monster not of this world."

"Judging from the evidence and based on your shared experiences in hunting that beast down, I would say it is safe to assume so," agreed the Wizard.

"Is there a chance the Dark Lord's *pet* had somehow been resurrected?" asked Kal-lel.

"In the realm of magic, especially if the powers of the forbidden arts were to be invoked, anything is possible," decided Lindras. "However, I am baffled by the origin of this new beast, for none but Beyilzon and his cronies, those witches of old, had the power to create such a monstrosity of an animal."

"The Dark Lord was slain," stated Markus. "We made sure of it so there is no way it could have been the same creature."

"And lest we forget, the witches of the north have scattered, their numbers in decline," reminded Arerys. "And remember, the dreaded Book of Spells had been destroyed."

"All this is true, but then, how do we account for this beast?" queried Joval. "Everything we know of this creature tells us it is as deadly and as difficult to kill as the Dark Lord's *pet.*"

"At this time, we can only speculate as to its origin," responded Lindras. "I recommend we be prepared to assume the worst."

For a moment, there was profound silence as the group contemplated the possibilities that the Dark Lord Beyilzon was somehow embroiled in the appearance of this new and deadly creature.

As though they shared a common thought, Arerys, Markus and the Wizard shook their heads to dispel this possibility. They were there on Mount Hope, leading the campaign to destroy this evil. In this final confrontation, Markus had beheaded the Dark Lord with the special sword forged by the Elves of Wyndwood and blessed by the Elven elders and the oracles of Mount Isa. And Lindras wasted no time to use his powers over the element of earth to imprison Beyilzon for all time.

The trio came to the same conclusion, muttering with more hope than with absolute certainty, "No… that cannot be. The Dark Lord is no more."

"If it was so, it would require dark magic powerful enough to resurrect that entity, allowing him to release that monster from his prison in the netherworld," reminded Kal-lel.

Lindras shook his head, releasing a great puff of pipe smoke as he responded, "If Beyilzon was released from his prison, we would be the first to know about it. His siblings, the Watchers on Mount Isa, would have warned us of this."

"But suppose the magic of the dark arts cloak Beyilzon's intentions so the Watchers are not aware of his return?" queried Arerys.

"If it were true, I sense Beyilzon would have wasted no time to hunt those of us down he knows were directly responsible for his banishment from this realm," replied Lindras.

"Beyilzon was never known for being subtle; neither in his words nor his actions. His dealing with those in Imago had always been exceedingly cruel as he lashed out against humanity," stated Kal-lel. "And even if he did not make his presence immediately known, improved relations with those in Talibarr would have garnered reports of any sightings. They would have betrayed the Dark Lord's presence."

"That is what we would like to believe," argued Cullen. "However, not every Talibarrian can be trusted to do so. It is a well-known fact there are still pockets of resistance; naysayers of the peace accord instituted by my King and accepted by the general population of this country. These rabble-rousers are few, but there are still enough to provoke an insurrection."

"I believe your distrust of these people taints your opinion," countered Markus. "The Talibarrians were betrayed by the Dark Lord, deceived by his promises. They feared and despised him. Their past experiences under the shadow of his rule would have been enough to dissuade them from ever forging a renewed alliance with that evil soul."

"Granted the vast majority will require little, if any, prompting to reject the Dark Lord and whatever promises he can use to entice them, however, I know there are malcontents who will gladly switch allegiance. If it served their purpose, if there were personal gains in doing so, these people can be swayed," argued Cullen.

"Contrary to what you choose to believe, captain, not all Talibarrians are self-serving fools," retorted Arerys.

"Well, excuse me, my lord!" grunted Cullen, his eyes rolling in frustration. "Who am I to listen to, anyway? Oh, yes... I am the voice of reason in the face of madness! Unfortunately, it is obvious there is no reasoning with any one of you."

Before the captain could be subjected to further ridicule, Joval spoke up in Cullen's defense. "Perhaps we should not be so quick to dismiss Captain Bristow's warning."

Cullen's eyes narrowed in suspicion, glaring at the Elf as he questioned Joval, "What is going on here? Why are you suddenly siding with me?"

"I am *not* siding with you," explained Joval. "I am merely suggesting that we consider your reasoning, for there is some truth to it."

"Are you suggesting that someone in Talibarr is hiding the Dark Lord?" queried Kal-lel.

"I believe we should not dismiss the possibility. A man, whether he be from Talibarr or any other country for that matter, can be persuaded to do the unthinkable. All it would take is one vulnerable man in a desperate situation. It could be enough to convince him to attempt such a dangerous thing," answered Joval.

"I knew we were of like mind, Master Stonecroft!" Cullen exclaimed proudly, giving Joval an affable pat on the shoulder.

Joval's eyes shifted down to Cullen's hand. With this unfriendly glimpse, the captain was prompted to act, hastily removing his hand from the Elf's shoulder.

"No, we are not," disputed Joval, rolling his shoulder as if he was shrugging off this mortal's touch. "I can see beyond the obvious. And though we may have come to the same conclusion on this matter, we came about it in a different manner."

"The point being; there is a chance, as remote as it may seem, that the Dark Lord is up and about," countered Cullen. "If that is so, he could have changed his strategy, opting to be discreet as he plots his revenge."

"The only way Beyilzon can be unleashed from his prison is through the magic of the forbidden arts," reminded Lindras. "If this was so, only the dark powers contained within the Book of Spells could aid him to do so and we all know what happened to that dreadful thing last autumn."

"Do you know for certain that book was destroyed?" questioned Kal-lel.

Joval, Markus, Arerys and Cullen were present along with Lando, Nayla and the four Wizards when the great ice palace housing the Book of Spells was demolished in a trap meant to destroy them. This towering, monumental structure of solid ice was conjured up by the magic the madman Draven Eldard had extracted from an incantation in this book. When he lured them to the north, using Prince Carstian as the bait, his attempt to kill them in the collapsing palace forced an explosive reaction. Shards and boulders of ice were scattered far and wide, as far away as the Sea of Storms and in the calamity, Draven Eldard was killed. There was no way anyone or anything that could have survived that disaster.

"The Book of Spells was sealed in the same pillar of ice that trapped Draven," answered Arerys. "We know for certain he was killed by the bits and pieces we found of him amongst the ruin. Though we never did recover the book, we assumed it had met the same fate."

"If, by chance, that cursed book survived the calamity and had fallen into the hands of those capable of deciphering the ancient runes, there is a very real possibility a new creature was conjured up by this magic," disclosed Kal-lel.

"But what are the chances there is someone capable of reading that ancient dialect of Elvish?" queried Markus.

"We can rule out the elders of Wyndwood and members of my family," replied Kal-lel. "There is nothing to gain in using the powers of that evil book."

"And the infamous Fairy that once haunted Spirit Wood is no more," added Cullen, making no mention of the fact he was directly responsible for the demise of the last known Fairy to dwell in this realm.

"That would leave only the Wizards," deduced Joval.

"Yes, it does," agreed Lindras. "However, I will be the first to say I have no desire to use the dreadful magic festering in that book, nor does it have any appeal to my brother Wizards."

"Hmph! So you say, Master Weatherstone!" grunted Cullen. "I would not be so quick to rule out the Wizard of the East. You saw how Firestaff fought Draven Eldard for possession of that cursed book just before that ice palace collapsed around us."

Lindras' face scowled in disapproval as he responded, "I will have you know, Eldred Firestaff saved our lives on more than one occasion during that quest. And if you remember correctly, Captain Bristow, he battled Draven for the Book of Spells so he could destroy it once and for all."

"Or so he would like us to believe," sniffed Cullen.

The Wizard's efforts to redeem himself was ignored by many, including Cullen, for his dubious and murderous reputation during his time as the Sorcerer left an indelible mark in the hearts and minds of those less forgiving.

"You can believe what you like," dismissed Lindras, as he glared at Cullen. "Before you jump to the wrong conclusion yet again, you should know that Eldred Firestaff has been spending much of his time with Tylon Riverdon in the Cathedral Mountains for the past few months. He has been nowhere near Talibarr since we departed from the north after rescuing Prince Carstian."

"How do you know he did not sneak away from the watchful eyes of the Wizard of the North?" questioned Cullen. "I am sure even Master Riverdon must sleep from time to time."

"Now you are being rather preposterous!" snapped Lindras. "And even if Eldred did *sneak away* as you so eloquently put it, just how did he come and go from this place so quickly?"

"His orb!" answered Cullen, pointing to the magical crystal mounted atop the Wizard's staff.

"You fool! Even Eldred would require the powers of at least three crystals to transport himself in that manner. The only person capable of travelling swiftly to and fro between here and there would be Tor Airshorn, and that would have to be accomplished on the wings of his dragon."

"Aah-ha, another possible suspect!" offered Cullen.

"What is wrong with you, Captain Bristow?" groaned Arerys. "Why are you so suspicious of the Talibarrians *and* the Wizards?"

"The better question is, why are you not suspicious enough?" countered Cullen. "Between the Talibarrians and their unscrupulous ethics and the Wizards and their powers to control and manipulate, it would serve each of you well to be more suspicious of those you choose to align yourselves with."

"Perhaps we would be wise to shift our suspicions to you?" suggested Markus. "There is a chance you conjured up this ferocious beast so you can revel in the glory of capturing and killing this creature."

"I mean no disrespect to you," responded Cullen; "but I will be the first to admit I lack the smarts to embroil myself in the lost art of deciphering antiquated languages to create incantations. Nor do I possess the cunning to mastermind such a daring plot."

"I know," said Markus, with a smug smile. "I just wanted to hear you say it with your own words."

Before the situation could deteriorate into an all-out verbal fisticuff, Kal-lel spoke up, "Anticipating the worst, if this creature was somehow summoned using the forbidden arts, whether it be by Beyilzon's hand or someone employing the powers from the Book of Spells, I recommend focusing our attentions on capturing that creature before it kills again."

"I believe we are all in agreement," stated Arerys. "Now that we have some idea of what we are dealing with and more importantly, how that creature can possibly be killed, we should resume our hunt."

"Something comes our way!" warned Joval, raising his armed bow as the loud crashing of branches and thrashing of leaves sounded behind them.

Just as the Elf drew back his arrow, a horse and rider burst into the clearing. The horse reared up in fright upon seeing Joval. Wheeling about, it pitched the man from its back before bolting. As the horse galloped away, the rider scrambled to his feet.

"Help! Help me!" cried the Talibarrian; raising his hands before him to show the Elf he was unarmed. "The beast! It killed again!"

"When?" asked Markus, hoisting the frightened man back onto his feet as Arerys motioned a squire to fetch him some water and a warrior to retrieve the frightened horse.

"In the wee hours of this morn, it attacked without warning!"

"Where did it strike?" questioned Lindras.

"Over there to the east!" exclaimed the stranger, his trembling finger pointing toward Mount Hope. "On the south slope, near the lake."

"So the creature still lurks in that area," determined Kal-lel.

"How many did it kill?" queried Arerys.

"One… It killed my son, an' it would've killed me, too," gasped the man, gulping down a mouthful of water the squire delivered to him.

"You were able to drive it off?" asked Cullen; surprised this small, wiry man would be able to fend off the powerful beast when others could not.

"That creature? Are ya crazy? I'm only here now 'cause it ran away, like it was being called off."

"It retreated?" repeated Markus, frowning with confusion.

"Yeah, ya know? Like someone was callin' it home. It took off, chargin' up the mountain when a horn sounded in the distance."

"This is sounding all too familiar," responded Lindras, thinking back on how Beyilzon's hound would viciously attack, and then obediently retreat on its master's command.

"Did you see anyone calling this animal off?" probed Arerys.

"If someone was there, I sure as hell wasn't gonna stick around ta find out. All I heard was the horrible screeching of a horn far away. I took off as fast as I could. Ran my horse all the way ta here jus' ta get away from that crazy beast."

"Is there anything else you can tell us about the creature? Anything that will help us hunt it down?" asked Kal-lel.

"What can I tell ya? It was huge! It had massive teeth that were yay big," replied the trembling man, his quaking hands demonstrating the size of the monstrous fangs. "It moved like a ghost. Here one minute, gone the next. An' I wasn't stickin' around ta get better acquainted either! I'm gonna put as much distance between me an' that *thing*."

Before Kal-lel could offer food and more water to the Talibarrian, the man ran toward his horse that one of the Elven warriors managed to corral and deliver back to their camp. Without so much as a farewell, thank-you or a good luck, the man threw himself into the saddle, his heels sinking into the horse's flanks. As quickly as the Talibarrian had appeared, he was gone, charging westward.

"Typical Talibarrian! A lot of help he was," grunted Cullen, shaking an angry fist as he watched the swaying branches left in the wake of the man's hasty departure. "I suppose we should be on our way. If things go as planned, we shall be burying this creature's sorry carcass next to the one King Galan killed."

"Even if we kill the beast, this will not be possible," disclosed Lindras.

"Hold on, Wizard," said Cullen. "You said King Galan killed the original monster."

"He most definitely did, however, when we exhumed the carcass the next day to burn it, the animal was gone," revealed Lindras.

"Gone as in it came back to life and had dug itself from the grave to return to Beyilzon?" questioned Kal-lel.

"The one thing we were certain of was that the creature was killed. It was deader than dead, which is why we buried its carcass," stated the Wizard. "We wanted to make sure it stayed dead by cremating it, just as a precaution."

"Then what happened?" asked Arerys.

"When we returned the next morn, there was a depression in the ground where we had hastily buried the beast. It was as though the earth sank like the creature's body rotted away beneath it. When we dug up this grave, there was nothing there: No bones, not hide nor hair... nothing."

"What do you suspect happened to the creature?" queried Kal-lel.

"It is a shared belief amongst the Talibarrians that Beyilzon had robbed this grave to steal away with his pet. Many believe he could not stand to be parted from his beloved creature that in his bitterness and grief, he consumed the flesh of his pet to be one with it. Others say he sent the creature's soul to the netherworld to await him. They say he had plans to resurrect the beast once he attained greater powers in his bid for world domination."

"I pray this creature is languishing in the same hell we banished the Dark Lord to," hoped Markus, drawing a deep breath as he contemplated this confrontation. "If luck is with us, we shall be sending this beast to meet the same fate as the other."

"Just keep in mind, whatever this creature is that we are faced with, it is larger and just as deadly," reminded Joval. "And it is obvious this is no hound we are dealing with, for this animal takes to the trees with incredible ease."

"It would suffice to say that given what we know of this creature's nocturnal habits, its agility on the ground and in the trees, and the manner in which it attacks, we are dealing with a type of cat; one that is much bigger than the Dark Lord's hound," surmised Kal-lel.

"And yet, it is eerily reminiscent of Beyilzon's pet of old," stated Lindras. "A creature spawned from hell and set loose on these lands."

"But for what reason? And by whom, if this is not the Dark Lord's doing?" questioned Cullen.

"That remains to be seen," replied Kal-lel. "The most pressing matter at hand is that the creature must be stopped immediately, for others unaware of the danger may be travelling directly into its path."

The colour drained from Arerys' face as an overwhelming sense of fear and foreboding seized his heart.

Nayla was due to return from Orien any day now. This beast was still roaming free and it was last seen in the general vicinity where those travelling from Orien through Talibarr and on to Darross would venture. They were going to follow this new trade route from the Iron Mountains that rounded the base of Mount Hope, through the Valley of Shadows and cut directly across the Plains of Fire to the mountain trail that would deliver them to Rock Ridge Pass.

"Arerys, did you not say that Nayla and Lando could be expected at any time?" questioned Markus, noticing the ashen pallor of his face.

"I must warn her to turn back!" responded Arerys.

"It may be too late," said Joval, thinking back on her last correspondence and estimated arrival time.

"Suppose she and Lando already crossed the Iron Mountains? What if they are heading directly toward this creature?" asked Markus.

"We must send a falcon to Aspenglow, from there; I can have Artel deploy Tori, Nayla's falcon. Her bird can be dispatched with a message to warn her," responded Arerys.

"Why not use your father's white falcon?" questioned Cullen, perplexed by the complexity of this order. "It is already here in Talibarr with us. It can deliver a message to her much faster."

"My falcons are trained to deliver correspondence between designated points, from castle to castle between Wyndwood, Carcross, Cedona, Darross and now, to the fortress city of Nagana to the east," explained Kal-lel, pointing to the white raptor perched near to his tent. "Nayla's little falcon not only flies to these destinations, her bird is trained to identify and locate her if Tori is set in the general direction Nayla is believed to be travelling in."

"Then, I suppose it does make sense to go this round-about way to speed a message to her," decided Cullen. "But are you not concerned the falcon will tire if made to fly from Aspenglow to the Iron Mountains, possibly beyond into Orien in search of her?"

"Fear not, Captain Bristow," responded Joval. "Falcons, Nayla's included, can easily travel three-hundred leagues in a single day if the conditions are favourable."

"So there is a chance this bird will find her today?" questioned Cullen.

"That will depend on many things, such as where Nayla is at this moment," replied Arerys. "Come what may, if my father's falcon reaches Aspenglow too late in the day, Tori will not be sent on her way until dawn. If she is released on this day, her search will end at nightfall."

"And what if Nayla has already crossed over?" asked Markus.

"If Tori can find her, then at least she has been forewarned. She, Lando and those in their company will be able to take the proper precautions to safeguard themselves from this beast," said Arerys, motioning for the squire to deliver parchment and ink to him. "That is all we can hope for."

straight into danger

"Nayla, if we leave now and ride hard, we should be able to reach Deception Pass by nightfall."

"I am eager to return home, too, Lando, but keep in mind, that is the last place we would want to spend the night."

"Who said we would have to spend the night up there in that icy hell-hole? With you leading the way, I am confident we can negotiate the mountain trail safely back into Talibarr, even in the dark."

"You have far more confidence in my skills than I am deserving of," responded Nayla, laughing lightly.

"Oh, come now, do not be so modest, Nayla. I know you can see almost as well as any Elf."

"Though I can see adequately in the most trying of conditions, I am more concerned for you and our Talibarrian friends. All it will take is one misplaced step to end this trek in tragedy. The way is treacherous enough by the light of day, there is no point in endangering lives, yours or the others, just to shave a half day or so from our travels."

"I suppose we would not be looked upon favourably if the delegates are harmed along the way," sighed Lando, glancing over his shoulder at the two men travelling with them as they readied their horses. These men were appointed by the new government to represent their people on this, the country's first, formal trade mission to Orien.

"I tell you what, Lando. We will ride as far and as long as the daylight holds. We shall sleep in the shadow of the mountain tonight. In the morning, we will begin our ascent."

"I suppose I can live with that."

"Yes, or chance *dying* in the mountain's icy embrace should the weather take a sudden turn. Besides, whether you freeze to death or take a fatal tumble stumbling about in the darkness on that mountain,

I dread the thought of having to be the one to break this news to your family. I hardly think Nakoa will regard me as a dear friend if you were hurt in my presence. She expects me to keep you safe."

"Oh, no, no, my dear little friend," chuckled Lando, shaking a finger of admonishment in her direction. "*I* am here to keep *you* safe from harm. I promised your husband to keep a watchful eye on you. I have every intention of keeping my word to Arerys."

"Well, you should know, your wife asked that I keep *both my eyes* on you, Lando. And I promised Nakoa that was exactly what I planned to do. So, do you honestly believe I would risk travelling that mountain at night with you stumbling about in the dark? I think not, my friend!"

"Now you are making me sound like I am an old, bumbling fool," groaned Lando, pretending to be wounded by Nayla's teasing.

"Bumbling perhaps, but never a fool, Lando. But if you recall, you are the one to regularly lament about getting too old to join the members of the Order on quests of derring-do."

"I will be the first to admit I am not as young as I once was, nor am I as fit and robust either," sighed the retired knight, patting his comfortably expanding girth. "However, this was a safe little trade mission we were engaged in, not some life-or-death quest – a daring adventure of epic proportions you are so used to, my friend."

"I never thought I would live to hear you, a knight of King Augustyne's prestigious court and a captain no less, saying that you prefer a ho-hum existence to a life of adventure," commented Nayla.

"A *retired knight* of my King's court," reminded Lando. "And though I am nowhere near as long-lived as you, I have certainly had my fair share of adventures and more battles than I care to remember. At this point in my life, a quiet, humble existence with my wife, surrounded by my three lovely children is about all the adventure I can handle. I would choose my vineyard and a sharp pair of pruning shears over my sword and shield any day."

"The love of a family certainly changes one's entire perspective," said Nayla, nodding in agreement as she thought upon Arerys and their daughter Carys, waiting for her to return to the enchanted forest.

"I take it, you miss the days when you roamed the lands of Orien in the company of the Kagai Warriors?" probed Lando, recalling how Nayla easily slipped into the customs and language of this land and its people. It was second nature whenever she became immersed in her mother's culture.

"I do miss my mother's people, particularly those who raised me," admitted Nayla, thinking back on her difficult childhood. It had been many decades since Joval Stonecroft had spirited her away from the fortress city to help her escape her father's cruelty. "Most of all, I miss my Kagai masters, but I do not miss the wars."

"There are some people who thrive on the sheer excitement of such battles," stated Lando, knowing how efficient and calculating Nayla was in dealing with matters of warfare.

"That is the type of excitement I can do without and it is not because I am feeling my age," replied Nayla. "I enjoyed my early days of training and the opportunity to test and hone my skills with my Kagai brothers, but I am glad the days of war are finally over."

"As I am, too."

"I must say though, it was good to go home to Anshen. I am grateful my master was able to spend the last years of his life knowing the days of peace had finally come," said Nayla, recalling her time with Hunta Saibon during his final hours.

"I do believe Master Saibon was grateful to see your face again," stated Lando. "I could tell he was pleased beyond words to speak to you, to see with his own eyes you were well and thriving in Wyndwood."

"I swear, when I first received news from Master Saibon's son that his father's health had taken a turn for the worse, I had serious doubts I would be able to return in time to see my mentor before he died. It was as though Master Saibon kept death at bay until I returned."

"I must admit, your arrival to Anshen was well timed," responded Lando, pleased his dear friend had an opportunity to spend a few hours with the old man prior to his passing. "During your time with your mentor, what did you and Master Saibon speak of?"

"It was as though time had slowed the moment I entered his cottage," replied Nayla, remembering how weak Hunta Saibon's grip was when she clasped his hand. "We chatted about how my life had changed since I had departed from Orien; about life in Wyndwood; and I also had a chance to boast about my charming, little daughter."

"That she is," admitted Lando, nodding in agreement.

"It was interesting how Master Saibon noted that Carys was so much like me in so many ways."

"In all the most positive ways, I must add," interjected Lando, knowing Carys' determined resolve to get things accomplished, her giving nature and humourous outlook on life were a reflection of her mother's character.

"Aside from talking about the changes in my life, Master Saibon also asked that I preserve his way of life on his passing," disclosed Nayla.

"You are speaking of Kagai warriorship?"

"It was the only way of life he and his descendents knew of. Master Saibon asked if I would help his son, as well as future generations of Kagai Warriors, in helping to keep the tradition of his people alive."

"I hope that does not mean the old chap anticipates more wars in the future as a reason to keep training the men," responded Lando.

"The time of the Elf-kind is drawing to an end in this realm and the fate of the world shall rest in the hands of mortal man. We can all hope for the best, but hope is not always enough to prevent a war from erupting, for whatever reason."

"I see your point," acknowledged Lando. "I will be the first to admit that left to their own devices; human beings tend to lean toward aggressive action than peaceful resolution when push comes to shove."

"Have you forgotten that you are a human?" queried Nayla, gazing with raised eyebrows at her friend.

"Look at me!" laughed Lando. With a jovial slap, his hand bounced off the paunch of his well-fed belly. "You have heard me moan and groan when the wind is too cold or the sun is too hot. You have listened to me grumble when my old body has sat too long in the saddle. How can I ever forget that I am a mortal man?"

"It was just that your remark pertaining to the human race was rather disparaging. And if I am not mistaken, by your words and tone, you seem to want to distance yourself from your kind."

"And rightfully so, but it is not so much from my kind as it is from my kind's *behaviour*. As it stands now, should another war break out during what remains of my mortal lifetime, I would definitely resist the urge to go to battle. In fact, there is no urge, whatsoever."

"Because you would choose to seek a peaceful resolution?"

"That… and I shall be too old and cantankerous to be enlisted into any man's army. Knights and soldiers will not tolerate being in my company for long as they listen to me gripe about saddle sores; cold, stale food eaten on the run; functioning on little sleep and enduring the elements as we are made to march to war."

"It is nice to see your sense of humour remains intact with the onset of *old age*," teased Nayla.

"You know where I stand when it comes to matters of war, Nayla. I take it Master Saibon was worried about this possibility."

"Master Saibon lived and died a true Kagai Warrior. He believed in always being prepared. But even if there were no more wars to be concerned about, the long history, the time-honoured traditions and teachings behind this level of warriorship prepares men for life as a whole, not just for battle."

"I suppose life in itself can be a battle at times."

"Indeed," agreed Nayla. "The discipline alone required to endure our rigorous training regimen can shape and define one's character. It can allow a dedicated disciple to view life from a perspective most cannot."

"I suppose you are living proof of just how character-building the arduous Kagai way of life can be. For one of such diminutive stature, you have more character in your little finger than most women, *and men*, have in their entire body," praised Lando, with a wry smile and a wink of his eye.

"Thank you... I think."

"Knowing you, my little friend, I sense you have every intention of ensuring the Kagai Warrior code lives on, even during times of peace," decided Lando.

"I owe it to Master Hunta Saibon, and all those who came before him, to keep this tradition alive. If it were not for these great Kagai leaders I had trained with, I would not be the person I am now. I truly believe I would not have survived in this world."

For a moment, Nayla's mind wandered back to the day when she first arrived at the secret Kagai enclave of Anshen. She was the mortal equivalent of a child of twelve years; a child without a mother, left to suffer at the hands of a cruel, uncaring father. Nayla could never forget how Joval Stonecroft had risked his life and standing in her father's army to secretly whisk her away from Nagana.

Her father, Dahlon Treeborn, as respected as he was amongst the Elves and mortals of Orien, harboured a secret known only to some within his inner circle. The few who did know chose to turn a blind eye and a deaf ear to this situation. Though Joval was aware of the vague whispering that echoed through the corridors of the palace in the fortress city of Nagana, he had no idea how Nayla truly suffered. It was quite by accident Joval had come across her, bound and gagged after enduring a vicious beating. She had been abandoned in an empty armoury, left alone to wallow in her pain and misery.

Nayla had been whipped with a bamboo cane for disgracing her father in the presence of the elders representing the council. When Dahlon failed to listen to her warnings after she learned the lives of their warriors would be placed in jeopardy if he did not alter his strategy that threatened to send them directly into a trap, she was forced to confront him before his peers. Such a personal affront, especially by a child – his daughter no less, was more than Dahlon could bear.

Nayla was the child he never wanted, but was forced to acknowledge before humans and Elves alike. It was bad enough he had fathered this child through an ill-fated affair with a mortal woman, but to have this half-caste besmirch his good name before those on council? He could tolerate no more.

Dragging her off where no one could witness his rage, Dahlon vented his wrath. When Joval happened upon her, she was a bloodied mess, whipped within an inch of her life. And more than her body had been tortured; her once exuberant spirit was shattered. Joval could never forget the look in her eyes that could no longer even weep for her own sorry plight. It was as though all she knew and felt in her young life was fear.

On her mother's deathbed, Lady Karida Treeborn had warned Joval that her husband Dahlon was heavy-handed in his dealings with Nayla. But for Joval, his love and respect for this great Elf he always regarded as an uncle, and then a father figure after his parents departed for the Haven, prevented him from acknowledging the true level of animosity Dahlon had long held for this child. It was only when he was forced to witness Dahlon's true level of cruelty was Joval compelled to act, freeing Nayla from a tortured existence and possibly death. He secretly delivered her to her mother's people in Anshen to be raised by a clan of Kagai Warriors.

"I understand your loyalty, Nayla, however, do you not feel you had already paid your debt to these people?" questioned Lando.

Nayla said nothing, staring to the east from where they had come, thinking about the life she had left behind.

Lando waved his hand before her face, "Hello! Are you even listening to me? Did you hear anything of what I had said?"

"Sorry, Lando. What were you saying?"

"I was saying, do you not feel that your debt to these people had been paid? After all, you have gone to battle far more often than many of the Saibon generations combined. What more can they ask of you?"

"It is not a matter of repaying a debt, Lando. As much as I do owe these mortals for taking me in when no one else would, and for teaching me all that I know, it is so much more than that. It is to honour my mother and to pay respect to the culture and traditions she held dear to her heart. It is my way of keeping her memory alive. And I suppose, in many ways, being a Kagai Warrior is so ingrained in my body, mind and soul, it is, and shall always be, in my blood."

"That is all fine and dandy, but do not go spilling this blood of yours for nostalgia's sake," warned Lando.

"I assure you, it is something far more important than nostalgia that motivates me to do so."

"But how do you intend to do that? You reside in the enchanted forest now. You are the consort to the Prince of Wyndwood."

"I was a warrior long before I became Arerys' wife. One is a way of life; the other, a life choice."

"I can accept that, but how do you plan to keep this warrior tradition alive when you are so far from Anshen?"

"All it will take is an annual visit; a chance to instill the values and teachings shared by my masters with the up and coming warriors. It will also be my opportunity to share my mother's world with Carys. I do not want her to deny that part of her being. It will be no different than denying who I am."

"So your motives for doing so are two-fold," determined Lando, as he nodded in understanding. Setting his foot in the stirrup, he hoisted himself onto the horse's back, easing his body onto the saddle.

"It is a long way to travel so I better have a very good reason to make the trek," explained Nayla, giving her friend a knowing smile. "And it is time for us to go. The others are ready to leave."

Winding their way through the lush bamboo forest, Nayla guided the group westward to the Iron Mountains. The monotony of the long journey was broken by intervals of rest for both horses and riders. Knowing the way intimately, Nayla timed each break to allow for adequate travel to get them to the foot of the mountain well before nightfall as she had promised to Lando.

As the sun passed over the Iron Mountains on its relentless journey westward, Nayla and the men in her company came to rest in the shadow of the great mountain.

Settling down as the twilight sky melted into the night, they gathered around a blazing campfire to share in a meal and conversation.

"So Master Slean, I take it your meeting with the elders of Nagana proved successful?" questioned Nayla.

The Talibarrian took a brief moment to select his words. "That is correct, my lady. It was very successful indeed."

He attempted to do away with his people's practice of using contracted words, making a conscious effort to enunciate each syllable he spoke than to allow the words to slur together.

"I couldn't believe their request fer iron ore an' coal, m'lady!" his

Talibarrian partner exclaimed with excitement. He suddenly stopped talking as Slean discreetly elbowed him.

Slean's partner, Merdak blushed with embarrassment, realizing his efforts to sound more civilized than the average Talibarrian fell to the wayside in his enthusiasm to share the details of their trade mission.

"I was most pleased the Taijins were eager to do business with us, my lady," said Merdak; deliberately slowing his speech so he can properly pronounce every word he spoke. "The promise of prosperity through commerce with these people shall give the Talibarrians renewed hope for a better life."

"Yes," agreed Slean. "Ever since King Sebastian's peace accord had been put into place, we had seen almost immediate benefits once our people were able to trade and sell freely with those in Darross and beyond. This new trading partner to the east holds much promise in the way of commerce for our people."

"Well, I am pleased the meetings were a success," said Nayla, sprinkling the dried tea mixture into a pot of hot water. "It would have been a long way to travel if things did not work out in your favour."

"And we must thank you and Sir Bayliss for allowing us to come along on this excursion – to guide us through these lands," said Slean, bowing his head in genuine gratitude. "Orien is a vast country. We would have been terribly lost if we attempted the journey on our own."

"And it was most fortuitous we were able to take advantage of this fair weather," added Merdak. "It allowed us to establish a trade agreement before others could improve on our offer and sway negotiations. The timing could not have been better!"

"I am certain those on council will be pleased with this news," said Lando. "Perhaps, it will finally end the discontented murmuring of those rabbles refusing to acknowledge this peace accord."

"The few rabbles you speak of, Sir Bayliss, do acknowledge this treaty," responded Slean. "However, they just refuse to accept a truce with those they have long regarded as the enemy. They are mired in the past; wallowing in self-pity and unable to relinquish old feelings of animosity."

"I suppose some habits and hard feelings do not fade away with time," said the retired knight, with a sigh of resignation.

"Very true! The pockets of resistance are concentrated to the north. There, trade and contact with those beyond the Aranak Mountains are restricted by distance and more so, by feelings of long-standing hostility," explained Merdak.

"And it is these people, isolated from the rest of the world, that are the most resistant to change," added Slean. "They trust no one, not even their fellow Talibarrians, unless they have very good reason to do so."

"You make it sound as if they are a completely separate race of people different from your own," noted Nayla, pouring the steaming hot tea for the men before serving herself.

"Those folks to the north are regarded as social outcasts by the rest of us Talibarrians. I guess they might as well be separate," grunted Slean. His head nodded in gratitude to Nayla as he breathed in deeply, enjoying the earthy aroma of roasted barley and dried jasmine flowers that mingled with the tealeaves. These fragrances blended harmoniously, becoming stronger, resuscitated back to life by the hot water.

"As it stands now, their numbers are small, but their influence can still be great if they chose to use it," added Merdak, "especially when those they attempt to sway to their way of thinking are simple people to begin with."

"I take it, the social outcasts you are speaking about are those who descended from the covens of witches from along ago," determined Nayla.

"That I do, my lady," acknowledged Slean, exhaling a cooling breath into his cup of tea before taking a sip.

"I thought the witches no longer existed," responded Lando, scratching his gray peppered beard as he contemplated this news. "I was always led to believe they were no more since the Dark Lord Beyilzon broke his covenant with them over one-thousand-years ago."

"True, that wretched being cast them aside once he got what he wanted from the infamous four," explained Slean. "However, witchery in Talibarr is like a religion. The teachings and philosophies have changed over time to suit the practitioners, but it always remains in one form or another, its roots intact."

"There are those still delving into the forbidden arts?" questioned Nayla, peering over her cup as she stared at the Talibarrians.

"If fortune-telling and herbal remedies are considered black magic, then I suppose so," answered Slean.

"I believe the lady was referring to the forbidden arts in the way of foul spells, evil curses and dark powers that can be used against the people – usually for the purpose of world domination," clarified Lando.

Slean and Merdak exchanged glances, and then they burst out, chuckling in nervous laughter.

"What?" responded Lando, staring at the Talibarrians.

"We do not mean to be rude, and we certainly do not mean you any disrespect, Sir Bayliss," apologized Slean, as he attempted to stifle his laughter; "but do you not think those witches of long ago, if they were still alive or their knowledge and powers were still intact, our people would have run rough-shod over those to the south by now? Darross and the other free countries would have fallen beneath their powers."

"Good point," conceded Lando.

"So, you are saying that the witches still do exist, just not in the numbers nor with the powers they once possessed?" questioned Nayla.

"That is exactly what I am saying, my lady." Slean nodded in confirmation. "Those still clinging to this arcane belief have dwindled drastically in numbers over the years and most certainly they have been left wanting in the strength of their magical powers."

"Yes, it would appear that ever since their comprehensive compilation of evil magic was lost over time, so too, were they depleted of their powers," added Merdak.

"This compilation of evil magic you speak of, would that be the Book of Spells?" questioned Nayla.

"It was a regular cornucopia of incantations and spells that could only be used for evil," responded Slean. "Fortunately, for many centuries that cursed book had been lost. Some believe that Eldred Firestaff absconded with it, fleeing far into these lands when he was a rogue Wizard. Since that time, the successive generations of witches and their powers diminished, becoming more and more impotent. They are merely shadows of their former selves and former greatness."

"Those who still survive and share their hexes and potions will never rise to their former stature of power or glory," stated Merdak. "They can certainly squawk and voice their grievances in a bid to rally other malcontents, but you cannot hope to win a battle if all you are armed with are angry words."

"And thank goodness for that!" declared Slean. "I, for one, have no desire to revert to the days of old. Prosperity for all without having been made to steal it and the end to the days of war are more to my liking."

"I suppose, over time, the remaining witches and their followers will pass into memory," decided Nayla. "After all, the Book of Spells will never fall into their hands again."

"I pray you are right, my lady," said Slean.

"Of course she is right," stated Lando. "We were there when that horrid book was destroyed – ripped apart to oblivion!. And I will tell you now, only the darkest of dark magic can resurrect that foul thing."

"That is reassuring to know," approved Slean. "As I understand it, the Dark Lord's influence and power lived on through the writings in that book. He was the very incarnation of evil and it would be a disaster if it fell into the wrong hands."

"I assure you, that will never happen again," promised Nayla. "The book is gone forever."

"That is a great relief, my lady," responded Merdak. "The citizens of Talibarr have begun a new era and we have no desire to look back. We finally have some hope of a better life without the constant threat of war. We now have the ways and the means to create permanent settlements with the promise of commerce. It is something our people could never do before."

Lando thought back on the small villages scattered along the way. Prior to King Sebastian's peace accord and during the years of war, most Talibarrians dwelled in temporary shelters that were quick and easy to assemble and take down. Forced to live a nomadic lifestyle, never settling in one place for very long, their lives and movements were dictated by the availability of food and the severity of weather.

Now, with the promise of true commerce and prosperity, the growing availability of scholars willing to educate the next generation of Talibarrians in the fundamentals of reading, writing and arithmetic became a reality. These people had opportunities like never before.

"Some changes are definitely for the better," remarked Lando.

"I agree," averred Slean. "I much prefer sitting here engaged in civilized conversation with you over a cup of tea than being made to engage in a swordfight."

"Believe me, Master Slean, it is Nayla you would not want to engage in a swordfight, not even a friendly little sparring match," warned Lando, with a lighthearted laugh as he winked at her.

"So there is some truth to the tales we have heard?" queried Slean, gazing over to the little warrior.

"What tales do you speak of?" responded Nayla.

"That you are skilled with this weapon," answered Slean.

"I have been known to wield a sword from time to time," confessed Nayla, giving the Talibarrian an affable smile.

"You are too modest for your own good, my friend," scolded Lando.

"To say she can *wield a sword* is a gross understatement, Master Slean. This woman put the *'war'* in warrior! Nayla is a master of the sword, bow, and a whole mess of other weapons you probably never knew even existed. In fact, I have seen her take ordinary objects and turn them into deadly weapons!"

"Now you are exaggerating, Lando," scoffed Nayla.

"And you continue to understate your own abilities," countered Lando.

"It is my understanding you once captained your own army," said Merdak. "Is that true, my lady?"

"That was over a decade ago, but yes, I did captain my father's army that was stationed in Nagana. Before that, I led my Kagai brethren into battle. However, that was another lifetime ago."

"How impressive!" exclaimed Slean. "One would never suspect a woman as tiny and beautiful as you would be capable of such an undertaking."

"That was part of the reason for my success, Master Slean. The enemy automatically underestimated my abilities."

"And that became their downfall," determined Merdak, listening with great fascination to this little warrior.

"Precisely."

"I do not mean to discredit you, my lady, but how is it that someone of your stature, a female no less, was able to do battle against men?" questioned Slean. "I can see some of the Talibarrian women doing this, for some are hulking brutes that can be easily mistaken for men, but you are obviously not."

"It had everything to do with my training as a Kagai Warrior," explained Nayla. "Our style of combat does not require strength to be effective against the enemy. It comes down to anticipating their moves, and then countering them; using their own energy to redirect their aggression as well as applying the simple rules of action and reaction and using them to one's own benefit."

"Your manner of warfare sounds very complicated," assessed Slean. "We are used to a more direct, hack and slash approach to combat."

"It is a matter of applying the method that works best for you," replied Nayla. "If I were to rely on this *'hack and slash'* style of fighting, the victor will be the physically stronger one. And I do not take well to losing, especially when it is my life on the line."

"So strength has nothing to do with the Kagai way of combat? It is not the determining factor in a bout?"

"Strength is always a factor, but one cannot always rely on it. I certainly cannot, as my opponents have been men and all have been notably larger and stronger. Believe me, I am not strong to begin with, nor do I waste my time engaged in long, drawn-out battles."

"Your words make sense, however, I do believe one must be trained in the Kagai way of warfare to truly appreciate it," decided Slean.

"That is very true," agreed Lando. "I have seen Nayla in battle before and not only is she quick and calculating in her moves, I have seen her using both her swords, one in each hand, to take the enemy down. Where you and I are taught to handle the sword with both hands on the hilt to deliver effective blows, Nayla can attack with lightning speed and with deadly strokes armed with her special swords."

The Talibarrians' eyes glanced over to the unique weapons Nayla carried with her. The typical swords carried by mortal men to the west and the Elven blades forged in Wyndwood were double-edged, had a larger hilt to accommodate a two-handed grip and were often adorned with a pommel as a counter-balance. Nayla always carried two single-edged swords; one full-size sword worn at her left hip and a short sword typically worn in front, held in place by the knot of her belt.

"And you can use a sword in either hand?" queried Slean.

"And just as competently?" questioned Merdak, his brows furrowing in skepticism.

"It is the Kagai way to be prepared," answered Nayla. "In a heated battle, there is nothing to say that your dominant hand will be safe from harm, or amputated all together. If you want to live, you best be able to wield a sword effectively in either hand."

"It would be like asking me to write or eat with my left hand," noted Slean. "I can just get by with using my right. I cannot imagine being made to brandish a sword in my left."

"It just requires practice," responded Nayla.

"Lots and lots of consistent, regular practice," added Lando, nodding his head judiciously as he considered the lifetime of training Nayla had endured.

"Given the option of dying unarmed or being able to take up my sword in my other hand so I can at least die fighting, if it came to that, I would choose to practice so I would be efficient using my sword no matter which hand it is in."

"Is this something you can teach us?" asked Slean.

"It can be taught to anyone willing to devote the time and effort required to master this technique," replied Nayla. "However, on this eve, the lessons must wait as the hour grows late. We have an early start in the morning."

"Finally, the weather has cleared!" declared Lando. He stared up to the towering mountain peak, its snowy pinnacle stabbing the bold, blue morning sky. "There is nary a wisp of cloud to impede the crossing."

"Let us hope it stays this way," prayed Nayla, scrutinizing the sky while ascertaining the wind direction before they ventured on. "After all, it is called Deception Pass for good reason, my friend."

"It's my understandin'…" The Talibarrian's words trailed off as Slean made a conscious effort to correct his spoken words. "I mean to say; *it is* my understand*ing* the weather can deteriorate rapidly up at that elevation."

"That is very true, Master Slean," confirmed Nayla, nodding in respect. She was pleased he was making a sincere effort to not only improve his reading and writing skills in accordance to his new position, but this Talibarrian continued to make an attempt to properly pronounce each word so he could speak the common tongue with a degree of sophistication. "The weather can change quickly and with little warning. This early in the spring it is still possible for a blizzard to blow in from nowhere to trap us in the pass."

"That can prove to be deadly," responded Slean, dreading the prospects of an icy demise.

"Yes, even for me," acknowledged Nayla.

She knew full well that being of mixed blood, she could tolerate temperature extremes better than her mortal comrades. She also understood the Elven blood coursing through her veins would not be enough to prevent her from freezing to death due to prolonged exposure to the harsh elements.

"Perhaps we should leave immediately, while the weather holds some promise of a safe crossing?" suggested the Talibarrian.

Mounting her mare for the next leg of the trek to deliver them to the gateway to the west, Nayla nodded in agreement as she urged Cloud on. "Come along, gentlemen. The east face of this mountain is a harder climb. We best make haste."

Venturing on, their horses plodded along at a steady pace. As they ascended to the halfway mark of this slope, their pace began to slow noticeably. At this elevation, the lush bamboo forests had long given way to the resilient pine trees. The higher they journeyed on, these great conifers gradually gave way to gnarled and stunted specimens that were forced to eke out an existence while enduring the severe elements and harsh growing conditions. Eventually, scant vegetation gave way to lichen-covered rocks and a growing layer of snow.

Pressing her mare on, Nayla glanced over her shoulder to see how her companions were faring. Drawing a long, slow breath in through her nose, she filled her lungs. Nayla was beginning to feel the chill in the air and the twinges of symptoms brought on by the thinning, alpine air. She knew these mortals would feel the ravages of this high altitude to a far greater extent.

Having made this trek several times before, and protected by the elements thanks to his Elven cloak, Lando fared better than his Talibarrian comrades. Other than his throbbing head, he was not about to let it slow him down. He was bound and determined to take the steps that promised to deliver him ever closer to home and family.

For Slean and Merdak, they visibly shivered. Their heads throbbed with agonizing pain as they fought to gulp down the cold, thin air. Wrapping their cloaks tightly around their bodies, they pulled it high around their necks and arched shoulders. The thick wool fabric was drawn over their mouths and noses to help filter out the numbing cold as a brisk breeze swept around them, tugging at their raiment.

Leading their horses on by the reins for the final push to breach the mountain, Nayla stepped lightly through the crisp mantle of snow. The Talibarrians followed close behind as Lando took up the rear, the soles of their boots crunching against the layer of frozen snow.

"It is a bloody good thing we did not attempt a crossing last eve," determined Lando, his eyes squinting under the sun's radiant glare.

"Indeed!" exclaimed Merdak and Slean, agreeing in unison.

"As cold as it is now, there is no doubt in my mind, last night would have been the death of us if we came by this way during the snowstorm," added Slean, the icy breeze catching in the back of his throat as his eyes took in this wondrous, but deadly sight.

As they entered the pass, a spectacular cathedral of ice and snow towered above them. Icy crystals glistened in the brilliance of the afternoon sun, blinding them with this show of light.

"Now this is truly magnificent!" marvelled Lando, his gaze spanning across the forests and plains of Talibarr. "It is a sight to behold!"

"You are an unusual one, Sir Bayliss," commented Merdak, smiling as his eyes took in the familiar landscape of his country. "Most of those to the south, or in your case, to the west of us do not generally welcome the sight of Talibarr."

"Perhaps when our countries were at war," responded Lando.

"However, once we breach this mountain and journey beyond this pass, we are all one step closer to home, wherever that may be."

"I do admit this trek was challenging," conceded Slean. "Yes, it will be good to return home."

"As challenging as this expedition was, keep in mind, Master Slean, the greater the challenge, the greater the reward," stated Nayla.

"Is that Kagai wisdom you impart on us?" questioned the Talibarrian, as he thought on the successful trade negotiations.

"No, I believe it is just old-fashioned common sense. I do believe it was Lando who once shared this with me."

"Indeed," admitted Lando. "I believe it is a common saying shared by most in the brotherhood of knights."

"Well, let us not keep you away from your family any longer than need be, Sir Bayliss," suggested Slean. "Let us journey on."

A bracing, cold gust of wind swirled through the pass to sweep up dry crumbs of snow. The glittering crystals chased each other, tumbling along like they were caught up in a mini cyclone, only to scatter on the frozen mantle of snow as the parting wind vanished, whispering a promise of an icy demise to all those choosing to linger for too long.

Nayla urged Cloud on, gently pulling at the mare's reins to coax her on. Without hesitation, the horse followed her master down the long, meandering trail that now scarred the slope of the mountain with growing traffic.

Trekking more than half way down, they left behind the chilling mountain air and conditions that made it difficult for horse and rider to breathe easy. Nayla motioned for all to stop. A small waterfall cascading down along this trail splashed noisily. Its water pooled before spilling over to continue its downhill journey.

Nayla dismounted. Instructing her companions to do the same, she took a moment to study the ever-changing sky. As though the sun's movement influenced the direction of the wind, with the cooling rays came a growing abundance of clouds. Having loomed on the horizon since early in the afternoon, the fleecy, gray formations seemed to follow the sun, but now, they had grown with the promise of unleashing a torrential downpour having spent a good portion of the day brood over the Sea of Storms.

"Allow the horses to drink, and then we move on," ordered Nayla. "If we continue our trek at this pace, we shall reach the base of this mountain before nightfall. We can set up camp well before the rain comes."

"If we make good time and the light of day continues to hold, I suggest we journey on," recommended Lando. "A little rain will do us no harm."

Knowing that Nayla had far greater stamina than them, the Talibarrians believed her suggestion to rest was to accommodate them.

"Master Merdak and I agree with Sir Bayliss, my lady," stated Slean. "The journey down promises to be much less difficult. And we still possess the will and the drive to go on until darkness comes. Besides, if the clouds do open up, it will not be until later tonight."

"Are you positive?" questioned Nayla.

"I am quite sure, my lady. I am confident the conditions will be far more inviting the farther we are from these mountains. And remember, my friend and I are citizens of Talibarr. We are used to the rain."

"Very well," responded Nayla, hoisting herself onto Cloud's back once more.

As they followed the sun westward, this massive mountain gave way to the less conspicuous Mount Hope. Skirting this landform that protruded just above the tree line, Nayla's keen eyes scanned the mauve sky as the golden orb began its descent behind the Aranak Mountains. In less than an hour, this twilight sky promised to surrender to the night.

A sharp 'screee', this familiar cry, caused Nayla to search the southwestern horizon as a small speck hovered momentarily before winging its way in the general direction of the mountain from where they had just come.

"What is it, Nayla?" queried Lando, his eyes narrowing as he studied the deepening sky for what she scrutinized so intently.

"It could be nothing," dismissed Nayla. "Perhaps a wild falcon or a bird on the wing to deliver a message to the east."

"Ah, I see it now!" exclaimed Slean, pointing for Merdak to follow his finger as it traced a falcon's swift, fluid movements.

For a moment, they watched in awe as the thermals that allowed the bird to float effortlessly on this rising bank of warm air dwindled as the sun's waning light no longer heated the earth.

"Either it is a falcon on the hunt or a messenger bird that is terribly lost," noted Lando, spying the raptor as it hovered, circled and then glided on before repeating this unusual flight pattern.

"The sun will be setting in less than an hour," determined Merdak. "Perhaps the bird is searching for a safe place to roost for the night."

"You may be correct," agreed Nayla. "These birds do not take to flying at night. I recommend we take the falcon's advice and find a place to rest for the evening, too. We should get settled before darkness descends."

"I believe we are all in agreement," responded Lando, shifting uneasily to ease his weary back as Slean and Merdak nodded in consensus.

"Very good, then," said Nayla. Coaxing Cloud onward to the stand of pine trees that fringed the Valley of Shadows, they followed the trail curving around the base of Mount Hope. "Let us find a suitable clearing to set up camp."

As the sun slipped behind the distant mountains, Nayla glanced skyward again as the same falcon cried out as it circled high overhead. Its tiny form stood out against the building cloud cover. The falcon's sharp eyes fixed onto the movement on the ground below as it attempted to determine if one of the people below was her master.

"Well, this is a surprise. It is *my* falcon!" exclaimed Nayla, her eyes now able to identify Tori as she wheeled above them. The bird descended ever closer with each revolution.

"What is she doing here?" asked Lando, staring at the bird that he could now ascertain was a falcon, but had no way of knowing if it was indeed Tori.

"No doubt, she delivers word from Wyndwood," assessed Nayla, whistling loudly as she raised her arm for the falcon to land on.

"Arerys knew we would be returning about now. I wonder what is so urgent he could not wait?"

"We shall soon find out," responded Nayla, following Tori's movement as the graceful falcon circled one last time.

Certain she had found her master, Tori's wings folded close to her body as she plunged to the earth, her eyes set on Nayla's extended arm.

Unfamiliar with falconry, the Talibarrians backed away, watching in astonishment as Tori sliced through the sky at a frightening speed. Just as the falcon slowed as it made its descent to land, an explosion of feathers filled the sky as Tori tumbled to the earth.

"Good gracious! What was that?" gasped Lando. He stared in disbelief as the bird plummeted from the sky to land somewhere on the forest floor before them.

"Tori was struck down by something!" exclaimed Nayla, her eyes following the falcon's descent.

"An arrow?" asked Slean, perplexed by who would do this and if it was indeed an arrow. He could not think of one Talibarrian who was that precise a marksman.

"I do not believe so," answered Nayla, coaxing Cloud on toward the forest. "But I am determined to find out!"

"Was that really necessary, Gran?" Druen groaned in disgust. Her heart was saddened as she watched the beautiful, little raptor tumble from the sullen sky.

"Yep!" answered Ratha. She was as pleased as punch that even with only one good eye and a little help from the forbidden arts, she was still able to down the falcon with a rock. The old woman tucked into her pack the leather sling she used to unleash the projectile on the bird. "An' keep yer damned voice down, girl. The enemy's comin' our way."

"But two of those men are Talibarrians," protested Druen, recognizing their manner of dress. "They're the ones appointed by the council to represent our people."

"Those men ain't any better than the company they keep. An' they certainly don't represent *our* kind. They'd want nothin' more than for our covens ta all but disappear from these lands."

"We can be in big trouble if yer plan fails, Gran," whispered Druen. "They'll have us hung up by our necks if this doesn't work."

"Shut yer mouth!" snarled Ratha, crouching low behind a shrub as Nayla and those in her company neared, their eyes intently searching the forest floor for the downed falcon. "We ain't gonna fail. We've got more than luck on our side this time."

"Well, I ain't gonna stand here an' watch ya do any kinda killin'! I'll mix up batches of potions an' whatnot, but I don't want no part in murderin' people," argued Druen, backing away from her grandmother.

"You're useless! What kinda witch do ya think you're gonna make if you're not even gonna help yer own granny with this task?"

"Helpin' is one thing, killin' is another. I ain't gonna soil my hands with the blood of an innocent person."

"What makes you think they're so innocent? You're jus' makin' excuses. You don't wanna dirty yer hands, period! You jus' don't wanna work, ya lazy dolt," countered Ratha.

"Killin' folks ain't work, it's… murder!"

"Well, you're a genius! You best head back an' leave us ta do the deed 'cause right about now, you're useless ta me," grumbled Ratha, waving Druen away as the sounds of hoof beats grew louder.

"There she is!" exclaimed Nayla, hopping down from her mare. She raced over to the clump of feathers at the base of the tree, but her steps slowed as she came to realize that Tori was dead. The falcon's neck was broken. Her head was twisted back unnaturally; her wings were bent and crumpled beneath a shattered, limp body.

"Oh no, Tori… You poor thing," whispered Nayla, gently picking up the falcon in her trembling hands. "What happened to you?" Cradling the still-warm bird in one arm, she removed the metal vial from its jesses. Inside, a small parchment was rolled up. Her fingers unfurled the note as she read aloud the first few words, "Nayla: Be careful. There is danger as you head west…"

"A warning?" queried Lando, listening intently.

"Yes, from Arerys."

"The warnin' comes too late!"

As Nayla glanced up, her eyes were greeted by the sight of Lando, Slean and Merdak perched on their mounts, their hands help up high in surrender as a dozen men encircled them with spears thrust to their chests. The ominous creak of a bow being drawn caused Nayla's eyes to dart to her left.

A wizened, old hag stepped out from the shadows. She motioned one of her henchmen to keep his arrow trained on Nayla as she snarled her orders, "If you want yer friend ta live, you won't try anythin' stupid. An' if these men you're travellin' with don't wanna see ya killed, they'll do 'xactly what they're told."

"Do you know who you're accostin', ya fool?" snapped Slean, angrily pushing aside the tip of the spear pressed against his rib as he dismounted from his steed. His voice and words lost all shred of civility, slipping back into the manner most Talibarrians spoke as he confronted the haggard, stooped woman. "This is Princess Nayla of Wyndwood you're aimin' that arrow at. And Merdak an' I were appointed by the new government ta stop hooligans like you, ignerant folks that give the people of Talibarr a bad name, from takin' such action."

"I ain't no fool! I know 'xactly who that arrow's pointin' at. An' I'll give ya more than jus' a bad name ta remember me by!" scoffed Ratha. With a wave of her hand, one of her minions rammed the rusted spear through Slean's chest.

Groaning in agony, Slean's legs instantly buckled beneath him as his assailant forcefully wrenched his bloodied spear free. In a state of absolute panic, Merdak's heels sank into his horse's flanks. Horse and rider bolted away, abandoning Nayla and Lando, but his flight was short lived. A spear flew through the air to meet its mark in his back. Merdak tumbled from the saddle, crashing to the forest floor.

"So, you plan to kill us?" determined Lando, his eyes quickly scanning their surroundings for something – anything, he could use against these unexpected foes.

Lando knew he'd never be able to draw his sword faster than the man holding the bow can be stopped. The arrow would be unleashed on Nayla in a blink of an eye. And the tips of these many spears pressed up against his chest and back now dashed any hopes that she would be coming to his rescue.

"How can you be 'xpected ta deliver a message fer me if you're dead?" grunted Ratha, keeping a respectable distance from this woman warrior of legend.

"You want me to deliver a message to her husband? To Arerys Wingfield?" questioned Lando.

"If it gets the Wizards' attention, then the Elf Prince will do nicely," snarled Ratha, motioning one of her men to bind Nayla's hands together. "Krygor, tie her up!"

Just as the man was about to wrap the rope around her wrists, Nayla attacked. Seizing this rope, she wound it about Krygor's neck, pulling him against her body as a human shield as Ratha's crony with the bow struggled to take aim at her.

"If yer friend's life means nothin' to ya, then you go right ahead, missy," growled Ratha, daring Nayla to act as she nodded at the men encircling Lando to do her bidding.

To Nayla's horror, the largest Talibarrian seized Lando, yanking him down from his horse. As Lando fell to the ground, the men armed with spears spun their weapons about, slamming the butt end of the staff against Lando's chest, stomach and face as the burly Talibarrian slammed his boot down on his victim's throat. He pinned the knight to the ground as his comrades repeatedly struck Lando, waiting eagerly for the order to turn the sharp end of the spear on him.

"So what's it gonna be? Are ya gonna cooperate, or should I tell my men ta finish him off?"

"*Stop!*" pleaded Nayla, releasing the man she held in a strangling hold with his own rope. She watched helplessly as Lando groaned in pain, unable to fend off the blows as he struggled to pry off the boot pressing down on his throat. "I will cooperate. Please, let him go!"

Ratha's henchmen reluctantly ceased their attack, but their spears remained poised over Lando's body as they waited for orders to skewer him.

Nayla held forth her wrists to be tied together. Just as the sputtering, gagging man was about to restrain her once more, tying her wrists together, Ratha snarled in anger at her crony. "Ya fool, Krygor! Don't ya know this ain't no ordinary prisoner we have here. This is the one they call the warrior maiden of Orien. She knows a-hundred-an'-one ways ta kill a man, an' that's just with her bare hands. You best tie 'em behind her back unless you have a death wish."

"Not wishin' ta die any time soon, Ratha," grunted the man, yanking Nayla's hands behind her back. She winced in pain as Krygor wound the coarse rope around her wrists, pulling it hard to secure the knot.

"Please, I beg of you, take me instead," offered Lando, fearing the worst for Nayla. "Set her free."

"Such a grand an' noble gesture! But ferget it!"

"What difference does it make so long as you have a prisoner?" questioned Lando, attempting to negotiate for Nayla's freedom.

"It makes a big diff'rence. So, unless you're tellin' me you're a king – a powerful an' wealthy man who's worth somethin' ta me, then shut your gob!" demanded Ratha, eyeing the large Cedonan. "So, are ya a king?"

"I am not a king."

"Are ya at least a prince?" asked the old woman, assessing this man's potential worth.

"No, I am not," confessed Lando. "I am but a humble knight from my king's court in Land's End, Cedona, but I have close friends, many of them in places of power."

"If you ain't a king or even a measly prince, yer life ain't worth much ta me," scoffed Ratha.

"But I have some influence with those in power," reasoned Lando.

"Well that's a bloody good thing then, 'cause you're gonna use yer *influence* ta keep this woman alive," stated the hag, motioning for one of her minions to deliver the knight's horse back to him.

"What must I do?" asked Lando, accepting his horse's reins.

"You'll deliver this message," instructed Ratha, watching as Lando gingerly raised his aching body back into the saddle while the many spears still remained fixed on him.

"A message?"

"You're ta tell Prince Arerys ta summon the four Wizards. Tell 'em that if this woman's life means anythin' to them, they'll be up fer some tradin' with me."

"What is it you wish to trade with them?" questioned Lando, as he wiped the warm trickle of blood seeping from the corner of his mouth with the back of his hand.

"Tell 'em one life set free in exchange fer four magical, crystal orbs. Oh yeah, an' tell those Wizards I'll be needin' those crystals before the next full moon. Now be off! If you're lucky, maybe you'll run inta yer friends before nightfall."

Before Lando could ask the old woman what she meant by encountering his friends, one of the men smacked his horse's rump, sending the stallion bolting into the forest. Lando pulled hard on the reins, wheeling his mount about. Glancing back, the hag and her cronies were gone, and so too, was Nayla.

hunting evil

"Even a dragon would be easier to kill than this monster," groaned Cullen, growing weary as he endured this long pursuit.

"How would you know?" queried Markus. "You have never pitted your skills against such a creature."

"True. However, I have heard tales of yore; great adventures from bygone days when knights of old battled against these ancient beasts."

"And exactly how did these knights succeed in killing a dragon?" questioned Lindras, listening with interest.

"From all accounts I have heard, it was a matter of plucking up enough courage to confront these magnificent, but deadly, creatures head-on; waiting for the most opportune moment to strike. It would take plunging a mighty sword between the ventral plates of scales, deep into the beast's body," explained Cullen, his words spoken with confidence.

"Indeed! Timing is crucial," agreed the Wizard. "The brave soul must wait until the dragon rears up, drawing its head back to attack or to fill its lungs with air. At this precise moment, these scales stretch apart to expose the vulnerable underside. A perfectly placed blade to pierce its heart is what it takes to kill a dragon."

"See… That is what I said," stated Cullen. "A dragon would be easier to kill than this beast we hunt now."

"That is not necessarily true, Captain Bristow," countered Arerys. "Just like the dragon, the beast we seek has a weakness in its armour, so to speak. It is a matter of exploiting this weakness to our advantage."

"Where a dragon will recoil to attack, you must admit, they are not reputed to be especially swift in doing so," countered Cullen. "As for the beast we hunt now, it has demonstrated incredible speed, agility and cunning unsurpassed by any dragon I have ever heard of, Tor Airshorn's *pet* included. With this in mind, I stand by what I said."

"For now, we must be patient," said Kal-lel. "No matter how difficult or easy, we must hunt that creature down before others are hurt or killed."

"We have been tracking the animal all day," groaned Cullen, shifting about on his saddle to ease the pressure off his back. Rolling his stiff shoulders, he turned to address the Wizard. "I was so sure with you by our side, that foul creature would be dead by now."

"If we had encountered the animal, then yes, in all likelihood, it would be very dead," grunted Lindras, urging Tempest on. His grey stallion snorted loudly, tossing its luxuriant mane and tail as black as coal as though ordering the other horses to follow. "But of course, there is no need to remind you this is no ordinary creature we are hunting. I agree wholeheartedly with King Kal-lel, a measure of patience is required at this time, Captain."

"Well, this beast is testing my patience," grumbled Cullen. "If I did not know better, I would say that animal has us going in circles."

"That is because we are," stated Joval, studying the paw prints set in the earth before them. "It appears that while we believed we had been tracking *it*, the beast had been following *us*. It has been circling around us, moving in the shadows of this forest."

"That animal has been *following* us?" gulped Cullen, his anxious eyes widening in fear.

"I agree with Joval, however, it is more accurate to say the beast has been *stalking* us," responded Arerys, his fingers pressing lightly to test the freshness of the spoor Joval had pointed out.

"Bloody hell!" gasped Cullen, his frightened eyes nervously darting about the forest as the sun's waning light cast longer, deeper shadows across the lands. "For how long has it been lurking about?"

"I would say, it has been on our trail since shortly after we departed from its lair where we had rescued King Sebastian," replied Joval, glancing over to the west from where they had come.

Staring at the scattering of paw prints littering the forest floor, Cullen was baffled by the Elf's claim.

"How can you even tell? These tracks go every which way," countered Cullen.

"It is obvious this particular part of the valley is where the beast most often frequents," replied Lindras. "These paw prints you see are many and were made a few days to a few hours ago, if that."

"Are you now telling me the monster is skulking about very near to us?" whispered Cullen.

"For the longest time, it would appear the beast has discreetly maintained a respectable distance from us, enough so we could not easily detect its movements," warned Kal-lel, his eyes piercing the deepening shadows. "By the freshness of these tracks, the creature could be even closer than we suspect."

Without the Elf-kind's keen sense of sight and hearing, it caused both Markus and Cullen to draw their swords in case the creature attacked.

"I do not like the sounds of this," groaned Cullen, clutching his sword tightly once he was able to unsheathe it from the scabbard. "Why did you not warn us earlier?"

"Why bother sounding the alarm when there is nothing to be alarmed about?" replied Kal-lel. "At least, not yet."

"I mean no disrespect, Your Highness, but did I not hear you correctly? I could have sworn I heard you and Master Stonecroft both state that the creature has been on *our* trail, hunting us?"

"Indeed we did. Arerys confirmed what we suspected," confessed Kal-lel, nodding to the Captain.

"Well, personally, I find this *very* alarming," snapped Cullen.

"And as I said before, why cause undue stress and worry when it is not necessary? That animal follows, but the distance between us is such that there is no need for immediate concern."

"Perhaps not at this very moment," conceded Markus, trusting Kal-lel enough to lower the tip of his sword as he relaxed for the time being.

Stubbornly brandishing his sword, Cullen made it clear to all he was not about to let his guard down, "The moment can change swiftly. I will not chance an encounter with that beast while my sword idly waits in its scabbard. I prefer to be ready for an attack."

"There is nothing wrong with being prepared," responded Lindras. "Just keep in mind, there is no point in becoming so utterly consumed with dread and worry that one is unable to react if and when that time should come."

"Who said I was worried?" grunted Cullen, putting on a brave face. "Wary, yes! But *worried*? I have no reason to be, being that I am quite prepared."

"Wary or not, I assume we shall continue on well into the night, until the beast is captured and killed?" determined Markus, looking to Lindras for an answer.

"We all agreed the beast is neither diurnal nor crepuscular; that it is a creature of the night. As it prefers to attack under the cover of darkness, I suggest we pander to its nocturnal habits," suggested Lindras.

"Huh? Di-urinal and crespuscu- what?" grumbled Cullen. Unfamiliar with these terms, he stared quizzically at the Wizard.

"This animal shuns the daylight and even avoids the twilight hours of dusk and dawn, preferring to move at night," explained the Wizard. Attempting to ignore the fact this mortal had completely bastardized the proper pronunciation of these words; Lindras did not bother to correct the Captain.

"Ah, yes!" exclaimed Cullen, nodding in acknowledgement. He pretended he understood all along, repeating these unusual words to commit them to memory should he ever feel a need to impress his peers or the ladies with his eclectic and ever-expanding vocabulary. Unwilling to ask the Wizard to pronounce them again, he mouthed the words beneath his breath as best as he could remember, "Di-ur-in-al and cre-pusc… crepuscu… crepusculard."

"Let the beast come, I say," responded Lindras, after giving their situation much thought. "We shall set up camp."

"So we shall rest for the evening?" questioned Cullen, hoping for a reprieve from this arduous search that had taken them through much of the Valley of Shadows.

"You can rest if you choose to do so, Captain Bristow, but the rest of us will be watching and waiting for the creature to make its move," replied Lindras.

"Are you telling me you actually *want* that creature to hunt us down?" gasped Cullen.

"Yes and no," answered the Wizard. "Yes, we want it to come to us, but if we are prepared, we shall be the ones doing the hunting."

"Besides, there is no point in wandering aimlessly in circles, each following the other, until chance or accident allows us to cross paths," explained Arerys. "That can prove disastrous."

"It is better to allow the beast to come," said Kal-lel. "After all, it is apparent the creature has been stalking us. As such, at least to some extent, we can control this encounter and act accordingly in our favour."

"So we set up camp here?" asked Markus, glancing up to the sullen, twilight sky. He could feel a damp chill in the air, a sure sign of impending rain, as the sun's waning light dissolved from the sky.

"No, let us move on; set up by the lake," recommended Lindras, his finger pointing northward through the stand of trees to the small body of water at the base of Mount Hope.

"Why there?" questioned Cullen, puzzled by the Wizard's choice of location. "The sun has all but disappeared and night shall soon steal away with what little light there is. What is wrong with this place?"

"If this creature is some monstrosity of a cat, I do not know of one feline that is fond of water," answered the Wizard, his words matter-of-fact. "Most do not even like getting their paws wet."

"Oh... I see," said Cullen, nodding in approval. Considering Lindras' words, if the creature did choose to mount an attack, if the situation warranted it, he could at least retreat into the lake. In all likelihood, if the Wizard was correct in his thinking, the beast would not follow and therefore, he'd be safe. "Then, to this lake it is."

Cautiously weaving their way through the now-dark forest, they journeyed on toward the small body of water pooling at the foot of Mount Hope.

"How much further is this lake?" queried Cullen, his eyes staring into the deepening shadows of the forest made all the darker by the thick accumulation of clouds that prevented the light of the moon and the stars from shining through. "I cannot see a bloody thing!"

"Any further and both you and your horse will be standing *in* the lake," warned Arerys, as RainDance came to a stop near the water's edge.

Cullen abruptly reined his steed in as he questioned Arerys. "What do you speak of? I see no water."

"Trust me, Captain Bristow, the lake is there," assured Arerys. Snapping off a small twig from an overhanging branch, he tossed the bit of vegetation just past the mortal. It landed with a small, but audible splash only a few feet in front of where Cullen brought his horse to a stop.

"I believe that even if the moon was full and shining down upon us, I doubt that you would be able to see the lake adequately," stated Kal-lel.

"That is odd. How can that be so?" queried Cullen, trying to make sense of this Elf's words.

"By daylight, you would see what my father means. Not only is it a very deep lake, the water is very murky," explained Arerys. "With all the peat and pine needles that has gathered through the ages, steeping in its depth, it is darker than a pot of day-old tea."

"Good thing you warned me, my lord," said Cullen, bowing in appreciation as he cringed in disgust on realizing what could have happened. "Had you not said anything, I would not have thought twice about filling my water flask in this lake."

As Cullen was about to dismount, Joval cautioned him, "Be careful where you tread, Captain."

Glancing down, his mortal eyes could barely make out the fresh spoor marring the silty shore of this lake.

Large, muddy paw prints revealed they were on the right track and Joval was correct in his concern the creature had circled around them yet again. Amongst the myriad of prints, the freshest set that led them to the lake suddenly veered to the west.

"The beast is close to here," determined Joval, after carefully examining the tracks.

"Wonderful!" exclaimed Lindras, dismounting from Tempest. "This little clearing should do quite nicely for the night."

"If the creature is lurking that close to us, why has it not attacked?" questioned Cullen, discreetly maneuvering between Joval and Markus so he was less vulnerable. "It seemed to do so without provocation before. Why would it hesitate now?"

"My thinking is, the beast is taking the time to carefully select its next victim," responded Markus.

"You think so?" asked Cullen, looking momentarily aghast.

"No doubt," replied Markus, speaking with all certainty. "In all likelihood, the beast is setting its sights on the one in our midst with the leanest, most tender young meat to sate its appetite."

Cullen was silent for a moment as he scrutinized those in his company, including the Elven warriors. The youngest appeared to be several years younger than him, but in reality, this warrior had existed for well over four centuries longer. Cullen then scowled in resentment as it finally dawned on him that being the youngest in the group, Markus had actually singled him out as the beast's next meal. "Hey, you were speaking of me! You want that animal to kill me!"

With this moment of unexpected levity at Cullen's expense, all burst out laughing; even the staid King of Wyndwood.

"I was speaking in jest," chuckled Markus. "And I would never wish for that beast to kill you, Captain Bristow. Slightly maim and lightly maul you perhaps, but not actually *kill*."

The corner of Cullen's lips curled up in a smirk of a cynical grin as he laughed mockingly, "Har, Har! You slay me with your wit, Your Highness."

"Better me than that beast," quipped Markus. "At least, if I were to slay you, it would be much less painful than being ripped apart."

"There will be time for chatter later," said Lindras. "We best use this time to prepare for our vigil."

"Perhaps we should build a fire – a great, big bonfire," suggested Cullen, hoping the light and the flames would ward off the beast than to entice it over to investigate their presence.

"A brilliant idea, Captain," agreed Kal-lel. "If the idea is to draw the creature to us, we should make our presence abundantly known."

"Brilliant indeed," grumbled Cullen, his heart sinking with the prospects of inviting a deadly encounter.

The hours passed slowly as the men waited, huddled around the campfire under a foreboding night sky. With the very real prospect the beast was watching them, waiting for an opportune chance to attack, the men sat in a circle. Joval and the Elven warriors positioned themselves on the outermost ring. Their backs were turned to the fire as they faced the darkness surrounding them. Speaking in whispers, the Elves listened and watched, but the usual ambient sounds of the forest at night were nonexistent.

It was unnaturally quiet. There were no crickets chirping, no frogs chorusing, not even owls winging their way through the darkness on the hunt for a nocturnal meal. There was only a heavy, stifling quiet that smothered the deep forest, spreading out to the lake and beyond.

Icy rain suddenly pelted down from the sky to patter loudly, rolling off the leaves high in the treetops. Gathering to form fat droplets that slapped down on the earth, some drops popped and sizzled, landing on the burning wood to break this unsettling silence.

"Just our luck! So much for a warm, inviting fire," groaned Cullen, wincing as a chilling raindrop hit him square in the eye. He glanced up as thunder boomed, echoing through the night. "It is bad enough waiting for the beast to make its move, now it will be all the more miserable having to endure this cold rain."

"Do not be distracted by the weather, Captain," warned Arerys. "Keep your eyes fixed on the forest around us."

"Look on the positive side, Captain Bristow," urged the Wizard, shrugging off the rain as he resigned to the fact his pipe was useless in this weather; "better wet than dead!"

"We better not end up wet *and* dead," sulked Cullen, using the back of his hand to wipe away the rain from his face as the heavens opened up to unleash a deluge upon them.

The torrential rain effectively extinguished the fire, creating heavy, choking gray smoke in place of flames. Instead of rising up in a billowy column to dissipate into the night sky, this smoke spread out low to the ground, pushed down by the cold air and the driving rain. Thick and stifling, it made it all the more difficult to see in the darkness, even for the Elves.

"I have a very bad feeling about this," whispered Markus, rising up onto his feet in a bid to stand above this blanket of suffocating smoke rolling along close to the earth before being pummelled away by the lashing rain.

"Do you see or hear something? Is something out there?" Cullen whispered back to Markus, his burning, watery eyes staring into the curtain of rain beating down on them.

"I said I *felt*, not I saw or heard something," corrected Markus, straining to listen above the sounds of the raindrops slapping against the wet leaves and muddy puddles. "Something is not right…"

"Oh," mumbled Cullen, as he nodded in understanding. He discreetly shuffled over to position himself between the Wizard and the Elf King; the two people in their group the Captain believed would be most able to detect the creature before the others. In his mind, they, too, were also the most likely ones to be able to fend off an attack, thereby guaranteeing his safety.

"Just keep your wits about you," advised Kal-lel, drawing his sword. "The beast could be anywhere."

"Master Weatherstone," whispered Cullen, his eyes trying desperately to focus in this consuming darkness.

"Yes," replied the Wizard.

"If the creature attacks, you were saying that only the blade tainted with the blood of an Elf can kill the beast."

"So I did. If, and when, the animal shows itself, I shall lance my hand, as will the Elves, to draw blood. That is how we shall kill the creature."

"But you are not an Elf," pointed out Cullen.

"I know that, but being a Wizard, I am confident my blood will be just as lethal to the beast."

"That is all fine and dandy, but if that is the case, King Markus and I are *not* Elves. What are we to do? Give one of you a poke with our swords to *borrow* some blood?"

"I suggest the two of you stay clear of danger. Allow us to finish off the beast," recommended Lindras.

"Now that is bloody brilliant plan, Wizard!" exclaimed Cullen.

"Hush… Keep your voice down," urged Joval. "We are trying to listen for the creature."

"My apologies," whispered Cullen, pressing a finger to his lips as he motioned the warriors for quiet, even as they stood silent and motionless.

For the longest moment, there was an unnerving silence hanging heavy in the air. Only the occasional rustling of branches pushed about by the wind and the steady patter of rain falling, punctuated by the horses snorting nervously served to set everyone on edge.

"Master Weatherstone," whispered Cullen, his eyes glancing about uneasily, searching the consuming darkness.

"What now, Captain Bristow?" grumbled the Wizard, leaning wearily against his staff as the rain served to dampen everyone's spirits.

"That crystal orb atop your staff; is it good for anything else other than destroying things?" questioned the mortal.

"It is good for a great many things. Why do you ask?"

"If you have not noticed, Wizard, it is bloody dark here. Perhaps you and the Elves can see adequately in these dreadful conditions, but I sure as hell cannot."

"Scared of the dark, are you?"

"I am *not scared* of the dark. I am *concerned* that creature will sneak up on me. I would not even see it until it has taken a bite from my backside. If it is possible, a little light would be useful about now."

"Oh, I understand!" responded Lindras. He held forth the staff he had been leaning against. "I can shed some light on this situation, and then some."

Overhearing this conversation, Markus knew he had to intervene. Lindras preferred to reason with mankind than to intimidate and manipulate these beings through magic, but there were apparent consequences for this. His reluctance to master his skills had led to near disasters for Markus and his friends on more than one occasion when the Wizard was forced to use his powers.

"If your life means anything to you, do not encourage Lindras to use his magic," cautioned Markus, whispering into Cullen's ear.

Cullen nodded in understanding as he reasoned with Markus, "I am not asking for a demonstration of his magical prowess. I am only asking for a bit of light."

"You were warned…" whispered Markus, turning away.

"Be prepared to bask in the glory of my powers," announced Lindras, pushing up his sopping wet sleeves to make ready for this task.

"Whoa! Hold on there, old chap! The only thing I want to bask in is a little light, just enough to see."

"As you wish, young sir!"

Holding forth the crystal orb, with a whispering of an ancient incantation and a grand flourish of his hand, Lindras worked his magic. Instead of a flicker of light that gently swelled to steadily push back the darkness, a brilliant flash exploded from the magical sphere, washing everyone and everything in a dazzling white light.

All, with the exception of Cullen, anticipated the outcome of the Wizard's magic. They had already averted their eyes from this radiant show of light.

"Bugger me!" groaned Cullen, squeezing his eyes shut as blobs and smears of phantom lights branding his retinas danced before them. "I can't see! You've bloody well blinded me!"

"Oh, poppycock! I did no such thing!" dismissed Lindras, holding his staff on high to illuminate their drenched surroundings. "If anything, you did this to yourself! I did not tell you to look directly at my crystal."

"Neither did you warn me to look away!" snapped Cullen, his left hand frantically rubbing his eyes as the other one brandishing his sword haphazardly flailed about, forcing Lindras and Kal-lel to leap out of the way.

"I did not feel there was a need to warn you of the obvious, after all, it is apparent this crystal is no candle and I did say *bask!*" grunted Lindras, the magical orb now glowing steadily.

"Before you impale someone, just calm down, Captain Bristow," urged Kal-lel, pushing the tip of Cullen's weapon away with his own sword. "You are not blind. Your vision is merely hampered from the sudden show of light in this darkness. Your sight will adjust to normal in time."

"Oh, come now, Your Highness, there is no need to lie to me. My eyes are ruined – burned to oblivion by the Wizard's magic!"

"If they were truly burned, I would be able to heal them quite easily," countered Kal-lel.

"Then do something about this," groaned Cullen, his hand waving in front of him to feel his way toward the high Elf.

"Trust my father," urged Arerys. "There is nothing that needs to be done. Your eyes will adjust in its own time."

"You are just trying to pacify me; to trivialize the severity of my injury!" groaned Cullen, his eyes blinking hard as they fought to see through the blur of light and shadow. "I am blind! Blind as a bat, I tell you!"

"Contrary to popular belief, bats are not blind," disputed Joval, his words terse.

"Who cares? The point is, I cannot see and none of you want to admit I am blind. You can tell me! I will take it like a man," argued Cullen. Everywhere he turned his head, whether his eyes were opened or closed, the phantom blobs of light danced before him, stubbornly refusing to disappear.

"For a *man and a knight*, you are whining like a *child*," admonished Markus. "It is no different than staring up into the dark night when a great flash of lightning breaks across the sky."

"And stop rubbing your eyes," advised Arerys. "It will do you no good, except to worsen your condition."

"I am not rubbing them," grumbled Cullen. "I am attempting to wipe the rain from my face."

"Well, you might as well desist, unless your efforts can make the rain stop falling down completely," countered Markus, nimbly side-stepping from the captain's sword as Cullen abruptly turned to face the direction of his voice.

"For pity's sake, Captain Bristow, either stand still or sit down before you hurt someone," ordered Joval, growing impatient with Cullen as he attempted to scrutinize the forest for approaching danger.

The sudden roll of thunder and a brilliant flash of lightning directly overhead rattled the trees and shook the earth beneath them. Cullen panicked, jumping with a start. His confusion was made worse by not being able to see and the growing fear the creature was closing in. Together, they wreaked havoc on his frayed nerves.

Again, just as another brilliant bolt of lightning illuminated the sky, this abrupt surge of energy exploding from the heavens struck a tree near to their camp. A large branch came crashing down to the ground with the rolling crescendo of thunder.

Cullen yelped with fright. Instinctively bolting away from the fearsome noise to hide behind one of his comrades, he tripped instead. Blindly stumbling forward, Cullen fell hard against the Wizard as Lindras' eyes were momentarily drawn to the smoldering tree damaged by lightning. Both tumbled to the ground, the glow of the Wizard's orb fading as the staff landed in a muddy puddle.

In the confusion, all eyes glanced over at the mortal and Wizard floundering about in the puddle. Just as Lindras was about to push Cullen off of his body, he suddenly thrust the mortal into the puddle once again. The Wizard lunged forward to reclaim his staff as the beast landed smack-dab in the center of their circle.

With incredible speed, the huge creature pounced down from an overhead tree, charging straight for Lindras and Cullen. Instead of going for either one of the men, the animal was instantly drawn to the Wizard's staff, snatching it up from the ground into its mouth.

With Cullen unable to see the immediate danger, Lindras seized him, yanking him down to shove his face into the puddle. Ducking low to the ground, the tip of the animal's spike-studded tail lashed out at them, skimming dangerously close over their bodies.

"Stay down!" shouted Lindras, scrambling to reclaim his staff from the creature's mouth.

Reacting quickly, the nearest Elven warrior dove forward, slashing the creature under its chin with his sword tainted by his own blood. Instead of plunging into the beast's throat, the blade missed. It cut into a tough, leather strap holding its armour in place to painfully nick the creature's skin, near to the unprotected part of the beast's neck.

The inflicted wound, poisoned by Elven blood caused the beast to unleash a blood-curdling roar. Dropping the staff, it bolted into the forest as Cullen blindly scrambled to upright himself. Wiping the mud from his eyes, he was startled to discover he had inadvertently placed himself between the creature and the many Elven arrows aimed at it.

"I told you to stay down!" snapped Lindras, snatching his staff from the ground as he admonished the Captain.

"Bloody hell! That beast could have killed me!" declared Cullen, the rain coursing down his face to wash away the mud.

"And we would have killed *it*, if you had not gotten in our way!" retorted Arerys, lowering his bow as the creature vanished into the deep shadows.

"In the way? The beast was coming for me!" argued Cullen, still trembling after the hair-raising encounter.

"It was not interested in you, Captain Bristow," responded Kallel, motioning his men to lower their weapons as Markus hoisted the Wizard back onto his feet.

"Well then, good for me, but unlucky for you, old man," said Cullen, shaking his head in pity at the Wizard.

"Clearly, it was after my staff," grunted Lindras, wiping the orb clean of mud to allow its light to shine brightly once more.

"What are you speaking of?" sniffed Cullen, in an incredulous tone. "What would an animal do with a magical staff? It is not as though it can eat it or speak to conjure up magic with an incantation."

"That is so," agreed Arerys. "It appears that whomever called up this beast is undoubtedly the one hoping to steal away with the staff and the crystal orb set upon it."

"What do we do now?" questioned Markus.

"I strongly recommend we aggressively pursue the creature," suggested Joval. "Set on it before it can double back. Chase it down before it can think on its next move."

"It is not good enough to pursue the beast," stated Lindras. "Instead, let us drive it on with purpose."

"Directly into a trap!" exclaimed Markus, knowing that look in the Wizard's eyes.

"Precisely," nodded Lindras. "We know how it moves, how it prefers to attack and more specifically, what it is now after. I say we take control and deliver the creature exactly to where we want it."

"I know the perfect place to devise such a trap and the perfect way to catch the beast," stated Joval.

"So it is time to take control of the situation than to allow the situation to control us," decided Arerys.

"Most definitely it is time… and time for a little blood-letting," responded Kal-lel, nodding to his son.

"The creature's blood, I hope," prayed Cullen, shivering as his drenched raiment clung to his cold, clammy skin.

"I am speaking of my blood," stated Kal-lel, unsheathing his dagger to lance his hand. "We now know for certain what Elven blood can do to that creature. A little bit of blood from a high Elf can tip many arrows. Even if a single, blood-tainted arrow does not pierce the beast's heart, it will definitely slow it down – enough that we will be able to kill it this time."

"Then let us prepare the trap and arm ourselves accordingly," suggested Lindras. "Before morning comes, the beast will be dead."

With dawn but a few hours away, Lindras knew the creature would mount another attack, if given the chance, before retreating to its lair or another hiding place. In a bold and calculated move, they would force the creature to react, pushing it relentlessly so it would not even have the opportunity to consider striking again, let alone retreat to find sanctuary.

Maneuvering swiftly through the dark forest, Lindras directed the Elven warriors to go wide, intercepting the animal to cut it off from its intended escape route in an attempt to herd it into a narrow ravine. Instead of advancing silently, they marched in noisy synchrony to make their presence abundantly known. Their swords hammered rhythmically on their shields as they turned the beast away, driving it on.

Whereas the animal's human prey had always fled, tiring easily, these Elves moved assiduously. They pursued the creature with dogged determination. With greater stamina than the beast possessed, the Elves swiftly closed in, pressing in on it.

Growing weary with being chased, but with no time to rest, the animal was forced to move, plodding through the forest in a bid to place as much distance between it and these persistent beings that had actually succeeded in inflicting it with pain. And though this pain was fleeting, the beast was now startled. There was mounting confusion as the growing din amplifying off the mountain slope to make it sound as though a small army was in direct pursuit, forced the creature to move on. Instinctively following the natural contours of the land, it headed east in hopes of finding sanctuary in a ravine. Deep and narrow, it would provide shelter from the intense glare of the impending sun that threatened to show its face in another hour or two.

"Are you almost done down there?" hollered Cullen, slapping his arms and stomping his feet to drive off the biting chill brought on by the driving rain that refused to relent. From this high vantage point, he could see Markus, Kal-lel and Arerys as they raced to help Joval create a system of traps needed to contain and kill the beast.

"We better be!" responded Joval, hearing the distant drumming of swords against shields heading their way.

He instructed the others to hastily scatter a generous layer of leaves over the ground. Raised in the east and familiar with the Kagai Warriors' method of warfare, this Elf employed the same type of traps used by the legendary warriors to ambush their enemy.

"The beast!" hollered Cullen, pointing to the northwest as leaves and branches thrashed, trembling in its wake to betray the animal's presence. In the distance, Cullen could not yet see, but could definitely hear the Elves advancing steadily to drive the creature on toward them and their awaiting trap. "It is coming!"

"Shut it!" responded Markus, sliding his index finger across his throat as he motioned for Cullen to stop talking. "And stay where you are. You are not to leave your post. Is that understood, Captain?"

"Yes, yes! I promise not to budge from here," grumbled Cullen.

In his heart, Cullen knew he was assigned to this less-than-prestigious task so the others could work on the trap to ensnare the beast. Though he was given this instruction under the pretense of keeping him safe, Cullen knew they wanted him out of the way. They were destined to revel in the glory of capturing and killing the beast, and for his part, the most Cullen would be able to boast about was that he was able to witness this event.

"They can try, but they will not steal my thunder!" Cullen growled beneath his breath. Determined to be part of this adventure, he took up a coil of rope into his hands, fashioning it into a noose. "I shall snare the beast myself if the chance should arise."

As the drumming on the shields grew louder, Cullen was able to clearly make out the large, dark shape plowing through the shadows just paces in front of Lindras and the Elves as they closed in on the beast. In tireless pursuit, they drove the creature on, funnelling it directly into the ravine.

"Wait for it…" Cullen whispered to himself. His gloved hands tightened around the coil of rope as his eyes strained to focus on the blur of movement rushing through the bushes toward this narrow gully. "Wait for it…"

Just as the beast burst from the forest to flee into the ravine, Lindras and the Elves immediately raised the wooden barrier, sealing off this entrance.

With this loud clatter as the gate went up, the creature whipped about to face its pursuers.

"Watch out!" cried Lindras, as the beast charged straight at them, running full tilt in their direction.

The animal released a squelched, guttural snarl. As it hurled its body toward the gate, its paws flew out before it as the beast slammed down onto its back, hitting the ground hard.

Cullen shouted in jubilation as he yanked on the rope, swiftly wrapping one end around an overhanging tree branch to brace himself against so he could string the animal up by its neck.

"*Woohoo!*" Cullen whooped gleefully as he pulled with all his might to hang the creature. "I've captured the beast!"

Cullen suddenly fell backward as the rope he gripped in his hands abruptly fell slack.

"What the?" Cullen muttered in surprise and bewilderment.

Following the limp line, he scrambled over to the edge of the ravine. Cullen abruptly gasped in fright. The beast had clambered up the wall to come nose to nose with him, roaring so hard Cullen can feel the blast of its hot, rancid breath bellowing into his startled face.

In response, Cullen screamed just as long and as loud at the beast.

They were so close, the heat of their breath mingled, condensing into a fog that dissipated into the cold, night air.

"*DUCK!*" hollered the Wizard, shouting at Cullen to get out of the way.

A brilliant bolt from Lindras' orb exploded forth, missing the beast. Instead, it smashed the wall of the ravine where the creature clung. Too slow to respond, the percussion of the blast propelled Cullen backward as the animal fell with the shower of crumbling earth and rocks, plummeting down to the floor of the ravine.

This thunderous blast sent Cullen flying back, tumbling head over heels down the rise he had been standing on. He yelped, groaning in pain each time bone and muscle smashed against the unyielding rocks as gravity made short work of him. Smacking his head, Cullen landed face first in a cold, fast-flowing stream. A black fog swallowed up his mind and stole away with all of his senses. Not even the chilling slap of the icy water against his face could revive him as the air slowly escaped his lungs, bubbling up to the surface only to be swept away by the current.

Shaking off the shock of the unexpected assault and the falling debris, the beast snarled in rage as its head slipped out of the loose rope that had ensnared its neck. It slowly turned to eye the Wizard and the crystal orb atop his staff as the sphere gradually swelled with light and power.

"Be ready, men!" ordered Lindras, summoning his magic in hopes that it would be set to discharge before the creature made another run at them.

With this order, the warriors who were not supporting the gate immediately drew their swords. Quickly lancing the palm of their hand to smear fresh blood onto the blade, the swords now protruded through the openings in the gate. If the creature chose to attack, there was a definite chance it would be hurt, if not killed on this assault.

The beast's sinewy, powerful body suddenly twisted about to face Joval as the Elf appeared before him, jeering and taunting it to give chase. With an angry snarl, the animal's massive claws sank into the muddy ground as it raced after the Elf.

Joval ran with all his might. His heart was pounding wildly; hammering in his chest as his legs pushed him forward over the slick, rain covered earth. In his ears, he heard a guttural roar erupting from deep inside the beast as it eagerly pursued him. Racing after Joval, its speed and agility allowed the creature to avoid the worst of the muddy earth to bounce off the walls of the ravine as it gave chase.

"*NOW!*" shouted Joval.

At this exact moment, Arerys and Markus yanked on the ropes to spring the trap. Beneath the layer of leaf litter, a multitude of sharp, wooden spikes sprung up from the floor of the ravine to impale the beast.

With impeccable timing, Joval dove over the deadly spikes, just barely clearing this obstacle. He rolled over his shoulder to somersault, landing gracefully on his feet as the beast instinctively gave chase. Undeterred by the spike-festooned floor, the creature leapt up high, its powerful haunches easily launching its body up and over to clear this trap.

Just as the beast became airborne, Kal-lel's sword came down. Slicing through two lengths of rope, his action released spike-studded logs suspended on high. They dropped from opposite directions, swinging down with incredible speed. Markus and Arerys automatically ducked, dropping low to the ground as the two logs passed over them to bite down on the monster.

As fate would have it, the log falling toward the beast as it attempted its escape was slightly heavier than the one swinging in to impale the creature from behind. It dropped with greater speed. Just as the beast twisted about in the air to avoid colliding with this weapon, one of the spikes tore into its neck. With a horrific bellow of pain, the animal was forcibly thrown against the ravine wall, just missing the other log as it crashed down, colliding together with the heavier one.

"Quickly! Before it attacks again," ordered Arerys, lancing his palm with the keen edge of his sword to smear fresh blood on the tip of the blade.

He charged toward the wounded creature as the animal struggled to its feet. Where one of the pointed spikes on the log had not only torn off the leather and steel armour protecting its chest, it stabbed through to tear into skin and flesh, onward to smash the collarbone, breaking and dislocating it.

The beast snarled in rage and agony as Arerys approached, brandishing his sword as he motioned his friend to safety, "Stay behind me, Markus!"

With another angry snarl, the beast shook off the pain. Fragments of shattered bone emitted an unnerving sound as they grated and struck up against each other. Mending rapidly, the clavicle magically realigned as a strange, gray vapour gushed from its wound and a black, blood-like substance oozed forth, stopping as the torn flesh healed together.

Arerys and Markus watched in amazement as the injured skin and flesh miraculously closed, repairing as if by magic.

"Bloody hell! What does that remind you of?" gulped Markus, recalling how the four warlords sent to slay him and those of the Order vented this same noxious steam from their wounds, rather than succumbing to their injuries.

"We have seen this before," whispered Arerys, undaunted by this bizarre sight as he edged closer, his sword poised in his hands.

"Careful now!" warned Kal-lel, as he and Joval raised their bows to take aim as the beast circled around Arerys and Markus.

"Into its heart... just one strike to the heart," Arerys whispered beneath his breath. He pointed the tip of his sword to the creature's chest as he crept ever closer.

The beast suddenly lunged toward Arerys and Markus, but just as it pushed off the ground to leap at them, the rattle of articulated armour running down the tail and terminating with a cluster of razor-sharp spikes whipped about as the animal abruptly veered away. It swerved around Arerys' torso, missing the Elf, but striking Markus in his back.

Markus screamed in pain as the tips of several spikes penetrated through his Elven vest of mail to puncture skin and flesh.

The tail flicked about as the beast spun around once more, yanking these projectiles from Markus' back. He stumbled against Arerys as the Elf caught him by his shoulders.

With a nerve-raking roar, the beast turned tail, fleeing back into the ravine as Kal-lel's arrow ricocheted off its armoured head, tearing through the tip of its left ear.

Infuriated by this assault, the creature raced through the narrow gully. It charged straight toward Lindras and the Elven warriors still manning the gate.

"Lindras! It is coming your way!" Arerys hollered in warning as he steadied Markus on his feet.

"Brace your selves, men!" shouted Lindras, motioning for the Elves to ready for impact as the animal careened around the bend of the ravine in a bid to crash through this wooden barrier. "It must not escape!"

With powerful strides fuelled by desperation, the beast lunged forward. It propelled its entire weight against this gate, but just as it smashed against the barrier, a bolt of energy surged from the crystal orb, striking the animal down.

With a wail of pain, the beast tumbled to the ground, but its rage was such, the Wizard's power briefly stunned it. It did nothing to hamper its movements. Pushing off the wet ground, the creature charged away in the opposite direction.

"Get down!" hollered Joval, hearing the mad raking of claws as the beast doubled back on Arerys and Markus. Yanking on the ropes to erect the spikes set on the ground, he hoped to slow the creature's bid to escape.

The beast sailed over these wooden stakes, leaping onto the logs that still dangled above this trap as Joval hurried to climb the rock wall to cut the ropes. It was his hope the creature would fall, becoming impaled on the sharp stakes below. The animal clambered about to avoid the sharpened branches as these logs swayed and rocked under this frantic scramble to make good its escape.

Kal-lel hastily nocked another blood-tipped arrow onto his bow, raising his weapon to take aim. In a blur of movement, just as Joval's sword sliced through the ropes, the beast attacked Kal-lel. Pouncing down from the collapsing logs, the creature's massive jaws clamped down around Kal-lel's neck and upper torso. Instantly, he could feel and hear the metallic crunch of huge fangs breaking through the links of his mail vest to sink into his body. As the beast's powerful jaws bore down on him, the blood that filled Kal-lel's throat muted his screams of agony.

Arerys and Joval wasted no time. Armed with their bows and swords, they gave chase, charging after the murderous beast.

"Lindras!" hollered Markus, watching in stunned disbelief as the creature darted off into the night with Kal-lel dangling helplessly from its jaws. "Quickly! It's got Kal-lel!"

Dropping the gate, Lindras and the warriors raced through the ravine.

"That way!" shouted Markus, pointing northward as Joval and Arerys disappeared into the forest.

"Fan out, there is a chance the beast will circle around!" ordered Lindras, directing the others on. "Markus, come with me!"

Listening above the sounds of their pounding hearts and the falling rain, the Wizard turned northeast, heading toward Mount Hope. "Quickly, Markus, follow me! I believe the creature will double back around to strike again."

As Joval and Arerys raced through the darkness, they followed the sounds of the beast as it crashed through the forest.

"Faster, Joval!" shouted Arerys, running with all his might.

"It will not get away from us!" vowed Joval, charging ahead of Arerys as his eyes followed a trail of black blood that vapourized into steam, only to be pummelled into the earth with this downpour.

In the distance behind them, Arerys detected the sounds of the warriors spreading out and racing through the forest to aid in this desperate search, but up ahead, there was now a foreboding silence.

Arerys froze. For the briefest instant, he stared through the forest, his eyes piercing the deepest shadows. He listened intently, straining to hear above the thundering of his heart. There was nothing, not even the snapping of twigs under foot or the creature's laboured breaths as it struggled to make off into the darkness with his father.

"We lost them…" gulped Arerys, his heart sinking.

"Look at this! We must follow this trail before it is washed away!" urged Joval, pointing to the traces of blood rising like steam from the forest floor. It was obvious by this evidence that Kal-lel, as wounded as he was, was still able to inflict the beast with injuries of its own.

"I hear it!" announced Lindras, his hand cupping his ear to better discern the noises before them. "It's coming this way."

"Could it be one of the warriors?" questioned Markus, nocking an arrow onto his bow. "Perhaps they got in front of us?"

"Elves can move swiftly, but not that fast," determined the Wizard; "not fast enough to get this far ahead of us. It must be the beast!"

Markus could hear the loud thrashing of leaves and branches. A creature of great size was crashing through the shrubs and weaving through the dark stand of trees, heading directly toward them.

"Whatever you do, Markus, do not miss," whispered Lindras, taking up the staff in both his hands.

As a large, shadowy figure burst out of the darkness before them, Markus let his arrow fly while a burst of energy erupted from Lindras' crystal to strike their quarry down.

"There it is!" shouted Joval, just as a strange show of light flared through the forest. In a small clearing, he spied upon the beast. It lay there, slumped to the ground, perfectly still.

Brandishing his sword, Joval rushed in to kill the creature, but Arerys charged past him, roaring in rage. Holding his sword on high, he attacked the beast with a vengeance. The blade of Arerys' sword repeatedly plunged into the animal wherever its armour had been torn away to expose its body.

There was no whimper of pain, not even the sound of the creature heaving its last, dying breath. Joval knew immediately it had died before Arerys had inflicted his wrath upon it. Grabbing a hold of the Elf Prince, Joval pulled Arerys off to end his assault.

"The beast is dead, Arerys. There is no need for this. You cannot kill what is already dead."

Yanking his sword from the lifeless body, a small movement just beneath the carcass caught Arerys' eyes. It was a balled fist slowly unclenching.

"Help me, Joval, quickly!" ordered Arerys, as he grabbed a hold of the beast by its massive shoulders.

As Arerys pulled and Joval pushed, they managed to roll the carcass off onto its side. From its bloodied chest protruded Kal-lel's sword, still embedded deep in the creature's heart. And pinned beneath this body was Kal-lel, he moaned in pain as he struggled for a breath of air as the weight of the beast was finally lifted from him.

"Father!" gasped Arerys, kneeling by his side to gently cradle his head. Leaning over Kal-lel's face, he shielded him from the pelting rain.

For a moment, Arerys struggled to collect his reeling senses. The shock of seeing his father in this state overwhelmed him with fear and guilt. From Kal-lel's forehead almost all the way to the back of his head, the left half of his scalp was ripped away, hanging by ragged threads of skin. The blood continued to course down his face as a tide of crimson surged with each beat of his heart, spilling from gaping holes on his neck and chest.

Where the weight of the animal bearing down on him and these injuries, the pressure served to slow the loss of blood, but now, the very essence of Kal-lel's life flowed freely, draining from his body even as Joval raced to heal these horrific wounds.

"Arerys, help me!" ordered Joval, his left hand pressing over the tear in Kal-lel's neck that bled profusely.

Instead, Arerys continued to cradle his father's head. Repositioning and smoothing out the torn scalp back onto raw flesh, Arerys' movements were rote.

"Arerys!" shouted Joval, giving him an abrupt shake to release him from the paralyzing hold of this shock. "Tend to the worst of his injuries; the ones nearest to his heart. Do so now!"

Arerys blinked hard, his breath catching in the back of his throat as the harsh reality that his father was terribly wounded struck every nerve in his heart and mind.

"Get to it, Arerys!" ordered Joval, his hand pressing over the horrendous tear to Kal-lel's neck. "Your father is dying as I speak!"

These words finally jolted Arerys into action. He tore off his leather gloves. Quickly placing his left hand over the puncture that gushed blood with each heart beat, Arerys called upon a healing incantation.

Working swiftly, he and Joval used their powers to heal, but even as flesh and skin mended, making Kal-lel appear whole once more, they could sense his life force ebbing away.

"We must get him back to Wyndwood," stated Arerys. "The combined powers of the elders can save him."

"There is no time," argued Joval. "If he is lucky, he will endure until the coming of dusk so he can leave this realm. There is hope he can keep death at bay long enough to enter the Haven."

"I will not rely on luck! It is not his time to leave this realm," snapped Arerys, refusing to accept this outcome. "We must do more. We must do everything we can to save him."

"We have done all we can. There is nothing more we can do for him. Your father's life is no longer in our hands."

"I will not stand by and do nothing!" cried Arerys, positioning his hand over Kal-lel's heart to administer more of his healing powers.

"Listen to me," ordered Joval, placing his hand on Arerys' so he would cease with this desperate display. "We have done all we can, but there is a chance he will be eternally bound to this realm."

"I will not allow fate to decide on his life. He will not be made to leave for the Haven before his time," argued Arerys, pushing Joval's hand away from his.

"And neither is my fate for you to decide, my son…"

"Father!"

"Listen to me, Arerys. I will not last… not even to see the coming of dawn."

"Enough talk. Save your strength to recover," urged Arerys, spreading his cloak over Kal-lel's trembling body. "You will be fine once we get you home."

"I am dying, Arerys. There is no going home… not for me. I have lost too much blood."

"Do not speak these words, father. Do not give up!"

"I am not giving up, Arerys. I am… accepting the… inevitable." Kal-lel struggled to squeeze out these words with each pained breath he drew in. "If I am to die in this realm, I am… ready."

"How can you say this? You must hold on, at least until this evening so you can enter the Haven."

"I have made peace with those I have wronged, and more importantly, I have made peace with myself… I am ready."

"But what of the Haven?"

"Nothing there for me… Better to become one with this realm… for my soul to bind with the energy that flows through our great forest."

"You speak as though you welcome death," whispered Arerys, unable to believe his ears. "You sound as if you want to die."

"I do not want to die, but if death stalks me… I will not run," admitted Kal-lel, drawing another slow, deep breath.

"I am not asking you to *run*; I am asking you to *fight* it!" argued Arerys. "It is as though you have lost all desire to live."

"I had lived my life as I saw fit… I had made amends where necessary… What more can I hope for?"

"This is madness!" denounced Arerys, unwilling to accept his father's words. "Joval, speak some sense to my father. Make him understand."

"I believe you are the one who needs to understand, Arerys," responded Joval. "Your father comprehends perfectly what is going to happen. You are the one unwilling to accept what your father foresees."

"You are not helping me!" snapped Arerys, glaring angrily at Joval.

"No, I am not. I am trying to help *him*. And your refusal to accept what your father already has is not helping him either."

"Leave us!" snarled Arerys. "If you cannot offer words to convince my father to hold off death until he can leave for the Haven, then go!"

"It is not in my nature to say words to appease," stated Joval. "All I can ask is that you give your father the peace of mind he needs."

"Go! Find Lindras!" ordered Arerys, waving Joval off. "The Wizard can help him."

With a curt bow to Arerys, Joval respectfully acknowledged the King as he backed away from the anguished Prince, "Peace be with you, my liege. I will honour your memory, in this realm and in the Haven."

"Arerys… listen to me," whispered Kal-lel, his hand gently squeezing his son's. "Do not be angry with Joval. You cannot begrudge him for accepting what you cannot."

"I am angry with you!" snapped Arerys. "I am angry you will not fight for your life."

"I would fight if I believed I would die leaving matters unfinished and lives undone because of my actions. I can now die in peace knowing I have made amends with the people and issues that truly mattered. It is far more than many can ever hope for."

"I fail to understand…" whispered Arerys.

"At this moment, you *refuse* to understand… In time, you will."

"Lindras can help you," decided Arerys, standing up to retrieve their friend, only to have his father clutch his hand. "Joval will find him."

"The greatest help you can offer me now is to just remain here by my side, Arerys," responded Kal-lel, sighing deeply as though surrendering to his predicament as the rain finally ceased.

With the blinding, powerful jolt erupting from the Wizard's crystal, the ground beneath their feet shook as a massive bulk of weight slammed down on to the ground. They could hear the thrashing of four legs flailing in the bushes as loud, painful snorts reverberated through the night air.

"Quickly, before it can attack!" hollered Lindras, rushing into the thicket where their quarry fell.

Nocking another arrow, Markus charged after Lindras. He readied his bow, drawing back as the Wizard used the end of his staff to push the branches aside for a clear shot.

Lindras and Markus gasped in disbelief. Before them was not the beast, but a horse. Wildly thrashing about on the ground, the frightened stallion convulsed in agony, its muscles involuntarily racked by spasms from the Wizard's power. And next to this horse was its rider. Markus' arrow still protruded high on his chest.

"Oh, my!" exclaimed Lindras, cautiously approaching the downed rider sprawled out next to his incapacitated mount.

"Good God!" gasped Markus. He stared in horror. The shock of recognition seared his heart as he stared at the man's face. "Lando… I killed Lando!"

a change of heart

Throwing down his weapon, Markus dashed over to Lando's body. Dropping to his knees, he pressed an ear to Lando's chest. He could hear the heart beating madly and a slow, deep breath as Lando sucked in the cold, morning air through teeth clenched in pain.

"Alive! Terribly hurt, but Lando is alive!" exclaimed Markus, greatly relieved by this discovery.

"While he is still unconscious, I recommend removing that arrow," suggested Lindras, crouching next to Markus.

"Perhaps you are right, Lindras. I suppose it is better to do so now while he is oblivious to his condition."

Just below Lando's left collarbone, the offending arrow was buried deep. Gripping the shaft as close to the body as he could, Markus eased the projectile out as straight as possible from the entry wound. As the barbed bodkin tipping the arrow hooked, snagging flesh and tissue, it also ripped through a major artery.

As the arrow was pulled free, blood suddenly gushed, surging and pulsating with each beat of Lando's heart.

"Bad idea!" declared Lindras, startled by this abrupt, copious flow of blood. It was apparent his suggestion only served to cause greater damage to Lando's wounded body.

"Good gracious!" groaned Markus, tossing away the arrow as he pressed the palm of his hand directly over the wound in a bid to dam the flow of blood. "He will bleed to death! We need an Elf, Lindras."

"Kal-lel or Arerys can heal this quite easily," determined Lindras, using his staff to upright himself.

"At this point, *any* Elf will do! Now hurry!"

Just as Lindras turned away to seek help, Joval suddenly appeared before them. He had followed the bright flash of light that swelled through the forest when the Wizard executed his magic.

"What luck!" exclaimed Lindras, motioning the Elf to follow. "You will do quite nicely."

"What happened?" queried Joval, rushing forward to aid Markus.

"It is Lando. I shot him with an arrow!" confessed Markus.

"Lando? Why did you shoot him?"

"It was an accident, but never mind that! He is bleeding to death, Joval. Do something! Save him," pleaded Markus, pressing down on the wound.

Without wasting another second, the Elf gently placed his left hand over the most obvious of wounds. Calling upon a healing incantation, immediately, Joval could feel the warm, tingling sensation that is synonymous with skin and flesh on the mend to stop the loss of blood.

"This wound is healed, but he does not wake," assessed Markus, troubled by the results.

"He was hit by only *one* arrow?" questioned Joval, looking doubtful as he searched for other telltale signs of injury.

"Luckily for Lando, it was all I had time for," replied Markus. "Mind you, his horse received a severe jolt from Lindras' orb."

"Perhaps it is Lindras' magic that holds him now," determined Joval, his left hand skimming lightly over Lando's body to locate a disturbance in the flow of energy.

"I do not believe so," responded Lindras, hoping to minimize his role in their friend's misfortune. "If anything, I certainly struck down Lando's horse, but in all likelihood, the poor fellow was injured when he was thrown from the saddle."

Sure enough, as evident by the growing goose egg and the manifestation of heat that concentrated to swell from the back of Lando's head, he was the sorry recipient of a concussion. Undoubtedly, he received this injury when he fell, striking his head on the unforgiving earth.

With a healing hand and a magical incantation, Joval worked quickly to dispel the pressure and bruising within Lando's skull. When he was done, Joval gently lowered Lando's head onto the ground, throwing his cloak over his prostrate body for added warmth.

"Given time, Lando will recover completely," promised Joval.

"Thank goodness, and thank you, Joval," sighed Markus, slumping to the ground in relief as this terrible burden was removed from his shoulders. "It was a bloody good thing you were close by to aid Lando. He is a lucky man."

"I wish I could say the same about Kal-lel," responded Joval, giving his head a dismal shake.

"You found him?" asked Lindras, his eyes brightening with hope.

"Yes. The King had succeeded in killing the beast. Sadly, it was not without great sacrifice. Arerys and I did what we could to heal him, but he had already lost so much blood."

"Are you saying Kal-lel is dying?" gasped Markus, slowly rising up to his feet.

"I would be very surprised if he has not already passed on. Arerys remains by his side as we speak."

"Joval, keep watch over Lando," instructed Lindras. "Markus, come with me!"

"Where are they?" asked Markus, snatching up his bow.

"Not but fifty paces west from where we are now," stated Joval, pointing the way he had come.

"Quickly, Markus, follow me!" ordered Lindras, as he rushed off. "We have not a moment to lose."

As the pale morning sun pushed against the darkness, the first light of day broke upon the lands. Markus and Lindras emerged into the small clearing where Joval had left Arerys and Kal-lel. Here, Elven warriors gathered around their fallen King. They stood in silent reverence, paying respect to Kal-lel.

Pushing their way through this circle of Elves, Markus and Lindras' eyes were greeted by a tragic sight. Kal-lel had died in Arerys' arms. Though he was made whole again by Arerys and Joval's healing powers, it was not enough to keep Kal-lel alive, not even until the coming of dawn.

"Arerys, I am so sorry," lamented Markus, kneeling by his friend's side as he bowed in sorrow and respect to the fallen King.

"As I am, too," sighed Arerys, gently lowering his father's head onto the ground. "I tried to save him… Joval and I both did."

"We know you did everything in your powers to do so," acknowledged Lindras. "However, there are times when our greatest intentions and most skilled efforts lay to waste against the powers of divine forces."

"There was nothing divine about the manner of my father's death! And there was no divine intervention that saw fit to deliver him to the Haven," snapped Arerys. "He was killed by evil; pure, unadulterated evil. The one who conjured up that beast will pay with his life!"

"I know nothing we say will offer you any comfort during this time of sorrow, Arerys. Just know your friends will stand by you in your hour of grief," vowed Markus.

"In twelve hours' time, my father will be interned to this realm for an eternity," said Arerys, struggling to pull his thoughts together. His mind was still reeling; coming to grips with the knowledge that only something of a profound nature would have caused his father to have this change of heart. Whatever it was to give him this *peace of mind,* it was enough to make him give up this fight for his life.

"Since Artel is not here, will you help me to ready my father's body, Markus?"

"Of course, Arerys. In many ways, Kal-lel was like a father to me. Whatever you want, just ask it of me. I will make it so," vowed Markus, bowing his head in respect and to honour this promise.

"For now, allow your warriors to deliver your father's body back to our camp," suggested Lindras. "While they tend to this, you must get word to your brother immediately. Artel must be told."

"Yes," agreed Arerys, his head nodding sadly. "This was not the way Artel would have wanted to become king, but you are right, Lindras. He must be told."

"While you deal with this matter, Markus and I shall take precautions to ensure that beast never returns again," announced Lindras.

"The beast is dead," averred Arerys. Though his heart was overwhelmed with grief, his eyes burned with hate as they glanced over to the carcass that had been pushed aside. "Make no mistake, my father saw to it."

"I intend to make sure that it remains dead," explained the Wizard. "Markus and I shall separate its head from its body. The head will be buried while the body shall be burned at a different location; hence, the two shall never come together again, in this life or another."

"I pray your plan works, Lindras," responded Arerys, making way as warriors delivered a litter to carry Kal-lel's body. "I shall send Captain Bristow to assist you with this onerous task."

"Say… Where is Bristow?" queried Lindras, his eyes glancing about, searching for the Captain. "Normally, his presence is irritatingly obvious."

"I have not seen him since last night, at the beginning of the hunt," noted Markus. "He did not follow you, Arerys?"

"I thought he was with you."

"Perhaps the Captain is still waiting atop the ravine," decided Markus. "After all, I did threaten him with his life if he even thought about leaving his post."

"I hardly think that would have stopped the fool," grunted Lindras.

"Since when has that mortal ever listened to our orders when it came right down to it?"

"Good point," agreed Markus. "He probably buggered off, thinking he can be a hero if he caught the beast on his own."

"Have any of you seen Captain Bristow?" questioned Arerys, addressing his warriors.

"No, my lord," replied one of the Elves, speaking on behalf of the others; "not since last night."

"This is truly bizarre," grumbled Lindras. "Captain Bristow vanishes and then Lando suddenly appears."

"Lando Bayliss? What are you speaking of, Lindras?" questioned Arerys, thoroughly perplexed by this revelation.

"We stumbled upon him, quite by *accident*, just before the break of dawn," explained Lindras. "Joval is with him as we speak."

"And Nayla? Is she with him, too?" asked Arerys, a spark of hope igniting in his troubled heart.

He watched as Markus and Lindras exchanged nervous glances.

"Where is she?" queried Arerys, his eyes suddenly darkened with concern. "Where is Nayla?"

"That is a bloody good question," gulped Markus, remembering now that Lando and Nayla were travelling together.

Cullen moaned, grimacing in pain. He slowly stretched as every bone and muscle in his weary, tortured body seemed to cry out, aching with the slightest movement. Even resting upon this thick, bearskin rug cushioned by a dense carpet of soft, dry moss, his battered body was hurting.

He forced his bleary eyes to open, only to squint at the brilliance seeping through. He blinked hard as the stark light of day stabbed through the shadows, shining through the narrow cracks of this lean-to. These pale sheets of gold served to illuminate every dark nook and cranny of this crude shelter.

How did I get here? Cullen wondered as his eyes glanced about these unfamiliar surroundings. Propping himself up on his elbow, he spied his boots and raiment hanging over a now-cold fire. He lifted the scratchy, wool blanket he had been sleeping beneath as he pondered this deepening mystery. *And how did I get naked?*

He turned with a start as a gentle sigh sounded next to him.

"What the…"

Slowly rolling onto his side, he suddenly realized he had not been sleeping alone. Cullen stared at the bare, milky white shoulder peeking out from beneath this shared blanket while the tantalizing nape of a slender neck peered provocatively through the long, dark wavy tresses.

"Now I know I am dreaming," mumbled Cullen, shaking the sleep from his foggy head as this vision of beauty lying by his side rolled onto her back.

Studying the exquisite features of her serene face as she slept, Cullen decided that if he were to be caught in this compromising position, at least this female was not ugly.

What fair maiden is this? I must be in Darross, thought Cullen; for in his mind there was no way this woman could be Talibarrian. *But if that is so, how did she get here? Come to think of it… Where is here?*

Alarmed and confused by these strange circumstances, Cullen eased his sore body to sit upright in this bed, trying to be as quiet as possible so as not to wake this woman.

"Well now, you're fin'lly awake." She spoke through a stifled yawn as she stretched.

Cullen winced, but not because of pain. This woman's distinct accent made it obvious he had bedded a Talibarrian woman. As beautiful as she was, there was no mistaking this less-than-impeccable use of the common speech.

"If I am not mistaken, I am in Talibarr. Is that correct?"

"Of course, you are. Where else would ya be?" she responded, propping herself up on her elbows.

"So, tell me if I am wrong, my good woman. You are Talibarrian?" queried Cullen, scrutinizing her captivating features.

"You're either a very silly man or ya must've knocked yerself on the head an' loosened somethin' up there," decided this young woman, staring with concern into Cullen's inquisitive, hazel eyes. "Don't ya remember anything?"

"I remember being on a hunt… I recall attempting to snare a horrific beast," responded Cullen, gleaning from his scattered memories to piece together the events leading up to this moment. "I do recollect seeing a brilliant flash of light and taking a terrific tumble, however, I certainly do not remember you, nor do I recall how I got to this place."

"Well then, you can't be all that badly hurt if ya remembered at least that much. I was the one ta get ya here."

"You were?"

"I most certainly did!" Her dewy lips smiled demurely at him.

"And just who are you?" questioned Cullen; suddenly feeling quite vulnerable beneath this maiden's prying eyes. He clutched the blanket, pulling it up high around his neck.

"This ain't fair," groaned his hostess. "This is *my* place so you should be tellin' me who you are. So, jus' who are ya, anyway?"

"My name is Sir Cullen Bristow of Darross, *captain* to King Sebastian's army." He made sure to emphasize his title so she knew he was more than just an ordinary knight.

"You're a knight *an'* a cap'n?" she gasped, surprised by this unexpected bit of news.

"That, I am. And just who are you, my good woman?"

"My name is Druen."

"*Druen...* Your name sounds strangely Talibarrian."

"That's because I *am* Talibarrian, but I ain't strange." Her words were defiant and proud.

"You certainly do not *look* Talibarrian," commented Cullen, staring at her eye-pleasing features.

"Hey, was that your way of sayin' I'm not ugly even though I'm from these parts?"

"I suppose it was," replied Cullen, nodding in confirmation.

"An' am I suppos'd ta be flattered or insulted by what ya jus' said?" queried Druen, staring at Cullen through suspicious, narrowed eyes.

"Flattered... definitely! You - you should be flattered," stuttered Cullen, realizing in hindsight his words could have been taken either way. "A lady of such sublime beauty is a rarity in Talibarr, or any other country when it comes right down to it."

"Well, you don't look like a knight *or* a cap'n, for that matter, so there!" Druen sniffed with indignation, sensing she had been slighted by this stranger even after his attempt to redeem himself.

"And just what did you mean by that?" grunted Cullen, scowling at her with a degree of annoyance.

"Aren't ya kinda young ta be a cap'n of *anything*, let alone be a knight?"

"Do not be deceived by my dashing good looks and youthful vitality, young miss. I will have you know I have been captaining my King's army for the past three or so years. With my great skills and ambitious nature, of course I would make my way up the military ranks faster than most."

"I suppose that's possible," decided Druen, her slight shoulders shrugging in response to downplay the fact she was actually impressed by his prominent standing.

"I would prove it to you, but undoubtedly, you had already made off with my sword; pawning it off for a worthless goat or probably less," responded Cullen, heaving a disheartened sigh.

"Do you mean *this* sword?" questioned Druen; reaching across Cullen's body for the weapon she left resting by his side as he slept.

Recognizing the ornate scabbard, he eagerly snatched his precious sword from her grasp. Cradling it in his arms, Cullen rocked the weapon like it was his long, lost love.

"No need ta be rude 'bout it!" scolded Druen, staring at her now-empty hand. "So much fer yer kind havin' such good manners. An' jus' 'cause I'm Talibarrian, it don't mean I'm a thief, if that's what you were accusin' me of."

"My apologies… It is just that King Sebastian gifted this special sword to me. There is none other like it in all the lands."

"It is pretty," admitted Druen.

"No, it is *handsome* and more importantly, this sword has great, sentimental value to me. Undoubtedly, this fine weapon has even greater monetary value to anyone happening upon it."

"An' therefore, you jus' assumed that I'd steal it from ya."

"Well, you must admit, it would be pretty damned tempting," reasoned Cullen, patting the hilt of his prized sword.

"In yer eyes, an' in the eyes of all Darrossians, I'm sure you'd be assumin' one of us would steal it. But I'll have ya know, Cap'n Bristow, we ain't all murderers an' thieves, though you'd like ta believe we are."

"I stand corrected. Only *some* are murderers while the vast *majority* are thieves."

"Think what ya like, Cap'n, but I know what's so. As needy as some Talibarrians are, there are some of us with morals. We don't all take ta stealin' from others. At least, I certainly don't!"

"I suppose you are right. I was wrong to assume you would be capable of such skullduggery," decided Cullen, realizing this young woman could have easily sold or traded this sword as he slept, or just claimed it as her own while pretending she had never even seen it.

"I *am right!*" snapped Druen. "Even a simpleton can see by yer dress an' 'specially by the manner of yer speech that you're one of those uppity folks from Darross. That alone would give the average Talibarrian good reason ta steal from ya! But, as you can see, I'm *not* the average Talibarrian."

She angrily thrust her thumb over her shoulder, pointing to all of Cullen's personal possessions she had left out to dry by the campfire. Each piece, present and accounted for.

"I can see now that you are indeed far from being like the average Talibarrian," Cullen admitted sheepishly. "Again, I can only offer my humblest apologies for assuming the worst, my lady."

"An' jus' ta prove we ain't all socially inept or mean-spirited, I accept yer apology, Cap'n Bristow," offered Druen, proudly sweeping her mane of dark brown hair off her shoulders.

"Well, that is good of you. Now, as I was saying; this sword was gifted to me by the King of Darross for exemplary service," explained Cullen, unsheathing the unwieldy sword to expose the smooth, stainless steel blade. "This is a prize gifted only to the knights of the most worthy standing, for committing an act of selfless bravery. And I will have you know, young miss, I am as selfless and as brave as they come."

"Even though you're from Darross, I think I can believe yer words. You have one of those trustin' faces."

"Of course I can be trusted, however, I believe after last night's accident – it was last night, yes?"

"Yeah, you took yer tumble late last eve," confirmed Druen, nodding her head as she winced in empathy as she recalled first discovering this man in the dark, rain-drenched forest.

"I believe after last night's accident, my face probably looks more battered and bruised than trusting."

"Yer face looks absolutely fine," assured Druen, offering this stranger a comforting smile as she placed a warm hand on his cheek. "You've got a nasty bump on the side of yer head, there's a small scratch here an' there, but other than that, you're lookin' pretty good ta me."

"Well, thank you," responded Cullen, flashing one of his disarming smiles as he sensed there was a come-on somewhere in her kind words and this soft, gentle touch.

"You're welcome," said Druen, her dark, sultry eyes shyly dropping away. She was momentarily caught off guard, overwhelmed by his bold, confident smile that oozed of charm. Pulling away from his face, Cullen clasped her warm, slender hand into his.

"So, I take it we did… You know?" inquired Cullen, giving her a coy wink of the eye.

"What did we do?" Her delicate brows furrowed in curiosity.

"You know?" repeated Cullen, with an evocative smile.

"What?" asked Druen, completely bewildered by his line of questioning. "What do I know?"

"No need to be shy, my dear! You know what I am speaking of," insisted Cullen, thrusting his hips in a suggestive manner. "The *deed!*"

He drew a blank stare from Druen, and then suddenly, she burst into a fit of laughter. It was as though this was absolutely the most hilarious and preposterous thing she had ever heard of in her entire life.

Cullen's face reddened. Flushing with embarrassment, he was made to witness this display and worse yet, be the object of this ridicule.

"I just assumed because we are both in this same bed, naked at that; something must have *happened* between us."

"You're so silly, Cap'n Bristow! When I found ya, you were freezin' ta death. You were gonna die from the cold. You were in no shape fer any kind of friskiness, if ya get my meanin'?"

"Then why in heaven's name did you strip me naked? This only happens when a woman wants her way with me."

"Good gracious! Ya make it sound like this is a regular occurrence fer ya!" gasped Druen, her brows arching up with an equal measure of surprise and disgust.

"For me, it happens all too often," sighed Cullen; "not that I am complaining about it."

"Well, sorry ta disappoint you, Cap'n. Nothing like that happened last night."

"So, you just make it a habit of bringing home strangers, handsome men you find in the forest and without their permission or knowledge, strip them bare and crawl into bed with them?" grunted Cullen, his tone unable to conceal the fact his ego was bruised by this strange, round-about rejection. It was something quite foreign to him.

"Do you take me fer some kinda trollop!" snapped Druen, frowning in revulsion at the knight. "I'll have ya know you're the first man I've ever shared my bed with, an' it was downright disppointin' ta tell ya the truth! You just lay there limp; like a cold, dead fish. All I was meanin' ta do was ta get you warmed up a bit."

Cullen cringed inwardly upon hearing the word *limp* being used to describe his condition. In his vocabulary, it was as bad as *flaccid.*

"Well, if it was that bad, then explain yourself, missy. If your intentions were completely innocent, you could have just propped me up by the fire! You could have thrown an extra blanket over me if your intention was to merely *warm me up.*"

"I'll have ya know; this was the fastest way ta get ya warm. Like

I said, you were so cold you were shiverin' up a storm. An' you were in no condition ta sit up by a fire, lest you wanted ta keel over inta the flames an' get yerself burned. Ta lie by yer side an' warm ya with my body was the fastest, easiest way ta drive off this chill. An' believe me; I derived no pleasure in cozyin' up next ta yer freezin' cold body."

"And that is all that happened?" There was obvious disappointment and doubt lacing Cullen's words. "We just *cuddled?*"

"You can say that. But come ta think of it, I'd say I was doin' the cuddlin' while you just lay there, dead ta the world."

"Goodness! That is a first for me… So nothing actually happened?" asked Cullen, pointing at her and then at his person to ascertain the facts.

"I assure you, Cap'n Bristow, *nothing* happened."

"If this is true, you are the first woman *ever* to successfully resist the urge to ravage me while I slept."

"My! You are so full of yerself, aren't ya?" admonished Druen, rolling her beautiful, brown eyes in dismay.

"But I speak the truth!" exclaimed Cullen, puffing his chest out in pride. "Women find me irresistible."

"Like I said, you were freezin' cold last night. There was nothin' to be ravaged, if ya get my drift?" Druen raised her pinkie finger, only to allow it to droop sadly to signify how thoroughly chilled he was from his ordeal.

"Well, with all that rain, it was excruciatingly cold last night," conceded Cullen, tucking the blanket around his nether regions to hide his shame. "I was freezing to death in this dreadful Talibarrian weather."

"Actually, I figured that you would've drowned before ya froze ta death if I hadn't of happened upon ya when I did," informed Druen, quickly changing the subject when it became apparent this knight was thoroughly embarrassed by her animated demonstration of one of his most prized body parts. "Ya landed face-first in a stream."

"I did?" questioned Cullen, his fingers gingerly touching the bump on his head as he tried to recall this mishap.

"Of course, you can't remember 'cause you were knocked out an' all, but I pulled ya out before you could breathe in the water."

"And you saved my life?"

"Well, I wasn't about ta jus' leave ya out there ta die. I managed ta get ya out of the stream an' dragged you over to my shelter," added Druen, her eyes glancing about her makeshift home. "I had ta get ya warmed up real fast or you would have died."

"Had I been conscious, the company of a little minx like you would have certainly got my blood flowing again," decided Cullen, giving her a coy wink of his eye.

"Did you jus' go an' insult me again?"

"Whatever do you mean?"

"Didn't you jus' call me one of those stinky, weaselly ferret-like critters?" questioned Druen, grimacing in disgust.

"No! I called you a *minx*. In Darross it means... oh, never mind what it means," groaned Cullen, flustered by her naïveté. "It was a compliment."

"Thanks... I think."

"I suppose I am the one who should be thanking you, after all you did for me," decided Cullen, grateful that she went through great effort to spare him from certain death.

"Yes, you should," agreed the young woman. Druen tugged on the blanket, yanking it back to expose Cullen's naked body.

"Whoa! Stop it! What are you doing?" snapped Cullen, struggling to pull the scratchy cover back up to conceal his body from her inquisitive eyes. "I was thinking of a hand-shake or maybe a hug."

"You're a funny man, Cap'n Bristow," giggled Druen. "I mean ta fix you up real good!"

"I am in no need of *fixing up,* young lady! I will be quite fine once I drive off this chill," insisted Cullen, his face flushing with embarrassment as he hastily wrapped the blanket around his waist to hide what little there was of his now-shrivelled manhood.

"Now, don't ya go movin'. Stay right where you are."

"Oh, I have no intention of going anywhere at this very moment. Would you be a dear and fetch me my clothes?" asked Cullen, pointing to his raiment and boots.

"Not until I'm done with you."

"And just what do you intend to do?"

"Jus' be patient. You'll see."

Druen stood up, naked as the day she was born. She casually sauntered away. As though she did not know the meaning of the word modesty, the young woman was unhurried as she wove her way around Cullen's scattered possessions. From one of the main poles used to support the lean-to, she removed an article of clothing she hung up to dry after last night's downpour.

Cullen could not help but admire the gentle curves of her nubile body as he watched the feminine sway of her hips and the golden sheen of sunlight streaming through the cracks of the shelter to dance on her creamy skin to give it a warm glow like liquid honey.

Druen could feel this man's eyes staring hungrily at her naked form as she nonchalantly slipped a simple frock over her head. To his disappointment, she pulled the dress down over her breasts and rounded hips to conceal her tantalizing body from his view. She wandered over to the cold fire pit to pick up a wooden bowl and a piece of bread that was mottled gray and green with fuzzy mold, delivering it to Cullen's bedside.

"I'm gonna fix you up so you're as good as new, Cap'n," promised Druen, balancing the bowl in one hand as the other seized the blanket, giving it hard tug to expose Cullen's naked body once more.

"You have already done quite enough, young lady! Now, unhand this blanket," insisted Cullen, pulling back on the cover with one hand as the other tried to hide his manhood that had involuntarily swelled, becoming turgid as he admired her seductive form parading before him.

"For shame, Cap'n Bristow! Quit all this fussin'! It ain't as though I haven't already seen ya naked," argued Druen.

"Well, I should say that you are the one who should be feeling some shame, for you have seen quite enough! And right about now, it would be more than you can handle," cautioned Cullen, attempting to will his erection to subside.

"Come on, stop being so shy! You weren't like this before."

"That is because I was unconscious. It is one thing for me to be naked, it quite something else when I am naked solely for your amusement. Besides, I fail to understand why I have to be naked to drink this medicine? And if you think I am going to *eat* that moldy piece of bread, then think again!"

Druen giggled, "It's not fer drinkin' an' eatin', you silly man! An' there ain't anythin' amusin' about all these cuts an' bruises on yer body, especially if infection were ta set in. That's what this bread is fer. I use it ta dress the worst of your cuts after I spread this honey poultice over yer wounds. The mold helps ta fight infection."

"That sounds rather disgusting."

"It's an old-fashioned remedy. Don't know how it works, but it does," attested Druen.

"I do believe I am recuperating quite nicely as I am now," countered Cullen, refusing to cooperate.

"Only 'cause I put a good dose of this medicine on yer body an' pressed chunks of this bread against the cuts while you were sleepin'," insisted Druen. There was something quite innocent, and yet, so very suggestive in the way she slowly stirred the sticky, honey mixture with her fingertip.

"You did?" He peered beneath the blanket to check her handiwork.

"Sure, I did. An' it was much easier when you were knocked out an' not makin' such a fuss about it."

"Why are you doing this?" questioned Cullen, searching her soul as he stared into her eyes. "Ultimately, you have no reason to help me."

"An' what reason do I have ta deny you help when my help is needed?" queried Druen, her long, dark lashes batting innocently at him.

"So, it makes no difference to you that I am a citizen of Darross; a knight and captain of the King's army, at that?" questioned Cullen, knowing that most Talibarrians despised those in the military whether they were responsible for the death of a kin in the past, or not.

"Jus' because our countries have been at odds fer longer than anyone can remember, that don't mean *we* have ta be. Things can change, but it's gotta start somewhere an' with someone. Why can't it start with us?"

"By God! You *are* a different breed of Talibarrian," noted Cullen, sensing her sincerity as he watched her dark tresses tumbled down around her shoulders to frame the exquisite features of her face.

"Diff'rent in a good way?"

"Most definitely!" exclaimed Cullen, tossing back the blanket with gay abandon.

"So you're not offended by my *Talibarrian* hands administerin' some healin' medicine to yer body?" asked Druen, as she smiled sweetly.

"By all means, use your healing touch, but be gentle with me. I am still hurting and I bruise easily," warned Cullen, lying back for Druen to slather his body in a great dollop of the poultice.

With her fingertips, she tenderly applied the herb and honey concoction to the worst of the cuts and scrapes coloured by purplish, mottled contusions rising up on his skin.

As the sun retreated from the horizon to wash the distant storm clouds in a purple haze, it withdrew the last of its defiant rays from the bruised sky.

With the coming of dusk, Arerys had no choice but to prepare for the internment of his father's body and soul to this earthly realm. Delivering Kal-lel to a rise on Mount Hope, with Lindras, Markus and Joval by his side, a solemn Arerys led the lament for the dead. The Elven warriors gathered, dropping down onto their left knee while bowing their heads as they paid final respects to the fallen King.

As the wan light on the western horizon was finally leached away, surrendering to the night, the silk shroud wrapped around Kal-lel's body collapsed, his physical form reduced to dust. A brisk, evening breeze whispered around them before sweeping up the shroud and the Elf's remains. They watched as the wind caught silk and dust, swirling it high up into the milky, twilight sky before blowing westward to deliver his energy back to the forest of Wyndwood.

"Artel and the elders will see to it the bells of Wyndwood sound loud and clear on this eve," announced Arerys, knowing this tradition was to call home the souls of Elves lost to this realm, to guide them back to the enchanted forest.

"Whatever I can say, I know you will take no comfort in my words," said Markus, offering his condolences. "Just know you have my sincerest sympathy on your father's passing, Arerys."

"Thank you, Markus."

"As difficult as all this seems right at this moment, you must take some comfort in knowing that Kal-lel died at peace with himself and how he chose to live his life," added Lindras. "It is more than what most can say."

"For now, I must push aside my grief," said Arerys, staring off to the distant as the wind swept the silk shroud high above the tree line, across the Plains of Fire and on to the south. "We must find out what had happened to Nayla and the Talibarrian emissaries she and Lando were travelling with."

"Lando was beginning to stir when I left his side to attend your father's service," said Joval. "Perhaps he is awake now."

"I am confident Lando can answer this question, and more," responded Markus. "Perhaps he even knows the whereabouts of Cullen Bristow."

"It is possible, but highly unlikely," decided Arerys, following his warriors down the slope back to their camp. "If I know the young Captain, I would say he has gallivanted off, returning to the safety of Darross. After all, both King Sebastian and Prince Garrick returned to their castle. He probably decided there was no more reason for him to continue on with the hunt for the beast now that his King was safely on his way home."

"Ah, but Captain Bristow being the man he is, I have no doubt his determination to be a part of this quest, to share in whatever perceived glory he thought there would be in killing the infamous beast got the better of him," surmised Joval. "I tend to believe his need to be front and center of this mission probably resulted in him somehow becoming separated and lost from our group. He probably runs about haphazardly through the forest trying to make his way back to our camp."

"You are probably correct, Joval," agreed Arerys. "As soon as we check on Lando, and discover where he left Nayla, perhaps we should mount a search for the Captain before he finds himself in serious trouble."

"Knowing that self-absorbed prig of a mortal, I sense Captain Bristow decided to abandon us to the hunt so he could seek shelter from last night's torrential downpour," decided Lindras. "Even as we speak, he is probably resting comfortably on his laurels somewhere in this forest."

"For his sake, I hope he is not hurt," said Markus, puzzled by Cullen's strange disappearance. "At least he has nothing to fear of that beast coming for him."

"For now, the only thing we know for sure is that Captain Bristow was not where we had stationed him," ascertained Arerys.

"There is a chance he will show up on his own," stated Joval. "At this moment, I suggest we concentrate our efforts on Lando and finding out what he knows of Nayla and her whereabouts."

"Yes," agreed Arerys. He drew in a deep, cleansing breath in an effort to remain focused and to push back the rising tide of fear that something terrible had happened to his wife. "The circumstances surrounding Lando and his abrupt arrival last night are more than just a little disconcerting. Hopefully, he can speak of this."

Suddenly, one of the Elven warriors rushed up to meet Arerys and his company.

"My lord, Sir Bayliss is stirring," alerted the warrior, his head bowing in respect. "I do believe he is starting to come to."

Arerys hastened his pace, eager to speak to Lando. Lifting the flap of the tent, he peered inside. Under the inviting glow of candlelight, he could see Lando was still asleep, but it was a restless sleep. The retired knight tossed about on the cot; his face contorting with a grimace as though trapped in a horrible nightmare there was no escaping from.

"Lando," whispered Arerys, giving his shoulders a gentle shake to ease him to consciousness. "Wake up, Lando."

"*NAYLA!*" Lando suddenly cried out, bolting upright to knock Arerys off his feet just as Markus and Lindras stepped inside the tent.

"Calm down, Lando," urged Markus, pushing his friend back down onto the cot as Lindras hoisted Arerys onto his feet. "You are safe now. You were having a bad dream."

Lando's heart was thundering in his chest. His eyes were wild with fear even as he gazed up at these familiar faces. A terrible sense of confusion overwhelmed his mind as panic seized his heart. Here he was, resting in the safety of this tent while somewhere out there in the forest, Nayla was defenseless and in grave danger.

"Nayla... Trouble!" he wheezed; his throat now parched from this long, unnatural sleep.

"Here, have some of this," offered Joval, appearing at the entrance of the tent with a cup of fresh, cold water to quench Lando's thirst.

"Drink, Lando," ordered Arerys, holding the cup to his chapped lips as Markus lifted his head.

Lando took a quick gulp of water. He then pushed the cup away as he spoke once more, his words tumbling out with urgency, "Nayla, she was captured – taken hostage!"

"Whoa! Slow down, my friend," demanded Lindras. "Take a deep breath and then share in the details – tell us everything you know."

"Try to remember as much as you can," requested Arerys. "Now start again, tell us exactly what had happened."

"Yesterday, no wait..." said Lando, as his dazed mind tried to make sense of the passing of time. "Was it yesterday?"

"If it is of any help, Lindras and I came upon you very late last night – almost at the approach of dawn," informed Markus. "We were in this forest attempting to capture a killer animal on the loose."

"We chanced upon you quite by accident, and I do mean it quite literally, by accident," confessed Lindras, glancing over at Markus, his co-conspirator in the incident that landed their friend on this cot.

"That was *your* arrow?" queried Lando, eyeing Markus with a degree of concern as his hand pressed up to the healed puncture wound just beneath his collarbone.

"So you remember me shooting you?" asked Markus, his face reddening with embarrassment and guilt.

"I recall being struck down by an arrow, but I had no idea it was *you!* Thank goodness for bad aim."

"If my aim was bad, I would have missed you altogether," countered Markus.

"If you were an excellent marksman, your arrow would have pierced my heart," determined Lando, giving his friend a forgiving smile.

"Well, for my part, I was the one to knock you off your mount," admitted Lindras, holding forth his magical staff. "But I must reiterate, it was very much an accident. We thought you were the beast crashing through the dark forest, heading directly toward us."

"The beast!" gasped Lando, his eyes darting over to the Elf. "Arerys, was that what you were trying to warn us about?"

"Tori delivered my message?" questioned Arerys, thinking back on Nayla's little falcon.

"Yes, this was when the situation went terribly awry," responded Lando, gathering his thoughts as he recalled the strange events leading up to his nighttime journey through the forest in his desperate search for help.

"What happened?" asked Arerys, anxious to learn more.

"Nayla's falcon located us as we were leaving the Iron Mountains, heading westward to take the trail through the Valley of Shadows. Just as Tori had ascertained it was Nayla she had found, on her descent, the bird was struck down from the sky, falling to her death. We were able to find the falcon as we entered this forest. It was just as Nayla was about to read your message of warning that we were taken by surprise."

"Go on!" urged Arerys.

"We were beset by a gang of thugs led by a crazy, old woman," revealed Lando. "With no hesitation and absolutely no remorse, in cold-blood they killed the emissaries sent forth by the new governing council. With that done, they forced Nayla to cooperate."

"Nayla? Cooperate with murderous thugs? Impossible!" disputed Arerys, bewildered by Lando's words. "She would rather fight than to give in to the likes of these people."

"Oh, believe me, Arerys, Nayla was doing just that when they turned the tables on her," confirmed Lando. "I was besieged by this woman's cronies, overwhelmed by sheer numbers. They savagely attacked me, threatening to kill me if Nayla did not cooperate. It was an impossible situation."

"That accounts for those other injuries on your body," noted Joval, recalling the deep purple contusions and cuts already present prior to Markus' arrow striking Lando down. At the time, Joval healed these wounds with little thought as to how this mortal had received these injuries.

"It certainly complicates matters," stated Lindras, pondering the dilemma they were now faced with. "I am acquainted with Nayla, well enough to know she would never let a friend come to harm, not if she could help it."

"Oddly enough, that old woman seemed perfectly aware of that. They forced Nayla's hand. Her cooperation in exchange for my life," explained Lando.

"Do you have any idea who these people were?" questioned Markus.

"I had never seen them before," stated Lando. "At first, when they thought nothing of killing the Talibarrians in our company, I assumed they were just regular malcontents opposed to the new government. However, this woman was very specific about her demands."

"What demands?" queried Arerys. "What do they want with Nayla?"

"After beating me until Nayla promised to do as she ordered, that wizened, old hag demanded that I ride off to deliver a message that will make its way to the Wizards."

"A message for me?" asked Lindras, frowning in curiosity.

"It was meant for you *and* your brother Wizards," replied Lando, struggling to sit up on the cot. "That crazy, old woman said that if Nayla's life means anything to you and your brothers, you will exchange your crystals orbs for her freedom. One life set free in exchange for four magical orbs, if I remember her words correctly."

"This woman wants our crystals in exchange for Nayla's life?" probed Lindras, seeking confirmation from Lando.

"Yes. And that hag made it perfectly clear the crystals were to be delivered to her before the rise of the next full moon."

"Does this make any sense to you, Lindras?" questioned Arerys, struggling to understand the motive for this violent attack and this woman's bizarre demand.

"Do you think her actions are motivated by political gains?" queried Markus.

"Since when has magic had anything to do with politics?" The Wizard responded with a question of his own as he pondered Lando's words.

"It is evident this woman and her followers were motivated by more than just mere politics," determined Joval. "My intuition tells me the powers vested in the Wizards' crystal orbs might give these people the power to alter the political landscape of Talibarr to their liking. Who needs a democracy when you can rule the masses with the threat of magic?"

"It could be just that, but I have a strong feeling their desires are much more basic than that," decided Arerys. "It is easy enough to mount an insurrection, to instigate political unrest in order to garner the backing of fellow Talibarrians opposed to the new government."

"Do you agree, Lindras?" questioned Markus.

"Why take the risk of capturing and holding Nayla hostage; a hostage who happens to be the consort to the Prince of Wyndwood, unless it was to make a personal statement or for personal gains greater than what can be derived by controlling the government?" responded the Wizard.

"In light of the fact Nayla's abduction coincides with the strange and sudden appearance of the ghastly beast that rampaged through this country, something unnatural is definitely afoot," surmised Arerys.

"What do you mean by unnatural? And what manner of beast do you speak of?" asked Lando, frowning in confusion.

"While you and Nayla were in Orien, the citizens of Talibarr were being terrorized by a mysterious creature," responded Arerys. "As best as we could tell; it was some enormous, monstrosity of a cat with a true penchant for blood."

"An unnaturally large mountain cat?" queried Lando.

"What was unnatural about this animal was that this species of *cat* died out many, many centuries ago," explained Lindras. "Only dark powers, magic unknown to mortal man or Elf could have resurrected such a creature."

"So that is what brought all of you to the Valley of Shadows," determined Lando.

"The new council had asked King Sebastian for his help in capturing this killer," responded Arerys; "but in the course of this hunt, King Sebastian was taken by the beast."

"King Sebastian is dead?" gasped Lando, his back straightening upon hearing this terrible news.

"Luckily, we were able to rescue the King from that creature," disclosed Markus.

"Unfortunately, by the time we were able to retrieve him, King Sebastian had suffered greatly," added Arerys. "We were able to heal his physical injuries easily enough, however, the terrible trauma he endured was more than his mind could cope with. Whether he will ever recover fully is still in question. For now, Prince Garrick handles the affairs of his country."

"Thank goodness King Sebastian survived that encounter," said Lando.

"Yes, however, King Kal-lel was not as lucky," stated Joval, bowing his head in sadness and respect.

"This beast had attacked Kal-lel?" Lando shook his head, unable to believe this tragic news.

"It attacked *and* killed my father," revealed Arerys; "but not before he killed the beast first."

"This is dreadful news all the way around! My sincere condolences, my friend," sympathized Lando, his great hand giving Arerys' shoulder a comforting pat. His heart sank as the terrible realization Kal-lel was unable to transmigrate to the Elf Haven saddened him.

"Thank you, Lando. But for now, my sorrow is outweighed by my concern for Nayla and what has happened to her."

"Understandably so," said Lando, gingerly standing on his feet. "We should organize a party to save Nayla from those murderous dogs. We must do so immediately."

"In due time," responded Lindras.

"There is no time! They will kill her!" argued Arerys. "We cannot leave her to their mercy."

"That, we will not do," vowed Lindras. "Her captors have a distinct advantage at this moment, so we can ill-afford to act in haste. Our actions, if hastily conceived and poorly executed, can place Nayla in greater jeopardy than she is already in. And do not forget, Arerys, Lando did say we have until the rise of the next full moon to meet their demands."

"At the very least, those murderous rogues will keep Nayla alive until this time," determined Joval.

"Then what do we do?" questioned Arerys. "I, for one, cannot stand by and do nothing."

"At this time, there are more questions than answers," replied the Wizard. "What has me truly concerned is not so much what this woman asked for in the way of the crystal orbs, but in the nature of its timing."

"You are referring to her request to possess these magical spheres before the next full moon," assessed Joval.

"Precisely! Further more, it does not bode well that we are at the place once known as the Witch's Hold," said Lindras, glancing back at Mount Hope where he and those of the original Order first confronted the Dark Lord Beyilzon over one thousand years ago.

"I will tell you now, my friends, I find it rather disturbing these events would coincide with the tenth anniversary of when I killed the Dark Lord at that very place," added Markus.

"I do believe it is high time to call upon my brother Wizards. There is a chance one them can shed some light on this matter."

"What do we do about Captain Bristow?" asked Markus.

"For now, the Captain can wait," decided Arerys. "And I am not just saying this because Nayla is my wife and Bristow is a royal pain."

"Something is definitely going on here; something much bigger than the mere fact Nayla had been taken hostage," surmised Lindras. "We must get to the bottom of this immediately."

"I agree," averred Arerys. "There is no point in wasting precious time searching for Captain Bristow if he is on his way to Darross. I would be more than just a little peeved if he could not even be bothered to forewarn us of his plans to abandon the hunt. I say we concentrate our efforts on rescuing Nayla, for we know for certain she is in danger."

"In all honesty, if this is so, I am thoroughly incensed that Bristow would scurry off as he did," grunted Markus. "For now, all I can offer that man is a small measure of pity if he is indeed hurt and languishing in his misery. If he is not, then he will pray for mercy when I get my hands on him."

"You poor man," whispered Druen.

Her sweet, sympathetic words and the skillful manipulations of her hands made Cullen's body unravel, drifting in a sense of relaxation he had never experienced before. It was as though his weary muscles were melting like the dripping wax oozing down the side of the candle illuminating this simple shelter. Druen kneaded away the knotted muscles on Cullen's aching back as he lay sprawled out on the bearskin rug, revelling in this attention. He would intermittently moan with pleasure each time a painful knot dissolved under her therapeutic touch.

"You're still feelin' so tense, Cap'n."

"I am feeling much better thanks to you, my dear, especially after you gently sponged off the poultice with that lavender scented water you had warmed to the perfect temperature," responded Cullen, sighing with contentment as he allowed Druen to nurse him back to health.

"The poultices an' salves can only do so much. There comes a time when it's best ta let nature take its course," said Druen, her fingers and thumbs kneading away at the muscles high on his shoulders. "Unfortunately, there's no medicine that can make these knots jus' disappear."

"True, no medicine will work; however, you are certainly doing wonders for me, my dear woman."

"You must be hurtin' something fierce," Druen sighed with pity, her thumbs applying steady pressure between the spine and his shoulder blades.

"After last night's ordeal, I *am* suffering," groaned Cullen, exaggerating his condition to squeeze out a little more sympathy and attention from this comely, young maiden. "I must have strained some muscles."

"The cuts an' bruises I can understand, but how did ya manage ta strain muscles?" queried Druen. Between the firm grip of her hands and the dexterous manipulation of her fingers, they worked in synchrony to undo the knots and kinks plaguing Cullen's body.

"I think it was when I had single-handedly strung up the monstrous beast by its neck," boasted Cullen, flexing his biceps for her to admire. "I had spent days hunting that damned creature down. I was determined not to let it get away."

"What beast are ya speakin' off? A wolf or somethin'?" questioned Druen; the delicate features of her face were softened by the glow of the amber light cast by the crackling campfire.

"Oh, this was no run-of-the-mill animal I am speaking of, my lady," stated Cullen. "It was a gargantuan creature with huge fangs as big as daggers and a nasty disposition to match. Surely, you must have heard of this rampaging beast terrorizing those in your country?"

"I've heard rumours of an animal runnin' amok, hurting folks..." said Druen. She suddenly stopped this massage session as she thought on this terrible creature on the loose.

"Little more to the left," urged Cullen, rolling his left shoulder that was craving her healing touch. "Hurting folks? That beast was maiming and killing people left, right and center!"

"So it killed whatever person it found?"

"Men, women, even children, fell victim to this monster. Anyone in its path was fair game."

"*Children?* Why would it kill innocent, little children? It shouldn't be doin' that!" Druen gasped in horror.

"One would think! But why would it care? That beast was indiscriminate in its attacks, thinking nothing of tearing the heads and limbs off its many victims. In fact, I swear the creature took certain pleasure in killing."

"That's terrible!"

"Terrible indeed!" Cullen agreed wholeheartedly, the grisly scene of dismembered bodies played over in his mind. "I never believed such carnage was possible off the battlefield."

"Well, I do hope someone is able to kill that animal," wished Druen, her eyes shadowed with worry. "It's not meant ta be."

"Fear not, my lady. Having done my part to detain the beast, I have no doubt my comrades had succeeded in doing away with the creature."

"I'm not so sure about that. When I pulled you from that stream, there was sure a lot of commotion comin' from the ravine. I'd swear that animal got away by all the runnin' and shoutin' I heard."

"Are you positive?" asked Cullen, rolling onto his back to gaze upon her troubled face.

"I didn't stick around ta see, if that's what ya mean. I'm jus' supposin' that's what happened based on what I heard. At the time, I was more concerned 'bout gettin' you ta a safe, warm place."

"Well, thank you for your concern and efforts, but now I am truly worried," confessed Cullen, pondering the outcome of last night's hunt.

"Why?" asked Druen, plopping down next to Cullen as the Captain scooted over on the bearskin to make room for her.

"If that creature is still skulking about, there is a bloody good chance it will be coming for us."

"No... We'll be safe here," assured Druen, smiling sweetly at Cullen.

His fingertip traced the outline of her face as he swept a tendril of hair from her eyes.

"I hate to tell you this, my lovely, but the walls and the roof of this flimsy shelter was enough to keep out the rain; however, it will not be strong enough to prevent the beast from breaking through. Its foul breath alone will cause this wall to collapse."

"You're 'xaggeratin', but don't worry. Like I said before, we'll be safe here," promised Druen.

"I mean no offense, but you are either extremely dimwitted or overly optimistic, my dear," chuckled Cullen, listening to her confident words. "You should know; none, save for King Sebastian and Prince Arerys, survived an encounter with that animal. I have seen it in action. The beast is more powerful than you can ever imagine. It will take more than several layers of twigs and branches woven together to keep that animal out."

"You jus' gotta trust me when I say we'll be safe."

"Oh, I certainly know I can trust you now, Druen," admitted Cullen, reaching for his sword. "It is the beast and its hideous, murderous nature I do not trust. At first light, we must move on."

"Why can't we just stay here? Jus' the two us… alone in our little hideaway. Away from everyone," pleaded Druen.

"Love to my sweets, however, you must consider this. These walls will do nothing to protect us if that creature comes skulking around."

"But we'll be safe here. As long as you're with me, you'll be safe," promised Druen, her hand squeezing his.

"First of all, I hardly think your lovely little hands are capable of wielding a great sword. And your beauty, as sublime as it is, will do nothing to spare your life from the beast's deadly maws," disputed Cullen, gently kissing the back of Druen's hands. "Second, there is safety in numbers. Until we ascertain the beast is dead, we are better to travel in the company of others so the creature can pick and choose its next victim, thereby reducing our chances of being mauled to death."

"So, you'll be going to go back to Darross?" asked Druen, as her heart sank.

"If the beast is dead, I will most certainly be going home. At this time, if that blasted creature is still alive, our best hope of survival is to seek out the Elves. They are the only ones that can kill the animal," explained Cullen.

"Well now, I hope you take no offense in me sayin' that you're the one who's dimwitted if you believe that's so. The Elves aren't the only ones able ta kill the beast."

"Of course they are," argued Cullen. "Or perhaps, it is better to say their blood is like poison to the beast."

"That may be so, but left in the sun long enough, that'll kill the beast, too," informed Druen, her words matter-of-fact.

Cullen frowned as he scrutinized her face. "Surely, you jest!"

"I'm not kiddin'. Why'd ya think the creature only moves at night an' shuns the daylight?"

"Hey! How did you know that this creature is neither diurinal nor crepusculard?" questioned Cullen, using these words to impress Druen with his ever-expanding vocabulary.

Druen stared at the Captain, momentarily baffled by his words. "Are ya sayin' it doesn't pee in the daylight hours or it's a fat creature that prefers ta roam during the hours of dusk an' dawn?"

"What are you talking about?" queried Cullen.

"I think ya meant ta say *diurnal* and *crepuscular*."

"That is exactly what I am saying. The beast is a creature of the night," explained Cullen, inwardly surprised this seemingly simple girl was familiar with these words only recently introduced to him by the Wizard. "How is it you know this? Was it just a lucky guess?"

For a lingering moment, Druen was silent.

"What is it, Druen?" probed Cullen, scrutinizing her pensive face.

"I've never been the lucky sort an' it's not a guess. It's just common sense an' common knowledge. That's all."

Cullen said with a shrug, "I suppose that is plausible."

"If ya mean ta say it's believable, you know I'd never out-an'-out lie to ya, Cap'n Bristow."

"Please, call me Cullen. After all we have been through together, I do believe we should be on a first-name basis by now," urged the Captain, his fingers tracing the lines of her slender neck.

"I could never address you so informally, good sir!" exclaimed Druen, her eyes shyly turning away from his. She could not deny she was revelling in this attention Cullen lavished on her. His fingertips brushing feathery soft against her skin served to seduce her.

"I insist," responded Cullen, beguiled by her loveliness and her obvious innocence.

"If you insist, Cullen."

"I most certainly do!"

Staring into her sultry eyes, his lips were irresistibly drawn to hers. Like the velvety petals of a perfect rosebud coming into bloom, he had to find out if they were as soft and tender as that. He was dying to taste her mouth, to indulge in a slow, long kiss with this maiden. Cullen could feel her gentle breath on his face, the tantalizing draw of these seductive, full lips brushing lightly against his caused his heart to pound like never before. Just as he leaned forward to kiss Druen, she suddenly pulled away, giving Cullen a shy smile.

"Hey!" Cullen groaned in disappointment as the promise of sweet treasures stored in a single kiss was stolen away. "It is not nice to tease me."

"An' it's not nice to tempt me," countered Druen.

"So… does that mean you *are* tempted by my charms?"

"An' so what if I was? I jus' get the sense you're used ta havin' your way."

"Yes, I am, especially when it comes to those of the feminine persuasion," admitted Cullen, giving her another disarming smile.

"I believe it," giggled Druen, smiling back at the Captain. "An' fer this very reason, I'm not gonna give in to your charms as the others do."

"You will deprive me of a kiss? A single, innocent kiss?" gasped

Cullen, stunned by her words.

"A kiss... an' a whole lot more!"

"But I am a wounded man! I might die. How can you do this to me?"

"I'd say you're recoverin' remarkably well," teased Druen. "An' jus' because those others girls gave themselves so freely to ya, maybe it'd do you some good ta be humbled fer once in yer life where those of the *feminine persuasion* are concerned."

"I will have you know I have felt the cruel sting of rejection once before," confided Cullen. "And I did not like it!"

"Only *once*?"

"Once was more than enough," sulked Cullen. "And it matters not how often one had been spurned in his lifetime, what truly matters is the level of the debilitating blow dealt by rejection."

"I find this hard to believe."

"To this day, so do I," admitted Cullen. "Sadly, it is the truth I speak. In fact, the woman responsible showed me a whole new world of hurt."

"So she broke your heart?"

"The lady, and I use the term loosely, whom I refer to soundly trounced on more than just my heart. She broke my face."

"This sounds quite intriguin'. Care ta elaborate?"

"What can I say? She was an exotic beauty not unlike you, but much shorter. She possessed a nasty disposition if you got on her wrong side."

"An' she struck yer fancy?"

"In the end, not only did she *strike* my fancy, she kicked it to high heaven," confessed Cullen, his hand absentmindedly rubbing his chin. "I thought she was just playing hard-to-get, but that demented little she-devil not only took great pleasure in humiliating me in front of her husband and male cohorts, she broke my jaw; knocking me unconscious in the process!"

"You made advances at a married woman? In front of her husband, no less?" gasped Druen, shocked by his brazen actions. "I think you got what you were deservin' of!"

"I suppose that is why her husband did not stop her from engaging in this contest of skills," responded Cullen, recalling how this diminutive female challenged him in a bid to prove her worth to lead them on a quest.

In what he first thought was a foolhardy move by arming him with a sword while she was armed with nothing more than her warrior training to combat him, Cullen spent more time mangled into the ground than he ever thought possible. His body endured a terrific beating and so did his ego. It was only when the toe of her boot clipped him on his chin, the blow rendering him unconscious, did her husband finally intervened to end his humiliation.

"I find it hard ta believe a woman can take ya on, an' beat you at that, but if it's true, then good fer her, I say," giggled Druen, feeling little in the way of sympathy for Cullen.

"This was no ordinary woman I speak of. It was Nayla Treeborn."

"The warrior maiden of Orien?" gasped Druen, her eyes opening wide in surprise as she heard him speak this name of legend.

"The one and only! However, that little she-devil had retired her sword and put aside her warrior ways when she became the consort to Prince Arerys of Wyndwood. Or at least, I thought she did until that woman soundly beat me before her male comrades. Now *that* was humiliating! Even though she cheated to best me, my pride still bears the scars of her beating."

"So your ego got a bit bruised," dismissed Druen. "It could have been much worse ya know?"

"How can it be worse than that?"

"You could have been beatin' up by just an ordinary girl. At least this woman was a warrior of legend, reputed ta be a skilled a fighter as any man trained in arms."

"I suppose you are right," conceded Cullen, releasing with a disheartened sigh.

"Of course, I am. So you best stop mopin' about it."

"I will stop moping about it if you would be so kind as to distract me," responded Cullen, his lips puckering up for a kiss.

Druen giggled as she playfully pushed his expectant face away to see his lips droop into a pathetic pout of dejection.

"Come now, my dear, here is your chance to do a good deed!"

"A good deed?"

"Yes, you can help to mend my battered pride and feel good in more ways than one in doing so," offered Cullen, giving her a seductive smile.

"I'm young, but I ain't that gullible," scoffed Druen, prying her eyes away from his handsome face. "If I didn't know better, I'd say ya only want me 'cause ya can't stand me spurning your advances. Ta be twice rejected can be twice as hard ta bear."

For the longest moment, Cullen was silent as he seriously pondered her words. Here was this beautiful, young, resourceful woman, obviously wiser than her years and smarter than most. Even though she was Talibarrian, somehow, he was able to see beyond his stereotypical beliefs that served to taint his perspective. He appreciated not just her physical beauty, but also her defining qualities, most notably her sweet and caring nature. In spite of her innocence, she was grounded and had a good sense of self, perhaps even more than he did. There was enough dignity and scruples to warn her of roguish men who'd think nothing of taking advantage of a woman's good virtue.

By her words and actions, Druen was definitely not like the other women Cullen had ever encountered on his many travels. There were those who shamelessly threw themselves at his feet for a chance to partake in his company and inwardly, he knew it was a pathetic attempt to garner the attention of friends and family. It was a chance to impress them when they'd be seen adorning the arm of this dashing knight and captain. In retrospect, perhaps his actions were just as pathetic in allowing himself to be used in this manner, all for the sake of maintaining his manly pride before his peers.

Cullen drew a deep breath as he absorbed her words. One thing was for certain; there was no one here for Druen to impress. And she was definitely nothing like Nayla, and yet, she, unlike the multitude of other women, refused to be seduced by his good looks and charms alone.

"That's it, isn't it?" asked Druen, her inquisitive mind probing his for answers. "You jus' want ta have me 'cause I turned ya down flat. You jus' can't stand ta be rejected by a woman."

"In all honesty, Druen, though I am not accustomed to being the recipient of *any* form of rejection, I am quite taken by you because you are unlike all the others," revealed Cullen, surprised by his own revelation.

"You are?" responded Druen, stunned by his admission that he was truly fond of her.

"Well… yes! Very much so," confessed Cullen. "Call me daft, but I sense you are attracted to me, and yet, you have enough pride that you refuse to cheapen yourself by allowing me to have my way with you. Strangely enough, this is a refreshing change for me."

"It is?"

"Definitely! I have now come to the realization the days of tarts and trollops are finally over for me. Though you are obviously not a woman of refined breeding, you are definitely a woman of character and substance."

"Thank you… I think," responded Druen, as she considered this backhanded compliment.

"Indeed, plus, you are not one of these women that chatters incessantly. Part of your charm is that you are a woman of few words."

"I am?"

"Point proven, my dear," said Cullen, with a smile. "To engage in intelligent conversation is one thing; to maul off my ears with idle gossip and mindless chatter is another matter altogether."

"I believe it's only 'cause I said *no* an' your body wasn't preoccupied that you were forced ta talk ta me," teased Druen. "You were made to see that even though I'm not formally educated or as you put it, *of refined breeding*, I'm not some empty-headed girl incapable of intelligent thought or conversation."

"I must say; I was duly impressed by your knowledge of medicinal plants and the art of healing," admitted Cullen, recuperating nicely from his mishap. He was used to being surrounded by pampered, spoiled young women who had never known a day of hard work and whose greatest accomplishment was in knowing the latest fashion trends for the upcoming season. "Who taught you all of this?"

"I learned mostly from my granny, especially after my momma died."

"Well, by your skills, I would say the old woman is quite knowledgeable. She must be a healer of great renown in these parts."

"I suppose you can say that."

"I would like to meet her acquaintance, if possible," said Cullen, pondering his next course of action.

"Why would you wanna do that?"

"Well, if I intend to woo you, to court you properly, it is only right I meet your kin-folk for their blessings in doing so. To simply whisk you away to Darross will undoubtedly lead to a false accusation that I stole you away from here. It can lead to political upheaval and a possible confrontation between two countries, being that I am the King's champion after all."

"We can't have that happen," sighed Druen.

"There you go! It is settled then," exclaimed Cullen. "After we seek out my hunting party and see to it that the beast is dead, we shall meet with your grandmother."

"That's a very bad idea, Cullen."

"How can it be a bad idea? I was the one to think it up."

"My granny's known fer many things, but bein' reasonable ain't one of them, especially when it comes ta matters concerning those from Darross," revealed Druen, speaking with conviction.

"What is there to reason about? Do you not think the very thought of her darling granddaughter having a chance at a better life would appeal to her senses?" queried Cullen. "Surely, she has the wisdom to know when her granddaughter has been offered a chance of a lifetime with the man of her dreams."

"You'd think," Druen responded drearily. "But truth be told, once ya meet her, there'll be no love lost between the two of yous."

"Because I am a knight and a captain from Darross," determined Cullen. "As an outsider, so to speak, she is sure to hold some disdain for me."

"Ta put it bluntly, yeah. You can say that. Mind you, practically everyone in the village is of like mind"

"If I can win you over, I am confident I can charm your grandmother enough to do the same."

"No… If she knew I had saved *yer* life, she'll have *mine*. As it is now, she wants nothing ta do with me anymore, all because I've turned my back on her way of life."

"So the old woman is a bit disgruntled with you…"

"Disgruntled with me? It's way more than that! I've been banished from her village."

"Banished?"

"Well… Truth be told, I fled for my life before she could force me ta have a change of heart," confessed Druen.

"Aah… family troubles," determined Cullen, with a thoughtful nod of his head; "a little strife between blood relations."

"More trouble than you can imagine, an' more strife between blood gone bad than you'd ever thought possible. But I'm not lookin' back. I ain't goin' back to that place either!"

"Alrighty then, it is better we make some good out of a bad situation."

"How can anythin' *good* come out of this?" queried Druen, the corners of her mouth drooping in a sad frown.

"When it comes right down to it, who needs the complication of in-laws?" decided Cullen, grinning broadly as a wave of sudden optimism washed over him.

"Are you sayin' ya mean ta marry me?" questioned Druen, her breath catching in the back of her throat as her delicate brows arched up in utter surprise.

"Only if I can sweep you off your little feet with my charming charisma," answered Cullen, giving her a dashing smile; "as there is little else you will allow me to use at this time to seduce your heart."

"This is rather sudden... You really don't know me as you should."

"I would know you better if you had allowed me to, but strangely enough, my growing respect now prevents me from taking advantage of you," confessed Cullen. "Given what I do know under these circumstances, I am most enchanted by your beauty and beguiled by your spirit. It is bizarre, but in your presence, you send my heart a-flutter. It is a sensation I have never felt before."

"Could be nothin' more than indigestion," countered Druen. In her heart, she dared to hope Cullen was speaking the truth.

"Do not tease, my lady," groaned Cullen, clutching his chest as though her words were like knives being thrust into his heart. "I reveal my most intimate thoughts, spilling my heart out to you and in return, you see fit to mock me?"

"It's not my intention to tease you. I'm just sayin' that if you really knew me, you'd think twice 'bout wishin' ta court a woman like me. I'm not what ya think I am."

"Who cares what I think? I am more concerned with what I *believe* and how you make me *feel*."

"An' jus' what do you believe you're feelin'?"

"Your beauty is obvious to see, but are you saying that your show of kindness to me was merely an act? That I was wrong in believing that you are a gentle, compassionate soul?" questioned Cullen.

"I ain't sayin' that... I'm saying that if you knew *everythin'* there is ta know about me, 'specially stuff about my family, you'd be thinkin' otherwise."

"Never mind your family," dismissed Cullen. "If your grandmother has no say over you and how you live your life anymore, then who cares? I know above all else, where you are concerned, your heart is pure and kind. If anything, you are like a precious gemstone."

"I am?" Druen's cheeks burned, blushing with heat from these adoring words of flattery that were never before spoken to her.

"Mind you, you just need a little polishing up to bring out your full brilliance. And as lovely as you are, you are most definitely unique – unlike any woman I had ever known, and I have known many. Your exquisite beauty is enhanced by an intelligent mind and a truly caring nature."

"Well, thank you, Cullen," responded Druen, smiling shyly.

"You can thank me later, my dear. Just understand that you know me only as well as I do you, so you must trust in your heart. Given time, I believe you will see beyond my noble carriage and my prestigious title. You will discover I am much more than just a handsome face with a bloody good body to match."

"I'm not one to judge a man by his title or appearance. In time, a title can be taken away an' one's appearance eventually fades with age," stated Druen, nodding thoughtfully. "I prefer a man with substance – real integrity. Qualities that will stand the test of time."

"I do not mean to boast, but I have substance galore and more integrity than you can shake a stick at!" claimed Cullen, hoping to win over her heart.

"Tad bit humble is nice."

"Oh, yes," agreed Cullen, with a nod. "Of course, I am much too modest to tell you how humble a man I truly am."

"An' I'd fancy a man sensitive enough ta share what is truly in his heart an' on his mind. I admire a man who is man enough ta shed a tear without feelin' ashamed."

"I am just that man," stated Cullen, his lower lip trembling as he attempted to squeeze a tear from his eye. "And it breaks my heart to know you cannot see that beneath the armour I am made to wear in the name of my King, I am a sensitive, sensitive man. I am merely forced to be in complete control of my emotions as a knight and a captain, for the lives of many depends on my ability to remain composed under times of great duress."

"You surprise me, Cullen," said Druen. She was touched by his confession, realizing that a captain weeping under the pressures of battle would hardly inspire his men to fight.

"I surprise me, too," sighed Cullen, dabbing away the tiny teardrop. "All I ask is that you take the time to discover the man I can be just for you, because of you."

"I suppose I've got some time ta spare," responded Druen, giving him a coy smile.

"Aha! So, I was correct!" exclaimed Cullen, beaming with delight. "You *do* like me!"

"I admit to likin' you, but that's a far cry from sayin' I'm in love with you. You do know the diff'rence don't ya?"

"I do believe with you by my side I can come to learn, my dear," stated Cullen, staring dreamily into Druen's eyes. "For some reason I just cannot explain, you are causing me to reassess my life and gain a bearing on my moral compass, so to speak. I can only attribute this feeling to my growing love for you."

"You are serious…" determined Druen, her heart racing as she listened to his words.

"Well… either that or I am completely mad. I prefer to believe I am *madly in love*. It is a strange sensation… unnerving really, but strangely satisfying at the same time."

"Now you are babbling!" teased Druen.

"Bloody hell!" cursed Cullen, rubbing his chin in thought. "That is what my friend Brandis Blackmer did when he met the woman of his dreams! He babbled like a fool, running at the mouth like a teenage boy besotted with love. He was rather pathetic, trying to say everything and anything under the sun to win her heart… Oh, dog's bollocks! I *am* pathetic! Damn you woman! Look at what you are doing to me!"

"Pathetic never looked so good on you," sighed Druen, charmed by this revealing confession.

"You think so?" asked Cullen, his eyes a-blazed with renewed hope. "If it pleases you, I can babble on some more."

Druen suddenly fell silent. She was overwhelmed with guilt the more she realized Cullen was being completely sincere.

"What is it, Druen? Did I say something to offend you?" queried Cullen, staring into her sad eyes. "Did I say too much?"

"You didn't say anything that'd upset me, Cullen. It's jus' that once you come ta know me better, you'll be changin' yer mind about me. I know ya will."

"Now that is complete and utter rubbish! You are Talibarrian, but I will not hold it against you, after all, you cannot help where you were born. What I do know is that you are the sweetest, kindest and the most caring woman I have ever chanced to meet. Not to mention the fact that you are extremely pleasing to the eyes."

"You're only sayin' that 'cause I saved your life."

"I am deeply touched you had risked your life out there to save mine," admitted Cullen; "and even more so now knowing that you spared my life in spite of the fact your kin-folk would react harshly to your show of kindness to me, a man they still regard as the enemy."

"I do believe your sense of admiration fer me is nothin' more than gratitude," dismissed Druen.

"As grateful as I am, it does not change the fact you have many redeeming qualities worthy of admiration, my dear Druen. And if anything, as the recipient of your rejection in my foiled attempts to seduce you, at least you did so with grace and tact. You did not resort to using physical violence on my person to spurn my advances."

"I could never hurt anyone like that, especially you!"

"I know! Another one of your endearing qualities, my love."

"That's very sweet of you ta say, but here's somethin' you won't find endearing at all," responded Druen, turning away from Cullen.

"Come now, do not be so hard on yourself," scolded Cullen, his hands resting lightly on her trembling shoulders. "Nothing will change the way I feel about you."

"I'm a witch," confessed Druen, in a sad whisper.

For a moment, Cullen was silent as he tried to digest these three, small words. "Look here, my love, we all have bad days. I am sure, from time to time, you might feel like an absolutely bit– "

Before he could finish his sentence, with eyes brimming with tears, Druen interjected, "I didn't say *bitch.*"

"Say again," gulped Cullen.

"I come from a long line of witches. They once ruled over Talibarr."

"Oh… So my ears did not deceive me," responded Cullen, his eyes suddenly turning cold as he looked upon her in this new light.

the witch's hold

"This way," ordered Lando, urging the others on. They rode through the mist veiling the forest as the light of the morning sun pushed against the darkness. "It is not much further."

Not far off, they could hear the raucous cries of ravens and crows as they squabbled in the treetops. These scavenging birds grew louder as Lando escorted his comrades in their direction to begin their search for Nayla.

In the pale light of the dawn sky, Joval's sharp eyes detected the subtlest of movements on the forest floor.

"What do we have here?" queried Joval, dismounting from his horse for a better look.

What Markus' mortal eyes had initially noticed, he had dismissed as being nothing more than small, dried leaves tumbling along, carried by the wind.

"What is it, Joval?" questioned Arerys, bringing RainDance to a stop.

"Feathers…" He held one up for Arerys to inspect. "Falcon feathers to be exact."

"It could be from Nayla's bird," determined Arerys.

"It can also be a feather molted from a wild falcon," suggested Markus, scrutinizing the soft plumes.

"A feather shed during a molt does not have blood on it," disputed Joval, spying the dried splash of crimson; "not like this."

"This is near to where Nayla's falcon was downed," disclosed Lando, recognizing a gnarled, moss and lichen covered tree trunk damaged long ago by a lightning strike.

"If we follow this trail of feathers I am confident it will deliver us to the exact location of Nayla's disappearance," said Lindras.

With the wind as their guide, they traced the scattering of feathers swirling and dancing along the forest floor.

"Here! Over here!" called Arerys, hopping down from his mare to inspect the remains. On the stained earth, a clump of feathers clotted with dried blood and a single talon chewed to the bones and still adorned with the now-tangled leather jesses were all that remained of Tori.

"It would appear nature has taken its course. A fox has benefited from the little falcon's death," stated Lindras, taking note of the small, distinct paw prints left behind in the earth.

In an explosion of ebony feathers, the flock of battling crows and equally boisterous ravens took to the sky as Lando and his comrades neared too close for comfort.

"Ooh, this is an ugly sight," groaned Lando, momentarily averting his eyes from the grisly scene. Where Master Slean had fallen to an enemy spear, the feeding birds mutilated the exposed flesh, particularly on his face.

Vacant, bloody orbs that once housed his eyes displayed the worst of the carnage inflicted by the ravenous scavengers on a feeding frenzy. Their sharp, pointed beaks pecked and tugged away at the softest tissue first to gain access to the *meat* hidden within the hard skull.

Their attention turned to a bold crow as it hastily snatched away a piece of flesh from Slean's dead comrade before taking flight as the Wizard approached, driving it away.

"So this is where you were confronted?" queried Arerys, his eyes searching for clues of what became of Nayla.

"Yes, this is exactly where that crazy, old woman and her cronies took us by surprise. Nayla had ridden on just ahead of us to find her falcon. That is how they were able to get the jump on her."

"It makes sense," nodded Joval. He took note of the disturbed earth where Lando had been engaged in a great struggle, only to be overwhelmed by numbers. "The only way to contain a warrior of Nayla's calibre is to separate her from the group."

"Which way did they go from here, Lando?" questioned Arerys, scanning their surroundings for evidence. "Did you see?"

"By the time I gained control of my horse to turn about, they were gone. They had vanished like phantoms into this forest."

"You saw nothing?" probed Markus.

"They disappeared, as though by magic," reiterated Lando. "I saw and heard nothing!"

"Why did you not try to follow them?" asked Arerys, staring

accusingly at his friend. "Why did you not try to stop them from taking her?"

"I did the only thing I could do," justified Lando. He was appalled that Arerys was blaming him for Nayla's plight.

"Then what you did was not enough," snapped Arerys, his fear for Nayla rising in his heart.

"Do you not think I tried to save her? Do you not think I would trade my life for hers to keep her safe?"

"Stop it!" ordered Markus. "If it is their intention to turn friend against friend, they have succeeded."

Arerys' face was momentarily flushed with embarrassment as he humbled himself before the retired knight.

"Forgive me, Lando. I did not mean to lash out at you. I spoke out of fear for Nayla. You must know I do not hold you accountable for these people's actions."

"I understand," said Lando, sympathetic to Arerys' plight. "There is no need to ask for forgiveness, my friend. And believe me, if there was a way I could have rescued Nayla at the onset, I would have done so. I would never have shown up before you without her safely by my side."

"I know."

"Good!" declared Lindras. "Now that we have cleared the air and apologies have been dispensed all around, I strongly recommend we begin our search for Nayla."

"Most definitely," agreed Lando. "I only ask that we take the time to bury these two men. I had come to know both Masters Slean and Merdak well during our travels and I grew to respect them. I dread the prospects of those birds and other wild creatures returning to further desecrate their remains."

"Of course," said Arerys, nodding in agreement. "But we shall have to be quick about it."

"I will help Lando with this task if the rest of you wish to look for clues pertaining to Nayla's possible whereabouts," offered Joval.

As the morning dragged on, so too, did the search. The higher the sun climbed into the sky, Arerys' concern for his missing wife grew accordingly. Their meticulous inspection of the immediate area of Nayla's abduction expanded. Combing the area in a radius from the point of her disappearance, they hunted for clues to ascertain her captors' movements. This work was tedious and time consuming, but necessary.

During all this time, there was nary a clue to be had. It was quickly becoming obvious the culprits were not on horseback. The telltale hoof prints left by Nayla's mare revealed that Cloud had dashed off, making her escape southward. Spooked by these mortals, she bolted when the men attempted to corner her. In a state of panic, driven by a herd mentality, Slean and Merdak's horses instinctively charged after Cloud. The three horses galloped away, fleeing capture as the Talibarrians successfully contained Lando's mount.

"This will definitely make tracking them all the more difficult," sighed Markus, his eyes probing the earth for a sign of Nayla's passing.

"At least there is one good sign," responded Arerys, attempting to remain optimistic. "If they move by foot, there is only so far these mortals can travel in a single day before they tire."

"Yes," agreed Lindras. "Even if they were aware Nayla has the stamina of the Elf-kind, these mortals would not be able to endure a long, gruelling hike through this rugged forest as she can. They would be forced to take periodic rests."

"This is all very true," admitted Lando. "However, what difference does it make if those murderous scoundrels are one or one-hundred leagues away from where we are now? They have left barely a trace of their passing. They move like ghosts through this forest. We have no way of knowing which way they have taken Nayla."

"These Talibarrians are exceptionally clever," noted Joval.

"They are thugs! Murderous thugs," disputed Lando, his face contorting in anger. "There was nothing clever in the way they had attacked us. Brutal and remorseless in their actions, they were unprovoked when they killed Slean and Merdak."

"Divide and conquer; apply brute force; and then control the situation by way of emotional leverage to have both you *and* Nayla bend to their demands," reminded Lindras. "I would say they were *very* clever."

"It was not just their method of attack," explained Joval. "These people move like Elves."

"With the exception of the Kagai Warriors, I know of not one mortal that can move as an Elf does," countered Markus. "Even when I walk carefully, making a deliberate effort to keep my prints to a minimum, I still leave tracks."

"Granted, these people might not be light on their feet, but wherever they tread, they took great care in concealing their tracks," responded Joval.

"Either that, or they have found a way to harness the energy flowing through this dreadful place, just as the Elves do in the enchanted forest," suggested the Wizard.

"No mortal man has ever had the power to do so. None, but the witches of old, were capable of this," argued Arerys. "No offense, Lindras, however, I tend to think as Joval does. These mortals are using a more worldly tactic to cover their tracks, whether it be a simple tree branch to sweep over their footprints or they avoid treading where the soil is soft, I believe they are employing practical methods to conceal their movements."

"What makes you say that is what they did?" questioned Markus.

"As light as Nayla's steps are, Elven eyes and the eyes of a mortal trained in tracking would be able to spot her footprints," explained Arerys.

"Whoever these people were that had absconded with Nayla, they know how to move through this forest undetected, leaving nary a trace of their presence," added Joval.

"Let me assure you, Joval," said Lando. "Those villains were *not* Elves. By their manner of dress and their speech, they were most definitely mortals – Talibarrians to be exact."

"True, however, how many mortals, particularly Talibarrians do you know of are capable of slipping through these woods like an Elf?" queried Joval. "The majority of humans I know usually lumber or crash through the forest leaving obvious signs of their comings and goings."

"These particular people have left no footprints in the earth; no broken branches, or trampled vegetation underfoot in the wake of their passing," noted Arerys. "It is as though they are one with nature or go through extreme efforts to leave their natural surroundings unmolested."

A long, dreary sigh escaped Lindras as he digested these words.

"What is it, Lindras?" queried Arerys.

"The only Talibarrians I know of who are one with nature, or should I say, at one time *were* one with nature were the witches of Dreymoor."

"Dreymoor? Where is this place, Lindras?" asked Lando.

"It was a heathen village of long ago, inhabited now by only a small band of followers still devoted to this arcane and antiquated religion. It was situated just north of the Witch's Hold, the place we now refer to as Mount Hope."

"But the witches no longer exist," countered Markus. "Their population dispersed and their kind diminished over the eons when their fellow Talibarrians persecuted them for their alliance with the Dark Lord Beyilzon."

"The ones I speak of were a small, but powerful coven of witches. For years, they held court over the majority of those living in the north before the Dark Lord roamed these lands," explained Lindras. "And though these original witches have long expired from this world, it is said there are devout followers that still cling to the teachings and lore surrounding these four."

"Are you speaking of the Coven of Four?" questioned Arerys. "The ones my father and the members of the original Order led by King Brannon of Carcross encountered during the first battle against Beyilzon?"

"Yes, but of course, those wretched hags are long dead," confirmed Lindras. "I now refer to their kin-folk that survive to this day. It is my understanding there are still those practicing the old ways and the old magic."

"One thing is for certain, only the powers of the forbidden arts could have been used to conjure up that killer beast," reminded Joval.

"Even if these four witches were still alive, they do not have the power to conjure up such a monstrosity," argued Arerys. "Only a powerful entity like Beyilzon himself can do so."

"Or be used as a medium to manifest such potent, vile magic. And we all know what became of the Dark Lord," added Lando, sliding his index finger across his throat as a graphic reminder of Beyilzon's fate.

"I severed his head clean off with the Sword of Power," reminded Markus, thinking back on the violent confrontation when he faced Beyilzon on Mount Hope almost a decade ago. "And Lindras saw to it that the Dark Lord was entombed in a hell of his own making."

"If this was not the work of the Dark Lord, then the present-day witches have found a way to channel his powers," determined Lindras. "There is only one means possible to create such magic."

"The Book of Spells," offered Arerys.

"Yes," confirmed the Wizard.

"Impossible!" dismissed Lando. "That dreadful thing was destroyed. We saw to it!"

"When we rescued the young prince of Darross from the clutches of Draven Eldard, the book was destroyed when that madman was killed," said Markus, nodding in agreement at Lando.

"Consider this," offered Lindras, "by the blood and bits of Draven's remains that rained down on us when his ice palace was destroyed, we know for certain of his demise. If the Book of Spells met the same fate, then would it not stand to reason that we should have been showered with bits of parchment, too? It would have fallen from the sky like confetti."

"Bloody hell!" cursed Lando, his hand drawing down his woeful face. "Do not even entertain the notion that damned book still exists after all we had endured to see it destroyed."

"I prefer to believe the book had been annihilated; its pages shredded to bits like Draven was," reasoned Markus. "And being that the fragments of parchment were lighter, they were lost to the winds, nothing more."

"Perhaps you are being overly optimistic, Markus," responded Joval. "Nayla and I tried to destroy that book once before. Even throwing that cursed thing into a pool of molten lava did nothing more than singe its cover and pages."

"I do not like the possibilities," stated Arerys. "However, we would be wise to keep an open mind, for I sense strange magic is at work here."

"Of course there is," agreed Lando. "It could have nothing to do with the long-departed Dark Lord or the witches of old, but this is Talibarr. The land and its people are entrenched in their old, superstitious ways. They are just coming to terms with our modern world."

"What we must come to terms with at this moment is how to track Nayla and those holding her captive when there are no tracks to follow," reminded Markus.

"Markus is correct," said Lando, turning to Arerys. "If your Elven eyes have yet to find a trace of their passing, I hardly believe Markus and I are in a position to see something your eyes cannot. If it is not obvious to you and Joval, then any clues left behind by Nayla will be lost to us."

"That is it!" exclaimed Joval, his eyes flashing with a thought.

"What do you speak of?" asked Lindras.

"We have been so busy searching for the obvious, we forgot the most obvious thing of all," replied Joval, rushing back to where Nayla and Lando were first accosted.

"What is he talking about?" questioned Lando, running to keep up with the Elf.

"Your guess is as good as mine," responded Markus, in close pursuit.

"Joval!" called Arerys, bewildered by this Elf's abrupt action as he charged after him. "What did we forget?"

"Think, Arerys!" urged Joval. "Nayla is your wife, but long before she became your wife, she had trained and lived most of her life as a Kagai Warrior. This lifestyle is so ingrained in her mind, body and soul it would never leave her, even if she turned away from this life."

"So, you are saying we should think as she would? As a Kagai Warrior?" determined Arerys.

"Easier said than done," responded Markus. "Joval is the only one amongst us truly familiar with the Kagai way."

"Care to tell us what the *obvious* is that we had been missing, Joval?" queried Lindras.

"How do most people mark a trail?" responded Joval, with a question of his own.

"I, for one, tend to leave a trail of broken twigs or branches," offered Lando. "Easy to spot; easy to follow."

"And easy for Nayla's captor's to see what she is doing if she had resorted to that," reminded Arerys.

"Exactly," confirmed Joval. "Instead, Nayla would devise a more subtle method to show the way."

"What method would this be?" questioned Markus.

"Better to show than tell," responded Joval, rushing off again. "Lando, take me to the exact spot Nayla was standing when she was captured."

Lando charged on ahead. Stopping where the falcon's remains were found, his eyes quickly scanned the surroundings. He recognized where he was besieged and beaten by his tormentors. Lando was able to pinpoint where Nayla was standing when the old woman and her minion confronted and captured her.

"Here!" declared Lando, pointing to the exact spot he last saw Nayla. "She was right over here."

Joval glanced about, searching the immediate area as he spoke, "She was definitely not taken westward. Lando would have seen them as he was made to depart. South would deliver her closer to those they perceive as the enemy and to the east; they would be faced with the Iron Mountain Range and the lands of Orien. If they are aware of Nayla's connections to those in the east, they would never take her there unless they wish to be captured and punished by the Taijins as they still hold Nayla in high regard."

"So… they journey to the north," surmised Arerys.

"That is the most logical direction," said Joval, his eyes searching for a clue to confirm his words.

"If that is so, they are heading toward Mount Hope," assessed Lindras.

"But how do we know for sure?" questioned Lando. "I dread the thought that we charge off to the north while Nayla is taken in the opposite direction."

"That is what I am attempting to ascertain. Now Lando, do you recall if her hands were bound? And if so, were they tied to the front or behind her back?" queried Joval.

"If I remember correctly, her hands were bound behind her. Why? Does it make a difference?"

"It narrows down where I should be looking for this clue," explained Joval, as he scrutinized each bush at approximately Nayla's waist to hip level. He determined that at this height, if Nayla did indeed leave a sign, she would have done so with the utmost discretion, keeping her hand movements to a minimum so as not to draw unwanted attention.

"What clue?" questioned Arerys, watching as Joval dashed from one shrub to another.

"This one," answered Joval, pointing to the sign he had missed the first time.

Separating this branch of the shrub from all the others, Joval revealed the longest twig that was also the tallest on this particular branch. Near the end of this slender growth, the twig was deliberately bent, not broken

"This is intriguing," noted Lando, studying the subtle but important clue Joval presented.

"It is an old Kagai trick Nayla uses," revealed Joval. "A twig snapped in half is obvious, even to those who hold her. It would betray her actions."

"I can see why we did not notice this before," said Markus.

"The tip of the twig is the most resilient and flexible," explained Joval. "By applying steady pressure with warmed fingertips and what energy she possesses, the twig can be manipulated without breaking."

"So they journey northward," surmised Arerys, inspecting the evidence.

"Not only do Kagai Warriors mark the way using this method; the direction the tip of the twig is pointing reveals the route they are heading," stated Joval, speaking with all certainty. "Or in this case, the general direction Nayla believes they are taking her."

"The very tip is pointed directly toward the west face of Mount

Hope," determined the Wizard.

"Then that will be our destination," said Arerys.

"This is a bad idea," groaned Druen, trudging on half-heartedly in front of Cullen as she led the way back to the ravine where she first found him.

"I came up with it. How can it be a bad?" countered Cullen, frowning with bewilderment. He held Druen's hand as he guided her across the creek he had almost drowned in the night before. "If things go as planned, I will be a hero and you, my love, shall endear yourself to my comrades and the people of Darross."

"How can you be so sure?"

"Because the esteemed company I travel with is comprised of men of sound character and strong morals," explained Cullen. Scanning their surroundings to determine the fastest route to deliver them back to the camp Arerys' warriors had set up the night before.

"How sound?"

"These men possess unwavering moral scruples, so much so, it can be downright annoying at times. They always do the right and proper thing even if it can lead to their untimely demise."

"Hmph! They're truly men of honour, but will it be 'nough ta make 'em listen ta me?" questioned Druen. "Ta make 'em believe my words?"

"They believe actions speak louder than words, my dear. If your actions spare our realm from a major catastrophe, even at the expense of your people's fate, they will come to appreciate and recognize your desire to do the right and decent thing. They will know you mean to put an end to the plotting of those wishing to unleash this evil."

"An' they'll believe me? Even though I'm a Talibarrian *an'* a witch, they'll still believe me?"

"Admittedly, they are more liberal-minded than I am," confessed Cullen. "It will make no difference to them whether you are Talibarrian or not. As for being a witch, I would strongly recommend downplaying that fact or omitting this bit of information altogether. After all, it is neither here nor there at this point, considering you have turned your back on that way of life."

"I'm not gonna start lyin' ta yer friends," protested Druen.

"I am not saying to out-and-out *lie* to them. I am saying, if they do not request this information, why offer it up to them? It will just add fuel to the fire and we do not need that. Let us win their confidence first before we divulge this somewhat irrelevant bit of news."

"I'm jus' thinkin' that they'd be more inclined ta believe me if I'm upfront an' honest with 'em right from the start."

"Look here, my lovely, there is a time and a place for honesty. This will not be one of them. Just trust me. I will be the first to admit I am, or rather, I *was* not particularly fond of your kind –"

"My kind being witches?"

"I was referring to Talibarrians in general, but you can include witches on my list of dislikes. The point being, if I can be convinced by you, then believe me, my comrades can be swayed to believe the same. All they need to know are the facts and how those crazies intend to hatch this plot."

"I hope you're right," sighed Druen.

"I am Sir Cullen Bristow, captain to King Sebastian's army. Of course I am right! Prince Arerys and King Markus are such do-gooders, at the very least, they will give you the benefit of the doubt that you speak the truth. Your deeds will mean you shall be exonerated of any wrong-doing where your deranged grandmother is concerned."

"But even if they knew the truth, that don't mean they'll be able to defeat this evil," cautioned Druen.

"I assure you, we will find a way to put an end to this madness. With the Wizard by our side, we will confront and defeat whatever evil that witch and her cronies can conjure up."

"Wizard? A Wizard is here? Which one?" asked Druen, staring intently into Cullen's eyes as she bombarded him with questions. "Where is he?"

"Lindras Weatherstone is somewhere in this forest. Last I saw, he was leading King Kal-lel's warriors on the hunt, driving the beast to the ravine from where I fell."

"Why didn't ya say somethin' about him before?"

"About that old coot? Why? What difference does it make?"

"It makes a huge diff'rence! What's he doin' here ta begin with?"

"Wherever trouble is a-brewing, whenever it involves the sanctity of this realm or the safety of his friends, that old gaffer is smack-dab in the middle of the crisis."

"You should've said somethin' ta me!" scolded Druen.

"I thought I did."

"You didn't! We better hurry," ordered Druen, pulling Cullen along by his hand.

"Before darkness descends and the beast is on the prowl?" asked Cullen, sensing the urgency in her voice.

"The beast doesn't concern me."

"Well, it should! That monster does not discern between Darrossian flesh and Talibarrian," warned Cullen, dismayed by her indifference.

"At this very moment, what concerns me more is the Wizard an' his presence here."

"He is the one who is most opposed to this evil. He is here to help us," assured Cullen.

"Yes, yes! That may well be his intention, but we don't need none of his help. His presence will only make matters worse."

"Whoa! Whoa! Whoa! Hold on here!" ordered Cullen, coming to a stop. Staring into her troubled eyes he emphatically stated his point, "What do you not understand, Druen? Lindras: *Good*. Witches: *Bad*. He will put a stop to their evil plans."

"No!" argued Druen. "We must stop Master Weatherstone before he summons his brother Wizards to this place. We gotta stop him before it's too late!"

"Here is another one!" announced Arerys, waving his comrades over to investigate his latest find. Sure enough, he presented a slender twig, its pliable tip bent over to discreetly point the way.

"They are moving directly westward now," determined Lindras, examining the direction of the curved twig. "It appears they are skirting the base of Mount Hope."

"But why?" asked Lando. "I can understand them not wanting to head east or south, but west? If they are indeed witches, as you seem to believe, they would be scurrying off directly over the face of this mount to seek refuge to the north, probably fleeing as fast as they can beyond the Shadow Mountains."

"If anything, I do believe these people think they will find safety in their former stronghold," assessed the Wizard, glancing up the slope of Mount Hope. "They believe, like this mount they once knew as the Witch's Hold, is still a place of great magic and power."

"If they mean to take Nayla to the old witch settlement of Dreymoor, would it not be quicker to head directly over Mount Hope than to travel around it?" questioned Markus, as he mulled over these words.

Glancing to the west, Markus could see the sun setting lower in the sky with the approach of dusk. Between the stand of trees in the distance, he spied the golden rays of sunlight dancing and reflecting off the dark, murky waters of the lake they had camped at on the night the beast made its final, fatal attack.

"There is little in the way of trees to provide them with cover. I can only assume that is what prevented them from doing so. To brazenly cross the face of Mount Hope in the light of day would have put them in our full view," offered Joval.

"No... They were travelling by foot and if this indeed was the route they travelled, they would have come by this way during the dead of night so you would not have seen them," countered Lando.

"The lightning storm," determined Arerys. "That would have placed them here on the night of the great storm."

"Well, a bare mountain that offers little in the way of safe cover is the last place any creature, man or beast, would want to be caught during the height of a horrific storm," decided Lindras. "They were forced to trek around this mount, for they feared being struck by a bolt of lightning."

"Damn it all!" cursed Arerys, his frustration mounting. "So there was a chance we almost crossed paths with them on that night, totally unaware of their presence."

"At least we know Nayla is still alive," reminded Markus, trying to sound optimistic for his friend's sake.

"But for how long?" queried Arerys. "We already know they wantonly killed the Talibarrian emissaries. You know they will kill Nayla, even if they get what they want."

"You do not know for sure, Arerys," argued Lindras.

"There is a chance they will set her free," added Lando.

"I hardly think so," said Joval, his words matter-of-fact.

"So you believe those Talibarrians will kill Nayla?" asked Arerys, stunned by Joval's words. Of all those in their company, Arerys believed this Elf would cling to the hope Nayla would live through this ordeal when all others would simply give up.

"I mean to say; knowing Nayla, she will escape before they have a chance to kill her," explained Joval.

"Yes... You are right, Joval," decided Arerys, nodding in agreement. "Nayla is still a capable warrior. Even if she does not escape, she can still hold her own until we get to her."

"Then let us journey on," recommended Joval.

"Into the night?" asked Lando.

"For however long it takes," replied Arerys, determined more than ever to find his wife.

"I estimate they are at least half a day ahead of us," assessed Joval, scrutinizing the tip of the twig. By the way the slender, bent stem had almost completely up-righted itself back to its original form, he was able to determine the amount of time that had passed since Nayla manipulated this twig. "If we continue on by horse, there is a very real chance we will catch up to them before the midnight hour. Shall we move on, gentlemen?"

"I lack the stamina of an Elf and I am definitely nowhere near as young as I once was, but I am prepared to do so," stated Lando. Though he was already exhausted by the search that had started at the break of dawn, Lando was driven by guilt to help recover Nayla, no matter the cost.

"As I am, too," added Markus. "Let us go on."

"Night will soon be upon us," noted Joval. "Allow me to lead the way. Keep your eyes and ears open for danger."

"By all means," invited Markus, urging Joval on before him. After his ill-fated mishap involving Lando, he was not about to make the same mistake twice, especially now that he knew Nayla was somewhere out here in the impending darkness.

Taking the lead, Joval steered his mount on, guiding it through the forest that hugged the base of Mount Hope. His sharp eyes continued to hunt for viable clues to show the way.

As the milky twilight deepened with the coming of the night, the group ventured on at a steady pace as the trail of bent twigs directed them on past the little lake at the foot of Mount Hope, continuing westward.

"Now this does not bode well," said Lindras.

"What do you speak of?" asked Arerys.

Glancing about their surroundings, Lindras commented, "To me, it cannot be a coincidence these people boldly ventured through the night into the exact location the killer beast frequented. Now, when you consider every Talibarrian, far and wide, was aware of this creature and where it was last seen lurking about, why would these people brazenly enter its known territory lest they had reason *not* to fear the animal?"

"There is a chance they knew of a way to fend off an attack," responded Arerys.

"Perhaps they were hunting the creature for the bounty promised by King Sebastian?" offered Markus. "It was only by chance they stumbled upon Nayla and her party, taking advantage of the opportunity."

"No," dismissed Lando. He shook his head in disagreement. "Who in their right mind would go on a hunting expedition for such a deadly creature with an old woman in their company? If you ask me, when those murderous scoundrels came upon us, their actions were too deliberate, too well thought-out to be a random act to take advantage of an chance opportunity."

"I tend to agree with you, Lando," said the Wizard, nodding in consensus.

"So, do you believe they had something to do with that evil creature, Lindras?" questioned Arerys.

"If they did not, then I strongly suspect they know who did," surmised the Wizard.

"If we continue on in this direction, this trail shall lead us back toward the ravine where we had attempted to trap the beast," noted Markus.

"We shall find out soon enough where it leads," responded Joval. Through the growing darkness, he spied upon another twig discreetly twisted over to show the way. "Follow me."

With nothing more than the cold, celestial light of the moon and the stars to show the way, the Elf's keen eyes easily adjusted to the conditions, allowing him to guide them on.

Joval suddenly stopped. Raising his hand, all fell silent as they brought their horses to an abrupt halt. In the stifling darkness, the Elf listened through the ambient sounds of the forest.

"Someone comes our way," warned Joval, speaking in a whisper as he hastily armed his bow.

Lando, Arerys and Markus did likewise. They quickly dismounted from their steeds. Nocking an arrow onto their bow, they silently followed behind Joval. Lindras crept close behind, his staff clenched in his hands as they inched forward, heading directly to the sounds of footsteps rushing through the darkened forest. The loud crackling of branches and the noisy crunching of dried leaves underfoot betrayed a sinister presence lurking just ahead of them.

"Could it be one of your warriors?" whispered Markus.

"It is definitely not an Elf. Elves do not move so noisily," reminded Joval, cocking his head to one side as he homed in on the sounds.

"Careful now," warned Arerys. "It might be Nayla. She could have escaped her captors."

"Come what may, be prepared," ordered Joval, cautiously raising his bow to take aim. "Whatever it is, it is moving quickly, running in our direction."

"Ready…" whispered Arerys, raising his weapon.

"Aim…" said Markus, drawing back on his arrow.

"Hold your fire!" shouted Joval, immediately dropping his bow as a dark figure burst into the clearing to come face to face with this small barrier of weapons.

"Bloody hell!" cursed a familiar voice, holding his hands up high to show he was unarmed as he shouted. "I'm not the beast! I'm not the beast, I tell you!"

"Good gracious! Is that you, Captain Bristow?" queried Markus, stepping forward for a better look.

"Of course it's me!" snapped Cullen, his heart still thundering in his chest with the realization he and Druen were about to be fired upon.

"Good gracious, it *is* a beast!" remarked Lando, with a disgruntled sigh upon seeing the Captain. "It may not be *the beast*, but it is a beast nonetheless! Kill it, I say!"

"Har! Har!" Cullen grunted in mock laughter, as he lowered his arms. "If I did not know better, I'd say this comical bloke must be Lando Bayliss."

"Of course," responded Lando, stepping forward from the shadows. "The one and only!"

"I should have known it was you," grumbled Cullen, glaring at his nemesis of a friend. "But you'd think I would have smelled you coming from afar, old man."

"As charming as ever, I see," groaned Lando, "but I suppose this is as good as it gets, considering you are such a boar."

"You mean *a boor,*" corrected Cullen. "You mean to call me a boor."

"That, too, but as you already forget, I did call you a *beast*," reminded Lando. "I am merely clarifying the species."

"Only you would attempt to slay me with your wit when you have none," snorted Cullen.

"What are you doing here, anyway?" questioned Lando. "I thought you would be long dead by now; a casualty of your own reckless behaviour."

"Still witty as ever… in your own pathetic way," grunted Cullen, his eyes rolling in frustration. "But never mind that. What are *you* doing here? You are supposed to be retired. Can you not stay that way?"

"Enough chatter!" admonished Lindras, stepping between the two men. "There will be time enough to exchange salutations later. We have other pressing matters to contend with."

"Lindras is right. And just what happened to you, Captain Bristow?" questioned Arerys. He was clearly annoyed Cullen would suddenly show his face at the most inopportune moment. "Where did you go? Where have you been all this time?"

Peppered with unwanted questions, Cullen was quick to respond, deflecting this interrogation, "I had met with a terrible accident, but the better question is: Where did *you* go and why did you all choose to abandon me during my moment of dire need? I could have died out there, you know?"

"We did not abandon you," retorted Markus, sensing that Cullen was exaggerating his situation. "We thought you had had enough of the hunt and chose to take your leave; returning to Darross Castle to be by your King."

"Now how was I to do that when I was hurt and left to fend for myself with that dreaded creature still on the prowl?" snapped Cullen.

"The beast is dead," responded Lindras.

"It is?"

"Killed, carved and cremated," confirmed Markus.

"Well, that is a bloody good thing then," said Cullen, nodding in approval. "If I had caught up to that beast myself, I would have skinned it alive before killing it with my sword."

"Well, it is a bloody good thing *we* did not kill *you* traipsing about here in the dark, like the fool you are," retorted Lando. "I could have easily killed you on this night."

"Perhaps another time, old man," sniffed Cullen, dismissing Lando to address the others. "But listen to me, gentlemen! I come with news, terrible news from a most reliable source."

"What do you speak of? And who is this in your company?" questioned Lindras, spying the shadowy figure standing motionless and silent in a bid to remain concealed behind the Captain's back.

"Nayla?" called Arerys, stepping forward as the dark haired woman backed away, cowering behind Cullen.

"*Nayla?* Oh, no! This lovely, young lady is Druen," introduced Cullen, stepping aside to present her. "She is from a place just north of here. This is Druen of Dreymoor."

"A *witch!*" declared Lindras. His crystal orb glowed menacingly to shed some light on this woman.

Squinting hard, Druen was momentarily blinded, throwing her hands up to shield her eyes from this brilliant show of light emanating from the magic crystal.

Joval and Lando suddenly lunged forward to detain her, only to have Cullen immediately leap between them. He deliberately pulled Druen behind him, shielding her from their grasp.

"Hold on here! Keep your grubby hands off her! I said nothing about Druen being a witch, so back off!" demanded Cullen, pushing Joval and Lando away.

"I am no fool, Captain! You so much as declared her a witch when you said she is from Dreymoor," explained Lindras.

"I meant to say *was* from Dreymoor. But that is a rather broad and sweeping generalization you make, for one so enlightened."

"That is because the only citizens of Talibarr still residing in Dreymoor *are* witches," argued the Wizard.

"Come now, that is like saying he must be an Elf because he dwells in Wyndwood," dismissed Cullen, pointing over to Joval Stonecroft.

"That is because I *am* and I *do*," countered Joval. "In fact, all inhabitants of the enchanted forest are Elves."

"Alrighty then, so that was a bad example," responded Cullen. "The point being, just because she *was, and I repeat was,* from this place, it does not make her one of *them*. And if you just give her a chance to speak, you will learn she has some important news to share."

"News about Nayla?" Arerys asked hopefully.

"Hey, not everything is about your woman," admonished Cullen. "This is bigger than her! It concerns the evil that is about to be unleashed on this realm if we do not stop it."

For a moment, the men were silent upon hearing these strange, ominous words coming from the young Captain. They peered warily at this beautiful stranger shielded by Cullen.

"See, I told ya!" snapped Druen, shrinking under their scrutiny. "They're not about ta listen. They already think badly of me even though they know nothin' 'bout me."

"Calm down, Druen," urged Cullen, grasping her by the hand as she turned to leave. "As I said before, these are men of reason I travel with. They are just and honourable, so they will lend an ear to hear you out. Is that not so, gentlemen?"

When a swift answer was not forthcoming, Cullen prompted his company, "Or was I wrong about your good character?"

"Look here, Captain Bristow," said Arerys; "we are willing to listen, but it better be worthy of our time, for we are in the midst of something very important – a crisis if you must know."

"Let me assure you, Prince Arerys, the news I have is *not* good and it is far more important than anything you are currently embroiled in," vowed Cullen. "I beseech you; please, just listen to what Druen has to say. Give her a moment of your time."

"A moment is all we can spare, Captain Bristow," said Lindras. "We are willing to hear you out, but be quick about it. What is this news, young lady?"

Druen meekly stepped forward to look upon Lindras. "You are the Wizard of the West?"

"Yes, I am Lindras Weatherstone. And just what is this news you wish to share?"

"I don't suspect any of you are gonna believe me, but at least if I say what's on my mind, then I can't be blamed when this whole thing goes bad," decided Druen, screwing up her courage to withstand the scrutiny she was confident she was about to be subjected to. "At least I tried ta warn you all."

"Go on, Druen, tell them what you told me," coaxed Cullen, taking her by the hand to lead her into this small circle comprised of mortals, Elves and a Wizard. "Tell them of this evil."

"Very well," conceded Druen, drawing a deep breath as much to gather her thoughts as to regain her composure. "I know of a witch an' she's plannin' on doin' somethin' truly evil."

"Evil?" said Arerys. "That is rather vague."

"Exactly what do you mean by *evil*," questioned Lindras.

"This witch I'm speakin' of is plannin' on resurrectin' the Dark Lord Beyilzon," revealed Druen.

"How is *that* for evil!" snorted Cullen, nodding his head to encourage Druen to reveal more.

"That is impossible!" dismissed Lindras. "There is no mortal in this world with the power to do so; at least, not without being endowed with the magic of the forbidden arts."

"But she is!" insisted Druen, nodding her head vigorously. "You gotta believe me."

"I would be more inclined to believe this if there were indeed a witch vested with such powers, but none exist these days," countered Lindras. "Not since the Dark Lord Beyilzon roamed these lands centuries ago had there been witches endowed with such powerful magic rooted in the forbidden arts."

"This witch has the power an' then some!" exclaimed Druen. "It's downright scary, the magic she can conjure up."

"And just where would she derive such magic?" questioned the Wizard, still doubting her words.

"She's usin' the powers she's gettin' from a horrible, old book," answered Druen, her words unwavering.

"Say again?" gasped Lindras, perplexed and shocked by her claim.

"I'm speakin' the truth, Master Wizard!"

"What book is this?" questioned Arerys, his interest suddenly piqued by these curious words.

"Well… I don't know exactly what it's called, but I can describe the damned thing fer ya, if it helps," offered Druen.

"Please do," urged Arerys.

"Let's see. It's got a tatty, old cover of red leather…" She paused for a moment as she called to mind other details that stood out. "It's kinda singed on its spine an' along the edges – like it was in a fire."

"This cannot be a coincidence," responded Joval, recalling how the Book of Spells was damaged by extreme heat when he and Nayla tossed it into a pool of lava in a bid to destroy it many years ago.

"So it is singed and has a red leather cover… It can still be any of a dozen of books out there," stated Markus.

"Plus, it's got these strange symbols on the front cover," disclosed Druen, her fingertip carefully scraping an image into the soft earth of the runes branded on the cover. "I don't know what it means, but that witch sure as heck did."

"Goodness, no!" gasped Lindras. He was absolutely mortified as he leaned heavily on his staff upon reading these ancient runes.

"I recognize these characters!" exclaimed Joval, visibly disturbed to see these familiar symbols. "It *is* the Book of Spells."

"That cannot be!" gasped Lando. "It was destroyed during our last quest."

"Could it be we all wanted to believe it was destroyed?" Markus wondered aloud, greatly troubled and disheartened by this news.

"How did this witch come to claim the book?" questioned Lindras, eager to learn more about its fate.

"Last winter, we – uh, *she* was fishin' the Sea of Storms. It's said that when she cast her net out, not only did she catch fish, but amongst the fish she sought was this book. Apparently, it was frozen in a great chunk of ice. It was jus' floatin' out there like it was waitin' ta be found."

"Good gracious! That book has a will of its own!" groaned Lando. "It refuses to be destroyed."

"Is this possible, Lindras?" queried Arerys. "Could that book have survived the devastation?"

"As much as I would like to deny it, where that vile thing is concerned, anything is possible. Keep in mind; this book was once bound to the Dark Lord. It is more than evident it is still protected by evil magic," revealed Lindras.

"So this witch has possession of the Book of Spells," acknowledged Arerys, but still discounting her words with a shrug of indifference. "Even if it was so, there is no mortal existing today that knows how to read this ancient dialect of Elvish."

"That's what you think," countered Druen. "This old witch I speak of knows how ta do jus' that."

"That is absolutely preposterous! How can that be so?" argued Arerys. "None but the Wizard, the elders of Wyndwood and members of Elven royalty are still acquainted with this language."

"Well, this woman understands it. An' you should know, she comes from a long line of witches," explained Druen. "She's a descendent of the ones who once ran the coven at the place us Talibarrians still refer ta as the Witch's Hold."

"So, this woman's ancestors belonged to the Coven of Four?" queried Lindras.

"No, sir… her ancestor *was one* of the *four* you're speakin' of, Master Weatherstone," clarified Druen.

"Good gracious! The news only worsens the more you reveal!" declared the Wizard, pondering the possibilities. "Those hags did speak and write this ancient language; that is a well-known fact."

"So this woman is a direct descendant of the original witches of Dreymoor," said Markus, attempting to downplay the relevance of this news. "Those women are long dead, gone and forgotten. So, too, is this knowledge they once shared."

"We are inclined to believe this, but more so because we wish it to be true," responded Lindras, entertaining this possibility. "Do keep in mind, the privileged in all societies, mortal and Elf alike, preserve history, lore, myth as well as antiquated languages, handing this knowledge down to the next generation."

"There is nothing to say this society of witches did the same," concluded Joval, "even after the original four met their demise."

"That is what Druen has been trying to tell you!" exclaimed Cullen, his frustration obvious to see. "This wizened, old hag Druen has been speaking of has the ways and the means to decipher those spells!"

"Did you say a *'wizened, old hag'*?" questioned Lando, frowning with curiosity as he stared at the Captain.

"I did," replied Cullen. "I have not seen the witch with mine own eyes, but according to Druen, that is not such a bad thing. She claims this witch is a regular eye-sore, if you get my meaning?"

Not taking Cullen's words for anything, Lando turned to Druen, questioning her, "Tell me, young lady, does this witch you speak of have an ill-favoured look about her?"

"They all do!" grunted Cullen. "You must be more specific than that."

"Does she have a wild mane of gray hair? Does she appear to be twice as tall if she were able to stand upright?" continued Lando; "and she has twisted, gnarled hands; warty moles on her face and she appears to be blind in the left eye?"

"Yes! That's her!" confirmed Druen, her heart racing with dread upon hearing Lando's description. "Have you seen her? She isn't close by, is she?"

Lando suddenly lunged at the woman, seizing Druen by her wrist as he announced, "She is one of them! She knows where they've taken Nayla."

"Unhand her!" demanded Cullen.

Just as he leapt to Druen's defense, Lando plowed Cullen square in the face with a clenched fist. As the dazed Captain fell backward into Joval's arms, the Elf promptly propped the reeling Cullen back onto his feet.

"Why the hell did you do that?" sputtered Cullen, nursing his aching jaw.

"Shut it!" ordered Lando. "She is one of them!"

"What do you know of this witch? What does she intend to do with Nayla?" questioned Lindras.

Instead of answering, Druen struggled all the more to be free of Lando's powerful grip as she snarled, "You're hurtin' me! Let go!"

"Not until you answer our questions!" snapped Lando, holding steadfast to Druen. "Now, speak! Answer the Wizard."

Druen winced in pain as Lando squeezed her wrist to prompt a response.

"You big buffoon!" cursed Cullen, attempting to pry Lando's hand off her only to have the retired knight shove him aside. "You are hurting her! Get your damned paws off her this minute!"

Just as Cullen foolishly lunged at Lando once more, Joval intervened. He seized the angry captain. Effectively restraining Cullen, he subdued him in a constricting hold to prevent him from getting hurt in another altercation.

"Can you not see Lando is hurting her?" growled Cullen, struggling to be free of Joval's hold.

"*You* are the one who will be getting hurt if you do not desist," grunted Joval.

Cullen groaned in pain as the Elf raised him off the ground with his arms pinned behind his back.

"Please don't hurt him!" pleaded Druen. She stopped struggling as she watched Cullen grimace in pain as he strained against Joval's hold to come to her rescue. "I'll tell ya what I know if ya promise not ta hurt him."

"I assure you, my lady, I am merely restraining Captain Bristow," responded Joval. "Whatever pain he endures, that is his own doing."

"Please, I ask again, don't hurt him," begged Druen. "He's a good man! He's jus' tryin' ta protect me."

"Do you even know whom you are standing up for?" queried Markus, mystified this Talibarrian woman would be concerned for the well-being of this Captain from Darross, especially knowing how much Cullen despised these people to the north.

"Of course!" retorted Druen. "He's Sir Cullen Bristow, brave an' respected Captain to King Sebastian's army."

"Now this is truly bizarre," commented Lando. "Alright then, just what did the Captain promise to make you speak kindly of him?"

"He promised me nothing!" growled Druen, angered by their callousness. "He's a kind an' carin' man; a noble gentleman of good character. That's why I'm askin' you ta stop hurtin' him. He doesn't deserve this!"

"Hmph! That is not the Cullen Bristow we know," chided Lando, staring skeptically at this young woman.

"Then ya don't know him at all, do ya?" snapped Druen, glaring back at Lando. "Now, if ya stop man-handlin' him, I promise I'll tell ya what I know."

"Joval, release Captain Bristow," ordered Lindras.

"As you wish."

Immediately, the Elf's powerful grip relaxed. Joval dumped Cullen to send him sprawling onto the ground at Druen's feet.

"You brute!" Druen cursed at Joval as she wrenched free of Lando's hold. She knelt by Cullen's side, comforting him. "How do ya fare?"

"I am quite fine," responded Cullen, scrambling onto his feet in a bid to regain his dignity as Druen helped him up, brushing the dust and embarrassment from his raiment.

"Good, now start talking," demanded Arerys. "What do you know about this witch Lando had described? And what does she intend to do with Nayla?"

"First of all," snapped Cullen, shielding Druen behind him again, "why do you keep bringing up this witch and Nayla in the same sentence? What does one witch have to do with the other?"

"Listen up, Cullen," snarled Lando. "Nayla was travelling in my company as we escorted the emissaries sent by the governing council of Talibarr on a trade mission in Orien. On the eastern fringe of this forest, we were attacked. The emissaries were killed in cold-blood; I was beaten senseless while Nayla was taken captive."

"Whoa! Hold on here!" ordered Cullen, attempting to make sense of this all. "Let me get this straight. Are you saying that *the great* Nayla Treeborn was captured by *a* lowly witch?"

"A witch and her cronies to be exact! And it just happens to be the witch I had described to this woman, right down to the gimpy eye," reminded Lando. "So I ask again, where did she take Nayla?"

"Nayla Treeborn?" Druen frowned with obvious worry as she repeated this all too familiar name of legend.

In frustration, Lando seized her by her slight shoulders, turning Druen about to face Arerys.

"This gentleman, young missy, is Prince Arerys of Wyndwood," disclosed Lando, his words emphatic. "It is his wife, Nayla Treeborn this witch had taken. And being that he is the Prince of Elves and we are Nayla's friends, we do not take kindly to such treacherous actions."

Druen blanched as she stared at the Elf's worried face as he pondered the fate of his missing wife.

"Now where the bloody hell did that witch take her?" Lando demanded to know. "If you do not wish to tell me, then for pity's sake, tell Prince Arerys where Nayla is."

"Oooh, this is not good," groaned Druen. "Not good at all!"

"Speak!" snapped Lando, growing impatient with her. "What do you mean by that?"

"Lando, let her go," ordered Arerys, urging his friend to stand down. "You are scaring her."

"And deservedly so!" rebuked Lando, reluctantly backing away.

Arerys knelt before Druen, taking her hands into his. In a calm, steady voice, Arerys made a heartfelt appeal, "Please, I beg of you, tell me what you know of my wife's disappearance. If not for me, then for our daughter's sake; if you know something of Nayla's whereabouts, speak now."

"I had no idea that witch I was speakin' of was plannin' on takin' yer wife hostage, m'lord," said Druen. "She said she'd be takin' someone important, but I was thinkin' she was referrin' ta one of the emissaries."

"So this witch knew about the trade mission?" questioned Arerys.

"Who in Talibarr didn't know?" responded Druen. "Everyone watchin' ta see what this new council is about; waitin' ta see exactly what they're gonna do fer the people – if anything at all."

"I take it, the witch also knew the emissaries would be in the company of Lando Bayliss and my wife?" queried Arerys.

"I suppose so, but like I said, I never thought she'd dare take on the consort to the Prince of Wyndwood. That's jus' plain crazy!"

"But why? Why would she take Nayla hostage?" questioned Lindras, trying to make sense of this news.

"I suspect she was thinkin' that she'd get exactly what she wants an' faster, too, takin' someone of *real* importance," surmised Druen. "That's the only thing I can think of."

"Hey! You said nothing to me about that demented, old woman's plans to take Prince Arerys' wife hostage," exclaimed Cullen, glancing over at Druen.

"That's 'cause I didn't know that's what she'd be doin'. I took off when I realized that bad things were jus' gonna get worse if she kept messin' with that book. In fact, as soon as I saw her kill a poor, little falcon, I jus' couldn't take anymore of her wickedness. I knew there'd be more killin' ta follow, so I fled. I wanted no part of it."

"Are you speaking of my wife's falcon?" inquired Arerys, listening intently to her words.

"How would I know? I suppose it could've been," replied Druen, her shoulders arching in a shrug as she recalled the dreadful feeling that overwhelmed her with sadness when the beautiful raptor fell from the sky. "As soon as that *witch* slung that stone at the bird, I left."

"Aha! You were there!" declared Lando, charging toward Druen as Markus and Cullen moved to intercept the retired knight. "Nayla's falcon was felled from the sky by a stone! You have something to do with Nayla's disappearance!"

"Watch what you say, old man!" admonished Cullen. "Just because she saw what happened, it does not mean she was a party to this."

"She is guilty by association!" denounced Lando.

"How is it that you know so much about this witch and her plans, young lady?" queried Lindras. "Care to explain?"

"Truth be told, I am – "

"I am being honest when I say Druen had heard of this through others." Cullen was quick to interject, discreetly shaking his head to dissuade her from blurting out the truth.

"I'm not gonna lie ta them now," countered Druen, turning on Cullen. "If they can stop her, then they gotta know the truth or they'll never believe me."

"For pity's sake, Cullen, were you going to have this woman lie to us?" scolded Markus.

"Of course not, I was merely encouraging her to reveal information that is absolutely relevant to what is going to happen, as we are so pressed for time."

"He wanted her to lie," groaned Lando, shaking his head in disapproval as he glared at the Captain.

"To withhold the truth, a truth that is irrelevant to these events, is *not* lying," disputed Cullen.

"Oh hush!" scolded Lindras. "Allow the woman to speak."

"Thank you, Master Weatherstone," said Druen. "As I was sayin'; I know what's happenin' 'cause I know this witch."

"And just how well do you know her?" questioned Arerys.

"That woman is my gran'mother," revealed Druen, her head hanging low in shame.

"She is?" gasped Cullen, in an incredulous tone as he took a step away from her to distance himself from the backlash of her admission.

"You know I am," grumbled Druen, scowling at Cullen. "I told ya this from the start!"

"So you knew all along, Captain Bristow?" asked Markus, staring with raised eyebrows at Cullen.

"What do you know? I suppose I did. It must have slipped my mind," responded Cullen, trying to sound nonchalant about this revelation.

"A selective memory… How very convenient, Captain Bristow," sighed Joval, rolling his eyes in exasperation.

"As far as I am concerned, Druen's relationship to this witch is irrelevant!" declared Cullen. "Judging from Lando's description, they are probably not even related by blood. The important thing is, Druen is risking her life in disclosing this information to you. She feared banishment or worse by her people. There is no need to make her feel more miserable than she already does."

"Is this true, young lady? You have been banished by your people?" questioned Lindras.

"I chose ta banish myself. Given what I know, my granny would rather see me dead. In fact, I'll be deader than dead if she knew I was talkin' ta you all. Being blood relations don't mean nothin' ta her unless it serves her purpose."

"But why would you turn your back on a legacy? A family tradition that had lasted an eon?" queried Arerys. "Why this sudden change of heart?"

"Ain't nothing sudden 'bout it. I never wanted ta be a witch an' I certainly don't agree with what my gran is fixin' ta do."

"If this is the only existence you have ever known, I find it hard to believe you would so readily refuse this way of life," argued Arerys.

"I mean no disrespect ta you, m'lord, but are ya mad? Have ya seen what testin' all those potions an' stuff can do to a person?"

"If your grandmother is a testament to that, I can sympathize," said Lando, recalling the dreadful looking hag he had encountered. "But you cannot tell me that you would turn your back on your kin-folk for the sake of vanity?"

"You insensitive lout!" snapped Cullen, coming to Druen's defense. "That is an asinine thing to say!"

"You are the insensitive one, and if this woman does not know it yet, just keep talking," countered Lando. "She will know soon enough!"

"Stop it, you two!" ordered Arerys. "What is your real reason for turning your back on your people?"

"I won't deny I dread the outcome if I'm made ta remain in this vocation, but I was a Talibarrian long before I knew I was supposed ta become a witch. As far as I'm concerned, it's bad enough our fellow countrymen want nothin' ta do with us anymore, but between them an' my folks, I'm an outcast of an outcast…"

"So, if you can find favour with the general population, you will not have to be concerned about your grandmother's people," surmised Lindras.

"First, I gotta try an' save the general population, so there's one I can get lost in when my gran sends her folks ta get me fer doin' this," explained Druen.

"Which brings us back to the subject of what the witch is up to and what she plans to do with Nayla," reminded Joval, steering the conversation back on course.

"Well, I have no doubt your grandmother will be upset with you, but exactly what did you mean she intends to 'resurrect the Dark Lord'? And how does Nayla play into all of this?" questioned Arerys.

"Upset?" gasped Druen, her eyes widening in horror. "Mark my words, m'lord, she'll have me killed fer speakin' of this!"

"Not if we offer you protection and a safe sanctuary in exchange, Druen. Is that not so, Prince Arerys?" Cullen bargained on her behalf.

"Yes! Now speak! Tell us more," urged Arerys.

"Starting with the witch's plans for the Dark Lord," instructed Lindras.

"Well, at first when she came across this *book*, I didn't think much of it," confided Druen. "My gran was tellin' me of all the remarkable powers vested in the pages, but I thought it was jus' crazy talk 'til things started ta happen."

"What things?" questioned Markus.

"Well... Like that crazy beast you claimed ta have killed," revealed Druen.

"The witch conjured up that monster?" gasped Lindras.

"Straight up from the bowels of hell itself. She used an incantation from the book, but instead of callin' up the Dark Lord's hound of old, she wanted somethin' far more threatenin', more dangerous; a creature that had no loyalty to the Dark Lord so she'd have complete control over it."

"Hence that overgrown cat with the monstrous fangs," determined Lindras.

"Yeah! In fact, she used scrapings from a big, old fang of one of these cats that died out a long, long time ago," disclosed Druen. "She mixed up a batch of a strange potion and poured it on the ground where the rest of the animal's bones lay buried in the earth up on the Witch's Hold. With this an' an incantation from the book, that horrible creature came ta be."

"This is why the witch and her followers felt safe travelling through these parts with the beast roaming about," decided Joval. "The creature was called upon to do the witch's bidding; therefore, it viewed her as its master."

"Well, bugger me!" exclaimed Cullen. "That is why you kept telling me that I would be safe if I remained by your side!"

"Yeah," admitted Druen. "That crazy animal was told ta leave her people unharmed as it went on a rampage."

"And just what was the purpose of setting this beast on these innocent people?" probed Lindras.

"As far as my gran was concerned; if you ain't a witch, you ain't innocent. She said that unleashing this creature would cause such a level of grief and panic, it'd bring the four Wizards together in Talibarr ta hunt the creature down."

"What made her think the Talibarrian people would not just mount their own hunting expeditions to capture and kill the beast?" asked Markus.

"If it were the Dark Lord's hound, that probably would've been the case," responded Druen. "But that's why she went through all that trouble of conjurin' up that horrid thing. She knew it would cause such fear an' present such a danger, she was sure the people would call on the Wizards fer their help. When they failed ta act fast enough, that's when she decided on capturing yer wife, m'lord."

"The witch was almost correct in her thinking," nodded Arerys, as he glanced over at Lindras. "She managed to get one of the Wizards to Talibarr."

"But the question is why?" asked Joval. "What does she want with the Wizards?"

"It ain't so much the Wizards," responded Druen.

"The crystal orbs!" exclaimed Lando, recalling the witch's parting words to him. "Four orbs for one life spared! That witch wants the Wizards' magical orbs in exchange for Nayla."

"But for what reason?" said Lindras, gripping his staff tightly. "What does this witch plan to do with the orbs?"

"She said she needs the crystals ta bring back the Dark Lord," revealed Druen. "She claimed that the four crystals represent balance in this realm. And she said, jus' as there's good, there's evil too. One balances the other…"

"That witch intends to use the powers of our crystals to resurrect the Dark Lord!" said Lindras.

"This is insanity!" dismissed Arerys. "If this witch was descended from the original four, she would know the Dark Lord betrayed her ancestors. Why would she even consider resurrecting Beyilzon knowing that he will only betray her and her people once more?"

"That's jus' it, m'lord; my gran is familiar with all that history. That's why she intends ta betray *him*, first," disclosed Druen. "She said the only way ta steal away with all his powers is ta bring him back, ta do the deed right."

"Bloody hell… I do not like the sounds of this," groaned Cullen, staring at Druen. "I knew you said the crazy, old bat wanted to make off with the Wizards' crystal orbs for evil gains, but you did not say anything about the Dark Lord, for he is as evil as they come!"

"You were already so worried 'bout my welfare, I jus' didn't want ya gettin' more worked up than ya had ta be," confessed Druen, offering Cullen a comforting smile as she gave his hand a reassuring squeeze.

"That was considerate of you, my dear, however, how can I, or any man standing before me for that matter, not be worked up about this prospect?" countered Cullen.

"So that is why the old woman took Nayla hostage," determined Arerys. "Since the killer beast's bloody rampage did not result in the four Wizards converging in Talibarr as she had hoped for, she knew the one thing that would bring the four powers together was to save Nayla's life."

"That's 'bout the only thing I can think of fer her reasonin' to take yer woman, m'lord," responded Druen, sounding sincerely contrite for the peril Nayla was now faced with. "She believes the Wizards will come ta spare her life. Surely, if not ta save the King of Darross, she believed their close friendship with yer wife would bring them runnin' ta Talibarr – ta this very place."

"If that is what she wants, she will face our combined wrath!" vowed Lindras.

"If she remains true ta her plans, she won't be wantin' any of your wrath. She jus' wants yer crystals," reminded Druen. "So, if you know what's good fer all of us, you'd be tellin' yer brother Wizards to keep clear of Talibarr so my gran don't get her way."

"What do you think, Lindras?" asked Arerys. "Do you believe her? Or are her words too far-fetched to be reliable?"

"But I'm tellin' you the truth, m'lord!" declared Druen. "I swear on my life. An' if that don't mean anythin', I'll swear on Captain Bristow's life, instead."

"You should know, my good woman, in my eyes, your life is of far greater value than his," grunted Lando, glaring over at Cullen.

"Damn it all!" swore Cullen, as he turned to the Elf. His hand lay over his heart in solemn promise. "Then I swear, Prince Arerys, on my father's good name, Druen is telling you the God's honest truth,"

"Do you truly expect us to believe this woman, Cullen?" grumbled Lando, staring accusingly at Druen. "Perhaps your mind is influenced by these surroundings. Though this place is still be remembered by some as the Witch's Hold, I do believe it is this *witch* who has a *hold* on you."

"You miserable, old goat!" cursed Cullen. "I believe her and so should you!"

"Perhaps Lando is correct, Captain Bristow," noted Markus. "After all, it does go against your character to believe in the words of a Talibarrian."

"I can understand your doubt, but I believe *her* and it has nothing to do with what she is or any enchantment you may think is at work here."

"Then why this drastic change, Captain?" questioned Arerys. "It is so unlike you to abandon your beliefs, no matter how skewed."

"Because Druen saved my life," confessed Cullen.

"She did?" responded Arerys, glancing over at the young woman.

"At the risk of her own life and safety, she came to my aid when none of you were around to do so! And as far as I am concerned, that is bloody good reason enough to believe in her. If you choose not to, then she had spared my life all for naught, for we will all be doomed to the same fate. Either way for Druen, if she goes back to her people, she is dead. If she had said nothing of this matter to any of you; she will be dead, as undoubtedly, we shall meet the same fate."

For a moment, the Wizard and all in his company silently mulled over this revelation.

"Doom or no doom, they don't believe me," groaned Druen, with a disheartened sigh as she peered forlornly into Cullen's concerned eyes. "I said all I could. There's nothin' more I can do."

"There is one thing…" disclosed Arerys, after carefully considering his limited options.

"What's that, m'lord," asked Druen. "Jus' tell me an' I'll make it so!"

"Will you take me to Nayla? Can you lead me to Dreymoor?"

taking a chance

"Hold on, Arerys," urged Markus, staring with disbelief into the Elf's worried eyes. "Do you understand what you are asking of this woman?"

"I most certainly do." Arerys spoke with conviction.

"Let us not be hasty, my friends. Men of the Order, it is time for a meeting," announced Lindras, motioning his comrades to step aside with him. "Gather over here."

As Cullen stepped forward to join in the discussions, Lando abruptly and intentionally intercepted the Captain. He stood steadfast before him, shooing Cullen away.

"You heard the Wizard. He said '*men of the Order*'," stated Lando. "Unless you had somehow wormed your way into our circle during my absence, you are not included. So bugger off until we call on you."

"Very well then," conceded Cullen, sounding nonchalant as he pretended he was not bothered by Lando's dismissive tone. "Besides, someone must keep this young lady safe while the rest of you plot and scheme behind my back."

"Yes, make yourself useful for a change. Keep a watchful eye on her," approved Lando, turning away to join his friends.

"Are you confident she can be trusted, Arerys?" questioned Markus, speaking in a whisper as his eyes scrutinized the Talibarrian woman in Cullen's company. "You do realize we will, quite literally, be placing our lives in her hands in doing so?"

"Well, Captain Bristow did say she saved his life," reasoned Arerys, attempting to justify the request he made to Druen.

"So she erred in judgment," assessed Lando, with a shrug of his shoulders. "She cannot be faulted for doing a seemingly good deed."

Lando was thoroughly agitated by the Captain's presence. Even when he had no intention of venturing on another quest, by some strange and ironic twist of fate, there was Cullen Bristow, yet again. Like the proverbial, annoying pebble that refused to be shaken from one's boot, his presence was felt, but not appreciated. Lando's blunt comment was met with a quizzical stare from his friends.

"What do you mean by that, Lando?" queried Markus.

"I am saying you cannot fault the girl for having compassion enough to spare his sorry life. After all, faced with a similar situation, even I would be hard-pressed not to save a mangy, stray mutt from a death by drowning."

"I see your animosity to Bristow has yet to wane after all this time, Lando," decided Lindras.

"And rightfully so, Wizard! My attitude to that dimwitted sod of a captain will only be swayed if he was able to prove to me he has an ounce of integrity somewhere in that corrupt soul of his. Instead, Cullen continues to pretend to be a true knight living by a code of chivalry. If he were not so morally repugnant, I would think differently."

"Personal feelings aside, Lando, do you believe this woman can be trusted?" questioned Joval, peering over his shoulder to gaze at Druen as she quietly waited by Cullen's side.

"I hate to admit this, but I trust her more than that cad the poor girl has obviously and foolishly taken a fancy to," sniffed Lando.

"But how do we know she will not be leading us directly into a trap?" whispered Markus. "There is that possibility, you know?"

"I cannot deny I have grave concerns as she is the granddaughter of this witch we seek," admitted Arerys. "However, if this madwoman is intent on killing Nayla by the rise of the next full moon if her demands are not met, my options are extremely limited. I am willing to risk encountering a trap, for there is a possibility there will be none, whereas Nayla will most certainly be faced with death if I do nothing."

"Grant you that, my friend. Just be forewarned, we are speaking of a group of people even their fellow Talibarrians hold little trust for," cautioned Lindras. "Even if this witch and her followers did not go out of their way to set up traps to keep *us* away, I am confident a regular obstacle course of deadly contraptions already exists to keep others dwelling in the neighbouring villages from intruding on their little enclave."

"Is there a way of finding out for certain?" queried Arerys.

"The only other person to come to mind who would know this for certain is Tor Airshorn. Of all the Wizards, Tor had spent a good portion of his life in this realm attempting to enlighten these folks to the north," disclosed Lindras. "Aside from that, we are left with having to trust this woman."

"In my way of thinking, we are forced to venture to Dreymoor if we intend to rescue Nayla," stated Joval. "What difference will it make if there are traps, or not? Either way, we are taking a chance. If we are clever about it, Druen can warn us of any potential danger."

"If she is being used by this witch to lead us into a trap, why would she bother to warn us?" questioned Lando.

"I am suggesting that she not only show us the way, I recommend she actually *lead the way*," explained Joval, his voice was cold and calculating as he stated his case. "Placed strategically in a position amongst our rank that can jeopardize her own life if there is a trap to consider, she will either warn us in advance or she will fall victim to it herself. In doing so, she will spare us some grief either way."

"It is a plan. Though it seems rather cruel to use her in this manner, it is a plan nonetheless," responded Mark.

"That is true, however, in my mind, what has happened to Nayla is more so," justified the Elf.

"Joval is correct," agreed Arerys, wanting nothing more than to secure Nayla's safe release by whatever means. "If Druen is telling us the truth and she truly means to put a stop to this witch's evil, she will voluntarily expose the hidden dangers along the way. As cruel as this sounds, if she is lying, then her untimely demise will be deserved."

"In all honesty, I do not wish this woman to come to harm, for there is a chance she is telling us the truth," disclosed Joval; "however, that is what I am thinking. That is what I am willing to risk to save Nayla."

"And if she is speaking the truth, how will you justify her death if she falls victim to a trap while helping us to retrieve Nayla?" questioned Markus.

"The only other option is to call upon my brother Wizards," offered Lindras. "However, I have my suspicions to do so, we shall be playing right into this witch's hands. For now, it is a risk I would rather not take. I say we use the girl."

"Unfortunately, as much as I believe the powers gifted to the four of you can overwhelm this witch, I am more overwhelmed by a terrible sense of foreboding that if there is to be a trap, it will be no ordinary one. It will be designed specifically for the Wizards if her intention is to steal away with the magical orbs," agreed Arerys.

"With this in mind, I believe it is better for all concerned if your brother Wizards kept clear of Talibarr," recommended Markus.

"I have an idea," whispered Joval. "If there is a trap awaiting us, we should turn the tables, take this girl as *our* hostage. If she is related by blood as closely as she claims, I hardly belief her grandmother will risk her life."

"We trade her life for Nayla's?" questioned Arerys.

"Sure… Why not?" responded Joval.

"But what if she spoke the truth when she said she had fled for her life? That her grandmother would want nothing more than to see her dead for this betrayal?" queried Markus.

"Or the witch is a twisted, demented soul bent on acquiring this power, enough that she would forsake her granddaughter's life no matter what?" added Lando.

"I do not know about the rest of you, but unfortunately for this woman, it is a risk I am forced to take," stated Arerys, glancing over at Druen. "For Nayla's sake, I have no choice."

"So, it is decided," announced Lindras. He turned to face Druen and the Captain, waving for them to step forward.

"And what have you decided?" questioned Cullen, his eyes narrowing in suspicion.

"We have come to the conclusion that with Druen's willingness to reveal this witch's plan and to eagerly come to our aid in leading us to Dreymoor, we have no reason to question her honesty," replied the Wizard.

"So, you believe me?" questioned Druen, momentarily stunned by this turn of good news.

"We have no reason not to believe you," answered Arerys.

"Do you want me ta show the way right now? I can take you, but it'll be tricky at parts."

"What do you mean *tricky*?" asked Cullen.

"There'll be some obstacles ta overcome on our way ta the village," revealed Druen.

"Obstacles in the way of traps?" queried Arerys.

"Yeah, but I know where they are an' how ta get around 'em. I'll warn ya now, it can be kinda dangerous as we near Dreymoor, especially if you travel by night 'cause there'll be more traps ta contend with."

"I tell you what," responded Lindras; "we shall journey on until we can travel no farther on this night. When we are ready to move on in the morning, we shall time our travel so we will arrive at this village while the light of day still holds."

"That should do," agreed Druen. "After all, it'd be senseless fer me ta take you all ta Dreymoor in hopes of puttin' a stop ta this evil only ta have you all killed along the way."

"Good thinking, my dear!" praised Cullen. He was pleased Druen was still concerned about his safety.

"Let us be on our way," ordered Arerys, urging them to follow Druen. "We have already lost precious time we will never get back."

Glancing up to the cobalt sky, Cullen yawned wearily as he stared up to the near-full moon shining down upon them. Glowing brightly like a luminous pearl suspended high on this velvety canvas bejeweled with a multitude of sparkling, diamond stars, the Captain noted by the movement of this celestial orb and the constellations, they had travelled for well over four hours without a break for man or beast.

With Joval leading the way, Cullen was just grateful they were not made to walk the distance. He could feel Druen tiring, her warm body resting against his chest as she began to nod off. The steady plodding of hoof beats into the soft earth and the gentle swaying motion atop this mount while wrapped in Cullen's arms lulled Druen to sleep. He steered Markus' stallion on to catch up to Markus as he shared a ride with Arerys on RainDance.

"Can we stop for a brief rest, if not for the night," whispered Cullen, trying not to wake Druen.

"Are you getting tired?" questioned Markus, glancing over his shoulder at the Captain.

"*Me?* I can go on forever," grunted Cullen, speaking in a hushed voice as his passenger stirred. "It is Druen I am concerned about. We have been on the move since daybreak."

"What say you, Lindras?" queried Arerys, hearing this exchange. "Should we rest for the remainder of the night?"

Lindras brought Tempest to a stop. "Now is a good a time as any, I suppose. If we continue on at this pace I believe we shall arrive at Dreymoor late tomorrow afternoon."

"Do you think we will be safe for the night at this place?" asked Joval, dismounting from his steed as he glanced about their gloomy surroundings.

"The beast is dead and I believe we are still far enough away from the witch's village that we can rest easy for now," determined Lindras.

As Cullen reined Arrow in, this sudden stop to the horse's steady, rolling gait that had lulled Druen to sleep served to wake her.

"What's goin' on?" asked Druen, through a great yawn as she rubbed the sleep from her eyes.

"We are going to rest for what is left of the night," explained Cullen, dismounting first before helping Druen down.

"Is it because I fell asleep? If it is, I'm sorry."

"No, my dear, it is because we are all tired," responded Cullen, placing Druen gently onto the ground. "It has been an exceedingly long day for all."

Glancing about, Druen recognized their location in relation to the west slope of Mount Hope.

"We'll be safe here. We're gettin' close, but we're not too close," disclosed Druen, nodding in approval. "If we leave in the morn an' all goes well, we'll arrive in Dreymoor by early evenin' at the latest."

"That is the plan, young lady," said Lindras, whispering words of instruction to Tempest to remain close and to keep watch over the other horses to ensure they did not stray away too far.

"In case you were thinkin' about it, it's not a good idea to build a fire," cautioned Druen. "There's no point in letting them know we're headin' in their direction."

"We shall take heed of your warning, my good woman," responded Lindras, nodding in acknowledgement as he rummaged through his worn, leather bag for his trusty old, earthenware pipe.

Lando yawned as he stretched his weary muscles, twisting to and fro in a bid to loosen up his aching back made stiff by the long hours in the saddle.

"I see your age is getting the better of you, old man," teased Cullen, watching as Lando painfully trudged along past him and Druen to wearily plop down on the log next to the Wizard.

"Aside from your company, it is not my *age* that makes me suffer as I do," grunted Lando. "I am still recovering from my injuries."

"From the beating you received at the hands of the witch's cronies?" asked Cullen, removing his cloak to wrap it around Druen's shoulders to keep her warm.

"More so from the injuries I acquired *after* that confrontation," replied Lando. "But enough talk. The main thing is, I will recover."

"This sounds intriguing. Just what happened? Did you nod off and take a little tumble from your horse?" scoffed Cullen.

"Oh, you wish!" snapped Lando, shaking his head in dismay.

"In our friend's defense, Lando was wounded by an arrow before being thrown from his mount," informed Lindras, clenching the pipe's worn, wooden mouthpiece between his teeth.

"Good gracious!" exclaimed Cullen, surprised by this news. "Was it a Talibarrian arrow?"

"What difference does it make?" snapped Lando, wanting nothing more than to change the subject. He rubbed his shoulder that had mended beneath Joval's magical touch, but still ached as a result of this rapid healing process human beings were not accustomed to.

"Well, you are definitely not the skilled knight you once were," mocked Cullen, rubbing salt into Lando's invisible wound. "No doubt, you somehow shot yourself. The arrow probably misfired, remaining snagged by the nock to strike back at you."

"It was *my* fault," admitted Markus, in a bid to deflect the ridicule his friend was being subjected to.

"*You* shot Lando?" gasped Cullen, his brows arching up in disbelief as he gazed over at the King of Carcross.

"It was a series of strange and unusual circumstances that manifested into the resulting accident," explained Lindras, willing to accept his part in the near-deadly fiasco. "At the height of the storm and amid the ensuing madness in capturing the rampaging beast, Lando fill victim to our efforts. Not only was he a recipient of Markus' arrow, our poor friend and his steed were struck down by the powers of my crystal."

"Somehow, I am not surprised. Nonetheless, this is rather astounding in a bizarre sort of way," marvelled Cullen, eyeing both Markus and the Wizard.

"That we were the ones to accost Lando in this terrible manner?" queried Markus.

"No… Knowing your aim and the Wizard's reputation for manipulating his powers, I am astonished the old gaffer even survived this assault," explained Cullen, truly surprised by Lando's fortitude.

Lando merely grunted, rolling his eyes in response.

"It should come as no surprise this knight's resilience allowed him to endure such punishment that he stands before us now," attested Lindras, nodding in approval to his friend.

"You forget, Wizard, this chap is no longer a knight. Lando had been retired from his King's service for some time now," reminded Cullen. "For that reason alone, he has grown soft from leading such an easy life with so few demands placed on him. And make no mistake, I do not mean just soft around the middle, I mean both physically and mentally. He is definitely not the man he once was."

"Watch your mouth, you insolent, young whelp! I am more man than you will ever be!" snapped Lando.

"Yes, with that girth, you most certainly are, my corpulent friend," mocked Cullen, patting his belly as though he had an ever-expanding waistline. "I see you have gotten a little thick. Your midriff has gotten no smaller than when I saw you last autumn."

"I am *not* your friend and I see you have gotten a little *thick*, too," retorted Lando. Hiding his form from Cullen's critical eyes, he hastily wrapped his cloak around his sturdy frame to conceal the paunch of his belly that became more pronounced when he sat down.

"Once again, you are wrong, old man!" disputed Cullen, standing before his company to prove his point.

Cullen used the flat of his hands to smooth out his vest. Flattening his silhouette as he turned sideways, he stared at his shadow that disappeared, becoming one with the dark forest floor.

"I still cut a dashing figure. Unlike you, I have not gotten thick in the mid-section," protested Cullen, inhaling as he pulled taut his stomach muscles to streamline his profile for Druen to admire and for all to take notice.

"Who said I was speaking of your belly?" chided Lando, his finger flicking the back of Cullen's skull. "I was speaking of your thick noddle!"

"You are a moron!" denounced Cullen, wincing from the sharp sting of this assault as his hand rubbed the back of his head.

"Are you talking to yourself again?" queried Lando, glancing about as though Cullen was speaking to an invisible friend, if not himself.

"Here we go again," groaned Markus, rolling his eyes in frustration as Arerys, Joval and Lindras shook their heads in disapproval. "This is promising to be another long and torturous mission."

"Can someone please remind me why Captain Bristow continues to travel with us," requested Joval.

"Because you need my help for a monumental quest such as this," explained Cullen, speaking in his own defense.

Arerys leaned over to Joval, sharing these guarded words, "Remember, the Captain refused to allow Druen to show us the way unless he is able to personally guarantee her safety during this trek."

"Ah, yes," nodded Joval, as he whispered back to Arerys. "Can we be rid of him once we arrive at our destination? Perhaps we can send him off on his merry way when we have done so?"

"I have not already considered that, Joval," responded Arerys, speaking in a hushed tone so Cullen would not hear and be set off on another one of his angry tirades.

"Alright!" grumbled Cullen, glaring at the two Elves in private conversation. "What are you two talking about? No doubt you are slandering my good name and character."

"I hate to disappoint you, Captain Bristow, but not everything is about you," responded Arerys.

"Knowing you two and your continued liaison with Lando Bayliss, you were probably agreeing with his derogatory comments."

"Don't get yer feathers in a ruffle," urged Druen, pulling on Cullen's arm to make him sit. "Don't ya know Sir Bayliss was only teasin' you?"

"Teasing me?" gasped Cullen, flustered by her good and forgiving nature. "Teasing would imply this man has a sense of humour! He has none!"

"Then where is yer sense of humour? Of course he's teasin' you," reasoned Druen.

"Lando means to insult me before present company. That buffoon just called me an imbecile!"

"Come now, you know you're a smart an' clever man," insisted Druen, offering a disarming smile to soothe Cullen's ragged nerves. "In fact, you're the smartest man I've ever met, that's fer sure."

"You truly think so?" asked Cullen, puffing his chest out in pride as he looked to Druen to stroke his battered ego.

"I know so! If Sir Bayliss truly meant ta insult you, he wouldn't have called ya stupid ta yer face if you really were. He'd be sarcastic an' say the total opposite."

For a moment, Cullen quietly reflected on Druen's words, "Good gracious, Druen, you are quite right! If anything, Lando is just completely and utterly jealous of me."

Instead of making his usual, caustic retort, Lando's hand came up as though shielding his eyes from the intense glare of the sun. He squinted as he stared through the dark forest as though he was searching the landscape.

"What are you looking for, old man?" questioned Cullen, glancing about to see what Lando saw in the distance.

"Somewhere out there, a village is missing its idiot, methinks," answered Lando, speaking with all sincerity before bursting out in laughter.

"You are the idiot!" snapped Cullen, but his angry words were lost above the sounds of Lando snorting and chortling loudly as his friends snickered, trying to show some restraint for Cullen's sake.

Druen listened to this verbal volley between Lando and Cullen. "By chance, are you two related? You both seem so much alike."

"What?" Lando and Cullen simultaneously gasped in dismay at this insult. They stared at Druen, and then at each other as Arerys, Markus, Joval and Lindras chuckled at her insightful observation.

"You've got so much in common, you two."

Stunned, Lando and Cullen were momentarily rendered silent by Druen's comment.

"Come on now, gents! You're both great knights an' captains. You both have the same sense of humour," explained Druen. "If I didn't know better I'd say you're brothers."

The two men exchanged suspicious glances, and then Lando squeezed out a forced guffaw, "I take it we were supposed to laugh at that?"

"You are being funny, right, Druen?" questioned Cullen, intently studying her face.

"I'm quite serious! You two could pass fer brothers the way ya nit-pick at each other in the same way."

"Have you lost your mind, woman? How can you say we are like brothers? This old curmudgeon is a heck of a lot older than I am. And if we had the ill fortune of being related, it would be more like father and son. Or perhaps, he is closer to being my grandfather!"

"Oh, you're more alike than ya both care ta admit," teased Druen, giggling at this realization.

"And let us not forget, not only am I younger, I am more dashing and I exude genuine charm," added Cullen; "while Lando certainly exudes *something*, but it is certainly not that."

"Cullen, that's not very nice!" scolded Druen, her hand smacking the Captain on his shoulder.

"Oh my! On a first name basis, I see," noted Lindras, his brows arching up as he glanced over at Druen, and then Cullen. "I had no idea you two were so well *acquainted*."

Since the Wizard and his friends first became familiar with this brazen, young Captain, all with the exception of Lando openly addressed Cullen by his first name. Cullen always believed it was Lando's way of being on casual, friendly terms with him as the men of the Order were all on a first name basis with each other.

However, the retired knight only did so because he did not respect Cullen enough to address him as *Captain Bristow*. And unbeknownst to Cullen, where he believed these same men addressed him as Captain Bristow as a sign of their respect for him, in reality, it was their way of creating an invisible barrier between them. It was their way of politely maintaining a discreet emotional distance from this seemingly less-than-chivalrous knight of questionable reputation and dubious moral character.

"You seem surprised, Master Wizard," responded Druen, studying the quizzical look on Lindras' face. "We've become very good friends in this short span of time we've come ta know each other. In fact, the Captain insisted that I address him as Cullen."

"I cannot speak for Lindras, however personally, I am astounded," admitted Lando.

"Why's that?" queried Druen.

"Even women familiar in the *friendliest of ways* with this knight are not permitted to address him so informally," explained Lando. "It is always *sir* or *Captain Bristow*. It makes him feel good – more like a manly man."

"Then I should be rightly honoured," responded Druen, smiling over at Cullen.

"It must be quite the *friendship* you have struck up with him," determined Lando.

"Oh, yes! Cullen has been very good to me," confessed Druen, her voice and demeanor quite innocent.

"I am sure he has," smirked Lando, giving Cullen a contemptible glare.

"Hey! I do not like your tone. What are you implying, old man?" growled Cullen, scowling angrily at the retired knight as his hands balled into tight fists that quivered with mounting rage.

"Never mind, Captain Bristow," urged Markus, sensing the tension between the two was about to flare up once again. "Lando did not mean a thing."

"Do not stand up for this insufferable blowhard!" snarled Cullen, pushing past Markus to confront Lando. "How dare you besmirch this lady's good character?"

"It is just like you to jump to the wrong conclusion. How can you accuse me of such a thing?" argued Lando. "I do not know her character, good or bad. All I know is the type of person *you* are, not to mention your unsavoury reputation."

"Shame on you, Sir Bayliss! If you're tryin' to insinuate that Cullen is being friendly to me 'cause he had his way with me, you're so wrong!" admonished Druen, her delicate brows furrowing in anger. "How can you think such a thing of this kind an' gracious man?"

"I hate to say this, but we have had the misfortune of knowing Cullen for longer than you have, young miss," reminded Lando. "This *dog* is a creature of habit. I hardly think he would change so abruptly for you, or for anyone, for that matter."

"Aah, but you admit a man *can* change," responded Druen. "A man can do so if he puts his mind ta it?"

"Under the proper conditions, any normal man can be made to change, however, there is nothing normal about Cullen," remarked Lando, speaking with all seriousness as his comrades attempted to refrain from chuckling in agreement with their friend's comment.

"I will not even dignify your sorry words with a response," grunted Cullen, attempting to take the high road to impress Druen.

"I will have you know, Cullen Bristow has been an absolute gentleman in my presence," declared Druen. "He respects me far too much ta ever take advantage of me."

For a lingering moment, there was an awkward silence as the men stared at Cullen, dumbfounded by this unexpected news as their mouths hung open in stunned amazement.

Finally, Lando spoke up, "Alrighty, young miss, just what did you do to the real Cullen Bristow; the one I know and despise? And if this bloke is the one and the same, what enchantment did you cast on him to cause his moral compass to suddenly find its bearings?"

"If that's your way of tryin' ta warn me that Cullen is a womanizing cad, don't bother," sniffed Druen, coming to the Captain's defense as her hands wrapped around his arm as though it would protect him from Lando's insult. "Cullen has been totally honest with me right from the start. He told me everything 'bout his life. I know about all those women an' I'll tell ya now, it's not his fault."

"It isn't?" responded the men, speaking in unison.

"Of course not," stated Druen. "It's not Cullen's fault women find him irresistible. How can they not? I mean, look at the man."

"I'd rather not," grunted Lando, shuddering as he grimaced in distaste while averting his eyes from Cullen.

"With his rakish good looks an' his charms, of course there'll be plenty of women shamelessly throwin' themselves at him!"

"Well, thank you, my dear," said Cullen, nodding in appreciation. "I knew you were far more understanding than the average woman."

"What are you talking about, Cullen? No disrespect to this lady, but you do not even understand a single thing about women!" disputed Lando, speaking with all certainty. "Tarty trollops and harlots of ill-repute, yes. Genuine women of true integrity and substance, no."

"Now, now, Sir Bayliss, be kind!" admonished Druen. "Those women come sniffin' around him like a cat in heat. It's not Cullen's fault they all wanna bed him. He's just too polite ta know how ta turn 'em away without hurtin' their feelings."

"A simple *no* would suffice," offered Joval, failing to see what mortal women would find so attractive about this rogue and scoundrel who passed himself off as a knight by virtue of his peerage.

"Truth be told, I am not sure who has whom under an enchantment," decided Lando. "Either Cullen has charmed this lady so she is oblivious to the obvious or she has him in a spell to make him behave somewhat like a gentleman before her."

"You are an idiot!" cursed Cullen. "I said it before; I will say again! Druen *did not* put a spell on me. If anything, she makes me want to be a better man."

The men in Cullen's company were momentarily stunned by his admission, struck silent once again as they mulled over his words.

"Sweet mother of pearl!" exclaimed Arerys, staring with disbelief into Cullen's eyes. "You are in *love*! That is the enchantment you are under."

Cullen's face reddened with embarrassment, but he said nothing to admit or deny the Elf's claim.

"Is that true, Captain Bristow?" queried Markus, dumbfounded by Arerys' observation. "You are in love with Druen?"

"Come now, Markus, this is Cullen Bristow we are speaking of!" dismissed Lando. "A lover to many, but loved by none. You know, as well as I do, the only person this cad is capable of loving is himself!"

"Oh... Now that was harsh and uncalled for!" fumed Cullen, glaring at the retired knight as Lando denounced him before Druen.

"Though you're respected amongst your peers, Sir Bayliss, I do believe you an' your company owe Cullen, if not respect, the benefit of doubt that a man can change his heart," admonished Druen.

"Unfortunately for us, we have seen this man's true colours, young miss. Though he wears the tabard bearing the heraldic symbol of Darross and had been appointed the captain of King Sebastian's army, he is merely a knight by title; not by his deeds and actions if the code of chivalry means anything to you," explained Lando.

"An' if this code means so much ta you, then how come you don't abide by them yourself?" argued Druen, standing steadfast by her man. "If it means ta rise above the standards an' ta uphold the virtues more so than the ordinary man, then why do you feel you're justified in berating Cullen before those he holds in such high esteem? What is knightly about this conduct, Sir Bayliss?"

In the darkness, Lando was grateful his friends could not see how his face burned with embarrassment from the sting of Druen's words.

It was not because she was bold enough to brazenly confront him, but more so because this woman spoke the truth.

"You misconstrue my efforts to spare you personal grief, young lady," explained Lando. "A sheep can be sheared naked, but it does not change the fact that though it appears different, it is a sheep nonetheless."

"How dare you compare me to a living piece of mutton?" growled Cullen, thoroughly insulted by this comment.

"Calm down, Captain," urged Arerys. "Lando did not say you are a sheep. He was only making an analogy, nothing more."

"The point being, you are what you are in spite of what you claim to be," rebuked Lando. "And I find it personally appalling you would lead this woman astray; that you would have her, not to mention those who know your true character, to believe you are in love."

"It does not matter what *you* believe!" snapped Cullen. "What is more important is that Druen believes me."

"An' I do believe you, Cullen," acknowledged Druen, offering him a comforting smile as she gave his hand a reassuring squeeze. "Ta make this claim before all those who openly ridicule you before me makes me believe in you all the more."

"Bloody hell..." groaned Lando, shaking his head is dismay. "I have come to accept Cullen for what and who he is. In the same breath, what I cannot accept is the fact you will take the word of this womanizing scoundrel when he does not even know the meaning of the word love."

"I beg ta differ, Sir Bayliss," argued Druen. "If I can change, if I can forsake the life that was intended fer me, then why can't ya believe Cullen can do the same?"

"Perhaps we owe Captain Bristow an apology," suggested Lindras, more so to put an end to this debate than because he believed it was possible for Cullen to be truly in love.

"What?" gasped Lando, staring in disbelief at the Wizard.

"Well... it is possible," responded Lindras.

"That's so true, great Wizard," said Druen.

"Look here, young miss," grumbled Lando. "The Wizard said that it was *possible*; not that it was true. There is a difference, you know?"

"Since you refuse ta accept my words fer it, perhaps you all should follow yer own 'xample," admonished Druen. "Maybe it'll do ya some good ta look at your own lives an' loves."

"What do you know of this subject?" questioned Markus. "You have nothing to compare it to."

"Ta the contrary, Yer Highness. In our time tagether, Cullen had spoken a great deal 'bout you all. An' you should know; he has the highest praise fer the company he keeps."

"This should be interesting," sighed Arerys.

"Take you, Prince Arerys," began Druen. "It's my understandin' most Elf-men marry by their five-hundredth year of existence. An' yet you did not marry until you were the equivalent of a mortal in his thirty-fifth year."

"The woman is quite right, Arerys. You had turned down all of the elders' recommendations for a suitable maiden for betrothal," reminded Markus. "You had vowed to marry only for love and the love of your life did not come along until you met Nayla."

"And fer you, King Markus, it's my understandin' that you found true love, but yer wife died long ago. To this day, you have not loved another."

"But King Markus is a human being capable of love. Cullen is a... is a..." stammered Lando, searching for the words to best describe the Captain. "Well, you just cannot compare Cullen to this great King!"

"An' what about you, Sir Bayliss?" responded Druen, turning to look upon the retired knight. "Cullen told me that it wasn't until later in your life that you married and had a family of yer own. Cullen tells me that you had travelled all the way ta Orien, far ta the east, ta find yer true love."

"So I did," admitted Lando, thinking back on his first encountered with Nakoa, Nayla's former lady-in-waiting and close, personal friend.

"If that be the case, then why is it not possible fer Cullen ta have a change of heart an' fall in love, too?"

"So take that!" sniffed Cullen, placing his arm around Druen's shoulders to claim his prize. For the first time in his life, someone proudly stood up for him, dispelling with the ridicule.

For a moment, the men of the Order mulled over Druen's words.

"It is apparent to me that you two have spent a great deal of time talking, if nothing else," determined Lindras, glancing over to the Talibarrian woman and the Captain.

"Like I said; Cullen's been nothing but a gentleman in my company."

"I will be the first to admit that miracles do happen, even to this day," conceded Lando. "However, in the days to come, Cullen's actions shall be much more telling than his words. I will have to see for myself if this man is indeed a *gentleman*. Time will tell if he knows the true meaning of chivalry and behaves as a true knight should; one that knows the meaning of valour and self-sacrifice in the name of justice."

"So ya do believe me, Sir Bayliss?" questioned Druen, her eyes shining with hope. "You believe that he's a great knight an' hero?"

"A knight does not a hero make," corrected Lando, with all certainty. "As I said before; we shall see, as you will, too, what Cullen is truly made of. In the end, it will take more than his mere words for me to believe he has changed as you claim he has."

"Why do you insist on being so stubborn and difficult all the time?" snapped Cullen, agitated by Lando's negative attitude.

"It is my prerogative," sniffed Lando, his broad shoulders shrugging with indifference. "And it is better to be stubborn and difficult than be foolishly compliant and easily swayed."

"You are just jealous that someone as beautiful as Druen is in love with me!" growled Cullen.

"How can I be jealous? I am a happily married man," argued Lando. "I am just confused by this young lady's claim, for she does seem brighter than most of the women you have kept company with."

"Druen is extremely bright," averred Cullen; "bright enough to obviously see what *you* cannot."

"Alright, I will give her that. But just when was the last time you actually fell in love?" questioned Lando. "And I am not speaking of falling in love with yourself. I am speaking of a woman."

"There was never a last time," confessed Cullen, with a smug smile. "I admit in the past, I had been deeply *in like*, perhaps even rather *fond* of a maiden or two, but in love? Never! At least, not until now."

"I do not care to hear details of this mortal's love life, even if one truly exists. In fact, I am getting quite sick of it," grumbled Joval, as he spoke in a whisper to Lindras. "Why must we listen to these two men prattle on; badgering each other about such nonsense?"

"If you had not noticed, my friend, Lando and the Captain's heated discussions have helped to keep Arerys' mind preoccupied, even if it is only for a fleeting moment here and there," explained the Wizard.

"I must admit," Joval whispered back; "even on their best behavior, those two can be quite distracting when subjected to each other's company. They seem to bring out the worst in each other."

"As inane as their arguments have been at times, and as dreadful as it is to be caught in their verbal crossfire, if anything, it has been enough to take Arerys' troubled mind off of Nayla and what she may be subjected to while in the custody of that witch and her followers."

"I understand, Lindras," sighed Joval, realizing there were indeed times that even his own mind strayed away from his concerns for Nayla's safety; distracted by the two bickering mortals as they verbally jousted in an unruly show of one-upmanship.

"Gentlemen!" interrupted Markus, standing up to come between Lando and his young rival. "The purpose of stopping this eve is to rest. I do not know about you two, but I intend to do just that – to rest for the remainder of the night! Unfortunately, sleep will not come unless you both either desist in your spirited debates or at the very least, kept your voices down so the rest of us can be afforded some sleep."

"I can be quiet if Cullen can only keep his big mouth shut," snorted Lando, with a smug grin.

"And I can keep my mouth shut if only you can stop saying silly things meant to put me off," grunted Cullen.

"If we are to rest on this night, I can only do so if the two of you stay your tongues for the duration," groaned Markus.

"My dear, is there an enchantment or potion you know of that will remedy their wagging tongues?" wondered Lindras, growing weary of the constant bickering.

"What's wrong with yer magic?" queried Druen, gazing at the Wizard's great staff adorned with the crystal.

"I am afraid to use my magic to shut them up will be accomplished at the expense of their lives," explained Lindras. "It is a little too potent to administer on such trivial matters, if you get my meaning?"

"Well, there's a plant, the juice from its stems an' leaves can cause the tongue ta swell an' become numb so it becomes most difficult ta talk," offered Druen.

"Where can we get some?" asked Lindras, his eyes gleaming with hope.

"Unfortunately, it's too early in the year. This plant's only available late in the spring into the fall," disclosed Druen.

"Pity!" sighed Lindras, shaking his head dismally as Arerys, Joval and Markus turned away to leave the combatants to continue their war of words.

"See what you have done!" snapped Lando, watching his comrades depart to find some solitude. "You have driven my friends away."

"I did no such thing! They want to sleep and sleep is a better option than to waste their time listening to you," grunted Cullen.

"Well, I've had about 'nough from the both of you," decided Druen. "If you two can't at least be civil ta each other, then I'm leavin', too!"

"I am sorry, my lady," apologized Lando. "I do not know about this little blighter masquerading as a knight, but I can certainly elevate myself to be civil to him."

"As I can, too!" stated Cullen, not to be outdone by Lando.

"So, you both think you can speak an' not be at each other's throat?" queried Druen, her brows arched up in doubt.

"I can only speak for myself, but I most certainly can," vowed Lando, his tone exuding confidence.

"Bloody right you will not be speaking for me," sniffed Cullen. "And I will have you know, Druen, I can be civil to this man if I choose to be."

"Prove it," ordered Druen, her arms crossing her chest in defiance. "Let's see if ya both can be as civil as ya claim."

For the longest moment, the two men sat in complete and awkward silence, each waiting for the other to stick his foot in his mouth. After this prolonged hush, Lando finally spoke up, taking notice of the new sword dangling from Cullen's baldric.

"That is one fancy weapon," remarked Lando, his eyes scrutinizing the ornate hilt protruding from the equally lavish scabbard used to sheath the huge blade.

"About time you noticed, old man," snorted Cullen. He proudly patted his sword. "I was starting to think your feeble, old eyes were failing you, too."

"Oh, my eyes do not fail me. In fact, on more than one occasion they were almost poked out by that gargantuan weapon weighing you down. What are you doing with that thing?"

"Since you ask, it was gifted to be by King Sebastian," replied Cullen, carefully sliding the polished blade from the scabbard to reveal the engraved image of the dragon adorning it. "It was specially crafted and given to me by my liege for my part in rescuing Prince Carstian from the deranged Draven Eldard. It is a gift I wear with pride."

"It is a good thing you know that wearing it is about all you can do with that beast of a sword," responded Lando, watching with amusement as Cullen struggled to remove the tip of the blade from its scabbard. "Obviously, its draw-length is too great for you. It is obvious it was meant more for ceremony than battle."

"That is what you would like to believe. I will have you know, this is no toy or fancy trinket adorning my belt. Its blade is as deadly as that Elven sword gifted to you by Arerys' father."

"I hardly think so," dismissed Lando, with a chuckle.

"Think again, old man. Like the Elven blade, this formidable weapon, too, has a name," boasted Cullen, the silver blade swishing about, slicing through an imaginary foe.

"I would hate to hazard a guess," sighed Lando, rolling his eyes in dismay.

"Meet the *Eviscerator*; as lethal as it is handsome, much like its master," boasted Cullen, bolding brandishing his new weapon for Lando to admire.

"When the Elves bestow a name unto their swords, it is with the intention of defining its purpose," explained Lando.

"There you go then," responded Cullen. "Its purpose is to disembowel all those wishing to challenge me."

"First of all, you must be able to draw your weapon before your opponent cuts you down," scoffed Lando.

"That will come with practice," insisted Cullen, struggling to sheath the hefty blade.

"Or when you grow another hand-span or so," mocked Lando. "Gracious! Your skin is becoming a strange tint of green."

"It is?" gasped Lando, his hand coming up to feel his face.

"Yes, I believe it is called envy!" scoffed Cullen.

"And what would I have to be envious about?"

"This, of course," responded Cullen. He proudly held forth his grand sword for Lando to admire once more. "This weapon is the hallmark of a great leader, and in this world, only a special few are destined to become leaders. I am one of the few with the necessary charm and charisma to lead the people."

"What makes you say that?"

"A leader invokes change," replied Cullen. "That is what I do. Besides, who wants to be a pathetic follower?"

"To put it bluntly, you are an idiot," admonished Lando. "A leader is nobody without his followers. And a leader with nothing more to offer than his charismatic charm is ineffective."

"Hmm… Charming leader or pathetic follower," sniffed Cullen. "I prefer being a leader any day."

"Any fool knows a follower with the wisdom to prudently choose a wise leader can accomplish far more than to blindly side with a man who is nothing more than a token leader – a man that says and promises much, but does little," dismissed Lando. "Better an effective follower than a pathetic leader any day."

"Jealous…" muttered Cullen, sneering at the retired knight.

"Yes, I am so jealous I am tempted to smite you with your own sword," grumbled Lando, drawing his index finger across his throat.

"So much for civility..." sighed Druen, rolling her eyes in frustration.

"Well, I have had enough of his idle chatter for one night. Druen, remain here. I shall return momentarily," said Cullen, rising up to retrieve his bedroll and water flask.

"Do not get lost out there," called Lando, searching his bag for his pipe as Druen sat down next to him.

"Now that I've met you in person, I'm quite surprised, Sir Bayliss," stated Druen. "You're not quite how Cullen had described ya ta be."

"Knowing that insolent, young whelp, he undoubtedly used colourful expletives and the most disparaging of adjectives to denounce my good character," grunted Lando, compressing the pipe-weed into the ceramic bowl of his pipe.

"Quite the opposite, sir," countered Druen. "In fact, Cullen had nothin' but words of high praise fer you."

"He did?" Lando frowned in surprise.

"Cullen told me a grand tale of courage; how you and yer friends confronted and defeated the Dark Lord. He also told me of other adventures he had been on with you. He said your fierce loyalty to those you serve an' those you count as friends is legendary. Cullen claimed your deeds an' actions exemplified the very best of a true knight."

"Are you positive he was speaking of me?"

"There is only one Sir Lando Bayliss of Cedona. Cullen would never openly admit it ta yer face nor would he be pleased ta hear I repeated his words to ya, but you should know, sir; Cullen admires you. He said he could only aspire to be a knight as respected an' revered as you are."

"I find this rather astounding."

"Why do you say that?" questioned Druen.

"Come now, my lady, it is no secret there is no love lost between us," disclosed Lando. "Our character... our actions and reactions to the same situations differ greatly."

"You have the wisdom of age an' experience, Sir Bayliss. Cullen does not. He told me that he was appointed to captain his King's army at a young age. His responses an' actions are tempered by his own limited experiences with life in general. No doubt, it's jus' as yer views an' ideals have changed with time an' served ta shape the man you've become."

"Granted, he had been thrust into a position of great responsibility for one so young; still, it does not excuse him from choosing to adhere by the code of chivalry whenever it suits him."

"I understand it's a code that knights live an' die by, but ya must see that where you have the support of trustin' friends ta help ya through the difficult times, Cullen has no one but his own wits ta see him through. From what he told me, he said not even his father offered him the guidance an' encouragement a young man needs. I sense you're more of a positive example than his father ever was. That's why he badgers you as he does. Yer criticisms he takes ta heart an' tries ta reshape himself accordingly."

"I do recall a slip of his tongue when he addressed me as his father," said Lando, recalling their first mission together and how Cullen saved him from a lethal fall. It would have been a similar death Cullen's father suffered and during Cullen's struggle to pull him to safety, he accidentally called him *father.*

"An' there's more," revealed Druen, glancing about to see if Cullen was returning. "He envies this camaraderie you share with yer comrades an' he can only wish ta be a part of this. In many ways, though you share in the brotherhood of knights, Cullen *is* a knight, yet he feels alone an' excluded."

"And until that young man learns to behave as a true knight should, there he shall remain; on the outside looking in."

"I sense there's still hope for Cullen."

"You must care for him a great deal to have this kind of faith in him, my dear," determined Lando.

"Jus' as you do," stated Druen.

"I do?"

"Oh yeah, you only egg him on an' badger him as ya do 'cause you know he has potential if he'd only apply himself. Jus' like I know Cullen harangues you ta force ya ta put yer best foot forward. It's because he wishes ta aspire ta yer reputed greatness, but his greatest downfall is that he doesn't believe it's possible."

"Then why does he do and say what he does when he knows it will only annoy me?"

"I know this will sound strange, but fer a young man who didn't have the influence he needed from a kindly father-figure when he was a boy, in Cullen's mind, yer negative attention is better than no attention at all."

"Well that is rather pathetic," decided Lando, puffing on his pipe as he contemplated this woman's words.

"Pathetic, yes," agreed Druen; "but what is more pathetic is your response to Cullen. If you're still the great knight he claims ya ta be, you'd have it in yer heart ta show him some compassion."

"I suppose I have been a bit hard on the young bloke," admitted Lando, as he sheepishly chewed on the mouthpiece of his pipe.

"No more than he has been on you. In all truthfulness, Cullen looks ta you fer guidance, but his pride prevents him from askin' outright fer yer help ta become the knight he wishes ta truly be."

"I must say; you have much in the way of insight and wisdom for such a young woman," praised Lando, giving Druen an encouraging nod. "I can see why Cullen is so taken by you."

"Well, thank you, kind sir!" responded Druen, rising up as Cullen approached with his bedroll tucked beneath his arm.

"And just to prove you wrong, old man, here you go, Druen," offered Cullen, passing her the bedroll. "Go find some sleep – *alone, my dear.* I will be taking the first watch."

"Wakey, wakey, Princess! Rise an' shine!"

This gruff voice rumbled in Nayla's ears. The Talibarrian was just about to reach over to shake her by the shoulders when her eyes instantly snapped open. Her body bolted upright. She was wide-awake, completely lucid as though never asleep.

His hands abruptly recoiled; surprised by Nayla's quick reflexes and alert condition. She was like a high-strung cat that had been startled awake; a bundle of nervous energy ready to attack.

"I was made ta guard ya last night," complained the man, pretending he wasn't surprised by her abruptness.

Nayla stared up at the ragged looking mortal; his slovenly form backlit by the early dawn sky. She squinted through one eye as the pale light of the sun leached away the darkness. Scrutinizing this man, she immediately recognized him as the one who had eagerly took to binding her wrists to hold her captive after she tried to choke the life from him.

"I waited all night an' well inta the wee hours of the mornin' waitin' fer ya ta fall asleep jus' so I could get some rest myself," he grumbled with contempt. "But no… You jus' had ta stay awake all night, didn't ya? So, when did ya finally fall asleep?"

"That is pathetic. Obviously, you did not stay awake long enough to find out for yourself," taunted Nayla, glaring angrily as she boldly mocked this stranger looming before her.

Needing much less rest than the average mortal, she had finally drifted off into a dreamless sleep before darkness melted away to a pre-dawn sky. By her assessment, spying the sun peeking low on the eastern horizon to shine through a thick stand of trees, she had only caught an hour or two of sleep. As short as this duration was by mortal standards, it was enough to provide her with adequate rest for now.

"Never mind 'bout me," snapped the Talibarrian, standing before her with a chunk of stale, hard bread and a cracked, earthenware cup that steadily dripped its content of water at his feet. "All that matters is that you're still here an' as you can see, you ain't goin' nowhere!"

Nayla's chilled, aching body struggled to sit upright on this thin, dew-dampened layer of straw bedding. It did little to cushion her against the cold, hard ground. And the slender, but sturdy, pole that rested behind her neck and across her shoulders onto which her wrists were now bound, effectively prevented her from rolling to either side to find a comfortable position to sleep. She slowly flexed her fingers to increase the circulation of blood in her numb hands that tingled with a prickling sensation.

"Serves you right," snorted the scruffy-looking Talibarrian, watching his prisoner as Nayla's discomfort became all the more obvious to him. "If you hadn't tried markin' a trail fer yer friends ta follow, we wouldn't have trussed ya up like this. Lucky fer us though, we caught ya before you could leave a trail all the way ta our village!"

"Who said I was doing it for my friends?"

"You weren't?"

"Of course not. I was doing it for you, just in case you got lost, you moron!" retorted Nayla.

"Watch yer damn mouth, woman! Don't you go givin' me no sass!" growled the man, kicking at her in resentment.

The blow jarred her legs, causing the bones in her ankles to painfully strike together. Glancing down, Nayla realized her feet were still bound since arriving late last night. Tied together at the ankles, this same length of coarse rope was used to tether her to a stake pounded into the ground; an added precaution to ensure she did not escape.

"If you be wantin' ta eat an' drink this morn, you best learn ta cooperate with me," warned the man, glancing about to see if any of the villagers were stirring from their sleep yet. He held the cup to Nayla's lips, tipping the cold water into her parched mouth to allow her a drink. "If you be wantin' anymore water or a bite ta eat, you're gonna give me somethin' I want."

"If you want money or jewels, you know that witch already helped herself to what I had," snapped Nayla, taking another mouthful of water before the man could snatch away the cup.

"An' that old hag ain't about ta share with anyone either, but I'm bettin' you will!" He grunted as his filthy hand brushed the stray wisps of hair from Nayla's eyes as a lurid smile curled his thin lips. "I ain't ever had me an Elf-woman before."

"I hate to disappoint you, but if you are too stupid to see the obvious, I am *not* a full-blooded Elf."

"Full... half... Who cares? I'm getting me some of this," he snorted as his eager hands reached over to unclasp the buttons on her vest.

The man suddenly fell back as water sprayed from Nayla's mouth right into his stunned face.

"That will never happen!" hissed Nayla.

"Why, you little...." growled the man, wiping the water and spit from his eyes with the back of his hand. In retaliation, he lunged at his prisoner.

Before he could throw himself onto her prostrate body, Nayla's bound feet came up, slamming hard into his chest to bowl him over. He groaned in pain as he slowly stood up, rubbing the point of impact on his aching body.

"You bitch!" cursed the man, kicking Nayla's legs hard to prevent her from countering his assault. Reaching behind his back as he pounced on her, he straddled her body. Pressing the rusted, jagged blade of a knife to her throat, he snarled, "You'll be givin' me what I want or I'll be cuttin' ya up inta little pieces ta send back ta yer prince."

"As I said, if it is an Elf maiden you want, you will be disappointed," growled Nayla, feeling the cold bite of the blade against her throat. "I am only half Elf."

"Close enough!" snorted the man, taking another furtive glance at the witch's dilapidated cottage to make sure Ratha was still asleep. "I ain't that fussy, anyway."

Dismounting from her, the man quickly scooted down to her bound ankles. With the knife clenched between his teeth, he used one hand to pin her legs down as the other worked to loosen the knot. Tossing this rope aside, he seized Nayla by her ankles, forcefully yanking her legs apart.

Insinuating himself between her thighs, the man took the knife, ramming the blade into the straw and earth right next to Nayla's head. It was a harsh reminder that he was in power. He was the one in control of the situation.

"Don't ya fight me! An' don't ya scream or you'll be as good as dead," snarled the man, hastily loosening the leather belt to drop his trousers about his knees. For a moment, he revelled in the sensation of her silky, smooth skin; feeling the heat of her flesh pressing against his as he knelt before her. His heart began to race with lust as his manhood brushed against her inner thigh.

Leaning in over her body to kiss her mouth, Nayla's face grimaced in utter disgust. Repulsed by the powerful stench of his breath, she turned away from the stink rancid goat cheese caked between his teeth. The rank odour swirled around her like a suffocating, foul-smelling blanket of fog seeping forth from a dead dragon's mouth.

Angered by this rejection, his hands grabbed the pole Nayla's wrists were bound to. Bearing down with all his weight, his elbows locked as he used this piece of wood to pin her to the ground. He grunted in pleasure as he positioned himself between her knees. Through the snaggled strands of oil-clotted hair, Nayla could see his beady eyes gleaming with lust as his voice rasped in her ears, "So, ya wanna get right ta business, eh?"

Just as he moved over her body, Nayla immediately threw her legs up between her and her assailant. The force slammed the man's arms together as her ankles locked and she rolled to her side.

"Here's more business than you can handle!" snarled Nayla, exacting her revenge on this mortal as she used the end of the stick to repeatedly strike him on his head.

Unable to deflect these sharp blows, the man yelped and groaned in pain. His arms, now trapped between Nayla's knees, pressed together as her body weight sank down as she rolled forward to sit up. In this position, she applied excruciating pressure to his shoulders. It caused his chest to feel as though it was about to cave in as she leaned forward.

Just as she was about roll forward and in the process, shatter the man's arms at the elbow and dislocate them at the shoulder joint, Nayla abruptly lurched forward. Her body suddenly crumpled, growing limp.

Rendered unconscious, she flopped to the ground. Nayla collapsed next to her intended victim as an angry voice faded in her ears like a distant echo.

"Krygor! What the hell do ya think you're doin'?" The walking stick that had cracked Nayla on the back of her head came down with a vengeance to punish him.

to run a deadly gauntlet

"We'd cover greater distance if we rode the horses rather than walked them," stated Cullen.

He glanced up through the tree canopy to take a visual measurement of the distance travelled against the position of the sun. They had been on the move since daybreak, but to the Captain, at this rate, the glowing orb had travelled much farther than they had.

"True enough, Captain Bristow, and I want nothing more than to charge ahead to rescue Nayla," agreed Arerys. "However, consider this; if there are traps hidden in this forest as Druen had warned us, we are better to proceed with caution."

"Lest you have a desire to be snared or skewered, by all means, rush ahead, Cullen," invited Lando, waving the Captain on ahead.

"Well, excuse me!" grumbled Cullen. "I was under the assumption we were in a hurry to mount this rescue."

"We are, but what is the point of blindly rushing ahead if it gets us killed in the process? It will be no good to Nayla, or us, for that matter," replied Arerys, motioning for Cullen to keep moving as Druen led the way.

In single file, they cautiously crept behind her. Cullen remained directly behind Druen as Arerys followed behind the Captain. This Elf deliberately positioned himself between Cullen and Lando to keep their verbal sniping to a minimum. Behind Lando, Markus and the Wizard followed the procession as Joval took up the rear to safeguard Lindras and his magical orb against a possible attack.

"Stay behind me an' don't go wanderin' off this trail," warned Druen. "From here on, the way gets more perilous the closer we get to the village."

"Perilous in the way of deadly traps?" queried Cullen, his eyes glancing about nervously.

"That's right," confirmed Druen, creeping on along this twisting trail as her eyes searched for the telltale signs that would betray the presence of a trap. "You best watch where ya step."

"Is there anything in particular we should be wary of?" questioned Markus, scrutinizing the path before them.

"Definitely," answered Druen. "Watch out fer parts of the trail covered with dead leaves."

Cullen's eyes widened with fear. His eyes darted down to his feet, for beneath them lay a scattering of wilted and dried leaves flattened into the ground.

"Bloody hell!" cursed Cullen, freezing in his tracks in case he set off a deadly trap.

Glancing down, Druen giggled, "Not those leaves, Cullen. Those ones are trampled inta the earth. I mean stuff like this."

Picking up a long stick, she took several steps ahead to where a thick layer of leaves was scattered across the width of the trail.

"Looks innocent enough, but watch," ordered Druen, tossing the stick onto the blanket of leaf litter.

A line hidden beneath the leaves snapped taut. The crackling of branches and the rush of air immediately followed as a half dozen arrows exploded across the trail, slamming into the trunk of a nearby tree.

"Oh, my!" exclaimed Lindras, stunned by the effectiveness and ferocity of this trap as the feathers fledging these arrows continued to vibrate from the impact.

"Well tie me down and slap me silly!" gasped Cullen, staring wide-eyed in disbelief.

"That can be arranged, but for now, the abuse will have to wait," responded Lando, with a smug smile as he scrutinized the trap Druen had triggered. "Let us see what we have here."

"Now I know what you mean about being mindful of where we tread," acknowledged Arerys, grateful that Druen willingly alerted them of this danger.

"Don't jus' mind where you step," cautioned Druen. "Don't go tuggin' or pushin' aside any branches leaning inta or hangin' down over this trail. It can set off a trap or snare, too."

"We shall take heed of your warning," responded Markus.

"I recommend we leave the horses behind from this point forward," suggested Lando. "There is a chance one of them will step off the trail to inadvertently set one of these traps off on us."

"Leave the horses behind?" gasped Cullen, appalled by this suggestion. "If we do, just how will we get around?"

"By our own two feet, of course," answered Lindras. "And it is not as though we can ride them right now, anyway. I will instruct Tempest to keep this herd together. When we are in need of our mounts again, my stallion will steer them back to us."

"Fair enough," agreed Cullen, watching as the horses turned away, following behind the Wizard's gray steed.

"As a precaution, I recommend we disable the obstacles we encounter along the way," suggested Joval. "The warriors advancing with Artel to aid in this rescue mission need not be endangered needlessly."

"A brilliant idea," responded Arerys, nodding in approval to Joval. "Can you do that, Druen? Can you forewarn us so we can do just that?"

"Sure I can. But like I said, jus' be careful. I'll point out the traps I know of, but there ain't no guarantee I'll catch all of the new ones, if they've set up more than just the usual ones."

"Now that we have some idea what we are up against and what to look for, if we advance with the utmost care, we should be safe," decided Arerys.

"And you are suggesting to do so with Druen leading the way?" questioned Cullen. "You expect her to run a deadly gauntlet, knowing she could fall victim to one of these new traps?"

"We do not know for certain if there are more traps - ones that Druen is not aware of. Whatever the case, I will not *force* her to do this," replied Arerys.

"Don't worry, Cullen, I know what ta look out fer," promised Druen, giving his hand a reassuring squeeze. "I'll be careful."

"Are you sure of this?" asked Cullen, genuinely concerned for her safety.

"Of course I am." Druen spoke with confidence. "I'll be fine."

"You better be, or someone will pay," stated Cullen, glaring at Arerys for even making this suggestion to begin with.

"No need fer concern, Cullen. If anything, you an' yer friends have more ta be worried about than I do. I know what signs ta be aware of, where you men don't necessarily know."

"I suppose," conceded Cullen. "All the same, do be careful, Druen."

"I will," she promised as she ventured on.

With Druen leading the way, the men crept behind her, remaining on this trail. Since encountering the trap of arrows, within the first league they travelled they had disabled two snares, another barrage of arrows, and a hail of spears.

"I see what you mean about watching where we tread," acknowledged Cullen, gingerly stepping over the line of a freshly sprung trap.

"True, you gotta be aware of yer surroundings," reminded Druen. "But don't jus' concentrate on what might be on the ground."

"Of course," responded Cullen, brushing aside a vine draped across the trail.

"Look out!" Druen cried out as she pushed Cullen to the ground. The Captain fell backward, knocking Arerys down just as two wooden grates studded with metal spikes swung down. Slamming together like a dragon's jaws snapping shut to bite down on its intended victims, they froze, remaining close to the ground until the trap clanked and rattled to a noisy stop above them.

"That was close!" gasped Cullen. His heart was still thundering as he clutched Druen to his chest. He stared at the sharp, metals spikes that were meant to impale his body.

"Too close," agreed Arerys, as Markus pulled the Elf up onto his feet. "Druen is quite correct. We must be aware of the potential dangers in all its forms. We cannot fixate on the fact that up until now, the triggers to launch these traps have been hidden on the ground."

"Yes, we must keep in mind that danger is concealed all around us," reminded Joval. "We must keep our wits about us if we wish to survive this trek."

Venturing ahead, Druen came to an abrupt halt. Something was not quite right. Glancing about, her eyes came to rest upon the widest section of this trail. A conspicuously thick layer of leaf litter concealing this portion of the path lay before her.

"What is it, Druen?" questioned Cullen.

"There's somethin' here… Some kinda trap that wasn't here before."

"Careful now," cautioned Cullen, reluctantly releasing her hand as she inched forward.

"The trip-line has gotta be hidden near to the middle of these leaves," determined Druen, cautiously creeping ahead to inspect this large patch of dried foliage.

Cullen followed close behind as the others searched the surrounding shrubs and trees for an arsenal of concealed spears or arrows waiting to be unleashed from above or beside the trail.

Stepping onto the edge of this carpet of leaves, the earth beneath her feet abruptly sank. Druen screamed as the pressure sensitive trigger launched the concealed trap. It sprang to life before her. Rows of sharp, wooden stakes erupted from the ground, tilting forward to impale her as she stumbled.

Her heart raced, her breath catching in the back of her throat as the pointed teeth protruding from the ground rushed at her. Her falling body jerked to a sudden stop, just mere inches from a row of deadly stakes waiting to sink into her face and torso.

Securing his hold on her cloak he had snagged, Cullen yanked her back, pulling Druen to safety. He breathed a sigh of relief as he held her trembling body to his chest, holding her close.

"Thank goodness!" exclaimed Cullen, feeling her heart pounding hard against his. "That could have been the end of you, Druen. How do you fare?"

Gazing at her face, Cullen noticed the colour drain from her cheeks as she stared at her bloodied hands. As she fell, Druen's hands instinctively flew out before her to break her fall. In doing so, two of the pointed stakes pierced the palms of her hands, one biting clear through to the other side.

Druen began to shake as her eyes welled with tears as the initial fright and shock worn off to allow the horrific pain to rush to the surface. These wounds now throbbed with agony as the blood seeped from these punctures.

"Good gracious!" gasped Cullen. Believing he had spared her from harm, he was taken aback by the sight of all this blood.

He held Druen by her wrists as she stared at the hole in the center of her right hand. She could see clear through to the forest floor until the blood pooled in this puncture faster than it could drain through this gaping hole.

"Don't just stand there, Cullen! Make yourself useful," ordered Lando, rummaging through his leather pack to find a clean strip of cloth to dress her wounds.

"Oh my! That is rather nasty!" declared Lindras, catching sight of Druen's trembling, bloodstained hands.

"Arerys, take care of this," ordered Markus. "Heal these wounds."

"Joval, quickly!" called Arerys, motioning the Elf to step forward. "Heal her left hand. I will take care of the right."

Positioning themselves so the palm of their left hand rested over the worst of the wounds, they enveloped Druen's hands with their own. With a murmuring of a healing incantation, they set to work.

Druen's hands seemed to pulsate with a heartbeat of their own as they throbbed in agony. With the whispering of these magical words, she felt immediate relief from this pain as the Elves' power to heal worked to mend skin, muscle, tendons and ligaments damaged by the wooden stakes.

Manifesting into a warm, tingling sensation, this healing power soothed the ravages of these injuries. This strange sensation immediately distracted the woman from the initial shock of the trauma. For the first time in her life, Druen experienced the miracle of the Elves' magical powers to heal.

"Is that better now?" asked Arerys, as he and Joval released their hold on her hands.

Druen stared, astonished by the results. Without a trace of pain, she flexed and splayed apart her fingers. She rotated them from palm up to the back of her hands, and over again, to scrutinize this miracle. Where once there was torn flesh and skin, there was now a red scoring on the palm of each hand.

"As you are not an Elf, you will probably be left with a slight scar," informed Joval.

"I can live with a scar," nodded Druen. "I'm just grateful it healed so quickly an' there won't be a need to deal with an infection. For us humans, infections can be worse than the actual injury, ya know?"

"You will probably feel a slight tingling sensation for a day or two, but you will have full and pain-free use of your hands," informed Arerys.

"Thank you," said Druen, with a grateful smile as her fingers gingerly traced the scar. "Thank you both."

"No need for thanks, Druen," responded Arerys. "I just ask that you be more careful as we advance."

"An' thank you, Cullen. This time, it was *you* savin' my life."

"I suppose I did!" exclaimed Cullen, his chest puffing out in pride.

"Perhaps we should venture on, but avoid walking on this marked trail," suggested Lando.

"We can, but on either side the ground becomes extremely swampy," warned Druen. "An' if it ain't the swamp an' all the leeches, then you gotta watch out fer bramble bushes an' the thorny Devil's Club. One wrong step an' you tread on those low-growing branches; it'll whip forward an' smack ya real hard with its thorns. You'll get carved up real good in no time!"

"Hmph! I do not know what is worse," sighed Lando, pondering the limited options she presented.

"Well, I sure as heck wasn't expectin' that," commented Druen. She stared over at the rows of stakes protruding from the ground. "That's definitely a new contraption they've taken ta usin'. I ain't ever seen that kinda trap before."

"Perhaps it was set up to catch you unawares, Druen. It was meant to punish you in case you returned after fleeing from your village?" offered Cullen.

"Naw," said Druen, shaking her head vigorously. "They know I wouldn't be comin' back ta Dreymoor unless they caught me an' dragged me back against my will. Even at that, death wouldn't be dealt so easily. My gran would see me tortured first fer betrayin' her, 'specially if she knew of the company I'm keepin' now."

"What a *sweetheart* your grandmother is!" Cullen groaned in a sarcastic tone as he rolled his eyes in disgust. "Wait until I am done with her."

"I know you jus' wanna protect me, Cullen, but the sad thing is, she wasn't always this way," responded Druen, thinking back on simpler, kinder times.

"What do you mean?" asked Markus.

"My gran always used her knowledge an' powers ta help our people as well as outsiders lookin' fer herbs an' potions to fix their ills or the occasional hex or curse ta right a wrong. Since that blasted book came ta her, all she cares about is gettin' revenge fer some long-dead kin-folk."

"And to acquire the powers contained within its pages to do so," added Lindras. "Unfortunately, the Book of Spells is much like the Dark Lord Beyilzon. The power it wields is like a poison, tainting the hearts and minds of every being that ever tried to lay claim to it."

"Eldred Firestaff included," determined Arerys, recalling the Wizard's bout of madness.

"Yes, even my brother Wizard had fallen victim to the seductive allure of its powers."

"So, now what?" questioned Cullen, turning to Arerys. "If you think I will allow you to use Druen to lead us on this ill-fated march to our possible doom, you are mad."

"In good conscience, no, I will not subject her to this danger," replied the Elf. "As I now have a very good idea of what to look for in the way of traps and snares, I sense that with my exceptional sight and hearing, as well as Joval's, between the two of us, we should be able to detect the traps that even Druen could potentially overlook."

"Brilliant!" Cullen nodded in approval to Arerys. "By all means, lead the way, my lord. After all, it is *your* wife we are attempting to rescue."

"Bloody well 'bout time ya woke up!"

Nayla moaned in pain as the tip of a walking stick jabbed her ribs. Her eyes slowly opened, squinting under the intense glare of the sun. The pale dawn sky she last saw had transformed into a cloudless, azure blue.

"All this talk of you bein' such a great warrior!" The witch grunted in disdain as she glared down at Nayla. "It's bloody ironic that ya couldn't even fend off a blow from a little, old lady with a cane."

"I was a little preoccupied," responded Nayla, glancing over at her wrists that remained bound to the pole resting across her shoulders. "And though you are little and old, you are definitely *not* a lady."

"You watch that smart mouth of yers!" snapped the witch. "An' if you're as great as ya claim ta be, it wouldn't have made a diff'rence if you were armed ta the teeth or hog-tied. You'd still be able ta fight!"

"I was never the one to make that claim."

"Well then, why the reputation? It had ta have started somewhere by someone," grunted the old woman, as her cronies hovering over Nayla laughed in agreement with the witch.

"I am a Kagai Warrior. We know what we are capable of. There is no need to boast about our deeds or accomplishments."

"Well, warrior wench, you're a long way home from Orien an' yer warrior brethren," scoffed Ratha. "I'm guessin' 'bout now, you're wishin' you had stayed there."

"At this moment, *anywhere* is better than this dreary place," retorted Nayla. "And the present company is not helping."

"Aren't ya jus' the funny one!" snapped Ratha. Just as the end of her walking stick stabbed at Nayla once more, the tip of the pole used to restraint her wrists slammed down to deflect this blow.

"What do ya know, boys? She still got some fight in her yet," mocked the witch, pulling her walking stick away.

"She's jus' a girl!" snorted the man who had tried to assault her until Ratha had intervened. "She can't really fight. Sure, she can bite an' scratch an' do that girlie fightin', but jus' 'cause she's armed with weapons, it don't mean she knows how ta use 'em properly."

"Don't ya go under estimatin' this one, Krygor!" growled Ratha, cuffing him on the back of his head with her stick. "If I hadn't come along when I did, both yer arms would be in a sling, or worse!"

"Are ya daft, Ratha!" cursed Krygor, glaring in resentment at the witch as she humiliated him before his peers. "Yer prisoner jus' got lucky. That's all."

"Ya stupid buffoon! Don't you go disrespectin' me before my people! An' what's the matter with ya? Are ya too stupid ta see this one's dangerous! She was tied up, but she still gave *you* a thrashin'!" snapped Ratha, scowling in anger. "You're the one who got lucky that she didn't go an' kill ya an' luckier still that I didn't let her!"

Krygor's cohorts chuckled aloud, greatly amused by the witch's belittling comments as the much larger man cringed, visibly shrinking under her scathing words and caustic tone.

"Don't ya go 'xaggeratin', Ratha! I had everything under control," argued Krygor, attempting to save face before his male comrades. "This little wench was jus' testin' me. I was jus' about ta teach her a lesson."

"Maybe if she was gagged, blindfolded an' shackled you'd have had half a chance against this woman," scoffed one of Krygor's comrades, shaking his head in doubt.

"Aren't you the funny one, Terat?" growled Krygor, shoving his friend aside. "I'll have a go 'round with her this very minute jus' ta show you she can be put in her place."

"Don't ya even think of it, ya fool!" ordered Ratha, thrusting a gnarled finger at his scowling face to jab at his crooked nose. "You hurt or kill her, then our plan is all but dead. Ya understand, Krygor?"

For a moment, this bellicose man brooded in silence, mulling over this order.

"Do ya hear me?" The witch's bony elbow jabbed him in his ribs to solicit a response.

"Yeah, I hear ya, Ratha," grumbled Krygor. He sneered at her with obvious displeasure.

"But do ya *understand* me?" snapped the witch, using the crook of her walking stick to pick up a wicker basket by its handle from the ground. "If ya don't, I've got special spells an' potions that can help ya ta understand."

"I get ya, Ratha," sulked Krygor. He was more than disappointed that his opportunity to save face before his male comrades was now effectively quashed by this shrivelled, old prune of a woman.

"Good! Now that we've come ta an understandin', I've got some business ta take care of. An' while I'm gone, yer job is ta see to it that our prisoner don't escape. So do ya think ya can handle the task, ya simpleton? Or is it askin' fer too much from ya?"

"What do ya take me fer, Ratha?" growled Krygor, scowling in anger from the sting of her demeaning words.

"I take ya fer 'xactly what you are," snorted Ratha, jabbing Krygor in his ribs with the tip of her walking stick.

"Of course I can handle this runt of a woman. I'll make sure she stays right where she is. She won't be goin' nowhere – not on my watch."

"Ya better make it so, or I'll be using yer blood an' one of yer eyeballs ta mix up a batch of potion ta heal my bad eye," warned the witch, as she turned away.

"When will you be comin' back?" queried Krygor.

"When I'm good an' ready. Could be a few minutes; could be a few hours. I can't rightly say. It'll depend on where I can find me a good, fresh patch of wolfsbane this time of the year."

Ratha's answer was deliberately evasive. Not wishing to give Krygor and the other men left to watch over Nayla a precise time of her return, it was a way of keeping them on their toes and in her control. She knew they were less likely to disobey her orders if the fear that she would return unannounced, and when they least expected it, would be an effective deterrent to prevent them from going against her wishes.

Adjusting the crumpled, leather bag that was slung over one shoulder; with walking stick in one hand and the battered willow basket in the other, the witch departed, limping eastward.

"Don't ya let her escape now!" hollered Ratha, as she disappeared into the forest. "An' remember, if you mess with my prisoner an' she gets killed, you're all as good as dead!"

"Yeah, yeah! We hear ya!" responded Krygor, waving her off.

As the witch melted into the shadows of the forest, Krygor stood on his toes, craning his neck as he strained to see if she was well away from sight and sound.

"Oooh, Ratha sure tore a strip off of you, Krygor," teased Terat, "but I don't know what's worse; to be belittled by that old woman before present company or knowing this runt of a prisoner, a girl at that, beat the living daylight outta you?"

The other men laughed at Terat's comment, finding certain amusement in Krygor's embarrassing predicament. As they began to disperse, Krygor called them back.

"Ain't none of you was awake ta bear witness ta what *really* happened," rebuked Krygor, glaring at the younger man.

"We know what happened. We heard all about it," countered Terat.

"Ratha said that she had ta club this woman ta get her off ya before she tore your arms off."

"She's a liar!" scoffed Krygor, huffing in anger. "That old bat was 'xaggeratin' something fierce jus' ta embarrass me before you all."

"An' why'd she do that?" questioned the man standing next to Terat.

"Ratha's just jealous," explained Krygor.

"Jealous of you?" sniffed another man, his tone cynical.

"Well, more like she's jealous of her!" explained Krygor, kicking at Nayla's leg. "That old hag caught me in a comprisin' position with her. She couldn't stand the fact this pretty, little thing wanted me."

"You were not *with me!*" protested Nayla. "You were trying to force yourself *on me!* And I would rather run a rusted, dull sword through my body before I would ever offer it up to you!"

"Shut yer gob, woman!" snapped Krygor, jumping aside as Nayla's foot lashed out to kick him.

"Never mind her. As I was sayin', it's been ages since that old biddy got any of this," explained Krygor, thrusting his hips about in a suggestive manner as the men laughed at his lewd display. "When she saw me atop of her, Ratha got crazy jealous."

"Well, I wish me an' the boys can say we envy you fer being the object of Ratha's affections, but we can't," mocked Terat, as the men burst out laughing. At the same time, while cringing inwardly at the very notion of the old witch lusting after Krygor, or any man for that matter, they were equally repulsed as they were amused. "We can only offer our condolences to ya."

Not even when the witch would use a spell to fool them into seeing her as a beautiful, young maiden – even masquerading as her lovely granddaughter Druen, in a bid to seduce them, these men had quickly gotten wise to her tricks. Even lulled under this enchantment, once close enough to kiss her, the rancid stench of her breath alone was often enough to break the spell. It was as though the years of testing potions, sampling herbs and an array of odd animal parts used in creating these potent, magical concoctions, finally manifested into a foul-smelling odour that was evil unto its self.

"Har! Har!" grunted Krygor, in mock laughter. "Aren't you the funny one, Terat! Make fun if ya want, but it's the truth!"

"What a bunch of malarkey!" Terat laughed heartily as he mocked Krygor's claim, "Ratha must've whacked ya on the head but good or you're jus' out-an-out lyin' to us. Whatever it is, it don't take a clever man ta know you're feedin' us a bunch of rubbish!"

"Are you callin' me a liar?" growled Krygor, glaring at Terat as he stood toe-to-toe with the younger man. Nayla looked on with growing interest as Krygor angrily jabbed an accusing finger into Terat's chest. "Is that what you're callin' me?"

"Don't need ta. Ya already know 'xactly what you are," snapped Terat, defiantly shoving Krygor's finger away from his person.

"You *are* callin' me a liar!" declared Krygor, his beady eyes narrowing in condemnation.

Listening to this hostile verbal volley, Nayla hoped it would escalate into a physical altercation between the two men.

"*You* said it, not *me*," snorted Terat, refusing to back down.

"Well here's somethin' that's the truth!" declared Krygor, glaring down at Nayla with mounting resentment. "This woman wasn't beatin' me up when Ratha got wise ta our shenanigans. Look at her; all trussed up like this. Ain't no way she was beatin' on me. How could she?"

"It was all too easy," spat Nayla, twisting about to take a swipe at Krygor's knee.

The man jumped, but too late. The tip of the pole resting on her shoulder swung about, cracking sharply just above his left knee.

"Bloody hell!" snarled Krygor, stepping back as he favoured the welt rising beneath his hand that nursed this new injury.

"See! You are as clumsy as you are stupid!" taunted Nayla. "Even with me tied up like this, it took an old woman to rescue you from me."

"*Oooh!*" The men groaned in unison, grimacing at the brutal verbal assault she unrepentantly accosted Krygor with.

"Them are fightin' words, woman!" snapped Krygor, sneering at her in utter contempt and loathing.

He snatched up the rope. Once used to bind her ankles together, it was now tied around her waist, tethering her to a wooden stake pounded into the ground. Giving it a hard yank, he pulled Nayla up onto her feet.

"You're lookin' fer a beatin' ta throw words like that around!" growled Krygor.

"I merely spoke the truth. Now, if I were to say you fought like a little boy with *his hands* tied behind his back... then those are definitely fighting words," clarified Nayla. "Mind you, it is still the truth."

A collective gasp rippled through the growing group of men as Krygor endured another verbal lashing from this brazen little prisoner.

"Are ya challengin' me ta a fight, woman?" growled Krygor,

staring down into Nayla's dark eyes in a bid to intimidate her into submission.

"No," she replied innocently, unmoved by his threatening posture. "Are you?"

"I'm thinkin' you're in dire need of a lesson!" snorted Krygor, yanking on the rope to draw Nayla closer to his ugly, glowering face that creased all the more as he sneered in rage.

"And if we fight, what lesson will these men learn when I defeat you? Are you going to show them how to accept defeat with grace and dignity even when beaten by a woman?"

"Oh, you're askin' fer it now!" snarled Krygor, motioning for one of the men to untie the rope from the wooden stake.

"And you have no idea what *you* are asking for," retorted Nayla, a small but menacing smile curling her lips as she braced for a confrontation.

"Those are bold words comin' from one so puny," scoffed Krygor, tugging on Nayla's tether to lead her into the clearing located in the center of this cluster of huts. "Get ready fer the beatin' of yer sorry, little life, woman!"

"Are ya mad, Krygor?" questioned Terat, snatching the rope from his hands. "You ain't supposed ta fight her!"

"There'll be no fight," sniffed Krygor, watching as the other men backed away to form a semi-circle around him and the prisoner. "Think of it as jus' a little challenge ta settle the score."

"A challenge implies a contest," interjected Nayla. "There is no contest here, not against an empty-headed buffoon of a brute. You will be flat on your back and taking a dirt nap before you can even lay a single hand on me."

Her audacious retort educed a collective gasp of surprise from the crowd as an elderly man scolded her adversary: "What kinda man are ya, Krygor? Are ya gonna take that kinda guff from a woman?"

"Of course not!" snapped Krygor, angrily snatching the rope away from Terat's hand.

"Ya better calm down an' back off, Krygor," warned Terat. "If you do somethin' stupid that gets her killed, we'll all be up the creek fer it."

"Stop yer frettin'," ordered Krygor. "I'm jus' gonna put her in her place fer disgracin' me in front of you all. A man's entitled ta do that, ya know?"

"Fight! There's gonna be a fight!" announced one of the men, gleefully heralding all the villagers to witness this bout. He waved at

bystanders to take part as spectators, for this was the most excitement this sleepy little settlement had seen in a very long time.

"Krygor, you heard Ratha," warned Terat. "She'll have ya strung up by yer balls if this woman gets killed by yer hands. In fact, we'll all be in big trouble if she dies an' we jus' stood around an' watched ya kill her."

"Who said I was gonna kill her? I'll thrash her ta within an inch of her life, but I'll stop short of killin' her."

"Damn it all!" cursed Terat, mentally calculating the risk of his involvement in this altercation. "If we get inta hell from Ratha 'cause of you, Krygor, ya bloody well better make it worth our trouble."

"What do ya mean, worth our trouble? How?" questioned one of the men, intrigued by Terat's words.

"Who's up fer a wager?" hollered Terat, holding on high a tarnished copper coin for all to see.

The crowd erupted in cheer as Terat determined the odds and collected the bets from those willing to gamble on this contest. Much to Krygor's chagrin, because of Nayla's well-earned reputation as a warrior of renown, the odds were in her favour.

"Ya fools! What the hell is wrong with all of you!" cursed Krygor, angered that his own men were betting against him. "You're all a bunch of idiots if ya think this puny woman can beat me."

As bets ranging from pieces of copper to live chickens, fresh eggs, a mangy goat, chunks of smelly, aged cheese and other items considered of value quickly traded hands with Terat, even after Krygor's declaration of imminent victory, the majority still bet against him.

"Fine then! You'll all be sorry fer goin' against me! I'm bettin' everything I own that I'm gonna win," growled Krygor. "Let this contest begin!"

Just as Terat was about to untie Nayla's wrists from the pole resting across her shoulders, Krygor shoved him aside as he snarled, "Leave her be!"

"You're gonna fight her like *that?*" gasped Terat, staring in disbelief. "That's not fair."

"And what do us Talibarrians know 'bout bein' fair?" dismissed Krygor, pushing up the sleeves of his ragged shirt to make ready for this bout. "Now you best go an' adjust the odds, Terat. Someone's about ta get a severe thumpin' an' it ain't gonna be me!"

Knowing he could not dissuade Krygor from engaging in what appeared to be such a lop-sided contest, Terat called out to the boisterous crowd, "Anyone wishin' ta change yer bets; do so now! This is you're last chance!"

To Krygor's anger, disbelief and humiliation, the odds were still stacked against him. Only two more women and one of his men changed their bets, siding with Krygor while the majority of the excited audience was still confident Nayla could beat him, even with her hands tied. His only comfort was in knowing that those who did bet against this woman warrior had bet heavily in his favour to soundly defeat her.

Fuelled by anger and embarrassment, Krygor bellowed with rage. With every intention of knocking her down to size before all, he charged full bore at Nayla to slam his shoulder into her chest.

Instead, just as he neared to tackle her, with impeccable timing, Nayla pivoted, turning sideway to his attack. Bending at her waist, just as Krygor's shoulder missed its target, his body flew across her back. Nayla used his own momentum, simply twisting over to stand upright again. She sent Krygor somersaulting over her. With a loud groan, the man slammed down onto the unforgiving ground.

Cheers, gasps of surprise as well as sympathetic groans of pain coursed through the crowd of spectators that stepped back to make room for Krygor's hard landing.

"That's showin' her, Krygor!" mocked Terat, egging the man on to do battle. "Give her heck!"

Pushing himself off the ground, Krygor brushed off the dust and humiliation as though he merely tripped.

"We ain't done yet!" growled Krygor, shaking a trembling fist at her. "I'll get ya!"

"You can try," said Nayla, her hands wrapped tightly around the pole as she prepared to square off once more against this much larger man.

Cocking back his right arm to deliver a devastating punch to Nayla's face, she pivoted, angling away from this blow. At the same time, the right tip of the pole swung across to clip his chin before striking the man's clenched fist. The initial contact to his face stunned more than hurt him. Before Krygor could retract his smarting hand, she slipped the right end of the pole beneath his arm. Nayla quickly positioned this weapon at an angle so the tip came to rest at the small of her opponent's back. Stepping behind his body to steal away his balance, just as Krygor struggled to remain upright, Nayla's right leg swept back, striking him on his right calf while the tip of the pole pressed into the small of his back to topple him over.

Once more, Krygor groaned in pain as he fell backward, crying out as his assailant spun about to strike him on the chest with the left end of the pole.

"Nice move, Krygor! That's it, take her from the ground!" heckled Terat, as those betting on Nayla cheered, while Krygor's supporters jeered her efforts, booing loudly.

Taking Terat's advice, Krygor grabbed the loose rope dangling from Nayla's waist that was now caught under her foot. With a hard yank, the rope whipped out from beneath her, throwing Nayla hard onto her back. With her hands tied to the pole, she was unable to break her fall. The most she could do was to exhale to keep the wind from being knocked painfully out of her as she impacted with the ground.

A raucous chorus of *boos* echoed through the growing crowd as those favouring Nayla suddenly realized their fortunes were about to change as Krygor leapt up onto his feet to take advantage of this moment. Just as he was about to lunge to pin her to the ground, Nayla's feet came up, ramming hard into Krygor's chest to send him flying. The tight circle suddenly opened up as this large man somersaulted backward through the crowd, almost bowling over several men and women along the way.

Nayla kicked, her body snapping forward to land her back onto her feet. Lifting the pole off her shoulders and over her head, she grasped it in her hands before her body as she braced for another attack.

As the dust settled, Krygor loomed before her once more. He seemed larger than before as his chest heaved like an angry bull getting set to charge. Snorting loudly, he filled his lungs with air as he seethed with rage. The distended veins protruding from his temples throbbed, pulsating with each beat of his heart. His face, contorting with anger, was a deep hue of red; coloured more by this public humiliation than the level of the beating he was being subjected to.

Beads of sweat dripped and trickled from his forehead, leaving a salty trail down his dirt-smudged face as his smoldering eyes burned with pinpoints of fire. Krygor was now hell-bent on revenge.

Treating this pole no differently than a six-foot staff, Nayla turned so her left side faced the man. She presented the left tip of her weapon low to the ground before him.

Acting on instinct, he assumed this would be the end she would attack with. In retaliation, Krygor stomped down to hamper her movements and prevent her from dispensing a blow with her makeshift weapon.

Predicting this was exactly what he would do, Nayla whipped about. Pulling her left foot back, the pole's right tip swung about to strike Krygor across the left side of his head.

He dropped down on one knee as he yelped in pain; his ear burning with agony as crimson blood oozed from a wound inflicted by the sharp strike she delivered on him.

As Nayla swiftly angled about to bring the left side of the pole down to administer another strike, she staggered back. Krygor threw a handful of dirt into her eyes to momentarily blind her.

"Hey! That's cheatin'!" declared Terat, as those betting on Nayla roared in protest, booing her opponent's actions.

"Talibarrian rules! Ain't no such thing as cheatin' in my books!" countered Krygor. Brushing the dirt from his hands, he stood up to finish her off.

Before Nayla knew it, unable to hear his approach above the chorus of boos and cheers resonating through this exuberant crowd, Krygor grabbed Nayla from behind. His right arm wrapped around her throat, squeezing against her windpipe. Turning her head and forcing her chin down at the crook of his elbow, Nayla prevented him from stealing away entirely with her breath.

"Not much you can do 'bout this, is there, woman?" growled Krygor, leaning into her right ear to snarl his words of impending triumph.

In a display of superior strength for the villagers to behold, he lifted Nayla right off the ground as he used his left hand to brace and strengthen the constricting hold around Nayla's throat.

Tilting her head away from Krygor' sweaty face, she suddenly smashed the bridge of his nose with the side of her head. The blow stunned him, causing Krygor to reel before dropping Nayla to the ground, but he stubbornly refused to relinquish his hold on her even as the blood flowed from his shattered nose. In response, Nayla raised her weapon, bashing the middle of the pole against her assailant's forehead as he struggled to maintain his chokehold from behind.

Taking advantage of this seemingly impossible position, Nayla lifted the pole up and over her head to catch Krygor at the base of his skull. Before he realized what was happening, Nayla dropped down on her right knee, tipping forward to throw her assailant over her right shoulder.

Krygor moaned in pain as the curve of his spine met the unyielding ground once more.

"Ground fightin' only works if ya get yer opponent on the ground, too," teased Terat, watching in amazement as Nayla soundly trounced Krygor to his financial benefit.

"Do you wish to surrender?" asked Nayla, watching as this time, the man was slow getting back on his feet.

"I'll quit when you're good an' dead!" snapped Krygor, staggering toward Nayla as he spat crimson saliva at her feet.

"Keep this up and *you* will be the dead one," promised Nayla.

"Not this time, girlie!" snarled Krygor. Snatching the knife from its leather sheath, he turned the rusted blade at Nayla.

"Hey!" cried out Terat. "You can cheat all ya want, Krygor, but you ain't allowed ta kill her!"

"Try an' stop me!" growled the defiant man, pointing his knife at Terat, daring him to interfere.

Terat, and those in his immediate area, backed away. They could see the crazed look glazing Krygor's eyes. There was no coming between him and this prisoner now.

"It's jus' you an' me, girlie! There ain't nobody comin' ta yer rescue this time!"

Lunging at Nayla with the knife in his hand, she pivoted, stepping back with her right foot to angle away from the tip of the blade. To Krygor's astonishment, the left side of the pole swept down, and then up, striking him hard directly in the groin.

It was as though this pain she inflicted was so great, all the male spectators winced in unison, groaning as their knees locked together in empathy. Krygor moaned in agony as the knife tumbled from his grip. Cupping his battered manhood with his hands, his legs buckled beneath him. Krygor crumpled to his knees, collapsing before Nayla. She twisted around, using the right end of the pole to smack Krygor across his head once again. As his eyes rolled skyward to show the bloodshot whites of his watering eyes, Nayla's foot came up, kicking the man in his throat. Krygor toppled backward, unconscious to the world before he even hit the ground.

For the longest moment, the subdued crowd stood in stunned silence, staring at the downed man and the diminutive victor hovering over him. All Nayla could hear was the pounding of her heart and the steady rush of air in and out of her lungs as she caught her breath.

Those who had wagered against Krygor erupted into boisterous cheer while those betting against Nayla grumbled in disappointment, cursing at Krygor for losing this contest. Terat beamed with delight as he eagerly collected from the losers and paid out the winners, claiming the excess spoils of this gambling venture.

"She's comin'! Ratha's comin' this way!" warned a boy, sitting high on a tree branch. He was posted at the edge of the village to keep watch for the witch in case she made an early return. "She'll be here any minute!"

"Quickly! Tie the prisoner back up ta the stake," ordered Terat, passing the rope over to one of his comrades as he motioned for two other men to seize Nayla to make sure she did not escape or put up a fight.

"You better hurry!" shouted the boy, scrambling down from the tree. He scampered away to take refuge in his family's hut as branches and leaves parted in Ratha's wake as she trudged back to the village with her full basket.

Thinking that one of the men would help him prop Krygor up against a tree to make it look as though he was just taking nap, Terat swore at them as they scattered. The crowd quickly dispersed, rushing off before their presence could somehow implicate them in this contest that Ratha would clearly be against. Terat was abandoned to contend with Krygor's unconscious body on his own.

"Bloody hell!" cursed Terat. He grumbled beneath his breath as he struggled to drag this dead weight across the center of the village to the shade of a tree near to Ratha's hut. "Why'd ya weigh so much more? You're like a sack of wet horse shit."

"What's the meanin' of this?" A familiar voice snarled, making the hairs on the back of Terat's neck stand on end.

He abruptly dropped his load, letting Krygor flop to the ground as he spun about to face the witch.

"What do ya mean?" responded Terat, trying his best to look and sound innocent before her.

"You look as guilty as sin!" snarled Ratha, the tip of her walking stick poking at Terat's chest. "What're ya up ta?"

"Me? I ain't up to anythin'! Nothin' at all!"

"That looks like *somethin'* you're hidin' behind ya," grunted the witch, peering around Terat.

"Oh, him… I'm just helpin' Krygor," answered Terat, using his body to block Ratha's view as she tried to get a better look at the dishevelled heap of a man lying on the ground behind him.

"What happened?" questioned Ratha, poking Krygor with her stick to see if he was still alive. "Why's he all covered in blood?"

"While you were gone, Krygor got inta the ale," lied Terat. "He got stinkin' drunk an' took a nasty tumble. You know how clumsy he is when he's been drinkin'. That's how this fool got all bloody. Krygor ran smack-dab inta a tree. Knocked himself out, he did."

Ratha's eyes narrowed in suspicion as the one good eye scrutinized the young man. "You're a liar! If you're gonna lie ta me, you had better make sure it's a bloody convincin' one."

"What do ya mean by that?" questioned Terat, shrinking away from her haggard, scowling face.

"We ain't got no ale! We ain't had ale since the passing of the last full moon, you idiot! Now, what the hell happened to Krygor? An' don't ya go tellin' me he got drunk."

"There was a fight," admitted Terat, sheepishly.

Ratha growled with rage as her one good eye glanced over at Nayla. "I told that buffoon ta not mess with the prisoner! I'm gonna kill him now!"

"Actually, Krygor didn't fight her," explained Terat, lying to protect the unconscious man from the worst of the witch's wrath. "It was me. I got inta a brawl with that belligerent fool."

"You did?" queried Ratha, in an incredulous tone. "Fer what reason? I thought you two were the best of friends."

"We're friends, alright, but how good is a matter of opinion. I draw the line when he's being stupid."

"He *is* stupid."

"I mean stupider than usual," explained Terat. "I gave him a real thrashin' when he started bad mouthin' you; questionin' yer leadership."

"Bad mouthin' *me?*"

"Yeah! He was callin' you all sorts of terrible things."

"Like what?"

"Like an ugly, old witch."

"But I am," grunted Ratha. She was momentarily stunned this young man would think she was anything but an eyesore. "Everybody calls me ugly, old an' lest ya ferget; I *am* a witch."

Terat was quiet for a moment, and then he responded, "An' a great one at that! But it was the *way* he said it! Krygor said it in a real disrespectful way."

"Yeah, right! An' even if he did, I'm supposed ta believe you were suddenly able ta take Krygor on?"

"Sure, why not?"

"You're 'bout half his weight an' age," dismissed Ratha, her one good eye looking Terat up and down. "He's got more meat on one leg than you do on yer entire body."

"You're sadly mistaken, Ratha. Krygor's a tub o'lard! That meat you're speakin' of is jus' fat cushionin' his body ta make him *look* bigger. I'm leaner, but at least it's all muscles," argued Terat, flexing his meager biceps for Ratha to admire. "An' Krygor's gettin' slower 'cause he's gotten fatter an' older over time. As fer me? Not only am I in better shape; I've gotten better with my fists. I'm a lot faster than Krygor is. All it took was jus' a couple of good hits to his fool noggin."

"I don't believe ya!" growled Ratha, glancing over at Nayla. "Krygor picked a fight with that woman. Only a warrior like her can give a man his size such a thrashin'!"

Before Terat could stop her, the witch stormed off to confront her prisoner. Standing over Nayla, Ratha saw that she was still tethered to the wooden stake and her wrists were still tied to the pole resting across her shoulders.

"What do you want?" grunted Nayla, sitting up on the thin layer of straw scattered on the ground beneath her.

Without a word, she grabbed Nayla by a fist full of hair. The witch yanked back on her head to inspect her face for cuts and bruises. Failing to spy any contusions to indicate she had been in a fight, Ratha scrutinized her hands and knuckles, searching for telltale cuts and swelling.

"What do ya know? I suppose you did beat the senses outta Krygor," praised the witch, nodding in approval to Terat. "I'm very impressed, young man!"

"You are?" gulped Terat, shrinking away as this hag's arthritic hands wrapped around his arm as her gnarled fingers roughly fondled his muscles.

She gave the young man a seductive smile; drawing back her thin, cracked lips to reveal shrinking gums and crooked, stained teeth. Her best come hither look was truly frightening in a perverse sort of way. Terat was immediately put off with the suggestion of a spring/winter, or in this case, an early spring/dead of winter romance with this wretched, old woman. He had no intention of becoming her favoured one.

"Maybe I should have ya lead the men on my behalf, instead of Krygor?" offered Ratha, giving Terat a shrewd wink with her one good eye.

"Nah, I don't think so," responded Terat, with an adamant shake of his head as he pried her gangly, twisted hands off his arm. "It's bad 'nough he had been humbled before a crowd. No point in strippin' him of what's left of his dignity. He'll have nothin' left then."

"*Dignity?*" snorted Ratha, chuckling at this notion. "Krygor doesn't even know the meanin' of the word! An' worse yet, he's like a stupid, old dog that I have ta repeat instructions ta over an' over again ta make sure he understands. But you, Terat... I'll bet you can take orders as well as give 'em. I'm bettin' you can take orders real good!" With a coy wink of her eye, the old woman smacked her lips in his direction. Instead of welcoming her lewd advances, Terat visibly cringed at her come-on. He shuttered in repulsion as he watched her pale, slug-like tongue slowly drag over her thin, drawn lips as she eyed him like a tasty morsel to be hungrily devoured alive.

"Oh, no! Krygor's a better man than me fer followin' yer orders, Ratha," insisted Terat, backing away from her lurid gaze that made his skin crawl. "You best stick with him! I know he called you an ugly, old witch, but he also made it clear ta all he's mighty fond of old – I mean ta say *mature* women like you."

"Don't be silly! Given a chance, I'm bettin' you'd fancy older women, too. Why don't ya fetch my basket an' come back ta my cottage?" invited the witch, her broken, stained teeth peering through her parted lips as she gave him an enticing smile.

"*Aargh!*" yelped Terat. His reaction was quite visceral as he grimaced with revulsion at the mere thought of the witch's suggestion.

"Can't! Gotta go," replied Terat, walking away briskly to escape her rapacious eyes.

"Hey! Where are ya goin'?"

"Gotta tend to Krygor. I can't leave him lyin' in the open like that. Bloody crows an' ravens will start pickin' at him; thinkin' he's dead if he's jus' left like this."

"Serves him right! It'll teach him ta mess with you the next time," called the witch, waving Terat to come back.

Before Ratha could catch up to Terat to lure him to her den of iniquity, the young man dashed over to Krygor's side. Where before he was struggling to drag this unconscious man away from the witch's sight, he suddenly found strength he never knew he had. With incredible ease, he tossed the limp body over his shoulder to carry Krygor back to his hut. Terat's quick, deliberate strides carried him away from Ratha's lustful gaze.

Now, thanks to Krygor's ill-conceived plan to punish Nayla, Terat would be forced to run the gauntlet to avoid the witch's depraved attention.

"Maybe you can accompany me ta check the traps this eve?" called Ratha, extending this unwanted invitation to the young man. "There may be a Wizard or two trapped in 'em by now."

"Don't think so!" hollered Terat, wishing for nothing more than to get as far away from her as humanly possible. "Krygor should be wide awake an' ready to go by then! You should jus' wait fer him ta go with ya, otherwise, he'll be mighty disappointed, heartbroken even."

"Ya think so?" asked Ratha.

"You can bet his life on it!" shouted Terat, as he scurried away with his heavy load.

"Druen, you mentioned we should be arriving at the village by late afternoon," said Cullen, staring up to the sky to check the sun's ever-changing position. "Do you think it is still possible?"

Druen stopped. Glancing about, she compared their location in respect to the features on Mount Hope.

"I'm thinkin' it'll probably be closer to late in the evenin' now," determined Druen. "Because of my mishap an' because we had ta slow right down jus' ta move through this forest ta avoid those new traps they had gone an' set up, it's takin' longer than I first thought."

"Do not be concerned about the speed with which we travel," advised Arerys. "It is paramount we arrive at our destination safely. That is the most important thing at this time."

"Perhaps stealing into the village under the cover of darkness would not be such a bad thing," decided Lando. "We can sneak in while the villagers are fast asleep. We can rescue Nayla; be in and out in a blink of an eye."

"It'll be easy 'nough ta sneak in," agreed Druen, thinking on Lando's suggestion.

"Is the village not heavily guarded?" questioned Markus, puzzled by Druen's response.

"Not during the day. If there's guards posted ta keep watch, it'd be at night. There'd only be two or three men at the most though, but they're usually asleep – dead ta the world by 'round midnight if their dice game even lasts that long."

"That is rather strange," responded Cullen. "I thought there would be men galore posted everywhere to stand watch at all times. You would think they would be more vigilant than that."

"As far as my granny's concerned, there's no real need for constant watch. With all these traps an' deadly obstacles along the way, most unwelcome visitors don't survive the trek to Dreymoor. If they do, they usually die from their injuries soon after."

"You do have a point," said Joval, nodding in agreement. He used the scabbard of his sword to trip a line concealed beneath a scattering of dried leaves before him. With a loud *whoosh* and a nerve-rattling clatter, a heavy, metal grate mounted with numerous sharp, metal spikes dropped straight down to bite the earth.

"*Ouch!* That would have hurt!" declared Cullen, rubbing the top of his head as though he could feel the points of these deadly spikes sinking deep into his skull.

"Death would be instantaneous," said Lindras, eyeing the contraption.

"If anythin', by day, there may be one or two men posted ta sentry duty ta guard yer wife, if she's there. An' maybe even more come nightfall," disclosed Druen, looking to Arerys. "Other than that, there are no traps within the village itself. They'd pose too much of a danger ta those livin' there, 'specially the few young ones."

"There you go then!" exclaimed Cullen, his two fingers tip-toeing through the air. "We sneak in. Save the damsel in distress. We sneak out. That witch will not even know we were there."

"Not only must we remove Nayla from this dangerous situation, we must also remove the Book of Spells from the witch's hands," reminded Lindras.

"We do?" queried Cullen, frowning with concern.

"Of course we do," confirmed Arerys, nodding in agreement with the Wizard.

"Whoa! Whoa! Whoa! Hold on here. Why does our plan keep changing? I thought this was a mission to rescue your wife," snapped Cullen, glaring at the Elf. "We were supposed to save her and get the hell out of this god-forsaken place as quickly as possible."

"That was the original plan, Captain Bristow. That was before we discovered the Book of Spells was still in existence," reminded the Wizard.

"Lindras is quite right, Captain," said Markus. "As important as it is to rescue Nayla, we must get that book. We must destroy it once and for all, so the Dark Lord's vile magic is not acquired by another living being."

"You saw for yourself what this book is capable of in the wrong hands, Captain Bristow. It is far too dangerous to allow its continued existence in this realm," insisted Joval. "It must be destroyed."

Druen released a disheartened sigh as she listened to these foreboding words as this mission took on an added twist.

"What is it, Druen?" asked Cullen, staring into her worried eyes.

"That's gonna be the hard part; getting the book away from her," disclosed Druen.

"As far as I am concerned, if it is not locked away in a secured vault or stashed away in her knickers under her frock, it should not be that difficult to steal away with," countered Cullen.

"That ain't where she keep that dreadful book, but still, it'll be hard 'nough ta get to it," insisted Druen.

"How hard?" questioned Arerys.

"As much as I'd like ta see that thing destroyed, I'll tell ya right now; m'lord, it will be easier ta secure your wife's release than it'll be ta make off with that wretched book."

"I take it, it is well guarded – hidden away in a secure and secret place?" queried Lindras.

"It's not 'xactly secret, but if you call pryin' it from her hands as she uses it as a pillow while she sleeps as bein' well-guarded, then yup; I suppose it is."

"The old witch *sleeps* with the book?" gasped Cullen.

"Ev'ry night," responded Druen. "She won't let anyone touch it; me included. The only thing she'd let me do was ta copy the characters so they'd be big 'nough fer her ta read so she can use the incantations. Other than that, she keeps it on her cot, hidden beneath her pillow by day, an' beneath her head by night."

"She keeps the Book of Spells *that* close?" questioned Joval.

"If it ain't under her head when she sleeps, it's wrapped up in her arms like a lover," stated Druen.

"Hmph!" grunted Lindras. "That certainly poses a problem."

"If that is the case, how do you suggest we pry it from her grasp without her knowing?" asked Lando.

"I shall have to think on this," responded Lindras, pondering this dilemma. "I am confident there is a way."

"Well, think on it quickly, Lindras," urged Arerys. "I would like this to be a perfectly planned and well orchestrated raid; not a mad, last-minute scramble where chaos becomes the order of the day."

"And I recommend devising a method that will *not* require you to call on your powers, Lindras," suggested Markus. "There is no point in avoiding all these traps only to be killed by your magic."

"You must have faith in me, my friend," urged the Wizard.

"I do! In fact, where you are concerned, I have all the faith in the world; just not for your abilities in manipulating your powers," responded Markus, knowing first-hand how Lindras' magic had been, more often than not, a hindrance than help; at times even endangering their lives.

"But wouldn't it make sense ta battle magic with magic?" questioned Druen, looking to the Wizard of the West. "If my gran is gonna use the spells from that book ta fend you off, don't ya think you should use yer powers ta fight back against this kind of evil?"

"You would think," said Lindras, with a disheartened sigh as he glanced over with a look of disappointment at his friends.

"I mean no disrespect to this great Wizard, but consider this Druen," explained Arerys; "as powerful as Lindras is at manipulating the element of earth, through the eons, this Wizard has been less than diligent in mastering his skills."

"Yes, as powerful as his magic is, so too, is this power to destroy everything in its path," added Markus. "As well-intentioned as he is, to ask the Wizard to unleash his magic, especially under duress, can be as deadly as racing into battle without a weapon or armour."

"That's not good," decided Druen, surprised by this unexpected bit of information.

"Not good indeed," nodded Arerys. "But that is part of Lindras' charm, and I doubt any of his friends would have it any other way."

"I would," announced Cullen, vocally candid in his response.

"Yes, but you are *not* counted as his friend," reminded Lando, giving the Captain a smug smile of exclusion.

Cullen merely snorted in disdain, rolling his eyes in disgruntled annoyance at the retired knight.

"Come what may, we must devise a plan that will allow us to separate the book from the witch," advised Arerys.

"Dusk will soon arrive. Darkness will follow. I recommend we journey on while we think of a strategy," suggested Joval.

"You are quite right, my friend. There is no time to stop," said Lindras, nodding to the Elf in agreement. "Tomorrow night will mark the height of the full moon. We must rescue Nayla before this time and be rid of the book before the witch manages to harness more of its powers."

"We must hurry," urged Arerys. "Follow me! Stay close. Do not stray off this trail if you wish to live."

Venturing on through the forest, they moved with stealth as daylight faded with the coming of dusk.

"Do use extreme care, my friend," whispered Lindras, following behind Arerys as the Elf forged ahead.

"No need to remind me of that," replied Arerys, his eyes probing the encroaching darkness as tiny, white stars twinkled on high.

The party suddenly froze in their tracks. A huge, dark shape blotted out the stars shining in the night sky as it glided swiftly and silently overhead to cast a deep shadow over the travellers.

"Bloody hell!" cursed Cullen, startled by this immediate and profound darkness that enveloped them, only to disappear just as quickly as it passed over. "What was that?"

"Did you make it out?" Arerys whispered to Joval as he motioned to Cullen to lower his voice.

"By the time I took notice, it had already gone," answered Joval, his eyes scrutinizing the night sky in case whatever it was that had glided over them decided to circle back.

"What do you think it was, Arerys?" questioned Markus.

"Your guess is as good as mine," answered Arerys. "Whatever it was, make no mistake; it was big."

"*Big?* It was monstrous!" insisted Cullen, his eyes filling with dread. "It was of gargantuan proportions!"

"You do think your grandmother had used her powers to conjure up another hideous beast, Druen?" asked Lando.

"I'm hopin' not," answered Druen. "From the glimpse of its shadow that I caught, whatever that thing was, it sure as heck was massive. It was way bigger than the first creature she created."

"That is all we need," groaned Lindras; "another rampaging beast to contend with and one that can fly at that!"

"Perhaps it was an owl; a very *big* owl," suggested Cullen, hoping to offer a perfectly good, non-life threatening explanation as much to calm his nerves as it was to calm Druen's. "And the light of the moon cast its shadow in such a way, it made the bird appear much larger than it truly was."

"Nice try, Cullen," scolded Lando. "The shadow that had passed over us was far too large to be any kind of owl. You know that."

"Fine then!" snapped Cullen. He was thoroughly annoyed by the retired knight's know-it-all attitude. "So what do *you* think it was, old man?"

"From the fleeting glimpse I caught of it, I would say it was a dragon."

"A *dragon?*" gulped Markus, glancing nervously overhead for signs of danger. "Are you serious, Lando?"

"It was only a guess," replied the knight, his shoulders arching up in a shrug. "I can be completely wrong though."

"Let us hope you are," prayed Markus. After all these years, his fear of dragons had abated little, if any.

"Is it possible your grandmother had conjured up such a creature, my dear girl?" queried the Wizard.

"Her powers were enough ta create the beast ya killed. I don't see why she couldn't use the same spell to conjure up a dragon, if she really wanted to. All it'd take is the potion, the incantation an' the old carcass or bones of a dead dragon ta bring it back ta life."

"So she *can* make the dead come back to life once more!" gasped Arerys. "That witch has the power to restore life; possibly even the Dark Lord."

"Actually, she can resurrect a dead thing's physical form, but she can't restore its soul, so I can't rightly say if it's truly alive in every sense of the word," explained Druen.

"Brilliant! Absolutely brilliant! As far as I am concerned, if it can up and kill a person, it *is* alive," groaned Cullen, his hand slapping his forehead in frustration. "And we all know the Dark Lord does not have a soul to begin with, so it will not matter to him in what form he is restored."

"Even if this is so, Beyilzon cannot be resurrected until the height of the full moon," explained Arerys. "At this moment, the more pressing matter is the nature of the creature that flew overhead. That is what presents an immediate threat to our lives and this mission."

"Knowing that dragons once roamed the northern reaches of Imago in abundance before the coming of mortal man, I sense that it would not be too difficult for the witch to uncover a dragon's skeleton in its entirety if she put her mind to it," surmised Lindras.

"If that be the case, I suggest we continue on, and do so with utmost haste," recommended Markus. "There is no point in lollygagging about; idly waiting to become dragon fodder for the dreaded creature, if it is indeed hunting for us."

"Quickly, then," urged Arerys. "We shall move with speed."

"Just be mindful of the traps," warned Cullen, motioning for the Elf to escort the party on.

"Yes, of course," responded Arerys, nodding his head with obvious agitation; "just do not get ahead of me."

"No worries about that, my lord," assured Cullen, taking Druen's hand into his as he followed close behind the Elf. "Just lead the way."

"Druen, is there a chance we will encounter the witch on this night.

Will she be inspecting these traps along the way?" queried Markus.

"Usually, she'll check 'em the next day, if she can be bothered ta do so," replied Druen. "If anyone's gonna go sneakin' inta the village, it'll be at night. She doesn't mind letting the victims suffer 'til mornin'."

"Good for us; unfortunate for any sorry sod falling prey to one of these deadly contraptions," responded Lando. "At least there is a less likely chance we will have a run-in with the witch or her cronies on this eve."

"We can only hope," said Lindras.

"Mind you, if she's 'xpectin' someone, namely the Wizards, ta come stumblin' inta one of her traps, it's likely that she'll be checkin' 'em more frequently," warned Druen, pondering the possibilities.

"We are better not to take any chances," responded Arerys. "We shall proceed with caution."

"Will you hear their approach?" questioned Cullen, looking to the Elf for reassurance.

"Not if you keep talking," answered Arerys. "Other than that, I should hear their advance long before they are even aware of our presence."

"I recommend drawing arms, just in case," suggested Markus, pulling an arrow from the quiver to arm his bow.

All with the exception of Lindras and Druen did likewise, arming themselves in case of a violent confrontation.

"Just keep in mind, if the winged leviathan was indeed a dragon, and if it is hunting us down, swords and arrows will do nothing more than agitate the beast," cautioned Joval.

"That is very true, my friend," agreed Lindras, giving the Elf a judicious nod of his head.

"My sword will be useless?" gasped Cullen, his grip suddenly loosening on the hilt of his weapon.

"Joval is quite correct, Cullen. Even a mighty Elven sword would nary put a dent in its scales and a strong arrow would simply glance off that body of armour," noted Lando.

"If we cannot fight it, run I say," suggested Cullen. "Run as fast as you can. Scatter and flee. And remember, you need only be a tad faster than the person taking up the rear."

"Now there is another brilliant idea from a less-than-brilliant mind," mocked Lando. "You do just that, Cullen! Run amok like a deranged half-wit. We shall stand by and watch you at your best."

Cullen's eyes narrowed in suspicion as he stared at Lando. "This is not right... You would have me escape certain death while you stand about waiting to become the dragon's next meal?"

"Lando speaks in jest," responded Joval. "If you run in panic, it will excite the dragon to give chase. Fast, sudden movements usually imply a potential meal on the run."

"Truly?" queried Cullen, frowning with curiosity as he scrutinized Joval's face.

"You can always test Joval's words," offered Lando, a mischievous grin spreading across his face.

"You wish!" snapped Cullen, scowling with resentment.

"Aah… but seldom are my wishes granted," lamented Lando, sighing wistfully. "You can make this one wish come true, if you like."

"Oh, shut your gob!" growled Cullen.

"Both of you, shut it!" ordered Arerys. "Time is being wasted on idle chatter. We move on."

With Arerys leading the way and Joval taking up the rear, the intrepid party crept ahead. Using utmost stealth, they cautiously ventured on through the darkness.

Arerys came to an abrupt halt, motioning his comrades for silence.

"What is it, my friend?" queried Lindras.

"Do you hear that?" whispered Arerys, as he listened intently.

"That is odd…" answered Markus, his voice in a hush. "Strangely enough, I hear nothing."

"There is not a single sound to be had," added Lando, confirming Markus' observation.

"That is what concerns me," responded Arerys, his head cocking from side to side as he listened for a sound – any noise that would betray approaching danger. "It is *too* quiet."

This numbing silence was broken by a sharp *crack!* It was the sound of a brittle, dried branch snapping under foot on the dark trail directly ahead of them.

Arerys suddenly raised his hand, motioning all for silence. Raising his bow, his eyes strained to penetrate the all-consuming darkness enveloping this forest.

"Are you sure it is not one of your warriors?" whispered Markus, reluctantly taking aim.

"Positive," answered Arerys. Knowing an Elf would travel in relative silence, not clumsily trampling dried vegetation underfoot; he drew his arrow with deliberate intention.

"There! Over there!" shouted a voice. *"I see them!"*

"Now!" ordered Arerys. On his command, just as Lindras raised his staff to protect the girl, his comrades unleashed their arrows in the direction of this approaching voice.

As this hail of arrows sliced through the darkness, a blinding explosion of brilliant, white light erupted toward them. Its force shattered the projectiles into harmless splinters as the invisible shockwave bowled Arerys and all those standing behind and near to him off their feet. Collapsing to the ground, they convulsed with a paralyzing pain that coursed through their tortured bodies.

"Hurry! This way!" shouted a voice in the darkness, as hurried footsteps rushed toward Arerys and his downed comrades.

a question of trust

"Look… He is coming to."

These words hummed and droned. This voice was like the distant sound of agitated bees buzzing in Arerys' ears as the ringing subsided. Stirring from this unnatural sleep, his eyes slowly opened to stare into the cobalt canvas of a deep night sky.

Arerys bolted upright, suddenly aware of a presence hovering over him. He anxiously glanced about his dark surroundings. His eyes immediately darted over to a strange show of light looming before him. It shone against a dark shadow as this shape took form before his bleary eyes.

This bright point of light glowing before him swelled, causing Arerys to squint, shielding his eyes as this brilliance expanded to illuminate the face of Tor Airshorn the Wizard of the North. Tor smiled sympathetically at the Elf as Arerys breathed an audible sigh of relief to spy upon a friendly face in these unfriendly lands.

"Have a drink of this, my friend," offered Tor, handing Arerys a flask of fresh, cold water.

"What happened?" queried Arerys, allowing himself a small, rejuvenating sip as he sat upright. "And what are you doing here?"

"Tor did not come alone and what happened to you on this night was a near-deadly accident," responded Tylon Riverdon, kneeling down next to his brother Wizard to greet Arerys.

"So, it was the two of you we had encountered on the trail," surmised Arerys, staring over to the Wizard of the South.

"It was the *three* of us," corrected Tylon, bowing his head in salutation. "We arrived with Eldred. We were searching you out. Unfortunately, our efforts to discreetly intercept your party in a bid to avoid detection from those in Dreymoor did not work as well as we had hoped."

"I would say," agreed Arerys, becoming aware of Eldred Firestaff. He slowly stretched his aching muscles that had contracted violently under the Wizard's painful and unexpected assault.

"If it is of any comfort to you, it would have been much worse had it been Lindras to use his magic to repel your arrows," reminded Eldred, bowing his head in respectful acknowledgment to the Elf Prince. "Had it been so, you would all be dead or severely incapacitated for a much longer duration."

"Not to mention being forced to endure far greater pain if the magic did not kill you immediately," added Tor, more to ease his guilt than to quell any anger this Elf could be feeling toward him.

"I suppose you are right," responded Arerys.

"And I must apologize for greeting you in such an abrupt and harsh manner," said Tylon, sounding sincerely contrite. "Before we were able to announce our presence to you and your party, you had engaged your weapons. It was merely instinct that caused me to use my powers to repel the assault."

"Unfortunately for you, but luckily for the others in your company, you had received the worst of it, my friend," explained Tor, helping Eldred to ease Arerys onto his feet. "Standing at the lead, you had absorbed the brunt of the power unleashed by Tylon's crystal orb."

"*Orb*, you say?" queried Arerys. "Was that truly necessary?"

"I merely over-reacted… It was quite instinctive really," answered Tylon.

"With all those arrows flying toward us, he had little choice!" added Tor.

"I understand," said Arerys, allowing for another sip of water before handing the flask back to Tor.

"How do you fare now?" questioned Eldred.

"I have felt far better, but this too shall pass," replied Arerys, shaking the fog from his head. Suddenly, the Elf was completely lucid. His heart raced as the realization his comrades were conspicuously absent overwhelmed his senses. Their immediate welfare leapt to the forefront of his mind.

"Where are the others?" asked Arerys, his eyes anxiously searching about for them.

"Worry not, my friend," assured Tor, glancing over his shoulder to where Arerys' companions had taken refuge. "Your comrades recover nicely in the clearing just yonder. Lindras is in their company as they recuperate."

"None were severely hurt?" questioned Arerys.

"Relatively speaking, not badly," answered Tor, sounding rather sheepish.

"Unfortunately, all felt the force of my powers, however, none more so than you did, my friend," explained Tylon. "Other than rattled nerves and some aching muscles, they are fine."

"Thank goodness!" exclaimed the Elf, relieved to hear this news.

"Are you fit enough to join them?" queried Eldred.

"My present condition matters not," stated Arerys, brushing the dust from his cloak. "We must go on. There is no time to lose."

"Yes, yes, that we shall do," agreed Tor. "First thing first, my friend. Lindras told us what brought you and the others to this place."

"And let me begin by extending our deepest condolences on your father's passing," offered Tylon, bowing his head in regret and sympathy. "We were nothing less than stunned; deeply saddened by this tragic news we received from Prince Artel upon our initial meeting."

"My brother is here?" questioned Arerys, hope rising in his heart.

"Alas, no," responded Eldred, motioning Arerys to follow him to where the others were convalescing. "Prince Artel is not here."

"When we parted company, we left him and his warriors heading across the Plains of Fire toward the Valley of Shadows," informed Tylon. "They are about a day behind in travel. It will only be a matter of time before they catch up."

"That time will not come soon enough," stated Arerys. "We cannot wait for my brother to arrive with his army."

"We sensed just that," disclosed Eldred, parting the shrubs that led into a small clearing. "That is why we are here now."

Markus smiled, as did Lando and the others. They were pleased and relieved to see Arerys finally on his feet, up and about once more.

"You look none the worse for wear," greeted Markus, sliding over on the log to make room for his friend. "How do you fare?"

"I am alive and grateful for that," responded Arerys, taking a seat between Markus and Lando. "I am pleased to see all have survived the Wizards' unorthodox greeting."

"We are well in spite of the terrible jolt we endured," admitted Lando.

"Speak for yourself, old man. My head is still throbbing," grumbled Cullen. "I was standing the nearest to Prince Arerys when fate dealt us this blow. Royalty, or not, this Elf proved to be rather useless as a shield."

Arerys stared at Cullen with raised eyebrows only to see Druen discreetly elbow the Captain to elicit an appropriate addendum to his terse comment, "Of course, I mean no disrespect to you, my lord."

"Of course," responded Arerys, his tone dismissive; "but enough about you. What did I miss of this meeting?"

"In case my brother Wizards did not tell you, we had shared with them what we know so far of the situation we are faced with," informed Lindras.

"So the three of you are aware of the details of Nayla's disappearance?" asked Arerys, turning to look upon Tor, Tylon and Eldred.

"Yes," confirmed Tylon. "Lando spared no detail in recounting the horrific events leading up to Nayla's abduction."

"And let us not forget about the power-grabbing witch and the Book of Spells," added Tor, glancing over to the young, mortal woman who had shared the news of her deranged grandmother.

"Though this witch may be consumed with the need for power, do not be so eager to put any credence in the existence of that book," warned Eldred. He was more than willing to dismiss Druen's warning. "We all saw what happened to it when Draven's ice castle was utterly destroyed."

"Indeed we witnessed the annihilation of the *castle*, however, we were mistaken in assuming the Book of Spells had met the same fate as Draven did," countered Lindras.

"So we are to take the word of this mortal? A Talibarrian woman who is a stranger to us?" queried Eldred, scrutinizing Druen.

"She may be a stranger to you, but you are just plain strange when it comes to the power of dark magic," sniffed Cullen, coming to Druen's defense.

"I do not say this in disrespect to you, my dear woman," explained Eldred, as he chose to ignore Cullen's slight. "I merely recommend a measure of discretion, for common sense to prevail to prevent the others from jumping to the wrong conclusion."

"And common sense, if you do have any, Master Firestaff, will tell you to heed Druen's warning!" declared Cullen, standing defiantly before the Wizard of the East. "In fact, I will vouch for her good character."

"And who will vouch for *yours*, Captain Bristow?" questioned Eldred, his unyielding stare compelled the mortal to sit back down next to Druen.

"Let it be known that I believe in her," announced Arerys, speaking with complete conviction.

"Your wife's safety; her very life is in jeopardy. My intuition tells me that you are ready to believe this woman you have known for barely a day because you have little else to believe in," assessed Eldred. "I understand your need to gather information that will allow you to save Nayla, but do not allow desperation and personal grief to hold sway over good judgment and common sense, my lord."

"I can understand your doubt, Master Firestaff," acknowledged Arerys; "but consider this: Druen has nothing to gain in disclosing to us the information she had shared. In doing so, she stands to lose much, her life included, should this witch catch wind of her collusion with us."

"As convincing as your argument is, my lord, it makes no sense that she would turn against her own," cautioned Eldred. "How can you trust this woman, one who freely admits her close ties to the witch? Not only did she admit to being her granddaughter, but she confessed to being the witch's apprentice."

"She is an apprentice no more!" snapped Cullen. "And if it is a question of trust, I will tell you now, Master Firestaff, I have far more reason to trust Druen than I will ever have to trust in you. Not in a thousand years will I ever believe the likes of a deranged necromancer like you."

"Steady your tongue, Captain Bristow!" ordered Lindras, coming to Eldred's defense. "Be mindful of what you say of this benevolent Wizard."

"*Malevolent* is more like it. And I will not be silenced! Not this time," growled Cullen, glaring at Eldred in resentment as he addressed the others. "I may not speak for present company, but believe me when I say there are many like me, far and wide, who refuse to forget what this Wizard did when he launched his personal vendetta against humanity."

"That was in the past," reasoned Tylon.

"And the past should not be so easily forgotten, Master Riverdon," retorted Cullen. "The atrocities this rogue Wizard subjected both man and Elf to through the ages should neither be forgotten nor forgiven."

"And what becomes of humanity if there is no forgiveness, Captain Bristow?" countered Lindras, attempting to reason with this mortal. "It is the very essence of humanity."

"In my mind, humanity as a whole was doing quite fine before Firestaff went on his murderous rampage," argued Cullen.

"But it was the conditions brought about by human nature that caused our brother to go against mankind," explained Tor. "Not that it is justification for going berserk and seeking revenge in such an extreme manner, but we must not forget that the human race had a critical part in his downfall."

"Nor do you know Eldred as we do, Captain Bristow," added Tylon. "You do not know the Wizard he was before his faith in man was broken by those he sought to protect."

"And keep in mind; just as Druen's grandmother is bent on procuring power, she is being manipulated by evil, just as Eldred was under the evil influence of the dreaded Book of Spells," reminded Lindras.

"And *you*, Master Weatherstone, keep in mind there is nothing you can say that will influence my way of thinking where this Wizard is concerned," snorted Cullen. From the moment Eldred Firestaff swore he had turned his back on evil, nagging misgivings about this former Sorcerer had dogged him. "If anything, I have the courage to say aloud what the others only dare to think."

"Why must you – " Lindras' sentence was abruptly cut short as Eldred raised his hand for silence.

"Say no more in my defense, my brothers. Your well-intentioned words fall on deaf ears."

"As you refuse to defend yourself, of course we shall speak up on your behalf," responded Lindras.

"He does not defend himself because Firestaff's actions cannot be defended!" argued Cullen, his words adamant. "If there was absolutely no lack of trust, then why is it the Wizards speak on his behalf and still, I have yet to hear a single mortal man or Elf in this esteemed company leap to his defense? I have heard not one word from any of you!"

Cullen stared accusingly at Arerys and his companions, cupping a hand to his ear as he solicited the party to vocalize their proud and unwavering support of Eldred Firestaff, "Come now! No need to be shy. Speak up! Someone... anyone!"

"Captain Bristow, I strongly suggest you step down from your high horse before I take the liberty of knocking you down!" demanded Markus, so thoroughly annoyed by Cullen's remarks that he was confident they were meant to impress nobody else but Druen.

"Gladly, Your Highness, once I have secured an admission from at least one of you that beyond a shadow of a doubt, with absolutely no reservations whatsoever, that you have complete and utter faith in this once-rogue Wizard," responded Cullen.

"Come now, Captain, you were there when he helped to save my daughter's life," countered Arerys.

"No disrespect to you, my lord," said Cullen; "but from my perspective, I would say he was attempting to *save* his own hide and reputation in the guise of committing a good deed."

"Good gracious! Cullen, you skeptical sod, Eldred's efforts helped to restore order to your kingdom when King Sebastian was under the enchantment of the evil Sorceress," scolded Lando, thinking back to the second quest that brought them together with this hubris, young Captain.

"Not to forget his aid in helping us to rescue Prince Carstian last autumn," reminded Joval.

"Now this is odd…" noted Cullen, his tone smug as he wagged his finger accusingly at his company.

"You are the *odd* one," snorted Lando, taking an angry swipe at the Captain's condemning digit.

"Mock if you want, but I cannot help but notice that you have all listed this Wizard's good deeds of late, and yet, not one of you had stepped forward to say that you unequivocally trust in this soul," commented Cullen. "And I, for one, will not forget what he had subjected our kind to, not to mention all those who stood by the human race, during Firestaff's reign of terror through the ages."

"There is no need to question the good character or intentions of these honourable men, Captain Bristow," scolded Eldred. "You have no right to subject them to such scrutiny."

"It is not my intention to scrutinize or question their honour, for it is yours that is in doubt. I merely want the others to remember the atrocities committed by you, so they will understand my lingering mistrust for unsavoury characters, the lot of which you are well acquainted with. I do not want them to forget what you had done and what you are still capable of."

"I do not expect my atrocious deeds to be forgotten, Captain Bristow. For me, I will never be absolved of my crimes no matter how much I repent. In my heart, I know that for an eternity I will never forget my treacherous actions nor can the guilt I bear be expunged from my heart and mind," admitted Eldred, bowing his head in humility. "All I can do is to pray for some forgiveness, for it is something I cannot give to myself."

"Well, your efforts to deflect attention from your notorious past and to shine a positive light upon your deeds of late might have fooled these good people, but I refuse to be tricked," grunted Cullen, glaring at Eldred. "The saving of Prince Arerys' daughter when she was kidnapped by the demented Sorceress Taiko Saikyu, your apprentice no less, and taking part in the quest to rescue Prince Carstian does not change the true nature of the beast."

"Actions speak louder than words, Captain Bristow. And need I remind you that words are nothing more than intentions not yet fulfilled?" declared Lindras. "Every being has the God-given right to be measured by his deeds – by his actions. That is what gives shape to a man's true character."

"In my mind, Master Firestaff's past deeds greatly outweigh his actions of late," grumbled Cullen. "For all we know, this *Wizard* is on his way to reclaim the wretched Book of Spells."

"What an outrageous claim," dismissed Tylon. "Eldred is here to offer his aid – to help in this mission."

"To help himself to that book is more like it," sniffed Cullen, his tone resentful.

"How can you say such a thing?" snapped Lindras, challenging this verbally bellicose Captain.

"Easy!" grunted Cullen. "Lest you all forget, this Wizard tried to wrestle the Book of Spells from Draven's hands during our last quest."

"I was attempting to get it away from him to *destroy* the cursed thing," explained Eldred, speaking in his own defense.

"So you say," snorted Cullen, his eyes burning with contempt as he stared at Eldred.

"What is your problem, Captain Bristow?" queried Markus, annoyed and perplexed by Cullen's self-righteous and arrogant attitude. "As a knight and a decent human being, where is your sense of forgiveness and compassion?"

"It is reserved for those more deserving than Wizards-gone-bad, especially those trying to make a feeble attempt at redemption," replied Cullen, his words were matter-of-fact.

"These reservations you have are real, however, they are not warranted," assured Eldred. "Nonetheless, I can understand your sentiments, Captain."

"Good, for you best accept that my mind will not be swayed by anything coming out of your mouth," warned Cullen.

"I can only say that a person can change. I have changed. I am not the murderous Sorcerer of old. I am a Wizard reformed, thanks to the compassion of mankind and the innocence of a child."

"A few good deeds will do nothing to wash away a multitude of sins. If I am to believe you, which I do not by the way, then it would stand to reason that this woman, too, can change," argued Cullen.

"Druen chose to abandon those heretics before her grandmother could punish her for willfully denying her birthright."

"I suppose that is possible," admitted Eldred, nodding in agreement.

"You are bloody right it is possible! And let us not forget, Druen has never killed a single person in her life. Can the same be said of you, Firestaff?" questioned Cullen, his eyes still scrutinizing the Wizard. "I think not!"

"Cullen, there's no need ta be rude ta him," admonished Druen, her hand squeezing his in hopes of calming the Captain down. "When ya think about it, this Wizard's doubt fer me ain't no diff'rent than yours fer him. Give this Wizard the benefit of your doubt an' maybe he'll do the same fer me."

"Well, you must admit, at least this woman has enough sense to see what Cullen cannot," stated Lando, nodding in approval to Druen.

"At least I am not so gullible to believe in the impossible," growled Cullen, his words curdling with malice. "And you cannot make me believe a lifetime of evil can be so easily abandoned."

"Look here!" interrupted Arerys. "We can debate this whole matter of trust until the coming of the full moon, but we cannot. If you all wish to turn back now, then I will go alone. I have no intention of leaving Nayla to the mercy of her captors."

"What luck, Cullen! There you go," announced Lando, smiling with glee. "You are free to trot off back to Darross and leave us to this quest."

"My King has returned safely to his castle. By all rights, there too, I should be," said Cullen. "However, I will have you know that I am here to make certain Druen remains safe for her part in all of this."

"She would be safer without you," responded Lando, giving Druen a reassuring smile.

"I hardly think so," grunted Cullen. "She needs to be protected by someone possessing true skill with the sword; not some retired bloke whose sword is now used to kill his dinner than to combat the enemy."

"Enough! Arerys is quite right," agreed Lindras, jumping into this exchange before it digressed into a full-blown verbal fisticuff between Cullen and Lando. "We should be using this time to establish a course of action to see Nayla rescued from her plight."

"Whatever your plans were before, I suppose our sudden arrival has changed the strategy you had devised," determined Tylon.

"I sense much shall depend on whether the witch employs the power of the Book of Spell, if indeed it is in her possession," added Tor.

"Based on what I had been witness to thus far, I believe this witch of Dreymoor is using powers beyond her natural abilities and inherent skills," disclosed Arerys.

"There was no other way that horrific beast that killed so many, including King Kal-lel, could have come to be without the conjuring of some dark magic," reminded Markus.

"That creature was definitely not of this world," agreed Joval. "It could only have only been created by the powers of the forbidden arts."

"There is also the possibility the witch had used these powers to create another creature," warned Arerys. "We saw a winged beast fly over us on this very eve, just prior to encountering the three of you."

"Apparently, the *winged beast* you speak of was indeed a dragon, Arerys," revealed Lindras; "but this dragon came bearing my brother Wizards."

"It was you?" gasped Arerys, glancing over at Tor. "You arrived here on the wings of your dragon?"

"How else would we arrive at this place in such a timely manner? My trusty dragon delivered us not far from where we are now," disclosed Tor. "With so much swampland in this area, it was the only place Button could land. We were forced to walk a distance to meet up with you."

"Your dragon's name is *Button?*" asked Druen, her brows arching up in surprise as she addressed Tor Airshorn. "How unusual!"

"True, but trust me when I say Button is an unusual dragon," responded Tor, smiling kindly at this young woman.

"Don't ask about the origin of its name," Cullen whispered to Druen. "It is a long story that makes no sense unless you are an eccentric, old coot of a Wizard with a strange affinity for monstrous lizards."

"Unfortunately, we were unable to announce our arrival to you from above the trees without declaring our presence to all from here to the witch's village," explained Eldred.

"So tell me; what did you see in your travels to get here?" questioned Arerys, eager to learn of any relevant news that would help on this rescue mission.

"We know your small contingent, as earnest as you are, will be in no position to lay siege on the witch's village," noted Tor. "Where are the rest of the warriors that had accompanied you?"

"Two of my warriors were sent off to deliver news to the Talibarrian council of the demise of their emissaries; two were dispatched to Rock

Ridge Pass to meet with Artel and his battalion, which presumably they did," answered Arerys.

"Yes, they were escorting Prince Artel and the others to this place," nodded Tylon; "to follow in your steps in your search for Nayla."

"Two remain by the grave of the beast to take appropriate measures should that creature rise up once more," reminded Joval.

"The remaining six warriors to accompany us were instructed to journey north, taking a wide path to Dreymoor. They will then advance from the opposite direction to descend on the witch's village in case they attempt to escape with Nayla as their hostage," added Markus.

"That is clever plan," decided Tylon, nodding in approval. "They would never expect an invasion from the north."

"With this strategy, we will converge on this place in such a manner, it will make it difficult if they should try to flee," said Joval.

"And let us not forget, not only must we secure Nayla's safe release, we must also destroy the Book of Spells," reminded Lando.

"You know for certain this cursed book is in the witch's possession?" questioned Tylon.

"Obviously, with the exception of this young lady, we have not seen it with our own eyes," admitted Lindras; "however, we have every reason to believe Druen spoke the truth about this book's existence."

"But is *she* positive?" questioned Tor, glancing over to Druen.

"After all, the Book of Spells is one of a kind," added Tylon. "There is no mistaking it for another."

"Of course, Druen is positive," averred Cullen.

"We all know what the Book of Spells looks like. Based on Druen's concise description, it cannot be by coincidence such a book would come into the witch's possession unless it was *the book*," confirmed Arerys.

"And whether we saw this book, or not, we had been witness to the powers conjured up by this witch," averred Lindras. "There is no evil like it. Trust me when I say the Book of Spells exists; it was never destroyed to begin with."

Throughout this exchange, Eldred was silent, quietly contemplating the ramifications of this revelation.

"If this is so, the Book of Spells must be destroyed as quickly as possible," stated Tylon.

"And this time, we must make certain of its destruction," added Tor. "We must make sure it does not fall into the hands of another willing to exploit its powers."

Cullen glanced over to study Eldred's face. The Wizard looked pensive, wallowing deep in his troubled thoughts as he reflected on the presence of this powerful book of incantations.

"You have been unusually quiet, Master Firestaff," noted Cullen. "Do you not agree with your brother Wizards?"

"Agree?" repeated Eldred, frowning in momentary confusion. "Agree with…?"

"Do you not agree the Book of Spells must be destroyed?" questioned Cullen.

"Oh! Oh… Yes, of course!" nodded Eldred. "The book is dangerous in the wrong hands."

"Are you implying that it is *not* dangerous in the *right* hands?" queried Cullen, staring suspiciously at the Wizard of the East.

"Stored within the pages of that book are powers well beyond your limited imagination, Captain Bristow," warned Eldred, staring intently into this mortal's eyes. "It is capable of many wonderful things, but so too, can these same powers be used to destroy. Even a person with the best of intentions can be tricked; enslaved by the very power they seek to harness. I know all too well what that book is capable of."

"That damned book is the instigator of all evil in this realm!" declared Cullen.

"You are wrong," protested Eldred, glaring at the young knight.

"So, I was correct about you and your intentions where this book is concerned," sneered Cullen.

"You are wrong in believing the Book of Spells is the instigator of all things evil," argued Eldred. "Beyilzon is at the root of this! He created that foul thing. The book is nothing more than his tool. So yes, it must be destroyed."

"Alrighty then, at least we are all in agreement on this matter," nodded Cullen. "The book must go."

"It is not going anywhere," stated Joval. "It must be *destroyed*; absolutely, unequivocally destroyed."

"Well, at least we now know why the witch is in want of our magical crystals," said Tylon.

"That's why you've gotta get out of here!" urged Druen, her hands shooing the Wizards away. "If my granny catches wind that you four are about, she'll do everything she can ta steal away with those crystal orbs. She'll have you all killed if she has ta."

"Your grandmother sounds a tad bit deranged and somewhat delusional if she believes she can stand up to the powers of four mighty Wizards," denounced Tor, taken aback by this mortal's brazen claim.

"Oh, she's deranged alright, thanks to that damned book, but believe me when I say she's got powers. She'll use 'em ta get your orb away from you."

"Believe me, you Wizards do not want that crazy, old biddy to get a hold of your powers," cautioned Cullen. "If she does, it shall spell certain doom for all."

"The Dark Lord won't be at his full power when he's resurrected. All my gran wants ta do is ta steal away with his essence, the very evil that keeps him alive in the netherworld. Combined with the magic in the Book of Spells, she'll be more powerful than all the witches combined that once held court with Beyilzon."

"She will certainly be a terrible power to contend with should that happen," admitted Lindras; "however, I am confident we shall prevail."

"Since you are so sure and we have established that Druen's words are credible; that her dear, old grandmother is a witch and this witch has her hands on the Book of Spells, what do you propose we do about it?" queried Cullen, looking to the others for an answer.

"After we free Nayla, we shall steal away with the book and destroy the damned thing, of course," replied Lindras.

"Perhaps the better question is, just how are we to do that?" responded Cullen. "You heard Druen. She told us where that old witch keeps that book when she sleeps."

"Is she a sound sleeper?" questioned Tylon, turning to Druen.

"When she's in a deep sleep, she's hard ta wake. Mind you, if there's a strange noise, say a disturbance like the dogs start yappin' an' howlin' at an intruder, that'll wake up her fer sure. Other than that, jus' normal sounds won't even cause her ta stir."

"Those dogs will probably start barking as soon as we set foot in the village," determined Markus. "They will raise such a ruckus, it will not only alert the witch of our presence, but the entire village will be upon us in no time."

"Not if we keep those hounds from sounding the alarm in the first place," said Arerys.

"Kill the mutts?" asked Lando.

"Do we have a choice?" replied Arerys.

"You'll do no such thing!" scolded Druen. "They're good dogs. They'd be doin' what any dog would do. You can't go an' kill 'em fer that!"

"I understand your sentiments, Druen, but there appears to be no other way around this," argued Arerys, sensing her compassionate heart.

"Yes, there is," stated Druen. "Those dogs know me. They won't bark at me. If I went ahead, I can call 'em away. Lead 'em from the village an' tie 'em up somewhere so they'll be safe an' out of harm's way."

"That is certainly a better option than having to kill them," agreed Arerys. "Are you willing to do that for us?"

"Absolutely," promised Druen.

"And then what?" asked Cullen, soliciting the company for a decent plan of action. "We sneak into the village and...?"

"And then we shall quietly incapacitate those on guard duty while Arerys sets Nayla free," replied Markus.

"And while this is happening, Druen can direct me to the witch's abode," said Eldred. "There, I shall steal in. Make it so the witch and the book shall finally part company."

"I hardly think so," snapped Cullen, sneering at the Wizard. "Do you take me for a fool, Firestaff? I believe you mean to say that *you* shall steal the book and part company with *us*!"

"I assure you, Captain, I have no intention of doing that," argued Eldred. "I mean to see that book destroyed."

"I trust you as far as I can pick up that tub of lard and throw him," grunted Cullen, his thumb jabbing over his shoulder at Lando.

"Cullen, don't be rude!" scolded Druen. "Apologize to Sir Bayliss an' ta Master Firestaff this very minute."

"I will do no such thing," sniffed Cullen, his arms stubbornly crossing his chest in defiance.

"If you truly cared about me, you'll apologize immediately," demanded Druen, her lower lip pouting at him.

"I am sorry to disappoint you, young miss!" said Lando, glaring at the Captain. "Cullen only cares for himself and his own feelings. An apology will not be forthcoming in his lifetime or yours."

To Lando's surprise, Cullen sounded almost contrite as he bowed his head to the retired knight and the disgruntled Wizard, "Druen is quite right. An apology is in order. I am sorry."

"See! That wasn't so hard, Cullen!" praised Druen, her hands clapping together with glee as she planted a kiss on his cheek. "You're a bigger man than even Sir Bayliss believed."

"I do declare! This is an absolute surprise," noted Lando. "Who would have thought you would have it in you to apologize?"

"It was not hard. In doing so, I was able to watch you eat your words," Cullen muttered beneath his breath to the flabbergasted Lando. "And if I am lucky, you might even choke on them."

"Why don't you choke on this?' grunted Lando, waving an angry fist at Cullen's face.

Smacking Lando's clenched fist away from his face, Cullen growled: "Why do we not settle this like men?"

"Enough!" snapped Arerys, pushing the two bellicose mortals apart.

"You heard Prince Arerys, there is no need to get your codpiece in a twist," dismissed Lando, cuffing Cullen on the back of his head.

"Keep your grubby hands off me! And be careful of what you say. We are in the company of a lady," admonished Cullen.

"Before we digress further, I suggest we finalize our plan and how to best execute it," recommended Joval, growing impatient with Cullen's chatter that strayed away from the subject at hand as well as Lando's efforts to bait him on.

"We cannot leave the Book of Spells in that mortal's hands. Obviously, someone must retrieve it from the witch's clutches," said Eldred.

"And that *someone* will *not* be you!" snapped Cullen, his words terse as he glared at the Wizard of the East. "That is for certain."

"And who are you to decide?" grunted Eldred, staring down at this defiant mortal. "Though you may not trust in me, there are those here that do!"

"Fine!" retorted Cullen, turning to the others. "A show of hands! How many of you believe this Wizard can be trusted to retrieve the Book of Spells?"

After a moment of awkward silence, a look of shock and disappointment shadowed Eldred's face. There was not one hand raised in his support. Not even his brother Wizards raised a single finger of encouragement.

"See, Firestaff! No one in their right mind trusts you!" snorted Cullen. "Not even a person with an addled mind like Lando Bayliss trusts in you."

"Is that so, Lindras? Do you not trust me?" gasped Eldred, reeling from this emotional blow dealt by the Captain as he searched his brother Wizard's eyes for the truth.

"In all honesty, Eldred, I do not trust in the Book of Spells and the powers within," answered Lindras. "It has the power to taint the purest of hearts and to corrupt the sanest of minds. You know that. You are well aware of what it did to you."

"But I can fight it this time," insisted Eldred. "The book's power to control is fed by one's own lust for power. I have no need – no desire to be imbued with the power of its foul magic."

"This I believe," responded Lindras, speaking with all sincerity; "however, the Book of Spells is evil unto its self. To expose you unnecessarily to that vile magic is to put you at great risk. I cannot do that."

"It is a chance we cannot take, Eldred," added Tylon. "We cannot lose you to the power of that book again."

"It is better that one of us undertake this task," recommended Tor. He glanced over expectantly to Tylon and Lindras, hoping one of them would volunteer.

"Oh, great!" snapped Cullen. "That is all we need; another Wizard claiming the book and manipulating its powers. You blokes are powerful enough without it. I say this task should be appointed to a mortal man, one not already imbued with *any* powers."

"Well, you certainly are as powerless as they come, but I still would not entrust *you* with this task," grunted Lando, staring with raised eyebrows at Cullen.

"And just why not?" huffed Cullen, demanding to know.

"You are such a clumsy oaf. Knowing you, you'll probably drop it on the witch's head just as you are about to make off with it," answered Lando.

"Why are we wasting time arguing about who will take the book?" groaned Joval. "An Elf can move with stealth, more so than a human being. I will do it."

"I hardly think so!" growled Cullen. "You already failed once before in destroying that thing. What makes you say you can do it now?"

"Already the Book of Spells weaves its dark magic," groaned Lindras, with a dismal sigh as he listened to this bickering. "And we do not even have it in our hands yet."

"I'll do it," said a meek voice.

All eyes turned on Druen as she stood before the men of this company.

"I know where it is. I can get that book away from my gran... Or at least I can try."

"I will not allow this!" protested Cullen. "You already endanger your life by leading us to Dreymoor. I will have you do no more on our behalf."

"But what's the point of bringin' you all this far, only ta have this mission fail 'cause no one could get that book away from my granny?"

"Did you not say she will kill you for your betrayal?" asked Markus.

"That, I did," admitted Druen, nodding her head in confirmation. "Where she'll have no qualms about killin' any one of you, I'm bettin' she'll hesitate ta do so ta me. At least, long 'nough ta allow me ta escape with it."

"Now, my dear girl, you have the best of intentions, however, Captain Bristow is quite right," contested Lindras. "There is no need to place you in harm's way. You have done quite enough in your bid to assist us. I will undertake this task."

"No, you won't," argued Druen. "No disrespect ta anyone of you, but there ain't none of you Wizards that's gonna go near my granny."

"I understand you are concerned for the witch's safety, considering she is your kin," acknowledged Lindras; "however, I promise you, no harm will come to her if she cooperates."

"Though I don't wanna see her get hurt 'cause I know it's the book makin' her crazy, I'm worried 'bout the harm that will come ta you," explained Druen.

"I am quite capable of fending for myself, young lady," assured Lindras, his grip tightening around his staff.

"You don't understand, Master Weatherstone. If she knows you and yer brother Wizards are about, we'll all be doomed. You'll be 'xactly where she wants you all 'cause it's yer crystal orbs she's after. An' once she gets her hands on 'em, she'll unleash a terrible magic."

"Druen is correct," agreed Arerys. "We shall be playing directly into her hands."

"Where it was not so much a risk with just Lindras in our company, we have increased the danger to us by many fold with all four Wizards converging on this one place," reminded Markus.

"I do believe Druen offers our best hope of reclaiming that book," stated Joval, his head nodding judiciously.

"I believe she is our only option and our best hope in doing so," conceded Lindras, his hand running down his woeful face.

"Over my dead body will she be going in!" snarled Cullen, taking Druen by her hand to pull her away from the others.

"That can be arranged," offered Lando, sneering with annoyance at the Captain. "Just keep in mind, if we fail this mission, we will *all* be dead; you and Druen included."

"But I – "

"Enough said, Cullen," interrupted Druen, placing a finger over his lips. "I can do this. I know my way around the village an' around my gran's hut. I can get in an' out easier than the rest of you."

"The lady has spoken," said Lindras, accepting her courageous offer. "So be it."

"I will accompany her; keep her safe," promised Joval.

"Hey! That is my job!" snapped Cullen. "If you insist on sending Druen in, then I will be the one to keep her safe."

"Then it is decided," responded Arerys, wishing to proceed. "Let us move while it is still dark."

trapped

Under the pale glow of the moon, Druen used utmost stealth to lead the way to the very outskirts of the small village of Dreymoor. From where the party remained concealed by the shadows of the forest, Markus, Lando and Cullen could not see with any certainty. For Arerys and Joval, their keen eyes easily penetrated the darkness. They carefully scrutinized every detail of this settlement as they searched for Nayla and for signs of potential danger awaiting them.

The only light that burned in this sleepy village glowed from a single coal oil lamp. It was suspended from a skinny, wooden post situated in the center of what can only be described as the plaza, a small clearing in the middle of the run-down tumble of shacks and cottages. Not far from the steady glow of this lamp, wisps of smoke curled from a dying campfire, drifting lazily into the night sky. Huddled around the still-warm rocks that prevented the fire from spreading, one guard was embraced in a deep sleep, cuddling up next to his sword. Standing over this older man, another guard stood watch, leaning wearily against his spear as he struggled to remain awake.

Arerys and Joval noticed how this younger man's head would slowly loll forward. His chin would come to rest on his chest only to abruptly jerk, snapping up as his weary eyes suddenly flashed open, only to flutter close once more as he fought a losing battle to this bout of drowsiness.

Next to this guard's feet was a wooden stake. It was pounded into the earth, but where it protruded from the ground, a rope was knotted around this stake. Arerys' eyes followed the length of this course rope as it strayed from the fire pit toward a large, wooden pillar. To his horror, as a shadow took shape before his eyes, he realized the rope led directly to Nayla. It was wrapped around her waist, tethering her to the wooden stake while an additional length of rope was tightly wound around her arms and body to secure her to this pillar.

In a panic, at the very moment Arerys was about to rush from cover to save her, Joval spotted Nayla, too. He immediately seized Arerys by his shoulder, throwing a hand over his mouth to keep him from calling out to her.

"What is it?" queried Markus, his anxious eyes peering through the cover of the shrubs to see what the Elves could see.

"Nayla…" whispered Joval; removing his hand from Arerys' mouth once he was sure the Prince was not about to give away their presence.

"She is there, trapped by those two Talibarrians. We must save her," insisted Arerys, struggling to contain his excitement to see Nayla was still alive.

"In due time, my friend," promised Lindras, his hand patting Arerys reassuringly on his shoulder. "First, we have the matter of the village security to silence."

"The dogs…" determined Lando, his eyes searching about for hounds on the loose Druen had warned them about.

Pressing a finger to her lips for silence, Druen motioned the others to go no further. Taking the coil of rope from Cullen's hands, she gestured to them to remain here and stay low until she returned.

Nodding in acknowledgement, the men watch as Druen cautiously crept forward, stopping to test the direction of the breeze before she advanced any further.

"What is she doing?" questioned Cullen, speaking in a whisper. He was mystified as he observed Druen raising a saliva-moistened fingertip before her prior to moving on.

"She is determining the direction of the wind," explained Joval.

"This is no time to be concerned about the weather," groaned Cullen, shaking his head in dismay.

"It is not the weather she is concerned about," responded Joval. "The dogs will most certainly sound the alarm if they are startled by her abrupt appearance before they are able to recognize her, however, if they can scent her out first, they are less likely to raise a ruckus."

"Oh… I see," said Cullen, nodding in approval of her cautious actions. "Smart girl, that one."

"Shut it, Cullen," whispered Lando. "Or you shall set the dogs upon her with your big mouth."

Weaving through the stand of trees that engulfed her in deep shadows, Druen silently prowled through the darkness, making her way to the east side of the plaza where four weary hounds huddled together. Shooed away by one of the guards, the weary animals shared the warmth of their body heat in this chilling northern night, hunkering down to sleep next to a hut not far away.

Krygor stubbornly refused to share the warmth of the campfire with these flea-bitten, mangy creatures that spent more time begging for food than earning their keep by guarding the village from intruders.

Nearing the corner of the hut where the dogs were sleeping, Druen froze in her tracks as the old male, the leader of this small pack, slowly lifted its scruffy, scarred head. The mongrel's muzzle and the base of its ears and neck were liberally studded with dried scabs from healing wounds inflicted by the other dogs as well as old, infected flea bites. Druen dared not move as she was yet to be in a position where the dogs could easily scent her out.

To her horror, the hound scrambled onto its gangly legs. As it shook its body awake, its long, tattered ears and droopy jowls liberally slathered with saliva slapped about noisily as a cloud of dust billowed from its mangy coat. The other dogs barely stirred, snorting loudly and heaving a weary breath in response. They were immersed in a wild dream. Their legs twitched nervously as they hunted plump, succulent rabbits in their sleep.

For a brief instant, Druen feared the worst, as the leader of the pack stood alert like an animal intent on protecting its territory. Its old eyes glanced about, searching the shadows.

Druen crouched low to the ground, remaining motionless. She did not even breathe as the dog's eyes momentarily stared toward the corner of the hut she was hiding behind in the deep shadows. To her surprise, instead of coming over to investigate or patrol the perimeter of the village for intruders, the animal casually sauntered away, plodding over to the pillar where Nayla was tied. The dog stopped momentarily to sniff at her legs, and then meandered over to Terat as he stood guard.

Terat was completely oblivious to this dog, nodding off only to wake briefly as his knees abruptly locked just as he was about to fall over. Instead of coming wide awake, he drifted off once more, leaning heavily against his spear. Terat's sudden movements caused the mutt to nervously skitter away, but as this human posed no immediate threat, the dog wandered closer. Avoiding Terat, it cautiously approached the sleeping guard curled up next to the fire pit.

The dog waited for a moment to see if this human would issue another angry warning to be gone. Quite asleep, Krygor was completely unaware of his immediate surroundings as well as this canine's nocturnal activities.

The dog took a moment to sniff at the sleeping man lost in a dream. As its cold, wet nose grazed Krygor's cheek, this man's lips, still tender and swollen from Nayla's earlier assault, curled into a lewd smile as he muttered in his sleep, "Don't be a tease… C'mon, give me a kiss."

In response, instead of plying Krygor with a friendly lick, the old dog unceremoniously raised its hind leg. Releasing a torrent of amber urine, it splashed against the human's back.

Nayla watched with silent amusement. Even if she had been able to drive the dog off, she would not have done so. It was a form of passive revenge delivered by a full-bladder on four legs.

"Oh, yeah… that feels real good…" mumbled Krygor. His chilled back revelled in this unexpected warmth as steam rising from this doggie deluge mingled with the evening breeze.

As though the old mutt knew this wet heat would rapidly dissipate into the night to give way to a biting cold, the dog's hind legs hurriedly kicked up a bit of dirt on Krygor's sleeping form to complete this scent-marking ritual.

Sauntering back to the rest of the sleeping pack members, the hound suddenly froze. The hairs on its neck and shoulders bristled, standing up on end as it stared into the darkness. Its dingy fangs were fully exposed as the dog drew its lips back into a menacing snarl. With nostrils flaring, it sniffed the air for signs of a trespasser encroaching onto its territory.

"Scabs…" Druen called the dog's name in a whisper as she knelt down, patting her leg in a friendly invitation for the mutt to approach. "C'mon, boy."

The dog's head immediately cocked to one side, its ears pricking up and its lanky tail wagging enthusiastically as it came to recognize this human was not a stranger.

"Good boy," praised Druen, hugging and patting Scabs as the other dogs woke, joining their leader in greeting her. Working swiftly, Druen tied the dogs together, quietly and calmly leading them away into the forest to vanish into the shadows.

"Success! The deed is done," whispered Arerys to the others. "Druen has secured the dogs and the guards were none the wiser to her presence."

"Of course, success," stated Cullen, his words emphatic. "I told you Druen could do this."

"Let us pray the rest of this mission unfolds as smoothly," responded

Lando, staring into the shadows for signs of the young woman's return.

"Should we move now?" questioned Markus.

"We should wait until Druen returns," advised Lindras. "We do not want her to be caught up in the chaos if our plan goes awry."

"I like your strategy," praised Cullen, appreciating the fact that at least Lindras was concerned for Druen's safety.

"In the meantime, I suggest the four of you take your places," recommended Joval, looking upon the Wizards. "Remember, do not come together. Do not allow the witch and her cohorts to capture the four of you or to make off with your crystals."

"Of course," nodded Tor, grasping his staff firmly in his hand. "That will never happen."

"Just remember to maintain a safe distance from this place," reminded Joval. "We wish to avoid a deadly situation."

"We shall intervene only if the situation deteriorates and it becomes absolutely necessary," promised Tylon.

"Let us hope it does not come to that," responded Lindras. "Whatever happens, the Book of Spells must be destroyed this time."

"Absolute annihilation," stressed Markus.

"Absolutely…" repeated Eldred, his words soft, but resolute.

"That hardly rings of sincerity," sniffed Cullen, staring with accusing eyes at Eldred. "I would feel far more confident if you had volunteered to be the one to destroy the Book of Spells."

"It does not matter who destroys that cursed thing," retorted Arerys. "As long as it is destroyed, that is all that truly matters."

"Think of it as a gesture of trust and goodwill on Firestaff's part, if he had done so," responded Cullen.

"I hardly believe it would have made a difference to you, Captain Bristow," disputed Eldred. "You are biased where I am concerned."

"And rightfully so," snorted Cullen. "We would not be in this predicament now if you had destroyed that cursed text in the first place than to employ its dark magic for your own unscrupulous gains."

"I cannot change what I had done in the past. I can only steer the course of my future. Even if I had offered to sacrifice my life to destroy the book, I hardly think it would have altered your attitude toward me."

"Oooh, I am willing to reconsider if you were to make such a sacrifice, but I can hardly see that happening any time soon," grunted Cullen, dismissing Eldred's words.

"The point being, Captain Bristow," continued Eldred, "trust is not given, it must be earned. Even if I were to earn your trust, I believe it is in your nature to never fully trust *anyone* – not even yourself."

"Now that is absolutely preposterous! There is no one in this world I trust more than *me*."

"Interesting…" muttered Lando. He stared at Cullen with raised eyebrows as he pondered this claim. "A man who calls a man his friend must first and foremost trust in this person. It is no wonder you have no friends if the only person you trust in is *you*."

"Now you misconstrue my words, old man," retorted Cullen, glaring angrily at Lando. "I am merely saying that I do not trust in Eldred Firestaff and I am not the only one. In fact, let it be known that I speak for hundreds – even thousands of people of like mind."

"Now that is a scary thought; to know there are thousands of people roaming about thinking as you do," groaned Lando. "Frightening, really!"

"Your attempt at humour is still as pathetic as ever, old man!" snapped Cullen, sneering with disdain at Lando.

"Quit your incessant jabbering," ordered Markus. "We do not need your negative attitude to cripple us on this night, Captain Bristow. Can you just *pretend* to trust in this Wizard, if it will mean a successful end to this mission?"

"Sure, I can pretend as the rest of you do," offered Cullen, his shoulders shrugging with indifference.

Eldred looked momentarily aghast, inwardly reeling from the sting of Cullen's insult.

"Do not speak on our behalf, Bristow," rebuked Arerys. "We are quite capable of speaking our own mind."

"Think on it, my lord. How do you know this Wizard has not addled your mind to impair your judgment?" asked Cullen. "Suppose he has cast an enchantment on all of you to make you believe in him? To put so much trust in him when in reality, it is totally unwarranted?"

"I am about ready to *addle your mind*, and it will not require a spell," threatened Lando, waving a clenched fist to Cullen's scornful face.

"Gentlemen!" snapped Joval, growing impatient with this mortal's ability to stray from the real issue at hand. "This is not the time to be distracted. We must remain focused."

"Joval is quite correct," said Lindras, more than willing to divert attention from Eldred so they could continue with this task. Turning to his brother Wizards, he made his order, "Let us take our positions and do be careful, all of you."

"And remember, if we are found out, do not allow the witch to know you are near to us," ordered Arerys. "The last thing we need is for any one of you to be trapped by her."

"Of course," responded Lindras, as he and the other Wizards nodded in understanding. They parted company, heading off in differing directions just as they had planned.

"And remember, Lindras, *no* magic," reminded Markus, his words emphatic as he stared at his friend to make sure there was no misunderstanding.

"No magic…" the Wizard of the West repeated in confirmation. Vanishing into the shadows of the forest, he grumbled beneath his breath, "Unless it is absolutely necessary."

As the Wizards headed off to their appointed destinations, Cullen glanced about, his eyes anxiously searching the perimeter of the village for signs of Druen's return.

Lando frowned, perplexed by Cullen's behavior and the look of concern clearly etched on his face. "Are you worried about Druen?"

"Of course I am worried for her!" snapped Cullen. "Though it is none of your business, why do you ask?"

"You surprise me. It is unlike you to worry about anyone other than yourself. You must be quite fond of her."

"I am as fond of Druen as you are fond of food and eating," grunted Cullen, his eyes scouring the darkness for his ladylove.

"I *love* food… And I do love to eat," admitted Lando, his hand proudly patting his expanding girth with obvious contentment.

"Need I say more?" responded Cullen, grunting in disgust. "I just pray Druen is safe. I wonder where she is?"

"Wonder no more," replied a hushed voice.

Cullen turned with a start to see Druen creeping up behind them.

"Thank goodness," whispered Cullen, embracing her in a hug. "You were taking so long. I thought something terrible had happened to you."

"I'm fine," assured Druen. "I jus' had ta make sure the dogs were tied up a good ways away from here so they wouldn't kick up a fuss an' be heard."

"So we are good to advance?" questioned Arerys, eager to be on his way to Nayla.

"Yep, if you're real quiet, you should be able ta free yer wife with no problem. She's tied up over yonder by those two guards, but Terat keeps noddin' off an' Krygor's fast asleep. They're really useless 'bout now."

"Wonderful! Joval, you and Markus will come with me," ordered Arerys. "Lando, head off with Cullen and Druen."

"Here is a better idea. Why do *you* not take Lando and the Elf comes with me?" suggested Cullen.

"Brilliant," responded Markus.

Expecting to be met with protest, Cullen's eyes narrowed in suspicion as he glared at Markus. "Are you being facetious?"

"Me? Never!" exclaimed Markus.

"Good suggestion," agreed Arerys, wishing to circumvent a new round of bickering that was bound to erupt between the retired knight and the young captain if they were made to work together. "Lando, come with us."

"My pleasure!" responded Lando, pleased to be teamed up with his good friends than to be made to endure Cullen's company. "Just be careful, Joval. Do not fall victim to Cullen's reckless ways."

"Har! Har!" grunted Cullen, in mock laughter. "And just think; I will be much safer in Master Stonecroft's company than yours!"

"Not if you annoy Joval," countered Lando, with smug grin. "He has a twitchy sword hand, if you get my meaning?"

"Come, Captain Bristow," ordered Joval, motioning Cullen to follow. "While all is quiet, let us make our move."

"This way," whispered Druen, pointing in the direction of her grandmother's run-down cottage. Pressing a finger to her lips, she gestured for silence as she took Cullen by his hand to lead the way.

As Lando watched Joval melt into the shadows as he crept along behind Cullen, Arerys was already on the move.

"Lando," whispered Markus, tapping his friend on the shoulder. "Arerys is intent of freeing Nayla. We best keep up with him."

"Here we are," announced Druen, directing Joval and Cullen to the rear of her grandmother's humble cottage. "She's gotta be fast asleep by now."

Being the tallest, Joval discreetly peered through the cracks of the tilted shutters mounted to the crooked window. Inside, the flame of a single candle flickered and flared as the wick burned down, fighting to stay afloat on this molten sea of wax. The irregular light cast by this candle served to illuminate the cluttered interior of this wood and straw abode.

The centerpiece of this ram-shackled cottage was an old, blackened cauldron. It was liberally encrusted with an eon of soot and an indiscernible mixture of various potions that had bubbled over the rim to coagulate and burn. This large pot rested over a pile of smoldering firewood, the acrid smoke drifting high into the rafters to seep through the holes and cracks in the thatched roof that was falling to decay.

Dangling from the beams of wood supporting the layers of straw sheltering this hovel, a number of bloated, spiny fish hovered above. They had been hung up to dry in the constant draft flowing through this room. The regular presence of smoke wafting up to the ceiling helped to cure these odd-looking sea creatures.

Joval immediately recognized these desiccated specimens as the same type of fish used by the Kagai Warriors to create a lethal poison extracted from the fish's liver. He wondered if the old witch used them for the same purpose.

"What do you see?" whispered Cullen, standing on his toes in a bid to steal a peek inside.

"Other than utter squalor, not much," answered Joval, continuing his scrutiny of these dingy, cluttered surroundings. "Hold on… I see something."

"What do you see?" questioned Cullen, tugging at Joval's sleeve like an impatient child demanding to know.

"Quiet," ordered the Elf, his eyes probing through the disorder.

"Hush, Cullen," whispered Druen. "Allow Master Stonecroft ta finish lookin'."

Staring through the cracks, Joval's acute vision was able to discern the usual array of household items from those employed in witchcraft. On one side of the cauldron was a worktable. Its surface was buried beneath a plethora of dirty dishes, food-encrusted pots, stained and splintered wooden spoons as well as a stone mortar and pestle used more for concocting potions than to create edible recipes.

Next to the mortar, beneath the clutter, Joval spied upon Nayla's swords the witch had undoubtedly seized upon capturing her. The only other thing that caught his attention was a large toad making itself comfortable in a half-eaten bowl of broth as it waited for an easy meal of moths drawn to the candle's flame.

With an Elven eye for perfection, Joval could not help but notice the staggered rows of poorly placed, slanting shelves lining one of the walls. He could only assume this was attributed to the fact the witch has but one good eye. This effectively hampered her ability to visually line objects up in a straight, level fashion. On these shelves, a wide assortment of ceramic jars of varying sizes and shapes sat among the blanket of dust and tangle of cobwebs.

Adjacent to this wall, tucked into the corner of the room, a narrow cot creaked as a sleeping form restlessly shifted about on the worn, under-stuffed straw mattress.

"Well?" queried Cullen. "Is the witch about?"

"Indeed she is. As luck would have it, the old woman is fast asleep," informed Joval.

"And the Book of Spells?" questioned Cullen. "Is it with her?"

"From what I can determine, it is nowhere on the shelves or the table. I believe it is safe to assume it is exactly where Druen told us it would be... in bed with the witch."

"Then let us not waste anymore time. Let us sneak in. I will pluck the cursed book from her clutches," said Cullen, following Druen to the front of the cottage.

Tiptoeing onto the small porch, Druen pressed her ear to the door.

"Hold on," urged Druen. For a moment, she listened. Through the thin planks of wood, she could hear her grandmother release a slow, heavy breath, snorting as she finally inhaled deeply.

"And?" asked Cullen.

"My gran is dead ta the world."

"Are you speaking literally or figuratively? For if she truly is dead, but she continues to live and breathe, that is a whole new level of creepiness," noted Cullen, shuddering involuntarily.

"I mean ta say, she's fast asleep. We best move now while she's in a deep slumber."

"Good idea," nodded Cullen. Turning to Joval, he gave the Elf his instructions, "Stand guard, Master Stonecroft. Keep a watch for danger and do warn us if anyone is coming."

"Are you sure you would rather not stay here and allow me to accompany Druen?" questioned Joval.

"I am positive. She is my responsibility," answered Cullen, speaking with confidence. "Just keep a watchful eye out for us."

"I will do that. Just be careful where you tread in there," cautioned Joval. "It is not exactly a scene of domestic bliss."

"Yes, yes, I will be careful," assured Cullen, waving off the Elf's warning.

"And retrieve Nayla's swords while you are at it," urged Joval.

"I will do what I can," whispered Cullen.

Having quietly crept around the perimeter of the village, Arerys, Markus and Lando remained concealed in the shadows as they made their way to where Nayla was tied to the wooden post.

"Now what?" asked Lando, his voice in a hush as he stared over at the sorry excuse for guards. "Shall we overpower them, Arerys?"

"We outnumber them," added Markus. "It should be easy enough for us to accomplish."

"If we can free Nayla while avoiding a confrontation altogether, I would prefer to do that," responded Arerys, stealing a glance to assess the situation. "As much as I want Nayla freed, the Book of Spells must also be freed of the witch's hands. As of yet, it appears that Bristow is not in possession of that book."

"So we wait until then?" whispered Markus.

"No... We must proceed with the rescue, but we must do so without warning the entire village, and the witch, that we are here," answered Arerys.

"Then we shall have to kill those two *quietly*," suggested Lando, his hand resting on the hilt of his sword as he stared over at the Talibarrians on sentry duty.

"It is better if we left them sleeping," decided Arerys. "Sneak in and out while they are unconscious to the world."

"Easier said than done," assessed Markus. "One is obviously fast asleep so he is of little concern; however, the other guard is standing and struggling to fend off sleep. Even if he nods off, he will be easy to wake."

"There may be a need for a distraction," responded Arerys.

"What do you suggest?" questioned Lando, watching as the guard leaning heavily against his spear slumped forward only to abruptly straighten as he shook his head to fend off the tide of weariness threatening to consume him, body and mind.

"I am sure you can come up with something," answered Arerys, focusing his attention on rescuing Nayla.

In this darkness, they remained motionless and silent as the steady, repetitious peeping of tree frogs served to numb Terat's mind, lulling him back to sleep.

"Nayla... if you can hear me, lift your head, but do not look about," whispered Arerys, his soft words floating on the gentle night wind.

From where they hid behind the back of the cottage, they waited and watched for Nayla's response. Arerys held his breath as Nayla's head continued to droop, her chin resting on her chest as she long gave up on her struggle to be free of these bonds.

"Nayla…" Arerys whispered again, speaking just a little louder. "Can you hear me?"

Krygor remained asleep as Terat restlessly shifted his weight from one foot to the other as he fought a losing battle to remain fully conscious.

Slowly, Nayla raised her head, becoming acutely aware that she was not alone. Her heart raced with relief and elation as she came to recognize Arerys' soft voice, sensing his presence near to her. Arerys' heart raced just as fast and loud, rejoicing that she responded to his voice, but panicking that her reaction would somehow wake her captors.

"Nayla, pretend you hear nothing…" whispered Arerys. "I am here to free you."

He watched as Nayla discreetly nodded in understanding, lowering her head back down as though she had drifted off to sleep.

"Now what?" questioned Markus.

"Stay here with Lando," ordered Arerys, removing his dagger from its sheath. "I will sneak in, cut her free."

"Are you sure?" asked Markus, glancing about for other Talibarrians coming to replace these two drowsing guards.

"Positive," answered the Elf, for he knew he could move with greater speed and far more stealth than his mortal comrades.

"Do be careful then," whispered Lando, carefully drawing his sword in case of an altercation. "We will be here if you need us."

Arerys nodded in understanding as he crept off. Remaining in the shadow cast by the large pole Nayla was secured to; he froze in his tracks each time either guard stirred. With silent footsteps, Arerys advanced, inching his way to his wife. Hiding behind this post, he proceeded to saw through the thick, coarse rope with his dagger. He suddenly froze as the guard sleeping by the now-cold fire woke with a start.

"What the hell's goin' on here?" snarled Krygor.

As Joval stood guard, Cullen silently crept along behind Druen. Slowly releasing the latch, she eased the door open, lifting it slightly to minimize the squeaking of the rusty hinges. Following her inside the cottage, just as he stepped into the room, Cullen was forced to scramble, grabbing the door as its weight, the tilted walls and the forces of gravity combined to abruptly pull the door shut. He bit down on his lower lip, stifling his groan of pain as the door slammed onto his hand, striking it hard against the doorjamb.

Druen pressed a finger to her lips, motioning for Cullen's silence. He nodded in understanding, shaking off the throbbing pain from his battered hand. She flexed her finger, this time, gesturing him to follow. She guided him into the gloomy abode, navigating around the cluttered stack of firewood, a scattering of broken pieces of earthenware and what Cullen could only guess to be scraps of food that didn't quite make it into the witch's mouth. It was left on the filthy, wooden floor to feed the rat that scurried for the safety of the deep shadow beneath the table.

With the unsteady light cast by the dwindling candle, Cullen's eyes remained fixed on the floor. He carefully skirted around this obstacle course that was undoubtedly a regular condition of squalor for the witch.

Cullen froze as something brushed up against his forehead, scratching lightly against his skin before snagging onto strands of his hair.

Glancing up, this small, dark object came into focus before his eyes. Cullen abruptly recoiled. He drew his breath in with fright as Druen threw her hand over his mouth, stifling his scream. He had walked into one of the several bats tied to thin lengths of twine and left to dry amongst the smelly fish hanging from the rafters. He cursed beneath his breath while Druen frantically motioned him to keep his voice down.

Cullen grimaced in disgust as he handled the desiccated remains of the bat's shrivelled, leathery wings by the tips of his fingers. Shuddering in revulsion, he carefully pulled his hair free of the tiny, hooked claw that protruded from the apex of its wing.

"It's dead. Ain't nothin' ta worry 'bout," whispered Druen, glancing over to the far wall to make sure her grandmother was still asleep.

"True, it's dead, but it is a *bat* nonetheless," grumbled Cullen, his voice in a hush as he ducked to avoid the others dangling overhead to dry.

"Over here." Druen's words were barely audible as she crept across the room.

Tip-toeing behind her, Cullen followed Druen, taking great care to advance across the creaky floor. They came to a stop before a rickety cot pushed up against the wall. Before him, amidst the crumpled, tattered bedding he spied upon a wizened, gaunt form. In the most unladylike manner, the witch was sprawled out in a spread-eagle, her gangly limbs splayed as her head tilted away from them. Lo and behold, resting against her right arm was the infamous Book of Spells.

Inching in closer, Cullen momentarily hovered over this wretched excuse for a woman. He watched as her bony ribcage rose and fell with each slow, deep breath wheezing through her long, pinched nose and mouth that hung slightly agape. The witch was fast asleep, totally oblivious to their presence.

Taking decisive action, Cullen made his move. His fingers wrapped around the book, gently easing this weight off the witch's arm. Suddenly, the old woman's head rolled over to the right, her half-opened eyes staring directly at Cullen's startled face.

Fighting against the rising tide of panic, his eyes locked with the witch's. One orb was clouded over, the other glazed and rapidly darting to and fro in the most unnerving manner as though scrutinizing every pore and facial hair on Cullen's face.

Druen quickly clasped her hands together, resting her cheek against them as a sign to Cullen that the witch was still asleep, even though her eyes were open and moving about.

Unsettling as it was, Cullen slowly waved a hand in front of the witch's face to make sure she was still embraced in a deep slumber. Sure enough, there was no response, only another slow, deep breath as she exhaled.

Druen pressed an index finger to her lips as she motioned for Cullen to remove the book, but to do so silently as her other hand gestured to him to hurry up in case her grandmother suddenly woke up.

Once more, Cullen's fingers wrapped around the heavy book to lift it from the witch's gangly, stick-like arm. This unattractive appendage, like the rest of this woman's body, suffered from unnatural aging. Wilting muscles and loose, drooping skin clung to these bones.

Just as Cullen was ready to steal away with the book, this sudden loss of weight pressing down on her limb caused the witch to stir. She abruptly rolled over before Druen could pull Cullen away. To his horror, the old woman threw her spindly left arm around his neck. She pulled Cullen closer, pressing his face to her sagging, deflated flaps of skin that, in her younger days, once formed her breasts as she muttered in her sleep, "You ain't goin' nowhere, my love..."

The hag snorted loudly, gagging on her own saliva as she exhaled heavily into Cullen's face. Remaining motionless, he held his breath,

trying not to move or cough as the rancid stench emanating from deep within her throat gushed into his face.

Cullen recoiled in utter disgust as the witch's pale, slug-like tongue protruded from her thin, parted lips. It slithered about to catch the drool trickling down the right corner of her mouth while she dreamed her salacious dreams.

"Don't move," whispered Druen. She frantically searched about the room for something to slide into the witch's arms in place of Cullen and the book.

"As if I have a choice," groaned Cullen, muttering beneath his breath. He tried not to gag as another smothering tide of foul, spent air rushed from the witch's mouth to wash over his tortured face.

With each exhalation, the wisps of brittle, tangled hair that hung around the witch's haggard face blew into his, tickling his nose. Unable to reach over to brush aside these stray strands, Cullen puffed, attempting to discreetly blow away these offending hairs. Instead, the witch heaved another heavy breath, sending them right back into Cullen's face.

Just as Druen returned with piece of firewood that approximated the weight of the book, Cullen sneezed!

To his surprise, this abrupt blast of air rushing from his nose and mouth, even as he tried to stifle it, was barely enough to cause the witch to stir from her slumber. The hag's vacant eyes that had stared directly into his since the onset of this potentially deadly predicament shut completely. It was as though she had drifted off into a deep, sound sleep once more.

Cullen released a great sigh of relief.

Ratha's eyes snapped wide open.

For a fleeting instant, nose-to-nose, they both stared at each other's startled face in stunned silence: Cullen, not knowing what to do next and the witch, uncertain if she was caught up in a strange dream.

Arerys froze. He pressed his body to the post Nayla was secured to as the guard snarled in anger, turning on his partner.

"What's the meanin' of this!" snarled Krygor, scrambling to his feet.

"What the heck are ya speakin' of?" grumbled Terat, forcing his bleary eyes to open. They were greeted by Krygor's scowling face contorting in anger as the man scrambled to his feet to confront him.

"*This!*" Krygor was quivering with rage as he threw his wet cloak at Terat. "You did this!"

Terat caught the cloak, but without taking a deliberate whiff, his face instantly grimaced in disgust, recoiling from the pungent stench of fresh urine.

"What's wrong with you?" grunted Terat, abruptly dropping the soiled cloak to the ground. "Couldn't even wake up ta take a piss?"

"Ya fool!" bellowed Krygor, peeling off the cold, clammy shirt plastered against his back. "Ya gone an' pissed on me while I slept!"

"Are ya daft? If I really wanted ta piss on ya, I wouldn't have waited 'til now. I would've done it when that woman knocked you out cold this mornin'," scoffed Terat, as he glanced over at Nayla.

"Bad 'nough ya made a public mockery of me today!" snarled Krygor, seizing the younger man by the lapels of his vest to give him a violent shake. "I won't be puttin' up with none of yer insolence no more, ya moron!"

"You're the moron!" Terat used the staff of his spear to shove Krygor away. "If anythin', you brought the humiliation onta yerself, braggin' before ev'ryone about puttin' this woman in her place."

"I went easy on her... too easy. That's the only reason she got the upper hand."

"I'm thinkin' she's the one who went easy on *you*," mocked Terat. "I suppose ya might have half a chance of beatin' her now that she's completely tied up. Oh no, hold on there! I'm wrong. Her head's not restrained so she'll most likely knock ya out with hers, if ya get too close!"

"Shut yer gob!" Krygor's clenched fists trembled with fury as Terat continued to taunt him. "I can take her on, no problem!"

"Yeah, if that woman was already knocked unconscious ya might be able ta wrestle her to the ground... with some help."

"I'll be knockin' you unconscious, if ya don't shut yer gob!" promised Krygor, waving a threatening fist in Terat's face.

"You can try, but even if ya thrashed me good, it ain't gonna restore yer dignity," scoffed Terat. "Don't ferget, it's one thing fer a man ta get beat up by a man, but it's another thing altogether if a man is beat up by a woman... an' a puny one at that."

"Don't you go disrespectin' me an' my dignity!" hissed Krygor, his eyes burning with pinpoints of fire.

"What are ya speakin' of? She stomped on what little ya had. Oh, my mistake; that wasn't yer dignity; that was yer arse she was kickin' all about the village!"

"Ya think you're so funny!" growled Krygor, his nerves bristling with anger as he listened to Nayla giggling in agreement to Terat's comment.

"Actually, you're the funny one. We've never been so entertained or saw anything quite so funny when this puny wench beat ya silly! Some of us had bets goin' that she kicked yer backside so hard, you'd actually taste the leather of her boot in yer mouth!"

"I've had enough of you! I'm gonna wake Ratha – have her replace you on sentry duty."

"Go right ahead! Wake the old witch. I don't care," invited Terat, daring Krygor to do just that. "You'll be doin' me a favour. An' besides, I'd like ta see ya try an' escape her clutches when she tries lurin' ya inta her bed once you're in her home."

"Ain't gonna happen... not this time," insisted Krygor, shuddering as he fought back the memories of all those times the witch had succeeded in seducing him though magic. "I'm not gonna bed that old bag of bones."

"Yeah, right... You're *sweet* on that old biddy," scoffed Terat. Pulling his lips over his teeth to feign a gummy smile, he smacked his tongue about in a lewd fashion like he was an old, toothless woman in heat.

"Shut it!" Krygor snapped in disgust, grabbing Terat by his raiment to give him another angry shake.

Having had more than enough of Krygor's blustering, Terat shoved him aside as he growled, "No, *you* shut it!"

Krygor's anger and frustration continued to mount. He now truly understood how his ill-fated contest with this diminutive prisoner not only stripped him of his dignity in the public eye, but now, even his lowly subordinate had developed a total lack of respect for him.

"You insolent, young whelp! I'll be teachin' you some manners!" declared Krygor, his emotions boiling over.

"How can ya? You ain't got no manners ta begin with!"

Assaulted by words meant to demean him, Krygor raged. Their verbal exchange escalated into an exchange of blows as the men grappled for control.

Krygor and Terat suddenly stopped.

A long, lonely howl wailed from somewhere in the forest. This sound was joined by the not-too-distant cry of the village dogs as they began to bay, yelping and howling as though they were gathering for a hunt.

"Bloody mutts!" cursed Krygor. Glancing about, the dogs he had shooed away from the warmth of the campfire were nowhere to be seen. "Damn those stupid hounds! What the hell are they up ta now?"

"They're probably chasin' down a rabbit or a fox, but you better go an' investigate," suggested Terat, staring off into the shadows of the forest. "Could be intruders they're chasin' down."

"I'm stayin' put ta keep a watch on this prisoner like Ratha ordered. If ya know what's good fer ya, you're gonna be the one ta check out the ruckus they're makin'."

Terat rolled his eyes in frustration as he snapped, "Fine! If it gets me away from yer big, fat mouth, sure! I'll go see what those damned dogs are up ta. They're better company than you are, any day!"

"Hmph!" Krygor grunted in resentment. "I'd warn ya to be careful out there, but personally, you pissed me off so much today I really don't care what happens ta yer sorry carcass now."

"Well, at least my sorry carcass ain't the one that got *pissed on,*" retorted Terat, pinching his nostrils shut to protect his olfactory senses from the terrible stench emanating from Krygor's soiled raiment. Terat grudgingly took up the spear in his hands, marching off into the forest in the direction of the furor the dogs were making.

For a moment, Krygor watched as Terat disappeared into the shadows, listening as leaves and branches rustled in his wake. Once he had ascertained that Terat was out of earshot, Krygor turned his attention to his prisoner.

"Alone at last!" Krygor's gruff voice rasped in Nayla's ear. He leaned in close to smell her dark tresses. "Thank goodness, Terat's gone!"

"Yes," acknowledged Nayla, turning her face away from the sour stench of his breath.

Krygor grasped her by the chin, staring with obvious surprise into her eyes upon hearing this unexpected word of agreement.

"So ya do wanna be alone with me?" questioned Krygor, staring suspiciously at her.

"Yes, after all, you would not want your friend here to witness me stick my boots to you again," finished Nayla.

"An idle threat! You're the one all trussed up like a hen fer roastin', not me!" snorted Krygor, tugging at the rope wound tightly around his prisoner's arms and waist.

Unbeknownst to this Talibarrian, her intended rescuer was hiding in the shadows directly behind this wooden pillar. Where just minutes ago, Arerys was racing against time to saw through the rope holding Nayla captive, he now fought to hold the cut pieces in place so this mortal would not suspect anything out of the ordinary.

"There ain't a single thing you can do ta me all tied up like this!"

"Try me," dared Nayla. "Bring your ugly face a little closer. I will give you two black eyes to match your broken pug."

Krygor cringed inwardly. The humiliation and agony inflicted by this small woman when she effectively and painfully cracked the bone in his nose with a hard swipe from the side of her head was still painfully fresh. His eyes watered at the mere thought of this trauma. Now, more protective of this still swollen and tender injury, the Talibarrian took a precautionary step back, away from this bellicose prisoner.

Drawing his sword, he stood poised to attack as he growled, "I ain't fallin' fer that damned trick again."

"Then how about this one?"

Just as the man could step forward to mount an assault, Nayla's feet came up. The balls of her heels slammed against the inner thigh of each leg, connecting with the bundle of nerves in the muscles to send a painful jolt coursing right to the bones and straight through his body. Before he could stumble back from this blow, Nayla's right foot flew up, kicking Krygor in his groin, now all the more vulnerable as his legs splayed out beneath him from the initial strike.

"Not again," squeaked Krygor. Doubled over in agony, he clutched his manhood.

As the ropes fell away from her waist, Nayla strained at the ones still binding her wrists together to the back of this pillar. Arerys' dagger made short work of it, slicing through to finally free her as he sawed through the last of the coil wound around Nayla's throat.

With her hands now free, she worked with haste to untie the knot of the rope that still kept her tethered to the wooden stake on the ground. Nayla suddenly gasped in pain. A powerful hand wrapped around her throat, picking her up off the ground to slam her back against the pillar.

"You little bitch!" snarled Krygor, pressing the blade of his sword to her neck. "You ain't gonna get away with this. This time, you die!"

Krygor flinched as a sharp point pressed up against his side, straining to pierce through clothes and flesh.

"Let her go," ordered Arerys. He was quite prepared to run his sword through this mortal.

From the corner of his eye, Krygor could make out the Elf. Glancing down, he spied the deadly blade waiting to plunge into his body.

Refusing to yield to Arerys' demand, Krygor stood firm. Though nowhere near as sharp as the blade of an Elven sword, this Talibarrian's weapon still possessed a dangerous edge. Pressing his sword to Nayla's throat, Krygor retorted, "I can slit her throat before ya kill me."

"You will be as good as dead if you try," vowed Arerys, the tip of his dagger puncturing through the guard's raiment to prick his skin.

"If I die satisfyin' my need in killin' her, it'll be worth it," replied Krygor, his eyes were wild with revenge as his blade bit into Nayla's neck to draw a thin line of blood.

"Do not even think about it!" growled a voice from behind Krygor.

The guard gasped in surprise, feeling the cold bite of two razor-sharp swords pressing against either side of his neck to scissor against his throat.

Forced to act, Krygor leaned against his sword to slash Nayla's throat. She winced in pain as the jagged edge bit into the side of her neck, but the pain was fleeting. With a swipe of their wrists, the edge of Markus and Lando's Elven swords sliced clean through the Talibarrian's throat as Arerys' blade plunged through his side, up toward his heart.

Before Nayla's eyes, Krygor's defiant scowl of rage dissolved into an expression of dumbfounded surprise. Just as abruptly, the mortal's head tumbled from his shoulders as his legs collapsed beneath him, dropping him to his knees before her. There was no spray of hot, crimson blood gushing from this wound as Arerys effectively stopped Krygor's heart, piercing it with his dagger.

"We warned him not to move," grunted Lando, in feigned disappointment. He flicked the blood from his sword as he and Markus stepped forward to greet Nayla while Arerys embraced her in a great hug.

Safe in her husband's arms, a monumental sigh of relief escaped her as she smiled at her friends.

"How do you fare, Nayla?" questioned Arerys, his eyes scrutinizing her petite frame for signs of injury.

"I am all the better now for seeing you," she answered.

"And we are relieved to see you, my friend," greeted Markus. "Thank goodness Lando found us when he did. We followed your trail as soon as he was able to take us back to where you were captured."

"Thank you for coming back for me, Lando."

"You knew I would." Lando watched with concern as Arerys used his Elven powers to heal the fresh wound inflicted to her neck. "And I even brought reinforcements with me."

"Of the best kind," acknowledged Nayla, pleased to see Markus and Arerys in his company.

All turned with a start as an ear-piercing shriek rattled the air.

"Good God!" exclaimed Arerys, glancing across to where Cullen was last seen with Druen and Joval. "What was that noise?"

"*Aiyee!*" shrieked the witch. Bolting upright on her cot, she shoved this stranger away.

"*Argh!*" screamed Cullen, dropping onto the floor as the wretched features of this frightening, old hag came to life before his startled eyes.

With their ears ringing from this shrill auditory assault, Cullen and Ratha stopped screaming in each other's face as they both scrambled to seize the book.

"It sounded like a woman," announced Markus, glancing across to the row of rundown shacks.

"Cullen's in trouble!" declared Arerys.

"Markus said it was a *woman*," countered Nayla, bewildered by Arerys' response.

"Ever hear Bristow scream?" asked Lando, dashing along as the Elf led the charge.

Calling upon an incantation, Ratha clutched the Book of Spells to her bony chest.

"Oh no, you don't!" snapped Cullen, grabbing a hold of the book.

Instead of wrenching it free from her grasp, the witch's hands had a firm grip. Her stiff, arthritic fingers wrapped around as though these gnarled, bent digits were permanently locked around it.

"Let go!" shouted Cullen, tugging at the book.

Instead, Ratha's terrifyingly weather-beaten face scowled with anger. It accentuated the multitude of wrinkles as she hissed in response, refusing to relinquish her prized possession.

Grasping the edge of the cot, Cullen tipped it over. Dumping the old woman onto the floor, he trapped the witch between the wall and the bed.

"*Run!*" hollered Druen, sprinting across the room for the door.

Hearing the commotion, Joval rammed the door open. As he raced in, Druen dashed out, colliding against each other. She stumbled back as the Elf was bowled over onto the rickety stoop of the cottage, the door slamming shut on him.

"I've got it!" Cullen shouted in triumph as Joval returned, kicking the door open.

"And the witch, too!" announced the Elf, peering in to see the Book of Spells still in this woman's stubborn grasp as she struggled to be free of the tangled bedding.

"Get out!" hollered Druen, grabbing Joval's hand has he hoisted her to her feet. Fearing for their lives, she waved Cullen on to follow. "Leave it! Jus' get out before she kills ya!"

"*Druen!*" snarled the witch, outraged as the fleeing shadow took the form of her granddaughter. "How dare you?"

With vengeance on her mind and betrayal poisoning her heart, Ratha called upon a powerful incantation as her arms wrapped around the book, holding it close to her chest as Cullen fought to wrestle it free.

"She's an old woman, for pity's sake!" shouted Joval, as he snatched up Nayla's swords from the table.

"Old, but unnaturally strong," insisted Cullen, grunting as he tugged at the Book of Spells.

A powerful jolt emanating from the book coursed through Cullen's hands. This searing pain shot up his arms, forcing him to finally relinquish his grip. As the witch finished the incantation, Cullen stumbled back just as Joval rushed in with his sword drawn, but he was too late.

A great power, like an invisible tidal wave surged from the Book of Spells. It expanded forward to propel Joval and Druen out the door while Cullen was thrown off his feet as he dove behind the cluttered worktable for cover. The tremendous force sent Cullen smashing through the opposite wall, exploding out of the cottage with a shower of splintered wood. He landed in a dazed, dishevelled heap at Arerys' feet.

unearthing the past

"Hey!" hollered Terat, racing back with the dogs upon hearing the commotion. *"What's goin' on?"*

From where he stood, he watched in dismay as a body was forcefully propelled by an invisible power from Ratha's cottage to land at the feet of the village intruders. Terat dashed over to his comrade's side. At a glance, he could see the prisoner had been freed and she was on her way, along with her rescuers, to confront the witch.

"Wake up, Krygor! Ya bloody fool! Ya let her get away!"

Cursing, he angrily pulled at the man's shoulder to rouse him. Terat gasped. Reeling in horror as he rolled his comrade over, Krygor's head remained where it fell.

"Bloody hell!" exclaimed Terat, only now comprehending what had happened upon spotting the dark pool of blood staining the earth where this decapitated head and body lay. Snatching up the goat horn from his belt, Terat sounded the alarm, blowing with all his might.

Excited by this human's frantic attempts to muster the forces, the dogs pranced about, yelping and whining as they strained against the rope Druen had used to secure them.

"Go on, ya stupid mutts!" growled Terat. He yanked at the knot of the rope to unleash the small pack as he ordered them to attack, "Get 'em!"

The horn bellowed once more, its raucous shriek shattering the night air to summon the others to come to his aid as Terat watched the dogs tear across the plaza. Barking ferociously, they set their sights on the unwelcome prowlers.

Lando and Markus seized Cullen by his shoulders, hoisting the dazed Captain onto his feet as Druen and Joval raced over to join them.

"The book?" asked Arerys, gazing expectantly at Joval before turning about to hear the vicious snarls and frantic clattering of paws dashing across the packed earth, charging toward them.

"The witch still has it!" hollered Joval, glancing over through the damaged wall of the cottage to see the witch struggling with the tangle of bedding as she awkwardly clambered over the toppled cot.

"*The* Book of Spells?" gasped Nayla.

"No time to explain," responded Lando, giving Cullen an abrupt shake to rattle him to his senses.

"Follow me!" ordered Druen.

"We'll never outrun those dogs," said Markus, seeing the angry hounds quickly closing in on them.

"A distraction!" suggested Lando. "Leave Cullen! Those mutts can chew on his bony carcass."

"Ferget it!" argued Druen. "Over here! Get behind this shed!"

As Markus and Lando dragged Cullen's staggering form along, Joval, Arerys and Nayla darted behind the small, but high wooden structure. Druen raced about to the front entrance to confront the angry pack.

Just as the snarling jaws closed in, Druen shouted at the leader of the pack, "Scabs, quiet!"

"Is she talking to Cullen?" asked Lando, disgusted by the thought he was handling a person inflicted with some kind of skin condition as he and Markus propped Cullen against the shed.

Druen's harsh tone caused Scabs and the other dogs to immediately stop their barking upon recognizing her once more.

"Inside!" ordered Druen, as she held the shed door open. Tempted by the tantalizing aromas billowing before them, the dogs willingly bounded in. They yipped in excitement at their turn of good fortune as the young woman slammed the door to lock them in.

"That flimsy door will not hold them in for long," warned Joval, as Druen raced around to the other side to join her comrades.

"This is the smokehouse," informed Druen, her hand slapping the wall where meat and fish were hung to cure. "Those dogs will stay in there as long as there's a good feed of meat ta be had."

"Good plan!" Markus nodded in approval, grimacing in pain as the shrill shriek of Terat's horn raked at his ears. "But now what?"

"We escape, of course," moaned Cullen, shaking the fog from his head.

"Not without that cursed book!" declared Arerys.

"But the Book of Spells was destroyed," insisted Nayla, she frowned in confusion.

"So we thought," responded Arerys.

"My granny has it," confessed Druen.

"Your *grandmother?* What are *you* doing with *us?*" asked Nayla, warily scrutinizing this stranger.

"It is not what you think. Druen is trying to help us," explained Cullen, peering around the corner of the shed to spy upon the enraged witch.

In her mad scramble to vent her wrath, the old woman was tripping over the carnage created by her devastating power. The spilled cauldron, toppled stack of firewood and items that once cluttered the table now lay scattered across the already chaotic floor.

"You jest!" exclaimed Nayla, staring in disbelief at Cullen.

"Trust me, Nayla, she is here to help," responded Joval. "Captain Bristow speaks the truth."

"That is unusual," sniffed Nayla, scowling at the mortal.

"Ha!" grunted Cullen, smirking as he shrugged off her comment. "But what to do? That crazy old biddy is on the rampage!"

"With that book in her hands, it is obvious she has been imbued with greater powers," assessed Markus.

"We would be fools to confront her head on," decided Arerys, wincing in pain as the witch's high-pitched shriek echoed through the night.

"Oh, you say that now!" groaned Cullen. Still quaking from his terrifying encounter, his eyes rolled in frustration.

"Surely that woman cannot attack us simultaneously if we were to attack her from all sides," offered Joval, hearing the witch cursing and swearing as she tripped while negotiating the devastation. The large toad that had made its home on her table belched a final croak as Ratha's bony knee came down hard, crushing the warty, old amphibian.

"Forget the witch, we have company!" exclaimed Nayla, peering around the corner of the shed as Joval handed over the swords Ratha had confiscated from her.

As the women, children and those too old or incapacitated to fight scurried from their cottages to flee northward, a band of men, at least thirty strong, joined Terat. Armed with spears and halberds, they assembled under Terat's orders, hastily falling into crooked rows to confront these intruders.

"*Attack!*" hollered Terat, leading the charge.

"*Run!*" ordered Druen, tugging at Cullen's arm. "Run away!"

"I am a knight. I never run!" snorted Cullen, struggling to unsheathe his ungainly sword. "We stand and fight!"

"You're outnumbered!" gasped Druen, watching in horror as Terat and his men raced toward them.

"What's new?" grunted Lando, sizing up his adversaries as he brandished his sword.

"Remain here, Druen," ordered Cullen. "I will be back for you when we are done."

Just as he was about to join his comrades, Druen's arms wrapped tightly around Cullen as she whispered, "Don't ya get yerself killed. Ya hear me?"

"Not going to happen, my love! We are the heroes here," responded Cullen, speaking with utmost confidence. He flashed a disarming smile at Druen as he held her close.

Her warm, soft lips pressed against his, but this kiss was short-lived. Lando pried the lovers apart, grumbling, "Now is not the time!"

"I'll be back for more!" promised Cullen, giving her a reassuring wink as he dashed off to meet the enemy with Joval leading the charge.

With a bone-rattling cry, Markus, Lando, Nayla and Cullen hoisted their swords as they followed the Elf, racing forward to collide into battle as Arerys took up his bow. With deadly aim, each arrow unerringly met its mark as one Talibarrian after another reeled from the impact as they fell over dead.

As the battle ensued, amid the chaos as his comrades clashed, Arerys was forced to lay down his bow lest he strike down one of his own. Unsheathing his sword, he joined the fray.

With the enemy fully engaged in battle against her men, Ratha made her move. With her tattered leather bag slung over her bony shoulder and the Book of Spells clutched to her chest, she hastened away.

Trapped in the midst of this wild melee, Nayla was prevented from chasing the old woman down. And though these villagers were adequately armed and still outnumbered them, with the haphazard hack-and-slash method of fighting, it was apparent to Nayla and her comrades that these Talibarrians were used to free-for-all brawls rather than organized military maneuvers. Mayhem and chaos reigned supreme as the Talibarrians closed in on them while wildly swinging their halberds or thrusting their spears.

For a fleeting instant, as fighting erupted all around her, Nayla glanced about. As soon as their eyes met hers, the many villagers not already engaged in battle with one of her comrades, stepped back or used their fellow Talibarrian locked in a confrontation as a physical barrier to keep her away.

Having already been witness to the type of carnage Nayla was capable of dispensing, the Talibarrians prudently and deliberately steered away from her, turning their attention to the male opponents rather than be left to face this diminutive, but deadly warrior.

With so many to defeat and no time to give chase to make these men fight her, Nayla proceeded to help her comrades. Ducking beneath the back swing of a halberd intended to strike Markus, Nayla dropped down behind this enraged Talibarrian. His roar of victory as he raised his battleaxe to cleave Markus' head was replaced with a scream of agony as Nayla's sword sliced through his trousers to slash through the back of the man's knees. The Talibarrian wobbled to and fro, frantically fighting to maintain his balance. As his knees buckled beneath him, Markus drove his sword through the man's midriff, his boot coming up to kick his wounded opponent over to free his blade.

Before Markus could thank Nayla, she was already gone. Diving through the pandemonium, she rolled over her shoulder to come up behind a villager as he, lacking any finesse with the halberd, relentlessly hacked away at a piece of firewood Arerys used as shield. The Talibarrian's blows were frantic and many, as though he believed if he slowed his attack for even a second, as ineffective as they were, the Elf would use the opportunity to put his sword to him.

Just as his last blow shattered the piece of wood Arerys used to shield him from the axe blade, Nayla leapt straight up. The palms of her open hands whipped down with all her body weight to slap the man high on his shoulders as her fingernails raked him down the length of his neck. This stinging blow and the ferocious tearing of tender skin and flesh worked in tandem with Nayla's foot kicking the back of the man's knee to topple him backward. He gasped in pain and surprise as the blade of the short sword Nayla had propped up against a dead body on the ground behind him rammed straight through his back to protrude through his chest.

Nayla ducked as Arerys deflected the blow from a halberd intended for her. Wrenching her sword free, she spun about, her blade slashing at this man's thigh as Arerys lunged forward to stab him through his side. As the Elf leaned forward to execute this blow, Nayla's sword was thrust behind Arerys to stab a Talibarrian as he raised his spear to ram it into his enemy's back. Yanking her sword free, as Arerys confronted his next opponent, Nayla called out to Joval as another Talibarrian armed with a spear prepared to hurl his weapon at the Elf.

Above the raucous din, her warning went unheeded as Joval continued to parry the blows as two villagers decided to take on this imposing Elf together. As a third Talibarrian set his sights on Joval's back, drawing back his throwing arm for maximum force, Nayla took up her sword as though it, too, was a spear. With all her might, she heaved her weapon. The blade sliced through the air to pierce the Talibarrian in his chest. The man stumbled back, his spear falling from his hand as he fell over dead.

In a mad scramble, Nayla raced to reclaim her sword. She tugged at the weapon to extract it from the man's body, but just as the wound was about to release its hold on the blade, two powerful hands seized Nayla from behind, picking her clear off the ground.

The large man's bulky right arm, now slick with sweat, wrapped around her neck in a chokehold. His left hand brandished a dull, rusted dagger that still possessed a sharp point. As Nayla wedged her right hand into the crook of the Talibarrian's elbow to loosen his strangling hold, her left hand fought to push the tip of the dagger away from her throat.

His sheer strength overwhelmed Nayla, lifting her higher off the ground so she would have no leverage to execute a throw.

"You ain't gonna toss me like ya did ta Krygor," growled the Talibarrian, pulling his head away as his body arched backward so Nayla could not reach around to grab and throw him.

The man suddenly howled in pain. With her left hand still grappling for control of the dagger, Nayla's right hand had dropped straight down. Her fingers wrapped around skin and flesh on the man's inner right thigh, first yanking up and then tearing down and away.

Dropping her to the ground, his hand vigorously rubbed the searing pain inflicted to the nerves at the surface of the skin. Taking advantage of the moment, Nayla dove for her sword.

Snarling in rage, the man bellowed, "You ain't gettin' away from me!"

Lunging at Nayla to drive his dagger into her back, she felt his deadly intention surging behind her. It was like an angry tidal wave rushing in to pummel the shore. Without turning to face her opponent, she merely spun her sword about, thrusting the blade backward to impale the Talibarrian. His forward motion helped to drive the sword deep into his chest.

Glancing about for her next victim, she watched as Lando confidently wrung the blood of his last opponent from his sword as a large brute of a Talibarrian taunted him, daring this retired knight to attack.

For a fleeting moment, the men eyed each other, sizing each other up. With a mighty roar, they charged headlong into battle, sword against halberd. Just as Lando thrust forward with his weapon, the Talibarrian's axe swung down, knocking the tip of the blade away.

Moving toward each other so fast, Nayla was certain the two mortals were going collide. Instead, Lando's body pivoted ever so slightly. Their left shoulders grazed by each other, but just before the Talibarrian rushed past him, Lando's left hand caught his opponent by the crook of his elbow. Lando took advantage of their combined momentum, spinning the Talibarrian about in ever-faster, widening circles. With the increasing force exerted with each revolution, the man desperately hung onto his halberd that was now fully extended out to his side.

Seeing this deadly axe blade whipping by, Joval kicked his opponent in the chest to send the man stumbling back. The Elf ducked as the blade of the halberd struck the man in his neck, sending a jet of blood gushing into the air. This blow was so violent, the head tumbled from the shoulders as the man's body was sent rolling along the ground, knocking several Talibarrians off their feet as they fought against Markus and Arerys. The halberd followed through, flying from the man's grip to embed itself into the back of the villager Cullen was fighting against.

Lando released his grip to send his adversary flying. Tumbling head-over heels, the big brute of a man careened through the mayhem, bowling over the two Talibarrians closing in on Nayla.

"Fifteen to go!" Lando shouted in glee as he quickly assessed the damage he had inflicted.

Nayla flashed him a smile of appreciation as Lando turned to face his next opponent.

With the enemy numbers in decline, but still outnumbering Nayla and the men, there was no time to rest.

Cullen heaved a weary breath as the muscles in his arms and shoulders ached with the repeated slashing, thrusting and parrying motions used to counter the enemy blows. The weight of his ceremonial sword was now proving to be a very real liability. As the tip of this formidable weapon now sadly drooped in his weakening grasp and his winded movements slowing him down all the more, the Talibarrian he battled against took advantage of Cullen's vulnerability. With a great swipe of his halberd, he knocked the sword from Cullen's hands.

"Try fightin' now!" snorted the villager, hoisting his halberd aloft as he closed in on the unarmed man.

Cullen's eyes opened wide in fright as he pointed over the man's shoulder. "Look out!"

"What?" grunted the Talibarrian, glancing about to see if someone was sneaking up on him. Seeing that he was in no immediate danger, he growled in rage, thoroughly annoyed he had fallen for this old trick.

Turning his attention back to his opponent, his angry eyes were greeted by the sight of Cullen scrambling to reclaim his sword that now lay trapped beneath a fallen body.

"Ya rotten bugger! Now ya die!" declared the Talibarrian, bearing down with his battleaxe. As the halberd slammed down, Cullen rolled out of the way. He gulped as he stared at the blade biting into the earth where just seconds before, he had been kneeling down.

Leaping onto his feet, Cullen took evasive action. Rather than bravely standing his ground to fight, he sprinted straight for the smokehouse with his assailant in hot pursuit. It was only when Cullen made it to the shed did he realize that to hide behind this small, wooden structure it would only lead this enraged man directly to Druen. With his back plastered to the door, he could feel the hounds trapped inside, frantically clawing and pushing against the planks of wood to be free. Having devoured all the smoked meats within their reach that hung from the lower racks, there was no more reason for them to remain. They wanted out.

With these cantankerous mongrels on one side and the frothing mad Talibarrian racing for him with halberd in hand, Cullen braced himself for the inevitable.

"Ain't no one gonna save ya now!" snarled the villager, raising his battleaxe on high to cleave Cullen's head.

Just as the Talibarrian was about to slam down his great axe, Cullen yanked the door open to release the hounds.

In a tangle of gangly legs, whip-like tails and slobbering, snapping jaws, the dogs bounded out to freedom, bowling the man over as Cullen scrambled into the smokehouse. Slamming the door behind him, he took refuge inside.

"You're a dead man!" cursed the Talibarrian, kicking at the dogs as they pranced all around him, drooling, yelping and begging for more food. "You ain't got no where ta go! You're trapped!"

Yanking the door open, the man jumped inside the shed, brandishing his halberd to make short work of Cullen. Instead of killing his opponent with a single blow, the man's eyes were met with broken and fallen drying racks now stripped bare of smoked meats.

"Bloody hell… Where did ya go?" growled the Talibarrian. Just as he glanced up, the string of sausages Cullen was clinging to as he balanced on a narrow wooden rack high above suddenly snapped. Cullen fell straight down, landing heavily atop his adversary.

Wasting no time, Cullen clambered out of the smokehouse as his assailant groaned in pain, struggling to his feet to resume the chase.

As the Talibarrian stumbled outside, Cullen ambushed him. Whipping a string of smoked sausages about so they wound tightly around his neck; he gave the Talibarrian a hard boot to his backside, driving the man onto his hands and knees.

Humiliated and angered beyond words, the Talibarrian bellowed in rage as he fought to remove this tangle of meat from about his throat. Suddenly, he glanced up to the sounds of fierce growling that filled his ears. Before his eyes were four sets of gnashing teeth and drool-slathered lips, all drawn back in a hungry snarl. Having had a taste of these smoked delicacies during their brief incarceration, Scabs and his pack mates were more than determined to satisfy their ravenous hunger.

In a mad scramble, the Talibarrian was forced to run as the two younger, more fleet-footed hounds proceeded to give chase, snapping and snarling as they lunged at his neck while the other two remained, hungrily eyeing the bounty still in Cullen's hands.

"Nice doggies," praised Cullen, preparing to toss these links of hard, dry sausages at the salivating hounds circling around him.

Cullen suddenly groaned in pain as he was tackled. Knocked to the ground, a corpulent villager forcefully plopped down on his midriff to knock the wind out of Cullen. Straddling the Captain's body, he raised his dagger to slash his enemy's throat.

Cullen flinched, his eyes squeezing shut as his hands flailed about wildly, hoping to intercept the blade. With the tangled strings of sausages caught around Cullen's fingers, the Talibarrian chortled, laughing at his misfortune. This laugh was short-lived as Scab's mate, in this frantic struggle, snapped down on the villager's hand, mistaking his fat, sausage-like fingers for the real thing.

The man howled in pain, startling the dog into releasing her hold.

"Who's laughing now?" scoffed Cullen, freeing one of his hands to seize the Talibarrian by his wrist.

"Won't be you, once I slit yer throat!" growled the man, pressing down on his dagger once more.

"You are so dead!" snarled Cullen, pushing against the powerful hand wielding this weapon.

"You'll be eatin' yer words!" snorted his assailant, summoning all his strength to plunge his blade into Cullen's neck.

Just as the Talibarrian roared in triumph, he suddenly gagged. Cullen rammed a sausage into his open mouth and down his throat.

"And you'll be eating this!" retorted Cullen.

Throwing the remaining links around the man's neck, Cullen

whistled, drawing the attention of the dog that had snapped at this Talibarrian's fingers.

The meat-laden man toppled off of Cullen's prostrate body as he yanked at the string of sausages to be free of this dog bait while his feet frantically kicked at the ravenous hound to drive it away. The man's frenzied movements only served to excite the dog all the more, instinctively driving the animal to give chase as the gagging man dashed away from these snapping jaws.

Cullen chuckled mockingly as he shook a fistful of sausages in the direction of the fleeing man. "Who's laughing now?"

He glanced down as a savage growl rumbled from Scabs' throat as the dog prepared to lunge at him. Just as he turned about to run, the tip of a spear skimmed past his chest, tearing a button from his vest. Missing its intended target, the thrust of the spear carried it forward to pierce the tip of the dog's ragged ear just as it made a leap for the links of sausages draped over Cullen's shoulders like an ugly, lanky fur stole, minus the fur. With a sharp yelp of pain, Scabs veered away, but his hungry eyes were remained fixed on the smoked meats.

As Cullen turned to face his newest adversary, the tall, gangly villager grunted in disappointment that he had missed.

"But I have no weapon!" protested Cullen, holding up the string of meat to prove he was unarmed.

The man's defiant scowl transformed into a sinister grin as he ridiculed Cullen, snorting in laughter, "So what? That ain't gonna stop me from killin' ya!"

Standing his ground as the Talibarrian picked up another spear. He hoisted this weapon as Cullen defiantly waved one of the sausages, hard and dry from a long, slow smoking process, before his foe.

The Talibarrian chortled in mock laughter at this defenseless knight, "Whatcha gonna do? Feed me ta death?"

"Maybe!" snapped Cullen.

Armed with nothing more than a string of sausages, link by link, Cullen unleashed his wrath, spinning the meaty weapon like it was a length of chain. Circling faster with each revolution, Scabs pranced about excitedly, snapping at the sausages whistling past his salivating jaws, but missing each time.

As the Talibarrian stopped laughing long enough to position his spear to thrust at his opponent, Cullen suddenly stepped forward. With a flick of his wrist, he sent the end of the link whipping about. The string of sausages instantly wrapped around the Talibarrian's right hand that was positioned closest to Cullen on the staff of his spear.

With a hard yank, the weapon was jerked free from his hand. Cullen made his move, rushing to further incapacitate the man.

With one hand still trapped by this meaty weapon, the Talibarrian gasped in surprise as Cullen whipped the free end of the sausage string around the man's neck. The last sausage on this link struck him hard across the bridge of his nose. He squealed in pain and fear as Scabs lunged for the delectable necklace wrapped tightly around his throat.

With one hand tangled by the string of smoked meat, the Talibarrian used the other to frantically tug at the links as he fled the mongrel's snapping, yellowed fangs.

"Death by sausage to be delivered by that mangy cur," grumbled Cullen. Wiping the grease from his hands, he set off to reclaim his prized sword.

Under the rising moon, Ratha hoisted a ceramic jar filled with a magical potion. Reciting an incantation she had memorized from the Book of Spells, she hastily hobbled from one grave to the next, quickly and carelessly splashing a portion of the jar's dark contents onto the earth as a strange mist rolled low along the ground.

"I'll show them!" growled the witch. "With a little magic, I'll unearth the past ta give 'em the most formidable foes they'll ever chance ta meet."

Uttering the final words of this incantation to conjure the powers of the forbidden arts, Ratha's gnarled fingers groped beneath her tattered frock to fish out the vial hanging about her neck. Grasping this small container in her bony hand, her decaying teeth sank into the cork seal, wrenching it free from the mouth of the vial.

Immediately, thirteen tiny orbs of light were set free, but before they could escape into the night, the souls of the warlords trapped for an eon within this tiny, glass prison were sucked into the earth where Ratha had doused each grave with the potion.

Hugging her precious book to her chest, Ratha watched and waited as the cold light of the full moon burned through the gossamer wisps of cloud, shining down upon this old graveyard.

She was expecting some truly potent magic to take place. Anticipating a spectacular display, aside from the din of battle and the dogs barking from the village, a strange silence lay heavy on this foreboding landscape. The skies did not suddenly darken. There was no great crash of thunder or a jagged bolt of lightning to herald the coming of a spectral force. There was no violent quake to unleash the dark powers she had summoned.

Her one good eye glanced from grave to grave, impatiently waiting for the potion and incantation to work in tandem.

Instead, there was an underwhelming display as a thin miasma of fog slowly rolled along the ground while a tranquil calm smothered this old cemetery. It was a silence that was soon broken by the cheerful chirps of crickets in search of prospective mates.

Trembling with rage and disappointment, with a disgusted snort, Ratha spat on the grave. Cursing as her clenched fist pounded angrily at the book, the witch turned away to flee her village. Suddenly, she shrieked in surprise, falling to her bony knees as the ground trembled beneath her feet. It heaved and groaned. With a great tearing of the earth, one by one, thirteen skeletal hands erupted from the graves where the tiny orbs of light had vanished.

"It's workin'!" Ratha squealed with delight, her feet kicking in the air like a beetle on its back as she struggled to upright herself.

Taking in this macabre sight, her demented cackling greeted a small army of corpses as dead soldiers clawed their way out of decaying, decrepit coffins that now collapsed under the weight of the dirt.

Some were nothing more than an organized arrangement of bones from which torn and tattered rags clung to. Others still had flesh clinging to their skeletons, festering in various stages of decay and writhing with maggots and earthworms, but each reeked of the unmistakable stench of death and all were frighteningly real.

With the souls of the warlords housed within the bodies of these long dead soldiers, an eerie green aura swelled from these skeletal forms as they shook the clots of dirt from what remained of their clothing. Taking up their weapons that had been buried with them, these old halberds, swords and shields were now rusted with age and heavily encrusted with soil, but were still formidable tools of war, nonetheless. This army of the damned stood before Ratha. Those still possessing lips snarled at the witch, voicing their displeasure that their souls were now imprisoned within these rotting corpses.

Holding the book before her, Ratha growled as her gnarled finger tapped the red, leather-bound compilation of spells for the warlords to see.

"You've seen this book before! Ya know what powers I have at my disposal," warned Ratha, as she held up the glass vial that once imprisoned the souls of the warlords standing before her. "I can trap

ya again, or I can set yer souls free forever from this tiny hell you've been trapped in. So what'll it be? Will ya do my biddin'?"

"Look!" exclaimed Cullen, as he glanced about. "They are scurrying away like a pack of frightened rats!"

He ducked as the villager that had foolishly leapt onto Joval's back was impaled by the back-thrust of his sword. The Elf tossed the mortally wounded man over his shoulder to dispose of him, almost knocking Cullen over in the process.

To the surprise of Nayla and her comrades, Cullen was right. The nine or so Talibarrians that had yet to meet their demise had thrown down their weapons as they fled northward, retreating into the forest.

Markus and Lando watched, sighing in relief to see their enemies hasten to blend into the shadows of the night.

"This is too good to be true..." determined Nayla, her voice wrought with suspicion as she wrung the enemy's blood from her sword with a flick of her wrist.

"Don't be like that!" scolded Cullen. He was just glad this ordeal was over, especially as he had yet to reclaim his sword that was knocked from his hands. "You should be grateful those murderous miscreants turned tail to flee like the cowards they are."

"But why? They still out-numbered us," responded Nayla, wiping the blade clean on the edge of her cloak.

"*Why?*" snorted Cullen, his tone incredulous. "They are Talibarrians! It is what they do. It is in their very nature to bugger off when situations get too dangerous for their liking."

"Nayla is correct, Captain," argued Arerys, watching as the last of the villagers disappeared from his sight. "There were still more of them than us."

"Look around, my lord," invited Cullen, pointing to the dead scattered across the plaza. "We are still standing. These men are not. Those Talibarrians knew they were going to meet the same fate."

"I suppose that is possible," conceded Lando, mopping the beads of sweat from his forehead with the back of his hand.

"I say we hunt that witch down. Claim that blasted book before she can conjure up anymore of that dark magic!" suggested Cullen, speaking louder in hopes that Druen would hear him boldly rallying his comrades to complete this mission.

"Later! We have company," shouted Joval, watching as a strange show of sickly green light swelled from the forest to emerge at the edge of the village.

"Bloody hell!" exclaimed Lando, staring in disbelief at the grisly sight that filled his eyes with horror. "What is *that*?"

Cullen's brows arched up in surprise as he gasped in dismay, "They're looking a bit rough… like death warmed over."

"Because they *are* dead!" retorted Arerys, hastily taking up his bow.

"How can they be dead? The dead do not walk and wield weapons," argued Cullen, his eyes squinting into this eerie aura of light glowing from these beings. "This is all too bizarre! Those hideous *things* are moving toward us and they are armed to the teeth!"

"This is strangely familiar," gulped Markus, his hand tightening its grip around the hilt of his sword.

"Too familiar," agreed Arerys, hastily nocking an arrow as this ghoulish army steadily advanced.

He stared at the ghostly shadow of a warlord's face that was exposed where the skull of this host body was cleaved almost in half. From the crown of its head, curving down and to the right where the blade of a halberd had glanced off the bridge of its nose, the weapon had hacked off its facial features. Where its right eye and cheek should have been, the blade of a halberd had cut through bone and flesh. It was a blow that had killed this Talibarrian instantly and yet, here he stood.

"If you are trying to convince me the four warlords we did away with have returned with friends, I believe you are mistaken," countered Lando, not wanting to believe it was possible.

"We dispatched their physical forms," explained Arerys. "Obviously, dark magic still holds power over their souls after all this time."

"Are you telling me that they are *dead*, but they are *alive* at the same time?" gasped Cullen, scratching his head in thought as he considered the absurd.

"Indeed," responded Arerys, taking aim at the closest form.

"How the bloody hell do we kill these monsters if they're already dead?" questioned Cullen, grimacing in disgust as their new adversaries came into full view in all their grisly glory.

"Like this!" answered Arerys. The string of sinew slipped from his fingertips to unleash his arrow.

With deadly accuracy, the Elf's projectile slammed into the dead man's chest, piercing right through its heart. The warlord's physical form recoiled from the impact, but instead of disintegrating into a pile of ash, this creature snarled. A guttural laugh erupted from its throat to send carrion beetle maggots feeding on its decaying flesh to spew forth.

"That was disgusting!" remarked Cullen, grimacing in revulsion. The plump, translucent grubs writhed about, their undulating bodies worming their way back into the damp earth.

"It should have died!" gasped Markus, shaking his head in disbelief as he watched a set of bony fingers wrap around the shaft of the arrow. With a hard yank, the projectile was wrenched free from its chest, along with a shattered piece of breastbone and what appeared to be the shrivelled remains of the corpse's heart. "It should have fallen to ashes!"

"It is clear to see, these creatures are our familiar foes in spirit only. Some strange magic has placed their souls in these decaying bodies," determined Lando, in awe but horrified at the same time.

"There must be a way to destroy their physical form, if not their soul," determined Nayla.

Without warning, brandishing his sword, Joval charged straight over to the decaying form leading the twelve others. The warlord encapsulated in this dead body raised its sword to block the Elf's blow, but with Joval's greater reach and quicker reflexes, his razor-sharp blade easily sliced through rotting flesh and brittle bone just before the elbow to send the amputated limb flying, weapon and all.

They watched in horror as the fingers of the dismembered hand slowly unclenched. It proceeded to crawl, inching its way back to the rest of its body. The warlord snatched up this limb, cramming it back in place where the wound hissed as it healed, miraculously fusing together to make this arm whole once more.

Using this reattached appendage, the creature took up its sword as it snarled at Joval, daring the Elf to attack again.

"Brilliant! Now you have made it angry," snapped Cullen, staring in disbelief.

"Think you can do better?" challenged Joval, slowly backing away from this army. "If so, go right ahead, Captain Bristow!"

"They can't be killed by a livin' being, neither Elf nor mortal man! I made sure of it," scoffed Ratha, stepping out from behind her gruesome minions. Her crippled hands were wringing together in eager anticipation of the carnage to follow. "They're dead! An' yer turn's comin'!"

"Why kill us when we can negotiate?" questioned Cullen, sounding hopeful. He raised his hands in surrender as he addressed the witch.

"Do ya have the crystal orbs?" responded Ratha.

"Not on me," answered Cullen.

"Kill!" ordered the witch. With a wave of her hand she motioned the warlords to fight. "Kill 'em all!"

"Arm yourself, Captain!" shouted Nayla. Her foot pressed lightly on the shaft of an abandoned spear, rolling it back toward her. As it tumbled over the top of her foot, she flicked it up, catching it in her hand. She tossed the spear to Cullen.

"But the witch said these monstrosities cannot be killed," argued Cullen, snatching the weapon up in his hands.

"Then use it to keep yourself from getting killed!" snapped Nayla, her sword poised before her.

As Nayla and the men braced for a confrontation, the army of dead soldiers encircled them. There would be no escape.

"Get 'em!" snarled Ratha, waving them on to attack.

Jostling and shoving to get a crack at the living, the ghouls jockeyed for position, crowding around to kill their adversaries.

"Attack!" shouted Arerys, using his sword to drive back the living dead as Nayla fought by his side.

As their weapons clashed, Ratha gleefully pranced about on the outskirts of this battle, cheering her minions on as it became evident these immortals' unrelenting assault served to wear her enemies down. Even as limbs dropped and heads rolled, the warlords took advantage of the witch's magic to literally pull themselves back together each time they were dealt what should have been a death-delivering blow.

"We cannot keep this up forever!" gasped Markus, fighting to catch his breath. He thrust his sword through his foe's chest, bringing his foot up to kick this dead body over to free his blade.

"They are not even winded!" groaned Lando, his sword slashing straight through one of the more skeletal warlords to effectively smash its spinal column. The creature reeled back from the impact as its backbone re-assembled like the beads of a necklace magically stringing back together again.

"I am getting bloody sick of this!" snarled Cullen, deciding to take matters into his own hands.

Bellowing like a man gone mad, the young Captain charged forward, ramming his spear straight through one of the corpses. The weapon pierced the ghoul through the chest and its heart, if it still had one. Instead of falling over dead, it screamed in rage, seizing the shaft of the spear to drive it in deeper, pulling Cullen in so they were face to face. The Captain screamed in fear and disgust as more maggots spewed from the creature's gaping mouth, pelting him in his face as this creature screamed back, refusing to release its hold on Cullen's spear.

"You want it? You got it!" growled Cullen. Instead of pulling away to be free of this aberration, Cullen no longer resisted. The combined force of this monster as it pulled and this mortal as he pushed on the spear in the same direction sent the creature flying back.

With adrenalin coursing through his veins, Cullen roared in triumph. He ran full tilt with the warlord's physical form still impaled on this spear, coming to a stop only when the tip of this weapon rammed into the post Nayla had been tied to. For good measure, Cullen forcefully jammed the spear into the wood to make sure this monster was not going anywhere.

"That will teach you!" snapped Cullen, stepping back to admire his handiwork as he proudly wiped the dirt from his hands. "Now try to get your loathsome carcass out of this mess!"

To his horror, the warlord merely grunted in disdain. The creature yanked its body free, leaving chunks of putrid flesh and tattered shreds of ragged clothing on the post where the tip of the spear bit into the wood. It lurched forward, heading straight toward Cullen, walking the length of the spear to be free.

"Bloody hell!" cursed Cullen, backing away as his nemesis advanced, sword poised in its skeletal grip.

Scrambling away, Cullen wrenched a halberd free from a dead Talibarrian's hand as he raced back to the others. Strategically positioning himself between the Elves as they battled these ghoulish minions, he shouted at Joval, "This is not working. They refuse to die!"

"Because they are dead!" reminded Joval, decapitating his adversary only to have the warlord control its dead limbs to take another swing with its halberd at the Elf.

"If we cannot kill them, I know what can," shouted Arerys, stepping back into the protective circle of friends.

"What are you waiting for? Go to it!" demanded Cullen, his foot coming up to ram his adversary in its bony chest, only to see the creature get right back up, unscathed by this assault.

Arerys ordered Nayla and the others to stand their ground, to hold the enemy at bay. Closing his eyes, he focused on clearing his mind amidst this rampant chaos. As the sounds of clashing weapons became nothing more than a distant drone, the Elf recited an ancient incantation known only to Elves of royal blood.

"Whatever the Elf is doing, he's not doing it fast enough!" Cullen grumbled impatiently, ducking as a warlord's halberd swung over him to graze strands of hair from the top of his head.

"Shut it!" growled Nayla, lopping off another warlord's arm, knowing it would only serve to slow it down. "Give him time!"

"There is no time! He naps, while we fight!" snapped Cullen, watching as his opponent stood up once more to continue its attack. "Why do we not surrender now?"

"I should throw you to these dogs!" snarled Lando, the pommel of his sword poking Cullen hard in his back. "That should appease them until Arerys can summon for help."

Under the light of an opal moon, a white mist rolled in. This strange miasma seeped in from the forest to blanket the earth.

"What is this?" snorted Cullen, in a disgruntled huff as he watched the churning vapour roll in, swirling all around them. "This is not even scary!"

Ghostly shadows took form before their eyes as an army of one hundred Elves killed in battle, their souls trapped in this realm, rose from the mist.

"Oooh! Now *that's* scary!" yelped Cullen, leaping behind Nayla as this spectral force assembled before Arerys as he ordered them to attack.

Without hesitation, the legion of ghosts responded to Arerys' command, hoisting their shields and raising their swords in preparation to do battle with these demons.

"What – What's this? How can it be?" stammered Ratha, stunned to see this great phantom army conjured up by Arerys. "You're only an Elf!"

"An Elf *Prince*!" corrected Cullen, mocking the witch.

"And as we cannot kill your minions, *they* certainly can!" shouted Arerys.

"Fight! Don't jus' stand there lookin' at 'em! Fight!" snarled Ratha, waving the warlords on to face these new opponents.

The leader of the thirteen turned to face this Elven army when its body abruptly recoiled from the blow of an arrow striking it square in the chest. For a lingering moment, all waited to see what the result of this ghostly projectile would be.

The warlord glanced down at the Elven arrow protruding from its chest. Releasing a hideous laugh, its ghoulish comrades chortled at this failed assault.

The warlord abruptly stopped laughing. It screamed in agony as the arrow bore into its soul. In a flash, the green aura that glowed from this skeletal form vanished, consumed by a great white light that erupted from this wound. Just as quickly, the remains of this dead body fell to ashes, scattering along the earth to be swallowed up by the miasma.

The twelve remaining warlords looked aghast, staring down at where their leader just seconds ago was standing. For the first time, there was a look of panic on their decaying faces as it became clear this phantom army of Elves could indeed destroy them, body *and* soul.

"Yes!" Cullen shouted in triumph, his fist pumping the air.

The purveyor of that first deadly arrow stepped forth from the army to take aim once again. Instead of standing their ground to fight, the twelve warlords backed away, only to turn tail, running in fear.

As the leader of the Elven army lowered his bow, waving the others on to take pursuit, Arerys was momentarily stunned. Orchestrating this assault was his father, Kal-lel Wingfield, and standing next him was his first officer, Valtar Briarwood.

"Father!" called Arerys, as Kal-lel dashed by him.

For an instant, as though he recognized this voice from another life and another time, Kal-lel's ghostly formed stopped, glancing over his shoulder.

"It's me, father! Your son, Arerys."

Kal-lel did not speak, his head bowing in acknowledgement. He offered Arerys a small, comforting smile as Valtar waved him on to follow the others.

"Valtar!" hollered Joval, just as surprised to see his dear friend who was killed in battle two years earlier. "Wait!"

As the mist churned and roiled, rolling along behind them, Kal-lel and Valtar's ghostly forms disappeared with their army, dissolving into the forest as they pursued Ratha's minions.

With the last anguished cries of the warlords ringing through the night, an eerie silence hung heavy in the air as Nayla and the men turned to look upon the witch as she seethed in rage.

"Well, well, well, you old hag!" chortled Cullen, glaring over at Ratha and the cursed book still wrapped in her bony arms. "This does not bode well for you!"

"More so fer you," sneered the witch. "You're still gonna die!"

"One shrivelled, old woman against the six of us?" scoffed Cullen. "You are sadly mistaken, witch. You have no men – no army, dead or otherwise, to speak of to fight for you."

"But I have *this*!" snarled Ratha, thrusting the Book of Spells before her. A blue bolt of energy exploded forth. Its powerful magic sent a jolting pain coursing through her enemies, slamming them hard to the ground.

an end to all things

The witch cackled with demented delight as she watched her victims writhing in pain, unable to take up arms against her. As Ratha deployed this magic, the nine villagers that had fled and were hiding in the forest upon the arrival of her thirteen warlords, finally found their courage. They warily skulked back to to her side, snatching up whatever weapons they could get their hands on as they advanced.

"Not good," groaned Lando, through clenched teeth. Flat on his back from the excruciating pain, his right hand strained to reach for his sword that was knocked from his grasp.

"You're bloody right!" snapped the witch, hovering over Lando's prostrate body that trembled from the debilitating pain. "I told ya ta come back with the Wizards an' their crystals. I want 'em now! Where are they?"

"Damned if I know!" grunted Lando, refusing to divulge this information as his fingers crept closer to the hilt of his sword.

"Damned ya be!" snarled Ratha, yanking the halberd from her crony's hands as she shoved the book at him to hold for her. Without even flinching and without an ounce of mercy, the great battleaxe swung down.

Lando howled in agony. He felt the cold, sharp bite of the blade hacking through skin and flesh. Inside his body, he heard and felt the snapping of bones as the blade chopped through his wrist just as his hand finally managed to grab his sword. Clenching his wounded arm, Lando cradled it against his body to staunch the flow of blood as Nayla and her comrades looked on in horror, seeing his hand still grasping the sword, but it now lay detached from him.

"Now where are my crystals?" shrieked Ratha, demanding to know as the bloodied blade pressed down against Lando's throat. "Speak now or you'll never speak again!"

"Then kill me now, for I will tell you nothing!" growled Lando, as he dared to defy the witch again.

"What say you, boys?" asked Ratha, turning to her henchmen. "Should I let him be or should I let him have it?"

"Kill him! Kill him!" chanted the Talibarrians, their feet stomping in time as they gathered around Ratha to spur her on.

"Kill the bastard!" prompted one of her men. He deliberately speared Lando's amputated hand, cruelly waving it in front his tortured face before flinging it at the pack of hounds sniffing around the dead bodies.

Though well sated from their smokehouse feed, these mutts were eager for a new toy to rip into.

"Bloody hell!" cursed Cullen, staring in disbelief as Scabs and the other mongrels leapt onto Lando's bloodied hand, tearing at the fingers as they fought over this plaything. He struggled to sit up as he swore at Ratha, "You miserable hag! You've been more than cruel. Show some mercy, for he has suffered enough."

"I will," promised the witch, her gnarled fingers wrapping tightly around the handle of the battleaxe, "by killin' him quickly! An' if you're lucky, I'll do the same fer you!"

"No!" pleaded Nayla, fighting against the pain inflicted by Ratha's magic as she struggled to stand, only to have one of the men strike her at the back of her knees with the staff of his spear. She crumpled to the ground. Too weak to stand, her fingers scraped into the earth to drag her tortured body to Lando's trembling form.

"Do not do this!" begged Nayla. Pulling herself to his side, she leaned over his head to shield him as she pleaded for Lando's life. "Have mercy!"

"I'll show some mercy," snorted Ratha, snatching her book back as she shoved the halberd into the man's hands. "Gailus is stronger than me. He'll kill ya both with one, clean blow!"

"Stop!" hollered Arerys, staggering to his feet, only to fall to his knees before the witch. "I know where the crystals are!"

"Too late!" growled Ratha, kicking the Elf on his shoulder to bowl him over. "I grow impatient with yer games!"

She cackled as she stepped back, making room as her minion hoisted his halberd. Raising the blade while rising up on his toes to deliver a devastating blow, the Talibarrian took aim. Eyeing the back of Nayla's neck to determine the best angle that would allow him to cleave straight on through to Lando's, the Talibarrian adjusted his stance as Arerys looked on in horror.

Just as the man swung the halberd down, a bolt of energy ravaged his body. The man was thrown to the ground, convulsing in pain as his weapon flew from his hands. He collapsed next to Lando; writhing in agony as his fellow Talibarrians cowered in fear. They were about to abandon him and the witch until Ratha threatened them with their lives.

"Run an' you'll be as good as dead!" vowed Ratha, her fist pounding the cover of the book as a reminder to her men that she was still the one in power. "Stand an' fight!"

"Fight and you will die," promised Lindras, the light from his orb glowing intensely as he prepared to attack.

"So, Weatherstone, I see you've come after all," greeted Ratha, her one good eye gleaming with anticipation as it stared greedily at the sphere. "An' ya didn't come empty-handed!"

"This crystal stays with me!" countered Lindras.

"Not fer long! If it's a fight ya want, then it's a fight you'll be gettin'!" snorted Ratha. "Me an' my men can take ya on. An' I know all about yer measly *powers*, Weatherstone. Jus' cause you got a lucky shot in ta down this man, it don't mean you're gonna be lucky again."

"It was not *luck*," grunted Tylon, as he stepped out of the forest from the southern-most edge of the village. His orb glowed steadily once more after being discharged to down the halberd-wielding mortal.

Ratha's good eye glanced over to where the Wizard of the South stood, poised to attack. "Lovely! Now all I need is jus' two more of ya miserable, old toads ta complete my set! Now hand over those crystals!"

"We will do no such thing," stated Lindras, standing firm as his hands wrapped around the staff.

"You will if their lives mean anythin' to ya," snapped the witch. She swung at Nayla, the book striking her hard across the side of the head to bowl her over. With the little warrior no longer hovering over to protect him, Ratha's boot stomped down on Lando's wound. He howled in pain once more as she ground his injured arm into his chest.

"Enough!" hollered Tor, his glowing sphere pointed to Ratha's back.

The witch glanced over her shoulder to spy upon the Wizard of the North as he attempted to sneak up behind her.

"Hmph!" grunted Ratha, her thin, cracked lips leering in scorn. "You're here, Airshorn, but where's Firestaff? I'll be needin' his crystal, too."

"That will never happen!" scoffed Lindras.

"Aah… I see," snorted the witch, her head nodded in understanding as she scrutinized Lindras. "Firestaff's not here 'cause none of ya trust him 'round this book. You fear he'll be seduced by its dark powers an' turn on you all."

"We trust him," retorted Tylon. "It is you we do not trust!"

"I want that fourth crystal!" raged the witch. "An' I want it now!"

Her foot stomped down in defiance; the heel of her boot grinding into Lando's fresh wound as he bellowed in agony.

Unable to bear anymore of his friend's torment, ignoring the pain that still racked his body, Markus forced himself onto his feet, sword in hand as he staggered to Lando's defense.

He fell hard on his back as one of Ratha's men took an angry swipe at him. The blade of the Talibarrian's halberd came down with a vengeance, slamming hard against the edge of Markus' sword. Using every ounce of his strength, Markus blocked this blow. It was just enough to deflect the battleaxe so it narrowly missed his throat, but it caught him high on his shoulder. The Elven vest of mail protected Markus from the bite of the blade; however, the blow still jarred him to the bones, knocking Markus flat on his back.

With a snap of Ratha's gnarled fingers, the villagers closed in on Nayla and the men, their weapons poised to attack on the witch's command.

"So what'll it be, Wizards?" she cackled. "If you're wise, you'll be gettin' Firestaff here before the full moon is at its height. If not, you'll be in fer one helluva bloodbath!"

"Enough blood has been shed on this night!"

Ratha slowly turned in the direction of this voice. From the forest to the east, a great shadow emerged.

"You heard me, witch!" growled Eldred. "This madness stops now!"

"I think not!" sneered Ratha, her arms wrapping tightly around the Book of Spells.

"You are surrounded!" shouted Lindras, as he and his brother Wizards crept in closer. "You cannot hope to escape."

"Don't need to. I gotcha 'xactly where I want you all," sniffed Ratha, her voice oozing with confidence. "But I'd recommend surrenderin' those crystals ta me before you're forced ta escape fer yer miserable lives."

"*Now!*" shouted Lindras, as he and his brothers discharged a bolt of energy from their orbs. Aiming low in case she ducked, the Wizard unleashed their magic on the witch. Ratha's men immediately dropped, pressing their bodies low to the ground as Nayla and her comrades shielded their eyes from the brilliant show of light and the dazzling explosion of white sparks as the Wizards' magical powers collided together.

Instead of striking the witch down, Ratha squealed in delight. Hoisting the book high over her head, the magic she conjured lifted her out of the way; levitating her above the volatile force of the Wizards' combined powers.

As she floated back down to the ground, she laughed to see the bolt of energy discharged from Lindras' crystal a fraction of a second after the others, deviate from its intended path, deflected by the explosive percussion. It veered to the north, striking down two of her men before bowling Tor over with its force.

"You, Weatherstone, are makin' this much too easy!" scoffed Ratha, her lopping gait delivering her to where the downed Wizard had dropped his staff and the crystal she was intent on claiming.

"Oh, no you don't!" growled Tylon, dispensing another charge from his orb as Ratha closed in on Tor's staff.

With unnatural agility for one so bent and decrepit, the witch twisted about, using the power emanating from the Book of Spells. Holding forth the book to deflect this bolt, Ratha sent it careening back toward Tylon.

Before Tylon could dart out of the way, in a flash, he was bowled over by his own devastating magic. His body involuntarily convulsed as this debilitating power painfully surged through his entire being.

"Lindras! Eldred!" hollered Arerys, using his sword to prop himself up onto his feet as the pain of Ratha's magic began to subside. "Run! Get away before she gets your crystals."

"Two is good! Four is better," growled Ratha, picking herself up from the ground after the impact of Tylon's magic ricochetting off the book sent her tumbling head over heels. "I'll manage all right with two orbs."

"You will get not one!" shouted Lindras. Not waiting for Arerys and the others to regain their senses to mount an assault, he rushed toward the witch. His staff was poised in his hands as he neared to ensure his aim did not miss this time.

Scrambling to beat Lindras to claim Tor's staff, and more importantly, the crystal sphere mounted atop, Ratha glanced over her shoulder to see the Wizard gaining on her.

Before Lindras could mount an attack, the witch turned to face her nemesis. Her voice hissed, curdling with malice as she called on an incantation, slamming the Book of Spells onto the ground before her. The shockwave rippling through the earth from this impact sent a great tremor surging toward Lindras. It bowled the Wizard off his feet, causing him to fall on his back as the dissipating quake travelled on past him to Nayla and the others, including Ratha's minions. They all struggled to maintain their balance while Lando, Cullen and Markus were forced to their knees once more.

With one arm wrapped around her book, Ratha's free hand lunged forward to claim Tor's staff.

She shrieked in pain as the tender, arthritic joints of her fingers bashed against Eldred's staff as the tip slammed down onto the earth, blocking her bid to claim the crystal.

"Out of my way!" hissed Ratha, crawling on her hands and knees as her gnarled fingers strained to reach Tor's staff.

"You will die before you claim that orb," vowed Eldred, pressing the crystal sphere atop his staff to Ratha's throat.

Instead of putting up a fight, the old woman uttered a pathetic whine of defeat as she rolled onto her back, the Book of Spells clutched to her chest as she sobbed.

"Give me the book!" demanded Eldred, holding his hand out expectantly as the other continued to press the crystal to her throat.

"Here," whimpered Ratha, lifting the book off her gaunt chest. "Take it. It's yers."

Just as Eldred leaned forward to reclaim the collection of incantations, Ratha swung out with all her might, bashing the Wizard's staff with the book.

Eldred bellowed in pain and anger as the conflicting magic surging from the book and the staff met head on. In a thunderous crash of light and sound, his staff shattered on impact, the crystal orb exploding with a brilliant white light as it flew from its mount to tumble to the ground.

"You witch!" snarled Eldred, throwing down the broken remnants of his staff as he lunged at Ratha.

"That's what I am!" growled the hag, frantically struggling to push the Wizard off as she enveloped her bony arms around the book.

"Let go!" ordered Eldred, the fingers of his trembling hands wrapping around the worn leather cover. "It is mine!"

"It *was*, but it's mine now! An' you'll learn ta bow down ta me yet!"

"*Never!*" raged Eldred; yanking with all his might to extricate the book from this unnaturally powerful grip she had on it.

"Kill them! Kill them both!" hollered Cullen, staggering back onto his feet. Fearing that the powers of this book had poisoned the Wizard's heart and mind once more, he frantically waved Lindras on, motioning him to unleash his power, no matter how haphazard, to destroy them both.

"You want it don't ya, Firestaff?" sneered Ratha, watching as Eldred's eyes darkened as his face contorted with a grimacing scowl. "You can feel its great powers consumin' yer black heart, can't ya?"

"I feel it!" admitted Eldred. His voice was deep and resonating, rumbling forth as though he was possessed by evil. Just as an explosive energy erupted from the book, he wrenched it free from Ratha's hands as he shouted, "But I do not want it!"

They both tumbled to the ground. Eldred, too rattled by the power still coursing through his muscles to flee with the book, managed to toss the cursed thing away. The book landed with a heavy *thud* at Cullen's feet.

"Don't just stand there looking at it!" scolded Eldred, struggling to reclaim his crystal before the witch had a chance to pounce on it. "Take the bloody thing! Destroy it!"

Cullen reluctantly picked up the book. As the witch's minions turned on him, he ran with all his might, away from this encroaching mob.

Ratha shrieked in utter rage, her talon-like nails clawing at Eldred's hands to pry the orb from his grip so she could use it to strike Cullen down. Tenacious and vengeful as she scratched and kicked at the Wizard, she ordered her men to stop Cullen as he fled.

Holding the cumbersome book at arm's-length in case a strange magic erupted from the pages within, Cullen ran toward Arerys as Nayla and Markus fended off the blows of halberds and spears so Joval could heal Lando's limb at the point of amputation.

Unarmed and with nothing more than the book to shield himself and to club his adversaries out of the way, Cullen managed to duck and dodge flying weapons as he shouted to the Elf to take the wretched book off his hands, but Arerys was embroiled in a battle of his own as the Talibarrians pressed in on them.

As Cullen desperately darted about, nimbly avoiding the enemy weapons, from the corner of his eye he spotted Druen struggling to remove his prized sword from where it was trapped beneath a body so she could arm him once more. Suddenly, Cullen spied upon a

Talibarrian bearing down on Druen, battleaxe clutched in his hands.
The man rushed up behind her as she ran toward him to deliver his
sword.

"Look out!" Cullen hollered as he tossed the book to Arerys. In one
fluid movement, he grabbed Druen, pulling her out of harm's way.
Snatching up his sword, he thrust the blade into the man's midriff.

Druen screamed in fright as the dying man lurched forward. The
blade of his halberd swung down as his body folded with the impact
as the sword pierced through his body. The battleaxe, still gripped in
the Talibarrian's hands, fell hard. With an audible *crunch*, the blade
shattered Cullen's ribcage, penetrating his chest, as the Talibarrian
stumbled forward, the axe no longer in his hands.

For a moment, Cullen stared in stunned disbelief at the halberd
protruding from his chest. His knees suddenly buckled beneath him.
He fell against Druen as he collapsed to the bloodied ground.

"No! Oh, no!" cried Druen, the colour draining from her face. She
glanced up to find an Elf to come to Cullen's aid, but Arerys, with
book in hand, was helping Nayla and Markus to fend off an attack as
Joval rushed to heal Lando's wound in the midst of this battle.

With aid not forthcoming, the only thing Druen could do was to
protect Cullen from Ratha's minions until she was able to find help.
She struggled, dragging him behind the smokehouse, away from the
madness.

"What do you know? Firestaff didn't want the book after all," said
Cullen. Along with the shock of this horrific assault, he was stunned
by this revelation that Eldred did not turn to evil as he had expected
he would.

"Hush, don't speak. Keep still," whispered Druen, tearing a strip
from the hem of her cloak to dam the flow of blood as she prepared to
pull the blade of the halberd from Cullen's chest.

"Don't look," warned Druen, her voice quaking as her trembling
fingers wrapped around the handle of the axe.

Instead of averting his gaze, Cullen's glazed eyes stared at the
weapon protruding from his chest. As the shock of the assault still
gripped his body and mind, he mumbled to himself as though it had
still not registered this halberd was buried in *his* body.

"Cullen, look at me," urged Druen, gripping his chin to turn his
face to hers. "Look in my eyes. Don't look away."

Shoving a stick between his teeth, she made him bite down on it.
"Whatever happens, don't scream or Ratha's men will find us both."

With adrenalin still coursing through his body, it was as though his senses were dulled and his mind, numbed. Cullen's response was rote as he complied with her order. He clenched the stick between his teeth, bearing down as he stared vacantly into Druen's worried eyes.

"Don't move," instructed Druen. Wrapping her hands firmly around the handle of the halberd, as swiftly and smoothly as she possible, Druen yanked the weapon free from his torso.

The sound of bone grating against metal raked at her nerves as a whole new level of pain swept through Cullen's body. It was as if the removal of this blade was somehow worse than when it entered his chest. Cullen spat out the now-broken stick as he howled in agony. The colour immediately drained from his face as he groaned, trembling as the true intensity of the pain abruptly surfaced. The extrication of the halberd served to release the blood. The hot crimson bubbled forth, spilling from this wound.

"Bloody hell!" groaned Cullen, through clenched teeth as he flinched, his senses reeling from the trauma of the wound. "Not supposed to happen... not to *me*."

"Why did you risk your life like this?" wept Druen, as the seriousness of this injury became all too apparent. Panic rose in her heart as she pressed her trembling hands over the wound in a bid to staunch the steady flow of blood.

"Love... it'll do that to a man. Had to... A chance to prove my worth," whispered Cullen, gasping for his breath as his lungs filled with blood.

"You had nothin' ta prove ta me!"

"I know... to myself. And you're worth dying for, my love."

"You're not gonna die! You'll be fine. I'll have one of the Elves fix you up. Jus' hold on. Promise me you'll hold on, Cullen."

"I will... for a kiss," whispered Cullen, his fingertips gently wiping the tears trickling down her cheeks. He put on a brave face, giving her a weak smile to calm her shattered nerves.

Druen held Cullen close, the blood soaked strip of cloth no longer able to absorb anymore as she tried desperately to stem the flow. Her anguished sobs were drowned out by the noises of battle as Nayla and the men clashed with the enemy, rallying back as Ratha wrestled the Wizard of the East.

Snarling and gnashing her teeth like a deranged animal, the witch attacked Eldred with a vengeance. As though driven by supernatural forces, this bag of bones still posed a formidable foe to the Wizard as his pain-racked body struggled to grapple control of his crystal orb from this old, mortal woman.

Just as Ratha wrenched the magical sphere from Eldred's hands, she turned the orb down, thrusting it to Eldred's chest as she snarled in victory.

"Ya know it's better ta be evil," sneered Ratha. "You can still be my henchman if ya co-operate."

"I would rather die!" Eldred snorted in disgust, his pained, quaking hands fighting to push the deadly crystal away from his chest as the orb glowed unnaturally.

"Then die!" grunted Ratha, bashing at the Wizard's hands as the light in the heart of the sphere began to swell with her growing rage.

Ratha suddenly gasped in surprise. She froze as the smooth, cold surface of a crystal pressed up against her throat.

"From this close, you know I will not miss," growled Lindras, thrusting this weapon to her neck as the crystal pulsated with light, its energy waiting to be unleashed on his command.

"Please, have mercy," begged Ratha, her voice a pathetic whimper as she cowered from the magic waiting to be released from Lindras' crystal. "You wouldn't want ta hurt a little, old lady, would ya?"

"Back away from Eldred! Give me that crystal!" ordered Lindras, his one hand still pointing his staff at the witch as he extended the other to collect his brother's orb for safekeeping.

"As ya wish." The witch's sharp shoulders drooped in defeat as she surrendered. "I'll give it to ya."

Ratha suddenly attacked. Lunging forward, she struck Lindras hard in his chest with the crystal. The Wizard doubled over in pain, dropping to his knees as she rushed in to claim her second sphere and to finish Lindras off for good.

Raising Eldred's crystal in her bony hands, Ratha took careful aim at Lindras as he coughed and sputtered, trying to catch his breath that was knocked out of him.

"Now, you die," grumbled Ratha, as the light in the orb intensified as she crept toward the downed Wizard.

"Witch!" hollered Arerys. "I have your book. Step away from Lindras if you want it."

Ratha froze. She turned to face the Elf as he threw the Book of Spells to the ground.

"Give it to me!" snarled Ratha.

"Come and take it!" shouted Arerys, daring her to try.

With a gnashing of teeth and a loping gait, Ratha charged toward him. The orb, still clutched in her hands, swelled with light as she set her sight on Arerys; determined to strike him down. Shrieking in surprise, the witch stumbled. The crystal flew from her hands as Lindras reached out with the end of his staff to trip her.

Ratha shrieked, scrambling on her hands and knees. She crawled like a desperate animal as she rushed toward the precious book. Suddenly, she stopped as her blood ran cold, watching as Arerys drew his dagger from its holster.

"What are ya doin'?" gasped Ratha, panic filling her black heart as she watched the Elf.

"This!" responded Arerys, as he quickly lanced the palm of his hand. Clenching it into a tight fist, he squeezed the blood from this wound, allowing the crimson drops to fall onto the Book of Spells. "If my father's blood was powerful enough to kill that monster you conjured up, then my blood should be enough to destroy the evil within these pages."

As the droplets pooled on the red, leather cover, it began to sizzle and dance like cold drops of water falling into a sizzling hot frying pan of grease. Taking his dagger, Arerys deliberately rammed the tip of the bloodied blade through the leather cover and into the sheets of parchment, giving the dagger a hard, deliberate twist to work his blood into the pages.

Ratha screamed, raging as she watched the book quivering as though in the throes of death beneath the point of the dagger as an eerie red glow swelled from the pages. Suddenly, a brilliant flash of crimson light erupted from the book as it burst into flames, the parchment curling and disintegrating into ash before Ratha's angry face.

"It is done!" declared Arerys, leaping back as the rapacious flames engulfed the Book of Spells, devouring the pages to destroy the ancient runes transcribed within.

Instead of weeping in defeat, Ratha began to cackle, laughing like a demented soul as she mocked Arerys, "No... You are done! You an' yer ne'er-do-well cohorts will die on this night!"

"The Book of Spells was destroyed," retorted Markus, brandishing his sword as he edged closer to the witch. "Your foul magic has been undone! The evil has been vanquished!"

"*Vanquished?* It is coming!" snarled Ratha, threads of saliva spewing from her mouth as she raged. "It has only jus' begun!"

"How can that be?" asked Nayla, shaking her head in disbelief. "You are mad!"

"That may be so, but I ain't stupid!" snapped Ratha. "With the comin' of the night, I set inta motion the magic needed ta release the Dark Lord from his prison. It began workin' as soon as the sun went down. Beyilzon is still comin' as I planned. Except this time, I won't be there ta contain him an' his powers with that book ya foolishly destroyed!"

"You did what?" gasped Eldred, shoving Ratha to the ground.

"You heard me!" snorted Ratha, trembling with anticipation. "You're dead! I'm dead! Soon, we'll all be dead! The Dark Lord will be unleashed ta vent his wrath upon the world."

"We can still stop Beyilzon!" declared Lindras.

"Ha! You'll never get there before the height of the full moon!" scoffed Ratha. "You'll be too late. The Dark Lord will have already risen! It'll herald the end of all things as ya know it!"

"There is still time!" grunted Tor. Staggering to his feet with the help of his staff, the Wizard released a loud whistle.

"*NOOO!*" Ratha shrieked as she glanced up.

Descending from the deep night sky, massive wings blotted out the moon.

Ratha's scream was instantly squelched as the dragon's incredible bulk crashed down on her, smashing her brittle bones and squashing shrivelled muscles into the earth.

The witch's scream was followed by a profound silence.

It was broken by a loud snort of disgust as Button proceeded to drag the pad of his clawed foot on the grass to wipe the smear of human off like one would clean off his boot after into a steaming, fresh heap of cow dung.

Tor fell onto his still quaking knees before his dragon, giving Button instructions, "Take Lindras, fly due south. Listen to him, Button, for now he is your master. You will do as Lindras commands."

Button's massive head cocked sideways as the black, slit-like pupil floating on a fiery-red orb dilated slightly as the dragon stared at Lindras through this one, unblinking eye.

With a jet of warm, spent air snorting from its nostrils as a sign it understood, the tip of the dragon's lower fang carefully snagged Lindras by his cloak, lifting the Wizard by the scruff of his neck to lower him onto its back. Using its powerful haunches to launch off the earth and its great, leathery wings to thrust it skyward, Button ascended into the night with Lindras clinging on.

"Go, Button! Make speed to Mount Hope!" ordered Tor, waving his dragon on as Joval helped the dazed Wizard back onto his unsteady legs. "And do be careful, Lindras!"

For the longest moment, Nayla and those in her company stared into the night sky, their eyes following the shadow of the great dragon until it became one with the darkness.

"He should not have gone alone," said Arerys, his eyes no longer able to track Lindras and the dragon against the deep sky.

"Yes," agreed Tor. "However, look at us… We are unfit to face the Dark Lord should he arise. We will only be in the way. And you… you and your comrades have fought for too long and for too hard. You have already faced Beyilzon once before. In this condition, none of you will stand a chance against the Dark Lord."

"We should have tried," said Markus, his sword drooping in his weary hands. "We could have tried to help Lindras."

"Tor is correct. Your good intentions will only hamper Lindras," responded Tylon, groaning in pain as Nayla helped to pull him onto his feet as the Wizard leaned heavily on his staff. "Lindras has no choice but to face Beyilzon, alone."

"Then we have sent Lindras to his doom," said Joval, shaking his head in regret.

"We sent him with our prayers, my friend," stated Eldred. "Now is the time we must put all our trust and hope in Lindras. We must believe he will not fail."

Staring off toward to the stark outline of Mount Hope silhouetted against the night sky, each said a silent prayer as the sounds of their battle long faded to give way to the serene sounds of a calm, spring night as crickets chirped and tree frogs peeped once more.

This tranquility was broken by the sounds of gentle sobs carried on the night wind.

"Do you hear that?" asked Lando, wrapping his arm in his cloak more so to hide away his injury from his own eyes than from his friends.

"Druen!" gasped Arerys, turning toward the smokehouse. "She may be hurt!"

Rushing off to where Cullen had left her to hide, they rounded the corner of the small building.

"Oh, no…" groaned Lando, dropping to his knees next to Druen as she cradled Cullen's head, her tears falling onto his ashen face as she wept.

Immediately, Arerys knew they were too late. What blood there was had all but drained from Cullen's shattered body and what did not gush out, filled his lungs, causing him to drown in his own blood.

Cullen was dead.

"How can this be?" gasped Nayla. Rattled to her very core, she shook her head in disbelief and sorrow. "People like Cullen Bristow do not just die."

"He tried… he tried ta save me," sobbed Druen. "He was a – a great man."

"Yes, he was, and I believe it was *you* who saved *him*, Druen," said Lando, forcing down the hard lump catching in his throat. His hand gave Druen's trembling shoulder a gentle squeeze, offering her some comfort. In Lando's heart, he knew the true valour of a knight that seemed to elude Cullen for so long had finally rose to the occasion at the cost of his life.

"He died an honourable death – a true warrior," praised Joval, his mind trying to make sense of Cullen's tragic demise. "His soul will now find peace with his forefathers."

"Look! It is the midnight hour!" announced Eldred, his finger pointing to the full moon as the great luminous sphere ascended to the highest point in the sky to flood the lands in its silvery light.

"Lindras!" cried Arerys, his eyes darting over to Mount Hope. "What of our friend –"

His sentence was cut short as a resounding boom shattered the night and an explosive show of pure, white light expanded from the mountain as the earth trembled beneath their feet.

"That cannot be a good sign," decided Markus, his eyes straining to pierce the consuming darkness that followed.

"We must get to Lindras!" ordered Arerys.

As the impending sun leached away the darkness of night to extinguish the dazzling glow of the diamond stars, Nayla and the men of the Order, as well as the three Wizards in their company, journeyed on. They left Druen behind at the base of Mount Hope to grieve, remaining by Cullen's body as they cautiously made their way up the slope.

"It is strangely quiet," noted Joval, listening as his keen eyes searched their peaceful surroundings under the predawn sky.

"I hope it is a good thing," whispered Lando, searching for signs of the Dark Lord's presence. "I sense if Beyilzon had escaped from his prison in the netherworld to run amok in ours, he would make his presence abundantly known."

"Especially to us," added Markus, wondering now if the Stone of Salvation would have served its purpose under these conditions, had they been armed with it.

As the group neared the entrance of Beyilzon's former lair, immediately, they saw the rusted iron gates that once barred the mouth of this den were ripped clean off the hinges from the percussion of the explosive show of light.

"Look!" exclaimed Markus. He rushed over to where the hilt of the Sword of Power he used to defeat the Dark Lord ten years earlier remained in the ground. Here, Lindras had conjured his powers to seal the torn earth to trap the evil soul. "It is still here after all this time."

"But where is Lindras?" questioned Nayla. Her eyes scanned the immediate area for signs of the Wizard as she picked up the abandoned staff now devoid of its crystal sphere. "And where is the orb?"

"The ground... It is as though incredible heat had scorched the earth," remarked Arerys, his fingers feeling the ash that was once grass and weeds that grew around the embedded sword. It crumbled to dust beneath his light touch.

"The burn follows the crack in the ground that swallowed up the Dark Lord," noted Lando, his one good hand tracing the seared earth.

"Well, I do not believe Lindras was able to use this sword," said Markus, grunting as he pulled with all his might to extract the weapon from the earth.

"And for good reason," responded Joval, his fingers probing the soil to reveal the steel blade was solidly embedded. The portion of the blade that pierced the ground just before the cross-guard had melted under incredible heat to become one with the earth as it cooled.

"What could have done this?" queried Tylon, looking on in amazement.

Tor glanced up to the pale sky to spy his dragon circling high overhead. Button glided on the thermals as the golden rays of the early morning sun peered over the Iron Mountains to warm the landscape.

"Perhaps Lindras ordered my dragon to use its fire to do this," offered Tor, grateful to see Button had escaped the explosion that had rocked the earth.

"My power over fire could have easily done this; melt solid rock to a molten state to hardened once more," said Eldred, palming his crystal orb that was now devoid of its staff. "If this was Lindras' doing, he would have required special magic to do so."

"Whatever the case, I believe Lindras had somehow circumvented Beyilzon's release from the netherworld," decided Arerys, pointing to the perfect impression of Lindras' crystal. "This circular indentation in the soil is proof enough his magic was at work here."

"And this is all that remains of him," said Nayla, wistfully as she held forth the Wizard's soot covered staff.

"Whatever he did, he had sacrificed his life to prevent Beyilzon from escaping into our realm," said Markus, with a disheartened sigh.

"I think he used his orb to become *one* with his element," determined Tylon, taking Lindras' staff from Nayla's hands to wipe it clean. "He did this to seal the Dark Lord in his prison... forever."

"So, what now?" questioned Lando, as the shrill songs of wrens echoed through the valley to herald the start of a new day. "What are we to do?"

"What *is* there to do?" responded Tor, with a weary, but relieved sigh. "The witch is dead, the book was destroyed and Beyilzon has yet to show his face, if indeed he did return."

"But what about Lindras?" asked Nayla. "Should we not look for him... just in case?"

"Look for him?" repeated Tylon, pondering Nayla's question. "There is no need, my dear. He is near to us. I can sense it."

"But Lindras is not here," responded Nayla.

"Lindras is all around us, my dear woman," said Tylon, with a reassuring smile.

Nayla and her friends gazed to the formidable Iron Mountains to the east. The towering spires pierced the sky as the brilliant spring sun crested the peaks. Their eyes turned to follow the mountains' great shadows creeping across the vast lands of Imago that Lindras loved, gazing westward toward the vibrant greens of the enchanted forest of Wyndwood.

"I believe you are right, Master Riverdon," said Nayla, nodding in agreement as her hand patted a granite boulder that had stood firm and unchanged on Mount Hope for an eon, weathering the ravages of time and the elements for as long as this mountain stood. "Lindras is still here."

"So this is the end?" asked Markus. He breathed a weary sigh as he surveyed the vista rolling out before his eyes as the sun climbed higher into the morning sky.

"No..." replied Nayla, giving her friends a knowing smile as she spoke with utmost certainty. "Being a Kagai Warrior, I believe the end only signifies the start of a new beginning."

"For now, let us deliver Lindras' staff to the Watchers for safekeeping and return Cullen to Darross so he can be put to rest in his rightful place," suggested Arerys, nodding in approval to Nayla. "And then we will go home to our loved ones until we are called together again."

"I suppose if there is ever a quest to search Lindras out, I will now be ousted from the brotherhood," lamented Lando. "The Order has no use for one permanently disfigured and disabled as I am now."

"To lose a hand is not the end of all things, my friend," offered Arerys, attempting to ease Lando's grief and self-pity.

"It is easy for you to say, Arerys," countered Lando, drawing his cloak around his amputated limb so none could see his shame.

"A man is not defined merely by his physical attributes," stated Markus. "You are more than just your missing hand, Lando."

"If a man cannot protect his family or even save his own life, he is not a man," argued Lando, unable to reach across to draw his sword even if his life depended on it.

"God has given you two hands for a reason," responded Nayla. "I have Kagai brothers who have lost a left or a right hand in battle, but it has not stopped them from handling their swords."

"Yes… you spoke of this before," said Lando, recalling her conversation on their journey home with the Talibarrian emissaries. "And they are still able to wield a sword?"

"Well enough to do battle if called to war," stated Nayla. "It is just a matter of adapting."

Just as all assumed Lando was about to wallow in self-pity, he turned to Nayla with a request. "Then teach me to fight as the Kagai do. Allow me to be a man again."

"I will make it so, my friend," promised Nayla. With a kind and understanding smile, she pressed her short sword into Lando's left hand. "When we return home, we shall begin with this."

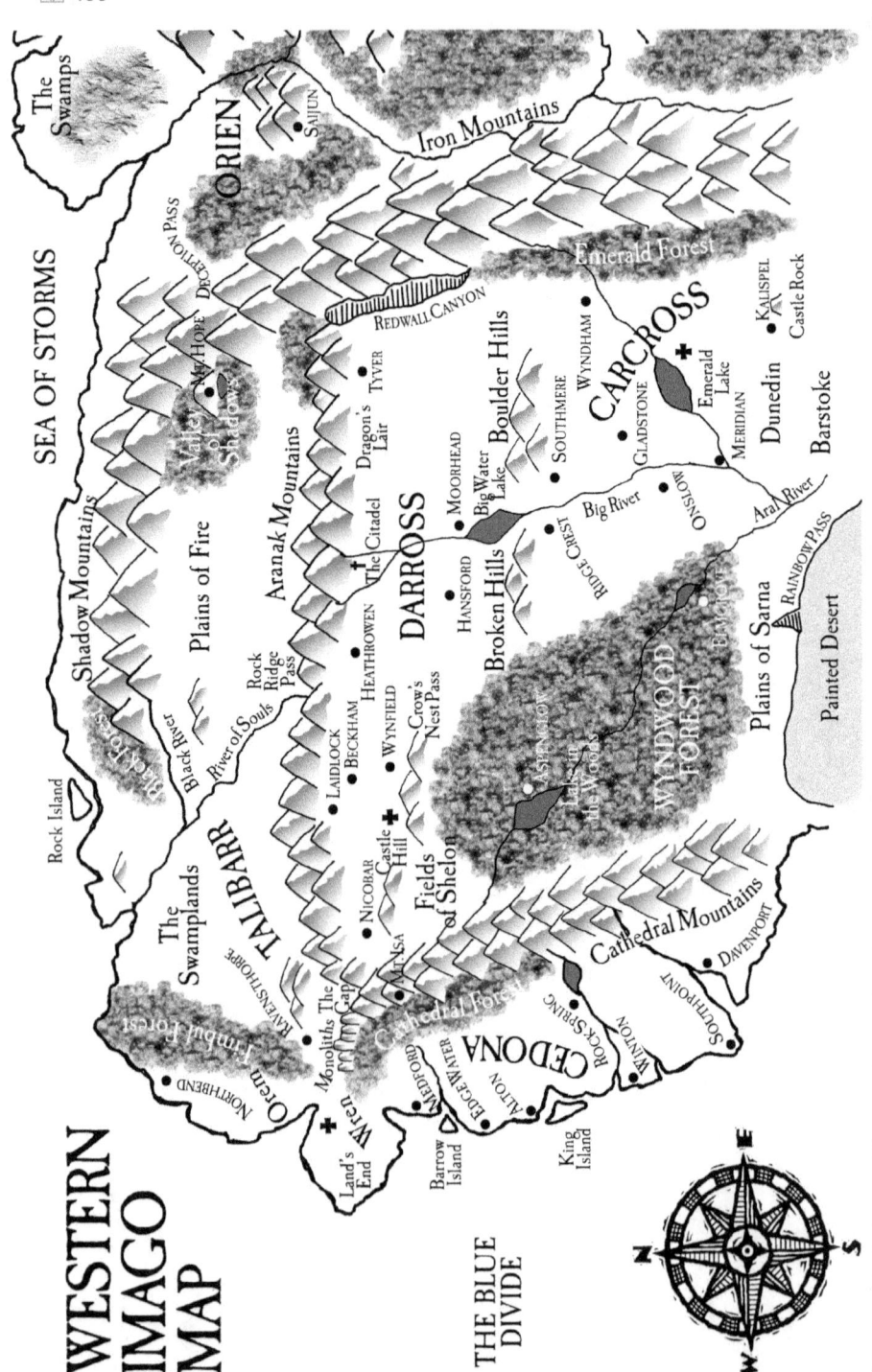

466

WESTERN IMAGO MAP

THE BLUE DIVIDE

SEA OF STORMS

The Swamps

ORIEN

SAJUN

Iron Mountains

Emerald Forest

DECEPTION PASS

NEW HOPE

Valley of Shadows

Shadow Mountains

Plains of Fire

Aranak Mountains

REDWALL CANYON

TYBER

Dragon's Lair

The Citadel

DARROSS

MOORHEAD

Big Water Lake

Boulder Hills

WYNDHAM

CARCROSS

SOUTHMERE

GLADSTONE

Emerald Lake

KALISPEL

Castle Rock

DUNEDIN

BARSTOKE

MERIDIAN

The Citadel

HANSFORD

Broken Hills

RIDGE CREST

Big River

ONSLOW

ARAN River

RAINBOW PASS

Black River

River of Souls

Rock Ridge Pass

HEATHROWEN

BECKHAM

LAIDLOCK

WYNFIELD

Crow's Nest Pass

Plains of Sarna

Painted Desert

Rock Island

The Swamplands

TALIBARR

NICOBAR

Castle Hill

Fields of Shelon

ASPEN CROFT

Elves in the Woods

WYNDWOOD FOREST

BAYPORT

RAVENSTHORPE

MANSA

Cathedral Forest

Cathedral Mountains

DAVENPORT

SOUTHPOINT

Orem Timbal Forest

Monoliths The Wren's Gap

CEDONA

ROCK SPRING

WINTON

NORTHBEND

Land's End

BEDFORD

EDGEWATER

ALTON

Barrow Island

King Island

EASTERN IMAGO MAP

ARASHE SEA

KANSAI BAY

USAGE

ESAN

HEGASHE

KEKAI

SHESAKE

KESO

MEDORE

ERO

HETAI

Henan Hills

Plains of Yasai

Yasai River

Hanmai River

Borai Mtn.

Kaisheke Hills

Medore Lake

MEDORE FOREST

NKPU FOREST

Magare Valley

ESSHU ROAD

KOTAI

Sheyat Ridge

MEDARA

NAGANA

Bando Lake

Lake Anzan

SAIYO

NSHEKO

Reyu Falls

Hebeku

FUREKO

MESAI

Safiya Lake

TAKAI FOREST
(The Great Bamboo Forest)

The Swamps

Reyu River

SAIJUN

Reyuzan River

adult fantasy series
(in reading order)

Imago Chronicles: Book One, A Warrior's Tale
Imago Chronicles: Book Two, Tales from the West
Imago Chronicles: Book Three, Tales from the East
Imago Chronicles: Book Four, The Tears of God
Imago Chronicles: Book Five, Destiny's End
Imago Chronicles: Book Six, The Spell Binder
Imago Chronicles: Book Seven, The Broken Covenant
Imago Prophecy (Prequel to Imago Chronicles series)
Imago Legacy (Sequel to Imago Prophecy)

YA fantasy series
(in reading order)

The Dream Merchant Saga:
Book One, The Magic Crystal

The Dream Merchant Saga:
Book Two, The Silver Sword
(Publication date: 2011)

about the author

L.T. Suzuki is a fantasy novelist, script-writer and
a practitioner and instructor of the martial arts system,
Bujinkan Budo Taijutsu; a system incorporating
six traditional samurai schools and
three schools of ninjutsu.

For more information, please check out L.T. Suzuki's
*official website at: **http://web.me.com/imagobooks***

www.ingramcontent.com/pod-product-compliance
Lightning Source LLC
Chambersburg PA
CBHW070541030726
47505CB00001B/119